Did she really believe her dad could help her bring focus and order to her chaotic mind and emotional field? Or was that just wishful thinking?

A part of her yearned to flee to Azaana and never leave. Surrounded by the other Suulh, she wouldn't have to fear her abilities. She couldn't harm them without harming herself.

But Reanne wouldn't rest until she'd tracked her down. She couldn't allow that threat to destroy the sanctuary she'd fought so hard to create for the three hundred Suulh. Or abandon all the Suulh still living on the original homeworld to whatever grim fate Reanne had in mind.

One way or another, eventually she'd have to face her enemy.

The question was, when that day came, would she be prepared?

THE LEGACY
OF TOMORROW

Starhawke Rising Book Four

Audrey Sharpe

Ocean Dance Press

THE LEGACY OF TOMORROW

© 2020 Audrey Sharpe

ISBN: 978-1-946759-93-1

Ocean Dance Press, LLC
PO Box 69901
Oro Valley AZ 85737

Visit the author's website at:
AudreySharpe.com

To my brother, with love. My playmate, my protector, my friend. You're the Luke to my Leia, and the best interstellar co-pilot a sister could ask for. This one's for you.

Want more interstellar adventures? Check out

these other titles in the Starhawke universe.

Starhawke Rising

The Dark of Light

The Chains of Freedom

The Honor of Deceit

The Legacy of Tomorrow

Starhawke Rogue

Arch Allies

Marked Mercenaries

Resurgent Renegades

One

Just keep breathing.

The rattle of machinery and drone of motors muffled the sound of Aurora Hawke's footsteps as she made her way down the planked dock of the shipyard. Dock workers in coveralls supervised the loading and unloading of smaller shipping crates from terrestrial freighters while at the water's edge massive cranes lifted containers the size of train cars out of the cargo bays of interstellar vessels moored at the winged support platforms.

No one paid Aurora any attention. And why would they? To them, she was nobody. Insignificant in their daily lives. They had no idea her existence had the power to destroy everything they held dear.

"You're not a weapon."

"That's exactly what I am. And Reanne Beck seems to be the only one who understands that."

A shiver skipped over Aurora's skin, but it had nothing to do with the pre-dawn mists swirling across the bay, dampening the glow from the lights overhead. A foghorn blew in the distance, a melancholy moan.

She'd created this waking nightmare. Her relationship with Reanne had set the stage. And while the reasons behind Reanne's actions were as ephemeral as the mists, her desire to bring a galaxy's worth of pain and suffering down on Aurora was clear as glass.

"Kreestol is the rightful leader of the Suulh. You, Aurora, are a worthless mongrel. One I will take great pleasure in bringing to heel."

Reanne had spoken those words with malicious glee. Even through the vocal modulator, Aurora had heard it. But she hadn't sensed any emotions from her former friend. Reanne had always been a blank slate to her.

Was that because Mya's supposition was true, that Reanne was half-Teeli? Aurora had never met a Teeli. The Admiral and Knox had made sure of that. Would she be unable to read their emotions?

The Teeli had been hunting her family ever since her mom, Marina, and Gryphon had fled the Suulh homeworld. Was Reanne's presence in Aurora's life part of the Teeli plan? Were they using her to finally capture the fugitives that had eluded them for decades? Or was Reanne using the Teeli to enact her personal vendetta?

The second option fit better with Reanne's obsession with power. She wouldn't willingly act as a pawn in someone else's game. But it didn't explain how she'd gained control over the Teeli fleet. Or the Suulh homeworld.

How had she learned of their existence? And how had she made the connection to Aurora? Or tracked down Aurora's aunt, Kreestol?

The manic ecstasy on Kreestol's face while she'd pinned Aurora in the river, intent on killing her, had haunted her dreams, contributing to her insomnia. It had also been the driving force behind her decision to leave her childhood home in the middle of the night. If Reanne could turn her own aunt against her—a Sahzade who was supposed to protect all Suulh—then it would be a small matter to manipulate the Suulh Mya had encountered on the homeworld into an army with one goal—destroy her.

To have a fighting chance at stopping them, she needed help. And only one person could provide it.

"Your dad is alive."

That revelation had rocked her world. She barely remembered him, just a vague shadow in a half-forgotten dream. She couldn't picture his face.

"I think he could help you with your reaction to the Suulh, perhaps teach you to control your empathic response so it's not so debilitating. His empathic abilities are incredible. Possibly stronger than yours."

Was Mya right? Could her father teach her how to manage the emotional overload she encountered with the Suulh, and the physical pain that came with it? She'd always assumed she'd inherited her empathic talents from her mother, her Suulh half. Accepting a paradigm in which her father was alive and well, and possibly holding the key to overcoming her greatest weakness, took some mental adjustment.

So did the revelation regarding her older brother, Micah. The brother she'd been encouraged to forget.

A tremor worked up from her toes, making her teeth chatter. She stuffed her hands in the pockets of her jacket and quickened her pace. More than anything else, she longed to see her brother, to feel the elemental connection they'd once shared. But as she'd stared at the spot in her room where his bed had once sat, she'd realized she couldn't allow that to happen.

"If he was near you, and especially when he touched you, your abilities went off the charts."

If what Mya had said was true, Micah was the last person in the galaxy she should go anywhere near. Her abilities were already lethal. If he enhanced them, her power to destroy could become cataclysmic.

Cade had proven that.

Tension radiated out from her chest, digging claws into her ribcage. She halted, squeezing her eyes shut as the image of him lying beside the river rose in her mind's eye.

She shoved it away, banishing it back to her mental lockbox along with all the other images of Cade that fought to get out. He was in danger because of her. In danger *from* her. She couldn't allow him to be part of her present. She loved him too much to put him in harm's way.

Rounding the corner of a large warehouse she arrived at her destination, a loading platform outside a smaller hangar. A terrestrial cargo freighter sat at the center of the open space, the side hatch open as workers maneuvered pallets of crates up the loading ramp.

A woman wearing a billed cap, her hair pulled through the opening into a ponytail, stood beside the ramp checking items off on a tablet as they were loaded. She glanced up as Aurora approached. "Can I help you?"

"Captain Roberts?"

"Yes."

"I'm Commander Hawke." She showed the captain her Fleet credentials from the *Argo*.

Captain Roberts stood a little straighter. As a freighter captain, she probably didn't meet too many Fleet personnel of Aurora's rank. "What can I do for you, Commander?"

"I understand you're on your way to Hawaii."

"That's right. We depart in twenty minutes."

"I'd like to catch a ride in your jump seat."

The captain's brows lifted. "It's not a comfortable way to travel. Wouldn't you rather take a Fleet personnel transport?" She gestured over her shoulder. "The passenger terminal must have a flight out today."

"Not until late this afternoon. I don't want to wait." If she gave herself time to think about her actions, she might change her mind. Or Mya might track her down and insist on accompanying her. She needed to get in the air now.

Roberts scrutinized her for a moment, clearly puzzled.

Aurora opened up her empathic senses, tuning into the other woman's emotional field. She sensed confusion, but more than a little curiosity, too. "It's a personal matter."

That tipped the scales. Roberts shrugged. "Well, I can't vouch for the accommodations, but if you don't mind, you're welcome aboard."

The tension in Aurora's chest eased slightly. "Thank you." She glanced in the direction of the freighter. "Is there anything I can do to help?"

"Nope. We've got it covered. Just head on up to the cockpit. Jump seat is behind the co-pilot's chair. We'll join you shortly."

Aurora stepped to the side to make way for the next load of pallets, then followed the dock workers into the cargo hold. The freighter's layout reminded her a little bit of *Gypsy*, Nat's shuttle, but twice as large.

She hadn't given the young pilot much thought since leaving her at Troi. She'd had more pressing issues on her mind. But she wished her well. Hopefully Nat had found whatever she'd been searching for on that planet. The hope and determination she'd projected as she'd stood in front of the windows of the *Starhawke*'s observation lounge had temporarily pushed back the permanent gloom that had settled over Aurora ever since she'd unmasked the Sovereign.

She slipped into the cockpit, lowered the jump seat and sat, exhaling on a weary sigh. Closing her eyes, she leaned her head back against the bulkhead. The lack of sleep was catching up with her. So was her impulsive behavior.

Normally she analyzed every situation before making a decision, but in this case, she'd acted on emotion-driven instinct. She'd packed her bag and left without a word.

Well, that wasn't exactly true. She'd left Mya a note. A one sentence explanation. But no details. Because she didn't have any to give.

She'd also addressed the note to *Lelindia*. Not sure why. Maybe just to make a point. But she'd always think of her as Mya. When Micah had been yanked from their lives, Mya had been little more than a child herself. It was unfair to hold her responsible for the deception. Or the fallout.

Which is why she'd put Mya in charge of the *Starhawke*. Guaranteed Reanne's minions would be tracking the ship while Reanne came up with a new plan of attack. Mya understood better than anyone what they were facing, what was at stake. She needed the freedom of movement the ship would give while Aurora was away.

With a sigh, she opened her eyes. The cockpit was warmer than outside, especially in the little nook where she was tucked. Standing, she slipped off her jacket and draped it over her lap as she sat back down. Pushing back the sleeve of her tunic, she switched on her comband. Now that she'd secured transport, she needed to move on to research.

"Commander?"

She glanced up.

A man about her height with curly dark hair and deep brown skin stood at the entrance to the cockpit. He stuck out his hand. "I'm the co-pilot, Dawson."

Aurora shook his hand. "Pleased to meet you."

"Can I get you anything? Coffee, maybe?"

"No, thank you. I'm fine."

"If you change your mind, we have a small galley by the head. Help yourself."

"Thanks."

While Dawson settled into the co-pilot's seat and began the pre-flight check, Aurora returned her attention to her comband.

Her mother had told her that her father and brother worked at the university on Oahu. She'd start there.

But a search of the university's database didn't produce any results for a professor named Brendan Hawke. Her heartbeat picked up. Surely her mother hadn't lied to her about that?

She tried typing in only his first name.

One result. Brendan Scott.

She pulled up the bio, inhaling sharply as an image appeared.

"Everything okay?" Dawson glanced over his shoulder.

"Fine." She rotated her wrist slightly to keep the image concealed.

He gave her a quizzical look but nodded and returned his attention to his work.

Aurora's gaze dropped to the image and held as if magnetized. The blue eyes staring back at her seemed to look into her soul. She saw herself in those eyes.

Her father.

His sandy blonde hair was several shades darker than hers with a touch of grey, parted on the side and swept over his high forehead, making him look rakish. His expression was arresting, penetrating, with a hint of a smile at the corners of his mouth.

That secret smile fit with her vague memories. The one thing she'd remembered about her father was he loved to laugh. If this picture was any indication, he still did.

At least now she had an image and his full name. His bio stated he had PhDs in psychology and sociology, was the head of the psychology department, and had an impressive array of accolades. Locating his office on campus would be easy.

He taught classes in psychology and metaphysics, with an emphasis on the untapped potential for the human mind-body connection for enhancing communication, healing, and strength. With her mother as inspiration, he would have developed a unique viewpoint on the possibilities.

What about Micah? Had he gone into psychology, too? She'd probably find his bio listed under Micah Scott, rather than Micah Hawke.

She typed in the first three letters of his name and stopped, her hand hovering over the comband. Did she really want to know more about her brother? To see an image that would taunt her with what she couldn't have? Coming face-to-face with him was far too dangerous, especially now, but accepting that logic intellectually did nothing to dampen her emotional yearning. It gnawed at her insides. If she uncovered details about the man he'd become, it would only make her decision to stay away even harder. Why torture herself?

"Loading's complete." Captain Roberts stepped into the cockpit and settled into the pilot's seat. She glanced over her shoulder at Aurora. "All set?"

Not at all. "Yep."

As the ship lifted off, self-preservation won out. She deleted the search.

Two

The boy's footsteps pounded on the hard-packed dirt in a steady rhythm, pushing forward, climbing, descending, then forward again.

His muscles worked to keep the rhythm going as the path turned away from the clouds blocking the setting sun, his dark skin and clothes blending in with the encroaching shadows. He'd only passed two other runners tonight, the bite of the wind coming off the ocean driving everyone else away.

He didn't mind the cold, or the push of the wind as it buffeted his body and made his shirt ripple against his chest. The thrill of the outdoors brought him here after school day after day, rain or shine. No winter squall was going to dampen his mood.

He'd started running shortly after his thirteenth birthday, on the day he'd told his family he wouldn't be submitting his application to the Academy. He'd shocked them all.

Since he was a child, he'd accepted that he would carry on the family tradition, make his grandmother and father proud by becoming a Fleet officer, like them. But his heart had never been in it. He didn't look to the stars and wonder what was out there. He wondered why anyone would choose to leave the beauty of Earth behind.

The natural world fascinated him. Which is why he ran outdoors. And painted. And sculpted. And drew, trying to capture the essence of that beauty with his hands.

The beat of the music playing in his ears matched the steady fall of his feet and his rapid breathing. He was almost to the big hill now. One more push, a hairpin turn, and the gradual descent to the end of the trail. He'd been running this path for two and a half years. He knew every rock, every tree, every shrub. The lengthening shadows and dark sky didn't concern him. He could run this course blindfolded.

He started up the hill.

He'd been lucky. His family had understood why he was changing the plan. Even his grandmother, the Fleet Admiral. And she'd supported his passion for art ever since. This spring, he'd be applying to the most challenging art schools around the globe. With hard work and a little luck, this time next year he'd be in a residence program abroad.

Almost to the top now. His calves and lungs burned as he forced his body up the incline. Keeping his focus on the clouds helped. This was always the do or die moment in the run. If he'd wanted to, he could have taken the loop the other way, starting with the climb, but it was a lot more rewarding to make it to the top of the hill at the end of the run.

Five more steps. Four, three, two, one...

He reached the top, his lungs working like a bellows as he scanned the vista for a few moments. The dark shadows changed the scene into a breathtaking alternate reality. Who needed to leave Earth to see new worlds?

He captured the view in his mind's eye before starting down the other side, following the hairpin along the edge of the dropoff to his right.

Maybe when he got home, he'd paint—

Sudden movement to his left made him jerk to the right. He stumbled, his shoes scraping on the small pebbles along the path's edge. A split second later something solid slammed into his left shoulder. His foot struck a tree branch lying across the path.

A branch that shouldn't have been there.

Pain streaked out like lightning from his shoulder, his eyes flying wide as his body pitched sideways. He tried to regain his footing and failed.

A scream tore from his lips as he plummeted over the edge into the darkness.

Three

I feel the way you look, my friend.

Mya Forrest rested her palm against the scarred bark of the giant redwood, the tallest tree in the woods behind her parents' house.

A swath of bark had been blasted off one side of the five-meter-thick trunk, the pieces scattered on the ground like shrapnel, barely visible in the hazy light of dawn. The exposed wood showed blackened scorch marks, and heat radiated from glowing embers. But the lightning bolt of energy that had struck the tree hadn't come from the sky. It had come from Aurora.

The massive tree had been Aurora's favorite spot in the woods ever since she was a child. She'd often gone there to play, think, or read. Now, it had become a soldier caught in the crossfire of a terrible battle.

Mya engaged her energy field, the rich green wrapping around the trunk and sinking into the open wounds. The tree's lifeforce responded to the healing touch, drawing on the cool energy she offered as the flow pressed deep into the rings where the fire still burned. She couldn't heal the tree in the same way she could people—the processes for growth and development were quite different. But she could nurture and invigorate new growth, helping the tree to heal itself.

Taking a wider stance, she spread her hands apart, expanding the energy field. The crisp December breeze brushed her cheeks as she worked, though the chill didn't bother her. She'd never been temperature sensitive, especially when she generated her energy field. The hooded sweatshirt and jeans she wore provided plenty of protection.

Dropping into the meditation of healing, she lost track of time. Soothing the angry marks on the tree's exterior was her primary goal, but focusing on the tree also helped to calm her inner turmoil.

Aurora had left, fleeing in the night. No explanation, no hint of where she'd gone. Only a cryptic line on a sheet of paper. *Until I return, the ship is yours.*

The note had given her two bits of information. Aurora hadn't retreated to the *Starhawke*. And wherever she'd gone, she planned to come back.

That fact was the only thing keeping Mya from full-fledged panic. Aurora wasn't impulsive. And she wasn't the type to abandon her friends. The uncharacteristic move had set off a plethora of flashing red warning lights.

What was she thinking? *Was* she thinking? Or had she reacted from emotional overload?

Mya could relate. She'd left the house before sunrise, seeking the solitude of the forest. She wasn't in any condition to face Libra. Or her parents. Not yet. She needed time to process.

The choices Aurora's mother had made had put them in this position, but Mya couldn't say with any certainty that she would have acted any differently. She wanted to keep Aurora safe just as much as Libra did.

And Aurora wanted...

She paused, the ridges of the bark under her palms drawing her attention as she shifted her stance. What did Aurora want? That answer used to be obvious. She wanted to be captain of her own ship, to help the Suulh, and to have Cade by her side.

But now? She'd closed herself off from Cade and turned the ship and the responsibility for the Suulh over to Mya. Which left a gaping void. For both of them.

A weary sigh slid from her lips. Seeing her name, *Lelindia*, written on the envelope had cut deep. Aurora had never called her that. As a toddler, before Micah had been taken away, they'd both called her Leelee. Her full name had been tough for them to pronounce. It shouldn't matter, but she hated the idea that Aurora would start using her given name instead of Mya. Only her parents called her Lelindia.

At least Aurora still trusted her. She wouldn't have left her in charge of the *Starhawke* unless that were true. The years of deception hadn't completely destroyed their connection. And she'd do everything she could to repair the damage as soon as Aurora returned.

Speaking of damage, the heat from the tree had dissipated, replaced by the healthy glow of regeneration. Releasing her energy field, she stepped back and surveyed the scarred trunk.

The bark was still shallow in the areas Aurora had struck, but the new growth was well on its way to establishing a protective covering over the bare spots, melding with the dark burns. In time, the tree would complete the process, though the scars would likely remain for years.

She'd never forget the look on Aurora's face when she'd learned the truth about her father and brother. Shell-shock. Fury. Betrayal.

The last had hit Mya like a blow. She'd never wanted to deceive her friend, but the choice had been made by Libra, and enforced by her parents. It hadn't been her secret to tell. Not until last night. The explosion that followed had been as violent as she'd feared. The tree was living proof of that.

"I'm glad you were here for her," she murmured, giving the tree a gentle pat.

But when Aurora had walked back into the house hours later, the fury had been replaced with emptiness. She'd looked like a wraith, just as she had after her encounter with Reanne Beck. In some ways, that lack of emotion had been worse.

Drawing in a shaky breath, she glanced in the direction of the house. Nope, still not ready to face Libra or her parents. She needed a plan first.

Stepping away from the tree, she moved over to the path and continued deeper into the forest.

The redwood had been Aurora's favorite spot in the woods, but Mya's was quite a bit farther. She'd discovered it not long after Brendan had left with Micah. The vivid memory of that morning was as fresh as if it had happened yesterday.

She'd moved into Aurora's room to keep her company, sleeping in Micah's bed. Aurora had woken her from a deep sleep in the pre-dawn hours, screaming Micah's name at the top of her lungs. *My-a! My-a!*

The anguish in Aurora's cries had torn Mya's heart to shreds. She'd been eight at the time, old enough to understand the actions of Aurora's parents in separating Aurora and Micah. Witnessing the devastating effect on Aurora, however, had driven her to the breaking point.

It had taken a couple hours to soothe Aurora back to sleep. Even though her cries would have been audible in Libra's bedroom down the hall, she hadn't come to check on her. And with good reason. Her presence only made Aurora's hysteria worse. Mya's parents couldn't help, either. She was the only one who could calm Aurora down, and only if they were left alone. That was another reason she'd moved out of her bedroom in the Forrest wing and into the bedroom Micah had shared with Aurora.

But calming Aurora had left Mya emotionally drained and on edge, unable to sleep. As soon as the sun had risen, she'd escaped into the peace and quiet of the woods.

Without a destination in mind, she'd meandered, finally coming across a group of trees deep in the forest that had grown close together. Their trunks formed a hollow that naturally filled with plant material, creating a cushioned bower. She'd climbed inside and stretched out on the leaves, gazing through the treetops far, far above her. In that moment, it had felt like the most peaceful spot in the world. And the perfect cure for her distress.

Over the years, she'd used the bower as her meditation and contemplation nook, especially when she had thorny problems to work out, or emotional upsets to work through. This trip qualified on both counts.

The leaves crunched under her boots as she reached her destination and stepped into the rough oval. The cold, hard ground wouldn't provide as much cushion this time of year, but that was okay. The whisper of the wind through the trees and the dappled sunshine in the blue sky were all she needed.

Settling onto her back, she rested her head in her palms and gazed up at the patterned brown bark of the trees and the sun-lightened green of the foliage. The energy of her surroundings called to her, drawing the tension from her muscles.

"I'm sorry, Sahzade," she whispered. She'd meant it last night, and she meant it even more now. But *sorry* wasn't going to get her anywhere.

Closing her eyes, she drew in a slow breath, focusing on the image of Aurora in her mind's eye. *Sahzade, where are you?*

To her surprise, the response came through within moments—an image of white sandy beaches, swaying palm trees, and the sparkle of sunlight on cresting waves.

But before the vision had fully fixed itself in Mya's mind, it dissipated like fog in sunlight. Aurora had closed the connection.

Understandable, considering. But she'd given Mya an answer.

She'd gone to Hawaii to find her father and brother.

But if that was the case, why had she chosen to go alone? And to leave so abruptly? Mya had offered to go with her, expecting that Aurora would welcome the emotional support. Apparently not.

Which left her with a choice. Follow Aurora against her wishes and risk another confrontation, or accept the role Aurora had given her and return to the *Starhawke.*

She stared at the shifting patterns of light and shadow as the two scenarios played out in her mind. If she showed up uninvited, Aurora would likely take it as a sign of overprotective behavior. That wouldn't improve their current situation. And it wouldn't help Aurora focus on getting the help she needed from Brendan.

And she did need him, desperately. After Brendan had left with Micah, Aurora had been forced to teach herself how to control her empathic abilities. She'd done a decent job, considering. But the appearance of the Suulh had changed the rules of the game. Without Brendan's guidance, Aurora's strength would become a weakness.

And Mya's presence wouldn't help.

Fine. She'd put her faith in Brendan. She hadn't seen him since she was a child, but she'd loved him like a father. His optimistic, compassionate nature, and ever-present smile, had been sorely missed.

He'd given up so much to keep Aurora safe. She had no doubt he'd do everything humanly possible to help her now.

But it wouldn't be a quick fix. It might take weeks, or even months, for Aurora to master the skills she needed. Which left Mya in the driver's seat. What should she do in the meantime?

In the plus column, she had the *Starhawke*, the crew, and money in their accounts thanks to the return of Admiral Schreiber. In the minus column, she had a grandmother living as a captive on the Suulh homeworld, the Galactic Council caught in the grip of a potential overthrow plot, and Reanne Beck building a Suulh and Necri army.

She hadn't trained for problems like these. She was a doctor, not a tactician. Aurora's abrupt departure had pushed her so far out of her comfort zone she'd need a telescope to see it.

So, she'd do the only logical thing. Call in the cavalry.

Four

On the southern California coast, the early morning sun struggled to warm the crisp ocean breeze blowing off the ocean. Waves crashed onto a small beach, the water racing against the pull of gravity. Small rocks and bits of shell tumbled along as the water stretched translucent fingers toward the lone figure walking along the damp sand.

Cade Ellis barely noticed the gurgle and sigh of the water. His gaze was on the horizon to the north, his thoughts hundreds of kilometers away.

I'm here, Rory. Can you hear me?

Only the rumble of the waves and the call of seabirds answered him.

When Aurora had first cut off all communication following the confrontation with Reanne, he'd done his best to accept Mya and Justin's advice. He'd been patient, giving her time to work through the trauma she'd endured while his team made the return journey to Earth in *Gladiator*, their newly acquired compact fighter.

But when they'd arrived at Sol Station, she'd shut him out again, refusing to even see him. Avoiding him was one thing. Banning him from access to her ship had a finality that had hollowed out his chest.

He wasn't an empath, but he knew Aurora. Every instinct told him she was fighting to keep her head above water. He wanted to be there to support her, comfort her, love her.

But she believed her presence put him in danger. Maybe she was right. So what? He'd gladly suffer a hundred painful deaths rather than live a long life without her. And in his heart, he knew she felt the same way. Ironically, that's why she'd sent him packing. To insure he wouldn't end up dead.

Well, he had news for her. He'd faced death more times than he could count, and would continue to do so as long as he led the Admiral's Elite Unit. Being cut off from her only made it harder to concentrate on his job.

Shoving his hands in the pockets of his jacket, he sighed, his gaze shifting to the cliff overlooking the water. Wallowing in self-pity like a lovesick teenager wasn't going to help. His team and Admiral Schreiber needed him.

Turning, he trudged across the loose sand to the stone stairway that curved up the rocky incline. As he climbed the steps, he focused on leaving his personal issues down on the beach.

By the time he reached the stretch of lawn that led to the Admiral's house, he'd succeeded in reasserting mental discipline. Well, mostly.

To his right, he spotted the Admiral through the wall of windows that made up most of the back of the house, working at the large wood desk in his study. Justin Byrnes, Christoph Gonzalez, and Tam Williams were in the kitchen to his left, laughing and joking while they prepared enough food to feed an army.

He headed for the double doors that opened onto the middle of the patio. Stepping inside, he found Bella Drew curled up on one of the plush couches in the living room, a datapad in her hand and a small frown line between her brows. She glanced up. "Have a nice walk?"

Her words were innocuous enough, but the empathy in her blue eyes indicated she'd figured out the real reason for his beachside stroll. His entire team knew he wanted to crawl out of his skin. "Yeah. Where's Reynolds?"

"She went for a run, but said she'd be back by oh-eight-hundred."

He glanced at the antique clock on the mantle over the fireplace. Seven fifty-seven. If he knew Tracy Reynolds, which he certainly did, she'd be walking through the front door in exactly three minutes.

He shifted his attention to Bella's datapad, which showed a neatly organized chart with the names of the five members of the Galactic Council she and Justin were in charge of investigating, along with detailed notes next to each. "Anything to report?"

"Nothing unusual so far. If Reanne had any dealings with these delegates, there's no trail to follow. Not that I'm surprised. She's good at covering her tracks."

"Yes, she is." Too good. "She also might not have bothered making contact with the delegates from the northern quadrants, especially those in the Outer Rim. They wouldn't have a tactical advantage for her, being so far from Teeli space and on the doorstep of the Kraed."

"Except her ship showed up at Burrow. That's in the northern Outer Rim."

"True, but the Council had no idea we were there. Reanne didn't find out our location through them." He still wasn't clear on exactly how she *had* tracked them, and that nagged at him. Reanne's semi-omniscience regarding ship movements in Fleet space was one of the puzzles he wanted solved.

"Hopefully Gonzo and Reynolds will have success tracking down Reanne's ties to the delegates in the southern Rim quadrants."

"Especially the one from Q4," he agreed. "That whole arrangement between the Etah Setarips and the admin at Gallows Edge had Reanne's influence written all over it.

And that quadrant adjoins Teeli space. I have to believe she has the delegate under her thumb."

The chime of the front door opening was followed by a melody from the antique clock announcing the hour.

Reynolds appeared in the foyer, her short blonde hair and the collar of her shirt damp with sweat. She spotted him and strolled over, mopping her brow with her sleeve. "Good morning."

"Good morning. How was your run?"

"Stellar. Nothing like the sea air on your face and terra firma under your feet."

Except the glitter of stars and the power of a starship under your fingertips. But Reynolds wasn't as entranced with space travel as he was.

"Breakfast will be ready in ten!" Gonzo called out amid the clatter of pans.

"I'll be showered in five!" Reynolds called back, nodding at Cade before heading toward the hallway connecting the bedroom suites. The Admiral's house had four guest rooms, so Reynolds and Bella were sharing a room, as were Gonzo and Williams, while Cade and Justin had their own rooms.

Several years ago, when his unit had stayed here prior to their first mission under his command, he'd offered up his room to the team, content to sleep on one of the many couches in the living room. He hadn't gotten any takers. In fact, Gonzo and Reynolds had made it clear they preferred sleeping on the floor, claiming it kept their senses sharp. He'd argued and lost, eventually accepting this would be the standard arrangement whenever his unit was in residence.

"I'm going to check in with the Admiral."

Bella nodded, her gaze returning to her pad.

The Admiral's lined face creased in a smile when Cade entered the study. "Beautiful morning for beach walking."

"Yes, it is." But he didn't want to talk about the weather. "Are we going into HQ today?"

"That was my plan." The Admiral leaned back in his chair and steepled his hands. "Any objections?"

"Concerns." He settled into one of the chairs across from the Admiral's desk, the ocean visible through the floor-to-ceiling windows to his right. "We have no idea how deeply Reanne's people have infiltrated the Galactic Council or how much influence she can exert on members of the Fleet."

"Such as Admiral Payne."

"Yes. She's a career Fleet officer with a spotless record, yet she knowingly sent Aurora's crew on a mission to Teeli space that would have resulted in an ambush and possible capture by Reanne."

"Do we know that for certain?"

"I think we do. Aurora knew Payne was lying about the mission details, and now that Reanne's connection to the Teeli has been established, is there any question that Payne was sending them into a trap?"

"No. We're in agreement. But we have no evidence."

And that was the sticking point. Aurora was the only one who had seen Reanne during the battle. One person's testimony wouldn't sway the Council to investigate the Teeli, especially with Reanne's moles working to manipulate them.

Cade stood, walking to the windowed wall and watching the rolling waves in the distance. "So, what do we do?"

"We continue to play Reanne's game while we gather information to prove our case."

"Which means going into HQ like nothing's wrong."

"Correct."

"What about Magee? Have you been able to reach her?"

"No. Her personal contact number has been disconnected."

"Disconnected?" The Admiral's PA had been reassigned to the Teeli delegation while the Admiral had been an unwilling guest of the Setarips. Protocol had made it impossible for Cade to contact her, but he'd assumed the Admiral would be able to get through. "Why would her personal number be disconnected?"

"I've been looking into that. And on whose authority she was reassigned. According to the official record, she requested the transfer."

"What?" He stared at the Admiral. "I don't believe it. She wouldn't do that. Certainly not while you were gone."

"I agree. Which means either the documents were forged, or she was coerced."

"Just like Payne." He fisted his hands, envisioning them circled around Reanne's neck. "Reanne's minions might have used your absence as leverage to convince Magee your safety was dependent on her cooperation."

"Possibly. Or it may have been more subtle. I've studied the Teeli for years. Their ability to bend others to their will is remarkable. Terrifying, but remarkable."

"So Magee may not have known what she was doing?"

"In a way. Her actions may have seemed perfectly logical to her at the time."

"And now she's locked away with the Teeli delegation."

"With no way for us to reach her. Yes."

While simultaneously giving Reanne a direct line. "Is she a security risk?"

"Not with regards to the Fleet. But if the Teeli can manipulate her into sharing what she knows about me, personally? Any information is dangerous in Reanne's hands. And she's not above using Magee in an attempt to manipulate me."

Cade started pacing in front of the glass. "Everywhere we go, Reanne's snares keep tripping us up."

"True, but we still have one important advantage. She has failed to capture Aurora."

"Not for lack of trying," Cade muttered. And now he didn't even have the comfort of knowing Aurora's plans.

"Aurora's unmasked her. That gives us a position of power we've been sadly lacking. If anyone can outmaneuver Reanne Beck, it's Aurora."

He glanced at the Admiral. "Have you spoken to her since you left the *Starhawke*?" The Admiral had remained with Aurora until they'd reached Sol Station.

"No. And I have no plans to do so. She needs time to heal."

So had the Admiral, although his wounds had been physical not emotional. The engine room explosion on the Setarip ship had almost killed him. Looking at him now, it was impossible to tell he'd suffered any injury. They had Mya Forrest to thank for that.

Hopefully the good doctor could work the same magic with Aurora, helping her heal from her emotional trauma with Reanne.

"What about the troll they assigned in Magee's place? We should be able to get some information out of him." Sharing air with the slimeball in a human suit would be unpleasant—one encounter had been more than enough—but interrogating the man would lighten his mood considerably. Especially if they could establish his connection to Reanne.

"Unfortunately, that's not an option."

Cade stopped pacing. "Why not?"

"When Sol Station received my credentials, they notified HQ of my arrival. I received a packet from my new PA last night—Lieutenant Valenzuela." The Admiral called up the Lieutenant's Fleet profile, complete with photo. It showed a woman in her forties or early fifties with dark hair and eyes.

"What happened to the man I spoke to?"

"I've been unable to find any documentation relating to him. As far as HQ is concerned, Magee held the post until Valenzuela took over five days ago."

"What? How can that be? We knew Magee had been reassigned more than a month ago."

"Which illustrates the bigger problem. Falsifying secure Fleet documents is not a simple task. It would require a high-level clearance and technical systems knowledge that rivals Drew's. As soon as she and Justin have finished their investigation of the five delegates they were assigned, I want them to begin digging into the paperwork."

"What about Payne? Could she have engineered this?"

"She has the necessary clearance, but not the skill set. If she's involved, she didn't do it alone."

Cade stared at the PA's image while his mind whirred. How many tentacles had Reanne wrapped around the GC? The Fleet? When would they start to squeeze? "Who do you still trust completely?"

"Besides your team?"

The assurance in that question chased away some of the chill. "Yes."

"Kathryn."

The Admiral was probably the only person besides President Kathryn Yeoh's wife who called her by her first name. Cade had only met the Galactic Council president once, but he'd been impressed by her sharp mind and keen observation skills. "Does she know anything about the Teeli threat?"

"Oh, yes. She was a newly-elected member of the General Assembly when the Teeli applied for membership in the Council. One of the few who argued against the fast-tracking of their application. We worked together to convince the Council, but ultimately failed."

"I'm surprised that didn't hurt her career, taking such an unpopular stance."

The Admiral's smile was self-mocking. "Kathryn was much more diplomatic than I was. Cool, level-headed. I learned a great deal about self-control from her."

Cade's brows lifted. He couldn't imagine the Admiral lacking self-control. In his world, the Admiral was the walking definition. "Have the two of you talked about the Teeli situation since then?"

"No. I considered broaching it after she was elected President, but I couldn't share the information I'd gathered regarding the Teeli without implicating Siginal and the Kraed. And without proof, I'd be placing Kathryn in a compromised position."

"Which brings us right back to square one. We need proof of what Reanne and the Teeli are doing."

"And thanks to Celia Cardiff, we have a start on that."

"What do you mean?"

The Admiral pulled up a vid file. "She recorded this while she was on the Suulh homeworld."

The video started playing, revealing a panorama of a landing pad at the edge of a peninsula, with ground transports disgorging Teeli personnel. A ship about the size of *Gladiator* glided into view, descending to the landing pad like a giant owl with wings unfurled.

Cade's teeth clenched. Reanne's ship.

The Teeli formed two rows on either side of the ship as the ramp descended. Armed figures stepped out, their bodies covered in mesh fabric to conceal their features. But Cade had seen those same uniforms on Gaia., covering the Etah Setarips.

A cloaked figure emerged next, the thick brown fabric obscuring any detail of shape or size.

Didn't matter. Now that he knew what he was looking for, Cade recognized Reanne's movements, the haughty way she carried herself. In his presence, she wouldn't be able to hide behind her cloak any longer.

The cloaked figure and several of the Setarips entered the vehicles, and then the video froze.

The Admiral pointed at the image. "This doesn't help us with identifying Reanne as the leader, but it does provide a clear link between the Teeli and the attack on Gaia. The Setarips who died during the fighting wore those same mesh suits. They're in storage with the other evidence we gathered."

"Is this video enough of a link to bring our case to the Council? We also have four eyewitnesses who were on that island with Reanne." Assuming Mya and Clarek would agree to testify. He had no doubts regarding Reynolds or Cardiff.

The Admiral echoed his thoughts. "I would need to speak with Aurora and Mya before making that decision. This is their homeworld we'd be revealing, which has major implications for their futures. And I'd want to check with Siginal and Jonarel, too. But this is enough that I can speak to Kathryn, let her know about Reanne and the Teeli link to Gaia. I have a meeting scheduled with her for two o'clock this afternoon. And you'll be joining me."

Five

The throng of students and instructors flowed past Aurora in a bustling current. Holiday music piped through the building's speakers provided a festive background to the babble of voices and the thump of footsteps.

But Aurora tuned it all out, pressing her back against the wall to avoid being jostled, her focus on the door across the corridor. *Psychology* was stenciled in bold black letters across the opaque glass panel, with the office hours listed underneath.

According to the information she'd gathered at the Administration building, her father's office was located behind that door.

Taking a deep breath, she reached out with her senses. The emotions of the people passing by danced around the periphery of her awareness, but she discarded them easily, seeking a stronger emotional field, the touch of something familiar. Would she recognize her father's field if she felt it? Would he recognize hers?

Seconds passed into minutes as she sorted through the multitude. But as her frustration mounted, she finally admitted defeat. If her father was in the building, she couldn't pinpoint him. Which left her with only one option.

Open the door, Aurora. Go inside.

She'd come so far. Why was she struggling to cross the last three meters? Her heart pounded in her ears, but her feet refused to move. What if he didn't want to see her? What if he sent her away?

What if he didn't?

A young man paused in front of the door. He checked the tablet in his hand, then reached for the doorknob and swung the door open, giving Aurora a peek inside.

A long counter ran parallel to the door. A man and woman about Aurora's age sat behind it. They looked up and smiled as the young man entered.

The cement blocks encasing Aurora's feet crumbled. Cutting across the wave of students, she caught the door in her right hand before it closed, pushing it back open.

The man behind the desk met her gaze, his smile warm and welcoming. His lips formed the words *Can I help you?* but she couldn't hear a thing over the roaring in her ears. Three more steps and she was in front of the counter. She leaned on it for support.

"Professor Scott?"

The young man frowned.

And no wonder. In her mind she'd said the words, but she was pretty sure she hadn't opened her mouth.

She cleared her throat and licked her lips—a pointless gesture since her tongue was devoid of moisture. She tried again. "Professor Scott?"

This time she'd produced sound, but the man's frown shifted to a look of apology.

"I'm sorry, he's out of the office today. Would you like to speak with his TA?"

He wasn't there.

She barely stopped herself from smacking her forehead on the countertop. How stupid could she be? This is where her impulsive behavior had gotten her. At the very least she should have called to make sure he was on campus.

"Do you know when he'll be back?"

The man checked the information on his screen. "He's giving a lecture on Maui, returning late tomorrow."

Not ideal, but she could work with it.

"Unfortunately, his schedule's pretty full the rest of the week with finals, but I see a three o'clock opening on Friday. Would that work for you?"

Three days. If she had to schedule an appointment and wait three days to meet her father, she'd go insane. Her plan, if she could call it that, needed major revisions. "That's okay. Thanks, anyway." She turned and then paused. "What about his son, Micah? Is his office here?" She hadn't thought to ask the Admin staff, but it would be good information to have if she wanted to avoid him.

The young man shook his head. "No, he's a professor for the Marine Biology department."

"Oh." Micah was a marine biologist? If she'd listed her top ten guesses for what profession he'd gone into, that one would have been around fifty-seven. For some reason, she'd assumed he'd follow in their father's footsteps. Or maybe have a passion for the stars like she did. Instead, he was studying marine life. "Well, thanks."

Her feet carried her out of the room much quicker than they'd carried her in. She was down the hall and out in the late afternoon sunshine before she'd registered where she was going.

The ache in her chest flexed its muscles, bringing her to a halt. She rested a hand on the nearest wall and drew in air in long, ragged breaths.

What had she been thinking? Well, that was the point, wasn't it? She hadn't been thinking. She'd reacted, rushing to get here, for all the good it had done her. Diving in had resulted in a faceplant.

Should she try to book passage to Maui? Her Fleet credentials had garnered her a free ride on the freighter with minimal fuss, but if she played that card again, she might start to attract attention. The last thing she wanted to do was alert Reanne or any of her moles in the Galactic Council to where she was or why she was here.

Thanks to the Admiral's arranging payment for her crew, she had funds. But it might be the last payment she'd see for a while. She needed to be frugal.

The tension in her chest moved into her temples, making her head pound.

More than anything, she needed sleep. The smart move was to go back to her hotel and take a nap. Clear her head so she could come up with a new plan. A logical one. Impulsive clearly didn't work for her.

At least she'd made brief contact with Mya. When Mya's mental link had reached out to her earlier, she'd sent a mental image of the island. Hopefully that had calmed her friend's fears. She didn't have the bandwidth for anything more. She didn't want Mya to worry, but she needed time apart right now, to focus on the task at hand.

Bringing Mya hadn't been an option. After the years of deceit and half-truths, she needed the mental and emotional clarity she could only achieve alone. Mya's presence would have muddied the waters.

The walk to her hotel seemed to take forever, but eventually she made it through the lobby and up to her room. Opening the sliding door, she stepped onto the balcony, which was enclosed by the trees and palms that surrounded the hotel. Rooms on the opposite side looked out on the water, which she would have loved, but she'd settled for basic accommodations. Even so, the energy of the plants drifted over her in a balmy wave, easing the tension and calming her mind.

Moving back into the room, she slipped off her boots, tunic, and pants, and stretched out on the bed, falling into a deep sleep as soon as her head touched the pillow.

Six

Mya entered the house through one of the doors off the back porch rather than the front door, which gave her quicker access to the staircase and her bedroom.

Not quick enough.

"Where have you been?"

Mya glanced at the front archway of the Forrest wing, which led to her mom and dad's home office. Her mom stood with her hands on her hips.

"Taking a walk."

Her mom glanced toward the closed door. "Aurora's not with you?"

"No."

"Do you know where she is? We missed you both at breakfast."

"I haven't seen her this morning." And wouldn't be seeing her anytime soon, either.

Her mom stepped closer, making the tension lines around her eyes more visible. "What about last night? Did you talk to her when she came in?"

"Yes."

"How did it go? Libra's worried about her."

No doubt. During the blowout the previous evening, they'd all been tossed around like sailors caught in a typhoon. "She's upset. But I think she understands why Libra made the choice to send Brendan and Micah away."

Her mom exhaled on a sigh, her shoulders relaxing. "Good. I had a feeling once the shock wore off, she'd be able to view the situation objectively."

And run off into the night, leaving only a note. "She just needs some time." Like weeks. Or maybe months. "I need to check in with the *Starhawke*." She pointed toward the staircase.

Her mom made a shooing motion with her hands. "Go, go. Don't let me keep you."

Climbing the stairs without rushing took effort, but she didn't want to tip her mom off that anything was wrong. She picked up the pace when she reached the second floor, hurrying to the privacy of her room. Closing her door, she snagged her comband off the bedside table and slipped it on. Two taps connected her with the *Starhawke*.

Celia Cardiff's face appeared as a 3D holo image above the comband, looking as beautiful and composed as a model.

"Celia, I—"

"Hold on a moment." Celia held up a hand and turned away from the camera. "Star, switch us to a secure connection."

The Nirunoc's voice drifted over the line. "Connection secure."

Celia turned back to face Mya. "Okay, what's wrong?"

Mya blinked. "How do you know something's wrong?"

"Because you hate vid calls. If you need a visual connection rather than just audio, something's very wrong."

And that's what came from having friends who knew you better than you knew yourself. "Aurora left."

"Left? She's on her way here?"

"No." Mya took a deep breath and launched into a summary of the events from the previous night, and the conclusions she'd drawn from her morning walk.

Celia listened intently without interrupting, her gaze locked on Mya's face.

"So, what do you think?" Mya asked.

"I think you and Aurora need a vacation."

Celia's unexpected response drew a soft chuckle. "Yeah. Don't we all. But I don't think a vacation is what Aurora has in mind."

"Neither do I. Can her dad help her?"

"If he can't, no one can."

"Then let's hope he's up to the task." Celia's lips thinned. "Where does that leave us? Do you want to wait here for Aurora?"

"No." She'd considered that possibility and rejected it. "There's no way to know how long that will be. I don't want to be sitting on my hands."

"Me, either. And keeping the *Starhawke* at Sol Station where Reanne's minions could start trouble isn't a good tactical move."

A trill of fear zipped through her stomach. "I hadn't thought of that." But Celia lived and breathed tactical strategy. "Any recommendations?"

"Avoid Fleet installations. And any place Reanne or the Teeli are likely to show up."

"You think we should go into hiding?"

"I think we should find a fortified position while we make our plans. We came here to deliver the Admiral and to give you and Aurora an opportunity to talk to your parents, which you've done. Is there any reason you need to stay with them?"

Mya chewed on her bottom lip. Was there? Much as she agreed with Aurora's assessment that Reanne Beck was someone to fear, it wasn't like Reanne could bring a Teeli warship to Sol Station. The Teeli claimed to be pacifists. Showing up with armed battleships would blow their cover and trigger an equally aggressive response. Earth was peaceful, but far from defenseless. The system was heavily fortified to deter Setarips.

Besides, up to now, Reanne had been working through manipulation and deceit. A full assault on Earth's defenses to reach Aurora wasn't her style. And it would take time for her to figure out another sleight of hand attack, especially when she had no idea where Aurora was.

"No, I don't need to stay. But I don't feel good leaving Aurora, either."

"Sounds to me like she expected you to."

"Maybe."

"And maybe this isn't about Aurora. Maybe it's about you."

"Me?"

"Yes, you. You've got to stop acting like a mother hen whenever Aurora has a problem."

That ruffled her feathers. "I'm just concerned. Until she learns to control her reaction to the Suulh, she's vulnerable."

"And she's working to correct that. If her dad's as powerful as you say, she'll succeed. And if Micah's presence boosts her abilities, even better. She's exactly where she needs to be."

Celia's calm logic deflated her indignation balloon. "You're right."

"Of course I am." Celia's self-deprecating smile coaxed an answering smile from Mya. "So, the question is, where do you need to be?"

Where indeed? An image of the tropical island on Azaana called to her. Raaveen and Paaw deserved to know about the new developments, about what she'd learned on the homeworld. But more than that, she needed to start asking the Suulh the tough questions she'd been avoiding while they healed from their emotional and physical trauma.

But that wouldn't be the only stop. She also needed to start gathering forces that could help her in the fight against Reanne. Against the Teeli. She needed *warriors.*

"Celia, alert Kire I'll be returning this afternoon. And tell him to assemble the crew in the conference room as soon as I arrive." She wanted backup when she announced to Jonarel they were leaving the station for Kraed space—without Aurora.

Seven

"Leaving? What do you mean you're leaving?" Libra Hawke's frown matched the same expression Mya had seen on Aurora's face a thousand times.

"I'm returning to the *Starhawke*."

Libra shot a look at Mya's mom, who stood on the other side of the raised kitchen counter.

"What about Aurora?" Mya's mom asked. "Is she going, too?"

"She's already gone."

"Gone?" Libra's mouth sagged open. "She went back to the ship?"

"No, she went to Hawaii to find Brendan and Micah. She left during the night."

Twin moons surrounded the irises of Libra's blue-grey eyes. Her hand flailed, making contact with a nearby stool. "That's why I haven't been sensing her nearby." She sank against the stool like her bones had gone liquid. "She went to Hawaii?"

"Yes. And left me in charge of the *Starhawke*."

"Left you in charge?" she parroted again. The shock slowly faded, replaced by steely determination. "You have to go get her."

Exactly the response she'd expected. "No, I don't."

Libra's brows snapped down. "What do you mean you don't? Of course you do. She needs you. You can't abandon her."

For most of her life, arguing with Libra had been unthinkable. Not anymore. "I'm not abandoning her. I'm giving her what she needs—time with Brendan to learn how to control her empathic abilities. I can't help her with that. He can. Besides, I have my own job to do."

"Which is what, exactly?"

She fought to stand tall under Libra's intense scrutiny. "Talk to Siginal Clarek." She didn't want to get drawn into an argument about her plans to talk to the Suulh on Azaana, so she left that part of the plan out. "He was in charge of the original expedition to Teeli space that located our homeworld and uncovered the Teeli subterfuge. We'll need his help if we're going to free the Suulh." Her grandmother's face appeared in her mind's eye. "All the Suulh."

Her mom straightened, her gaze troubled. "You're going to—"

"What about Reanne?" Libra interrupted. "If she's as focused on capturing Aurora as you believe, what's to stop her from tracking Aurora down and launching another attack?"

Mya reined in her irritation. Libra's desire to control Aurora's movements was now spilling over onto her. "Reanne's previous assaults have been methodical, well planned. She won't leave Teeli space half-cocked, and she can't bring her warships here. Besides, she has no way of knowing about Brendan or Micah. Until Aurora learns to control her empathic response to the Suulh, she's far safer on Earth with her dad and brother than on the *Starhawke*."

"But they can't protect—"

"She doesn't need protection!" The heat in her voice surprised her.

It surprised Libra and her mom, too. They both stared at her in disbelief.

"Reanne has tried to capture her three times, and three times she's failed. Aurora can handle herself." What she couldn't handle was her reaction to the Suulh. Or the specter of collateral damage from a confrontation. When Aurora had avoided all contact with Cade after she'd accidentally electrocuted him, her actions had made it clear she didn't fear Reanne half as much as she feared herself.

"What about you?" her mom asked, worry lines creasing her forehead. "You won't have Aurora to protect you, either."

"I know. But I'm tougher than I look." She'd learned that on the Suulh homeworld. "And I'll have Celia and Jonarel backing me up," she added, to ease her mom's fears. Her friends would die before they'd allow anyone to harm her.

Her mom stepped around the counter, stopping in front of her. "Do you want me to come with you?"

The offer was so unexpected it took a moment to process. When it did, a lump lodged in her throat. To her knowledge, her mom hadn't left Earth since before she and her dad had mated. "Thank you, but no. Whatever happens with Brendan and Micah, I'd like you both to be here if Aurora needs you."

"We will be." Her mom pulled her into a hug, squeezing until Mya's lungs started to protest. "You be safe."

Her dad took the news of her departure in stride, packing her a lunch for the trip down the coast. Libra gave her a parting hug, but it lacked warmth. Mya didn't take it personally. Libra was caught in an emotional whirlwind, buffeted by forces beyond her control, chief among them the fear that her daughter would never forgive her for her deception. Blaming Mya for leaving was easier than facing the mountain of blame and guilt she was heaping on herself.

Her mom's hug at the monorail station lasted an eternity, interrupted only when the pre-departure whistle sounded.

She eased away from her mom. "If Aurora or Brendan contact you, you'll let me know?" She didn't want to leave Aurora hanging in case her training took less time than she expected.

Her mom nodded, her smile shaky but genuine. "Be careful out there," she whispered, wiping moisture from her eyes.

She gave her mom a quick hug before stepping toward the platform. "I promise." Although since Kraed territory was in the opposite direction from Teeli space, the odds of encountering any trouble were slim.

Eight

It was early afternoon when Cade walked with the Admiral into the antechamber for President Yeoh's office suite, located in the presidential residence six blocks from GC administrative headquarters.

He'd seen plenty of images of the interior, but never set foot inside. The pictures had captured the clean, simple lines of the décor, but not the open, airy feeling of the space, or the almost Zen-like calm that pervaded every room.

A staff member led them into a formal sitting room. "The President will be with you shortly," she informed them before exiting.

Cade's gaze swept the room. Artwork of Asian influence predominated, a mixture of ancient and modern, depicting mountains and gardens. One wall had been painted with a trompe l'oeil mural of a wooden bridge spanning a sunlit stream that was so real he reached out to touch the wall to convince his brain it was an illusion.

He snatched his hand away when the wall pushed back, revealing a discreetly concealed side door that swung open on noiseless hinges.

President Yeoh appeared in the opening, her intelligent gaze meeting his. The sparkle in her dark eyes made it clear she'd timed her entrance to catch him off guard. "Very lifelike, isn't it?"

"Yes. Surveillance camera?" He nodded to the door. Her timing was too perfect to have been an accident.

"Something much simpler. Squeaky board." She stepped on the spot where he'd been standing. Sure enough, the board gave an audible high-pitched squeak.

"Ah."

"If you're limber enough and know the right spots, you can play music on these floors."

An image of the President leaping and twirling around her sitting room rendered him speechless.

The Admiral saved him. "President Yeoh was trained as a professional dancer before she decided to go into public service. I had the honor of watching her perform once."

She smiled. "That was a long time ago." She held out her hand to Cade. "It's a pleasure to see you again Mr. Ellis."

He returned her firm handshake. "I'm surprised you remember me."

"Four years ago. Dedication ceremony for the *Argo*. You attended as a guest of the Admiral and Captain Schreiber."

Sharp mind and excellent memory. "That's right."

She turned to the Admiral and extended her hand. "You're looking spry for a man who was on medical leave for two months, Will."

He clasped her hand in both of his. "Keeping track of me, Kathryn?"

"Trying to." She gestured to the seating circle before settling into one of the plush chairs. "What have you been up to?"

Cade took the seat opposite President Yeoh while the Admiral sank into the chair to her left with a sigh. "That is a very long story."

"I thought it might be. Luckily for you, I've cleared my afternoon."

"Then we'll need to start with Gaia." The Admiral launched into a detailed account of the attack on Gaia, neatly omitting any mention of Aurora's and Mya's abilities or their connection to the Necri-Suulh, but explaining Cade's role as the leader of the Elite Unit. "The investigation Knox and I completed on Gaia didn't produce any conclusive evidence that was actionable, but events since that time have filled in the blanks. The woman who masterminded the attack is Reanne Beck."

The President's sculpted brows lifted. "The former Director of the Rescue Corps?"

"That's right."

"Why attack Gaia? What was she hoping to gain?"

"She's commanding the Teeli forces."

A deafening silence filled the room. President Yeoh went perfectly still, but her eyes revealed the lightspeed processing of that piece of information. She drew in a slow breath. "How long do we have?"

Right to the point.

"I don't know. The *Starhawke* went on an information gathering mission into Teeli space—totally off the record, of course—and located the planet where the Teeli are abducting the Suulh to turn them into Necri soldiers. The entire planet is encircled by a sensor web and lethal defenses."

"I understand you arrived at Sol Station on the *Starhawke.* Were you onboard when they entered Teeli space? Is that why you put yourself on medical leave?"

"No. I had traveled to Gallows Edge to track down the Teeli connection to the Setarips and ended up as a prisoner on a Setarip ship. The *Starhawke* crew rescued me when they returned to Fleet space."

"What did you learn about the Setarips?"

"Reanne stranded the Etah leader in a junker in the Gallows Edge system and commandeered his ship and crew for the attack on Gaia. The Ecilam faction is also working for her."

She tilted her head, clearly puzzled. "Why would Teeli and Setarips work for a human?"

Cade spoke up. "We have a theory that Reanne may be half-Teeli. She definitely has the ability to manipulate people into doing her bidding, which seems to be a Teeli trait. I saw the effects firsthand on Gaia when the two RC officers under her control turned on each other and then themselves. She was able to use a simple suggestion to convince one of the officers to kill herself. We're guessing she's doing something similar with the Setarips."

"But what about the Teeli? Why are they following her? If they're the source of her manipulation abilities, they shouldn't be susceptible."

"We don't know. We're not even certain if they're aware she's human. She wears a thick cloak and uses a vocal modulator that conceals her identity."

The President's gaze sharpened. "You've seen her?"

"Yes, during the battle to rescue the Admiral."

"You were on the *Starhawke*?"

"My unit was involved, yes."

Her gaze held his, assessing. She clearly knew he was withholding details, but he couldn't say more without opening himself and his team up for potential prosecution. They had, after all, stolen *Gladiator* out of a junkyard. The fact that the owner of said junkyard was an underhanded slimeball who'd probably stolen the ship from somebody else was beside the point.

President Yeoh turned her attention to the Admiral. "What do you anticipate as Reanne's next move?"

"She favors sneak attacks where her opponent is outmatched rather than a blunt assault. I don't expect her armada to show up in Sol system anytime soon. Our planetary defenses are too strong."

"But based on her pattern, she might try to gain control over those defenses."

"And over the Council. Gaia was definitely a test. She's gauging our response, searching for weak points she can exploit."

She folded her hands, the picture of calm composure. "What actions do you propose we take?"

"First, we'll be looking for unusual behavior, orders or requests that are outside standard protocol, or abrupt changes in staffing in the GC and Fleet to figure out who is already compromised. As Director of the Rescue Corps, Reanne had interactions with a wide array of personnel in both. She's clearly used those opportunities to weaken us from within. Lt. Magee's transfer is a prime example."

"I wanted to ask you about that. I visited your office during your absence, hoping to get an update on your condition, but she wasn't there."

"According to official records, she requested a transfer to the Teeli delegation while I was gone."

"I know. Ensign Barr claimed ignorance of her whereabouts. I had to track down the transfer order in the GC database."

Cade sat up straighter. "Ensign Barr? Is that the name he gave you?" A name would give him a lead to track down the troll who'd been squatting in the Admiral's office.

Her gaze shifted to him. "You met him?"

"So oily you wanted to take a shower afterward?"

"That's the man." She turned to the Admiral. "I couldn't imagine he was your choice to replace Magee. And her transfer didn't make any more sense than your illness, so

I sent an encoded message to Knox. His reply indicated any digging on my part might put you in danger, so I backed off."

The Admiral nodded. "Ensign Barr took control of my office after Reanne's minions coerced Magee into transferring. I'll have Cade do a search when we get back to HQ, but I doubt there are any Fleet service records for him."

"I wasn't able to locate any in the GC files, either." She sat forward, gaze intent. "Are you saying Reanne Beck successfully installed someone in your office without being questioned and then scrubbed all data related to that person from the records?"

"That seems to be the case."

President Yeoh's lips flattened to a line, the first visible sign of tension. "Where is she now?"

Cade fielded that one. "In Teeli space. Or at least her ship is. One of the *Starhawke's* crew attached a tracking device to the hull." He owed Celia Cardiff for that one. She'd shared the tracking information with Reynolds, who had been monitoring the signal ever since. Unfortunately, they'd lose the signal whenever the ship was in an interstellar jump. They'd know if Reanne's ship left Teeli space, but not where she was headed.

She turned to the Admiral. "What about proof of her involvement? Do you have evidence I can bring before the Council?"

"Not regarding Reanne's role. I do have a video that ties the Teeli to the Setarips who attacked Gaia, but I don't have permission to make it public. I hope to obtain that permission soon."

"And when you do?"

"That depends on what we learn regarding any influence Reanne has exerted on members of the Council. If the Council's integrity has been compromised, bringing any information to light wouldn't help. It would only tip our hand."

"And give Reanne Beck more ammunition." She took a slow breath, her gaze focusing on a distant point. "Who do you suspect is compromised?"

Cade waded in. "My team is working on that right now. I hope to have their preliminary reports this evening."

"I'll have my preliminary report ready in a week."

He blinked. "You're going to investigate the Council?" He hadn't expected her to get involved until they had evidence to present. Her job didn't exactly leave her a lot of free time.

"Does that surprise you?"

"A little."

President Yeoh's dark eyes glinted with a soldier's resolve. "Perhaps I'm overly sensitive, but when a half-Teeli megalomaniac attempts to destroy the integrity of the Council—all it stands for, all we've worked for—I tend to take it personally."

Nine

When the monorail glided into the station near Fleet Headquarters, Mya exited quickly and made her way to the hanger where she could catch a shuttle to Sol Station.

This time, she wasn't on a private shuttle with the rest of the crew. Instead, she claimed her seat on a Fleet personnel shuttle. The woman seated by the window on her left gave her a tight smile before returning her gaze to the transportation crews moving in the hanger. Her insignia identified her as an ensign, and the fidgeting of her fingers on the armrest and at the collar of her uniform labeled her a novice.

"First assignment?" Mya guessed.

The woman glanced at her. "How did you know?"

Mya smiled. "Experience."

"How long have you been with the Fleet?"

"My first assignment was seven years ago." And in many ways, she'd been as innocent when she'd boarded the *Excelsior* as the ensign. She and Aurora both.

The woman sighed. "I hope I make it that long."

Mya rested her hand on the woman's sleeve and squeezed, allowing a gentle flow of soothing energy to surround her. "You will."

The woman's smile relaxed. "Thanks."

Mya settled into her seat and closed her eyes, the hum of the engines providing a subtle background as she sank into a meditative state. Space travel had never bothered her, but she didn't get excited about it the way

Aurora did, either. She heard the ensign's sharp inhale as the shuttle launched, felt the brush of her sleeve as she gripped the armrests. The contact allowed Mya to send another ribbon of energy to the woman, calming her anxiety as the shuttle escaped the pull of Earth's gravity.

"What is *that*?"

The ensign's startled exclamation pulled Mya out of her mental cocoon. She focused on what the ensign was pointing to outside the window.

The *Starhawke*.

"It's beautiful." The awe in the ensign's voice matched the comments from several other passengers.

The ship was anchored to the C terminal by an airbridge, but the Kraed-designed hull turned the exterior into a glittering field of diamonds on black velvet in the vague shape of a frozen waterfall.

As the shuttle glided past, the other passengers shifted to get a better view, clearly as fascinated as the ensign.

Mya hid her smile. She'd reacted the same way the first time she'd seen the ship. Jonarel had created a technological wonder encased in a stunning mobile sculpture.

Not unlike Jonarel himself. A brilliant mind contained in a breathtaking body of incredible power.

Memories of him carrying her on his back while climbing a tree on the Suulh homeworld rose unbidden, but she suppressed them. Those were not the kinds of thoughts she wanted to be having right now. Or ever. Her attraction to the *Starhawke*'s engineer was inconvenient, especially at a time when she needed to keep her wits about her and take command of the situation.

Convincing Jonarel to leave Aurora behind while they traveled to Azaana and his homeworld wouldn't be easy, but the note from Aurora tucked in her pocket was her ace in the hole. When he objected—and he would—she'd make it clear Aurora had made her the acting captain of the *Starhawke*. No matter his personal feelings, Jonarel would never disobey a direct order from Aurora, even tangentially.

And she needed his help. Siginal Clarek had a wealth of information about the Suulh and the Teeli, but she wasn't at all convinced he would willingly share it. He'd kept his knowledge and motivations hidden from her and Aurora while acting as their friend, including Jonarel as a key figure in his manipulations and placing him in a no-win scenario. She still wasn't clear on Siginal's endgame, which put him in limbo between adversary and ally. Only Jonarel could guide her in determining the truth.

The shuttle settled onto the deck of the landing bay, the engines powering down.

"First step," the ensign murmured, unstrapping her harness and standing.

Mya did the same. "That's always the hardest."

The ensign returned her smile. "Safe travels."

"You, too." Mya snagged her pack from the storage compartment on the way to the ramp, following the other Fleet personnel off the shuttle and out into the station.

They'd docked at B9, which put her a short hike from the *Starhawke*. The mix of Fleet personnel and civilian passengers flowed steadily as she made her way to the C concourse and the security scanner for the *Starhawke*'s berth. The outer door for the airbridge parted after she was granted access.

The ship's hull didn't resemble black velvet from this angle, but rather the gunmetal grey of the airbridge. It also looked seamless, but as she approached, a doorway materialized, opening before she reached it.

Star appeared on the other side as Mya stepped through. Her dark hair was swept back in a braid that looked remarkably similar to the style Aurora favored but longer, falling halfway down her back. Apparently the Nirunoc was experimenting with her visual projection. "Welcome back."

"Thank you. Has Kire gathered the crew?"

"Yes. They are waiting for you in the conference room."

"Does Jonarel know Aurora's not with me?"

Tension lines formed around Star's mouth. "Not yet."

That would be a fun conversation.

She sent an encrypted message to Aurora's comband before heading up to the conference room, giving her a projected timetable for the journey to Kraed space, but didn't receive a response. Not that she'd expected one. Aurora wasn't likely to be in the mood to talk yet.

Jonarel looked up when Mya entered the conference room on the command deck, his golden-hued gaze sweeping over her and then glancing behind her into the corridor. The corners of his lips turned down. "Where is Aurora?"

He and Kire sat on either side of the conspicuously vacant chair Aurora normally occupied at the round table, with Bronwyn Kelly next to Kire and Celia beside Jonarel.

Might as well start as she planned to proceed. Mya slid back the vacant chair and sat. "Aurora won't be joining us for this trip."

Jonarel's transformation from calm engineer to growling guard dog made her flinch. "Where is she?"

"With her father."

Kire jerked in his chair. "Her father? But he's dead."

Mya shook her head. "He's alive. So is Aurora's brother, Micah."

Kire blinked. "She has a brother?"

"Yes."

"Did she know?"

"No."

Kire let loose with an earthy swear word, a rarity for him. "More damn secrets." His eyes narrowed, assessing. "Is he older or younger?"

"Older."

"Then did you know about him?"

"Yes."

He smacked the table with his palm, his normally jovial expression transformed by the heat of anger. "Why the hell didn't you ever tell Roe?"

"I was forbidden to say a word. Libra swore us all to secrecy. To protect Aurora."

A low growl made her turn. Jonarel's lips had pulled back from his teeth, but his expression indicated pain rather than menace. He had personal experience keeping the truth from Aurora under the guise of protecting her. And he'd seen how strongly she rejected those behaviors.

"I don't understand." Kire rested his forearms on the table. "Why did Roe need protection from her dad and brother?"

"That wasn't the reason." She drew in a slow breath. Repetition of the story wasn't making it any easier. "Micah doesn't share Aurora's shielding abilities, but he enhances her skills, making her more powerful. Before Aurora was two, they were already drawing attention in our community. My mom and I often had to use our abilities to calm the energy outbursts Aurora and Micah would generate when they were playing. Even with our help, the odd occurrences were getting harder to explain to anyone who witnessed them, so Libra had curtailed how much she took Aurora and Micah out in public."

"Huh." Kire cocked his head. "For some reason I'd assumed Roe had always been keeping her abilities secret."

"Hardly. As a toddler, she loved using them when she was with Micah because the results were impressive, though erratic. I was working with her to help her learn control, just as my mom had worked with Libra when she was a child. But Aurora was... precocious." Willful, stubborn, and mischievous also applied, at least until Brendan had taken Micah away.

"She still is." Kire said, the faintest wisp of a smile on his lips. "What made her dad and brother leave?"

"The Teeli. When they made contact with the Fleet, Libra was terrified. She believed that if Aurora and Micah stayed together, news of their unusual behavior might reach the Teeli. She convinced Brendan that the only way to keep them safe was to split them up. Brendan took Micah to Hawaii."

Kire's thin brows drew together. "Damn. Roe must have been devastated."

"She was." Memories of those long days and longer nights still haunted her.

Jonarel's chair creaked as he leaned back, his hands folded over his taut abdomen. "Aurora did not remember she had a brother?"

"For a while she did." She swallowed past the constriction in her throat. Admitting her role in the deception wasn't easy, either. She glanced at Celia, who gave her an encouraging nod. "She'd cry out his name, which she couldn't pronounce fully. She called him My-a."

She peeked at Jonarel. A look of understanding lit his golden eyes, but she didn't see any condemnation. At least not yet. She plowed on.

"I moved into the room they'd shared and did everything I could to help her deal with her grief. Over time, she started to associate the name My-a with me, something

Libra encouraged. Once Aurora started calling me Mya, memories of her brother blended into her memories of me."

"And the rest is history," Kire murmured.

"Yes."

He studied her for a moment, his gaze thoughtful. "Well, at least she'll finally get to see Hawaii."

Leave it to Kire to find the silver lining.

"How long is she planning to stay?"

"I don't know. She's hoping Brendan can teach her how to control the empathic reaction she has to the Suulh. If she has to fight Kreestol, or any of the other Suulh, she wants to be prepared."

"Why would he be teaching her instead of her mom?"

"Because her empathic abilities come from him, not Libra."

"Really? That's not part of being the Sahzade?"

Mya shook her head.

"Fascinating." Kire tapped his index finger on the tabletop. "So, where does that leave us? Are we waiting here?"

"No." Mya reached into her pocket and pulled out the envelope containing the note from Aurora. "She left me in charge of the ship." She turned to Jonarel. "We're going to Azaana and Drakar."

Surprise quickly shifted to wariness on Jonarel's handsome face. "Why Drakar?"

Mya folded her hands to hide a slight tremble. "Because I'm not going to leave my grandmother and the rest of the Suulh to whatever fate Reanne has in store for them. I'm tired of stumbling around in the dark and falling into her traps. The Admiral indicated your father coordinated the secret expeditions into Teeli space when the Teeli applied for Council membership. We need to learn everything he knows about the Teeli so we can figure out how Reanne managed to gain power over their forces." She paused. "Unless you already have those answers?"

The question wasn't meant as an attack, but he flinched anyway. "I do not. My father shared what he knew about Aurora and you, but very little regarding the Teeli. And nothing about Reanne."

"I doubt he knew of her involvement. The Admiral certainly didn't."

Reanne had hoodwinked them all. Aurora had been so close to stopping her. And if Mya had been there, backing her up, she might have succeeded. But Mya had chosen to save the Admiral's life instead. That decision had allowed their adversaries to escape to Teeli space.

Aurora didn't blame her. In fact, she'd made it clear she would have given the same order if she'd known. But her understanding didn't let Mya off the hook.

Jonarel's gaze shifted to the viewport, where the blue-green curve of Earth hung below them. "I should remain with Aurora."

Yep, she'd seen this coming. "To protect her?"

"Yes."

"No."

The force of her denial made him turn.

"Aurora can protect herself."

His full lips pinched, his dark brows drawing down. "What about Reanne? She could—"

"Reanne has no idea where Aurora is. And no knowledge of Brendan or Micah. If we leave Earth, Reanne will logically assume Aurora's with us on the *Starhawke*. We'll be drawing attention away from her true location, which will give her the time she needs with Brendan. Your presence in Hawaii would be a neon sign flashing *look here*."

Jonarel's scowl deepened, but her logic was irrefutable. He didn't voice any more objections.

She glanced at Celia, Kire, and Kelly. "Any questions?"

Kire lifted his hand. "When do we leave?"

"As soon as we get clearance from the station."

Ten

Cade shortened his stride as he and the Admiral joined the congested flow of Fleet and Council personnel entering and exiting GC Headquarters. Passing through the spacious lobby, they continued to the lifts, stepping off at Fleet HQ on the tenth floor.

One of the security officers at the sign-in station broke into a wide smile when he spotted the Admiral. "Admiral Schreiber! Wonderful to see you back, sir."

The Admiral held out his ID for scanning. "Wonderful to be back, Mr. Dorn. How are the kids?"

"Rowdy as always. Michael lost his first baby tooth the other day." He pressed his palm to his chest. "Gets me right here when he grins with that big gap."

"I'll bet."

Cade held out his ID, the one that identified him as a Fleet Commander.

Dorn scanned it. "Thank you, Commander."

Cade followed the Admiral through the hallways. The Admiral responded to the well-wishes expressed by those they passed. Clearly his absence had been a cause for concern for many Fleet personnel.

The door to the Admiral's office suite stood open as they approached, the interior lights on. Cade recognized the woman behind the reception desk from the photograph the Admiral had shown him.

Lieutenant Valenzuela rose as soon as her gaze settled on the Admiral. "Admiral Schreiber. It's a pleasure to meet you, sir."

The Admiral extended his hand and she moved forward to shake it. "You as well, Lieutenant. This is Commander Ellis, one of my most trusted officers."

"Nice to meet you, Commander."

Cade shook her hand. She had a firm grip and a steady gaze. No sign of recognition for his name or face. If she was part of Reanne's network of informants, she was hiding it well.

She turned back to the Admiral. "I've been unable to locate any information or communications in Lieutenant Magee's files relating to the past six weeks. Do you know if she moved them offsite while you were on medical leave?"

The Admiral's poker face gave nothing away. "She may have. I'll check with her. In the meantime, please find out if Admiral Payne is in her office. If so, I want to see her in ten minutes."

"Yes, sir."

Valenzuela returned to her desk while Cade followed the Admiral into his office. As soon as the door closed, Cade removed the handheld device Drew had given him and began scanning the interior.

The Admiral settled in at his desk but remained silent. The only sound in the room came from a soft ping when Valenzuela sent a message. Cade glanced at it as he passed the device over the desk. Payne would be arriving on schedule.

Five minutes later, he'd finished his sweep. Three dime-sized, deactivated audio-visual transmitters now sat in a pile on the Admiral's desk.

The Admiral's brows lifted.

Cade nodded. "The room is clean."

"Whoever was tasked with monitoring these feeds will know we found them."

"And may attempt to replace them. Or gain access another way." He glanced at the ceiling and floor. "Maybe from above or below."

"Very possible. But that doesn't concern me. My day-to-day activities won't provide scintillating viewing. This meeting, however, could."

A chime sounded. The Admiral acknowledged it with a tap. "Yes?"

"Admiral Payne has arrived."

Cade gathered the transmitters and slipped them into his pocket.

The Admiral stood. "Send her in."

Cade retreated to the far wall and faced the door as Payne entered, his muscles tightening in battle-readiness. Admiral or not, she was a threat. She'd deliberately sent Aurora into an ambush. He wanted to know why.

Despite the fact that the top of her head wouldn't even reach his chin, her commanding presence made her appear statuesque. She'd earned the respect and admiration of her peers during her long career as a Fleet officer and captain of the *Excalibur.* He'd observed her at several Fleet functions over the years, but never been formally introduced, since the Admiral liked to keep the members of his unit under the radar as much as possible.

Her dark-eyed gaze leapt from the Admiral to him and back again, a small tell she quickly concealed. But her bright smile looked brittle. "Welcome back, Admiral. Good to see you looking well."

Cade watched her as the Admiral delivered his opening gambit.

"Thank you. I understand you've had some challenges recently, too. I was sorry to hear your grandson was hospitalized. How is he?"

Payne's smile faded, tension pinching her lips. "The doctors were able to stabilize him, but he's still in the ICU."

"Was it an accident?"

"Yes." Payne swallowed, her voice growing hollow. "An accident while running."

"What's the prognosis?"

"Uncertain." A muscle in her jaw twitched. "He has severe brain trauma, internal bleeding. They're keeping him heavily medicated for the pain. My son's still deciding whether to proceed with surgery. His vitals are weak. There's a good chance he wouldn't survive the operation."

"How old is he?" the Admiral asked.

"Almost sixteen."

Sixteen. Far too young to be in a fight for his life.

The timing was too convenient for coincidence, and Payne's delivery too practiced for believability. She'd been coached on what to say. Or more specifically, what *not* to say.

Cold steel wrapped around Cade's ribcage as Reanne's foul presence settled into the room like a wraith. He had no doubt she'd been responsible for the boy's supposed accident, a strong-arm move designed to prove to Payne she meant business. She was holding the teenager's life in her hands to keep Payne dancing like a puppet on a string.

The grim expression on Admiral Schreiber's face indicated he'd reached the same conclusion. "I know an exceptional doctor who specializes in trauma. I'd be happy to arrange for her to give a second opinion."

Or a healing that would restore the boy to complete health. Mya Forrest had that power.

Payne's jaw continued to twitch. "I'd have to check with the trauma unit first. But thank you for the offer."

Her reluctance indicated Reanne might have told her she'd kill the boy outright if Payne tried to intervene.

The Admiral seemed to get that message too, because he didn't push. "Just let me know." He gestured to the chairs in front of his desk. "Please, have a seat."

She chose the chair farthest from Cade and closest to the door. Her gaze drifted to Cade in a move that was meant to be casual but came off as furtive. "I don't believe we've been introduced."

Cade gave her a closed-mouth smile. Now that they understood how compromised she was, Admiral Schreiber would need to decide what information to reveal. "No, we haven't."

Her dark brows rose at his non-answer. She glanced at Admiral Schreiber.

He folded his hands, his smile warmer than Cade's. "Commander Ellis is here at my request."

"Commander?" Payne looked Cade up and down, clearly trying to place him.

She wouldn't be able to. All of his Fleet records were classified for the Fleet Director's eyes only, as were those of his entire unit. A search of the Fleet database would reveal nothing except his security clearance. Only his service in the Rescue Corps was part of the public record. But since Reanne already knew his identity and the details of his work with the Elite Unit, there was no harm in telling Payne his name and rank.

Admiral Schreiber cleared his throat, drawing Payne's focus back to him. "I called you in to discuss the survey mission you assigned to Captain Hawke and her crew."

Payne's mahogany skin greyed slightly, but her gaze didn't waver. "I'm sure you had your reasons for pulling them off of it. However, we missed a rare opportunity." Her tone had a bite. The attack on her grandson had probably been punishment for her failure to deliver Aurora and the *Starhawke*. "And caused an incident with the Teeli delegation. They were outraged that we accepted their generous offer and then ignored it."

And Payne's grandson had paid the price. Her conflicting loyalties between her family and the Fleet had to be tearing her apart.

"I understand. I'm sorry for putting you in a difficult position. I take full responsibility." Genuine regret lined the Admiral's face. "I assure you, the reassignment was necessary and unavoidable. However, I'm hoping all is not lost. I would like to apologize to the delegates in person. Do you think they'd be open to a meeting with me? Perhaps I could convince them to allow us to go forward with the survey."

Cade almost swallowed his tongue. Had the Admiral lost his mind? He was seriously considering sending Aurora into Teeli space?

Payne straightened. "It might take some convincing, but I believe that could be arranged." A glimmer of hope lit her dark eyes. "They were eager to see what the *Starhawke*'s advanced technology could reveal about the system."

And get their hands on Aurora and her ship. Reanne's minions would leap at the chance to set another snare. What was the Admiral's plan?

"If you can arrange the meeting with the Teeli delegates, then I will speak with Captain Hawke about rescheduling the mission, perhaps for after the new year."

Payne rose, her gaze shifting briefly to Cade before answering the Admiral. "I'll contact the Teeli as soon as I return to my office."

Cade kept his expression neutral, but his mind raced at lightspeed. A meeting with the Teeli would mean a trip to the embassy. The Teeli never left the grounds except to attend Council meetings. All other business involving the Teeli was conducted in their personal sanctum.

The official explanation was that the light from the Sun was too intense for their eyes and skin. He'd bought that explanation until Reynolds had filled him in on the *Starhawke*'s visit to the Suulh homeworld. She'd described the Teeli's buildings of glass and metal, and how they'd paraded down the Suulh streets like they owned them, abusing the older Suulh who worked as slave labor. Exposing themselves to sunlight certainly had *not* been an issue.

He could guess the real reason for the seclusion. It gave the Teeli the perfect setting to keep their activities hidden from the Council and any nosy humans who might start asking uncomfortable questions. Or realize they weren't the benevolent pacifists they claimed to be.

The Admiral stood as well. "That's wonderful. This week would be preferable."

"I'll see what I can arrange."

Cade waited until the door clicked behind her and her footsteps faded before he turned to the Admiral. "You want to send Aurora into Teeli space?"

The Admiral's brows rose. "Good heavens, no. Why would you think that?"

Cade blinked. "Because you just said—"

The Admiral waved him off. "Oh, that. I wanted to buy Payne some breathing room while we figure out a way to keep her grandson safe."

"I see. How do you propose we do that?"

"With Dr. Forrest's help, of course. Unfortunately, the *Starhawke* just left Sol Station."

"What?" Aurora was gone? His gaze shot to the ceiling—a ludicrous reaction—but one he couldn't control. "Why did they leave?"

"The message from Commander Emoto didn't specify, just that they were leaving the system and could be reached through the Kraed network."

"When did he send it?"

"While you were securing the room."

"And you waited until now to tell me?"

The Admiral tilted his head, the look in his eyes questioning Cade's tone.

He backpedaled. He needed to start thinking with his head, not his heart. And remember that the Admiral was his commanding officer. "I'm sorry. I just hate not knowing where she is." No need to specify which *she* he was referring to.

"I understand. Neither do I. But I learned a valuable lesson about Aurora during our captivity onboard Tnaryt's ship. Her bottomless well of empathy for those she loves is her greatest strength. It's also her greatest weakness. She does a much better job of taking care of herself when we stay out of her way."

Cade opened his mouth to object, then closed it. The Admiral had a point. If Aurora hadn't been so distraught over accidentally electrocuting him, would the shock of Reanne's betrayal have hit her so hard? Could she have succeeded in capturing Reanne if she hadn't been worried about him? Was he a liability to her, instead of an asset?

The Admiral came around the desk and rested a hand on his shoulder. "Don't overthink this. I'm not saying you should leave Aurora alone. Far from it. You give her strength when she needs it most. I'm just saying we both need to give her some space and let her decide when to ask for our help."

Cade grimaced. "What if she doesn't?"

The Admiral chuckled. "Patience, Mr. Ellis. When she's ready, she will. Thankfully you have plenty to keep you occupied until then. Like meeting with the Teeli delegates."

"I was wondering about that."

"Assuming they take the bait—which I'm sure they will—you'll be coming with me."

"Entering the Embassy is a big risk, given the Teeli's ability to manipulate people. You and I would be prime targets."

"Targets, yes. Risky, no." The Admiral moved back to his chair and sat down. "We're immune."

"Immune?"

"Absolutely. If we weren't, Reanne would already have control of the Fleet."

Cade frowned. "I'm not following."

"Reanne has already tried to manipulate me and failed, although I didn't understand what she was doing at the time. Whatever power she wields to affect behavior, it has no effect on me. Or you, apparently. If it did, she would have taken advantage of the situation while you were on Gaia."

The importance of what the Admiral was saying sunk in. "If that's true, something's changed."

"Changed?"

"I was susceptible to her during my Academy days, back when Aurora and I were first dating. She turned me against Aurora. I don't even remember exactly how, just that I was consumed with suspicion and jealousy. It sucked the joy out of our relationship until only anger and pain remained." An echo of that pain reverberated in his chest. Reanne was still a toxic presence in their relationship, pushing Aurora to keep her distance from him.

"Interesting." The Admiral tapped the tips of his fingers together. "So Reanne's influence can be overcome. I'd feared it was an all-or-nothing proposition."

"It can't be. She wanted information from me while we were on Gaia, but I felt no compulsion to give it to her. Quite the opposite."

"Do you recall specifically what she said or did when you were together?"

He called up the memory, replaying it like a private movie in his head. "She asked me questions about Aurora. Wanted to know if being around her again was difficult."

"How did you respond?"

"I answered her questions with questions." A small smile tugged at his lips. "She didn't like that."

"I can imagine."

"She said she was worried about me. I'm not sure I even believed her at the time. She told me that if I needed to talk, she was there for me."

The Admiral lifted one brow. "And you didn't respond?"

"No. I'd confided in her regarding Aurora once before, and everything had gone to hell. I wasn't about to do it again."

"What did she do?"

"Got right in front of me and put her hand on my arm, acting concerned and sympathetic."

The Admiral's gaze sharpened. "And what did you do?"

"I pulled away."

"Did that surprise her?"

"Sure. She seemed..." He trailed off as he caught the thread the Admiral was dangling in front of him. The memory crystalized in his mind. "She touched me. Got up from her desk and created an excuse to touch me."

"How did you feel in that moment?"

"Like she was trying to crawl under my skin. The sensation was familiar, but in a negative way. I knew I didn't want to be there again. That's why I stepped back."

"And prevented her from influencing you."

He held the Admiral's gaze. "Do you think that's how she does it? With touch?"

"I think that's when she's strongest. I suspect she also gives off some kind of pheromone that subconsciously makes people more susceptible to suggestion."

Lightbulbs went off. "Like the RC guard on Gaia. She was in physical contact with Reanne, holding her hostage. Reanne kept talking to her, telling her it was hopeless. At the time, I thought Reanne was trying to convince her to let her go. But she was actually planting a subconscious suggestion. Seconds later the guard shot herself."

"Eliminating a potential witness to her crimes."

A thousand tiny spiders crawled over Cade's skin. "So why would those same manipulations now act as a repellent on me?"

"Her influence cost you precious time with Aurora. You couldn't see it then, but the trauma of your separation from Aurora seems to have forced your body to imprint the sensation of Reanne's influence as negative. Now you subconsciously avoid it, rather than being drawn to it."

"That's good news." He'd harbored a secret dread that Reanne would have the power to regain control over him. "Do you think I'd have the same reaction to all Teeli manipulation?"

"I believe so, based on your description of your experiences. That's why I want you with me for this meeting."

Cade braced his palms on the desk. "Why are you immune?"

"That's a question I can't answer. I've spent long hours in close proximity with the Teeli delegates and with Reanne, and have never suffered any ill effects, even when we came in physical contact with each other. Perhaps some people have a natural immunity."

"Aurora certainly does. Reanne must have tried to influence her a thousand times while they were roommates, especially after Aurora started to distance herself, but it clearly didn't work."

"Which is another piece of good news. Aurora under Reanne's control would be a worst-case scenario."

He hadn't even considered the possibility.

The Admiral obviously had. "Thankfully, that's not something we need to worry about. And we have other items in our favor regarding Reanne. She and the Teeli have no idea the *Starhawke* visited the Suulh homeworld, or that Aurora knows about Reanne's connection with the Teeli. That gives us an advantage."

"But no proof of their hostile intentions, or of Reanne's connection to the Teeli."

"We have Aurora's testimony. She saw Reanne, confirmed her identity."

"After she ignored her Fleet-assigned mission from Payne, helped my unit steal *Gladiator* from a junkyard, and met up with a smuggler on Gallows Edge while looking for you. There's no way we could allow those facts to come to light. It would put you both in a compromising position."

The Admiral leaned back in his chair. "I see your point."

"We need proof, an irrefutable link between Reanne, the Teeli, and the attack on Gaia."

Too bad Reanne had learned from her mistakes. On Gaia, his unit had been able to recover the bodies of the dead Setarips, unknowingly connecting Reanne to the Etah faction. But the guards who'd died defending Reanne during the recent jungle battle had become gelatinous and unrecognizable as humanoid, let alone Teeli, by the time he and Justin had checked on them. Scans had indicated the mesh cloth covering them from head to toe had released some kind of corrosive agent after they'd died, which had rapidly dissolved their bodies.

The Admiral nodded. "I'm hoping our meeting with the Teeli will move that goal forward. Unfortunately, in exposing Reanne, we also risk exposing Aurora's abilities and the existence of the Suulh. Reanne will never go quietly."

Cade massaged his forehead, where a tension headache was building steam. "So, what's our next move?"

"That will partially depend on what we hear from Payne and what your team has learned regarding the Council delegates."

Cade checked the chronometer on his comband. "They're due back at your house by eighteen-hundred hours. That gives us an hour."

"Which I'll spend attending to Fleet business." He glanced toward the closed door to the reception area. "I need to find out what other personnel changes have been made in my absence."

Cade stood. "And I'm going to learn a bit more about your new PA. I'll meet you in the lobby in an hour."

The Admiral nodded, already pulling up personnel files on his desk.

Lieutenant Valenzuela looked up as Cade exited the Admiral's office. "Does the Admiral need something?"

Cade gave her his most affable smile. "Just me out of his hair. He has a lot of catching up to do."

Valenzuela returned his smile, the friendliness in the gesture making her look at least ten years younger than the age listed in her Fleet file. "I understand. I was a bit surprised by the disarray in the files. The Admiral strikes me as a man who prefers order."

"I think his absence and Lt. Magee's transfer created some communication breakdowns."

"Well, I'll have it all shipshape in no time."

"He'll appreciate that." He gestured to a picture on her desk that showed a dark-haired boy and girl who shared her dark eyes and copper skin. "Cute kids."

Her smile widened. "My grandkids. My son and daughter-in-law moved to this area earlier this year. I grabbed the opportunity to put in a transfer request so we could be near each other. I didn't expect it to be approved so quickly." She glanced at the closed door. "Or to be taking over as the Fleet Director's PA."

"What was your last posting?" He already knew, thanks to her personnel file, but he wanted to keep the conversation going.

"PA for the Head of R&D in the Singapore office."

"Impressive. You must have a science background."

"Engineering."

"Then you'll do well with the Admiral. Engineering is his specialty, too."

But her family connections could be a vulnerability, as Payne's situation had demonstrated.

She nodded. "I know. I studied his service record after I received the assignment."

Detail-oriented, too.

"What about you, Commander? Which department are you with?"

Not a question he could answer. He shifted away from the desk. "Long story. I'll let the Admiral fill you in." Or not. Trust wasn't a luxury the Admiral could afford at the moment. "I've gotta run." He gave Valenzuela a wave and exited through the open door.

Eleven

Aurora awoke to the soft patter of rain on palm fronds. A quick glance confirmed the sun was still up, although the chronometer on her comband indicated she'd been out for hours.

Her stomach grumbled, reminding her she'd gone almost twenty-four hours without eating.

Another sign she wasn't acting sensibly.

The comband also showed a message from Mya. She hesitated for a moment before opening it.

Sahzade, we're going to Azaana and Drakar to talk to the Suulh and Siginal about the Teeli. Back in two weeks or less. I hope you're finding the answers you need.

Interesting. Mya wasn't wasting any time making a plan to move forward. And she must have convinced Jonarel to go along with it. She'd half expected Mya to show up at her hotel room. Or to send a message asking her to return to the *Starhawke.* Instead, she was gathering the troops and leaving the system.

A small smile tugged at her lips. Good thing she'd stipulated in her note that the ship was only on loan until she returned. Mya was getting a lot more comfortable taking command.

After a quick shower, she dressed in clean clothes and headed down to the street. Her neutral-toned long-sleeved tunic, pants, and boots didn't blend with the lightweight, brightly-colored clothing worn by most of the people she passed, although it wasn't as incongruous as it would have been in summer. If she wasn't able to connect with her father tomorrow, she'd need to look into some alterations to her wardrobe.

She caught a ride on one of the trams, stepping off when it arrived at the beach. A cart vendor fulfilled her food needs with a sandwich and fresh fruit, which she took with her as she walked through the sand toward the water.

Settling onto an open space among the other beachgoers, she gazed out at the vista as she ate. She'd always loved the ocean—the rumble of crashing waves, the briny scent in the air, the tactile pleasure of the water racing over her toes. Saltwater was a great purifier too, both physically and energetically.

But after her recent experience in the saltwater river, there was no way in hell she was going anywhere near the waterline, no matter how much she craved its soothing touch.

Maybe she'd generate her own saltwater with a workout later.

Surfers dotted the rolling waves, their darker shapes easily visible against the aquamarine water. A group of three women and two men drew her attention. It didn't take long to realize that their skills at navigating the waves far surpassed those around them, but it was the vibrant joy and playfulness of their emotions that called to her. While the general emotional resonance around the beach was one of happiness and contentment, what she sensed from the group was much stronger, more intense.

Their laughter carried on the breeze. Their shouted comments were unintelligible over the crashing waves, but their easy camaraderie brought a lump to her throat. It was so achingly familiar, reminding her of what she'd lost.

She'd had that with her crew, in the beginning. Before the lies had surfaced. Before the shadows had descended. Before the weight of the cosmos had fallen on her shoulders.

She swallowed, almost gagging as her throat constricted. *Get a grip, Aurora.* Yes, the future seemed bleak, but that's why she'd come here in the first place. She needed to rally whatever forces she could muster so that the next time Reanne's minions attacked, she'd be prepared.

The food in her hand had lost all flavor, but she polished it off anyway. She needed the energy.

Brushing the crumbs from her fingers, she slipped off her boots and dug her toes into the sand. Better. The tickle of the tiny granules streaming over her feet grounded her. Standing, she picked up her boots and strolled along the beach, staying well clear of the wet sand.

The group of surfers she'd been watching were coming out of the water toward her. Four of them, anyway. One of the men had remained behind, paddling back toward the waves.

"Hey, Stone!" one of the women shouted over her shoulder. "Don't you know when to quit?"

"One more run!" he yelled back, his arms stroking into the water.

Aurora paused to watch as the other four surfers drew closer.

The dark-haired woman who'd spoken glanced at her as she set her board upright in the sand near a pile of towels and a cooler. "Do you surf?"

"No, just observing."

"Well, you picked a good time. Stone can't resist performing for an audience."

"Oh?"

"Yeah. He's the best surfer on the island."

She'd already pegged him as the most talented member of the group, but the woman's emotional field indicated she was about to see something special.

Facing the water, she watched as he moved into position to catch an incoming wave. But as it rolled in, she spotted six other dark shapes in the curl of the water. "Are those—"

"Dolphins? Yep."

The man rose onto his board with fluid grace, three of the dolphins on either side of him as he caught the wave.

Aurora held her breath as he glided along the edge of the wave, his body and the board moving as one, dipping and pivoting, the dolphins adjusting their paths so they stayed in near perfect formation, their silver bodies glistening in the sun. It looked like a choreographed ballet, the epitome of grace and harmony. And the fierce joy pouring off of him nearly drowned her.

Aurora's heart pounded as the performance reached a crescendo and the wave broke, bringing the dance to an end. When the surfer reappeared, he was lying on his belly on his board, coasting in toward shore.

"Show off!" the woman called out, grinning.

His answering laugh made Aurora smile, too. He slid off his board and stood. "Hey, just because you can't do it Birdie, doesn't mean I shouldn't."

"Yeah, yeah." The woman shook her head in mock disgust as the other surfers joined in the good-natured ribbing. Clearly the group had played out this scene before.

Aurora tried not to stare as the man emerged from the water and strode toward her, but it was a challenge. He was gorgeous—about her age, with a tanned, muscular body. He shook his head, flinging water droplets off like a dog, which spattered his friends, and her.

He stopped when he noticed her. "Oh. Sorry." He ran a hand through his wet hair, flinging more water down his back. "Did I get you?"

"A little. But I won't melt."

He grinned, showing perfectly straight teeth that would make any dentist proud. "Glad to hear it." His chin dipped as he looked her up and down. "You're not exactly dressed for the beach."

"This was a spur-of-the-moment decision."

"Best kind. When'd you get in?"

"How do you know I'm visiting?"

One brow lifted. "Anyone from the islands would have a swimsuit in their pack or under their clothes. I'm guessing you don't."

"Correct." And he was incredibly perceptive. "I take it you're a local?"

"Yep. I grew up on this beach." His easy-going manner fit that image.

"That explains why you're such an amazing surfer."

"I do all right." He stuck his board in the sand and accepted a towel from one of his friends, running it briskly over his hair. "You know anything about surfing?"

"Not a thing. I grew up in California."

He settled the towel around his neck. "There's surfing there."

"Not on the northern coast."

"And you never went south?"

"Not as a kid." Her mother had always found reasons to go north or east on their rare trips.

"What about as an adult?"

"I've been a little... busy."

"Hmm." He pursed his lips. "How long are you here for?"

"I'm not sure."

"Well, if you can find a couple hours in the afternoon day after tomorrow, I'd be happy to take you out and show you the basics." His grin reappeared. "Hawaii's where surfing was started. It's the best place for a first experience."

She grinned back. She couldn't help it. His attitude was infectious, even if the thought of stepping in the water gave her chills. "Would the dolphins be joining us?"

She hadn't noticed them before they'd appeared for the big finale, but maybe they'd been out there all along.

"They don't usually take an interest in beginners. But they'd probably make an exception for you."

"Why's that?"

His grin widened. "Because you're pretty."

She laughed. "Flattery will not help your cause."

"Hey, you can't blame a guy for stating the obvious."

He was flirting with her, but completely without guile. She hadn't tuned into his emotions intentionally, but they flowed over her just the same. He was enjoying her company as much as she was enjoying his.

"Don't let him fool you," the dark-haired woman said. "The dolphins always show up when Stone's here."

Aurora glanced at her. "Really? Why?"

"They have a thing for him."

"How so?"

The woman gestured to Stone. "Why don't you explain it, Professor. After all, you're the marine life expert here."

A tremor zipped up Aurora's spine.

Oh, no.

He faced her. "It's simple, really. I talk to them."

The tremor turned into a quake as she stared at the man in front of her, really looking for the first time. Blond hair. Square jaw. And green eyes that exactly matched her own.

Twelve

Micah.

She recognized the shadow of a small boy in the man standing before her.

The intense emotions. The pull of connection. Why hadn't she realized?

She backed up so quickly that she tripped over her own feet and fell onto the loose sand.

"Are you okay?" He took a step forward.

She was quicker, scrambling up like he was coming at her with a machete. If he touched her...

"Fine," she mumbled, snatching her boots from where she'd dropped them. She could feel his confusion like it was her own. The power of the link, the pull he exerted on her, threatened to root her to the spot.

She had to leave. Now.

She avoided his gaze as she backed away. "I just remembered I have to be somewhere." Lamest excuse ever, but it didn't matter. She had to put distance between them.

She pivoted, plowing her way up the beach as quickly as her feet would take her through the loose sand. Which wasn't nearly fast enough. She sensed his approach before he called out to her.

"Hey! Hang on."

"I have to go." She picked up the pace. Or tried to. Only a few more meters to the sidewalk.

He was closing in. She could feel it. She wasn't going to make it.

She jerked her arm away on instinct, spinning around to face him.

His hand passed through air where her arm had been a second earlier. Close call.

She took a step back, staying out of reach as his emotions buffeted her. Confusion. Concern. And scariest of all, awareness. He was sensing something from her, too.

He halted, his gaze locking with hers. "Have we met before?"

He asked it as a question, but his emotions said he already knew the answer. He just hadn't figured out the source.

How to answer? "I know your father." What was she thinking, telling him that? She mentally smacked her forehead with her palm.

"Oh. Are you one of his students?"

No, I'm his daughter.

The words almost slid from her lips before she caught them. She'd never felt such a strong compulsion to tell the complete and unvarnished truth. It was like he was a human lie detector set on maximum strength. Misleading him was the best she could manage, and it took every iota of willpower she possessed. "At one time." Her dad must have taught her things when she was a child.

"I see."

Except he didn't. And it was bothering him. A lot.

"I have to go," she repeated, taking a tentative step back.

He took a step forward, though it seemed to be more instinctual than a conscious choice. "Wait." His brows pulled down, his gaze searching hers. "Please. Who are you?"

Aurora. Your sister.

Every cell in her body wanted to scream it. But she wrestled the impulse to the ground. "It's a long story."

He ran a hand through his damp hair, the same shade of dark blond as their father's. "I'd like to hear it."

She shook her head. "I really have to go." *Please, Micah. Don't push me.*

His gaze grew more intense, almost as though he'd heard her. "All right. Would you meet me for dinner later? You can tell me then."

She started to shake from the effort of keeping her distance and her silence, clutching her hands at her sides. The pull to reveal the truth, to reach out and touch him and complete the connection, was so strong it stole her breath. "That's not a good idea."

"Why not?" His lips quirked up. "I have excellent table manners."

His flash of amusement swept over her, catching her off guard. A smile rose unbidden to her lips. "I can't." *But I want to, more than you'll ever know.* Which proved just how much danger she was in. She backed toward the sidewalk.

He followed. "How about tomorrow? Are you free for lunch?"

Yes! No! The longer she talked to him, the more ground she lost. "You're persistent."

His smile widened. "And you're hard to pin down. Come on, you'll have fun. I'm a nice guy."

She didn't doubt it. "I can't."

He folded his arms. "Your words say no, but I'm hearing yes."

"Then you're not listening."

"Yes, I am. Listening is one of the things I do best." The intense scrutiny returned. "Does my dad know you're here?"

"Not yet." Why, oh why, had she said that?

"But you'll be seeing him?"

"I don't know."

"Then maybe—"

"Hey, Micah!"

The shout made them both turn.

The other man from Micah's group was striding toward them. "We're heading over to The Shack. You coming?"

"Yeah. Can you snag my board?"

"Already got it. We'll meet you at the tram."

Aurora took advantage of the distraction to move onto the sidewalk and slip on her boots.

Micah turned back and lifted one brow. "Sneaking off?"

"I told you, I have to go."

"So you said. And so do I. I won't keep you any longer." He leaned toward her, gazing at her with a devilish half-smile. "But one way or another, I guarantee you'll be seeing me again."

Thirteen

Aurora flopped onto the bed in her hotel room with a sigh.

What a disaster.

Not even a full day into her mission and she'd already failed completely. Her father was off the island, but she'd managed to run into her brother without trying.

Stupid, really. Why hadn't she caught on sooner? The emotions she'd sensed on the beach had been so intense as she'd watched the surfers. It should have clued her in. Mya had said Micah amplified her abilities. Logically, that included her empathic senses as well. But she'd been so caught up in the moment she hadn't seen the danger.

She rolled onto her side and stared out the sliding door at the palm fronds swaying in the breeze.

She'd talked to her brother. *She'd talked to her brother!*

The unreality of their interchange settled over her. And the incredible strength of their bond. Even though he was at least a few kilometers away, she could still sense him. His energy field must have been calling to her ever since she'd arrived on the island, drawing her to the beach like a magnet. She just hadn't recognized it for what it was.

She could probably locate him blindfolded. Could he do the same with her?

Scary thought. If he could, she'd never be able to avoid him.

She'd never been this aware of another person in her life. His behavior proved he'd felt it, too. He clearly had no idea why he was drawn to her, only that her bizarre behavior and evasive answers had piqued his curiosity.

Well, he'd certainly caught her attention. His impact on her was even more extreme than she'd feared, challenging her for control. She didn't want to imagine the horrors that could occur if she engaged her energy field while he was by her side.

At least now she'd know when he was nearby. He might be able to track her, but she could also use the connection to avoid him. Move and countermove, like pieces on a chessboard. But could she keep him at a distance and still figure out a way to meet with her father?

Rolling off the bed, she paced in front of the slider. Her energy field danced under her skin, begging to be turned loose, to explore this new reality. But she didn't dare give in. The last time she'd engaged her field, she'd scarred the beloved old redwood behind her mom's house. She didn't trust herself to control her actions, especially without Mya's calming presence to keep her contained.

She glanced at her comband sitting on the bedside table. Mya had offered to make this journey with her, to help her face these challenges. But instead of taking her up on that offer, she'd abandoned her in the middle of the night, running away like a headstrong teenager. Foolish and impulsive. Not exactly the behavior of a friend. Or a leader.

And now Mya and the *Starhawke* were on their way to Kraed space without her.

She sat down on the edge of the bed. What was wrong with her? Ever since she'd uncovered Reanne's identity, she'd been acting like an infected computer component. Finding out about her father and brother had only expanded the scope of the malfunction.

Did she really believe her dad could help her repair the damage? That he could bring focus and order to her chaotic mind and emotional field? Or was that just wishful thinking?

A part of her yearned to flee to Azaana and never leave. Surrounded by the other Suulh, she wouldn't have to fear her abilities. She couldn't harm them without harming herself.

But Reanne wouldn't rest until she'd tracked her down. She couldn't allow that threat to destroy the sanctuary she'd fought so hard to create for the three hundred Suulh. Or abandon all the Suulh still living on the original homeworld to whatever grim fate Reanne had in mind.

One way or another, eventually she'd have to face her enemy.

The question was, when that day came, would she be prepared?

She'd left Stoneycroft because her presence posed a danger to everyone she cared about.

But she couldn't escape the danger she posed to herself.

Fourteen

"Report." Cade settled next to Williams on one of the couches in the Admiral's living room, his attention on Gonzo, who sat across from him, and Reynolds, who stood behind Gonzo. A fire crackled in the fireplace to his right, harmonizing with the patter of rain outside.

Gonzo looked unusually grim. "I think it's safe to say several of the Southern Quadrant delegates have been compromised."

Reynolds folded her arms, her lips curving down. "Council records show multiple visits by Outer, Central, and Interior Quadrant delegates to the Teeli Embassy during the past six months."

"Visiting the Embassy doesn't prove they're compromised," Cade pointed out. If the Admiral got his wish, they'd both be making that trip soon. "What did the logs give as the reasons for the visits?"

"Trade route negotiations, mostly. A few Setarip sightings."

"But you don't believe they're legit?"

"Prior to the attack on Gaia, you could count the number of delegates who visited the Teeli Embassy in a year on one hand. The number of visits by delegates has tripled. That can't be a coincidence."

"No, it can't." He glanced at Justin and Bella, who sat on the couch to his left. "Did you dig up anything that could tie Reanne to the Teeli?"

Bella shook her head. "Not only is there no link between her and the Teeli, her official record is spotless.

Nothing that would indicate she was anything but a hard-working civil servant."

"Spotless? I find that hard to believe." When Reanne rubbed someone the wrong way, she could generate a lot of friction. Kire Emoto was a prime example. "No record of incidents with co-workers or supervisors?"

"Not a one."

"Which means those records are also falsified." Williams' voice rumbled with banked anger. "I have a friend who served with Reanne several years ago. I thought he'd said once that he'd had an altercation with her, so I contacted him. He confirmed that he filed a complaint against her for unprofessional conduct, which his supervisor upheld. Reanne was given a formal reprimand. Now there's no record of it in her file."

"Interesting."

"I also took a look at her RC medical file. Not only does it corroborate the diagnosis of PTSD that allowed her to resign from the RC Director's position gracefully, but I couldn't find any clues that would indicate a Teeli genetic profile."

"So, we're wrong about her half-Teeli heritage?"

"I think we're right, but she's scrubbed her medical records just like she's scrubbed her service records."

"I tend to agree." He glanced around the circle. "What about the other delegates?"

Bella lifted her hand. "I'm still investigating one of the Northern Rim delegates. I can't put my finger on why, but something in the records doesn't match up. And since that's the quadrant that houses Burrow and borders Kraed space, having a mole there would have benefited Reanne."

"What did President Yeoh have to say?" Justin asked the Admiral, who stood to Cade's right, gazing into the fire.

He turned his head. "She's as concerned about the Teeli threat as we are. But there's very little she can do until we present her with solid evidence."

"Which brings us back to square one." Justin grimaced.

"Not necessarily. Mr. Ellis and I have a plan." The Admiral briefly outlined their discussion with Admiral Payne. "I have no doubt the Teeli will agree to the meeting, if for no other reason than to perpetuate their veil of innocence. When they do, we will need to take full advantage of the opportunity."

A gleam lit Reynolds' eyes. "I already tried to access the Embassy's security system, but it's a closed loop with paranoia-level defenses. However, I can outfit you with surveillance devices you can plant on the personnel inside, something they won't be able to remove or detect."

Cade's brows lifted. "Oh, really?"

"They're a little project Cardiff and I were working on while we were on the *Starhawke*. Integrated Kraed tech."

Cade managed to hide the flinch her words triggered. The Kraed were still a touchy subject for him. So was Aurora's ship. "What's the range after it's been deployed?"

Her smile had a Cheshire Cat quality. "If a pin drops there, you'll be able to hear it here."

"Good to know. Coordinate with Justin and Drew so they'll be able to get the feed as soon as it's active." He focused on Justin. "How's your Teeli?"

Justin made a face. "Getting there. I'm still working on mastering the updated vocabulary and grammar Emoto compiled during the *Starhawke*'s stint in Teeli space. I had to unlearn everything I was taught at the Academy."

A second jab. He'd love to go five minutes without anyone mentioning Aurora or her ship. He was having enough trouble pushing her to the back of his mind already. "Take whatever time you need over the next few days. That's your primary task. Assuming we get the surveillance devices in place, we'll need you to translate."

Justin nodded. "I'll be ready."

He turned to Gonzo next. "I want you to work on an extraction plan, just in case the Teeli make a move on the Admiral while we're there."

"Unlikely," the Admiral said. "This is a high-profile visit."

"Yes, but the Teeli are masters of manipulation. I'm not leaving anything to chance." He met Gonzo's gaze. "Have any discreet weapons I can get past security?"

Gonzo ran a hand over the dark hair of his goatee. "Possibly. I picked up a few tricks while we were on the *Starhawke*, too."

This time, he did flinch. There was only so much he could take. "Let me know what you come up with." His gaze swept the circle. "Let's get to work."

Fifteen

Her sleep schedule was completely jacked up.

After two hours of tossing and turning, Aurora gave up. Pulling on her clothes, she grabbed her jacket and comband and headed out the door.

A cool breeze greeted her in the lobby, but it was downright balmy compared to what she was used to at Stoneycroft. She slipped her jacket on as she passed the desk clerk in the atrium, stepping onto the sidewalk and turning south toward the water. Very few people were out this time of night, which suited her just fine. She quickened her steps, willing her muscles to loosen up as she breathed in the sea air.

When she reached the edge of the beach, she paused. Ambient light from the pathway cast a faint glow on the water, but otherwise, the ocean stretched out into pitch black. The starlight twinkled overhead, but the new moon had already risen and set with the sun.

Taking a seat on the block wall, she stretched her legs out, rested her weight on her palms, and closed her eyes.

The steady rolling of the waves provided a soothing background beat as she focused on her breathing, bringing it in sync with the moving water.

With her eyes closed, she could almost convince herself she was on Azaana. She hadn't spent much time on the island's expansive beach—she'd been too busy helping to build the settlement—but she could picture the azure water and pristine sand. Maybe Raaveen was down there now, gazing out at the water, or playing in the surf with Paaw and Sparw.

Justin had sent her an update during their stopover at Troi, letting her know he'd heard from Raaveen. Work on the settlement was nearly finished. He'd also said Raaveen had asked when Aurora would be returning, hoping she and Mya could be part of the planned festivities to celebrate the settlement's completion. He said she was eager to show them what the Suulh had accomplished in their absence.

Well, Mya was already on her way. That would have to suffice for now. Much as she'd love to spend a couple weeks with the Suulh, she had a task of her own to complete.

Too bad she didn't know her next step.

She drew in a deep breath and opened her eyes. No time like the present to figure it out.

Brushing the sand from her palms, she stood.

Taking a more circuitous route back to the hotel gave her time to think.

Waiting until Friday to see her dad wasn't an option, so she'd have to track him down after he returned to the island, preferably at home. Ambushing him outside one of his classrooms wasn't the kind of first meeting she'd had in mind. She wanted to be alone, not surrounded by a thousand curious gazes.

Maybe she could locate his address in the public records. If not, she could always do the amateur sleuth move—wait outside his office and follow him home.

Assuming he didn't sense her first. Which, if he was as empathic as Mya had indicated, he might. That could blow a hole in her plan.

She sighed. *And I thought locating him would be the easy part.*

The murmur of the surf grew fainter as the buildings closed in, but the walls amplified a new sound.

The steady fall of footsteps behind her.

She hadn't noticed anyone else by the beach, but she hadn't been paying attention, either.

Turning right at the next corner, she continued down the walkway.

The footsteps turned as well.

Probably a coincidence.

She slowed down, pretending interest in the brightly-colored clothing and beach paraphernalia in the darkened storefronts. The footsteps slowed as well.

Her heartbeat sped up. *Don't be paranoid. Probably just another insomniac out for a stroll.*

She continued on, turning another corner that took her away from the direction of her hotel.

The footsteps came around the corner, keeping perfect pace with her.

Tension gripped her chest, but she forced air into her lungs. She was definitely being followed. But by whom?

Certainly not Micah. His energy shone like a candle in the darkness about two kilometers to the northwest.

Opening her empathic senses, she focused on her pursuer. Pinpointing the emotional field of her unknown tracker would be a piece of cake with so few people on the streets.

Or it should have been.

She couldn't get a reading.

A vise clamped down on her throat. Only one person was a blank slate to her. Reanne Beck.

If she'd followed her here, a trap awaited somewhere in the darkness.

She broadened her empathic search, seeking any indication of Kreestol's presence, or the unnatural energy of

Necri soldiers, but came up empty. Had Reanne figured out a way to block their emotional resonances?

Didn't matter. She had to get away from the city. An open fight against Reanne's forces would hurt a lot of people.

She couldn't go near the beach. No way would she risk contact with the water.

She'd have to make a run for the parkland to the northeast.

Taking a deep breath, she broke into a sprint.

"Aurora, wait!"

The male voice didn't stop her. But the emotions that wrapped around her like a bear hug halted her in her tracks.

Pain. Loss. Hope.

Love.

Her body shook like a fault line as she pivoted.

A male figure strode out of the darkness toward her, his steps slowing as he drew closer. He was dressed in dark slacks and a blazer, which made him appear imposing. Powerful.

"Do you know who I am?" he asked as he stopped in front of her.

She opened her mouth, but her first attempt at speech produced a harsh croak as the words backed up in her throat.

He held her gaze, his emotions surrounding her in a warm cocoon as he waited.

She swallowed and tried again.

"Hi, Dad."

Sixteen

He released his breath on a sigh. "Your mother finally told you?"

She nodded, her mind struggling to form complete sentences. Her father was here, standing in front of her, as real as the surf pounding in the distance. If she reached out, she could touch him.

That thought helped her string a few words together. "How did you find me?" *And why couldn't I sense you?* Was he so skilled at controlling his emotions that he could create an emotional void?

The hint of a smile curved the corners of his mouth, which was framed by a close-cropped blond goatee sprinkled with grey. A change since his faculty picture had been taken. But the same light of amusement lit his eyes. "Somehow I didn't expect that to be the first question you'd want to ask me."

"It's a start." Especially while her brain continued to process the abrupt switch from nightmare vision to dreamlike reality.

The breeze ruffled his hair, sweeping it off his forehead. He was only half a head taller than she was, but the intensity of his presence made him seem larger than life. "I suppose it is." He glanced in the direction they'd come. "But the middle of the sidewalk isn't the right place for this discussion."

No, it wasn't. "My hotel's a few blocks from here."

He nodded. "Lead the way."

They traversed the distance in silence, while she kept sneaking peeks at him. Her father, in the flesh, walking beside her down the street like it was the most natural thing in the world.

"I'm sorry I scared you," he said as they entered the atrium of the hotel and continued to the elevator.

"You didn't."

His steady look called her lie. *Right. Empath.* She couldn't hide her feelings from him. She wasn't used to someone else having that advantage.

She passed her keycard over the scanner and the doors closed.

He faced her as the elevator rose. "To answer your question, I sensed your presence about eight hours ago."

"But weren't you on Maui?"

"I was."

"Then how did you sense I was here?" He wasn't a Suulh. He was human. Given the distance, his assertion seemed improbable.

"Your emotions hit me like a wave. I was nearing the end of my afternoon lecture. My TA thought I was having a heart attack, even after I recovered from the blow."

So he hadn't sensed her this morning when she'd arrived. It had been in the afternoon, probably when she'd encountered Micah on the beach.

"I convinced her I was fine, but I'd never felt anything that strong before, or that complex. A lot of conflicting information. It took a while to sort it out, and even more time to convince myself that my instincts were right. That I was sensing you."

"Oh." *Brilliant response, Aurora.* But she couldn't come up with anything better, not without bringing Micah into the discussion. And she wasn't ready for that.

The elevator doors opened onto the hallway to her room.

She led the way, unlocking her door and pushing it open. "Come in." She gestured to the chairs by the slider to the balcony. "Have a seat."

He stepped past her, shrugging out of his black blazer and draping it over the back of one of the chairs before sitting down. The long-sleeved shirt underneath was also black. Not a common color choice on this island, from what she'd seen. Appropriate for a funeral, though. She'd certainly been going through a mourning period recently. And now her father was back from the dead.

She slipped off her own jacket before claiming the other chair.

His gaze moved over her face, studying her. "I still can't believe you're really here."

"That makes two of us." But now that he was a hand's breadth away, her tension level was shooting through the roof. *Keep breathing.* "I came to find you."

"Because there's a new threat."

She blinked. "How could you know that?"

The look in his blue eyes was so bittersweet it made her heart bleed. "Because I know your mother better than anyone. Only a serious threat to your safety could have forced her to reveal the truth."

He'd nailed it. Her mother had fought every step of the way, only giving in because not telling her would have put her at greater risk.

He leaned forward, lacing his fingers together. "What happened?"

Where to start? "How much do you know about my life?"

"I know you have your own ship. And that you and Lelindia discovered the Suulh weren't all killed off as your mother and Marina had believed."

Her mouth dropped open. She closed it. "Mom told you that?"

"No, Marina did. She and Gryphon keep me informed. Talking to your mom would be... difficult."

Difficult. Biggest. Understatement. EVER.

But the word clearly meant something very different to him than it did to her. The elemental nature of his pain flowed over her, catching her by surprise and constricting her lungs. "You miss her."

His voice roughened. "Every moment of every day." Such yearning in those words. "But seeing you..." He drew in a slow breath. "I can see her in your eyes."

Her chest tightened a few more notches. Talking to her mom wasn't difficult for him because they argued. It was difficult because he was still in love with her. "I'm sorry."

"For what?"

"I'm just... sorry."

"Me, too."

Silence hung in the air for several beats as they stared at each other, casualties of a war neither had chosen to fight.

He sighed. "What scared Libra into telling you the truth?"

"Her sister, Kreestol, tried to kill me."

He sank back in his chair, his face a mask of shock. "She's alive? She's here? On Earth?"

"No. I encountered her on a planet near the Outer Rim."

His hand trembled as he ran it through his hair. "But Marina said the Teeli were in control of the Suulh. Caging them, turning them into mindless soldiers."

"For some that's true. They've also manipulated Kreestol into believing I'm her enemy. She doesn't know the truth and the Teeli, and wouldn't listen when I tried to tell her."

"How could she not know?"

"She's convinced Mom abandoned her. And her rage has been fueled by Reanne, a former friend of mine who has a connection to the Teeli. They want to destroy me."

"Why?"

She shrugged. "I wish I knew. Reanne's unstable, power-hungry. And she's turned this into a personal vendetta against me."

"Did she hurt you?" Parental concern overrode his initial shock.

"Not directly." *She just ripped my life into shreds.* "But fighting Kreestol is the hardest thing I've ever done."

"I can believe that. Does she have your shielding ability?"

"Yes, but that's not the problem. She's much weaker than I am in that regard, and not a skilled fighter. I could defeat her. The problem is our empathic connection. I feel her pain—the pain of all the Suulh—as though it's my own. When I hurt them, I hurt myself."

She'd expected a reaction, but not the one she got.

He nodded. "I've wondered if that would happen."

"You have?" It had been news to her.

"From the day you were born, it was clear you had inherited my empathic abilities. Whatever your mother and I were feeling, you would mirror it. And with Mi—" He cut off abruptly, his gaze dropping to his hands.

"Micah?" she finished for him.

He looked up. "Your mom told you?"

"No. Mya—Lelindia—did."

His gaze intensified. "Did she also explain why I brought him here?"

"Yes. For the same reason I had planned to avoid him during this visit. Being together is dangerous. He proved that this afternoon when we accidentally ran into each other at the beach."

He grunted. "That explains it."

"Explains what?"

"Why I was able to sense you from so far away. And why I was getting so many conflicting emotions. He was amplifying yours, turning up the volume so to speak, until I heard you. And you were channeling his emotions as well as your own." He leaned back in his chair. "Running into him was no accident."

"What do you mean?"

"Ever since you were born, the two of you have behaved like magnets. Micah rarely left your side, to the point where he would crawl into your crib with you. And once you could walk? Wherever one went, the other soon followed."

He'd just confirmed what she'd suspected. Her brother had a built-in GPS tracking device to locate her.

"When he was a child, he asked me at least once a week if we could take a trip to northern California to see the redwoods. I thought it was because he had residual childhood memories from living there. But then not long after you left your mother's house to attend the Academy, he changed his mind and started asking if we could spend the winter break learning to ski. In Colorado."

Where she'd been.

"I asked him why he'd chosen that location, but he never came up with a solid answer. Just that it seemed like a good idea. But the answer was you."

Moisture gathered behind her eyes. He'd wanted to be near her. Just as he'd wanted to keep her from leaving today.

"Thankfully, that was around the same time he got serious about his surfing. It's a year-round sport here, so leaving for a week would have put him behind the competition. Before long he stopped talking about vacation spots and focused on places where he could compete."

And she'd been focusing on earning an officer's spot on a starship. "Did Marina tell you I begged Mom to take me to Hawaii for vacation?" She'd assumed after meeting the Suulh that her strong desire for tropical island surroundings was tied to them, to her homeworld. But what if it was an unconscious yearning to be where Micah was? "She always said no, claiming she couldn't stand the humid heat."

He nodded. "I made similar arguments about the cold dry air to dissuade Micah."

Which brought her to another important point. "I get not wanting to tell Micah about me, but what about you? Why didn't you make contact with me after I graduated from the Academy? You could have overruled Mom's dictate once I was an adult. Told me the truth." That last part came out as more of an accusation than she'd intended.

His flinch proved it, as did his flare of emotional pain. But he didn't evade the question. "I wanted to. Please believe that. Being separated from you, not being able to watch you grow up..."

He sighed, staring at the swaying palms outside. "When I met your mother, she was plagued by fear and anxiety, but she was also strong and self-reliant. She never asked me for anything, not until the Teeli made contact with Earth. We'd been so happy together, with you and Micah. To see her joy crumble back into fear—it broke my heart. Reaching out to you would have meant betraying her. I couldn't do it, not after all she'd been through. Not when staying away seemed like the best way to protect you both."

How could she argue with that?

He met her gaze. "But I didn't expect you to share that fear. The full-blown panic I felt from you today—it really shook me up. It's what drove me here to find you." He rested his elbows on his knees. "What exactly happened when you saw Micah? Why did being near him terrify you?"

And now to the nitty-gritty. "I've had some experiences lately that have shown me just how lethal I can be."

He pulled back, his eyes wide. "Lethal?"

"I almost killed—" Her lover? Her friend? The man she wanted to spend the rest of her life with? "Someone. It was an accident, but it was still my fault. I electrocuted him. Stopped his heart."

The shock faded, replaced with compassion. "But he lived?"

"Yes, he's fine. Mya—Lelindia—was able to correct the damage." But *she* would carry the emotional scars from that experience forever.

"Then if it was an accident, what—"

"He could have died!"

His brows lifted at the vehemence in her voice.

She adjusted the volume. "My abilities pose a threat to everyone around me. Being near Micah would only make it worse."

"Are you afraid you'd hurt him?"

"No." Strangely, she had a sense that she couldn't hurt Micah, almost like he had a natural immunity to her energy. "But you said yourself that he amplified my emotions to the point that they affected you like a blow while you were an island away. If he can do that with what I'm *feeling*, imagine what he could do with my shield? Or my electromagnetic energy? It would be catastrophic." For all she knew, the two of them could level this city in the blink of an eye.

"Or maybe he could help you."

Her brain came to a screeching halt. "Huh?"

"He's an amplifier for your abilities, but that doesn't mean chaos, which is what you're implying. What if Micah's enhancing effect is exactly what you need to handle Kreestol and the Teeli?"

Seventeen

In all the doomsday scenarios Aurora had painted regarding her brother, it had never occurred to her that their connection might help her defeat Reanne. She'd assumed he'd turn her into a nuclear bomb with a millimeter fuse. "That seems unlikely."

"Why?"

"You felt what I went through when I saw him. I was completely out of control."

"You were caught off guard."

"It's not like it got better the longer I talked to him. He was drawing my power out without even trying. The urge to engage my energy field, to make that connection, was so strong..."

"It scared you."

"Horrified me."

"You wouldn't have hurt anyone."

"How do you know? I could have—"

"I know. Yes, you have power, and with Micah you have more, but that doesn't make you dangerous."

"Of course it does."

"No, it doesn't."

"But—"

"Aurora, listen to me." He lifted a hand, silencing her. "Your ship has weapons capable of great destruction, correct?"

She eyed him warily. "Yes."

"Do you consider your ship inherently dangerous?"

"Well, no." She didn't even consider Star dangerous, even though the Nirunoc had proven she could fire the ship's weapons if she chose.

"You're the captain of that powerful ship. You could use it to destroy. But you wouldn't fire those weapons at an unsuspecting target. Just as you wouldn't use your energy abilities to kill, either."

"Not intentionally. But if I lose control, then—"

"Did you lose control when you electrocuted the man who almost died?"

"No. I was fighting Kreestol in a river. I didn't realize it was saltwater, and sent an energy blast to break her grip. Cade had a foot in the water at the time."

"Cade?" His eyes narrowed. "You mean the man you're involved with?"

Her dad knew about her relationship with Cade? Exactly how much information was Marina sending him? "Yes."

"He's the one you electrocuted?"

Memories of that moment flooded her, clamping down on her vocal cords. She nodded.

His expression shifted, understanding dawning. "No wonder you're terrified." He reached out, clasping her hand in his.

It was like being caught in a game of freeze tag. She couldn't move.

His voice touched her with the same gentle caress as his fingers. "Hurting those we love is heart-wrenching and debilitating, doubly so when your empathic abilities allow you to feel their pain as your own."

The force of his compassion pushed tears against the back of her eyes. She blinked them away.

"Does Cade blame you for what happened?"

She shook her head. "Not at all. In fact, he's been on a campaign to change my mind ever since I told him we couldn't be together anymore."

The hint of a smile touched his lips. "Smart man. But you're resisting?"

"Of course I am! If you'd seen him lying by the river..." A tremor worked its way up from her toes.

His grip on her hand tightened, offering comfort. "You're afraid you'll hurt him again."

"Or he'll get hurt because he's with me."

He shifted closer, holding her gaze. "What if you're wrong? What if you could save him?"

Save him? "What do you mean?"

"You're the Sahzade. A born guardian with incredible strength. You believe he's in danger because of you. And maybe you're right. But wouldn't he be safer from your enemies if he's by your side, rather than on his own?"

"He's not on his own. He has his team. And he's a trained special forces commander."

"Okay. But judging by what you've told me, he's also a man in love. And right now he thinks he's lost you. He'll have a hard time maintaining his focus if you've cut off all communication." His grip loosened, the pain in his emotional field resurfacing. "I have firsthand experience with that."

Aurora rocked back in her chair, realization striking like a gong. Her dad had just held up a mirror. Her mother's face gazed back at her in the reflection. History repeating itself.

Her mom had sent her dad and Micah away in order to keep everyone safe. And now she was doing the same thing.

She hung her head. "I am my mother's daughter, after all."

His palm cradled her chin, applying gentle pressure until she met his gaze. "And that's a good thing. Your mother has a lot of gifts to share. But you're also *my* daughter. And more courageous than you realize. You wouldn't be here if you didn't want to overcome your fear and reclaim what you've lost."

Her lip trembled. He was offering her a precious gift of his own. Hope.

"I'm not saying it will be easy, but I can help you." His thumb stroked her cheek, brushing away a tear she hadn't even felt fall. "If you'll let me."

A leap of faith.

She took a ragged breath, her entire body quivering. "All right."

His blue eyes brightened, a small smile creasing his cheeks. "That's my girl." He exhaled like the weight of a mountain had just slid off his shoulders.

Releasing her, he pulled out his comm device. "I have to catch a plane back to Maui in about five hours to finish the symposium, but I'll be back this afternoon. If you're willing, when I return, I'd like you to come stay with me."

Butterflies danced in her stomach. "Stay with you?"

He nodded. "I have a house on Diamond Head. Plenty of space and a view of the ocean. It's quiet and private. We can work there."

She hesitated. "What about Micah?"

"His place is in town, but most likely he'll show up within a few hours of your arrival, whether I say anything to him or not."

"Does he know about me? That he has a sister?"

The light in his eyes dimmed. "He knows he had a sister. But he thinks you died when you were two."

"Oh."

"I'll leave it up to you to decide how you want to handle it. But I suggest we tell him the truth."

If Micah knew the truth, there would be no going back. "I'll think about it."

"Fair enough." Standing, he picked up his blazer. "I'll send a car for you at four this afternoon. Micah has a heavy teaching schedule today, so you shouldn't have to worry about him showing up in the lobby in the meantime."

"Doesn't matter. I'll know if he heads my way."

He paused with one arm in the sleeve of his blazer. "So you can sense him? Consciously?"

"Now that I know what his energy feels like? Yeah. He's that direction." She pointed to the west.

"You're sure?"

"Yes."

"Do you know how far?"

"A couple kilometers."

His half-smile returned. "Amazing."

"What?"

"That you can so clearly pinpoint his location. His condo is two kilometers to the west."

"But you can do that too, right?"

"Not exactly. I can use the intensity of emotions I sense to help guide me in finding someone. It's how I located your hotel, but it took a couple hours of wandering the streets to triangulate the exact spot."

"Oh." So their empathic abilities weren't exactly the same.

"You and Micah can thank your mother for your internal GPS. She could find me in the middle of a forest with her eyes closed."

Eighteen

Mya exited the lift and walked the short distance to Jonarel's cabin, passing her own on the way. Having only a bulkhead separating their quarters was one of her personal daily challenges. When Aurora had made the cabin assignments, she'd had no way of knowing the arrangement would place Mya in her own private hell.

Celia would swap with her if she asked, which would put her on the opposite side of the corridor, but she'd never come up with a plausible reason for the switch. She didn't want to make Jonarel or Aurora suspicious of her motivations.

So, she'd learned to live with the low-grade discomfort. Spending very little of her free time in her cabin helped. She preferred the solace of the greenhouse, anyway.

Halting in front of the carved wooden door outside Jonarel's cabin, she touched the panel. The soft chime within announced her presence, but it took a while before the doors parted.

When they did, she stifled a groan. *Should have used the comm.*

Jonarel stood on the other side of the door, his thick dark hair damp and curling around his shoulders. His *bare* shoulders. No shirt, just a pair of lounge pants slung low on his lean hips. His feet were bare, too.

Hold it together. Don't stare!

She couldn't help it. The muscled perfection of his chest rivaled the carvings of Michelangelo, although Jonarel wasn't made of cold marble. Far from it. Warm flesh, richly-colored in deep green with tendrils of brown tempted her to reach out and touch.

"Mya?"

She met his gaze. "Uh-huh."

"Did you need me?"

Always. "Um, yeah. Were you in the shower?" She bit the inside of her cheek as soon as the words left her mouth. She didn't want confirmation, or the visual her mind would generate as a result.

"I was finished. Come in." He stepped back, gesturing for her to enter.

Keep it cool. Just a simple conversation.

Right. With a half-naked Kraed god.

She gave him a wide berth as she walked into the room. The subtle scents wafting off his skin and hair set her nerve endings tingling anyway.

She chose one of the freestanding chairs next to the coffee table and sat down. Knowing his penchant for close physical contact, she couldn't sit on the couch. He would sit right next to her and her mental circuits would fry.

He settled onto the couch with the grace of a panther, his long legs almost touching hers. "Is this regarding Aurora?"

Naturally he'd leap to that conclusion. She didn't exactly make a habit of visiting him in his cabin. And their private conversations were always about Aurora. "Not exactly." She folded her hands together and kept her gaze slightly averted. "I've been thinking about our trip to Azaana. I wanted to know if there's a way to keep our arrival secret from your father."

His brows lifted. "Why?"

She took a fortifying breath and met his gaze. "Correct me if I'm wrong, but he's not likely to be happy that we left Aurora on Earth, is he?"

He tilted his head slightly. "I believe that is a fair assessment."

"I thought so. The last time we were on Azaana, he was there to meet us. If he did that again, it could make things... complicated."

"How so?"

"First, he'll want an explanation for why Aurora's not there. He also might decide he needs to be there when I'm talking to the Suulh. That's not going to help."

Jonarel frowned.

She pressed on. "Don't get me wrong. I'm incredibly grateful for his help. The Suulh wouldn't have Azaana if it weren't for him. It's just that I need—"

"Time alone with the Suulh."

She nodded. "This will not be an easy discussion for them. Or me." A slight chill traveled over her skin. She rubbed her palms over her upper arms. "I'm concerned that if he's there, he'll..." She circled her hand in the air, unwilling to put her feelings into words for fear she'd insult him.

He captured her hand in both of his, freezing her in place. "I understand." His thumb brushed over the back of her hand, a soothing gesture.

She was the polar opposite of soothed.

"My father can be a bit... intense. That is not what the Suulh need. Or you."

What she needed was for him to stop touching her. The seismic activity he was generating was off the charts. Her gaze traveled along his muscled arm, pausing briefly at his pecs before lifting to his face. Not even a hint of awareness showed in his golden eyes. That was good, right? "Is there—" She cleared the huskiness from her throat and tried again. "Is there a way to hide our arrival?"

He released her hand and stood. "Tehar."

The Nirunoc's image appeared standing to Mya's left. "Yes?"

"Can you alter the hull camouflage to prevent detection by the *pitar*?"

Star glanced at Mya. The understanding in her eyes made it clear she'd heard every word of their conversation. "I will begin working on it right away."

"Thank you. Alert me if you need my assistance."

Star nodded, her image already fading.

Mya turned to Jonarel. "What is *pitar*?"

"The security network that allows us to track all ship movements within our borders."

Mya's eyes widened. "*All* movements."

He seemed amused by her surprise. "Is that so difficult to believe?"

"Within your home system, no, but you're talking about—" She spread her arms wide, unable to come up with the right terms. She wasn't an astronomer. She had no idea exactly how much territory the Kraed claimed, only that it was vast. How could they monitor all ship movements within that range?

Now he was definitely amused. "We have been exploring space far longer than humans or Suulh. And unlike humans, we were methodical. Setting up monitoring beacons as we expanded our territory seemed prudent for the safety of our ships, and to help us gain insight into any lifeforms we might encounter."

"I guess." Although she'd had no idea her request would mean outmaneuvering such a complex system. She'd been worried about the tracking buoys and defensive systems the Kraed had put in place to protect Azaana. No wonder Star had gotten right on it.

Jonarel settled back on the couch, his full mouth flattening to a line. "Now I have a query for you."

She knew what was coming even before he spoke.

"Will Aurora be alright?"

Yep. Nailed it. She held back a sigh. At least the change in topic threw cold water on her physical reaction to his nearness. "She's exactly where she needs to be. And her father is a good man. He'll do everything he can to help her."

Some of the tension eased from Jonarel's lips. "You trust him?"

"Completely. He would give his life to protect Aurora. He already gave up the woman he loves to keep them both safe."

Pain flickered in Jonarel's eyes. And maybe empathy. He understood self-sacrifice better than most. "Then I am glad she has found him."

"Me, too." Although she'd feel even better if she knew for certain that Brendan could help Aurora overcome her weakness with the Suulh. If he couldn't, Aurora's connection to the Suulh could become her Achilles' heel.

Nineteen

"Is this your first trip to the island?"

The driver's question pulled Aurora's attention off the swaying palms and snippets of aquamarine water visible out the vehicle's side window as they made their way toward the base of the rocky promontory of Diamond Head. She'd expected an automated transport to pick her up and deliver her to her dad's house, but this jovial man with a stout figure and easy smile who'd identified himself as Kai had greeted her when she'd exited the hotel and ushered her into the front passenger seat. "Yes."

"You been out in the water yet?"

"Not yet." And she still had no plans to do so, no matter what her dad or Micah said.

Kai must have picked up on her reluctance. "You really should. Hard to find a nicer place for a swim. And the surfing's phenomenal. Brendan's son Micah is the top ranked surfer on Oahu."

"So I heard." She shifted to face him. "Have you known them long?"

His round face scrunched up in thought. "We've been good friends about fifteen years now, I guess. My daughter Iolana met Micah at a surfing competition shortly after we moved here from the Big Island, and they've been catching waves together ever since."

Which meant Iolana could have been one of the women she'd seen with Micah the previous day. Maybe even the one she'd spoken to. Her coloring and easy smile matched Kai's.

"The way they act around each other, you'd think they were siblings. They bicker and argue, but it's always in good fun. Brendan and I can't keep up with them in the water, but we still get out there whenever we can, especially at the luau."

"Luau?"

"He hasn't told you about that?"

She shook her head.

"Well, you're in for a treat. He hosts a blowout beach luau for friends and colleagues on Christmas Day. As his newest student-in-residence, you'll definitely be invited. Micah and Iolana give surfing lessons in the morning, followed by an informal competition in the afternoon. The main feast and entertainment start at sunset. It's the most popular event of the year."

And only a couple weeks away. She forced enthusiasm into her voice. "Sounds like fun." In another lifetime, she would have been thrilled to attend. But parties held no place in her current reality. Especially parties near an ocean of saltwater.

"No better way to celebrate the season. And the four of us always spend Christmas Eve together." He glanced at her. "But maybe you'll be celebrating with family."

She almost laughed. Almost. He had no idea how right he was. "I'm not sure. We didn't set a definite time for how long I'll be here." And she saw no reason to disabuse him of the idea that she was a student. If her dad had chosen not to tell his good friend Kai that she was his daughter, she'd happily go along with that decision.

"I see." But his tone and emotional field indicated her answer had confused him. He slowed the vehicle and flipped on his turn signal, gesturing to the left. "We're here."

She peered past him to a curving driveway leading up from the base of the hill. He made the turn, the steep incline drawing her attention to the robin's egg blue sky and the bright magenta blossoms of the shrubs lining her side of the hillside. As they climbed, the tops of the palms to their left gave way to a view of sunlight sparkling on the ocean, interspersed with brightly colored sailboats.

Near the top of the hill, the driveway curved to the right and leveled off, revealing a cream-colored two-story house with wide windows. Kai guided the vehicle past a waterfall fountain built into the rocky hillside and surrounded by lush vegetation, stopping in front of the carved stone entrance to the house.

"You're gonna love the views," Kai said as he exited the vehicle, snagging her bag from the back seat before she'd even opened her door.

Stepping out, she stared up at the structure, taking in the location and dimensions. She wasn't an expert on real estate by any means, but this house had to be worth a fortune. Way more than a university professor's salary would cover. Which begged the question of how her father had paid for it.

The disparity reminded her of how little she really knew about him.

Kai rested a comforting hand on her shoulder. "I know it can seem intimidating, but you'll love it here. I promise."

He'd mistaken her hesitation for uncertainty. His worry drifted over her like mist.

She met his gaze, summoning a reassuring smile. "I'm sure I will. I just wasn't expecting something so breathtaking."

He chuckled. "Brendan's full of surprises. He'll definitely keep you on your toes. In a good way," he added when her smile slipped.

A few months ago, she would have been all for surprises. But she'd experienced an avalanche of them since then, most with dramatic repercussions for her present and her future. Steady and boring sounded far more appealing at the moment.

Kai slung her bag over his shoulder. "Come on."

He led the way through the opening in the stone and turned right. Glass doors provided a view into an expansive room beyond, with a couple couches and bistro tables arranged like a sidewalk café. She almost expected a barista to appear holding a coffee carafe.

A section of the natural stone hillside made up most of the wall in the far right corner of the room. The house had clearly been built to flow with the existing landscape, rather than altering and dominating it.

Kai pushed open one of the oversized doors and held it for her. "We're here!"

The scent of baking bread and simmering vegetables reached her first, followed by footsteps on the slate tile. Her dad appeared through the archway at the far end of the room, a dishtowel in his hands.

"Aurora!" His face lit up with a smile as he draped the towel over his shoulder, but his emotions didn't come through, just as they hadn't the previous night.

She paused, uncertainly grabbing hold of her.

His steps slowed, a small frown turning down the corners of his lips. It vanished a moment later, as did the emotional wall she'd sensed. He pulled her into a quick hug, love and joy flowing over her like warm caramel. "Sorry," he murmured in her ear. "Shielding my emotions is an ingrained habit." He released her before she could respond, turning to Kai. "Thanks for getting her here safely."

"My pleasure." But Kai was looking at them strangely.

She'd be willing to bet her dad had never greeted another student so enthusiastically.

Her dad nodded toward her. "I've been waiting a long time to train this one. I was beginning to think I'd never get the chance."

Kai accepted the explanation with a nod and a smile, but her dad's words were clearly meant for her. A little ribbon of warmth curled in her belly. Nice to feel wanted.

"Can you stay for dinner?" her dad asked Kai as he took the bag Kai held out and set it on the floor.

"I'd love to, but Iolana's coming over this evening to help me put up my holiday decorations."

Her dad laughed, the warm rich sound cracking the seal on a long-forgotten memory. Her mom and dad, curled up on the couch in front of the fireplace in the main room at Stoneycroft, talking and laughing. She and Micah lying on a bed of blankets inside the tent Micah and Mya had built out of old sheets and boxes. The glowing fire casting everything in a dreamy softness.

A memory of contentment. Safety. Love.

Her dad winked at her, no doubt picking up on the tenor of her emotions. "You mean Iolana's not willing to let you go another year without some acknowledgment of the season?"

"I'm a big fan of the season." Kai planted his hands on his hips. "It's putting up decorations I'll be taking down a few weeks later I don't like."

"Change is good, my friend." He rested a hand on Kai's shoulder. "Keeps you young."

Kai harrumphed. "I see your tree's already up."

Aurora followed his gaze to the open living room that ran parallel to the main entrance. An enormous holiday tree covered in glittering ornaments stood proudly in front of an expansive wall of floor-to-ceiling glass. The stone deck beyond the glass doors led to a pool with an unobstructed view of the ocean.

"Of course. I started my decorating in November."

Just like her mom. Maybe he'd picked up the habit from her. Or she'd picked it up from him.

"We're not all wired that way." Kai motioned to her. "I mentioned the luau."

A fissure of surprise passed through her dad's emotional field. He glanced at her. "Would you consider joining our party?"

The question held enough weight to topple an elephant. "I'll think about it."

He gazed at her for a long moment. "I'd love for you to be there."

Disappointing him wasn't part of her plan. But neither was blindly agreeing. She might not even be here by Christmas. "We'll see."

He gave a brief nod, then turned to Kai. "Thanks again for acting as chauffeur."

"My pleasure." He smiled at Aurora as he hooked a thumb in her dad's direction. "Watch out for this one."

Her dad whisked the towel off his shoulder and snapped it in Kai's direction like a whip. "Don't be putting the wrong ideas in her head."

Their laughter surrounded her as Kai strode to the door. "She'll find out soon enough," he shot over his shoulder.

"Yeah, yeah." Her dad was still chuckling as he faced her. The laughter faded as silence descended. Stepping forward, he pulled her into another hug, holding on more tightly this time. "I'm so glad you're here."

She hugged him back. Amazing how natural it felt. "Me, too." And since he could feel what she was feeling, he'd know just how true her words were.

When he released her, his blue eyes sparkled with a sheen of moisture. "Let's get you settled." His voice was a little husky, too.

She followed him down a short hallway and up the stairs to the second story.

"My bedroom's there." He gestured to a door on their right. "Micah's old room is over there." He pointed across the expansive loft, which contained three couches in a conversation grouping around a coffee table. "This will be your room." Leading her through an open doorway on the opposite side of the loft, he continued along the corridor beyond.

Framed pictures covered the walls on both sides. She stopped as soon as she registered the subject of those images. "Space."

Everything else she'd seen in this house had reflected the tropical ambience of the islands. This did not. Nebulas, galaxies, and planets surrounded her, most of the images as familiar as old friends. She pivoted slowly, taking it all in, and catching her dad studying her with the same intensity she was giving the pictures.

"Why did you—"

"A father's wishful thinking."

She frowned. "I don't understand."

He took a deep breath, let it out slowly. "Even as a toddler, you loved the stars. You could sit for an hour on the back porch, gazing up at the sky in rapt wonder. I wasn't the least bit surprised when Marina told me you were applying to the Academy. But I couldn't be a part of that."

The depth of his loss, his frustration, swept over her, stealing whatever words had risen to her lips.

"This room gave me a way to feel connected to you, to share your dream in some small way."

The hope within that idea was a light in the whirlpool of sadness. She tried to speak and failed. Swallowed, and tried again. "I wish I'd known."

"I wish I could have told you."

They stared at each other for several long moments, as the years that had separated them filled the chasm.

His crooked smile broke the tension. "But you're here now." Motioning her forward, he continued down the corridor. "Bathroom and closet are through that door." He pointed to the right then disappeared through the opening in the wall on the left.

She turned the corner and came to a halt, the air exiting her lungs.

She knew the bedspread. It exactly matched the one on her bed back home, except this one was still a deep navy blue, unfaded from wear and repeated washings, the starfield shining brightly. The bedframe matched the one at Stoneycroft, too, as did the other furniture items. It was like her childhood room had been transported here.

Except for one thing. A meter-and-a-half wide painting of a starship hung in a dark wood frame above the bed. The image drew her across the room. She knew the ship's shape, identified it even before she was close enough to read the name stenciled on the hull. "It's the *Argo*." Her old ship, the one she'd been first officer on before she'd become captain of the *Starhawke*.

"Yes." Her dad moved beside her. The huskiness was back in his voice. "I commissioned it the day Marina told me you'd become the youngest Commander in Fleet history."

Pain and joy played tug-of-war in her chest. Her mother had barely managed a few words of congratulations when she'd heard the news, too afraid of the risks her daughter would face as Commander on the Fleet's flagship.

But her father had honored her achievement with this painting.

She'd yearned for this kind of approval and encouragement for her dreams since she was a child. Marina and Gryphon had tried to fill the void, but they couldn't offer too much open support without drawing her mother's ire. Yet her father had been silently cheering her on, creating this haven for a daughter he never expected to see.

She wrapped her arms around her torso to ward off a sudden chill.

"Hey." His arm slipped around her, pulling her close in a sideways hug. "It's okay."

She couldn't speak. Couldn't do anything but stare at the painting and the room that housed it.

He held her, not saying anything, silently offering his love and support.

When she finally found her voice, she asked the only question she could think of. "You did all this for me?"

"No." His grip loosened as he shifted to face her. "Mostly I did it for me. Who do you think sat beside you on that porch while you gazed up at the stars?"

Fragments of memory tugged at the edge of her consciousness, elusive in their details. But looking at his face now, they started to gain focus. "You wanted to travel the stars, too."

"Uh-huh. Had planned to do just that, in fact, before I met your mother. She had no interest in leaving Earth. Neither did Micah. But after you were born, I began to imagine sharing my dream with you when you got older. Then things got... complicated."

"Yeah." Her gaze returned to the painting. "You would love the *Starhawke.*"

"I have no doubt. I already love the captain."

He said it so easily.

She couldn't. Accepting such unconditional love from someone who was in many ways still a stranger took effort. Openly returning those feelings? That would take time. She was still struggling to come to grips with her new reality.

He released her, clearly sensing her emotional turmoil. "I need to go check on dinner. Why don't you take a little time to get settled, and then join me in the kitchen."

"Okay."

After he left, she inspected the room a little more closely. The far wall that ran parallel to the bed had French doors that opened onto a small balcony. A quick peek confirmed the balcony was inside the house, directly above the rock formation in the room below. She spotted a matching balcony at a ninety-degree angle, which was connected to Micah's old room.

Micah. She'd kept tabs on him for most of the day, except when she'd been catching up on much-needed sleep. As her dad had predicted, he hadn't ventured near her hotel, her sense of him placing him on the campus of the university. But was he still there?

Tuning into his unique vibration, she rechecked his location. Yes, still on or near the campus. But if her dad was correct about their magnet-like bond, he might head this way when his workday ended. What should she do if he showed up? Moving to this house had torpedoed her plan to avoid him. She needed a new strategy.

Maybe her dad would have some suggestions.

Picking up the bag he'd set on the bed, she carried it into the bathroom and began unpacking her toiletries. She hung up the few items of clothing she had, but they looked puny in the expansive closet. And inappropriate. When she'd packed on the *Starhawke*, she'd expected to spend a couple days in the cooler climate at Stoneycroft. An extended tropical vacation hadn't been on the agenda.

She'd deal with that issue in the morning. For now, the scents wafting up from below drew her out of the room and down the stairs, her stomach rumbling in anticipation.

Reaching the main floor, she continued along the corridor toward the kitchen, but paused just short of the doorway.

Her dad was singing.

She stood absolutely still, catching snatches of phrases as he moved about the room, pans and utensils clanking together in time to the music. She didn't recognize the tune, but it was upbeat, something about the rain disappearing and a bright day filled with sunshine.

He put more emphasis on a particular phrase, which described a future with a blue sky. A brief pause, then in the same sing-song voice he called out, "Come out, come out, Aurora." A soft chuckle followed.

Heat rose in her cheeks, but she obeyed, stepping into the kitchen. "I didn't want to interrupt."

His blue eyes sparkled. "Your presence is never an interruption." He handed her a ladle and a couple soup bowls. "Do you like to sing?"

"Uh, sure." But it wasn't something she'd been inclined to do while serving on Fleet starships. "What were you singing?"

"*I Can See Clearly Now.* It's an old tune, but I've always liked it."

The lyrics certainly fit with his current attitude.

He gestured to a large pot on the stove. "Go ahead and dish us up. I'll get the garlic bread out of the oven."

Pulling the lid off the soup pot, she dunked the ladle in. Hearty chunks of vegetables nestled in a thick broth of tangy herbs tantalized her nose. The scent was very familiar. She took a closer look. "Is this—"

"Gryphon's vegetable stew recipe? Yes." He set the tray of lightly browned bread halves on the counter and grabbed a basket lined with checkerboard linen. "He taught me everything I know about cooking."

"Really?" For some reason she hadn't made a mental connection between Gryphon and her father. Up to now her dad had only mentioned communicating with Marina. But of course her dad knew Gryphon. They'd lived in the same house for years.

"Before he took me under his wing, the most exotic thing I could make in the kitchen was peanut butter and jelly sandwiches." Placing the bread in the basket, he snagged a bowl of salad greens in his other hand. "And I taught Micah. He's the really creative cook. He'll blow your socks off."

A frisson of fear streaked up her spine, but it was followed by a flare of excitement. She'd missed so much time with her dad and brother. Was it foolish to hope they could find a way to be together without putting anyone else at risk?

Her dad nodded toward the archway where she'd entered. "If you'll carry the bowls, we can head outside. I've set us up at the table on the pool deck."

"Right behind you." Balancing a bowl in each hand, she followed him along the corridor and down the five steps to the living room with the Christmas tree. He'd turned the lights on, a combination of white, blue, fuchsia, and green that blended beautifully with the tropical fish ornaments swimming through the pine boughs. She paused. "I didn't expect your tree to be a pine."

He glanced over his shoulder. "It's a Norfolk pine, the one variety that can grow on the island. I pick one up from the local farm every year."

And it looked gorgeous against the breathtaking backdrop of the teal and azure ocean visible through the window. The sun had dropped low on the horizon, the clouds above starting to take on a pink undertone that matched the lights on the tree.

Another chuckle drew her attention to where her dad stood beside a stone table with a white umbrella at the center. "I take it you like the view."

Ungluing her feet from the floor, she joined him, setting down the bowls on the woven placemats. "It's lovely." And surreal. Two days ago this scene would have ranked about three thousand and twenty four on her hypothetical "what will I be doing for dinner" list, right after a formal invitation by the President of the Galactic Council to dine with her and her wife at the presidential residence.

"I prefer to eat out here when I don't have students staying with me."

"I can see why." She sat down and pulled a piece of bread from the basket. "How often do you have students here?"

"I host long weekends for a couple students a few times a year, and larger gatherings in the summer, but not all the attendees stay here. I didn't have anyone scheduled over the winter break." He grinned. "You have excellent timing."

She grimaced. "Mom would disagree."

His grin faded. "Would you rather be spending the holidays with her?"

She shook her head. "That's not what I meant. I haven't been home for Christmas in years. But it's Mom's favorite time of the year, and my two most recent visits have blasted a gaping hole in the celebratory mood."

"Not your fault."

"I know." And technically her mother deserved a hefty portion of the blame for putting her in this situation in the first place. She sighed. "I just wish things were different."

His hand covered hers. "They will be. Give it time."

A small smile tugged at her lips. "Are you always this optimistic?" He had as much reason to be sullen as her mother, yet like the song he'd been singing, every moment seemed to be filled with sunshine.

Her gave her hand a squeeze and then reached for a bottle of uncorked red wine, pouring two glasses half full. "Pretty much."

She could believe it. Just being in his presence was lifting her spirits.

He handed her one of the glasses while raising his. "A toast. To my daughter Aurora, the dawn of my day, the blue sky of my life, and the stargazer of the future."

She opened her mouth to respond, but nothing came out. He kept stunning her into silence.

He clinked his glass with hers and winked. "Cheers."

"Cheers," she murmured, taking a sip of the ruby liquid.

As it slid down her throat, a bubble of warm anticipation filled her, an almost giddy joy. She set down the glass, but the feeling remained, slowly intensifying. It took a moment to figure out why.

Drawn with the pull of a magnet, she turned her head in the direction of the road. "Micah's here."

Twenty

Micah Scott gripped the handlebars of his bike as he raced along the road toward his dad's house. He'd passed a few other cyclists on the way, but traffic in this area was light. Good thing. His mind was only partially focused on his surroundings.

He hadn't been able to stop thinking about the woman he'd met at the beach the previous day. He'd even dreamt about her, but in a convoluted mashup of images. At one point, she'd looked like a little kid, standing on a stairway at the far end of an enormous room. Then they'd been running together through a forest of trees, but not palms or banyans. The huge trunks had looked like redwoods. Toward the end of the dream, he'd found himself on his board riding a wave. She'd been walking on the beach, her back to him. He'd battled the wave, trying to get closer to the shore, but inexplicably the water had carried him out to sea.

He'd woken with a knot in his stomach and the powerful urge to ditch his classes and spend the day tracking her down. But sanity had prevailed. He couldn't abandon his students during finals week.

Making it through his classes and the previous day's exams had challenged his patience, but he'd finally cleared his desk and hit the road. She'd told him she knew his dad. That seemed the best place to start. And the closer he got to the house, the faster he pedaled.

Building up speed around the last curve, he made the turn across the road and onto the driveway, rising to pump the pedals as he climbed the steep incline.

It wasn't just that she was pretty. Pretty women were plentiful at the beach, and most wore a lot less than his mystery woman. But physical beauty had never been a deciding factor in any of his relationships. The easy banter she'd lobbed at him when he'd accidentally sprayed her with water had appealed to him a lot more. And while her strange behavior afterward had intrigued him, that wasn't what drove him, either.

He couldn't shake the sensation that she was... familiar. Looking into her eyes was like catching a snippet of a song he recognized but couldn't place.

Cresting the hill, he swung the bike to the left, coming to a stop in front of the entryway. The scents of food and the murmur of voices from the pool deck on the opposite side of the two-story stone wall made him pause. He hadn't considered that his dad might have company. Should he—

"We're out here, Micah," his dad called out.

Internal debate over. His dad had already sensed him.

He stripped off his biking gloves and helmet and left them inside the alcove with the bike. Pushing open the glass front door, he went down the stairs and crossed the living room to the open door to the pool area. But his feet ground to a halt as he stepped outside and recognized his dad's dinner guest. "You."

His mystery woman stood beside his dad, facing him. Her outfit today was very similar to what she'd worn the day before—long-sleeved tunic, pants, and boots—an odd choice for the tropical climate. Her blonde hair was pulled back in the same neat braid, although a few wisps had pulled loose to curl around her face.

And she was watching him like a doe watching a wolf.

He glanced at his dad. "Am I interrupting?"

"Not at all." His dad waved him forward. "We were expecting you."

"You were?" News to him.

"Yes. Have you eaten?"

"No. I came straight from work."

His dad smiled at the woman standing like a soldier at the front lines. "Told you."

She didn't smile back. "So you did." Her inflection made it impossible to tell whether she thought that was a good thing or a very bad thing.

He shifted his weight. "I can leave you alone if—"

"Nonsense." His dad rested a hand on his shoulder and turned him toward the house. "Come inside and we'll get you set up."

Micah glanced back at the woman. She hadn't moved a centimeter, her gaze still locked on him like he might pull a gun at any moment. Why was she so afraid of him?

"We'll be right back," his dad told her.

As soon as the door closed behind them, Micah lowered his voice while they headed for the kitchen. "Dad, I don't think she wants me here."

"Not true. She's just nervous. It's not what you think."

"I don't know what to think. I came over here to ask you about her, but I never expected to find her here. I met her at the beach yesterday, but she ran off like her tail was on fire. Now she's looking at me like I'm a serial killer. Why? Who is she?"

His dad pulled a bowl and wine glass from the cupboards. "It's her story to tell." He gestured to the drawer underneath. "Grab a placemat, napkin, and utensils."

He fetched the items as his dad filled the bowl with stew from the pot on the stove. "Will she tell me?"

"I hope so. She needs your help." His dad fixed him with a pointed stare. "But be patient. If you push, she'll push back."

"I wouldn't—"

"Yes, you would. You shine lights in all the dark places."

Had he just been insulted?

"No, I didn't mean it as an insult."

"Then what did you mean?"

"A warning. This is very hard for her. She needs to know you're on her side."

Tension drew his shoulder blades together. "Who is she, Dad?"

His dad's jaw worked, his eyes getting the far-off look he had when he really focused on his empathic senses. His lips parted, but then he shook his head. "Let's go." Picking up the bowl and wine glass, he headed back outside.

Micah followed, but at a slower pace, giving himself time to process. Whoever his mystery woman was, she was important to his dad. Which made her important to him.

Taking a deep breath, he stepped out onto the deck.

Twenty-One

This close to Micah, Aurora could feel every emotion tumbling through him—confusion, anxiety, even a little fear. Whatever their dad had told him in the kitchen, it had made him almost as wary of her as she was of him.

She hated being the cause of his discomfort. When he'd arrived, she'd sensed excitement, curiosity, and determination. She'd risen from the table without even realizing it, as if to greet him at the door. But when he'd appeared in front of her, his dark blond hair tousled where he'd run his fingers through it and his green eyes glowing with joy and recognition, a whirlwind had swept over her, alternately shoving her toward him and yanking her back. As a result, she'd stayed rooted to the deck.

"Let's eat." Her dad gestured to the table.

Returning to her seat, she picked up her wine glass and took a fortifying swallow, the dark liquid sloshing against the sides of the glass as her hand shook. *Breathe, Aurora.* She hadn't done much of that in the past few minutes. In addition to the tension gripping every muscle in her body, her head felt like someone had stuffed it with cotton.

While Micah laid out his place setting to her left and pulled out his chair, she focused on the ocean, counting to four as she inhaled, held the breath, and exhaled. A few repetitions slowed her heartbeat so it wasn't pounding in her ears.

Her dad gave her an encouraging smile as he reclaimed the seat across from her. "I understand you two met at the beach yesterday."

"Briefly," she replied. Her dad was trying to ease her into the conversation, but there wouldn't be anything easy about it.

"But I never got your name." Micah accepted the breadbasket and salad bowl their dad passed him.

Keep breathing, keep breathing. She clenched her hands in her lap in an effort to stop the internal quake rising from her core. "Hawke."

Micah's brows lifted. "Hawke? That's an unusual first name."

She shook her head. Micah obviously didn't know their mom's full name. Otherwise he would have reacted differently. "That's my last name."

"Oh. What's your first name?"

Don't tell him! Panic gripped her with icy fingers as she stared into his green eyes. If she took this step, there would be no going back.

An image of her mother flashed into her mind. Her mother had set this scene in motion all those years ago and had been dominated by her fears ever since.

Is that who you want to be?

No. No, it wasn't.

But the syllables still leaked out in slow motion. "Aurora."

Micah gazed at her, a frown pulling down the corners of his mouth. "Huh. That's interesting."

The wave had started to gather momentum. It was only a matter of time before it crested. She could either swim with it, or be sucked under.

If she was going down, she'd go down fighting. "Why's that?"

"I had a sister with that name."

Surging now. She could sense the emotional shift as his subconscious pulled pieces together—questioning, considering, analyzing.

Taking a deep breath, she started paddling for all she was worth. "No, Micah. You *have* a sister with that name." Reaching out with trembling fingers, she made contact.

Twenty-Two

Micah's ears rang like he'd been clocked by his board after a wipeout. Maybe he had, and this was all a fantasy conjured from delirium. That was more believable than the information his senses were sending him.

A sparkling pearlescent glow shone like a corona around the woman seated beside him. It gave off no visible light, casting no shadows, but a soothing warmth traveled up his arm from the point where her fingers encircled his wrist. Her touch held him transfixed as the glow enveloped him, wrapping him in sensations that danced over his skin, making his body tingle and lifting the small hairs on his arms and neck. The experience was incredibly... familiar.

How was that possible?

He stared at her, and she stared right back, like she was reading his mind. Or his soul. Her green eyes were familiar, too, as was the stubborn determination emphasized by the strong jut of her chin.

But his sister and mother had died when he was a child. "You can't be my sister."

Defiance flashed in those eyes. Also familiar. "Wanna bet?"

And then things got even stranger. An image appeared in his mind, playing out like a scene from a movie. He was looking out through the eyes of a little girl with long blonde hair who was standing on a staircase, screaming a name. *My-a!* A woman with short blonde hair stood on the ground floor, tears streaming down her cheeks. His mom? A little boy he recognized as his four-year-old self was on the ground floor too, with his father, who lifted him off the ground and carried him away from them. He struggled and called out to the little girl. *Ror!*

"I didn't die, Micah."

Was she speaking out loud? Or in his head?

"We were separated. Our dad brought you here. I stayed with our mother."

The image shifted, still in the same room, but now the little girl was at least ten years older, standing beside the blonde woman as they decorated an enormous Christmas tree.

Pressure built in his chest, making it difficult to breathe. More images assailed him. But these weren't being projected into his mind. They were crashing through the walls of his own memory.

Playing hide and seek in the redwood forest with his sister, which quickly turned into a game of tag since neither could hide from the other for long. An older girl with long dark hair teaching him how to swim in the nearby creek. Boisterous gatherings in the big room with his dad, mom, sister, the older girl, and two adults he couldn't quite picture clearly.

"That's right, Micah. That's home."

His focus moved away from the internal images, returning to the present. And the grown woman gazing at him with tears shimmering in her green eyes. "Ror?"

"Hey, My-a."

He didn't remember moving. One moment he was frozen in his chair, the next he'd hauled her out of hers and crushed her against the wall of his chest.

She let out a yelp that was half surprise, half laughter, the sound smothered against the fabric of his shirt.

"You're alive." He pulled her tighter, one hand on her back the other on her hair, as if she might vanish in a puff of smoke if he didn't hold her in place. But she was as real as the sensations surrounding them. The strength, the power, the intensity of their connection overwhelmed him.

"Nnoformmshlgr."

"What?" He pulled back.

She lifted her head, gasping and laughing at the same time. "Not for much longer. You're suffocating me."

"Oh." He eased up his death grip. "Sorry."

Her smile warmed him as much as her touch. She hugged him back. "I've missed you, too."

The breeze blew a stray tendril of hair across her eyes. He brushed it back. "Aurora." He stroked his hand along her silky hair, needing the tactile assurance that she wasn't a figment of his imagination. "My little sister, Aurora. You're really here."

She turned her head and pressed a sweet kiss on his palm. "I really am."

And yet, he couldn't believe it. Not fully. Not until his brain caught up with the images she'd shown him, what she'd said. Hope and fear warred in his chest. "Our mom?"

"She's fine. Still living with Marina and Gryphon."

The names nudged more long-forgotten memories to the surface. The parents of the girl with dark hair. "What about the dark-haired girl?"

"Mya?"

"What?"

She blinked, then shook her head. "Sorry. Not you, My-a. Lelindia."

"Lelindia?" He frowned. That didn't sound right. His subconscious tossed out an alternative. "Leelee. I called her Leelee."

She tilted her head, like he'd jogged a memory loose. "Yes, you did. We both did. She's fine, too."

"Oh. Good." He stared at her, his mind still processing. His sister was alive. And he'd had no idea.

As the initial shock began to wear off, a pang struck his chest, making him flinch. He didn't recognize the sensation, but it wasn't pleasant.

A bubble of heat followed it. Not the warmth from his sister, but something more primal. It built rapidly, flowing into his limbs and up his throat to his face.

Her grip around his torso tightened. "Micah, don't—"

The heat erupted, searching for a target. He pivoted, dragging her with him, his finger stabbing the air like a knife aimed at his father's heart. "You *lied* to me!"

His dad hadn't moved from his chair. He absorbed the blast of anger with a wince. "I know."

"How could you?"

"I had to."

"*Had* to?" He released Aurora and planted his fists on the tabletop, bringing him eye-level with his dad. "Why would you do that to me?"

The color leeched from his dad's skin. "It was the only way to protect the family. Your mother—"

"My mother was alive! And my sister! But you said—"

"Micah, stop!"

The sharp command brought his head around.

"He didn't have a choice." His little sister looked like a general or Fleet captain—head high, the tension in her shoulders giving off a subtle warning. But he also saw pain flashing in her eyes. He hadn't inherited their dad's ability to feel the emotions of others, but apparently she had. And by attacking their dad, he was hurting her, too.

He straightened, his voice softening. "Why didn't he have a choice?"

She glanced at their father. "That's going to take a while to explain." Her gaze moved to the open bottle of wine. "And we're going to need more wine."

Their dad stood. "I'll fetch another bottle."

Aurora's gaze flicked to Micah. then back to their dad. "Better make it two."

Twenty-Three

Two and a half bottles of wine later. Micah's head was spinning, but not from the alcohol. Thanks to his high metabolism, he could drink most people under the table. He'd won a fair share of bar bets.

But he was beginning to wonder if it wasn't just his metabolism that gave him that edge. He scrubbed a hand across his face. "You're saying I'm only half-human?"

"I'm saying we're *both* half-human." Aurora clasped his free hand and entwined their fingers. "Our dad is fully human, and our mom is fully Suulh."

Suulh. She'd said that word several times during the tale she and his dad had told him. He was still struggling to accept that the term applied to him.

He spread the fingers of his free hand in front of his eyes, turning his wrist to examine it from all sides. Completely normal. "But I look human."

"I know. So does Mom. It's parallel evolution. Biologically, the two species are almost identical."

He lowered his hand, gazing at her. "Almost?"

"The Suulh have abilities humans don't."

"Like that glow you generated." At the time, he'd been so focused on how familiar it had seemed, he hadn't questioned its existence. He was doing a hell of a lot of questioning now.

"Yes. Our family line developed the ability to produce a physical shield, and to manipulate electromagnetic energy. That ability gets stronger with each generation."

He frowned. "Then why can't I do that?"

She ducked her head, looking a little sheepish. "Because you're male."

"What does that have to do with it?"

"Most abilities in the Suulh flow from mother to daughter, particularly in the Guardian and Healer lines."

"So there's no way I could have inherited the shielding ability?"

Aurora shook her head.

He untwined their fingers and sat back. "That doesn't seem fair."

His dad picked up the open wine bottle. "Your mom was stunned that she gave birth to a son at all." He filled Micah's glass, then Aurora's. "From what she told me, sons in the Guardian and Healer lines are unheard of. And you seemed completely human. She'd expected—" He cut himself off, the bottle poised above his own glass as a shadow passed over his face.

"Expected what?" Micah prodded, although the sharp stab of pain in his chest gave him a pretty good idea.

His dad met his gaze, an equally pained look in his eyes. "A daughter."

Micah held his dad's gaze for a long time. "She didn't want a son, did she?"

His dad poured wine into his own glass, set the bottle down, then took a healthy swallow. "That's not it. She didn't think it was even a possibility. Her family always had daughters."

Micah ran his finger along the edge of his placemat, his gaze shifting to the ocean beyond. "I must have been quite an unpleasant surprise. A son without Suulh abilities."

His dad reached across the table, resting his hand on top of his forearm. "You were a gift. Never doubt that. She was surprised, yes, but your mother loved you from the moment you were conceived. She would face the fires of Hell to protect you."

The conviction in his dad's voice eased some of the tension in his chest.

Aurora placed her hand on his other arm, offering her support. The connection reminded him that she was dealing with the same situation he was, but from the opposite side. He wasn't alone.

His dad settled back in his chair. "And don't believe for a second that you were left in the shallow end of the gene pool. You act as a powerful amplifier for Aurora's abilities. That's why your mother was so determined to separate you." A small smile played around his lips. "And Aurora can't talk to animals."

Ah. He'd forgotten about that.

Aurora's eyes rounded. "You can talk to animals?"

Her curiosity made him smile. "Yeah."

"I didn't know that."

"Neither did I until I was six or seven. I thought everyone interacted with them the way I did. Even after I realized it was an unusual talent, I assumed it was an adaptation of Dad's empathic abilities. I had no idea..." He gestured to her and shrugged. "Besides, *talk* is a misnomer. It's more like image sharing." Kind of like the memories Aurora had shared with him. "Well, except for the dolphins."

"The dolphins?"

"They're very talkative."

Her head tilted. "Is that what they were doing while they were surfing with you? Talking?"

"More like goading me."

"What do you mean?"

"Compared to most people, I'm an excellent surfer. But compared to a dolphin, I'm a novice. And they delight in pointing that out."

The corners of her lips turned up. "Really? They tease you?"

"Mercilessly. It's why they're usually there when I surf. I'm the first human they've encountered who can understand them. It's a game for them, trying to break my concentration by pointing out my mistakes and weaknesses."

"I had no idea. It looked like a perfectly orchestrated performance."

"Sometimes it is. Depends on their moods. Yesterday they had an audience, so they were showing off a bit."

She grinned. "So were you."

"Hey!" He gave her a light swat on the arm. "No picking on your big brother."

The grin turned into a belly laugh. "Well, you were."

"Yeah, yeah." He shook his head, his smile fading as he gazed at her. Time for his second hardest question. "So, what made Mom tell you about us after all these years?"

All traces of laughter vanished like smoke, replaced by a haunting dread that made his chest ache. "There's a new threat, not just from the Teeli, but the person who's in control of their forces. And the Suulh." She glanced across the table at their dad. "I need help."

Saying the words seemed to cost her something. He got the distinct impression his little sister wasn't in the habit of asking anyone for help, let alone a father and brother she hadn't seen in nearly three decades.

"How can we help you?" She had the ability to create an energy shield and manipulate electromagnetic energy.

What could she possibly need from him?

Twenty-Four

Aurora took several slow breaths before she trusted herself to speak. For the second time in as many days, she found herself surrounded by unconditional love and support. Emotional overload seemed imminent.

"My empathic abilities give me an unusual connection with the Suulh. I don't just sense their emotions, I *feel* what they're feeling physically, in my own body. If I hurt them in any way, I hurt myself, too."

Micah's brow furrowed. "Why would you want to hurt them? Aren't you their Guardian? That Sayzee thing."

"Sahzade. Yes. And in normal circumstances I would never harm a Suulh. But when they were turned into mindless Necri soldiers, they attacked me. I was defending myself." And then one of the Necri had plummeted to her death. The shared suffering of the Necri's body breaking apart, without the release of losing consciousness, was one she never wanted to repeat.

She shuddered. "We don't know how many Necri soldiers the Teeli have created. Or how they plan to use them. But before our next confrontation, I have to figure out a way to fight them without debilitating myself."

He turned to their dad. "You're going to teach her to control her abilities?"

"That's right. Her skill level now is remarkable considering she's self-taught, but I can help her achieve the mastery she needs."

"Okay." Micah met her gaze. "But what can I do?" He spread his hands. "I can't sense emotions."

"I know. But Dad thinks you might be able to help me anyway."

"How?"

Her dad cradled his wine glass in his hands. "Your connection to Aurora is unique. We already know you amplify her abilities. But I suspect you'll be able to help her focus them as well."

Micah glanced at her. "But I don't know how you do what you do."

The corner of their dad's mouth quirked up. "Let's test that." He turned to her. "I want you to generate a shield ten centimeters in front of your body and block me from touching you."

An odd request, but she did as he'd asked. Lifting her hand, she summoned her shield. The pearlescent glow surrounded her, forming a solid barrier.

"Good." Her dad set down his wine glass, then reached across the table like he was going to clasp her hand. His own met with the shield and stopped. He placed his palm flat against the surface, pushing against it in several places, but without effect.

Maintaining the shield took no effort on her part. She'd deflected cascading boulders without breaking a sweat. If she hadn't been watching him, she wouldn't have even been aware that he was trying to break through.

He sat back, folding his hands over his stomach. "Now Micah, I want you to try it."

Micah looked as confused by the request as she was, but he dutifully reached out toward her hand.

And made contact with her skin.

They both jerked back as their connection flared.

She checked the shield, but it was still in place. Micah's hand and wrist had somehow pushed right through it.

"I don't understand." She stared at their joined hands, then turned to their dad. "How did he—"

"Natural immunity." Her dad's smile lit up his blue eyes. "From an energetic point of view, you sense Micah as an extension of yourself, no different than your arm or leg. And just as you can't use your shield to sever your own limbs, you can't use it to block him, either."

How could that be?

She returned her attention to their hands. The evidence was right there, but she couldn't quite believe it. She met Micah's gaze. "I'm going to push the shield toward you." A flare of alarm streaked toward her. "But I promise to stop if it hurts you."

"You can't hurt him."

She shot her dad a look before focusing on her shield. He seemed so certain, but she wasn't.

Keeping the shield completely solid, she pushed it outward. It traveled along Micah's arm like it wasn't there, then passed through his torso and legs before meeting resistance from his chair. "Hmm." Micah now sat completely within the shield. And that wasn't the only change. The power flowing through her from their joined hands resembled a nuclear reactor. An asteroid could probably fall out of the sky, leaving a kilometer-wide crater around them, and they'd be just fine.

The image produced a bolt of panic. She yanked back from Micah's grip like his hand had morphed into a viper, dropping the shield.

He lurched toward her. "What's—"

"Don't!" She shoved out of her chair. It clattered to the pool deck as she put three meters between them, backing toward the house.

"Aurora—"

"Just... give me a moment." Her pulse beat behind her eyes, her breath rasping in and out. She tried to slow it down, but the image in her head kept pushing it back up. The potential devastation, the horror...

"Stop."

The command, spoken with the quiet authority of a parent, brought her gaze to her father.

"Aurora, whatever you're thinking, just stop. You're conjuring nightmares where they don't exist."

"But we could—"

"Stop." He stood, walking toward her with steady, measured steps. "Uncertainty leads to fear. Fear leads to rash action. But you have nothing to fear."

Like hell I don't! Her gaze darted to Micah. He looked stricken, like she'd backhanded him. But recognizing that fact helped her get out of her head and back into her surroundings. She could sense his fear and anxiety swirling through her.

Was he afraid of her?

The tenor of his thoughts brushed her consciousness. No. He was afraid he'd somehow hurt her.

Drawing in a shaky breath, she released it on a sigh.

Her dad stayed in front of her, his arms loose at his sides, giving her time to collect herself. "Better." Not a question, because he could feel the shift in her emotions.

"Much better." She glanced at Micah. "Sorry."

He raised his hands, palms up. "No apologies." His mouth pinched. "You okay?"

"Yeah. Just freaked myself out." But for the first time, she'd had someone who could handle the situation, talk her down. Too bad her dad hadn't been handy when she'd electrocuted Cade and uncovered Reanne's identity.

Those memories brought their own tremors, so she shoved them back in her mental lockbox. She'd deal with them later.

Her dad stepped forward, resting his hands on her shoulders. "We'll get through this. I promise."

She drew strength from his touch, and the steady flow of his emotions. No fear. No anxiety. Not even worry. Just determination, hope, and love. Such a contrast to the emotions she battled whenever she was around her mom.

She placed her hand over his and squeezed. "I think I'm going to call it a night."

He squeezed back. "A good night's sleep can do wonders."

She wouldn't know. It had been a long time since she'd slept well. She met Micah's gaze. "Will I see you tomorrow?"

"Do you want to?"

His uncertainty nicked her heart. "Yes. Definitely."

The uncertainty faded like shadows fleeing from the sun's rays. "Then I'll be here as soon as classes are over."

Twenty-Five

Walking into the Teeli Embassy reminded Cade of entering an underground cavern, even though the building wasn't subterranean.

The original structure had been a three-story boutique hotel, converted into the Embassy after the Teeli became Council members. The renovation had eliminated all the windows on the first two stories, leaving only a few dormer-style windows on the third floor, visible from outside. Interior lighting was provided by wall sconces spaced at two-meter intervals along the wall, creating shadows that made the space appear ominous or protective, depending on your point of view.

The Teeli had waited almost a full day before they'd sent word to Payne that they would agree with the Admiral's request. Perhaps that's how long it had taken to get word to Reanne and a response back. The meeting had been scheduled for the following day at nine-hundred hours.

His team had made good use of the time. Drew had pulled the building's blueprints and helped Gonzo and Reynolds come up with an exit strategy. Cade had memorized the layout and was using the micro-surveillance devices attached to two of his fingertips to send images back to the team.

The long corridor was devoid of doors or ornamentation except the sconces, creating a narrow chute with the front entrance at one end and the security station at the other. He didn't see any indication of hidden weaponry or defenses, but the metal door beyond the security station looked sturdy enough to serve as a starship's exterior hatch. Once closed and locked, it would probably be easier to blow a hole through the exterior walls than open the door.

One of the security guards posted near the security scanner moved in front of it, blocking the path, his hand resting lightly on his weapon. Apparently any humans who worked for the Teeli didn't have to pretend to be pacifists. "Name?" His gruff voice made the word come out as more of a command than a question.

The Admiral halted, giving the guard a warm smile. "Admiral Schreiber and Commander Ellis to see Delegate Bare'Kold."

The guard flicked three-fingers at the guards standing behind him without taking his gaze off the Admiral and Cade. "Check it."

"Checking." The woman at the display didn't sound quite as anti-social as the human roadblock standing in front of them, but there was no interest or warmth in her voice or expression, either. "Confirmed. Schreiber and Ellis scheduled at nine-hundred hours."

The guard took one step to the side. "Through the scanner. You first." He pointed at the Admiral.

The Admiral obeyed, stepping through the scanner, which remained silent. Another guard, even more muscled than the one standing in front of Cade, stopped him on the other side. "Wait here."

The first guard motioned to Cade. "Now you."

Nice to meet you, too. Cade kept the comment to himself as he stepped toward the scanner. He needed to be as invisible as possible during this meeting, although thanks to Reanne's knowledge of his unit's activities, he couldn't be the proverbial fly on the wall.

The only item in their favor was Reanne's ignorance of the link they'd made between her and the Teeli. She would assume the Admiral's visit was a diplomatic mission to maintain cordial relations with the Teeli and smooth over the faux pas regarding the *Starhawke*'s failed mission. She also knew Cade regularly accompanied the Admiral on fact-finding missions, so his presence wouldn't draw undue scrutiny from her.

He walked through the scanner, which thankfully didn't make a peep despite the weapon concealed in his clothing. Gonzo's newest toy had successfully evaded detection.

The third guard shifted to the left so that he blocked Cade's path as well as the Admiral's. "Stay here."

Shall we sit, too? Another comment he kept to himself. Monosyllable Guard wasn't likely to appreciate his sense of humor.

A faint pop of a broken seal preceded movement behind the guard as the hatch-door swung outward. A woman appeared, dressed in a neutral-toned pantsuit, her straight auburn hair pulled back in a simple ponytail.

Cade blinked. "Magee."

The woman smiled, her gaze shifting from the Admiral to Cade. "Admiral. Commander. Good to see you. Follow me."

The Admiral didn't move right away, apparently as stunned by his former PA's appearance as he was.

Magee glanced over her shoulder. "Admiral?"

He gave a barely perceptible twitch, like he was coming out of a waking dream. "Yes, lead on." He didn't look at Cade, but the tension that radiated from him was palpable.

Cade's mind raced while the pads of his index fingers itched. The two microscopic surveillance devices rested against the skin on each hand, held by a bonding agent that would attach them to another person's skin with the correct application of pressure. He'd been planning to affix them both to Bare'Kold, but Magee's presence gave him a rare opportunity that would be so much better.

Following her and the Admiral through the security doorway, they turned a corner into another long corridor that seemed to run the length of the building to the back, with doors opening off to the right.

"I was surprised by your transfer request, Isabeau." The Admiral's voice held just the right note of wounded pride and curiosity. "What prompted the change?"

"The opportunity of a lifetime." Her smile seemed cheerful enough as she glanced at them, but Cade had seen Magee's natural smile too many times to mistake this for the real thing. It was a close approximation but not quite right, like watching a clone imitating Magee. "In a couple weeks, I'll be traveling with Delegate Bare'Kold to the Teeli homeworld."

Cade almost swallowed his tongue. "You're leaving Earth?"

Her gaze met his, her hazel eyes looking ever-so-slightly glazed. "Oh, yes. It's an incredible honor. Few humans have seen Ways'lend."

He was willing to bet *no* humans had seen it.

She stopped in front of the last door before the corridor turned another corner. Opening it, she gestured them inside.

Cade didn't move.

Neither did the Admiral. "I can understand your excitement, Isabeau. It's a rare opportunity. But I would have appreciated some notice. And an explanation before you left. We've been friends a long time."

Her smile slipped a notch, a tiny crease appearing between her brows. "I know. And I'm sorry. It all happened very quickly."

One of the doors they'd passed opened and a figure stepped into the corridor.

His shoulder-length white hair and pinkish-grey skin blended with the muted grey of his clothing, which flowed around him as he strode toward them with the authority of a king. His oversized ice-blue eyes focused briefly on Cade before moving on to the Admiral and Magee, taking in the situation with cool efficiency. "Is there a problem?"

His Galish was easy to understand, though accented with a heaviness that made the words ponderous.

Cade had only seen pictures of Delegate Bare'Kold. They didn't do him justice. His features gave a vague impression of a featherless snowy owl—one intent on making Cade and the Admiral his evening meal.

Hard to imagine the Teeli as pacifists, now. Everything about Bare'Kold screamed predator. But his reaction to the Teeli might have been different a few months ago, before he'd learned the truth.

The Admiral stepped forward while Cade edged closer to Magee. "No problem, Delegate Bare'Kold." The Admiral held out both hands, palms up, in the Teeli gesture of greeting.

Bare'Kold clasped the Admiral's hands in his, their gazes locking briefly before they stepped apart.

The Admiral nodded toward Magee. "I haven't seen Lt. Magee since my return. I understand you're the one who lured her away from my office."

Bare'Kold's expression did not change. "Admiral Payne introduced us during your absence. I was moved to offer her a position on my staff. She accepted. Her skill set has proven invaluable."

And her knowledge of the Admiral even more so, no doubt. Cade watched the Admiral's reaction.

He responded with a sad smile. "She is invaluable. And a dear friend. It's difficult to say goodbye." He faced Magee. "You will be missed, Isabeau."

The small line reappeared between her brows. "Thank you, sir."

Bare'Kold moved next to her, cupping her elbow in his hand in a manner that looked more personal than professional. "That will be all for now, Ms. Magee."

She glanced at him, her lids lowering in a slow-motion blink. "Yes, sir."

She pivoted just as slowly away from Bare'Kold toward the back of the building.

Cade grabbed the opportunity as she passed him to clasp her right hand in both of his, pressing his index finger to the outside of her wrist as he held her hand. "Safe travels, Magee."

She tilted her head in acknowledgment, the movement robotic, giving no indication that she'd registered the extra pressure on her skin. She was clearly under the spell of Teeli influence, and completely unaware of it. "Thank you, Commander." Without another word she disengaged her hand and strode away, the click of her footsteps on the tile floor fading after she rounded the corner.

We'll see you soon.

"I do not believe we have met."

Cade turned back to Bare'Kold, who was sizing him up with those arctic eyes.

He'd extended both his hands in welcome. Now that Cade suspected that the Teeli manipulated through touch, that gesture took on a whole new meaning.

"Commander Ellis." Reaching out, he clasped the Delegate's hands, paying close attention to the mental and emotional reaction the connection produced.

The urge to back up hit him immediately, but he'd anticipated it and shoved it away, focusing on cataloguing the tactile sensations. Bare'Kold's hands felt cool and smooth to the touch, not just on his palm, but on his entire hand. It also felt padded, the bony structure underneath difficult to discern, plumped up in a way that on a human would indicate excess fat cells, although Bare'Kold's weight seemed proportional to his size.

He met the Teeli's gaze. "It's a pleasure to meet you." It gave him the opportunity to press the second surveillance device to the outside edge of Bare'Kold's hand.

"The pleasure is mine." Bare'Kold maintained the connection much longer than he had with the Admiral, his pupils dilating to eclipse the blue iris, as if he was watching for a response he wasn't getting. Perfect. He was too busy trying to influence Cade's emotional state to realize he'd just been tagged.

Cade stared back until Bare'Kold released his grip.

The Teeli turned to the Admiral, a haughty lift to his chin. "Please, join me." He led the way through the open door into the room beyond.

Cade hung back for a moment, glancing toward the corner where Magee had disappeared. How long did the effect of successful Teeli manipulation last? He'd witnessed her reaction to Bare'Kold's touch. Did she have moments of clarity when she realized she was a prisoner? Or was she living in a permanently compliant state?

She'd been more like a daughter than a PA to the Admiral, working closely with him for years. Seeing her under Teeli control had to be tearing him up inside. But with the two surveillance devices in place, they had a chance to find a way to break her free—assuming they could get it done before Bare'Kold whisked her off to Ways'lend.

Cade followed Bare'Kold and the Admiral into the informal conference room. Three long angular couches in a U-shape surrounded a rectangular coffee table made of metal and glass. The overall impression was sterile and uninviting, further emphasized when Cade sat beside the Admiral on the center couch. The cushions were cold and hard as a rock.

Bare'Kold didn't seem to find them unpleasant. He lounged on the far couch, his arm draped over the metal rail along the back. "Admiral Payne informed me you wished to apologize."

So much for small talk. Bare'Kold's patronizing attitude and indulgent smile put Cade's teeth on edge.

The Admiral sat forward, steepling his fingers between his knees. "Yes, I do. I deeply regret any inconvenience my actions caused you and the Teeli. Admiral Payne made it clear your scientists were invested in the study of the binary system, and that this was a wonderful opportunity for cooperation between our two peoples."

"Yes, it was." Bare'Kold's smile turned decidedly chilly. "And yet you called off the ship that accepted the mission. You insulted my people after we extended a gesture of generosity and goodwill. Your actions are inexcusable."

"You are correct." The Admiral tapped the tips of his fingers together. "That's why I'm here. To ask if you would consider allowing the *Starhawke* to complete the original mission."

The gleam that lit Bare'Kold's pale eyes didn't thaw the ice in his words. "You rejected our offer once. Why should we make it again?"

Because your goal is to capture Aurora and her ship. Cade kept his expression neutral, watching for Bare'Kold's tells. Cracking that icy façade would be his pleasure.

The Admiral opened his hands, palms up. "Please, do not let this be a black mark in the history of our two species. The fault is mine alone."

Bare'Kold's stony expression didn't change. Apparently he was going to play hard to get.

The Admiral pressed on. "I would hate to see Captain Hawke and her crew miss out on this opportunity, and for your people to lose out on the cooperative benefits that could result."

Bare'Kold's gaze flicked to Cade. "What is your role in this, Commander?"

He had his answer ready. "I served as an interim pilot for the *Starhawke* on their first mission to Gaia. I'm familiar with the captain and her crew. Since they could not be here to plead their case, I offered to come in their stead."

The arrogance quotient in the air rose fifty percent. "What is so important that they could not make their request in person?" His gaze bored into the Admiral. "Another classified mission?"

The Admiral waved away the jab. "Nothing like that. They had personal matters to attend to, but I expect them back at Sol Station by the first of the year."

"I see." The Teeli's eyes flared wide, his body going still.

Cade had spent too much time dodging predators not to recognize Bare'Kold's reaction for what it was—the Teeli believed he'd cornered the canary and was preparing to snap his jaws on its throat.

"I will, of course, need to confer with my superiors regarding any overtures of reconciliation." Bare'Kold's fingers stroked the metal of the couch like he was stroking a cat's fur.

The Admiral nodded. "I understand."

"A recording of your deepest apologies would go a long way to smoothing the path."

Cade suppressed a growl. Bare'Kold wanted the Admiral to beg.

The Admiral didn't seem the least bit ruffled. "I can record it now if you wish."

"By all means."

Bare'Kold reclined against the cushions with a satisfied smirk as the Admiral lifted his comband and activated the recording feature. After reiterating what he'd already said to the delegate, he closed with a plea for understanding and his best wishes for a positive outcome to the incident.

Switching off the recorder, he tapped his comband. "I have sent you a copy."

Bare'Kold inclined his head. "I will see that high command receives it." He rose, his body language and tone indicating they were being dismissed.

"Thank you." The Admiral stood.

Cade followed as Bare'Kold walked them to the end of the corridor where a guard was waiting for them, arms crossed like a bouncer at a bar.

"See our guests out." Bare'Kold nodded to the guard before turning to Cade and the Admiral. "Until our paths meet again." He held his palms up in a Teeli farewell, then pivoted and strode down the corridor.

"Come with me."

The guard's gruff command drew Cade's attention off Bare'Kold, to where a meaty hand was reaching out to propel him forward. He stepped aside before it fell on his shoulder, walking with the Admiral through the hatch-door where they'd entered, back through the security checkpoint, and out onto the sidewalk.

The bright sunlight blinded after the muted artificial lighting inside the building. The sun had burned off the morning's grey marine layer.

Cade tapped his comband as they walked along the tree-lined pathway to the transport platform at the bottom of the hill, summoning the Admiral's personal vehicle. It glided silently to a stop in front of them, the driver and passenger doors swinging open.

The Admiral slid behind the wheel while Cade claimed the passenger seat. Neither of them spoke until the Admiral had set the auto-controls and the vehicle had exited the gated embassy grounds. "Were you successful?"

"Yes. Magee and Bare'Kold are both tagged." Cade sent a message to Bella and Justin, confirming they were monitoring the feed.

"Well done."

Cade glanced at the Admiral.

The muscles of his jaw flexed beneath his weathered skin, his gaze on the flow of traffic as they headed toward the road that would take them to HQ.

But Cade doubted he was seeing his surroundings. "We'll get her back, sir."

The Admiral's gaze met his, turbulent emotions swirling in the hazel depths. "Without tipping our hand regarding our knowledge of the Teeli manipulation and secret agenda?"

A tall order, but his team had waded into difficult waters before and come out on top. "We'll find a way. The team's already monitoring the video feeds."

"I appreciate your willingness to help, but retrieving Isabeau isn't our top priority, much as I would like it to be. Considering Bare'Kold's hold on her, she might even put up a fight if we tried. I think her presence today was meant to convince us that her acceptance of this new position was genuine, to allay our suspicions or concerns, to get us to stop digging. Or it might have been orchestrated to put her in a more receptive frame of mind for manipulation. If her subconscious accepts this situation as normal, she'll be more pliable."

"Then getting her out of there *is* a priority."

"Not at the expense of the long game. Aurora is, and always will be, our top priority. Whatever they convince Isabeau to say or do isn't as critical as Aurora's safety. Your mission is to find out what Reanne and the Teeli plan to do next."

Twenty-Six

Much to her surprise, Aurora slept like the dead. By the time she awoke, sunlight was streaming through the east facing window of her room. Sliding out of bed, she padded to the bathroom, pausing in the corridor to listen for sounds in the house.

Nothing.

After splashing water on her face, pulling her hair back in a loose braid, and getting dressed, she walked barefoot out into the loft. The door to her dad's bedroom was open. A quick check confirmed he wasn't inside, and his bed was neatly made.

Continuing down the stairs, she turned left into the kitchen. The scent of coffee and bread hung in the air. She spotted a note tucked under the fire engine red pepper mill sitting on the island counter.

Aurora, I'll be at the university most of the day, but you can reach me on my comm.

He listed the number and the time he expected to be home.

A friend's delivering a few things for you this morning. Open them when they arrive.

Huh. What would he be sending her that he couldn't just bring home with him? Maybe he had study materials he wanted her to go over before their first session. He was a professor, after all.

The house is yours for the day, so make yourself at home. See you soon. Love, Dad

Such a simple, ordinary note, yet it managed to bring a coating of moisture to her eyes.

Leaving the note on the counter, she moved to the cupboards, scrounging around under she located a container of cinnamon spice loose leaf tea and a loaf of freshly baked zucchini bread. After the tea had steeped and she'd sliced off a chunk of bread, she took her breakfast out onto the pool deck, settling into the same chair she'd used the previous night.

The azure blue and turquoise green water of the Pacific undulated in gentle waves, the palm trees swaying in the breeze. Quite a difference to the chilly December mornings at Stoneycroft. Or trudging through the snowbanks to reach her classes at the Academy.

But very similar to the view from the Suulh settlement on Azaana.

While she sipped her tea and nibbled her bread, her gaze followed the rise and fall of the water in the distance. She'd pushed all thoughts of Azaana to the back of her mind in the past few weeks. Putting Justin Byrnes in charge of keeping in close contact with Raaveen had worked out fine while she'd been with Cade. Now that she wasn't talking to him anymore, she'd created a problem for herself.

Since Azaana was in Kraed territory, she'd have to go through the Kraed communication network to reach the Suulh. Which meant going through Siginal Clarek. She wasn't ready to tell anyone where she was, least of all Jonarel's father.

He'd used Jonarel's clan loyalty to keep tabs on her movements for years, without any thought for her right to privacy. The Admiral had indicated their actions had been motivated by a desire to protect her, but no matter how well-intentioned, their overreach into her life was still wrong. She'd worked through her anger with the Admiral, but she still had an explosive emotional grenade with Siginal's name on it. She'd have to let Mya take point with the Suulh until she was prepared to deal with him.

He'd have to wait in line.

Finishing her tea and bread, she stood and gathered her dishes, then paused. What next? She didn't have anywhere to be, or anything specific to do. In fact, the entire day stretched before her like a giant question mark. Not a good thing. She wasn't used to being idle.

If she had exercise clothes and running shoes, she'd go explore Diamond Head, but she was still stuck with her long-sleeved tunics and boots.

Her gaze strayed to the pool, the surface rippling as the waterfall on the far end tumbled crystal-clear water over the smooth stones and into the basin.

The water in the pool didn't contain any salt. And she was all alone.

But she didn't have a swimsuit.

Maybe...

A quick check confirmed the pool area wasn't visible from any of the surrounding homes. And anyone on the ocean would have to use binoculars to see her.

Feeling like a kid with her hand in the cookie jar, she moved to the lounge chair near the steps. Slipping off her clothes and leaving them in a neat pile on the chair, she dipped her toe in the water. Cool, but warmer than she'd expected. The sparkle of the sun on the surface created a sea of fire opals, beckoning her. Taking a deep breath, she dove in.

She curved along the pool's bottom before breaking the surface near the base of the waterfall. She'd never skinny-dipped in her life—had never had the opportunity or inclination—but she could instantly understand the appeal. Unburdened by material clinging to her skin, she glided through the water like a seal, spinning and flowing like she'd been born with fins instead of fingers.

She swam the length of the pool and around the perimeter, mostly underwater, losing track of time as she immersed herself in the soothing caress of the water and sunshine.

The tips of her fingers had pruned by the time the hum of a vehicle coming up the driveway pulled her out of mermaid mode.

Her dad's friend had arrived.

And she was still nude.

Swimming to the shallow end, she put her foot on the first step and froze. She'd forgotten to grab a towel!

Impulsive behavior biting her in the butt again.

Using her hands to squeeze the water from her braid, she climbed out onto the pool deck. The breeze hit her skin, making her shiver, but it also helped her as she whisked moisture off her body with firm strokes. She bypassed her underwear and bra and pulled on her tunic and pants. They clung in unpleasant places, but at least she was fit to venture back into the house to answer the door.

A young woman with light brown skin and thick dark hair piled in a haphazard topknot stood on the other side. She grinned when she saw Aurora. "Shower or pool?" she asked as soon as Aurora opened the door.

Her light-hearted attitude smoothed away any embarrassment. "Pool."

The woman nodded. "Looks like Brendan was right."

"About what?"

The woman's brown eyes twinkled. "You'll see." Turning, she hefted one of two matching half-meter square cardboard boxes, handing it to Aurora.

The box was light for its size. Definitely not books or anything electronic. What on earth had her dad sent over?

"And the second." The woman held out the matching box.

Aurora set it next to the first, noting the logo of a sea turtle stamped on the side above the name *Hawksbill Surf Shop*.

"Surf shop?"

The woman nodded. "We supply all Micah's clothing and gear."

"But I—"

"Trust me." The woman looked her up and down with another grin. "I picked it all out myself. You'll love it. And I added a few other items you'll need. But read this first." She handed Aurora a small envelope. "Enjoy!" With a toss of her head and a wave, she trotted off.

Enjoy what?

Only one way to find out.

Opening the envelope, she unfolded a notecard with a tropical scene on the front. Her dad's neat handwriting filled the interior.

You'll need to be comfortable to work. Keep whatever you like and put the rest back in the box.

Kneeling beside the first box, she popped open the lid. A kaleidoscope of color hit her—aqua, fuchsia, plum, teal, lime, and a plethora of colors she couldn't name. Reaching inside the box, she pulled out the first item, a teal T-shirt with a drawing of an umbrella and beach towel on the front and the phrase "Life's a beach" below. A stack of at least twenty other shirts in similar styles lay underneath, along with shorts and lounge pants in matching or complimentary colors. Under those, she found assorted packages of underwear.

Her dad had provided her with a new wardrobe.

Lifting the lid off the second box, she found an array of tank-style swimsuits, both one piece and two piece, socks, and six boxes of running shoes.

She checked the label on the first pair of shoes she pulled out. Her exact size. Either her dad had a very good eye, or he'd been in communication with Marina since she'd arrived.

She hadn't thought to ask him if he planned to notify Marina she was here. Or what that would mean if he did. Would Marina share that information with her mom? Did she want her to?

What she didn't want to do was think about the emotional turmoil her mom was dealing with right now. Didn't want to imagine her mom tackling the holiday rush at Hawke's Nest while she struggled to block out the knowledge that her daughter was with her husband and son. And all the ramifications of that reality.

A popping sound brought her focus back to her surroundings. She glanced at the shoebox in her hand, which now had a deep indentation in the lid where she'd squeezed it until it buckled. She unclenched her hand, and it popped back up.

Thinking about her mom was counterproductive, especially when her dad had just delivered such bounty. They could discuss how she'd pay him back after she'd determined what she'd be keeping.

Leaving the box of swimsuits, socks, and shoes, she lifted the second box and carried it upstairs. After a quick shower, she began pulling items out of the box to try on. Anything she liked went into the closet, anything she didn't went back in the box.

Twenty minutes later, she had a respectable number of clothing options in shades of blue, green, and brown at her disposal, including the fern-green T-shirt and lounge pant combination she was wearing. The clean underwear was a real bonus. She could hand-wash and rotate out the two bras she'd brought with her, but three pairs of underwear wouldn't have been as easy to work with.

Placing the remaining items in the box, she carried it out of the room, but paused at the top of the stairs. She still had quite a few hours before her dad would get home. Curiosity pulled her toward the room her dad had identified as Micah's.

Leaving the box on the floor, she walked to the open doorway. The corridor was lined with framed pictures just like hers, but these were all of aquatic animals and seabirds rather than space images. The bathroom to her left had a window facing west toward the lush green foliage of the hillside. The archway to her right opened into a mirror-image layout of her room, complete with interior balcony at a ninety-degree angle to her room, with the curved natural stone wall that sloped from the lower level creating an atrium effect.

The sea life theme continued with a painted mural that filled the west wall. The top half showed the Hawaiian shoreline with birds flying overhead and palms swaying in the breeze. The bottom half showed the view under the water, including a rainbow of tropical fish, sea turtles, and a dolphin that appeared to be swimming into the room, a mischievous look in its eye.

She'd be willing to bet Micah had given a lot of input to the artist on that one.

The oversized framed photograph hanging on the wall above the bed drew her attention next. The colors were almost as saturated as the mural's. It depicted a surfer in a black and pale green wetsuit riding a deep teal wave amid cascading white foam. His head was turned away from the camera as a dolphin leapt out of the surf beside him, backlit by the peach and grey of a pale sunset as sparkling water droplets streamed from its dorsal fin and tail.

Even seeing his body in profile, it was easy to identify Micah's blond hair and muscular form. She couldn't see the smile on his face, but she instinctively knew it was there.

She pivoted in a slow circle, taking in the feel of the space. Micah had grown up here, surrounded by the sights and sounds of this tropical paradise. And on some deeply subconscious level, she'd shared that experience. It explained why she always felt so at home on tropical islands, like the one she'd chosen for the Suulh settlement on Azaana.

Ever since she'd physically connected with him the previous night, she'd been aware of him on a more conscious level. She could sense his moods almost as clearly as if he was standing beside her. The playful joy that seemed to be his default emotional setting had added a buoyancy to her step all morning.

She glanced at the picture above the bed. Maybe his influence had been the push that had sent her into the pool without a swimsuit. She had no problem imagining him swimming in the buff on a regular basis. His full-throttle enthusiasm for life matched her own. They approached their experiences in very different ways, but she understood him, understood what motivated him.

Her dad was more of a puzzle.

Since her mom had never talked about him, she knew nothing about his life before she'd been born. Or how long he and her mom had been together before she and Micah came into the picture. She didn't even know how her parents had met.

Maybe the house could offer some insights.

Exiting Micah's room, she hefted the box of clothes and carried it downstairs. Setting it near the front door, she turned her attention to inspecting the lower level for clues to her dad's history.

And came up largely empty.

Oh, she'd found plenty of framed pictures of her dad and Micah, but they'd all been taken after they'd left Stoneycroft. She'd spotted her dad's friend Kai in a couple of the group shots, standing next to a much younger version of the dark-haired woman she'd met on the beach, the one Micah had called Birdie. Odds were good that was Kai's daughter, Iolana.

But she hadn't found any pictures of her dad when he was a kid, or any pictures of his parents or extended family. Were her dad's parents still alive?

She'd never given the concept of grandparents much thought growing up, since neither she nor Mya had them. But that was no longer true. Mya had met Breaa, her grandmother, on the Suulh homeworld.

Which begged the question of whether Aurora's grandparents were still trapped on the homeworld, too.

Twenty-Seven

Surreal.

That was the only word that could describe Micah's morning. When he wasn't bouncing off the walls at the thought of seeing his sister, he was watching the faces of those he passed, trying to decide if they were looking at him strangely.

Finding out you were half-human could do that to a person.

He'd expected that knowledge to keep him up most of the night, but instead he'd slept so soundly he'd almost arrived late to work. His TA could have handled supervising the final exam, but he'd always believed his students needed to see he was as dedicated to being there for their educations as they were.

He'd focused on grading yesterday's exams to keep his mind from wandering. It worked, kinda. But his gaze kept straying to his hands and arms, searching for any signs of abnormality, anything physical that would show that he was different.

Nope. Same tanned skin and blond hair. No tentacles sprouting from his fingers or chameleon color-changing ability.

Not that the interstellar alien species humans had encountered so far had those traits. The Kraed's skin looked very different from humans, with the patterns of brown on green, but as far as he knew they couldn't change color. Neither could the Teeli. Their albino white hair and grey-pink skin was distinctive, and they certainly didn't have tentacles.

He'd heard rumors that the Setarips had a more reptilian look to them, but he'd never seen a picture, if one even existed.

His sister might know. She'd indicated she worked as an officer for the Fleet, although he was still hazy on the details. He'd only been able to take in so much last night. Yesterday at this time, he'd been clueless about the identity of his mystery woman. Never in a million years would he have guessed the truth.

He wrapped up his second final in early afternoon and headed immediately to his dad's house. He'd contacted Birdie during his break between classes to let her know he wouldn't be meeting her for their planned surfing date. She'd rolled with it, not even asking any questions after he told her he was helping his dad with a project. But he'd promised they'd hit the waves together over the weekend.

Maybe he could convince Aurora to join them. She'd already met Birdie and they'd seemed to get along well. No surprise really, since Birdie was his best friend. In many ways, she'd become the sister he'd lost.

Only now his sister had been found. And he wanted to share his world with her. Which meant getting her out into the water.

Reaching the top of his dad's driveway, he swung his bike to the left and parked it by the entrance. He didn't see Aurora through the glass front doors, so he called out to her as he stepped inside. "Aurora?"

"In here." Her voice carried from the living room leading out to the deck.

He headed for the stairs, spotting her over the low wall. She was on the floor near the Christmas tree, her body contorted in a convoluted pose with back bent, one arm holding her leg, and the other stretched toward the ceiling. Soft music played in the background, a cheerful holiday tune.

"What are you doing?"

She smiled as she released her hold on her leg. "Yoga."

"Ah." He should have guessed. Several yoga groups gathered regularly on the beach, but he'd never paid much attention to the poses. "Nice outfit." She'd traded the darker clothes from the previous night for a green T-shirt and lounge pant combination that made her green eyes luminous.

She popped to her feet and brushed a hand over her shirt. "Dad sent them over from the surf shop."

He grinned. His dad hadn't been able to wait even a day to get her into native gear. And it looked good on her. "I'm guessing there was more than what you're wearing."

"Two boxes full, including running shoes and swimsuits."

His grin widened. "Great! Now you're ready for your first surfing lesson."

But instead of smiling back, her expression closed down like he'd flipped a light switch. "I don't think so."

"Why not?" The sudden change threw him off balance. He understood why she'd freaked out on the beach the first time she'd seen him. She'd just figured out who he was, and was dealing with the shock. But they'd worked through those complications last night.

"It's saltwater. It's not safe."

"Safe?" The word had no context. "Do you have some sensitivity to saltwater?" Maybe it made her break out in a rash.

"No, nothing like that." She rubbed her hands up and down her arms like she was cold.

He moved closer. When she didn't back away, he rested his hands on her shoulders. "Is it a phobia?" Some people were terrified of the ocean, although that was hard to believe with her. Her shielding ability would protect her from any danger.

"No." She gazed into his eyes, pain and sadness clear as daylight in hers. "I accidentally hurt someone I love." She blinked, like she hadn't expected to hear the words out loud.

He ached for her, but her answer didn't give him the clarity he needed. "What does that have to do with saltwater?"

"He was standing in a saltwater river. I sent a shock of electricity through the water and electrocuted him." Again, she seemed surprised that she'd spoken. The pain and sadness in her eyes shifted to fear and worry, her shoulders tensing.

He kneaded the tension with his fingers, the only thing he could think to do to help her. "Did he die?" That would traumatize anyone.

She shook her head. "Almost. But I brought him back."

Her answer made him smile, despite the seriousness of the moment. "Of course you did. You're amazing." Every second he was with her, she blew his mind. He continued the gentle massage, letting her know through his touch that he was there for her.

The anxiety in her eyes faded. "That doesn't frighten you?"

"Frighten me?"

"Yeah. That I almost killed someone?"

His fingers stilled as he gave the question his full attention. "Maybe it should, but it doesn't."

She tilted her head, studying him. "Why not?"

"I don't know." He sifted through his thoughts and emotions, making sure he wasn't telling her what he thought she needed to hear. Nope. He couldn't locate an iota of fear.

"You said it was an accident. It wasn't like you set out to electrocute him."

"No!"

The horror in that single syllable acted like a magnet. He drew her into his arms, tucking her head under his chin. "There's no reason to be afraid."

She didn't resist. In fact, as she wrapped her arms around his back, she released a small sigh, her muscles relaxing. "Thank you."

"For what?"

"For understanding."

He smiled, pressing his lips to the top of her head. "That's what big brothers do."

Her soft laugh warmed him like a ray of sunshine. "Then I guess it's a good thing I found you."

"Damn straight."

She giggled, sounding more like the little girl of his memories. She lifted her head, gazing into his eyes. "How do you do that?"

"Do what?"

"Always find the bright light in everything?"

He grinned. "Inherited it from my dad." He hadn't meant it as a loaded comment, but her expression grew serious.

"Yes, I suppose you did."

When she pulled back, he let her go.

She moved to one of the couches and sat, patting the cushion beside her. "I want to ask you some questions."

"Okay." He settled in next to her.

"Does Dad have any family? Besides us, I mean. Aunts or uncles? Siblings?"

He shook his head. "Not that I know of."

"What about his parents? Did you ever meet them?"

"No." And he hadn't thought about it since he was a kid. "They died before I was born."

"Are you sure about that?"

"Yeah. I—" He paused, her point sinking in. "Well, that's what he told me."

"How did they die?"

He sat back, stretching one arm across the top of the couch cushions. "Earthquake. They did a lot of humanitarian work. They were at New Athens, helping with a relief effort after a smaller earthquake had destroyed a section of the colony. They didn't anticipate it was the precursor to a bigger quake. More than a thousand people died, including our grandparents."

"How old was Dad at the time?"

"Early twenties."

"That must have been horrible for him."

"I'm sure it was. But he's not the type to wallow. He said at least they'd died doing something they believed in."

"And he doesn't have any other family?"

"Not that he's ever mentioned. He inherited this." He gestured to the room and ocean view beyond.

"Ah." She nodded. "I've been wondering about that."

He leaned in, lowering his voice to a conspiratorial whisper. "My place isn't nearly this posh."

She laughed, just as he'd hoped. "Well, mine's—" She paused, light and shadow flickering in her eyes. "Mine's quite different."

"I'd imagine so. I've heard the accommodations on Fleet ships can be a little cramped. Is your cabin bigger than a shoebox?"

A teasing light pushed the darkness from her expression. "Quite a bit bigger. I'd love for you to see it sometime."

He shrugged. "Send me an invite and I'm there."

Twenty-Eight

Aurora hadn't told Micah anything about the *Starhawke*, yet. With all the discussion the previous night regarding their pasts, she'd never gotten around to her present. He didn't even know she was captain of her own ship.

She could tell him now, but where was the fun in that? He'd said he'd come if she issued an invitation. Now she wanted to see the wonder in his eyes when he got his first look at her ship. "Consider yourself invited."

"Offer accepted."

With him, it was just that easy. No fuss, no debates.

Not so with her mother. She'd issued an invitation to her and been rejected, with an excuse that had turned out to be a lie, no less.

Micah had just been served up a world-changing paradigm shift, which should have put him on guard, but instead he was ready to show up on her doorstep at the first opportunity.

On impulse, she leaned over and kissed his smooth cheek. "You're the best."

His startled laugh was followed by his arm hooking around her torso as he hauled her against his side. "And you're precious."

Her laugh turned into a shriek when he started to tickle her. "No fair!" She squirmed, pushing ineffectively at his muscled arms, her laughter blending with his. She engaged her energy shield, but his fingers pushed right through it.

He waggled his eyebrows. "Your shield can't defend you from the tickle monster."

"And you..." She gasped for air. "Don't have a shield." She went on the offensive, her fingers connecting with his abdomen as she tickled him back.

"Hey!" He jerked away from her touch with a chuckle, releasing her. "You didn't know how to tickle when you were two."

She grinned. "I've learned a lot since then."

His eyes narrowed in a mock glare. "I'll just bet you have."

"Oh, you'll find I'm full of surprises."

"Truer words were never spoken."

His happiness flowed into her, through her, blending with her own in a seamless tapestry. How had she forgotten this? Forgotten him? Replaced his memory with Mya? She loved Mya like a sister, but their relationship growing up had never been like this. Life with Micah was just... brighter. Simpler. And oh so much fun.

A door closed, their dad's voice carrying down to them. "Feels like a party in here."

"Gettin' there!" Micah called back. "Care to join us?"

Their dad appeared at the half wall that separated the main level from the living room. "You're inviting me to a party in my own home? How generous."

Micah's Cheshire Cat grin made Aurora chuckle. "What can I say. I'm a generous guy."

Her dad lifted one brow, his gaze shifting to her. "See what I put up with?"

"He gets it from you."

He pressed a hand to his heart like she'd shot him. "And the damsel backs the dragon instead of the valiant knight. All is lost."

She gave him an assessing look. "I think the valiant knight can handle this dragon just fine." She hooked a thumb in Micah's direction.

"Hey!" Micah pouted. "Turncoat."

"Neutral observer."

"No such thing."

She stuck her tongue out at him.

He mirrored her.

Her dad's laugh made them both turn.

"Good to know you can now settle your differences like adults."

"She started it." Micah reached a hand toward her side, tickle fingers at the ready.

She dodged, bouncing up off the couch. "And I'll finish it, too." She pointed a warning finger at him.

He grinned at the empty threat, lounging against the cushions.

When she was certain he wasn't going to try a sneak attack, she turned to their dad. "Thank you for sending the clothes. I can pay you back—"

He waved her off. "No, you won't."

"But—"

"Aurora, please. I've missed so many holidays, so many birthdays. Let me do this."

The yearning behind his words weakened her resolve. "Okay. Thank you."

He smiled. "You're welcome. I see you found at least one you like."

"Quite a few, actually. How did you know my shoe size?"

"I asked Marina."

Butterflies took wing in her belly. "So, Mom knows I'm here?"

"Yes."

And she couldn't get a read on how he felt about it. That part of his emotional field was behind the wall she'd encountered before.

"Would she come down here?" Micah asked.

"No." She and her dad said at the same time.

"She's not ready for that." Her dad rubbed his chest, like he was easing tension there. "At least, not yet."

"Oh." A pained sadness seeped into Micah's emotional field.

She understood why. He'd believed their mom was dead, just as she'd believed the same thing about their dad. Knowing the truth had dropped them into limbo. She'd gotten out when she'd connected with their dad. But Micah was still trapped there. "It doesn't mean she doesn't care."

He met her gaze. "Then why—"

"She's not like you. Or Dad. Fear drives her actions."

"What's she afraid of?"

"Me, for one. Our last interaction wasn't exactly cordial. I'm sure she's afraid that I'll bite her head off if she shows her face. Or that you might. That we'll blame her for the choice she made. For all the years we've missed."

"Which we wouldn't, right?" Anxiety pinged his field.

"No." She sighed. "But she doesn't know that. And even without that obstacle, she'd still be motivated by an overriding fear for our safety. It's been her governing principle for decades." And the main source of friction between them. "I can't see her tossing it aside and hopping a plane down here. As long as she believes keeping her distance will insure you and I are safe, that's what she'll do."

"Even though we're now together?"

She shrugged. "When it comes to me, logic doesn't factor into her decision-making process very often."

"She's a very complicated woman."

They both turned to their dad, who was gazing at Micah.

"But if you'd seen the look on her face the day you were born, the wonder and joy, you'd know how deeply she loves you. Both of you." His gaze swept to Aurora, determination darkening his blue eyes. "Don't worry. I won't let her hide in her cave forever."

She believed him. But he was setting himself up for the battle of the millennium.

Twenty-Nine

The sun was setting over the water by the time Cade returned to the beach house with the Admiral and Williams.

While the Admiral had spent the day attending to Fleet business, Cade had met with Williams at the hospital where Payne's grandson was in the ICU. Their surveillance and investigation had confirmed Payne's story, and the foul stench of Reanne's influence.

Unfortunately, there was nothing they could do to help the boy at the moment. He wasn't stable enough to move, even if they could come up with a plan to sneak him out past the minions who were continually watching the room.

Appearing to go along with the research mission in Teeli space would buy the boy time. And when the *Starhawke* returned to Sol Station, they'd have Mya Forrest's talents to bring to bear on the problem.

"Justin?" Cade called out as he, Williams, and the Admiral entered the house from the garage.

"In here." Bella's voice drifted out of the media room to their left.

Cade and Williams followed the Admiral into the room, where Justin and Bella were ensconced on one of the couches. Her gaze was on two videos playing on the oversized screen, while his eyes were closed, his fingers moving rapidly across the keys of his laptop, headphones over his ears.

Bella glanced at Cade. "Nice job with the surveillance tags."

"Thanks. What are we getting?"

She motioned to the screen. "Nothing usable from the images yet, but Justin's recorded all of Bare'Kold's conversations since you planted the devices. He's working on the translation now."

"What about Magee?" the Admiral asked, his gaze on the screen.

"She's alone in what looks like her office." She pointed to the image on the right, which showed a closeup view of a smooth metallic surface, with sections of digital files becoming visible as Magee moved her arm.

The Admiral stepped closer to the screen. "What's she working on?"

"Messages, mostly. I caught a glimpse of Bare'Kold's official schedule when she entered an appointment for him."

Cade looked at the other image, which showed a woven pattern of grey cloth. "What about Bare'Kold?"

"He's even tougher. He doesn't move his hands much. Mostly static images of his clothing and an occasional glimpse of the blank wall."

"Stimulating."

"Oh, yeah. Puts you right to sleep."

Cade glanced at Justin, who still had his eyes closed, his fingers tapping away. He knew better than to disturb his number one when he was focused on a translation, especially with a language as challenging as Teeli. Accuracy was as much an art as a science. But Justin could also push himself too hard, lose track of time.

He met Bella's gaze. "Make sure he takes breaks."

She nodded. "I will."

It wasn't the first time he'd given her that assignment. Or Justin. They were both driven by passion for their work, but their concern for each other's wellbeing made them perfect partners. Telling one to watch out for the other was more a reminder than an order, making sure neither of them would work too hard.

He turned to go, his gaze falling on the Admiral, who was still watching the video feed from Magee's device, furrows gathering on his forehead. He looked like he wanted to reach through the screen and pull her into the room.

The Admiral wasn't wrong about priority one, but that didn't mean Cade wouldn't do everything he could to get Magee away from the Teeli.

Thirty

"Are you ready for your first session?"

Aurora met her dad's gaze over the table on the pool deck. Discussion topics had been lighter while they'd prepared and eaten dinner, but he seemed ready to get down to business. "Now?"

"End of the day is the best time for an evaluation."

"Evaluation?"

"Before you receive any training, I need to assess the scope of your abilities."

"But I told you what I can do." She glanced at Micah for backup, but he shook his head.

"He needs to determine what type of empath you are."

"Type? Aren't all empaths the same?"

His lips tilted up. "Ah, young one, you have much to learn."

They hadn't even started, and he was already teasing her. "All right Mr. Know-It-All, what types are there?"

Her dad stood, picking up his empty plate. "We'll go into that after the evaluation. First I need to talk to Micah alone." He motioned to her brother, who gathered the other remaining dishes and followed her dad into the house.

Aurora stayed in her chair, but couldn't resist tuning into their emotional fields as they disappeared up the stairs toward the kitchen. Her dad's excitement came through clear as a bell. She sensed amusement from Micah until a sharp pang of anxiety spiked and disappeared. What was her dad telling him?

Her dad returned to the back door a moment later. "Come on in." He directed her to one of the couches in the living room.

Micah had settled into the couch facing her, a tablet in his hand. Her dad claimed the other couch at the bottom of the U-shaped configuration. She got the distinct impression they'd teamed up like this before.

"Micah will take notes while I focus on you," her dad confirmed.

Micah winked at her.

She rolled her eyes.

"Focus, children," their dad chided, but he was smiling.

"Yes, sir," Micah replied, pivoting to face him.

Aurora did the same.

"I want you to close your eyes. Take a deep breath in, releasing it on a four count."

She followed his instructions, the muscles of her chest and shoulders automatically relaxing as oxygen flowed into her lungs and through her bloodstream.

"Take another breath in for four, hold it for four counts, then release it for four."

The rhythm matched her yoga practice, her mind and body flowing with the soothing repetition.

"Good. Allow your breath to proceed naturally, but maintain that calm focus. If you lose it, repeat the four count breathing sequence until you return to that state. When I ask you to, use your empathic senses to tell me what emotion I'm expressing. Do you understand?"

"Yes."

"Then we'll begin."

A wave of emotion flowed over her a moment later. "Joy, happiness." It buoyed her spirits, lifting her up.

"Maintain calm focus," her dad instructed. "Don't allow my emotions to become yours."

Right. Focus. She went through the four count sequence, allowing his emotions to swirl around her but not overtake her. Another wave struck. She inhaled sharply. "Anger." An emotion she'd never sensed from her dad. It caught her off guard.

"Maintain focus," he repeated, even as his anger circled her.

Her throat tightened. She forced in another breath. And was hit with a wave that sucked the air right out of her lungs. "S-Sadness," she stuttered, struggling against the deep sense of loss pulling her down.

"Focus, Aurora."

How could she focus when he was dragging her into a black hole of despair?

Fear hit her next, a scorching bolt that cut through her midsection like a scythe. She flinched, her voice coming out as a whisper. "Fear."

"Breathe, Aurora." The soothing tone of his voice didn't match the emotional cage he'd flung her into, but she did as he instructed, forcing air in and out of her lungs.

The wave shifted, a sense of isolation overtaking her, like she'd been pulled into the black of space without a star, planet, or ship anywhere in sight. She recognized the sensation. She'd experienced it for months after her dad had taken Micah from her, and again when Cade had rejected her at the Academy. "Loneliness." Ironically, she handled that one better than any of the previous emotional tsunamis. Maybe her trials by fire had boosted her resilience.

The next wave rolled over her, and her stomach bottomed out. Thanks to her mom, she'd had plenty of experience with this one, too. "Shame." And she'd learned to deflect it. If she hadn't, she never would have made it to the Academy or earned her first post with the Fleet.

The wave swirled again, the next emotion striking her from all sides like a battering ram. Her shield flared to life around her, adding warmth but failing to scratch the surface of the blade. "Pain," she muttered through gritted teeth.

It vanished as quickly as it had begun, replaced with the first emotion she'd sensed. Her breath released on a sigh as she embraced the sensation. "Joy."

It cut off in a nanosecond, leaving her unbalanced. She put a hand on the couch cushion to steady herself as her body swayed. When she opened her eyes, she jerked back.

Her dad was crouched directly in front of her. She hadn't sensed him at all.

"My emotions aren't your emotions, Aurora. Remember that. If you let the boundaries cross, you'll lose yourself." He sighed. "Maybe now would be a good time to talk about empath types."

"Okay." She tried to keep her voice neutral, but she couldn't shake the feeling that he was disappointed in her. That she'd failed.

The lack of emotional resonance subsided as he settled onto the couch beside her, the flow of love she'd come to expect from him surrounding her. Sliding his hand under hers, he cupped it between his palms. "This is my fault, not yours. Don't go beating yourself up."

"Hard not to."

"Hey." He gave her hand a squeeze. "You did great. Amazing really. You're the most sensitive receiver I've ever met. Which is part of the problem."

"Receiver?"

He nodded. "That's the first type of empath, the one most people associate with the term. Receivers can pick up on the emotions of others. Some can only sense emotions when they're making physical contact, while others can detect emotional resonance from great distances. There's also a range on the types of emotions receivers can sense, as well as how strong the emotion needs to be before it comes through."

"So, I'm a strong receiver?"

"That's an understatement." Micah held up the tablet. "You broke Dad's scale. All his prior students ranked between one and eight on a ten-point scale. You're a twelve."

"Meaning what?"

"Meaning," her dad said, "that you can sense the full range of emotions at even the lowest levels. More than I can. I'm a ten on my scale. I kept dialing it back with each new emotion, and your sensitivity didn't change."

"It didn't feel like you dialed it back." Each new emotion had struck like a right hook.

"I know. That's why I had to adjust my scale. No student has ever responded like that at the beginning of the test. Usually I don't see reactions that intense until I switch to projecting."

"Projecting?"

"That's the second type of empath, the one that's less commonly known. Projectors don't sense other peoples' emotions, they project their own emotions outward, almost always unconsciously. There's a commonly known term for it. Charisma."

"Charisma? How is that linked to empathic abilities?"

"Because charismatic people draw others into their emotional states. Only a receiver could sense what's really happening. To everyone else, the person just seems dynamic or charming in an undefinable way. Most people have no idea their own emotional states are being supplanted by the projector's."

"Huh." She frowned. "I guess that makes sense. Except you said you could switch to projecting. I thought you were a receiver, like me."

"I'm both. And I suspect, so are you."

"Both?"

"That's the rarest type of empath, a receiver-projector, one with the ability to receive *and* project."

Her head was starting to swim. "I don't think I can project." And wouldn't want to if she could. Sensing the emotions of others was one thing. Supplanting their emotions with her own? No thank you.

"Don't be so sure. It's a hereditary trait. With Micah's help, we can test it and find out." He stood, motioning Micah to take his place.

She shifted on the couch, unable to sit still. "What do I have to do? Try to project my emotions to Micah?" That might not be so bad.

Her dad smiled as he sat across from them. "After he shows you how it's done, yes."

"Shows me how it's done?" Her gaze swung to her brother, who looked like the cat who'd eaten the canary. "You're a projector?"

"That's right. It's why you find me so devilishly charming."

She froze in mid-laugh. "Did you just project that to me?"

He grinned. "See how easy that was?"

"Yes." Too easy. She wasn't laughing anymore.

His grin turned into a frown. "I didn't mean to worry you."

"I know." She drew in a breath and rubbed her palms on her thighs, where her skin had pebbled with goosebumps under her lounge pants. "I just don't like the idea of someone overriding my emotions."

He tucked one leg on the cushion so he was facing her full on. "It's not like that. I'm a nine on Dad's projector scale and he's a six. Most projectors range between one and four. And we don't override emotions. We influence them. I can't make you feel something you don't want to feel."

"And remember your connection with Micah makes you more open to his projections." Her dad picked up the tablet Micah had set down and typed something on the screen. "Which should also make him more open to yours."

"Is that supposed to be reassuring?" Because she wasn't feeling reassured.

"Informative. Right now we're just assessing what is. We'll talk about how to deal with the implications after I have all the facts." He lowered the tablet. "It's going to be okay. I promise."

Butterflies continued to flit around in her stomach, but she focused on calming them down. After all, this was why she was here, wasn't it? To figure out the extent of her empathic abilities and learn to control them. "Okay." She faced Micah and pulled her shoulders back. "What do I do?"

Thirty-One

His little sister had courage by the truckload. Micah didn't need to be a receiver to know what she was learning was scaring the stuffing out of her. But that would change when she had more pieces of the puzzle. Right now she was wandering around in the dark. His job was to shine light on her path.

"Close your eyes and start your four count breathing cycle."

As soon as she complied, he glanced over at his dad, who nodded.

Start your engines. He'd ease her in with the most straightforward emotion, the one she was least likely to resist projecting.

"Allow your mind to drift back until you come to a time when you experienced intense joy. Put yourself back in that place. Feel what you were feeling then. Bring that emotion into the present."

A small smile appeared on her lips, indicating she'd latched onto something. But he wasn't getting any increased sense from her of that emotion, just the low-grade awareness that he'd come to accept as their normal connection. A quick check with his dad, who shook his head, confirmed she wasn't projecting yet.

"Feel it bubbling inside you, filling you with so much joy you could burst. Can you feel it?"

"Yes." Her smile grew as she did as he instructed. His dad held up two fingers, indicating he was getting a projector level two from her.

A good beginning, but he doubted it even scratched the surface of her abilities.

"Allow the emotion to expand, pushing out from your body and steadily filling the room."

The smile disappeared, replaced by a thin frown line between her brows.

He glanced at his dad. He sliced his hand through the air, indicating Aurora had cut herself off from the emotion she'd been building. As his dad had anticipated, they had an uphill battle on their hands.

"Are you still focusing on the emotion?"

Her mouth worked, the frown line deepening. "I've lost it." She opened her eyes. "Sorry."

He gave her an encouraging smile. "It's not a test. It's an assessment. You can't fail." *But you can dodge and block.* Which was exactly what she seemed to be doing. "Let's try again. Close your eyes and focus on your breathing."

She dutifully followed his instructions, but tension remained in her shoulders, her hands clasped tightly in her lap.

"Allow each inhale to calm your mind, and each exhale to release any tension."

She nodded in understanding, but her body language didn't change very much.

His dad's lips pursed, his frown almost identical to Aurora's. He motioned for Micah to continue.

Micah focused on his sister. Switching to a more forceful emotion, one she'd have more trouble holding back, might help. "Now I want you to let your mind drift back until you encounter a moment when you were angry, so angry your body shook and your skin flushed."

Judging by how quickly her neck muscles tensed and her lips flatlined, she didn't have to go back very far.

His dad smiled, holding up four fingers.

Good, they were getting somewhere. He wouldn't make the mistake this time of telling her to consciously project. That was when she'd shut down. He'd just let her do it naturally.

"Be in that moment. Feel what you were feeling then—the sights, the sounds, the smells."

Her hands separated and curled into small claws against her thighs.

A good sign that she was well and truly plugged into the emotion.

His dad flashed five and one.

She was up to level six now, on par with their dad.

He couldn't sense her emotions directly as his dad could, but his connection with her made the experience intense in a different way, like being plugged into a high-voltage circuit. Just how powerful was she?

"Visualize the person or persons who triggered your anger. See them seated in front of you."

Her lips pulled back from her teeth in a grimace.

His dad lifted another finger. Level seven.

"Nod if you can see them in front of you."

A curt movement of her head.

"This person has crossed your boundaries. Triggered your anger. Without words, express to them how you feel."

Pressure built inside him for a moment, then vanished in an instant as Aurora visibly jerked back.

Shutting down. Closing off her ability.

He'd promised his dad he wouldn't allow that to happen, that he'd push her if he had to. For her own good.

Without giving himself time to think, he slapped his hands on her knees and shouted one word into their subconscious connection. *Project!*

Her arms jerked up as if to block a blow.

A moment later her eyes snapped open. blazing with indignation as she blasted a wall of heat right through him. "What the hell!"

Thirty-Two

Micah had just slammed into her!

Not physically, but her body had reacted as though he'd hit her like a battering ram.

She shoved his hands away from her legs and backpedaled on the couch. "What was that?"

Micah at least had the grace to look uncomfortable. "I gave you a push."

"A push? More like a full-body tackle!"

He winced. "Is that what it felt like?"

"Yes!" Although on reflection, it was more the surprise of it rather than the force that had struck her. He'd knocked her emotional control right out of her hands.

His misery swept over her. "I'm sorry, Aurora. Our connection must have made the suggestion a lot stronger than I'd intended. I just wanted to keep your emotions flowing. You were blocking yourself, closing off your projection before you'd reached your potential."

He'd just pegged her, which made it harder to hold onto her indignation. That was exactly what she'd been doing.

She crossed her arms over her chest and huffed.

Her dad appeared in her peripheral vision, kneeling beside the couch. "Don't blame Micah. I'm the one who asked him to do it."

So it had been a group effort. "What did you learn from your little experiment?"

Her dad and Micah exchanged a glance, but it was her dad who answered. "You're a projector. At least as strong as Micah, if you allow yourself to access your full potential."

The news didn't improve her mood. Projecting emotion still seemed dangerous. "You could have warned me."

"Not if we wanted an authentic reaction. You've had years to develop your emotional blocks. I can't train you until we've pulled them down. To accomplish that, I have to know how extensive they are."

"But those blocks keep other people safe!"

Her dad sighed, his head drooping for a moment. When he looked up at her, his blue eyes seemed grey. "No, sweetheart, they don't."

She started to protest, but he held up a hand, silencing her.

"Blocking emotions inflicts damage, building emotional scar tissue. You've clearly been doing it a long time, which might be another reason the Suulh have such a powerful impact on you. You have to learn to harness your emotions, work with them, channel them, not block them. I can teach you how to do that."

His steady gaze bored into her soul. She wanted to believe him. But after the slew of betrayals and revelations she'd endured in the past couple months, she was operating on a trust hair-trigger. "No more sneak attacks."

He clasped her hands, giving them a gentle squeeze. "I promise."

She allowed his comforting love to surround her, but a thread of sadness wound through her as well. She glanced at Micah.

He was still sitting on the couch, more drawn into himself than she'd ever seen him. The sight tore at her heart.

She held out her hand. "Come here, you goofball."

The sadness washed away as his palm touched hers. But he didn't stop there. Pulling her forward, he wrapped his arm around her shoulders, burying his face in her hair. "I'm so sorry, Ror."

"I know." She could feel it. "It's okay. You were trying to help." They both were. She was the one reacting defensively. Like she did with her mother. She'd grown accustomed to everything being a constant battle, especially when it came to her abilities.

Oh, the irony. She'd finally found two people who wanted her to reach her full potential, and she was the one fighting to stay behind walls.

She pulled back with a sigh. "So, what's next?"

Her dad gave her an assessing look. "I have all the information I need to get started."

And then the real work would begin. "But not tonight." A blanket of exhaustion had settled onto her shoulders.

He gave her hand another squeeze and then pushed to his feet. "No, not tonight. I have one more final to give in the morning and then I'm done for winter break. We can schedule your first training session for tomorrow afternoon, if you'd like."

She glanced at Micah. "What about you?"

"Two finals, but I'll be wrapping up by three. I can come over then." He paused, uncertainty creeping into his voice. "If you still want me here."

"Of course I do." Her defensive fear had put up a wall between them. She wanted to obliterate it. She punched him lightly on the arm. "Who else will keep me honest?"

He smiled, though with less enthusiasm than normal. "Just me."

"That's right. So you better be here, or I'll track you down."

The light of his smile turned up, filling her world with its glow. "I'll be here."

Thirty-Three

"I translated the message Bare'Kold sent to Teeli space."

Cade's fork halted halfway to his mouth, his gaze snapping to Justin's as his number one strode into the kitchen's dining nook. He looked like he'd slept on the couch in the media room, and probably had. "Did he contact Reanne?"

"I don't think so. I don't know the Teeli translation for *Sovereign*, or whether that's what the Teeli call her, so no way to know for sure, but I think the message was addressed to someone called Lur. Or *Lur* might be an honorific of some kind. Hard to say."

Cade set down his fork and pushed his plate aside, his appetite gone. "What did the message say?"

Justin pivoted one of the dining chairs and straddled it, running a hand through his unruly hair. "I'm working with an incomplete Teeli dictionary and vague grammar and syntax rules. It took two passes just to stop myself from applying the bogus structure I'd learned at the Academy. But I think he told them the *Starhawke* is away from Sol system for two weeks. He was requesting instructions."

"That doesn't sound good."

"No, it doesn't."

"Did he say anything else?"

Justin shook his head. "Bare'Kold's not exactly verbose. We were lucky he recorded an audio message, rather than text. Emoto and I haven't tackled a rework on the Teeli written language yet. He did include the Admiral's message regarding the *Starhawke*'s aborted science mission with the request to reschedule it."

"I wonder how Reanne will react to that. I can't see her trying to set the same trap twice, especially now that it's so high profile. But she'll definitely try to turn the situation to her advantage. Did you learn anything else about Bare'Kold?"

"He's incredibly arrogant, treating the staff like mindless drones. Including Magee."

Tension pulled at Cade's skin. "Is she okay?"

"Depends on your definition. She's living in the equivalent of a coat closet in the Embassy. Spent the entire evening and night there without moving after Bare'Kold visited her office and told her to go to her room and sleep. One of the Teeli woke her about ten minutes ago and told her to get dressed and go to the dining hall. It's like she's a robot who can only accept simple commands."

"Have you learned anything from her video feed?"

"Nothing obvious. She doesn't talk to anyone except Bare'Kold or her handler, and they don't say much." He stifled a yawn, pushed to his feet, and headed for the half-full coffee pot on the counter. "Bella's running the vids through pattern recognition software to see if she can catch any data that way."

Cade drummed his fingers on the table. "So, I guess we wait."

Justin poured coffee into one of the mugs on the counter and took a sip. "Guess so." He studied Cade over the rim. "Any word from Aurora?"

"No." He was still having trouble accepting that she'd taken her ship and left without a word. It didn't seem possible that she was out in the cosmos somewhere, far, far away. In his heart, she felt very much closer to home.

Justin turned his chair around to face the table and sat back down, steam rising from the mug in his hands. He took a sip and exhaled on a sigh, his eyelids drooping to half-mast. "Give it time. She'll be back before you know it. And she'll want to see you."

It was exactly what he wanted to hear, but that didn't make it true. "How can you be so sure?"

Justin chuckled. "If there's one thing I've observed about the Suulh, it's the intensity of their emotions. They don't feel anything halfway. Her head may be saying *stay away*, but her heart's all in. She won't be able to hold out forever."

"Hold out for what?" Gonzo asked as he and Williams entered the room.

Cade shot Justin a look.

Justin grinned. "My body." He nodded toward Bella, who had just appeared from the media room, looking rumpled and sleepy. "She's got it for me bad."

"In your dreams, Byrnsie," Bella shot back as she joined them, accepting the mug of coffee Williams handed her.

"Oh, come on, Bella. You know you want me."

"I do. For your mind."

Justin caught her around the waist as she passed his chair, bringing her to a halt. "My mind isn't my only worthwhile attribute."

She met his gaze, a twinkle in her blue eyes. "Oh, really?"

"I also make a very comfortable chair." He pulled her onto his lap.

She laughed, the cheerful sound brightening the room. She looped an arm around his shoulders. "I'll be the judge of that."

Justin waggled his eyebrows at her. "By all means."

She glanced around the room. "Where are Reynolds and the Admiral?"

Cade motioned to the front door. "Out running together."

Gonzo's brows lifted as he claimed one of the other chairs around the table. "He can keep up with her? He's in better shape than I thought."

"He can't." Williams took a drink from his coffee mug. "She didn't want him going out alone."

Cade nodded. Reynolds had been tactful when she'd suggested the Admiral run with her, clearly not wanting to injure his pride, but the Admiral hadn't argued. He knew the stakes.

"Any new info regarding the GC?" Justin asked Gonzo and Williams.

Gonzo gestured to Williams. "We're building a case against the five delegates we identified as Teeli puppets. We've also ascertained that at least fourteen members of the General Assembly seem to be under the control of the Teeli, with another twenty-six in the maybe column, including the Prime Minister."

"The Prime Minister?" Justin's gaze darted to Cade, concern creasing his forehead. "Did President Yeoh indicate that might be the case?"

"No, but until we brought the recent events to her attention, she wasn't looking for potential Teeli collaborators in the GC. Might be worth another visit to get her input." He focused on Gonzo. "How much hard evidence do you have?"

"Very little. Mostly circumstantial at this point. We can see the connections because we know the patterns to look for, but it wouldn't hold up in a Council chamber debate, let alone a court of law."

"Keep digging. If this comes to a head, we'll need to provide the Admiral with as much data as we can find. And you two." He motioned to Justin and Bella. "Go get some rest. I'll monitor the video feeds this morning."

Justin lifted Bella off his lap, setting her on her feet as he stood and stretched, several popping sounds from his back and shoulders accompanying the motion. "If you insist." He slid his arm around Bella's shoulders. "Come on, you. Time for some shuteye."

She punched him playfully in the gut. "Don't get any ideas, Byrnsie."

His grin was pure mischief. "Who me? I'm a perfect gentleman."

"Yeah, yeah. Come on, you big knucklehead." She tugged him out of the kitchen toward the guest rooms.

Cade watched them go, the weight on his heart lightening. Their interactions always had that effect.

"Think they'll ever figure out they're crazy about each other?" Williams murmured under his breath.

Cade turned, meeting Williams' amused gaze. "If they're lucky." *And even luckier if they're able to stay together.*

Aurora's smiling face appeared in his mind's eye, making his throat clench. For a brief time, he'd known that kind of bliss, sharing a life with the woman he loved. But the odds of experiencing it ever again were stacked against him, regardless of what Justin believed. As long as Reanne Beck and the Teeli posed a threat, Aurora would keep her distance.

And his heart would continue to bleed.

Thirty-Four

After her dad left for work the next morning, Aurora pulled on her new pair of running shoes and hit the trails around Diamond Head.

Running outdoors was a rare treat. The simulators onboard Fleet starships were decent, but they couldn't recreate the tactile experience of the breeze brushing across her sweat-dampened skin, or the tang of the sea air on her tongue. The elevated track in the *Starhawke's* gym came closer, but any type of illusion, no matter how technologically advanced, was a poor substitute for the press of terra firma under her feet.

The uneven terrain and unfamiliar surroundings kept her mind focused, pushing away the anxiety that had been building since the previous night.

Her dad had assured her that they'd start off slow, but she was still entering uncharted waters. And while she normally viewed the unknown as an exciting challenge, this particular ocean was personal. She knew the monsters that swam in its depths, and the bite of their razor-sharp teeth.

The last time she'd felt this unprepared for an encounter, she'd been standing outside the door to the *Argo's* gym. She'd debated with herself about whether to ask the ship's best hand-to-hand combat fighter to train her.

That had turned out well. Not only had she found a mentor, she'd made a friend.

And two years later, Celia had agreed to be the *Starhawke's* security chief. If she hadn't, Aurora wouldn't have been able to come here. Celia was the one person she trusted to keep Mya and the rest of the crew safe during her absence.

Pushing to the top of a rise, she paused to catch her breath and enjoy the view. The dark fronds of the local flora framed the turquoise water shimmering in the distance. If she was going to face monsters, she couldn't ask for a better setting.

Clouds drifted overhead as she circled back to the house. The long climb up the driveway made her calves and lungs burn. She welcomed the physical challenge. It was child's play compared to what she'd face this afternoon.

She followed up the run with a swim in the pool, this time wearing the royal blue and aqua tank swimsuit she'd chosen from the selection her dad had provided. Gliding through the water relaxed her muscles, the burble of the waterfall and call of sea birds greeting her each time she surfaced. She could get used to this.

After about a dozen circuits, she climbed out, grabbed the towel she'd draped on the lounge, and headed inside. Showered, dressed, and hair braided, she left her room, stopping in the loft. What next?

The longer she stood there, the more the silence pressed in, growing louder with each passing moment.

What time had her dad said he'd be home? She checked the clock. Two hours to go.

She needed a way to counteract the oppressive silence. Pulling up the listing of holiday tunes on her dad's audio system she'd used yesterday during her yoga stretches, she turned up the volume. The cheerful jingle of sleigh bells and voices singing about winter wonderlands filled the house.

Much better.

She hummed along as she made herself a salad for lunch, choosing to eat at the island counter rather than outside. Straightening up the kitchen brought her to within forty-five minutes of her deadline. Now what?

She wandered through the house, searching for something—anything—to keep her brain occupied. But she'd already gone over the entire house the day before. It wasn't like she expected to find something new. And she was too agitated to work up enthusiasm for a yoga session.

Idle time had never been an issue while on the *Starhawke*. Or during her years with the Fleet. Or while studying at the Academy. Come to think of it, she couldn't recall a time when she'd had nothing specific to do. No tasks to complete, no responsibilities to attend to. Even when she'd had down time, she'd always had plans to work out or puzzles to solve.

Right now, she desperately needed something to focus on. Her free-floating anxiety was pushing her over the edge.

The music cut out abruptly, replaced by a female voice. "Incoming text message for Aurora from Brendan Scott."

Her dad was sending her a message? Was there a problem? Was he running late?

Walking over to the comm panel in the foyer, she brought up the message.

It was short and to the point.

Breathe. Relax. I'll be home in thirty minutes.

She closed her eyes and gritted her teeth. Her inability to control her emotions had projected them to her dad. Great. Not the way she wanted to start off their session. She typed out her reply.

I will. See you soon.

Moving to the living room, she settled onto the floor facing the Christmas tree. Taking slow, deep breaths, she focused on the earthy scents of pine and sap, the sparkle of the delicate, brightly-colored ornaments, and the glow of the lights.

Knowing her dad was tuned into her emotional state helped her maintain her focus until she sensed him coming up the drive. She met him at the door. "I'm sorry I disturbed you."

He shook his head, a bemused smile on his face. "I've been jittery all morning, too. Starting your training is a dream come true for me, so I hadn't realized how anxious you were about it. I should have had you come to the campus with me, rather than leaving you here alone."

She shrugged. "I didn't know how anxious I was until I got back from my run."

"Ah." He set his satchel on the kitchen island, then drew her into a hug. "There's nothing to fear. I promise." He kissed the top of her head before releasing her. "And the sooner we get started, the sooner you'll discover that for yourself."

She drew in a shaky breath. "Okay."

"Okay." He glanced down at his tailored slacks and button-front shirt. "Give me a few minutes to change clothes and I'll meet you in the loft."

She followed him up the stairs and perched on the couch facing toward Micah's room while she waited, her hands pressed against her knees to keep them from bouncing. Why was she so nervous? She'd endured Setarip captivity, battled with her aunt, and even faced down her mom without falling prey to anxiety. Why did the idea of working with her dad make her quake like a raw cadet called up to the captain's office?

"I won't bite."

She glanced up. He'd changed into lounge pants and a snug navy-blue T-shirt, the kind of outfit he probably wore when he worked out, which clearly he did. Not a bit of flab or paunch to be found. If his beard wasn't liberally sprinkled with gray, he could pass for Micah's older brother.

"What?" He looked down, running a hand over his shirt. "Is there something on my shirt?"

"No. It just looks good on you." If only her mom could see him. After so many years apart, she might have convinced herself he wasn't as wonderful as she remembered. She'd be dead wrong.

"Oh. Thanks."

His delighted smile warmed her heart. He probably thought of her mom when he looked at her, too. And wondered if her mom thought about him.

"So, how do we begin?"

He settled onto the couch opposite her. "I'll take you through a guided meditation first. Have you ever done one before?"

"All the time." It had been a required part of her Academy training program, a way to help crewmembers cope with stress. She had several of her favorite meditations loaded on her comband.

"Excellent. Then get into a comfortable position and close your eyes."

Pushing her back into the cushions, she tucked her feet into a yoga lotus pose and closed her eyes.

"Breathe in, feeling the air working from the top of your head down to your toes, releasing any tension along the way. With each exhale, allow the tension to pass out of your body and into the cosmos."

Her body responded to the timbre and richness of his voice, the sense of safety her subconscious attached to it. She relaxed against the cushions, anchored by his voice.

"As the tension drains away, as your body relaxes, I want you to visualize a very special place. This is one of your own design. It is your domain. Here, you are omnipotent.

You can control everything about it—its shape, size, the colors you see, the objects around you, the lights and sounds—adapting it to fit your needs. It can be indoors, outdoors, or anything in between. It is your resting space, your sanctuary."

An image took shape in her mind—a packed earth floor, textured walls, an open doorway, and a thick carpet of grass leading to a gurgling stream beside an evergreen forest.

"This space is also your playroom. You can use it to explore, experiment, and energize."

Her energy field fluttered under her skin, begging to be set free. She reined it in.

His voice changed, deepening. "While you are in this space, there is no danger. Nothing to hide. Nothing to fear. In this space, you can be exactly who you are."

She got the unspoken message. He'd sensed her pulling back.

Inhaling through her nose, she released the breath on a sigh and allowed her energy field to engage.

Its comforting warmth embraced her like a long-lost friend.

"Keep your focus in your space."

Right, her space. The stream beckoned to her, drawing her outside onto the grass.

"Feel how the space nurtures you, giving you strength. Giving you comfort. Allowing you to relax fully."

She sat on a boulder beside the brook, the sun warm on her back, her muscles growing pliant, her body fluid.

"As you feel your body settling into this space, begin to visualize a specific color, a color that symbolizes peace and calm to you. Safety."

An image sprang to mind, but she hesitated. The pearlescent glow of her energy field had been her grounding source all her life, but it also triggered conflicting messages of danger and fear, especially now.

She could use the rich green of Mya's field, but that was a complicated choice, too.

Her dad must have sensed her waffling. "Choose a color that protects you. That grounds you."

That did it. She'd go with her pearlescent white. This was just a meditation, after all, not a life or death decision.

"When you've found your color, visualize surrounding yourself in a sphere that matches that color."

Easy as generating her shield.

"Make the sphere large enough that you can reach out your hands and feet without touching it. It extends into the ground and out in all directions."

In her mind, she reached out her hands, the curve of the sphere just beyond her fingertips.

Her dad's voice sounded closer. "This sphere is your emotional shield. It protects you from the unwanted emotions of others, just as your physical shield protects you from the unwanted actions of others. When outside emotions encounter the sphere's smooth surface, they will slide off and return to the universal energy."

This sounded a lot like the way she'd taught herself to deal with her empathic abilities before encountering the Suulh. She'd just never visualized her emotional barrier as a sphere.

"Within this sphere you are protected. You are safe. Outside emotions cannot reach you as long as you maintain the sphere."

Yeah, but what about the Suulh? Sensing their emotions wasn't like sensing others. Blocking them didn't seem to be an option or a choice.

"When you have successfully established the sphere, and given yourself time to study it, let it go and return to your sanctuary."

The pearlescent glow dissolved, replaced by the view of the trees and the flowing water.

"Look around your space. Like the sphere, it is yours. You can summon it anytime you wish. It will always be available to you."

She'd never considered creating a mental sanctuary, but she could see the potential benefits for calming mind and body. Whether it would help with her reaction to the Suulh was another story. Her gaze moved over the sun-drenched view toward the vague outlines of the domed structure where she'd started. It looked a little like a mini Stoneycroft.

"Allow your sanctuary to fade as you prepare yourself to return to the present."

Good. She had questions she wanted answered.

His voice held a hint of laughter. "I'm going to count backward from five to one. With each number, you will slowly leave your space and return to this room. Five. Your sanctuary is fading into the distance."

The structure, trees, and brook began to recede.

"Four. Take a deep breath and release it."

She drew in a slow breath, exhaling on a sigh.

"Three. The sounds of this room are returning to your conscious mind."

She caught the gentle whisper of a breeze through the trees outside.

"Two. Focus on your physical body, the textures and sensations it feels."

An itch started on her right thigh. She fought the urge to scratch it.

"One. Come fully into this time, this space. When you're ready, open your eyes."

She drew in a breath, letting it out slowly as her eyelids fluttered open. The sunlight that had seemed subdued when she'd sat down now shone like a spotlight in her eyes. She rubbed them with her hand.

"You enjoyed that?"

Her dad stood beside her. When had he moved? "It was interesting."

His smile looked exactly like Micah's. "See? Nothing to fear."

She held his gaze, an answering smile tugging at her lips. "Nothing to fear."

Except her anxiety still sat in the corner, waiting. This had been a baby step, free from the trauma she'd expected, but she was still at base camp. She'd hold off any judgment until she'd seen the rest of the mountain she was climbing.

Thirty-Five

Free at last.

Micah drew in the sea air as he pedaled up the driveway to his dad's house. He always looked forward to winter break. More time out on the water with Birdie, the big Christmas luau, and the New Year's Eve celebration. And this year he had a much more powerful reason to enjoy the season.

Not that he didn't love teaching. Watching the *aha* moments flash in his students' eyes was a natural high, which is why he planned excursions whenever possible. Marine biology was best understood by observing creatures in their aquatic environment rather than in a simulation or video.

Parking his bike, he headed inside. "Dad? Ror?" His connection to Aurora pulled him to the stairs before his dad's voice drifted down from above.

"Up here."

He climbed the stairs two at a time. His dad and Aurora were in the loft, seated on the couch closest to Aurora's room.

His dad glanced over his shoulder. "Perfect timing. We just finished Aurora's preliminary meditation."

He met his sister's gaze. "How'd you like it?" Most students loved the guided meditation, but his sister wasn't most students.

"Interesting." Her shoulders were no longer up around her ears like they had been the previous night. A good start.

He settled onto the couch on her other side. "That meditation has helped me focus before surfing competitions."

And control his projecting ability. "What color did you choose for the sphere?"

"Pearlescent white. What about you?"

He stared at her like she'd sprouted a horn in the middle of her forehead.

"What?"

"That's the color I chose."

"That's the color of my energy field."

He blinked. "You're right." He hadn't made the connection, but now that he thought about it, the color he visualized during the meditation looked *exactly* like her energy field. "Freaky." His subconscious must have held onto the sense of protection his child-self had associated with that imagery.

"Very." But she looked more excited than freaked out as she gazed at him.

The sensation of connection—of belonging—that was uniquely theirs surrounded him. How had they lived apart so long without realizing it was missing? Although it hadn't really been missing, had it? Despite time and distance, their bond had remained unshakable. Muted, yes, but being together again had turned up the volume.

He glanced at his dad, whose grin confirmed he was enjoying the heck out of their interaction. And sensing everything they were feeling.

Micah cleared his throat. "So, what's next on the agenda?"

His dad adopted a more studious manner, but his eyes still twinkled. "Now that you're here, I'd like to try a sphere test."

Aurora looked back and forth between them. "What kind of test?"

"Now that you understand the concept of the sphere to block external emotional input," his dad said, "I want to see if you can use it to block Micah's emotional projections. His close connection to you makes him the ideal test case. If you can block him, you can block anyone."

She nodded. "Okay. How do we begin?"

"For starters, I'll take you back through the meditation but at an accelerated pace. Once you have your sphere established, Micah will project a low-level emotion and we'll see if you can block it with the sphere."

Her shoulders stiffened, her spine straightening. "Okay. I'm ready."

Micah exchanged a glance with his dad. Aurora looked like she was preparing for battle. He draped an arm over the back of the couch, resting his fingers on her shoulder. The zing of connection pulsed like a jolt of electricity. "It's not an assault."

"Oh." But the muscles beneath his fingers remained taut.

"The more relaxed you are, mentally and physically, the easier it is to achieve your goal," his dad confirmed.

Her brows drew down. "Okay." But now she looked confused.

"Think of it like your yoga practice." Micah slipped off his shoes and sat cross-legged on the couch, facing her. "In yoga, if you tense up, it's difficult to get into the poses, right?"

"Yeah."

"But when you relax, you allow your body to flow into them. Same idea here."

Her lips compressed, but she nodded. "Okay."

Resistance was normal for all new students. She'd feel better about the process once she'd gone through it a few times.

While his dad took her through the opening sequence of the meditation, Micah focused on her physical reaction. Closing her eyes seemed to have an automatic calming effect, the tension between her shoulder blades easing. The rhythmic breathing unlocked the tightness in her jaw.

His dad met his gaze, giving a brief nod.

Shifting his focus off Aurora, he called up the visualization that helped him project sadness, the emotion that was usually the easiest for students to identify and block.

"Focus on the sphere," his dad instructed Aurora. "It surrounds you, providing a barrier like your shield. Inside the sphere, the only emotions are yours."

Another nod from his dad.

Keeping his gaze on Aurora's face, he pushed the emotion outward, directing it at her at the lowest level he could sustain.

The muscles around her eyes twitched, her breathing stuttering.

"The sphere is your emotional shield. It can deflect anything that comes from outside of you."

The twitching stopped, but her breath still seemed strained.

He increased the emotional volume a notch.

Her lips compressed.

"The emotion you're sensing is not yours. Give it a color, a shape that is distinct and separate from you. Don't allow it to penetrate the sphere. Visualize it rolling down the outside."

She was struggling. The frown line between her brows told him that, but he also sensed it on an elemental level that had nothing to do with her physical tells. Instinct told him to back off, even though he was barely projecting. Most students couldn't even sense his emotions at this level, let alone have trouble blocking them. If she couldn't handle this, what would she do when he really let her have it?

"See the sphere blocking the emotion like rain on a windowpane."

She drew in a slow breath, her face pinching in concentration. But it didn't seem to help.

"The sphere is yours to command. You can use it to block any emotion, any intensity. You are the calm at the center of the storm."

The slightly defiant lift to her chin made him smile. Her locked jaw did not.

A quick glance at this dad, another nod.

You can do it, Ror. Projecting with laser focus, he raised the bar again.

Thirty-Six

The emotional ebb and flow of sadness washed over Aurora, pushing her like a boat caught in the current.

"Focus on the sphere, Aurora. Use it."

Her dad's voice kept her focused, but it didn't make any difference. She couldn't separate Micah's sadness from her own emotions. Since the sphere wasn't working, she decided to engage her energy field. Maybe it would provide a barrier.

Nope. The sensations intensified.

"See the sphere, Aurora. Shield yourself. The emotion you're sensing is not yours."

Intellectually she agreed with him. But her empathic senses begged to differ.

And then the sadness was gone.

Like a whale surfacing after a prolonged dive, she pulled oxygen into her lungs. Her muscles released the built-up tension, and she flopped against the back of the couch like a ragdoll. "Well, that went well."

"Ror?" Micah's voice was tight and reedy.

She cracked her eyes open, turning her head to meet his gaze. "Sorry. I couldn't do it."

"I know. I'm sorry, too."

"Not your fault." She'd failed. Simple as that. He'd projected and she'd collapsed like a house of cards. Why had she ever thought that they could help her?

"Neither of you has anything to be sorry about."

They both looked at their dad.

"I had a feeling we'd encounter a problem with Micah as the projector. That's why I wanted him to test you."

"Why? So you could confirm I'm a hopeless case?"

"Aurora." He gave her a chiding look and rested a hand on her forearm. "You are far from hopeless. What I sensed from you during this session was unlike anything I've ever experienced. Rather than two distinct emotional elements meeting, I felt a blend from the very beginning, like you were absorbing Micah's emotions as he generated them." His gaze searched hers. "It explains why you're having so much trouble dealing with the Suulh. Your empathic side literally can't separate what's yours and what's theirs. There's no division. You experience it all equally."

She stared at his hand on her arm, hope fading. "Then you can't help me."

"Yes, I can."

She glanced up, meeting his gaze.

"We'll just approach this in a different way."

Hope peeked around the corner. "How?"

"Before I explain that, I want to focus on the problem. During the test, you engaged your energy field. Why?"

"I was hoping it would insulate me."

"But it made the experience more intense, correct?"

She frowned. "Yes."

"I believe that's because your Suulh energy field is linked to your human empathic abilities. If you weren't an empath, blocking Suulh emotions wouldn't be an issue. Your mother never had this problem. And if you were an empath but not a Suulh it wouldn't be an issue, either. It's the combination that makes you unique, and creates the direct line that enhances both. You cannot use one without increasing the sensitivity of the other."

"So, engaging my field will always result in increased emotional input?"

"That's right. Especially with the Suulh."

She let her head fall against the back of the couch. "Then it really is hopeless."

"No, it's not."

"Why not? You just said I can't use one without enhancing the other. Any time I use my shield or energy abilities around the Suulh, I'll be opening myself to emotional overload. I can't fight or defend under those conditions."

"Unless you learn to control your emotions."

The conviction in his voice made her sit up. "Control them how?"

"The night I followed you back to your hotel, you couldn't sense my emotions. Do you know why?"

"You said something about shielding them. Were you using the sphere?"

"No. What I use isn't shielding the way you're thinking of it. More like a circular river I can pour my emotions into. As a receiver-projector, I needed it, especially after..." He shook his head, dismissing the train of thought. "It's a technique I came up with years ago to maintain emotional equilibrium and increase my focus."

She'd bet money he'd come up with it to deal with the devastating loss of connection with her and her mother. "Have you taught anyone else this technique?"

"I've never had a student who needed it. You're the first person who could even detect the emotional stasis it produces."

She glanced at Micah. "You can't sense when he's using it?"

He shook his head. "I'm a projector, remember? Not a receiver. Although I'm curious whether I'll be able to sense when you're using it."

He might. Their connection was extraordinary. "Maybe." She turned back to her dad. "Emotional stasis, huh?"

"That's right. The concept is simple. Mastering and maintaining it is not, especially under pressure."

And she'd certainly be working under pressure when dealing with the Suulh. Which brought up another point. "If you're right about how my empathic side can't separate my own emotions and those of the Suulh, then why didn't I have a problem when I was living with Mom? Or Mya, Marina, and Gryphon, for that matter?"

"It's not that your mind can't distinguish between what's yours and theirs, or that you can't maintain your own emotions while feeling theirs. Clearly you can, or you and Micah would always be in emotional sync. It's separating them that's the problem. As long as you're willing to feel both, you're fine. It's when you want to shut theirs out that you're struggling."

"Huh." An intriguing idea.

"You said you first realized your direct emotional connection to the Suulh when you injured one of the Necri. Pain drove the point home because the sensation was so new to you and was clearly not coming from you."

"That's right." She rubbed her thigh as the memory took hold.

"You wouldn't have had that type of experience with your mother because she can shield herself from injury. And Marina and Lelindia can heal themselves within seconds. The only person who might have triggered a similar revelation is Gryphon, but he would have had to be severely injured at a time when you were with him but Lelindia and Marina weren't."

"Which never happened." She could probably count on one hand the number of times she and Gryphon had been totally alone together. Marina or Mya had always been with them. And she couldn't recall any injuries. "But what about their other emotions? Anger, fear, sadness? Why didn't I make the connection from sensing those emotions?"

"They're not as startling or debilitating as pain. Or as localized. You could have easily shrugged them off as normal empathic reactions, not realizing how much more intensely you experienced emotions coming from Suulh compared to other people."

"Until Gaia." She'd never forget crumpling into Mya's arms on the island when the Suulh were reunited with their children. The tsunami of their emotions had flattened her, and she'd been helpless to stop it.

"Like I said, when their emotions are in line with yours, it's not a problem. But with the Necri, you were completely out of sync physically and emotionally. You could see the power they exerted on you."

"Huge understatement," she muttered.

"Learning to use emotional stasis will give you the strength to protect yourself. To reclaim your power without fear."

"How will we know when I'm ready?"

"When you can maintain emotional control while working with Micah. He should be your toughest opponent. However, your connection is also unique, which could throw in a few variables we haven't accounted for. If you want a completely objective test, we'd need a willing Suulh." He lifted his brows. "Any chance Lelindia could pay us a visit?"

"Not for a while. She's on a mission for a couple weeks."

"Then that gives us a couple weeks to work."

She turned, meeting her brother's gaze and giving him her best captain's stare. "My toughest opponent, huh?"

His lips twitched. "Guess so."

Pulling back her shoulders, she made the sound of an imaginary bell ringing. "Round one."

Thirty-Seven

By the time the *Starhawke* reached Azaana, Mya was dancing on pins and needles. Not only was she concerned that Star's anti-detection methods might have failed, alerting Siginal to their presence, but she was also battling her inner demons regarding her upcoming discussion with the Suulh.

The *Starhawke* had received a message from Justin Byrnes while they were still at Sol Station, confirming he'd been in contact with Raaveen and that all work on the Azaana settlement had been completed. All Kraed ships and personnel should have returned to Drakar, although the Azaana system would now be included in all standard Kraed patrols of the area.

Contacting Paaw and Raaveen directly when the *Starhawke* reached the system would have made sense under normal circumstances, but their current situation wasn't normal. Mya didn't want to risk a transmission that might act as a flare to alert Siginal to their arrival.

Instead, she kept the *Starhawke*'s hull camouflage engaged as they entered the planet's atmosphere and glided toward the ocean of deep blue. The lush tropical island home of the Suulh rose from the water in the distance. The dormant volcano peak stretched to the sky, the settlement nestled at its base, and the sandy beach wound along the shore.

Not that she could see the settlement itself. The Kraed architects had done a masterful job of blending the buildings with the surrounding terrain and foliage. The image on the bridgescreen showed abundant greenery, the sparkle of waterfalls and rivers, the protrusions of rock, but no sign of habitation.

Well, unless you counted the people swimming in the aquamarine shallows and frolicking on the sand.

She spotted at least thirty Suulh, mostly children, with a few adults scattered in the mix. She couldn't hear their laughter or the splashing of the waves, but she could feel their energy as it surrounded her, drawing her in.

Had it always been this strong? Or was it her perception that had changed? Perhaps she was more in tune with them after visiting the Suulh homeworld. The subconscious pull of Suulh energy had helped her to locate Sanctuary, the prison disguised as an island paradise on their homeworld. Many of the Suulh below had once lived there. And suffered there.

Her grandmother's face flashed into her mind's eye. *"They are our end."*

That's what her grandmother had said when she'd asked about the two hooded figures she'd seen on the island. At the time, she hadn't known she was asking about Reanne Beck and Aurora's aunt Kreestol. Now that she did? She wished she'd pushed harder to get answers from her grandmother.

It still made her chest hurt every time she thought of the look of despair in her grandmother's eyes, and the emotional wall her grandmother had erected to drive her away. It wouldn't have worked if Reanne's ship hadn't taken off, necessitating their mad dash to follow in the *Starhawke*.

Not that she regretted her decision. If they hadn't left, Aurora would have faced Reanne and her forces with only Cade and his team as backup, a fight they couldn't win, especially while Reanne was holding the Admiral's life in the balance. Aurora would have been forced to make an impossible choice—the Admiral's freedom, or her own. Her bone-deep desire to protect others might have pushed her to give Reanne exactly what she wanted, becoming a pawn in Reanne's twisted game.

"Dr. Forrest?"

Bronwyn Kelly was the only person on the crew who called her Dr. Forrest. Right now, the young pilot was looking at her expectantly. Had she asked a question? "Yes?"

"Did you want me to set down close to the island, or farther out?"

Yep, she was definitely repeating the question, having failed to get a reaction the first time. Unfortunately, Mya wasn't sure of the best answer. "Which would you choose?"

Kelly didn't bat an eye at the unusual question. "Close to shore would shorten shuttle time, but farther out gives more flexibility for takeoff. I assume Lt. Clarek will be piloting the shuttle while I stay here?"

She hadn't thought that through either, but it was the logical choice. "Yes."

"Then I'll put us down well offshore."

While Kelly guided the ship down, Mya switched on her comband. The device was one of the few tech tools on the ship the Clarek clan hadn't provided, and therefore couldn't monitor. She opened a channel to Paaw. "Mya to Paaw."

The response came through immediately. "Nedale! You are here?" Paaw's excitement bubbled out of the device. "We did not expect you."

"I know. I'm sorry for the abrupt arrival but—"

"No apologies. You are the Nedale. We are grateful for your presence."

Mya bit down on her tongue. Paaw and Raaveen weren't as obsequious as most of the Suulh, but they still treated her with a reverence that she hadn't figured out how to handle. "It will be a brief visit, but it's imperative that I talk to Zelle and Ren. Can you please ask them to join us in the Great Room?"

Worry crept into Paaw's voice. "Is something wrong?"

"Not exactly. I'll explain when I see you."

"Very well. Raaveen and I will meet you at the landing pad."

"We'll be there shortly." She closed the channel and turned to Kire at communications. "Do you want to come with us or stay here?"

"I'll stay." He leaned back, interlacing his fingers over his stomach. "Help Star and Kelly keep an eye on things."

She caught the undercurrent of tension despite his casual pose. "And alert us if any Kraed arrive?"

He inclined his head in acknowledgment.

"Thanks." She pushed out of the captain's chair. "Celia?"

Celia slid out from behind the tactical console. "I'm with you." The focused look in her brown eyes as they strode to the lift made it clear she'd appointed herself as emotional backup.

Jonarel seemed equally protective. It was probably her imagination, but when he met them outside the shuttle bay, his muscles seemed to bulge more than normal. He also walked closer to her than was comfortable, tantalizing her senses but not quite touching.

During the flight to the settlement she kept her attention on the island, rather than the pilot, as she mentally reviewed the questions she needed to ask Zelle and Ren. Celia sat in the main cabin, having declined Mya's offer to take the co-pilot's seat. Her innocent smile had said it all. She wasn't going to miss any opportunity to shove Mya out of her comfort zone, especially where Jonarel was concerned.

Paaw and Raaveen stood at the head of the pathway for the landing pad as the shuttle descended. It had only been a month and a half since she'd last seen them, but she found herself staring at them as she walked down the ramp.

Paaw came forward first, clasping her hands and then enveloping her in an enthusiastic hug. "Welcome, Nedale."

The confidence in the gesture took her by surprise, triggering a soft laugh. As she hugged Paaw back, she noted the young woman's fleshed out and toned physique. Quite an improvement over the whip-thin, malnourished teenager she'd met on Gaia. Now Paaw's long blonde hair shone like silk, and her blue eyes sparkled with joy and excitement. "How are you, Paaw?"

"I am very well." She practically glowed, even though her energy field hadn't engaged. "We have missed you."

"I've missed you, too." Being this close to the Suulh made her feel like she'd been plugged into an electrical current.

Raaveen approached, a frown line between her dark brows as she glanced behind Mya to where Jonarel and Celia waited. "Sahzade remained on the ship?"

"She's not with us. She had an important task to take care of."

Raaveen and Paaw exchanged a worried glance. "But she is well?" Raaveen asked.

"Yes. We hope to rejoin her soon."

"And Justin? Is he here?"

She'd forgotten that Raaveen and Paaw had formed a friendship with Cade's number one. "He's not with us, either."

Paaw bit her bottom lip and darted another glance at Raaveen. "Has something gone wrong?"

Hopefully something was going very right, at least where Aurora was concerned. "Not at all. Cade's unit is working with Admiral Schreiber right now, so we haven't been in touch since we left Sol Station."

The tension eased from Paaw's shoulders.

Mya gestured to the path. "I'm eager to talk to Zelle and Ren." Her biggest challenge still lay before her, and the clock was ticking.

"Come." Raaveen took the lead, with Mya, Paaw, and Celia behind, and Jonarel bringing up the rear.

"We have completed all construction." Raaveen glanced over her shoulder. "We hope you will be pleased."

"I hope *you're* pleased. This is your new home."

Raaveen's frown returned. "It is lovely. But we wish for you and Sahzade to be happy here, too."

Mya let out a sigh. How did you climb down from a pedestal when everyone kept shoving you back up? "Aurora and I will always be happy when we're with you."

Raaveen fell silent, apparently digesting that bit of information as they wound their way up the path to the settlement. The babble of excited voices reached Mya as they drew near. Rounding a curve, the pathway opened to reveal a wall of Suulh lining each side of the packed earth walkway leading to the central structure. A large group had gathered on the covered porch near the main entrance. Ren, Raaveen's father, Zelle, Paaw's mother, and Paaw's younger sister Maanee stood at the front, with more Suulh filling the branching paths to the nearby buildings.

A hush fell.

Mya stopped, gazing at the hundreds of eager, expectant faces. She didn't need Aurora's empathic abilities to feel the joy her arrival had brought to the group. It echoed in her own heart. Switching from Galish to the Suulh language, she addressed the crowd. "It is wonderful to be with you again." Her throat constricted, turning the last two words into a harsh whisper.

The Suulh responded by engaging their energy fields, the burst of color brighter than any rainbow. The sheer intensity stunned her. The last time she'd seen their energy fields, they hadn't been nearly this strong. Clearly a month and a half in the nurturing environment had restored the former Necri soldiers to vibrant health.

Her energy field flared to life without conscious thought, weaving in and out of the Suulh fields like a ribbon through braided hair. The feeling of joy swelled, pushing tears from her eyes.

She focused on Zelle and Ren as they strode toward her. Yes, even Ren's field was a rich red, not as brilliant as Raaveen's, but no longer the anemic grayed out version she associated with him. The physical changes were even more pronounced. His muscles were filling out, his clothes showing definition rather than hanging on his skeletal frame. His dark hair had grown in, the same shade as Raaveen's with a similar wave that curled the locks around his face and nape. The withered old man who'd arrived on the island in a catatonic state had vanished, replaced by a Suulh in his prime who exuded the same inner strength as his daughter.

He greeted her with the traditional Suulh hand motions of welcome. "Nedale. We are honored to welcome you."

He held out his hands, and she clasped them in hers, the joining of energy wrapping around her like her father's bear hugs. "I am delighted to see you looking so well."

The smile that spread across his face was another change. He glanced at Zelle. "I have received excellent care."

Zelle's pale cheeks flushed a soft pink as she met Mya's gaze. "My daughters and I have helped him, but his dedication to his healing has made the difference."

Quite a difference. And unless she was misreading Zelle's blush, the two were developing a relationship that went beyond friendship. That would be a blessing. Ren's mate had died on Gaia, committing suicide to escape the Teeli imprisonment. At the time, Ren had been so mired in his Necri existence he hadn't even known about the loss. The shock had come later, after they'd arrived here on Azaana. Raaveen had been the one to tell him about her mother's death.

Zelle had suffered a similar tragedy. The bits and pieces Mya had learned about Zelle's mate indicated he'd been tortured by the Teeli to find out just how much damage they could inflict before the Suulh couldn't heal. Their experiments had resulted in his eventual death, leaving Zelle as a single parent for Paaw and Maanee.

If the two families could find comfort with each other, it would go a long way to healing their emotional wounds and strengthening the interconnection of their leadership for the Suulh.

Zelle looked past Mya's shoulder to Celia, who stood with Maanee. The blonde-haired adolescent gazed up at Celia with obvious hero worship.

Zelle smiled. "You are also most welcome," she said, switching to Galish so Celia could understand her.

Celia stepped forward and grasped Zelle's outstretched hands. "I'm honored to be here." Since Celia had been responsible for liberating and protecting Zelle's daughters on the Necri slave ship. Zelle held her in very high regard.

Ren turned to Jonarel. "Son of Siginal, we are grateful for the bounty your clan has bestowed upon us." He spread his arms to indicate the settlement. "What is ours is yours."

His Galish had a strong accent, not nearly as fluid as Zelle's, but remarkable considering he'd been catatonic a month and a half ago. Apparently he'd been getting language lessons during his recovery.

Jonarel inclined his head. "Thank you."

To anyone else, Jonarel seemed the picture of composure, but Mya could see the fissures of discomfort threatening to break through. Talking about his clan was the last thing he wanted to do right now.

Zelle motioned them forward. "Come. We have refreshments waiting."

Stepping through the front entrance of the domed structure was a surreal experience. She'd watched the building come together during construction, maintaining an emotional distance without much effort. But that was before she'd seen the original version on the Suulh homeworld.

She paused, taking it all in. The great room was four times the size of Stoneycroft's, but the layout was the same, with the kitchen and gathering spaces at the center and the massive staircase at the far end leading up to the gallery and residential rooms on the second floor. The half-moon shaped wing to the right was designated for the Sahzade, while the matching wing to the left was meant for the Nedale.

In this case, Zelle, Paaw and Maanee had accepted the responsibilities of healers, so they were in the Nedale wing. Raaveen and Ren were standing in for Aurora, so they had quarters in the Sahzade wing.

The grandfather clock that stood near the staircase at Stoneycroft was conspicuously absent, as were all the evergreen decorations that filled the house this time of year. This space overflowed with ferns and flowering plants, cultivated from the tropical landscape outside. The air had a sweetness to it that was similar to the greenhouse on the *Starhawke*. She took in a deep breath, allowing the air to fill her lungs and ease the tension from her neck and shoulders.

The wood furnishings had a decidedly Kraed feel to them—graceful lines worked from native trees and plush cushions covered in the wondrous and colorful fabrics that only came from Drakar.

Several of the Suulh hurried to move the furnishings into a small conversation circle while others brought over trays of food and drink. Mya accepted one of the mugs, thanking the Suulh as she settled onto the couch facing the Sahzade wing, the same vantage point she usually chose at Stoneycroft. Jonarel sat beside her, near enough that his elbow brushed her arm as he took a drink from his mug.

For the first time she welcomed the distraction he provided. It kept her from obsessing about what was to come.

Zelle and Paaw sat across from her, Ren and Raaveen to her left, and Celia and Maanee to her right.

She wrapped her hands around her mug, mentally fortifying herself for the difficult discussion ahead. "This won't be easy, so I'll get right to the point." She spoke in Galish so Celia and Jonarel could follow the conversation. "I recently learned the location of the original Suulh homeworld."

Zelle and Ren visibly stiffened.

"We took the *Starhawke* there."

Zelle's eyes widened. "You were on Feylahn?"

Feylahn. Of course. Now she remembered. She'd heard the name before, from her parents, but not since she was a child. "Yes. And don't worry. We weren't detected by the Teeli."

She gave them a moment to process the initial revelation before throwing another log on the fire. "We visited a village of Suulh who were working to provide food for the Teeli, supposedly in exchange for protection from the Setarips. We also found the island the Suulh call Sanctuary."

Ren jerked like she'd taken a swing at him. Raaveen clasped his hand in hers, engaging her energy field to surround them both. Zelle and Paaw looked equally shaken.

Raaveen spoke first, her voice reedy. "How close were you to the island?"

"We were able to bypass the security and land a shuttle in the water inside the perimeter. We saw the Suulh running drills on the beach. I also spoke with my grandmother."

Zelle pressed a hand to her chest. "You saw Breaa? She is alive?"

"Yes. She was very relieved to learn you were all safe." But Zelle's reaction seemed very personal, almost familial. "Did you know her well?"

Zelle nodded like a puppet on a string. "I was her apprentice."

Thirty-Eight

Another piece of the puzzle clicked into place. No wonder Zelle had been able to survive the Necri incarceration better than the rest. She'd recovered from her physical trauma quicker than the other Suulh because she'd been trained in advanced healing by Mya's grandmother. "What can you tell me about your experiences with her?"

Zelle's throat moved in a convulsive swallow. "My family was brought to the island two years after Maanee was born." She glanced at her younger daughter, who was snugged hip to hip with Celia, her hands fisted in her lap. "We had been convinced by the White Hairs, the ones you call Teeli, that a terrible war was being fought against the Pebble Heads."

Pebble Heads. The term the Suulh used for Setarips.

"They would recruit the Suulh with the strongest abilities to help in the fight. I was to train with the Nedale, whose daughter had been lost in the fighting."

Not lost. Mya's mother had fled with her dad and Libra to Earth.

"Or at least, that is what we were told." She met Mya's gaze briefly, before continuing. "I was needed to help the Nedale train the other Suulh on the island in healing. We would send our best students to the front lines to care for the injured." A shudder wracked her body. "I didn't know we were sentencing them to torture and death."

"Did Breaa corroborate the Teeli story?" *Please say no.* She didn't want to think of her grandmother as a traitor to her own people.

Zelle shook her head. "She never spoke of it. If I brought up the war, she grew silent, her eyes haunted. I assumed it was because she had seen the horrors of war up close. And in a way, she had. I did not realize she knew what truly awaited those we trained."

And yet her grandmother had done nothing to stop it. Why? "How long did you work together?"

"Eight years."

Eight years? How could her grandmother have stood by for *eight years*, knowing what awaited the Suulh?

Heat and pressure built in her chest. She shoved it down, keeping her focus on Zelle. "And then you left the island?"

Zelle gave a tight nod.

Paaw wrapped an arm around her mother's shoulders, taking up the thread of the story. "We had been told the Setarips had devised a new weapon that was devastating our people. They needed the strongest healers at the battle site to treat the injured. My mom and I were happy to go, even though it meant leaving Maanee and my father behind. I was so excited that I was finally old enough to help." She paused, drawing in a slow breath. "We knew nothing of space travel. They kept us in windowless rooms onboard the transport, so we had no way of knowing we had left the planet, or that we had docked at a larger ship. All we saw were the corridors, our rooms, and the wounded they brought to us."

"Were they Necri?"

"No. It was not that." Paaw's jaw worked, moisture making her eyes shimmer. "What we saw there I had never seen before, or since. The destruction to their bodies was like a sickness that ravaged their cells like fire eats wood. They bled from their noses and mouths, had terrible fevers, developed sores and burns on their skin, and lost hair in clumps."

Mya closed her eyes, her stomach rolling. She knew exactly what caused those particular symptoms.

"While studying the texts I borrowed from Dr. Williams during our time on Burrow, I figured out what we had been treating. They had radiation poisoning."

But how would a Suulh get exposed to that much radiation? To overwhelm their natural healing ability, the source would have needed to be intense and prolonged. "Do you know what they were exposed to?"

"We never found out."

"None of the Suulh told you?"

Zelle answered. "When they arrived in the infirmary, they were too weak and disoriented to say anything coherent. Whatever words we understood could have meant anything. The Teeli supervised their care very closely, never leaving us alone with them. We did not think anything of it— the Teeli were our protectors, or so we believed. As soon as any of the Suulh healed enough to speak, they were removed to a recovery ward."

"And you never saw them again?"

"Sometimes we did. They would return with the same symptoms and injuries, just as delirious as they had been before. The Teeli told us it was because they had insisted on going back to the front lines to defend our homeland from the Pebble Heads' weapon."

"But you weren't on the homeworld?"

"Definitely not. After traveling to Burrow and then here, I now realize we could not have been on our world. It took a long time to reach our destination—days, if not a week or more. But with no windows or chronometers, we had no way to mark the time."

"How did the Teeli explain the long journey?"

"They said we had to move slowly and with care to avoid detection by the Pebble Heads."

Of course they did. The Teeli had a lie for every occasion.

Celia spoke up, her voice soft but direct. "When did you go from being healers to captives?"

"After the weapon was supposedly destroyed." Zelle's mouth twisted in a grimace. "We stopped receiving injured and returned to Sanctuary for a few months. Breaa broke down when she saw us. She held me so tightly I could not breathe. Her tears soaked my shirt. It was the only time I saw her cry."

Mya had seen her cry once, too. "She probably never expected to see you again."

"And the Teeli noted her reaction. They used it against her when we were taken to the slave ship."

Mya inhaled sharply. "How?"

"The Teeli came to tell us we had been chosen for another special mission, one where we would not have to leave Maanee and Reepaar, my mate, behind." Zelle swiped a bead of moisture from the corner of her eye. "I foolishly believed that was a good thing."

Mya braced herself, even though she knew how the story ended.

"I was shocked when Breaa argued with the Teeli, told them I could not leave again. She was the Nedale, the healer of our people, yet she was trying to prevent me from helping. I knew she was afraid I would get hurt, but I did not understand her fears. It never occurred to me that they would take Reepaar and—" She broke off, her hand covering her mouth, muffling a sob.

Paaw pulled her mother close, rubbing her hand on her back. Maanee stood and moved to Zelle's other side, the two girls engaging their blue energy fields and surrounding their mother in the glow.

"I am okay," Zelle said, sounding lightyears away from okay. "I just wish I had known—"

"It wouldn't have changed anything." Celia leaned forward, her gaze intent. "If you hadn't gone willingly, the Teeli would have coerced you with threats, just as they did when you became Necri soldiers."

Zelle met Celia's gaze, tears streaming down her pale cheeks. "I know. But my mate is still dead."

Mya swallowed past the constriction in her throat. She'd never had a mate, but it wasn't hard to imagine how she'd feel if Jonarel died at the hands of the Teeli. "Did Breaa try to physically stop you from leaving?" The power of the energy blast her grandmother had delivered when Mya had refused to leave the island was still fresh in her mind.

"Yes. We argued. I thought she was dishonoring the Suulh. When the Teeli came to take us, she tried to stop them, until the Sahzade intervened."

Sahzade? It took a moment for the words to track. "You mean Kreestol, don't you? Aurora's aunt?"

Zelle blinked slowly, as though Mya's words weren't clear, either. "Aunt? Kreestol is not her mother?"

A harsh laugh shot from Mya's lungs. "Mother? Hardly. Aurora's mother is Kreestol's older sister, Libra."

"*Older* sister?" That comment came from Raaveen, who looked as stunned by the information as Zelle and her daughters. "Where is she now?"

"On Earth with my parents." She tried to say it without sounding defensive. Didn't work out that way. It was getting harder and harder to think of her relatively happy life on Earth while staring at the harsh evidence of the

Suulh suffering on the homeworld her parents and Libra had abandoned.

"Do the Teeli know they are there?" Raaveen asked.

"They do now."

"Now?"

And they'd reached the heart of the matter. She looked around the small group. "Did you ever have contact with someone called the Sovereign?"

Judging by the harsh inhalations and wide-eyed looks on all their faces, they had.

Raaveen found her voice first. "You know of the Sovereign?"

"Yes. We saw her on Feylahn." No need to mention that Reanne was Aurora's former roommate, or that she'd recently used the Etah Setarips as pawns to capture Aurora. The Suulh were dealing with enough trauma.

"Her?" Raaveen's dark brows drew down. "How do you know the Sovereign is female?"

"She's someone we already knew." She gestured to Jonarel. "Aurora unmasked her during a battle. Her real name is Reanne Beck. She attended the Academy with us."

Raaveen stared at her in shock. "That cannot be."

She understood the sentiment. Coming to grips with the truth had taken her a while, too. "There's no doubt. The attack she engineered on Gaia was a trap she set specifically to catch Aurora, and possibly me. You were the bait that drew us in."

"Did Sahzade capture her?"

She flinched. "Uh, no. Reanne got away." Because she hadn't been there to back Aurora up. Guilt still clung to her like cobwebs.

The hope in Raaveen's eyes faded.

Jonarel spoke for the first time, the deep rumble of his voice soothing her like a cat's purr. "What were your experiences with the Sovereign?"

The five Suulh exchanged distraught glances. Zelle finally took the lead. "She is a mind-bender."

Jonarel stiffened. "Explain."

"I do not know how, but she could make us do things that were illogical, against our best interests."

Mya leaned forward, resting her elbows on her knees. "Like what?"

"Like entering the cages. And wearing the flight packs." Zelle's chest rose and fell like a runner climbing a steep hill.

Memories of the jetpack straps embedded in Zelle's skin played through Mya's mind.

"She did not use force. Or even coercion. She just talked in her mechanical voice. I do not remember what she said. Or why I responded as I did. But as she led me to my cage and I stepped inside, it seemed natural, logical. It was only later, when I became cold and hungry, and realized my daughters were not with me, that I began to question what I had done, and why." Her voice fell to a whisper. "By then, it was too late."

"Yes," Ren echoed in the same low tone. "Much too late."

The story was hauntingly familiar. And reminded her of something she'd noticed about Reanne. "When she walked you to the cage, did she touch you?"

Ren and Zelle's gazes met, both growing unfocused, as if reliving a shared memory. "Yes," they said in unison.

"She had her hand on my arm," Zelle clarified. "But not pulling me. Just resting there, like she was offering support."

Celia gave a derisive snort.

Mya had to agree. Whatever Reanne had been doing, she most definitely had not been offering support. "Is that the only time you saw her?"

"No." Zelle stared at her hands, twisting them in her lap. "She returned to the ship a few days later. Breaa was with her. So was Reepaar." Her voice came out guttural. "It was the first time I had seen him since I had been locked away. He looked strange. Disconnected. Like he was sleepwalking. And his body..." She swallowed. "I could sense the depth of the injuries he had sustained. For a moment, I thought Breaa was there to free us, but then I saw that her hands were bound. The Sovereign made her stand outside my cage. And then the Teeli—" The words choked off, her body shaking.

Mya rose from the couch and knelt in front of her, covering Zelle's hands with her own and engaging her energy field. Healing emotional wounds wasn't like healing physical wounds, but she'd do what she could. "What happened, Zelle? What did the Teeli do?"

"They tortured him. He did not resist. Not for a moment. He shrieked as their weapons scorched his skin. His eyes rolled back, but he did not try to run. Did not fight." She shook her head. "I screamed at Breaa to help him, and she did, sending out her energy field even with her hands bound. And that is when the Teeli shot me."

Mya sucked in air. She didn't want to hear any more, but she had to.

"Breaa flung herself in front of my cage, blocking the weapons. The Teeli did not fire on her. Instead, they fired on Reepaar. I watched from the floor of my cage as he crumpled to the deck. And the Sovereign laughed. *Laughed.*"

The horror in Zelle's voice echoed in Mya's soul.

"That voice. So cold. Lifeless. No empathy. No mercy." Zelle swiped at the river of tears streaming down her cheeks.

Mya's cheeks felt wet, too.

"As they dragged Reepaar's body away, the Sovereign told Breaa that if... if she ever challenged her again, she would—" Zelle's breath stuttered, the words choked off by the pained panting of hyperventilation.

Mya increased her focus on Zelle's physical well-being, easing the stress on her lungs and airways.

Paaw finished for her mother. "She told the Nedale that she and my mother would be forced to watch as they tortured and killed me and my sister. Slowly."

A dagger slid between Mya's ribs, stealing her breath. No wonder her grandmother had given up hope. And sent her away so forcefully. Reanne had used Breaa's love for Zelle against her. If she'd gotten her hands on Mya, no telling what Reanne could have convinced her to do.

But they'd never find out. She wouldn't suffer Zelle's fate. She was the Nedale. Her powers were far stronger than Zelle's. Or Breaa's. She'd never mated, so she didn't have any children who could be used as pawns in Reanne's sick games. And most important, Reanne couldn't get to her without going through Celia, Jonarel, and Aurora.

She was the most well-protected Suulh in the galaxy.

Thirty-Nine

"My brain is fried."

Aurora stood and stretched her arms over her head, working out the kinks in her neck and back. She'd spent two hours the previous evening working with Micah and her dad, and another three hours this morning. Concentrating that hard for that long had turned her mind to mush.

Her dad finished tapping notes on his tablet. "You're making good progress."

She grunted. Yes, she'd grasped the basic concept of the emotional stasis, but pouring her emotions—and the ones Micah was projecting at her—into a virtual holding tank where she could study them objectively, was another matter.

She'd had some success with loneliness and shame at very mild levels, but joy had kicked her butt. She'd resisted separating herself from it. Yesterday, sadness and anger had taken her down immediately, but this morning she'd managed a few seconds of stasis with each.

She still hadn't tackled the two emotions that worried her the most—fear and pain.

Micah slung an arm around her shoulders, pulling her into a hug. "I think it's time you got out and had some fun."

His grin was infectious. "Is that so?"

"Yep. And I know just the thing. An afternoon on the beach."

Her muscles locked up.

"Not in the water," he added, loosening his grip, "unless you want a surfing lesson."

No, she did not. Crowded oceans of saltwater were still on her banned list. "Not today." Or maybe ever. "But I wouldn't mind hanging out on the sand and watching you."

His grin widened. "As long as you cheer wildly when I do something amazing."

She laughed, her muscles relaxing. "That's a requirement?"

"You bet."

"Then I accept."

"Dad? You game?"

"Absolutely."

"Hang on." She placed a hand on Micah's arm, stopping him as a possible wrinkle occurred to her. "Will Iolana be there?"

"Birdie? I don't know. We didn't have any definite plans, but she's usually there on Saturdays. Why?"

She hesitated to cast any shadows on his happiness, but too much was at stake not to say something. "If she is, how will you introduce me?"

Micah glanced at their dad, then back at her. "Uh..."

"As my newest student?" their dad offered. "That's what I told Kai. And it's the truth."

Micah nodded slowly, his brow furrowing. "Yeah, I could do that."

But he didn't want to. She could feel it. Keeping secrets from his best friend, especially a secret that carried so much emotional weight, would be hard for him. "Are you sure? We could stay here instead. I don't want you to be uncomfortable."

He gazed at her for a long moment, his mouth setting in a determined line. "No, I'll be fine. I'm not sure I'm ready to tell her I'm half-human, anyway."

He had a point. That would be a tough conversation. But his willingness to sacrifice to her wishes both warmed and pained her. "Then lead the way."

Forty-five minutes later she stood on the warm sand, surveying the folding canopy her dad and Micah had set up. They'd handled the job with the efficiency of a Fleet crew, leaving her to arrange the folding chairs and cooler once the canopy was in place.

They'd just sat down when a familiar voice called out a greeting.

"Hey, Stone! Where've you been hiding?"

She glanced over her shoulder.

Just the people she'd been hoping to avoid.

Iolana and her dad, Kai, were striding across the sand toward them, carrying a cooler, beach chairs, and two surfboards. Iolana looked pretty much the same as the last time she'd seen her, but Kai had traded in the tailored knit shirt and pants he'd worn when he'd driven her to her dad's house and was now dressed in a bright purple t-shirt and matching swim trunks.

Micah popped up out of his chair and took the surfboards from Iolana. "Us important professor types had work to do." He gave Aurora a wink, though it looked forced. "No time for play."

Iolana pushed her sunglasses to the top of her head and rolled her eyes. "Sell that story to someone who's buying." She turned as Aurora stood, her eyes widening in recognition. "Oh. Hi, there."

Kai glanced between them. "You've already met?"

"On the beach a few days ago." Iolana held out her hand, her gaze assessing. "Nice to see you again. You must be Brendan's new student. I'm Iolana."

"Or Birdie," Micah chimed in.

Iolana shot Micah a look. "Only to you, Stone."

"I'm Aurora." She shook Iolana's hand, relieved that Kai had already established their cover story, freeing them from having to repeat it.

Iolana nodded. "Right. My dad told me."

Thank you, Kai.

Her dad shot her an encouraging look before taking the chairs from Kai. He plunked one down next to his and the other beside Micah's before facing his friend. "I thought you were working today."

"I had a last minute cancellation." Kai's gaze swept over Aurora's tank swimsuit and shorts. "I see you found the surf shop."

She glanced down at her clothes. "Yeah, what I brought really wasn't working for me."

"I'll bet. And how are you managing these two characters?" He motioned to her dad and Micah, who were finishing rearranging their setup to make room for the new arrivals.

She returned his easy smile with one that felt almost natural. "We're doing just fine."

"I take it you've earned an afternoon off?"

"Uh-huh."

"She's been working hard," her dad said as he maneuvered the two coolers into the center of the circle of chairs as a makeshift table.

"That I believe." Kai settled into the chair beside her dad with a sigh, and the two began dispensing drinks.

Aurora reclaimed her chair and turned to Iolana, some of her tension easing now that the preliminaries were over. "I'm curious. Why does Micah call you Birdie?"

She made a face. "Because my name means *soaring like a hawk.*"

Aurora gave an involuntary jolt, her gaze snapping to Micah's. "Did you know that when you two met?"

The significance seemed to have struck him, too. "No. I looked it up later."

Was it just a bizarre coincidence that he'd been drawn to someone whose name meant *hawk*?

"What am I missing?" Iolana's gaze darted between them.

Aurora answered her. "My last name is Hawke. With an e."

"No kidding?" She lifted her glass in Aurora's direction. "Then I guess we're destined to be friends."

I hope so. She returned the gesture, touching the rim of her glass to Iolana's. "I'd like that." After all, this was the woman Micah had claimed as a surrogate sister.

"Any woman who can handle Stone is okay in my book."

Which begged her next question. "Why do you call him Stone?"

"Payback. Mica is a stone. But that was my second choice. When he first started calling me Birdie, I called him Animal."

Now it was Micah's turn to make a face. "Stone. Definitely Stone."

She grinned. "He threatened to use my board for bonfire wood if I didn't stop."

"And for good reason. No serious scientist is nicknamed Animal."

"But Birdie is okay?"

"You're not a scientist."

"I could have been. Maybe it was my nickname that held me back."

Aurora hid her smile as the banter continued. They'd clearly had this argument hundreds of times, and enjoyed the verbal sparring. It was also calming the anxiety that had been spiking from Micah ever since Iolana had called out to him.

"It's always something with these two," Kai confirmed. "Ever since they were teenagers. You'd think they were related."

Right idea, wrong pair.

"At least they're not waking each other up before dawn on Christmas morning anymore," her dad said, taking a sip from his glass. "I recall one year at our house when you almost tossed them both in the pool after they woke you at four in the morning."

Kai groaned. "After they tried waking you and found you'd locked your bedroom door. I hadn't, foolishly believing they were too old for such antics."

"You didn't factor in that they'd asked for new boards that year."

Kai nodded, turning to Aurora. "If you haven't noticed, they're a bit excitable when it comes to surfing."

She gave Micah a sidelong glance and deadpanned her answer. "I hadn't noticed."

Kai chuckled. "I knew I liked this one," he told her dad.

"Yep. She's a keeper."

The undercurrent of her dad's emotions let her know he wasn't as relaxed as he seemed. Micah, thankfully, seemed to be finding it fairly easy to settle into familiar patterns with Birdie, his exuberance returning to the fore.

"You see how they're talking about us like we're not even here?" Micah affected a hurt expression. "And slandering our good names."

Iolana nodded, curling her lip in a childlike pout. "I know when I've been insulted."

"I'm sure Aurora never would have woken me at four a.m." Kai raised his brows. "Am I right?"

This was one question that was easy to answer honestly. "Sorry. I would have been right there with them." She and Mya had never been able to wait for dawn, either.

Kai threw up his hands. "What's the world coming to?"

"Chaos, apparently," her dad said, his blue eyes twinkling.

Iolana leaned over and gave Kai a kiss on the cheek. "And on that note, I'm hitting the waves." She rose. "You coming, Stone?"

Micah hesitated for only a fraction of a second, his gaze darting to Aurora before he stood. "Right behind you."

As Micah and Iolana gathered their gear and headed toward the surf, Aurora topped off her iced tea from the jug in the cooler. "So, is this the setup you have for the Christmas Day event?"

Kai's booming laugh made several of the nearby beachgoers turn. "Hardly. Brendan's roughing it today."

She looked to her dad. "This is roughing it? Just how big is this event?"

"It's... substantial."

"That's an understatement." Kai stretched his legs out in front of his chair. "You'll love it." He took a sip from his drink. "What does your family do for Christmas?"

Kai's question was innocent enough, but it hit her like a jab. She gazed at Micah and Iolana in the water as she answered. "My mom loves celebrating holidays. She starts decorating in November, with lights and wreaths and bows all over the house, and a huge tree in the main room."

"What about your dad?"

She swallowed as her father's emotional field flickered. Not an easy topic for either of them to discuss. "I haven't spent many holidays with him."

"He and your mom aren't together?"

She met the stormy blue of her father's gaze. "Not at the moment."

"But he loves the holidays, too," he murmured.

A tremor raced down her spine. She shot a look at Kai, but he was focused on her dad.

"You know her dad?" Kai asked him.

"Yes. And he's incredibly grateful Aurora's here."

But he couldn't claim her as his own. Couldn't tell his best friend the truth. The bond of secrecy her mother had imposed on him all those years ago held him captive.

She had the power to free him. To free them both. Her mother's decision had imprisoned her just as securely as her father, changing the course of their lives and keeping them apart.

She was tired of secrets, lies, and deceptions created and guarded with the best of intentions. From the moment she'd arrived, her father and brother had shown her a world filled with light and joy. If she wanted that world for her future, she had to break the chains that bound her and make a leap of faith.

Taking a deep breath, she turned to Kai. "Which is why I'm so happy to be spending the holidays with him and my brother this year."

Forty

"So, what's the deal with Aurora?"

Micah glanced at Birdie as they paddled out toward the rolling waves. "What do you mean?"

"First she shows up on the beach dressed for a mountain climb rather than a swim, then she freaks out and runs off for no reason, and now she's staying at your dad's house as his newest student. What gives? Who is she?"

Micah kept his gaze forward as he stroked through the water. He was the world's worst liar, and Birdie could read him better than anyone except his dad. And Aurora. "She's an empath."

"I *know* that. She wouldn't be working with your dad otherwise. But who is she? What's her background?"

Keep your head down. "What don't you ask her?"

"Because I'm asking you. She's only been here a few days, but you and your dad are acting like she's family. I don't get it."

"I'm friendly with all my dad's students." He pivoted his board, watching the incoming swells, searching out one that would take him in and interrupt the interrogation.

"Not like this, you aren't. The way you look at her—it's weird."

"What do you mean, weird?" He shifted, keeping his back to her so she couldn't see his face.

"Like she's your birthday and Christmas presents all wrapped into one."

An apt description. And not a comment he wanted to respond to.

He shifted his weight as a wave approached. It was smaller than the ones he usually rode, but he couldn't wait for a better one. Rising to his feet, he caught it. So did Birdie.

He tried to focus on the rolling water and his board, but his mind churned in opposition. He dumped into the drink as his concentration broke before the wave did.

Clasping his board, he bobbed in the water, shaking droplets off his face.

And found Birdie right in front of him.

"Are you dating her?"

"What? No." Talk about getting the wrong impression.

"But you want to?"

"No! Definitely not. It's nothing like that." Not that Birdie would be upset if he did. They'd never been the least bit attracted to each other in that way.

"Is she a family friend?"

"Not exactly."

She threw a hand in the air, flinging a trail of water that pattered his board. "Then what?"

He wanted to tell her. She'd been his surrogate sister and best friend since the day they'd met. And he understood her concern and confusion. If she suddenly showed up with a guy that she treated like a long-lost brother, he'd feel the same way. "I can't tell you."

Her eyes widened. "Can't? Or won't?"

"Can't."

"Huh." She studied him for a long moment before pulling herself onto her board. "I take it she'll be at your birthday party tomorrow night."

His birthday. In the excitement of Aurora's arrival, he'd forgotten all about it. "Yeah, she'll be there." At least he hoped she'd agree to come. They were holding it at his favorite restaurant and all his friends would be there. He wanted her to meet them.

And how exactly will you be introducing her, genius? If Birdie's reaction was typical, there'd be a lot of odd looks and speculation going on. As an empath, that could make the evening unpleasant for her.

He and Birdie paddled back out in silence, the voices of the other swimmers and surfers making their sudden awkwardness more pronounced.

As she turned her board around, she faced him again. "Answer me one question, if you can."

He nodded.

"Do you trust her?"

"With my life." Literally. His sister would sacrifice herself before she'd let anyone hurt him. And he'd do the same.

The tension around Birdie's mouth softened. "That's good enough for me."

They stayed in the water for a few more runs, but he wasn't able to find his rhythm, and their usual jokes and jibes were conspicuously absent. When he suggested heading back to the tent, she didn't offer any objections.

As they approached, Aurora stood, her gaze locked on him. No doubt she was sensing his unease. She intercepted him when he ducked under the canopy. "It's okay. You don't have to cover for me. I told Kai the truth."

His gaze darted to Kai and his dad, who both looked a lot more serious than when he'd left. "What truth?" His sister was a labyrinth of secrets. He didn't want to inadvertently reveal one she had on lockdown. Or implicate himself.

"The one that's been ruining your afternoon." She stepped over to Birdie and stuck out her hand. "We need to do this again. I'm Aurora Hawke, Micah's sister."

Micah's jaw hinged open.

So did Birdie's, her arm freezing in mid-handshake. She glanced at Micah, then back at Aurora. "Sister?"

"That's right. We haven't seen each other since I was two and he was four. That's why I reacted so strangely when we met on the beach. I'd just figured out who he was."

Clearly Aurora had been sensing his emotions while he was surfing. And Birdie's, too, judging by the directness of her explanation.

"I came here to find my dad. Reconnecting with Micah was unexpected."

Birdie blinked, her brown eyes twin moons against her tanned skin. "Wow. I figured it was something but... wow."

"I know." Aurora's smile held a touch of irony as she released Birdie's hand. "I've been saying that a lot the past few days."

Birdie turned to him. "I thought you told me your sister died."

"That's what I believed. But it wasn't true."

Birdie frowned, her gaze shifting to his dad. "You lied to him?"

"As I said to Kai earlier, it's a long story." He glanced at Aurora, then back at Birdie. "And this isn't the place to tell it." Standing, he gestured to the tent. "Let's pack up. We can continue this discussion at my house."

Forty-One

"How much do you want them to know?" Aurora's dad asked her as they rode along the winding road toward Diamond Head.

She turned away from the window, where the sun was creating ribbons of silver on the water. "How much can they handle?"

Her dad glanced at Micah before answering. "As much as you're willing to share."

Which was what, exactly? Her mother's warnings echoed in her head. The more people who knew about her Suulh heritage, the more the target on her back would expand.

She'd believed that voice most of her life. Where had it gotten her? The Admiral and Knox had figured her secret out and kept that knowledge from her, maneuvering her through the Fleet to keep her away from the Teeli. Siginal Clarek had known as well, and had convinced Jonarel that he should mate with her to pull her under the umbrella of the Kraed, whether she wanted their protection or not.

And then there was Reanne. She'd never said a word to her roommate, but that hadn't kept her secret safe, had it?

Her father's voice spoke of a different reality, one in which she stood tall and proud, declaring and defending her heritage, reclaiming the parts of herself she'd kept locked away for so long. In his vision, she wasn't isolated. She wasn't hiding. And she wasn't cut off from her family.

She pivoted in her seat so she could see both her dad and Micah. "I can't go back to the way things were. I want this," she gestured to the three of them, "to continue. The only way to make that happen is to stop pretending to be something I'm not." She held Micah's gaze. "But I'm not the only one who would be affected." Micah was half-Suulh, too. Standing beside her and claiming her as his sister would make his life harder. And more complicated.

He reached out, clasping her hand, his emotions surrounding her in a gentle embrace. No fear. No anxiety. Only love and joy. "I don't want to deny who I am. Who *we* are. And I won't give up what we have together." The intensity in his green eyes made her heart pound. "Face it. You're stuck with me, sis."

Joy flooded her, both hers and his. Maybe she should try to channel it away, but now wasn't the time. Instead, she grasped it with both hands and held on tight.

Letting out the breath she'd been holding, she turned to her dad. "Then I guess we're telling them everything."

His soft smile filled the air with light. "That's my girl."

They gathered in the living room, the lights of the Christmas tree casting a kaleidoscope image on the walls. Iolana and Kai took one couch, Micah and her dad took the other, and she settled in facing Kai and Iolana. Taking a deep breath, she launched in. "It all began on a planet many lightyears away."

Once she got started, the words flowed with surprising ease. Her dad filled in a few points regarding his early days with her mother, but mostly he and Micah kept silent. Iolana asked a lot of questions, particularly after she realized Micah and Aurora were only half-human. Micah fielded the questions he could answer, bouncing those he couldn't back to Aurora.

Kai spoke up a couple times, focusing on why her dad had not made any effort to contact her. "You let your own daughter believe you were dead?" The rebuke in the question wasn't subtle.

Her dad winced. "I know, it's bad."

"Damn right it's bad, Brendan. You had a responsibility to her, but you let your wife talk you out of it. How could you? You're a better man than that."

Her dad's pain cut into her chest, making her breath hitch.

"You knew Aurora was an empath, and that she'd need training. You let her flail around on her own rather than standing up for her."

"I couldn't—"

"Please, Kai, don't blame him."

Kai's stormy gaze swung to her.

"He was protecting me the only way possible. Staying away was the best of two terrible choices."

"It's kind of you to defend him, but—"

"I'm not defending him. I'm telling you the facts. My mother put him in a no-win scenario. Believe me, I know what that's like. She did the same thing to me when I chose to join the Fleet."

"How?"

"She was dead set against it, to the point that she refused to give me any money for tuition. She thought that would stop me. She was wrong."

Kai studied her. "You made it through on your own?"

"With honors. And the help of grants. But it cost me. She never approved of anything I did after that." Her gaze met her father's. "And it probably reinforced her determination not to tell me about my dad and Micah. Or to allow my dad to contact me."

"Hmm." Kai crossed his ankle over his knee, leaning back into the couch cushions. "Your mother sounds like a formidable woman."

"That's putting it mildly."

"Also sounds like she met her match with you." The corner of Kai's mouth tilted up.

Heat rose along Aurora's neck. "I guess so."

"Brendan's damn lucky to have you for a daughter."

The warmth reached her face.

"Yes, I am." Her dad's soft words drew her gaze. "Thank you."

She glanced away and cleared her throat. "I'm just glad the secret's out."

"And I'm glad you told us." Kai gestured to Iolana. "We'll keep this to ourselves."

"I appreciate that, but that won't be necessary for long. I plan to have my dad introduce me as his daughter starting tomorrow night. And as soon as I've learned to control my empathic response to the Suulh, I won't be keeping my heritage a secret anymore, either."

Forty-Two

Be careful what you wish for.

Mya sighed, resting her cheek on her folded arms as she gazed out at the shadowed trees swaying in the evening breeze, the air sweetened with the scent of fresh rain.

She'd gotten the answers she'd been looking for, filling in the blank spaces regarding the Suulh. But that knowledge had sunk into her like a virus, making her ache all over.

She'd pushed aside the discomfort during the festivities. The Suulh had put together a feast to celebrate her return and the completion of their settlement. They'd also insisted on taking her and the crew on a tour of every building and the gardens. She'd marveled at how homey and welcoming the spaces felt, but it had also reminded her of how much they had all lost and endured.

When the party broke up and everyone went to bed, she'd retreated to the back deck, seeking solitude.

"You have been quiet this evening."

Jonarel's deep voice made her turn.

He stood on the deck behind her, the warm glow of soft light through the back windows of the main building making his dark hair shimmer like flames. She hadn't even heard him come outside.

He gestured to her perch on the steps leading down to the pathway that circled the central building. "May I join you?"

She nodded, scooting over to give him plenty of room before drawing her knees back up to her chest.

He settled right beside her anyway, his hip and shoulder brushing against hers.

An involuntary shiver passed over her, but she couldn't summon the energy to worry about it. Her mind was too preoccupied with the haunting images of the Suulh's tortured past.

Jonarel didn't say anything, simply sat beside her and gazed out into the darkness beyond the halo of light. He'd been quiet all day, too, though that wasn't unusual when they were around the Suulh.

Mya drew strength from his reassuring presence, the solidity of his body beside hers. When he was with her, she felt safe. Hopeful. Protected. She treasured their moments together, even though they caused her pain.

Resting her cheek back on her folded arms, she asked the question that had been tormenting her for hours. "How could anyone be so heartless?"

A sigh that seemed dragged from his soul preceded his reply. "You are a healer, a being of light and love. It is understandable that you cannot conceive of such evil."

She lifted her head, but his gaze was still directed at the trees. She studied his profile—strong jaw, high forehead, arresting eyes. And an intangible quality that both thrilled and scared her. "But you can?"

"Yes." His mouth worked, like he was tasting his words, trying to decide which ones were palatable. "I have felt the touch of Reanne Beck's evil in my mind. In my heart. I remember the darkness she summoned. The darkness she unleashed."

It took a moment for her to figure out what he was referring to. "You're talking about your reaction to Cade."

He met her gaze, his golden eyes filled with banked fury. "She wanted me to kill him."

"Kill him?" Mya swallowed. "I knew you were furious with him, but you wouldn't have—"

"Only because Aurora stopped me."

Despite the open air, oxygen became a rare commodity. She'd seen the painful results of their fight, tended to their wounds, but had always believed Jonarel would have called a halt even without Aurora's intervention.

She'd been wrong. "But Reanne pushed you to do it."

"Like a hand thrusts a dagger into an opponent's heart."

That image would stick with her for a while. "Why did she want Cade dead?"

His gaze shifted back to the foliage. "I have given that much thought during our journey. My conclusion is she viewed him as competition for Aurora's attention. I was competition, as well. If I had murdered Ellis in cold blood, I would have been prosecuted, or at least sent back to Drakar. She would have eliminated both of us with one move."

Mya's teeth began to chatter. She clamped her jaw down. "That's... that's..." She couldn't even put it into words. Couldn't picture Aurora rooming with the psychopath who had sent Jonarel to commit murder for her own twisted purposes. Much easier to believe Reanne had become a monster after leaving the Academy.

Jonarel had just shattered that illusion. "The evil has always been within her." His fingers curled, the claws at their tips catching the light. He stared at the unsheathed blades, a snarl lifting his upper lip, exposing his teeth. "And her evil is infectious."

His anger could be directed at Reanne, and probably was, but she knew him too well to miss the self-recrimination. He was blaming himself for being her pawn.

Reaching out, she slid her hand into his.

The claws retracted immediately, disappearing into the pads of his fingers.

"Jonarel, it's not your fault."

He didn't look at her. "Is it not? Reanne manipulated me as she manipulated the Suulh. I do not even know if my anger and distrust for Cade Ellis is my own, or what Reanne wanted me to feel."

She finally got it. "You're scared."

He went very still.

Nailed it. "You're scared because you lost control. Because you weren't able to stop her from using you." She gazed at his beautiful face, darkened by shadows of the past. "You're afraid that it could happen again."

His fingers enfolded hers, enclosing her hand in his. "Yes." He finally looked at her, a tortured helplessness in his eyes. "I have focused all my efforts on protecting Aurora. And you. But Reanne has proven she has the power to control my mind, my actions. The next time we confront her, what is to prevent her from turning me against you?"

"Oh, Jonarel." She leaned into him, resting her head on his shoulder and engaging her energy field, offering comfort the only way she knew how.

He inhaled sharply but didn't pull away. Instead, he rested his cheek against her hair.

"I don't believe she could ever turn you against us." She paused, but he didn't respond, so she continued. "With Cade, you had a reason to dislike him. You planned to mate with Aurora, and you had also appointed yourself as her protector. You understandably saw him as a threat to both. I think Reanne played on that, fanning the flames of emotions you were already feeling."

His grip on her hand tightened a fraction.

She pushed on. "With Aurora and me, it's completely different. Your feelings for us are positive, nurturing." She thought over what Zelle had said, about how she'd reacted to Reanne. "I think her manipulation amplifies thoughts and emotions you already have. That's why she seeks out each person's weak points."

He growled.

Clearly his pride was still intact. She'd just dinged it by pointing out a weakness. "She preyed on your concern for Aurora's safety, making Cade out to be a dangerous threat. At the same time, she played on Cade's insecurities about his relationship with Aurora, making him jealous and distrusting."

He relaxed into her, rubbing his cheek against her hair. "You are very wise."

Snugged up against him like this, his voice rumbling through her entire body, had a predictable effect on her breathing. She cleared her throat. "Reanne could never convince you to harm Aurora. Or me. Or to stand idly by while someone else did. It would go against the core of your being."

"You are correct." He released her hand, wrapped his arm around her, and pulled her into a cocooning hug that set her brain on tilt. "I would die for you," he murmured, his lips nuzzling the curve of her ear.

Aaaaannnnddd this was the glaring problem with the nature of their relationship. To him, *you* meant *you and Aurora*, and his caress was a natural way for a Kraed to show connection and caring. There was nothing the least bit romantic or sexual about it.

Her body didn't get the message.

Boundaries. I need boundaries. And an oxygen tank. "I know." Giving his arm a reassuring squeeze, she pulled back, clearing several centimeters of breathing room. Not enough, but it was a start.

He released her, his stoic façade settling back into place.

She hated that she couldn't give him what he yearned for, the casual physical connection that was so elemental for the Kraed. But it would cost her more than she had to give.

She redirected the conversation. "I understand my grandmother's actions better now." She still wasn't clear why her grandmother hadn't fought to defend the Suulh in the beginning, before Reanne came up with her twisted Necri plan. Maybe she had. Or maybe she'd been manipulated by the Teeli.

One thing was certain. After hearing Zelle's story, she wasn't going to judge her grandmother harshly. She'd be willing to bet Zelle's husband wasn't the first Suulh her grandmother had watched die. The psychological toll had to be excruciating.

"Did you tell your mother?" Jonarel asked. "About seeing your grandmother?"

"Yes." It had been one of the better moments from that long, traumatic night. "She cried, but I think they were mostly happy tears."

"You gave her the one thing she has been denied for decades. Hope."

"I suppose so." But it had also raised the bar on the challenges they faced. Made it personal. "We'll be leaving for Drakar in the morning. Any recommendations on how to handle your father when we get there?"

He drew in a slow breath. "He will be displeased that Aurora is not with us."

She got the feeling *displeased* was a gross understatement. "I wasn't planning to tell him where she is."

"He will be displeased by that as well."

She quirked a brow. "You're not giving me much to work with here."

He shrugged. "My father is... focused. Single-minded when it comes to the clan and Aurora. The best course of action is to remain calm, not allow him to force you into playing his game."

"Hmm." An image of the chessboard Jonarel had given Aurora flashed into her mind. Siginal, like Jonarel, was an excellent chess player.

Mya had never developed a knack for the game. Strategy and counteracting an opponent were not her strong suits. And she'd never imagined going toe-to-toe with a ticked off Kraed.

But remaining calm under pressure? She excelled at that.

Siginal Clarek was about to meet his match.

Forty-Three

"The Teeli are setting up a rendezvous with Bare'Kold." Justin strode into the Admiral's study with Bella right behind him. "I just translated an audio message that gave the coordinates. It's in Southern Quadrant Four."

"Why am I not surprised?" Cade rested his hip on the corner of the Admiral's desk and folded his arms. "That entire quadrant seems to be Reanne's malevolent playground. Where are they meeting?"

"It's a multi-planetary system around a K-type star."

The Admiral leaned back in his chair. "When is this rendezvous taking place?"

"We don't have an exact timetable," Bella answered, "but Bare'Kold told Magee to pack for departure tomorrow morning. Based on the estimated speed of Bare'Kold's yacht, they should be able to reach their destination in three days."

Cade glanced at the Admiral. A slight tightening around his eyes was the only indication that he'd reacted to the news about Magee. "Bare'Kold's taking her with him?"

Bella nodded. "She seemed excited, the most animated she's been since we started watching the feed."

"She always loved to travel," the Admiral murmured, the look in his eyes growing distant.

If the *Starhawke* was still in orbit, and if Cade was still on speaking terms with her captain, they would be able to trail Bare'Kold out of the system without the Teeli ever knowing. Maybe even find a way to detain the yacht and get Magee back.

But Aurora and her ship were gone.

"We could take *Gladiator* to the rendezvous point and observe from a discreet distance." They didn't have the *Starhawke*'s camouflage ability.

"I've been working on some upgrades gleaned from things I learned from Jonarel," Bella said. "We might be able to conceal our presence, or at least make the ship harder to pick up on scanners and cameras."

"And watch for an opportunity to get Magee back," Cade added.

"No interventions, Commander." The Admiral fixed Cade with a steely stare. "Am I clear?"

He straightened. "Yes, sir." But following the order would cost him. He didn't want the Admiral to lose someone he viewed as family.

The Admiral's gaze moved to Bella. "How confident are you about these modifications? Will you be able to keep the ship disguised?"

She nodded. "I believe so. And if we do encounter trouble, *Gladiator*'s a lot more maneuverable than the Teeli ships when it comes to close contact flying. Once we make our interstellar jump, it doesn't matter if they're faster. But we do have a problem. It will take *Gladiator* three and a half days to get there."

Cade glanced at the clock on the wall. The day was already half gone.

"Then you'll need to get moving." The Admiral stood. "I'll see what I can do to slow Bare'Kold's departure."

Cade turned to the Admiral, his mind flashing on another important logistical issue. "We can't leave you alone."

The Admiral's brows rose, a sparkle of amusement in his eyes. "Believe it or not, I've been taking care of myself since long before you were born."

Cade shook his head. "That's not what I meant."

"I know. I'll be fine."

"That's not a given. The Teeli may not be able to manipulate you directly, but what if Reanne tries something more aggressive, like the accident she orchestrated against Payne's grandson?"

"That's a risk I'll have to take. You need to be at that rendezvous."

"But—"

The Admiral halted him with a raised palm. "This is not open for debate. Your unit will take the next personnel transport to Sol Station and depart for the rendezvous coordinates. Those are your orders."

A vise squeezed Cade's chest, his heart at war between his need to follow orders and his need to protect the Admiral. They'd already lost him once. He didn't want to go through that again.

The Admiral tilted his head, studying him. "If it will ease your mind, you may leave Ms. Reynolds behind."

Air filled Cade's lungs, the pressure releasing. "It would, and I will. Thank you."

"You're welcome. Now get going, Commander. Your ship awaits."

Forty-Four

"What do you think?" Iolana's voice barely carried over the spirited music of the live salsa band playing on the restaurant's small stage.

Aurora set her plate of food on the high-top table for two, along with the cocktail Iolana had insisted she get— a yellow-orange concoction with a wedge of fruit on the rim. "It's fabulous."

Iolana slid onto the other chair. "Stone and I have had many a celebration here." She set down her plate and matching cocktail and gestured to the band. "Do you dance?"

"Dance?" She hadn't even had time to notice the small dance floor. In the whirlwind since their arrival, Micah had introduced her to all the birthday party attendees. Once she'd passed fifteen or twenty names, they'd begun to blur together. Then Iolana had pulled her through the buffet line. She wasn't even certain exactly what items of food she'd heaped on her plate.

"Yeah." Iolana spread a napkin on her lap and picked up her fork. "Micah loves to dance. Do you?"

"Um... I guess."

"You guess?" Iolana pointed her fork at her. "What kind of answer is that?"

"The kind that means I'd probably like it a lot, but I haven't had much opportunity to find out serving with the Fleet."

"Fleet personnel don't dance?"

"Of course they do. But I was focused on other things."

Iolana shook her head and made a tsking noise. "That's just sad. We'll definitely need to fix that before the night is over."

A smile tugged at Aurora's lips. "So, I'm not a lost cause?"

"Nobody's a lost cause if they're willing to stand up and give it their best shot."

"I assume that applies to surfing, too."

"Absolutely. The learning curve is steep, and you spend a lot more time in the water than on the board in the beginning. But once you catch your first wave?" Her eyes gleamed. "Unbelievably magical."

No wonder Micah had been drawn to her. She was a kindred spirit in both her love of the water and her positive attitude toward life.

Aurora glanced over at the dance floor, where several couples and a few singles moved to the playful beat. "After we eat, I'm game to give it my best shot."

Iolana held her hand up palm out and Aurora returned the high five. "All right!"

"Whoa, whoa!" Micah appeared beside the table, an almost empty plate in his hand. "Looks like I'm missing out on all the fun."

"Not our fault you have to be the life of the party," Iolana teased, digging into her food.

"But that also makes me the master of ceremonies." He grinned at Aurora. "Having fun?"

"You bet."

"How do you like your drink?" He nodded to the glass beside her plate.

"I haven't tried it." Setting down her fork, she picked up the cocktail and took a sip. A sweet, fruity flavor slid over her tongue, followed by a warmth that spread down her throat and into her belly. "Wow. That packs a punch."

"They don't call it a Hawaiian Hurricane for nothing."

She took another sip, the mellow warmth expanding through her limbs. "Tasty."

Iolana shot Micah a mischievous smile. "After she finishes this one, I'm taking her out on the dance floor."

"Excellent. I'll meet you there. For now, duty calls." He lifted his fork in a salute and moved on to the next table of party guests.

Aurora watched him circulating through the crowd, sharing smiles and laughs with his friends and even stopping at tables of total strangers to say hello. "He's in his element, isn't he?"

"Oh, yeah. If he's not catching a wave, his favorite place to be is in the middle of a crowd. It's one reason he loves teaching so much. He gets a constant flow of newfound friends to talk with."

"I'll bet he's an excellent teacher."

"The best. I've sat in on a few of his classes and gone out on some of his field expeditions as well. You'd be hard pressed to find a teacher who's more passionate and enthusiastic about his subject. Or who does a better job of inspiring that same enthusiasm in his students."

Aurora propped her chin on her hand as she watched him, a soft melancholy weighing her down. "I've missed so much."

"Hey." Iolana rested her forearms on the table and fixed Aurora with a pointed look. "That's backwards thinking. You need to be facing forward. Focus on all the wonderful experiences you two can share now that you're reunited."

And just like that, the cloud lifted. Regret wasn't where she wanted to live. "I'm so glad Micah met you."

Iolana laughed. "You and me both. I didn't think I minded being an only child until I had him to pick on. Way more fun."

Aurora smiled. "I know what you mean. I don't know what I would have done without Mya."

"She's the one you grew up with, right? The one whose parents live with your mom?"

"Uh-huh. We grew up like sisters."

"Where is she now?"

Good question. "I left her in charge of my ship while I was here."

"She's your first officer?"

"No. I have my own ship."

Iolana's brows lifted and she slowly set down her drink. "You own a starship?"

"Yeah." She hadn't gotten to that part of her story during the discussion the previous day.

"But I thought you were with the Fleet."

"It's complicated."

Iolana stared at her for a long moment. "I'm beginning to understand that."

"I still haven't told Micah about my ship. I'd planned to make it a surprise. But maybe I should tell him before I take him to see it."

Iolana's smile reappeared. "Whatever you decide, your secret's safe with me." She glanced at Aurora's empty plate. "You ready to hit the dance floor?"

Picking up her drink, she took a healthy swallow, the warmth burning away any lingering nerves. "Let's do it."

Iolana led the way to the dance floor. Staking out a small section near the perimeter, she spent a few minutes teaching Aurora the basic movements for this particular style of dance.

Aurora followed her instructions, keeping time with the rhythm of the music. Thank goodness for her yoga training and sparring sessions with Celia. They'd taught her how to isolate and control her body movements and maintain her balance, which she needed to keep up with Iolana's spirited gyrations.

She sensed Micah's approach from the opposite side of the room. When he reached the dance floor, he caught her hand in his and spun her around to face him, a devilish grin on his handsome face. He moved effortlessly into step with her and started guiding her around the floor in a dizzying whirl.

"Shake it, Aurora!" Iolana called out over the music, giving her a thumbs up.

Aurora's laughter blended with Micah's as they danced in perfect unison. It was as easy as breathing. She could anticipate every move he made, and every move he wanted her to make.

The music reached a crescendo. "Big finish!" Micah's breathless words alerted her right before he took her through a series of spins that ended with her arched over his arm, head thrown back.

Her body tingled from head to toe like a million tiny fireworks. And no wonder. Her energy field surrounded them both.

Micah grinned down at her, his eyes impossibly green. Lifting her back to her feet, he gave her a hug. "Thanks, sis. That was awesome."

She hugged him back as moisture gathered behind her eyes. "Yes, it was." A moment in time she'd remember the rest of her life.

Forty-Five

A warm dampness tracked across Aurora's cheek and along the curve of her nose.

Opening her eyes, she gazed into the shadowy darkness of her room. Her stomach felt hollow, her body heavy. Touching a hand to her cheek, she traced the moisture to her eye. She'd been crying. A bad dream?

She sorted through the tendrils of memory, but came up empty. Maybe a reaction to the intensity of the evening, and the days that had led up to it. She'd experienced a compressed series of high highs and low lows, so dealing with emotional miscues was to be expected. Her subconscious would be working overtime during the night to sort it all out.

Pulling the comforter up to her chin, she burrowed deeper into the cozy nest of her bed. But the sensation stayed with her.

Let it go, Aurora. A bout of insomnia wasn't on her agenda. She needed her rest if she wanted to be prepared for her next training session right after breakfast.

She curled onto her side, fluffed the pillow, and focused on her breathing.

Nope.

The aching void pulled at her.

No way was she going back to sleep.

Shoving the covers aside, she slid out of bed. Maybe a cup of warm tea would soothe her cantankerous subconscious.

She made it to the bottom of the stairs before the intensity of the sensations forced her to pause. Pressing a hand to her abdomen, she leaned against the wall, tears spilling onto her cheeks. She swiped them away, but new ones took their place. What the hell was going on?

Tea no longer sounded like a good idea. She needed the breeze on her face, the smell of the salt air.

Padding along the hallway to the living room, she crossed to the door to the pool deck.

It was already partway open.

The ambient light from the pool revealed a figure in silhouette, lying on one of the lounge chairs, gazing up at the stars.

Realization clicked. The emotions weren't hers. They were her dad's.

She started to back away, but his voice stopped her.

"I woke you, didn't I?"

Pushing the door all the way open, she stepped onto the patio. "I didn't mean to disturb you."

He turned his head, meeting her gaze. "I think that's my line."

She took a few steps, then halted. "Do you want me to leave you alone?"

His sad smile was barely visible. "I think I've been alone long enough."

The emptiness in her belly grew, drawing her to him. "Are you okay?" Stupid question. Of course he wasn't. His emotional pain had woken her from a sound sleep.

He held out a hand. "Better, now that you're here."

She clasped it, perching on the second lounge chair. "Bad dreams?"

"No. I couldn't sleep, so I came out here. And got maudlin." He scrubbed a hand over his face. "It doesn't happen often, but after watching you and Micah having so much fun dancing together, I just—" He circled his hand in the air, unable to finish the sentence.

It didn't take empathic skills to figure out the path his mind had followed. "You've been thinking about Mom."

"Always." He laced his fingers through hers. "But not like this." His gaze traveled over her face, studying her. "Your emotional resonance is so similar to hers. For a moment tonight as I watched you, it almost felt like she was in the room with us."

That soul-deep ache spread, pressing against her heart. "Have you seen her? I mean, since you and Micah left?"

"Only once, at your graduation."

"You were there?" She'd had no idea.

"It was one of the best and worst days of my life."

Exactly how she would have described it.

"I didn't try to talk to her, but I'm sure she sensed me. That was a rough day for her. For both of you."

He would have sensed the emotional battle they'd waged that day. And been dealing with his own demons, too. "She'd hoped I'd never make it through the Academy." Her mom's fear had turned what should have been a day of celebration into a tense, stress-filled slog. Her dad's presence at the ceremony no doubt had added to that fear.

He held her gaze. "She was worried about what would happen when you joined the Fleet."

"I know." And her rational side understood the depth of those fears. But the old wounds still burned.

"If it's any consolation, her fear came from her absolute certainty that you'd succeed. That you'd become the leader you were born to be."

"I guess." Which made her fear a backhanded compliment. "She tried to talk me into applying for a teaching position at the Academy. Anything that would keep me planetside."

He was silent for a moment. "I can understand not wanting to let you go. I'm not exactly eager to send you back to your starship."

She squeezed his hand. "But you wouldn't try to talk me out of it."

He shook his head. "Never. You belong there. I always knew that. But that doesn't mean I won't miss you like crazy."

A pleasant warmth spread through her chest. "I'll miss you, too." In many ways, more than she missed her mom. Which circled them back to the reason they were out here, sharing confessions under the stars. "Why haven't you ever visited her at Stoneycroft?" The depth of his yearning would break most people in a day. He'd been carrying that burden for twenty-seven years. "After I joined the Fleet and left the house, you could have visited. I wouldn't have known."

His crooked half-smile did nothing to ease the pain in his eyes. "If I held your mother in my arms again, I'd never be able to let her go."

"Oh." His words punched her in the gut. She could feel his longing for the woman he loved but couldn't have. It was hard to reconcile that emotional intensity with the image she held of her mother, who'd always seemed a bit cold. "Have you talked to her?"

"A few times when you and Micah were young. But after the Teeli became members of the Galactic Council, she cut off even that small amount of contact. If it hadn't been for Marina and Gryphon..." He stared up at the sky. "I honestly don't know what I would have done. Lost my sanity, maybe."

"And you never tried to change her mind?" That didn't seem like him. Passive and yielding weren't two words she associated with her father.

He sighed, his gaze shifting to hers. "This may be difficult to understand, but I made a promise. And mostly I agreed with her. I would sacrifice anything to keep you and Micah safe. Even the joy of spending my life with the woman I love."

So much sadness. Emptiness. Loss.

And so much love.

Talk about a no-win scenario.

The part of her that was her mother's daughter understood the driving need to shield loved ones from danger. She'd felt the same impulse since becoming captain of the *Starhawke*.

But the part of her that resonated with her father's joyful enthusiasm for life wanted to stomp her feet in frustration. Her mother had made a decision that had cast a pall on all their lives, a storm cloud that hovered over them, blocking out the sun.

And she was sick and tired of living in the shadows.

Her energy field flared to life, its pearlescent glow surrounding them both. "What about now?"

He stared at her like she'd burst into flames, his gaze roving over the energy field and his throat moving in a convulsive swallow. "Now?"

"Yes." He was responding to her energy field, just as she'd suspected he would. His emotions came through in a complex jumble, with none of the calm control and focus she was used to. She wanted him to remember what it felt like to be a part of that field, to experience the joy of interconnection that was uniquely Suulh.

The connection he could have again with her mother.

He deserved to be happy, dammit, the way he had been when they'd been living together as a family. But she'd have to blast apart his outdated ideas to get him there.

"Micah and I know the truth, so there's no reason for you and Mom to stay apart."

Boom!

The dam exploded, the force of his emotional tidal wave crashing into her, making her tremble. But she held firm against the onslaught, tightening her grip on his hand, which shook as much as her own. "It's okay, Dad. You don't have to be alone anymore."

His chest rose and fell like a bellows, each breath audible, his gaze searching hers. "How—" His voice caught and his brow furrowed. He cleared his throat and tried again. "How do you know she still wants to be with me?"

"Are you crazy?" She gave his arm a shake. "Why wouldn't she? You're amazing. And she's still in love with you. Always has been. I just thought she was pining for a ghost." His emotions started to stabilize, so she pushed her advantage. "She's never shown the least bit of interest in anyone else. And believe me, several of her male customers have tried. She shut them down so fast it's a wonder they didn't get squashed flat."

He snorted. "Is that so?"

She raised her hand. "Cadet's honor." His soft smile lightened her heart. "I assume you still want to be with her? There's no one else?"

"There was never anyone else. After what I shared with your mom... well, let's just say no woman on this planet stood a chance of catching my interest."

The conversation had made a delightful U-turn. "Glad to hear it." And her mom could certainly use a healthy dose of her dad's optimism. He'd been the one to make her laugh before. He could do it again. "Then when you've taught me everything you can here, I'll take you with me to Stoneycroft."

He was silent for a long moment, gazing at her. "Has anyone ever told you you're as stubborn as your mother?" Tugging gently on her hand, he scooted over so she could sit beside him.

"All the time." It was one of her defining characteristics. "It's an important quality for a captain."

His lips curved. "Or the leader of the Suulh?"

"That, too." Although she'd been a little lax in those duties lately. "But if there's one thing I know for certain, it's this." She leaned closer, dropping her voice to a conspiratorial whisper. "You deserve to be loved."

"Is that so?"

"Uh-huh."

"And what about you?"

"Me?"

He arched his brows. "As I recall, there's a young man out there who's desperately in love with you. When will you be contacting him?"

Whap! Boomerang to the head. "Uh..."

"You deserve to be loved, too." He brushed a lock of hair away from her face. "Cade sounds like a good man for the job."

"Yeah, well... the thing is—"

"The thing is, you're scared. Am I right?"

She couldn't deny it, even to herself. "Terrified. I don't want him to get hurt because he's with me. Or *because* of me."

He nodded. "I understand. Probably better than anyone. But tell me this. Does being with him make you happier than being apart?"

"Yes, but—"

"But, nothing." He clasped her hands in his. "You've made some very good points tonight, given me a lot to think about. And I will. But it goes both ways. Your happiness is just as important to me as mine is to you. You know that, right?"

She nodded. His every word and action had made that abundantly clear.

"Good. So, I'll make you a deal."

She waited, her stomach doing backflips.

"I'll agree to go with you to Stoneycroft, but before we leave Hawaii, you have to agree to contact Cade to work out a solution to your problem."

Forty-Six

Informing Reynolds she was staying behind had been easier than Cade had expected. She'd apparently mentally appointed herself as the Admiral's personal guard already, so she'd latched onto her orders with both hands.

The team had bid her and the Admiral farewell and headed for the Fleet transport station, where they'd caught a crowded personnel transport to Sol Station.

During the long walk to *Gladiator*'s berth, Cade had fought to suppress memories of Aurora. Despite the crush of personnel moving through the corridors, the station felt oddly devoid of life without the *Starhawke* in residence.

Or maybe that was just the echo chamber in his chest.

The crew had fallen into the focused quiet that always preceded a mission. No one said a word until they'd passed through the security access for their airbridge and sealed *Gladiator*'s airlock behind them.

"Home sweet home," Bella murmured, glancing around the close confines of the main room with a smile of affection.

"It's good to be back," Cade admitted. *Gladiator* couldn't compete with the *Starhawke* in ability or luxury, but it did have one distinct advantage. It was his to pilot and command. "Prep the engines for departure. We'll take off as soon as we get clearance."

While Bella headed for the engine room and Gonzo and Williams stowed the gear, he and Justin moved to the cockpit. Memories of Aurora followed him there, too, taunting him with what had been. He shoved them aside. Until his unit returned safely to Earth, he couldn't allow any distractions, especially unproductive ones.

He slid into the pilot's seat. "See what you can do to get us a quick departure."

Justin claimed the co-pilot's seat to his left. "On it."

While Justin spoke with station control, Cade worked through his pre-flight checks. A subtle vibration under his boots alerted him when Bella brought the main engines online.

"Roger, Control." Justin slid his headset around his neck and glanced at Cade. "We're fourth in line for departure, estimated twenty minutes."

Not bad. He'd expected to wait at least half an hour. He checked the chronometer. That put their departure around twenty-one hundred hours GC Standard Time. But if the Teeli delegation left any earlier than nine hundred hours the next day, his unit would have trouble beating them to the rendezvous point.

"We're cutting it close," Justin said, echoing his thoughts. "But Reynolds said she would help the Admiral find a way to delay the yacht's departure." Justin grinned. "I think it may involve dusting off some old Fleet rules and regs."

"I'll take all the help we can get." While they waited for their clearance, Cade worked on the interstellar jump calculations that would take them to the rendezvous point. Their flight plan had them leaving in a perpendicular trajectory. After the small initial jump to clear the beacons around the Sol system, he'd be altering that plan, taking them through a different jump window to reach their destination.

He opened a comm channel to the engine room. "Engine status?"

"Main engines and interstellar engines good to go." Bella sounded positively giddy to be hands-on again with the ship.

He'd never quite understood why she got such satisfaction from being stuck in windowless compartments working on machinery when she could be gazing at a galaxy of stars outside the viewport. The points of light in the sea of black called to him like a siren's song. He'd hate not seeing them for hours or days at a time. *To each their own.*

"Roger, Control." Justin nodded to Cade. "*Gladiator* is cleared for departure."

Anticipation flowed through Cade's veins. Nothing beat flying a starship.

Well, almost nothing.

Grasping the yoke, he took the ship through the departure sequence, the docking clamps disengaging and the station sliding away as the starfield grew to fill the viewport. The ship gathered speed, the image of Earth rapidly shrinking in the aft camera.

As he watched the tiny blue dot disappear into the distance, a strong tug in the center of his chest caught him by surprise, making him suck in a breath.

"You okay?"

He met Justin's concerned gaze. "Fine."

Justin's eyes narrowed. "You don't look fine."

He rubbed the center of his chest. The sensation burrowing under his skin felt like a dull ache, or a sense of loss, like maybe he'd left something behind. "Any chance we left something important at the Admiral's house?"

"You mean besides Reynolds?"

"Yeah."

"Nope. I looked over our supply checklists twice. We're good. Why? Feeling anxious?"

"I'm not sure." He glanced at the aft camera view, but Earth was no longer visible in the blackness. "Just a weird feeling. Like there's something missing. Something I need."

"You're probably just worried about the Admiral. It hasn't been that long since we got him back. It's not easy taking off when we know he's still a target."

"I guess." Although that didn't feel quite right.

A light flashed on the console, alerting him they were approaching the jump window. Time to focus.

"Powering up interstellar engines."

The sensation remained, gnawing at him as he guided the ship to the jump window. Irritating, but tolerable. Maybe after they were in the second jump he'd take time to figure out what was bothering him. Or ask Williams to give him a onceover. His heart had been through a lot lately. In more ways than one.

Until then, he had a job to do.

He shifted *Gladiator* from main to interstellar engines. "Let's go shed some light on Reanne's next move."

Forty-Seven

Lesson Number One: Never debate emotions with a level ten empath.

Aurora stared at the image in the mirror over her sink as she braided her hair the next morning. Her dad had handled her like a pro, neatly flipping her words back at her, and extracting a promise she hadn't wanted to give.

Mostly hadn't wanted to give.

Okay, maybe some small part of her wanted to give.

Oh, who was she kidding? After talking to her dad, the walls she'd put up around her emotions regarding Cade had developed serious structural flaws. Her dreams had been filled with images of him, some quite... intense. And she couldn't shake them. Everywhere she looked she saw him, like an afterimage, just out of reach.

She'd picked up and set down her comband at least six or seven times, but words had failed her. What could she say? *Hi, Cade. I know I kicked you to the curb, but I had a long talk with my dad and he really thinks we should work things out.* Yeah, right. If she was going to do this, she needed a solid plan for the future, not a vague wish.

Besides, for all she knew he could be in the middle of a mission for the Admiral. He had *Gladiator,* so his team didn't need to rely on the *Starhawke* for transportation anymore. He could be halfway across the quadrant by now.

You're making excuses.

Yes. Yes, she was. And she'd keep making them until she figured out how to proceed.

Leaving her room, she headed for the kitchen.

Her dad was seated at the raised countertop, sipping a mug of coffee, his hair still damp from his shower. "Morning."

"Morning." She kissed him on the cheek before fetching a mug and the tea canister from the pantry. "How did you sleep?"

"Much better, thanks to you."

She met his gaze, an understanding stronger than words passing between them. She smiled. "So, what's on the agenda for today?"

"I've been thinking about that. Since Micah won't be able to join us until this evening, I thought we'd focus on the emotion we were both dealing with last night."

Not exactly a fun prospect, but a necessary one. "What's Micah doing today?"

"He's taking a group of students on a scuba expedition."

"He scuba dives, too?"

"Yep. Swims like a fish. Or more accurately, a dolphin."

"Do the dolphins show up when he's diving?"

"Not usually. They tend to avoid scuba divers. But they're almost always around when he free dives. He loves that. I've lost track of how long he can stay under—two or three minutes at least. That wonderful Suulh physiology seems to have given him an edge in controlling his autonomic breathing functions."

"Huh." She'd never tried a free dive before. Going exploring with Micah as her guide would be fun.

In the salty ocean?

Her thought train came to a screeching halt.

"What is it?"

The concern in her dad's voice pulled her back into the room. "It's noth—" She stopped her standard response, shaking her head. The truth. Only the truth. "I'm still terrified of going in the water. Of what might happen."

He came around the counter and wrapping her in a hug. "Getting over trauma isn't easy. You need to give yourself time." His hand stroked her back in a soothing motion. "Remember that you're not alone. We'll work through this. All of it."

A sigh escaped her as she allowed his comforting embrace to soothe the anxiety churning in her belly. "Thank you."

He leaned back, placing a soft kiss on her temple. "It's all going to work out, sweetheart. You'll see."

A smile slowly spread across her lips. Her dad was the ray of sunshine she'd been yearning for her entire life.

After breakfast, they returned to the loft, settling onto the couch.

"How will this work without Micah doing the emotional projections?"

"I'll do them." He set his tablet on the cushion in front of his crossed legs. "You're very physically expressive with your emotions. I won't need to sense them as intently as I do with most students. I'll be able to see your reactions on your face."

"Really?"

"That surprises you?"

"Kinda. I've often been told that my emotions are difficult to read because I'm reserved."

"Reserved?" His laugh filled the loft with rainbows. "Not a word I'd use to describe you, but then again, I've never seen you in uniform. Maybe you're different with me because you can be yourself."

"Good point." She certainly wasn't trying to hide anything from him. But at the Academy and in the Fleet, she'd been on continual alert, protecting the secret of her Suulh heritage.

Mirroring his pose, she rested her hands on her knees, palms up. "Ready when you are."

The opening of the meditation had become familiar, her mind grabbing onto the imagery like a favorite toy.

"Your emotions are a physical entity, a flow of water that you can direct, control, and contain. When they become too strong to process, you can pour them into your container so they cannot harm you. Visualize your container."

This part had become second nature, too. At first, she'd struggled to come up with a visual for her container that worked. She'd tried a steel water tank like the ones used on Fleet starships, a bathtub like the one in her bathroom at Stoneycroft, even a pool like the one on the deck outside. None of them had successfully given her the control she needed. She'd finally settled on a more elemental image—a circular earthen trench that flowed with a never-ending pearlescent river around her.

"Pour your emotions into the container. Observe them without judgment, without expectation."

Simple when her emotions were at a low ebb. That would soon change.

Sure enough, a deep melancholy pushed into her consciousness.

"As you sense new emotions, add them to the container."

His voice didn't match the emotion pulling at her. Intellectually, she admired the discipline it took to achieve that. Emotionally, she needed to focus before she got knocked out in the first round.

She allowed the melancholy to flow through her and out into the channel, joining the emotions already swirling there.

"Good. Remember to breathe."

She drew in air, letting it out on a sigh.

"Allow the emotions to flow into your container with each exhale."

The melancholy upshifted to an aching sadness, pulling and tearing at her gut.

Her fingers tightened on her knees.

"The emotion is not yours. You know this. Give it a shape, a form, a color. Then release it into the container."

Spheres of deep blue sadness appeared within her, pressing against her ribcage. One by one, she pushed them out, visualizing them joining the river's flow at her feet. They bobbed on the water for a moment, like monochromatic beach balls, before disappearing below the surface, leaving a sense of peaceful calm.

So far, she was having a lot more success than she'd expected. Maybe her talk with her dad the night before had helped her prepare for this challenge.

"You are in control. You are the center."

She concentrated on her breathing, waiting for what was to come.

Wrenching sadness slammed into her, latching onto her like a giant leech.

"Focus."

This mass was larger, heavier, more persistent. She couldn't push it away.

"Send the emotion to your container. Let it go."

Let it go? She wasn't the one holding on. The emotion didn't want to let go of *her.* It wanted to overwhelm her. Overpower her. Drain her dry.

So, she switched tactics.

Pearlescent tendrils rose from the river surrounding her, like slender appendages. They grasped onto the dark blue of the emotion that clung to her, sliding in between and steadily, methodically, pulling it away. The mass resisted for a moment before tumbling into the water's embrace, dissolving like sugar.

Her shoulders dropped, her breath evening out.

"Notice how you feel in this moment."

Peaceful. Serene. Grounded.

"This is your center. The core of your being. Remember this moment. Whatever you experience in this place comes from your authentic self. Trust it. Trust yourself."

Trust yourself. Such a simple concept. So hard to do.

Her dad began the countdown to bring her out of the mediation, the sounds, scents, and tactile sensations of the room moving back into her consciousness.

"One. Open your eyes."

Her eyelids fluttered. Her dad's soft smile caught her attention first.

"How do you feel?"

"Good." She stretched her arms out, arching her back until her spine popped. "Great, actually. Really relaxed."

He nodded. "You went a lot deeper this time than in the previous visualizations. And you were able to maintain control longer."

"I tried a new set of imagery." She described the challenge of the emotional leech, and how she'd dealt with it.

"So adapting your shielding imagery helped you regain emotional control. Fascinating. Not surprising, I suppose, considering you started shielding as an infant. It's your instinctive response for dealing with a perceived threat."

"Or was, until Mom drilled me endlessly so that I would *not* instinctively shield when threatened."

His brows rose. "She did?"

"Oh, yeah. She was terrified that I'd use my shield while we were out in public and give myself away. And her training worked... mostly." The day she'd met Jonarel was a notable exception. Although to be fair, she'd been protecting them both from an avalanche at the time.

"But when I was assigned to the *Argo*, I knew the dangers would be a lot more intense than what I'd faced before. I was afraid I wouldn't be able to control my shielding, which is why I sought out Celia to teach me how to fight hand-to-hand."

"Celia's your security chief?"

"Yes. She was assigned to the *Argo's* security team at the time."

"And did it help?"

"A lot. Our sparring sessions challenged me in ways Mom's training couldn't. And the confidence I gained in my ability to defend myself without my shield allowed me to raise the threshold for my instinctive reactions."

He studied her, absorbing that information. "Did you ever consider telling anyone about your abilities?"

"Only when forced to."

"Forced?"

"By circumstance. The day I met Jonarel, I saved him from a rockslide using my shield. I couldn't explain away what he'd seen." Thanks to her dad's contact with Marina and Gryphon, he already knew quite a bit about her friendship with Jonarel and Kire. "And Cade found out the first time we kissed."

Confusion clouded her dad's eyes. "You shielded when he kissed you?"

"No. My energy field engaged. He could see it."

His gaze sharpened. "He saw it?"

"Uh-huh. Described the pearlescent glow perfectly. But he's the only non-Suulh I've met who can. Well, besides you."

A speculative look passed over his face. "Did you ever meet Cade's parents?"

"No. They didn't want him to join the Fleet any more than Mom wanted me to, so they never visited the Academy. A lack of parental approval was one of the things we bonded over."

His lips pressed together. "I'm sorry you had to deal with that. Both of you."

She shrugged. "Not your fault."

"Partly my fault." His gaze shifted to the interior rock outcropping rising past the edge of the loft's low wall. "But I'm glad you found each other." The low murmur was as distant as whatever he was seeing beyond the stone.

"Me, too." Despite all the trauma she and Cade had been through, she wouldn't give up a moment of what they'd shared.

Her dad's gaze met hers. "That kind of love is rare."

He'd sensed what she was feeling. "I know."

"It's caused you a lot of pain. And fear."

Her throat constricted. Her dad didn't pull punches. But he also understood. "It's worth it."

The corners of his mouth slowly lifted. "I agree." Moving his tablet to the cushion behind him, he scooted closer. "I think it's time to clear some of that fear away."

The oxygen level in the room dropped by sixty percent. "I don't think I can."

"I *know* you can. You are so much stronger than you realize." He slid his hands around hers, their gazes locking. "Do you trust me?"

"Completely."

"Then let's do this."

Forty-Eight

"I'm scared." The confession leapt out of her mouth before she could stop it.

His blue eyes warmed like the sky on a sunny day. "I know." The brush of his thumb on the back of her hand soothed, comforted. "I'm here. You don't have to face this alone."

Which had always been her modus operandi, hadn't it? Never asking for help. Always taking the weight of responsibility on her shoulders even when others offered to share the load.

Her dad's solid presence shone a spotlight on the weaknesses inherent in that stance. "Thank you."

His answering smile spread warmth over her skin. "This isn't like the training we've been doing. I won't be testing your limits or pushing you in any way. Just follow my instructions as I guide you along. If it gets too intense, we'll stop. Okay?"

Not okay. Not anywhere close to okay. But she didn't want to let him down. Or prove to herself she was a coward.

Taking a deep breath, she nodded.

"Close your eyes."

His hands clasping hers provided a tether that kept her anchored as a whirlpool of anxiety swirled around her.

"Draw in a slow breath to the count of four, hold it for four, and release it for four."

She followed the familiar rhythm, the cord of tension between her shoulder blades slowly loosening as he led her through the opening sequence with infinite patience, giving her time to settle in.

"You are safe in this space. Nothing can harm you."

She focused on the warmth of his hands, the strength he gave her so effortlessly.

"Now, allow your mind to travel back in time to the incident in the river."

Her breath hitched.

"You are safe in this space. Nothing can harm you," he repeated, his grip on her hand tightening a fraction. "Visualize the river. You are fighting with Kreestol."

"I'm not your enemy."

Kreestol's arms pinwheeled as she lost her balance on the rocks. "Yes... you... are."

"No." Aurora took another step backward, drawing Kreestol into the middle of the river. "I don't want to hurt you."

"You want... what's... mine!"

"I want to help the Suulh." Aurora deflected the next blow. "All the Suulh. Including you."

Kreestol sneered. "I... don't need... help."

"You do if you're trusting the Sovereign."

"You know... nothing!"

Her father's voice overlaid the memory, directing her thoughts. "The fight takes a turn for the worse, putting you at a disadvantage. You're in trouble. You need a way out."

Kreestol changed her approach, lunging in a flying tackle.

Aurora sidestepped, but not fast enough. Kreestol plowed into her, knocking her off balance and tumbling them both into a deep pool in a flail of arms and legs.

Kreestol struck first, pinning Aurora to the rocks at the bottom. She was taller, with a longer reach, which gave her leverage as she held Aurora down. Underwater, she looked like an avenging nymph, strangely untouched by the water thanks to her shield.

Aurora kicked her in the shins, but the water stole the force from her movements. Kreestol's shield pressed down from above while the rocks to either side blocked her in, making it impossible to slide out of Kreestol's grip.

Her aunt's lips contorted in a malicious grin that matched the emotions pouring out of her. Whatever her weaknesses as a fighter, she'd taken full advantage of the situation. Her shield was open to the air, allowing her to breathe while Aurora was trapped underwater.

"You have to break free. There's only one option available to you, and you take it."

Her jaw clenched, bracing against the images that assailed her.

Drawing on the core of her power, she channeled energy into a blast that struck like a tsunami.

Kreestol's weakened shield deflected some of the energy, but she was no match for the assault Aurora had unleashed. Her arms flew out like wings as she fell backward, her body rigid with shock.

The agony racing through Kreestol's body echoed in Aurora's, locking her muscles and obliterating her shield. Water rushed into the void, soaking her skin.

"Breathe, Aurora."

Her body shook as she dragged in air.

"You defeated Kreestol. You survived. Allow yourself to remain in that moment."

She broke the surface of the river with a gasp. Air and cool water flowed into her mouth, choking her and setting off a series of hacking coughs that burned her windpipe. She placed a hand on the rocks to steady herself until the coughing subsided.

Droplets of water clung to her eyelashes. She brushed a hand over her face and blinked to clear her vision, searching for Kreestol. There. Clinging to a rock beside the pool.

As the image of Kreestol stuck in her mind like a video on pause, a tickle started at the base of her throat. Like a caterpillar climbing a branch, it worked its way up her esophagus, triggering a hacking cough that doubled her over.

"Focus on your breath." The calm, steady cadence of his voice flowed over her, never changing. "In for four, hold for four, out for four."

Each shuddering inhale eased the violence of her coughing. Seconds, minutes, hours passed before she straightened. She rolled her shoulders and tilted her head side to side to stretch the tight muscles of her neck.

"Are you ready to continue?"

No. The worst was yet to come. But if she ran from the truth now, her fear would gain another foothold. She couldn't allow that to happen.

She nodded.

"Visualize the river."

A tremor danced over her skin.

"You've defeated Kreestol, but the energy blast caused unexpected consequences. You hurt Cade, too."

The tremor expanded. She shivered.

Justin knelt at the edge of the opposite bank next to a prone figure.

Cade!

A strangled cry ripped through her throat. She clawed her way onto the rocks, slipping and sliding on the slick surface as she stumbled to Cade's side.

She sank to her knees and placed a hand on his chest. No heartbeat.

"The river flowed with saltwater. You didn't know. Could not have suspected. You were fighting for your life. And you had no idea Cade had stepped into the river."

The tremors became a quake that made her teeth chatter.

By sending a massive energy charge through a saltwater river, she'd electrocuted every living being in contact with that water. Including Cade.

A boa constrictor wrapped around her chest and squeezed.

"You used your energy field to save him. You brought him back."

She shook her head. Hard. He couldn't understand. She'd killed—

"You *saved* him!" His hands squeezed hers. "He didn't die. You—"

"No!" She shook from the force of the emotional hurricane. "Dad, I—"

Pain rained down like a summer monsoon, drowning out her words.

His strong arms enfolded her, gathering her against his chest and tucking her head under his chin. He stroked her hair, rocking her like a child. "I'm here," he murmured. "I'm here."

Time stood still. There was only this moment. This pain. This release.

Giving into her grief, she sank into the comfort he offered, her tears soaking his shirt.

Forty-Nine

By dinnertime, Aurora was physically and emotionally drained, but far calmer than she'd been since she'd arrived.

Her dad had taken her through the same memory regression sequence twice more in the afternoon. By the third pass, she'd been able to make it beyond the moment when she'd seen Cade prone on the ground, pushing through to where she'd restarted his heart and he'd opened his eyes.

The emotions erupting from her subconscious still had the power to bring a sob to her throat and force tears down her cheeks, but she hadn't turned into a quaking mass of goo like she had the first time.

She couldn't attain mastery over her responses to the Suulh until she dealt with the emotional blocks that triggered her own fears and pain. As her dad had said with his usual directness, "You can't clear someone else's junk when you're standing waist-deep in your own."

Waist-deep was being generous. Most of the time it felt like it was up to her chin.

"So tell me about Reanne."

She glanced at her dad, who was watching her from his seat across the table. They'd quit for the day and were enjoying a meal out on the patio by the pool.

She picked up her fork, swirling it in her pasta bowl. "What do you want to know?"

"Everything. How you met. How your friendship progressed. And any theories as to why she holds such hostility toward you."

She took a bite, chewing slowly, gathering her thoughts. "We met my fourth year at the Academy. Mya and

I had been roommates when we first started, but that year she moved into housing with the other med students. I was asked by my faculty advisor to room with Reanne, who was an incoming cadet. That was fairly standard practice—for older students to be paired with incoming students. We served as live-in mentors."

"How did you and Reanne get along?"

"Fine, at least in the beginning. She was young, both physically and emotionally, but she loved to socialize, so I introduced her to the people I knew and included her in activities when I could. We had similar interests and ideologies—or at least I thought we did—so we had a lot to talk about." She paused, taking a sip of her wine. "More than anything, I felt sorry for her. She'd been dealt a rough hand. She never went home during the holidays, and no one ever visited her, either. Her mom had flat out told her she was unwanted and that she wished she'd never been born."

"Ouch."

"Yeah. Reanne had worked hard to make it into the Academy so she could get away from her. I could relate to her drive to leave home, but at least I knew Mom's behavior stemmed from love. Reanne's mom seemed to hate her. I never heard any details about her dad. She said she'd never met him. I could relate to that, too."

Her dad flinched.

She pointed her fork at him. "No judgment."

His lips lifted. "No judgment." He plucked a roll from the breadbasket. "How long were you friends?"

"A few years. Things didn't start to fall apart until our third year together. She'd been accepted into a cadet exchange program with the Academy in London. She left for the fall semester, only a few weeks after I met Cade." She stabbed a spear of broccoli and popped it in her mouth, focusing on the mundane task of chewing to calm the emotions bubbling to the surface. "By the time she returned at the end of the year, Cade and I were spending most of our free time together. We'd even started talking about our plans for the future. When she tried to reinsert herself into my life, things got... awkward."

"Awkward how?"

"She couldn't accept that things had changed, that I couldn't give her as much attention as I had before. She started contacting Cade or showing up at his room unannounced on the pretext of wanting to talk about me. She'd also try to join us when we were together, flirting shamelessly with him the whole time. At first, it seemed harmless. Cade clearly wasn't interested in her. But then he started to act differently around me. Argumentative. Suspicious."

"And Reanne was feeding those behaviors?"

"Yes. She was doing everything she could to poison our relationship. I've never asked Cade for the full details, but from comments he's made, I think she convinced him I was cheating on him. Or if I wasn't, that I would dump him as soon as someone better came along."

"He believed her?"

"Not right away. It took her a year and a half to bring everything to a head. But once she figured out she could prey on his insecurities, she manipulated him every chance she got. It's one of her talents, actually, finding out someone's weak points and exploiting them. Unfortunately, I didn't figure that out until it was too late."

"What happened?"

"Cade accused me of having a fling with Jonarel, which was ridiculous. Jonarel was like a brother to me. But when I denied it, he didn't believe me. He told me he never wanted to see me again. I was devastated."

"I can imagine."

Yes, he probably could. "I wanted to salvage the situation, give Cade some time to calm down and then talk it through. But Reanne wasn't about to let that happen. She went straight to Jonarel and told him Cade had dumped me. She claimed later that she thought he would comfort me."

"I take it he didn't react well?"

"She knew exactly what she was doing. Being an overprotective Kraed, Jonarel accommodated her by hunting down and attacking Cade. It was awful." She shuddered at the memory. "Jonarel could have killed him if I hadn't sensed what was happening and intervened."

"You stopped them?"

She nodded. "I placed my shield between them." She stared out at the ocean, allowing the breeze to cool the heat rising from within. "That drove the final nail in the coffin. I could feel Cade's hatred, see the jealousy and fury in his eyes as he stared at us. I was never going to change his mind."

"And Reanne got her wish. You weren't with Cade anymore."

"No, but she didn't get what she wanted, either. I didn't want to be around her. I was still mostly in the dark regarding her role in the whole debacle, but I'd seen enough to realize she wasn't the friend I'd thought she was. When I started the two-year officers training program that fall, I requested a transfer to a suite with several members of my officer class. Reanne and I didn't see much of each other after that."

"Did she try to keep in touch?"

"She made a few gestures, like giving me birthday cards or Christmas presents, but I never encouraged it. She also met a guy who doted on her. I foolishly hoped that his presence would take her focus off me." She shook her head. "I was so very, very wrong."

"Hey." Her dad's hand rested on top of hers. "It's not your fault. You had no way of knowing how unbalanced she was."

"There were signs."

"In hindsight there are always signs. Take it from a professional. Nothing you've told me would have convinced me she was capable of the kind of full-scale vendetta she's executed. And there certainly was no way you could have known she had a connection to the Teeli, either."

"I wish I had. If I'd been able to read her emotions, I could have anticipated the problem with Cade before it got out of hand. But she's always been an emotional blank to me."

"A blank?"

"Like she's not there. It's not even a wall like what I feel when you're using emotional stasis to contain your emotions. With her, it's just... emptiness. A void."

"Interesting."

"Terrifying. I should have recognized the sensation when I encountered her at the river, but my mind couldn't make the leap. Even when I pulled off her cloak and was staring at her face, I couldn't accept what I was seeing."

"The most dangerous adversaries are those who hide under the guise of normalcy."

"Well, she can't do that anymore. Now I know who I'm fighting."

"How do you feel about that?"

"Feel?"

"Yes. Are you afraid of her?"

"No." The word leapt from her lips without conscious thought, firm and direct.

"No? You seemed pretty fearful when you arrived."

He was right. She had been. In fact, before she'd left Stoneycroft, when her mom had claimed she wasn't afraid of Reanne, she'd told her she should be.

But fear wasn't the emotion vibrating under her skin. No, the emotion rising to the surface spoke of heat and fire, of boundaries crossed, of wrongs to be righted.

Her hands curled into fists on the tabletop as the vibration intensified, her energy field flaring to life. "I'm not afraid of Reanne Beck. Or her Teeli and Setarip friends." Her voice came out deadly calm. Focused.

"But she should be afraid of me."

Fifty

"Your heart's in perfect working order." Williams brought up the results of Cade's scans on the display in *Gladiator*'s infirmary. "No scarring, irregularities, or evidence of trauma. In fact, Mya's healing session probably added ten years to its lifespan."

Cade rubbed a hand over his chest, trying to relieve the tension that had been building ever since they'd left Sol Station. "That's good news."

"Yes, it is." Williams switched off the display. "You're in the best shape of your life."

"Okay. Good." The knowledge did zip for relaxing his mind and body.

Williams scrutinized him for a moment, then moved to the med platform and sat beside him. "You want to tell me why you're concerned?"

Cade continued to rub his chest, where the ache sat like a cold potato. "My heart just feels... off."

"Any pain?"

"No. Not really. Just an ache."

"When did it start?"

"When I was piloting *Gladiator* to our jump window."

"Hmm."

Cade narrowed his eyes. "What do you mean, hmm?"

Williams shrugged. "I have a theory, but you may not want to hear it."

"Of course I want to hear it."

"Okay. I think it's Aurora."

Cade's hand stilled. "Aurora?"

Williams nodded. "Your feelings for her are powerful, strong enough to create physical symptoms that have nothing to do with your health."

Williams had been right. He didn't want to hear it. "You're saying this is all in my head?"

"No. I'm saying it's all in your heart. This is the first time since you two reconnected when you haven't been working together. I think that really bothers you."

"Of course it does. But we weren't together on Burrow and I didn't have this problem then."

"You were separated from her physically during that time, but you were still working on the same project—helping the Suulh. She was sending you updates, keeping in touch. You knew where she was and what she was doing."

"I know where she is now, too. On her ship in Kraed space." With Jonarel Clarek.

That knowledge triggered a different sensation, one he was quite familiar with. His jaw clenched rather than his chest.

"But you're not in communication with her."

"I haven't been in communication with her for a while. Why didn't I start to feel this earlier?"

"Denial, probably. It wasn't until we were on Sol Station, leaving on a mission without Aurora, that it became real. It drove the point home that you'd lost that connection."

His words were certainly driving the point home. And not helping the ache in his chest. If anything, it was getting stronger. "So, what's the treatment?"

"Time heals all wounds."

Cade rolled his eyes. "That's the best you can do?"

Williams stood, resting a hand on Cade's shoulder. "I can fix many things, my friend, but heartache isn't one of them."

"Wonderful."

"If it helps, remember you're not alone. Aurora has to be feeling the same way. She was rattled after what happened at the river, which is understandable, but she's a fighter. She won't allow Reanne to destroy what you two have found together. I'd bet money you'll be seeing her sooner than you think."

"I hope you're right." Living with this feeling for the foreseeable future was not a pleasant prospect.

Fifty-One

The journey to Drakar gave Mya two days to plan what she was going to say to Siginal Clarek when they arrived. Her list of questions grew with each passing hour. She replayed previous events in her mind, spotting inconsistencies that had gone unnoticed when she'd been in the dark regarding Siginal's involvement with the Admiral and the Teeli. Seen from her current perspective, and in light of his plans for Aurora and Jonarel to mate, his words and actions took on a whole new meaning.

Question One: Why didn't you warn us about the Teeli?

She could understand withholding that information while she and Aurora were still at the Academy. And their posting to the *Excelsior* after graduation had made any Teeli encounters virtually impossible. But when the *Starhawke* had arrived on Drakar following the attack on Gaia two months ago, he should have shared what he knew. Yet he'd remained silent. Why?

He'd even forced the same code of silence on Jonarel, who'd known the Teeli were responsible for the attack on her homeworld. Siginal had ordered him not to say a word. He hadn't even allowed him to speak up after they'd rescued the Suulh refugees and relocated them to Azaana.

If Knox Schreiber hadn't shared what he knew with Aurora during their talk on Osiris, they'd still be flailing in the dark.

She'd always viewed Siginal as a friend—an oversized, burly, alien friend—but now she wasn't sure if that term fit. He clearly had an agenda. And she wanted to know what it was.

When the doors to the lift parted, she stepped onto the bridge. Kire rose from the captain's chair as she approached, relinquishing it to her and moving to the communications console. During their mission to the Suulh homeworld, she'd resisted taking command, preferring to leave that role to Kire. He had command experience, after all. But she didn't feel that way now. Quite the opposite. She wanted Siginal to know exactly who was knocking at his door.

Kelly turned from the navigation console, the display backlighting her auburn curls. "We've entered the Drakar system."

Mya settled into the captain's chair. "Good. Celia, drop the hull camouflage." She'd debated lowering it when they'd left Azaana, but she'd decided she wanted to be within sight of Drakar before announcing their presence. The less time she gave Siginal to react, the better. She turned to Kire. "Send a message to Siginal, alerting him we'll be arriving shortly."

He nodded.

She pivoted back to Kelly. "Will you be able to land the ship?" Based on Aurora's description, docking on Drakar wasn't like landing on water or connecting to a spaceport. It was more like a controlled crash into the trees. She'd missed the spectacle last time, choosing to stay in the med bay rather than coming up to the bridge.

Star's projection appeared beside the young pilot. "We'll be fine."

"Incoming message from Siginal," Kire said.

"On screen."

The Kraed's image appeared on the bridgescreen larger than life, giving him the appearance of a fairytale giant. His gaze locked onto the captain's chair, his mouth curling down. "Where is Aurora?"

Not even a greeting. "It's good to see you too, Siginal." She kept her voice steady, plastering a close-lipped smile on her face. Jonarel had been right. Siginal's reaction bordered on hostile.

His dark brows drew down, his expression fearsome. "Hello, Mya. Where is Aurora?"

Her fingers curled. "Otherwise occupied. I'm here to talk to you."

"Will Aurora be joining us?"

"No. She's not onboard."

"Not onboard?" She might as well have said Aurora was boiling in a vat of oil. He doubled the volume. "Where is she?"

Stay calm. Follow Jonarel's advice. "She's fine."

"Where?"

"Taking care of a personal issue."

"You left her?"

"She told me to." Or at least her actions had implied she wanted to be left alone.

"What? Why?"

"She had her reasons. And I have mine." But she wouldn't get into it until they were face-to-face. "Are you free to meet this morning?" According to Star, the sun had risen at the Clarek Compound only thirty minutes ago. She had the whole day to wear him down.

He ignored the question, his gaze sweeping the bridge. "Jonarel is with her?" The words came out more like a growl than a sentence.

"No, he's in engineering, preparing for our arrival."

His lips peeled back, showing his white teeth. His piercing gaze moved to Star. "You hid the ship from us." A statement. And an accusation.

"At my request." Mya did her best to imitate Aurora's command voice, drawing Siginal's attention back to her. "I had a reason for that, too."

"Why?"

"We can discuss it when we meet."

Siginal stared at her, a cacophony of emotional discord playing across his features.

She waited.

"I will meet you at Tehar's berth."

A small victory, but she'd take it. "Looking forward to it."

His eyes narrowed before the image disappeared from the bridgescreen, replaced by the blue, green, and brown orb of Drakar.

"That went well," Kire said under his breath.

She glanced over her shoulder. "No worse than I expected."

"He's always been Aurora-centric, but this is a bit much. I guess hiding our arrival wasn't going to improve his mood, either."

"It was the only way to get uninterrupted time with the Suulh."

"I would have made the same decision." He shrugged. "He's not great at respecting boundaries."

Star turned to face them, her expression pained but resolute. "He is not displeased with you. He is displeased with us." She gestured at the deck, presumably indicating Jonarel in engineering.

Mya frowned. "That's not fair. None of this was your decision. It was mine."

"It does not matter. The situation has not progressed as he would wish it."

"Nothing lately has progressed as we would wish it." And if Siginal's initial reaction was any indication, she was in for a battle royal while they were on Drakar.

"We have not behaved as he expects. You must help him understand why." Star held Mya's gaze, a clear message in her golden eyes. "He does not see things as you do. For Aurora's sake, and yours, that must change."

Fifty-Two

The flight to the planet's surface stole Mya's breath. At one point a small shriek may have escaped despite her clenched jaw. But Star and Kelly acted like aiming the ship directly into the trees was completely natural.

After the *Starhawke* glided to a halt with nary a bump, Mya unclenched her fingers from the armrests of the captain's chair, wiggling them to restore circulation.

Kire appeared beside her and nudged her shoulder. "Were you worried?" His grin indicated he'd been watching her the whole way down.

"A little," she admitted. "I didn't expect it to be quite so..."

"Intense?"

"Terrifying."

He chuckled. "If it makes you feel any better, it gets easier the second time. I still flinched, but I didn't have the urge to scream *abort, abort, we're all going to die.*"

She laughed. "Yeah, that did cross my mind."

Kelly joined them on the lift, a decided bounce to her step and sparkle in her eyes. She'd obviously enjoyed the challenge of landing the ship.

"Well done, Kelly," Kire remarked as the lift descended.

"Thank you." The enthusiasm in her voice was unusual, too, though she'd reacted the same way during their last visit to Drakar. The opportunity to rub elbows with the best pilots in the galaxy seemed to strip away the mask of serenity she normally wore, revealing a more playful side.

They met Jonarel and Celia at the cargo entrance on the main deck near the doors to the observation lounge. Celia had volunteered to assist Jonarel in securing the ship.

As the entrance opened up, letting in a wave of moist heat, Star materialized in front of them. The green and brown tones of her skin, which matched the coloring of the trees outside, was such a perfect projection that it was easy to forget she was made up of light energy rather than cells. But when Mya looked at the Nirunoc with the healing vision that enabled her to see injury and disease, Star's form took on a ghostly quality that revealed her lack of physical substance.

Mya led the group off the ship. Jonarel and Star flanked her while Kire, Kelly, and Celia followed behind. Even this early in the morning, the warm humid air pressed against her skin like a moist towel from a hot spring. Before arriving in the system, she and the rest of the crew had changed into the garments Jonarel's mother had given them during their last visit. The cloth made a huge difference, whisking away the moisture with surprising efficiency.

She hadn't walked more than three meters when she spotted Siginal standing partway down the planked pathway, his expression far from welcoming. He was dressed in clothing similar to that worn by the crew, rather than the ceremonial clothing he'd worn last time. And he'd come alone.

Instead of stepping forward to greet them, he waited until they came to him, his gaze on Jonarel and Star while he studiously ignored Mya. Jonarel and Star went through the ritualistic greeting, but even to Mya's untrained eye it looked forced. When Siginal finally turned to her, his hug was perfunctory, a chill cutting through the dense warmth of their surroundings. His behavior was equally brief with the rest of the crew. "Come with me."

Mya glanced at Jonarel. His jaw tightened, his attention on his father's retreating back. When his golden gaze met hers, the intensity set her heart pounding, blasting through the layer of frost from Siginal. He gestured for her to follow Siginal, but not before his expression changed to one of puzzlement, the way he looked at her whenever he couldn't understand what she was thinking.

And what exactly had she been thinking? That he looked like a woodland god, beautiful and lethal. Which was completely inappropriate. Not that it was entirely her fault. Jonarel was a potent distraction at any time, but his home environment and native clothing brought out every sensuous detail of his physique, transforming him into a being straight out of her most vivid fantasies.

Stay on task! You have a job to do. And in case you forgot, he's still in love with Aurora.

Celia had recommended she tell Jonarel how she felt about him. And she'd seriously considered it after Celia had implied Jonarel was facing a lonely future following Aurora's rejection. But a lot had happened since then. They'd located the Suulh homeworld. She'd met her grandmother. She'd learned of Reanne Beck's betrayal. And she'd watched Aurora drop into a tailspin that still had her off balance.

Aurora's loss of self-confidence had resulted in a physical and emotional separation from Cade. And while Mya hoped that situation was temporary, especially considering how happy Aurora normally was when Cade was around, she couldn't ignore the possibility that the threat from Reanne and the Teeli forces might push Aurora to change her mind regarding a future with Jonarel. The Kraed would be powerful allies for the Suulh in a battle against the Teeli. A mating between Aurora and Jonarel would solidify that position.

The very thought made Mya's heart shrivel in her chest, as much for Aurora's sake as her own. But it was a practical consideration, and Aurora was a practical woman. She was also a born leader, who would willingly sacrifice her own wishes for the good of the Suulh.

As long as that possibility existed, Mya couldn't bring herself to reveal her secret yearning, no matter how badly she wanted Jonarel to look at her with the passion and love she saw in his eyes whenever Aurora entered the room.

The walk through the massive trees passed in uncomfortable silence. The thump of their footsteps on the wood planks and the cries of the creatures in the treetops provided the only sounds, like subtle background music in a minor key. As they reached the outskirts of the Clarek compound, several of the Kraed called out greetings, but the dour expressions on Siginal and Jonarel's faces kept the residents from approaching the group.

Mya recognized many of the Kraed, some from the gatherings during their prior visit to Drakar, and others because they'd helped build the Suulh settlement on Azaana.

The structure Siginal led them to blended seamlessly with the surrounding forest, as did all the houses and public buildings in the compound, giving the impression that they'd grown up naturally as part of the trees, rather than being constructed with advanced technology. It was one of the qualities she loved most about this place—the harmonious balance of native flora with the needs of the space-faring Kraed.

The doors parted as they approached. Daymar, Jonarel's mother, stood waiting for them. She clearly hadn't gotten the memo from Siginal regarding the freeze, because she greeted Jonarel and Star with motherly enthusiasm before hauling Mya into a rib-crushing hug. "I am so glad you are here."

Really? She'd always had great respect and affection for Jonarel's parents, but she'd never felt singled out for attention. That role had always fallen to Aurora. "Thank you for welcoming us."

Daymar stepped back, clasping Mya's hands in her own, the deep green and brown of her skin complementing the light tan of Mya's. "You are always welcome here. Always." She glanced at Siginal and Jonarel, who stood on opposite sides of the foyer like twin sentinels. "Do not allow their behavior to convince you otherwise," she added in an undertone.

Daymar's unexpected support brought a lump to her throat. "I won't."

"Good." She greeted Kire, Celia, and Kelly before addressing the group. "I have placed refreshments in the gathering room. Come."

Siginal looked like he was going to object, but a glare from Daymar silenced him. Mya followed Daymar into the spacious room which, based on the curve of the trunks visible as sections of the walls, sat in the open space between three of the enormous denglar trees.

Mya rested her hand on the smooth bark, soaking in the tree's vibrant essence, her entire body tingling. Aurora liked the tenrebac—the Kraed version of wine—that Daymar often served, but Mya found the plant life on Drakar far more intoxicating.

Daymar gestured to the seating arrangement, which had exactly the right number of chairs to accommodate their group, positioned in a conversation circle. Mya had seen enough of the tricks on the *Starhawke* to guess that the seemingly solid floor beneath her feet probably held a plethora of alternate seating and furnishing options that could be reconfigured on a moment's notice.

She chose a chair close to one of the trees. Siginal claimed the one opposite her, settling in like a king on his throne. He steepled his fingers in a gesture that reminded her of Admiral Schreiber, staring at her over his fingertips.

She stared back as Celia and Kelly took the chairs to her left and Jonarel and Kire claimed the ones on her right. Star remained just behind and to the right of Jonarel's chair.

Daymar balanced a tray loaded with wooden mugs, handing one to Mya first. "To what do we owe the pleasure of your visit?" she asked as she continued around the circle.

Siginal's expression didn't reflect the graciousness of his mate's question. In fact, he scowled when he accepted the mug she held out for him.

She didn't seem to notice.

Mya took a sip from the mug, which contained a flavorful, energizing tea she'd enjoyed during her last visit. She waited until Daymar had settled into the empty chair beside her mate before answering her question. "We need information about the Teeli forces."

"Teeli forces?" Siginal's gaze shot to Jonarel, anger flashing in his eyes. "You told her?"

To his credit, Jonarel didn't flinch under his father's accusing glower. "No, I did not. Knox Schreiber and the Admiral did."

Surprise overtook the tightly leashed anger. "You have talked to Will? When?"

"After Mya saved his life." He glanced at Mya, deep respect and admiration in his eyes.

Heat suffused her cheeks. "That's my job."

There was no admiration in Siginal's tone. "Why did he need saving?"

Mya fielded that one. "He'd been badly injured in an engine explosion on a Setarip ship."

"Setarip?" Siginal's eyes narrowed. "Which faction?"

"Etah. He was being held captive."

"Captive?" His nostrils flared. "Will's latest message said he had been detained, not captured, but had returned to Earth."

Admiral Schreiber, ever the diplomat. He probably hadn't wanted to light Siginal's fuse, either.

Siginal leaned back in his chair, taking a moment to process the new information.

Mya took advantage of his silence to fire off the question that had been buzzing in her brain for days. "Why didn't you warn us about the Teeli?"

Siginal deflected the hit with a shrug. "You did not need to know."

She'd been expecting an answer like that, but it still made her blood boil. "Didn't need to know? A supposedly pacifist race has been hunting Aurora's and my families for decades, and you didn't think we needed to know?"

"You were not in danger." His gaze shifted to Jonarel and Star, the corners of his mouth pinching. "Jonarel and Tehar were supposed to insure that." His tone made it clear they'd let him down.

She wanted to smack that disapproving look off his face. He had no idea how much Jonarel had suffered, or how hard he'd fought to protect Aurora. Or how valuable Star had been to the crew. Without her, they might not have escaped the trap at Burrow. Or pushed back Reanne's Teeli forces and saved the Admiral.

She shifted forward in her chair, setting down her mug and planting her palms on her thighs. "If it weren't for them, we wouldn't be here." The note of warning in her voice surprised her, but she pushed on. "Your refusal to tell us the truth is what put us in danger. We've been flying blind, trying—"

"There are things you do not understand."

"Things *we* don't understand? Then try this one on for size. We visited the Suulh homeworld. And discovered Reanne Beck is running the Teeli like her personal army."

Siginal froze like he'd been encased in carbonite. In a less serious situation, his open-mouthed expression would have been comical.

Daymar recovered before he did. "Reanne? How is that possible?"

"We don't know, but it's true. She tried to kidnap Aurora."

"Kidnap her?"

"She has a personal grudge to settle—most likely something she's created in her own mind. But she's wielding the full force of the Teeli and Necri in her determination to take Aurora down."

Siginal slammed his mug onto one of the side tables and shot out of his chair. He advanced on Jonarel like a pouncing panther, grabbing the front of his tunic in both hands and hauling him to his feet. "How could you leave her!" His roar filled the room. "Where is she?"

"She is safe!" Jonarel's roar matched his father's, but Mya caught the defensiveness and pain in the words.

"She is in danger—"

"No, she is—"

"You have failed—"

"She has every right—"

Mya couldn't let Jonarel face this alone. He'd been doing exactly what she and Aurora had told him to.

She leapt to her feet and grabbed Siginal's arm. "Stop it! He's—"

She didn't get to finish the sentence. The back of a hand the size of a bear's paw smacked her on the cheek.

The force of the blow drove her to the floor as stars danced in front of her eyes.

Another roar, this one far more primal, filled her ears, followed by a loud thud and the crash of splintering wood.

A shadow fell over her. She looked up into the blazing fury of Jonarel's golden eyes. But his touch as he brushed his fingertips across her cheek was featherlight.

"Are you all right?"

Her healing instinct had triggered her energy field a millisecond after the blow had landed. The sting had already vanished as coolness spread over the side of her face. But his touch generated heat in her belly. She pushed onto her elbows. "I'm fine."

Or she was until he slid his arms around her and lifted her off the ground. She squeaked as he cradled her body against his chest. "Jonarel, I'm—"

"Shh." He bent his head toward hers and brushed his lips against her hair.

She stilled, her brain and heart waging war over how to react.

He pivoted, giving her a look at the cause of the crash.

Siginal had climbed to his feet, but the chair he'd been sitting in hadn't fared so well. It lay in broken pieces, the remnants scattered on the floor. Small pools of spilled tea from his and Daymar's mugs also darkened the ground. He rubbed the center of his chest, wincing.

No wonder. It looked like he'd been hit with a sledgehammer. She could see three cracked ribs and a mass of tissue damage surrounding the point of contact. More minor injuries showed along his back and upper thighs where he'd collided with the chair.

She struggled to get down, her healing urge pushing her to help.

Jonarel tightened his grip. His voice came out in a low growl, the rumble in his chest transmitting to her. "You will never harm her again."

The threat wasn't implied. It was a promise.

Mya gaped at him, her brain struggling to catch up with the turn of events. A quick peek at Signal proved he was just as stunned.

Jonarel's gaze shifted to Daymar. "We will return after midday meal for a more civilized discussion."

Daymar nodded, her gaze moving between her son and Mya, a small line appearing between her dark brows.

Without another word, Jonarel carried Mya from the room.

Fifty-Three

Jonarel didn't loosen his grip until they'd reached the walkway outside. Even then, he set her on her feet with the care she'd reserve for sensitive medical equipment. He cupped her face in his large hands, his gaze moving over her cheek. "Are you certain you are all right?"

She didn't know what to do with his concern. She was used to him acting as her protector whenever Aurora wasn't around. But this? He'd just knocked his father into next week. Because of her.

She placed her hands over his and pulled, needing to break the intimate contact before she did something stupid. Something really stupid. "Yes. I'm a healer, remember?"

The tension in his hands relaxed a fraction, allowing her to disengage and step back, releasing her hold on his hands.

He continued to stare at her, a storm of emotions swirling in his eyes. "I apologize for my father's actions. He should not have struck you."

Celia stepped next to Mya. "No, he shouldn't have, but I don't think he meant to hurt her. Or even make contact. It looked like he was trying to shake Mya loose. He misjudged the force needed for the job."

Because he'd been busy getting forceful with Jonarel. The way he'd grabbed him had sent her brain into the red zone. But she wasn't a strong physical specimen like Celia. If she'd had a better grip on his arm, things likely have ended differently.

Jonarel's gaze flicked to the house, a muscle in his jaw twitching. "He knows better."

The low-grade anger burning in Celia's eyes indicated she agreed with Jonarel's assessment.

Mya hated being the cause. "But I'm okay. No harm done." Well, except to Siginal. Hopefully the Kraed doctors could heal the wounds without much fuss. She doubted he would accept her help. And Jonarel would definitely protest.

Which brought up the question of how he'd managed to crack three of Siginal's ribs with a single blow. The Kraed bone structure was extremely durable.

Her gaze shifted to his right hand. Abrasions on his skin showed where he'd made contact, but it was the deeper damage to his bones and tendons that made her eyes widen. It looked like he'd punched a cement pylon. "Jonarel, your hand!"

Cupping her palms on either side, she summoned her healing field, repairing the fractures and restoring the soft tissue within seconds. She glared at him. "Why didn't you tell me?" He'd been hauling her around with that hand. His overprotective streak had clearly overridden his common sense.

The anger faded from his eyes, replaced with a look she couldn't identify. "It was inconsequential."

She snorted, folding her arms over her chest. "No injury is inconsequential."

The look intensified. "You are correct. I apologize."

He was placating her, but she'd let it slide. They had bigger issues to discuss, and she wanted a more private venue where they could address them. "Let's head back to the ship."

Jonarel and Star led the way, although Mya was beginning to recognize the landmarks for the route. Each denglar tree was distinctive, the swirls of color on the trunks and branches creating abstract shapes that helped her identify them. The one near the walkway that led to the

Starhawke had a mark that looked like a bird in flight. Well, with a little imagination it did.

Stepping back onto the ship didn't lower her stress level as much as she'd hoped, but at least they were no longer drawing curious looks from the members of the Clarek clan. "Let's meet in the observation lounge. I need tea." And if that failed to settle her nerves, she'd spend some time in the greenhouse. "Anyone else?"

"I'll take some," Kire replied.

"Me, too." Celia followed her into the kitchen while the rest of the crew settled at one of the carved wooden tables in the lounge.

Mya pulled down the canister for her favorite herbal loose leaf tea and spooned a generous amount into the ceramic teapot Aurora had given her a few years earlier. The ship had a built-in tea machine that could do the work for her, including delivering the mugs to the observation lounge through the food service dispensers, but she loved the ritual of steeping and pouring the tea from an old-fashioned teapot.

Celia propped her hip against the counter while Mya poured in the hot water. "That was an interesting beginning."

Mya grimaced. "Not what I'd hoped for."

"I know, but I think it might work out in our favor."

"What do you mean?"

"I mean our Kraed engineer just drew a line in the sand regarding his father. I'm not convinced he would have done that without a strong incentive. Siginal's careless action gave him one."

Mya lined up three mugs on the counter. "He was just being protective."

"Yes, very protective."

The gleam in Celia's eyes gave Mya pause. "What?"

"You know what."

"No, I don't."

Celia cocked her head. "I would have expected that reaction with Aurora involved. But not with you. That is, unless there's more going on than you realize."

Butterflies fluttered in Mya's stomach. "Like what?"

"Like maybe his feelings for you are closer to how you feel about him than you think."

"That's ridiculous."

"Is it? You should have seen the look on his face when he scooped you up. It wasn't how someone who's at the friendship emotional level would look. More like he was defending his mate."

The butterflies morphed into a flock of birds banging inside her ribcage. Or maybe that was her heart. "You're imagining things."

"And you're overlooking the obvious. Jonarel's always cared about you. Now that Aurora's distancing herself from him, he may have started to take a look around, reevaluating his situation. He'd be a fool not to notice what's been right in front of him all along."

Fifty-Four

Celia's words followed Mya as she walked into the observation lounge. Kire and Jonarel had left a seat open between them, and their expectant gazes made it clear they'd meant for her to claim it.

It's because I'm the acting captain. But that's not how it felt, especially when Jonarel turned his golden gaze her way. *Damn you, Celia.* Now that she'd planted the idea in her head, every action Jonarel took would be filtered with that in mind. As if she needed one more thing to obsess about.

Setting her mug and Kire's on the table, she sat, lacing her fingers together to disguise a slight tremor. Meeting Jonarel's gaze at such close quarters took all the composure she could muster. "How do you recommend we proceed?"

His full lips turned down, drawing her attention to the pattern of brown lines woven across the dark green skin around his mouth. She could have a field day tracing those lines with her fingers.

Stop it!

What was wrong with her? She needed to get her head in the game. Jonarel had started to answer her question, and she'd missed the first few words.

"...amenable after what happened. Harming a guest who has been welcomed is a serious offense. Especially for a clan leader."

Oh. His words acting like a bucket of ice water, cooling her fevered brain. So much for Celia's theory. Jonarel's severe reaction hadn't been triggered by any feelings for her. He'd been motivated by a powerful cultural belief regarding the treatment of guests.

Kire rested his forearms on the table. "Will there be legal action against him?"

Jonarel's gaze remained on her. "If Mya chooses to submit a grievance, yes."

She shook her head. "I want his cooperation. Taking legal action against him would be counter to that goal. Besides, it was an accident. I don't believe he intended to hurt me."

Anger flickered in Jonarel's eyes, his gaze moving to her cheek. "Intention is not the issue."

"I think it's precisely the issue. Not just in this incident, but for all of his actions with regards to Aurora and me. I need to understand his reasons for hiding so much from us, for asking you to spy on us."

Jonarel fidgeted, clearly uncomfortable. His gaze moved to the floor-to-ceiling windows, where a grove of denglar trees and part of the walkway wound past the ship's exterior. "He believes his actions are in the best interests of the clans, our world, and the future of the Galactic Council. But one of his greatest strengths as a leader—his ability to remain dedicated to a particular goal and overcome obstacles to achieve it—is also one of his greatest weaknesses." He met her gaze. "He is very slow to change his mind. Especially when he believes he is right."

She took a moment to consider his words. "So, he's created a master plan that he believes will address the Teeli threat?"

"Yes."

"Do you know what it is?"

More fidgeting. "Only my role in that plan."

"Which is?"

His jaw worked like he was fighting to keep the answer contained behind his teeth. He also looked like he wanted to activate the floor separators and drop through the deck. Anything to avoid answering her question.

Which gave her the answer. The one she didn't want to voice either, but had to. "You're supposed to mate with Aurora."

He stared at her for an eternity, the tortured look in his eyes tearing her heart to pieces. "Yes. His entire plan depends on it."

She dropped her head into her hands and massaged her temples, unable to hold his gaze. What a nightmare. She had more questions, but they were likely to trigger additional pain. For both of them.

Celia spoke up, saving her. "Does he know about Aurora's involvement with Cade?"

"He knows they were together when we returned from Burrow."

"What about now?"

"They are not together now."

Celia lifted one brow. "Not physically. But emotionally they're still all in."

"That may change."

"Do you really believe that?"

Mya stopped breathing, waiting for his answer.

It was a long time coming, but he said the words without flinching. "No, I do not."

Stellar light. She almost fell out of her chair as her world tilted on its axis. After all the discussions they'd had about Aurora, after all the hours she'd spent tormented by his emotional outpourings, he'd finally conceded the fight to pair bond with Aurora.

Which opened up a whole new Pandora's box of possibilities.

Celia folded her arms on the table, her gaze shifting briefly to Mya before locking onto Jonarel. "Taking that fact into account, I'd say your dad's plan needs some serious revision."

Fifty-Five

By the time they returned to Siginal and Daymar's home. Mya was tied up in so many knots she could barely move.

Jonarel didn't seem to share her condition. He strode along with the fluid grace of all Kraed, his body exuding the coiled power of a wolf tracking a rabbit. Kire walked beside him, his lean form a sharp contrast to Jonarel's muscular breadth.

She and Celia followed behind, which wasn't doing anything to calm her racing heart.

Kelly had chosen to stay with the *Starhawke*. A couple of the Kraed she'd befriended on their last visit had come to the ship, offering to assist her with an upgrade to the navigation system. Star was staying to help as well, although she'd be checking in on their discussion with Siginal, too. One advantage shared by all the Nirunoc—they could appear at any location in the compound in the blink of an eye.

When the doors to the house parted, Daymar and Siginal both stood waiting for them. A quick glance at Siginal's chest revealed he'd received medical treatment for his injury, though the level of healing was far less extensive than what she could achieve. If things went well, she'd offer her services before they left.

Siginal moved to intercept her. Per Kraed custom, he dropped to his knees at her feet, just as Jonarel had said he would, and bowed his head.

She halted, holding out her hands, palms up, as Jonarel had instructed her to.

Siginal kept his gaze downcast as he rested the backs of his hands in her open palms. "I beseech your forgiveness, honored guest. The injury I caused you was unforgiveable. I place my fate in your hands."

Thanks to Jonarel's coaching, she knew exactly how to respond to his formal request. "Honorable host, I accept your humble petition and forgive the injury you caused." Cupping his hands in hers as best she could considering the size difference, she pressed his palms together. "I return your fate to your hands."

His gaze finally met hers, revealing lines of regret etched around his eyes. "Your graciousness honors me, as my behavior does not." He stood, but his gaze remained on her as he slowly opened his arms. "I welcome you to our home with joy."

Pressure built behind her eyes. This was the kind of greeting she was used to from him, not the glacial wall he'd erected when they'd first arrived. She stepped into his embrace, which was warm but a little tentative, like he was expecting her to pull away at any moment. Instead, she held on tight, pressing her cheek against his chest and her hands on his spine, sending a flow of healing energy to the bones and tissues of his chest, back, and legs, restoring them to perfect health.

He inhaled sharply, leaning away from her. "I do not deserve your gifts."

She held on and he stilled. "Yes, you do." She met his troubled gaze. "You are Jonarel's father. And my friend." Which was one reason his decision to withhold valuable information felt like such a betrayal.

His gaze searched hers like he was really seeing her for the first time.

Maybe he was. She'd never thought about it, but in all their past interactions, his focus had always been on Aurora, not her. That wasn't an option now.

He waited, his muscles still stiff, until she released him. "Come." He stepped back and clasped her hand, drawing her toward the gathering room.

The scene was set much as it had been that morning. The demolished chair had been replaced with one of similar design, giving weight to her theory regarding additional seating stored below them.

Siginal walked her to the chair she'd occupied last time, but instead of releasing his hold on her hand when she sat down, he took the chair beside her. The move was a bit unsettling—sitting there holding hands—especially when Siginal didn't give any sign that he intended to let go.

Jonarel claimed the chair on her other side, a warning in his eyes as he gazed at his father.

She expected Siginal to release her—Jonarel's look certainly made her want to let go—but Siginal shifted in his chair so that not only was he holding her hand, but his muscled forearm was now in full contact with her arm.

Okay, this was getting weird. She didn't want to become a pawn in a power play between father and son. She glanced at Jonarel, ready to yank her hand out of Siginal's grip to prevent another blowup. But Jonarel's reaction stunned her into immobility.

Instead of taking offense at what seemed to be a show of dominance from his father, he'd relaxed into his chair as though he didn't have a care in the world.

Huh? Why would... oh. She almost smacked her forehead with her free hand. *They're Kraed, not human.*

She'd been analyzing their behavior using human cultural standards, rather than Kraed. Jonarel had done such a masterful job of adapting to human customs that she routinely forgot how much restraint he showed in his interactions with her and the rest of the crew. The Kraed were a highly tactile species, even more so than the Suulh. Hugs could last minutes, and members of all ages and genders would regularly hold hands, cuddle, or show other signs of familial affection.

Suddenly Jonarel's refusal to put her down after she'd been hit—in fact, gathering her closer—made perfect sense. Celia had interpreted the move as a sign of deeper affection for Mya specifically, but Jonarel had simply been acting the way any Kraed would have in that situation. For the Kraed, close physical contact was a way of showing connection to the clan. His father had struck a guest, a serious offense to their moral code. By defending her and then pulling her into his arms, he'd been withholding her from his father, sending a non-verbal message that matched the spoken one—*you will never harm her again.*

Siginal's physical connection to her now was also a non-verbal cue. It showed an extension of his apology, letting Jonarel know that he would treat her with the respect that her role as a guest deserved. If she'd been a Kraed, he might have wrapped an arm around her shoulders, or pulled her onto his lap and cuddled her like a child, rather than just making contact with her arm.

Not that she would have minded either way, at least once she'd understood the reason behind his actions. As a Suulh and healer, she was very tactile, too. In fact, touch was her preferred sense. She could spend hours in the *Starhawke's* greenhouse with her fingers digging into the rich soil or stroking the leaves of the plants.

Maybe that's why she found Jonarel so captivating. He shared her passion for physical sensation, though he rarely allowed himself to indulge in it. She'd seen him in the greenhouse on several occasions, interacting with the plants in much the way she did. The most heartbreaking moments had been when she'd caught him staring at Aurora, the look in his eyes practically screaming *touch me*.

Aurora never seemed to notice.

Mya couldn't look away.

Shoving the thoughts aside, she turned to Siginal.

Daymar had taken the chair on his other side, their hands and arms entwined in a mirror image of his connection with her.

Mya drew in a slow breath before asking her first question, the one least likely to inspire a heated debate. "What can you tell us about the Teeli?"

Siginal licked his lips, like his mouth had gone dry. "The Teeli are an opportunistic race who believe they are inherently superior to all other forms of life."

"Not exactly what they teach at the Academy," Kire murmured.

Siginal nodded. "You are correct. The information in the public records portrays the Teeli the way they wish to be seen—as a benevolent race of pacifists and explorers who minimize interactions with other species to preserve the simplicity of their own culture."

Celia snorted. "If you call slavery and exploitation culture."

"The Teeli see nothing wrong with such behaviors. To them, it is their right to make use of any resources they encounter—animal, plant, or mineral—to grow their own population."

What a horrifying thought. And not what she would expect from intelligent, space-faring beings. Even the Setarips weren't that cold. They were opportunistic too, stealing and killing when it served their purposes, but the only race they were out to conquer was their own. "We saw large transport ships leaving the Suulh homeworld, loaded with raw materials and goods produced by the Suulh. They must have been headed for the Teeli homeworld."

"Unlikely."

"Why?"

"From what we have learned, only the members of the lowest caste in Teeli society still live on their homeworld. By our estimates, they account for more than two-thirds of the total Teeli population, but they scrape by with the meager resources their mostly arctic world produces, living in thermally heated underground caverns to escape the freezing temperatures. The middle and upper castes do not provide for them."

Kire held up a hand. "I don't understand. If the Teeli believe they're inherently superior, why would they allow two-thirds of their population to live in desolate poverty?"

The look in Siginal's eyes sent a chill racing down Mya's spine. "While they believe their race is superior to others, they also believe in a strict caste system. All members remain in the caste into which they are born. They cannot mate outside of their caste, and they cannot earn their way into a higher caste. Those in the lowest caste are viewed as the equivalent of drones in a hive. Their sole purpose is to provide labor and resources for the families in the middle and upper castes."

"You're talking about culturally sanctioned servitude!" Indignation fired Celia's words. "None of the members of the lowest caste question this practice?"

"Why would they? It is all they have ever known."

"But the Teeli have tremendous resources at their disposal! The sensor web and ships we've seen are exceptionally well built. If they diverted five percent of those resources to provide for their own people, they could raise the standard of living for all."

"What motivation do the leaders have to do that?"

"Common decency!"

"Unfortunately, that is not a trait that applies to the Teeli."

Celia grew quiet. "You're right. We saw how they treated the weaker Suulh."

Siginal's eyes narrowed, but he continued without comment. "All Teeli accept that members of the middle and upper castes are inherently more valuable and important to the survival of the race. But to keep possible disruption to a minimum, the higher castes also provide incentives to members of the lowest caste for compliance. For example, pregnant females are given the easiest tasks and shortest work hours, which encourages them to produce a lot of offspring quickly. Many females are pregnant before they're fully grown."

Mya's stomach rolled, bile rising in her throat. "So they spend their lives producing the next generation of servants."

"Until their bodies give out, yes. It is unclear what happens to them then, but there is no indication of older generations on the Teeli homeworld."

Just like in Faahn's village on the Suulh homeworld. Maybe the older females became garbage collectors on the Teeli ships. "What about the males?"

"They are considered more expendable, so they are given the most physically taxing and dangerous jobs. However, those who prove they can produce strong offspring are given special status, earning them easier workloads and shorter hours. This reward system ensures prodigious mating at a very young age and a steady supply of new workers."

Silence fell over the group, making the muffled call of the wildlife outside deafening by comparison.

Mya pressed her hand to her abdomen, pushing back a wave of nausea. Every time she thought she understood the depth of the horror that defined the Teeli, something new kicked her in the gut.

A strong arm settled over her shoulders, startling her. She glanced up into Jonarel's hypnotic gaze.

"We will stop this," he murmured.

How? Siginal's recitation was leeching the hope from her bones. How could they defeat a race that placed so little value on life?

"No wonder they didn't have any problem enslaving the Suulh." Celia flexed her fingers, like she wanted a weapon in her hands. "It's an extension of what they do to their own people."

"And Suulh are physically robust, even as children." Kire looked as sick as Mya felt. "Why do they need all that labor? What do the middle and upper castes do that's so damn important that they feel justified to enslave so many?"

"Important?" Siginal lifted a brow. "Nothing. The middle caste is educated to a level that allows them to perform administrative functions, provide assembly work during the construction of ships, and operate machinery and weaponry. The upper caste are the leaders, engineers, scientists, and teachers, performing any task that requires advanced schooling. However, they are allowed to buy their way out of the need to work." A growl rumbled in his chest. "The communications we have monitored indicate sizable donations to the military that allow many Teeli to choose a life of idle leisure instead."

Celia glanced at Mya. "Like the Teeli we saw in your ancestral city on the Suulh homeworld."

Mya didn't want to think about the beautiful domed building that had been her mother's and Libra's childhood home. Now, it was besieged by the harsh glass and metal Teeli houses surrounding it.

"They have luxury settlements on the other planets they have invaded as well," Siginal added.

Mya tightened her grip on his hand. "They've enslaved other races?"

"Enslaved? No. Only the Suulh. The other two planets where they've set up colonies do not have any sufficiently advanced animal species, though the animal and plant life on both have experienced extinction-level losses from the Teeli exploitation. It is the Teeli's main method for adding to their wealth."

Celia looked like she was having trouble sitting still. "So, let me see if I have this straight. The upper caste Teeli families, who are extremely exploitative, gather more money and then buy the right to do anything they please?"

"Correct."

"Wonderful system."

Pressure built in Mya's chest, but she wasn't sure if she wanted to scream or cry. The information Siginal was supplying helped her understand what they were up against, but that was small comfort when she imagined all the suffering the Teeli had inflicted, even on their own kind. And how much more would occur before she could do anything about it. "How do we stop them? How do we free the Suulh?"

Siginal met her gaze. "That is not an easy question."

"I know. That's why I'm asking it." After all he'd told them, she really wanted to hear the details of his master plan, the one with Aurora as the lynchpin. She had a feeling she'd hate it, but better to have it out in the open rather than being kept in the dark. "What's your plan? I know you have one."

Siginal's gaze flicked over her head to Jonarel.

She sat up straighter. "Don't blame Jonarel. This is about you, me, and Aurora. With all the maneuvering you've done at the Academy, with Aurora's and my careers, and then with the *Starhawke*, it's clear you have a master plan for dealing with the Teeli threat. How do we fit in?"

He held her gaze, clearly deciding exactly what to tell her. And what to conceal.

She ground her molars together while she waited.

"Aurora is the key."

"Okay. How?"

"As the first and only child of her mother's womb, she has received all the power of her family line, enhanced with the increased strength that is the gift of succeeding generations."

One sentence in and she'd already learned a valuable piece of information. Siginal had no idea Aurora had a brother. Or that her brother had been born first. She wasn't about to disabuse him of that notion until she found out what he had in store.

"That makes her the most powerful Suulh in the galaxy. For now."

"For now?"

His brows lifted, silently chiding her. "Has it never occurred to you that one of the reasons the Teeli hunted her mother and yours when they escaped the Suulh homeworld is because they knew the first child born to either of them would be stronger than any of the Suulh left on the homeworld?"

"I—" No, it hadn't occurred to her.

"And now they hunt you and Aurora."

"What exactly are you saying?"

"You and Aurora are not the end goal. The Teeli also want the possibility of your offspring."

Fifty-Six

Mya's mouth opened and closed, but no sound came out. The Teeli wanted her first child?

How could they have evil intentions toward a child she hadn't even thought about, let alone conceived? The idea was beyond creepy. And ridiculous. The only male who'd managed to stoke her fire in more than ten years was the golden-eyed Kraed sitting next to her. And the odds of the two of them ever conceiving a child together neared infinity, for more reasons than she could count.

But Aurora was another story. She was passionately in love with a man who felt the same way about her. And he was human. Compatibility for mating shouldn't be a problem. The possibility of their conceiving a child together was closer to single digits.

What if they did? What if Aurora gave birth to a daughter? Would she be more powerful than her mother? Or would her diluted genetics, only one quarter Suulh, make her weaker? Did it matter? Would the Teeli go after the child, regardless?

Suddenly Reanne's comment about putting Aurora in a cage and making her suffer took on an even more sinister meaning. What if Reanne's ultimate goal wasn't Aurora at all?

A tremor worked its way under Mya's skin. What if she—

"You understand the dangers."

Signal's softly spoken words yanked her out of the dark pit she'd been staring into. She swallowed, her throat feeling like sandpaper. "Yes, I do."

Aurora's shielding ability could prevent anyone from forcing her. And unlike humans, Suulh could only conceive a child by making a conscious choice to do so. Aurora had inherited that Suulh trait, as evidenced by her lack of the monthly cycle typical of human females. But as the situation with Tnaryt and the Admiral had proven, Aurora could be coerced into complying when others were in danger.

A flare of panic shot through her like wildfire. She'd left Aurora on Earth with only her father and brother to protect her! What had she been thinking? It had seemed logical at the time, but now...

"Where is Aurora?"

"She's—"

"She's safe." Celia cut her off, shooting Mya a look that didn't leave room for debate. "Reanne and the Teeli won't be able to find her."

Clearly her friend didn't think it was wise to share Aurora's location with Siginal.

"You cannot possibly know that."

Celia's mouth turned up in a cool smile. "Wanna bet?"

A growl rumbled in Siginal's throat.

Celia's expression didn't change. "Aurora is exactly where she needs to be. She doesn't want our protection, and she doesn't need it. What she *does* need is for us to craft a plan to take down Reanne."

Siginal's expression darkened. "You spoke of Reanne before. How can she be connected to the Teeli? She is human."

"Not entirely," Mya said. Her initial stab of panic had subsided, clearing her mind. Celia was right. Siginal had told them a great deal about the Teeli, but no details about his plan for Aurora. She needed to tread carefully.

Signal's attention swung to her. "What do you mean?"

"It's possible that her father is a Teeli."

He stared at her. "No. That cannot be."

"I know biologically it's unlikely, but—"

"No. You do not understand. No Teeli male would take a human female for a mate."

"Why not?"

"The Teeli view humans as grossly inferior. Having intimate relations with a human could be acceptable entertainment, but to mate with one and conceive a child would be unthinkable."

"I doubt the pregnancy was expected. Or wanted. Reanne certainly wasn't. She told Aurora that her mom couldn't stand to be in the same room with her." That fact had engaged Aurora's and Mya's empathy, making them more forgiving of Reanne's many faults, at least in the beginning.

"Who is Reanne's mother?"

"I don't know her name, but she's a wealthy socialite. Reanne claimed her mother had friends on the Council, but I don't know if that's true." Which brought up another question. "How would the Teeli react if they learned of the existence of a Teeli-Human child?"

Signal scowled. "They would treat the child worse than they do the lower caste Teeli. It would be enslaved, abused, or killed."

"What about the Teeli who conceived it? Would there be any repercussions for him?"

"Of course not. His family would not even acknowledge the child."

Pieces slid across the board, forming a new picture.

Kire sat forward. "If that's true, how did Reanne gain control of the Teeli fleet? They should have turned on her the minute she showed her face."

"I know how." The words left Mya's lips while her brain continued to process the repercussions.

Everyone turned in her direction.

"Blackmail." She met Siginal's gaze. "She's blackmailing her father."

"How?"

"Reanne is excellent at figuring out people's weaknesses and exploiting them. She must have gained access to information about her father he doesn't want revealed. If so, he'd do anything to insure her silence. Even place her in control of the fleet. And the Suulh."

"Even if that is true, to wield that much power, he would have to be an extremely prominent member of the Teeli upper caste. A military or governmental leader, or member of the royal family."

"Which fits. Their leaders spent time on Earth when the Teeli first made contact. He could have had an affair with Reanne's mother and left before she gave birth. Twenty-something years later, Reanne figures it out and plans her revenge. She must have obtained proof of her biological heritage from her mother and used her ability to manipulate people to gain access to her father."

Siginal frowned, clearly confused. "Why give in to blackmail? He could have killed her instead. No one would have questioned him."

The emotionless way he said it raised the hairs on Mya's forearms. She shook her head. "Reanne's too smart to leave herself vulnerable. She would have engineered the situation so that her father stood to lose everything if he killed her."

"What about the other Teeli?" Kire asked. "Why would they go along with her father's orders? Reanne doesn't look like them. She looks human."

"Which is why she wears a cloak and face mask. And uses a vocal modulator. It wasn't just to conceal her identity from Aurora. She's manipulating everyone, working from the shadows, gaining control through coercion. It's what she does best."

Siginal said something in the Kraed language she didn't understand, but it sounded like a curse. "If you are correct, our situation is more dire than I anticipated." His grip on her hand tightened. "Where is Reanne now?"

Celia fielded that one. "In Teeli space. At least her ship is. I was able to place a tracking dot on it before it left the Suulh homeworld."

"Reanne tried to kidnap Aurora while you were on the homeworld?"

"No, later. In Fleet space."

His gaze swung right over Mya's head to Jonarel. "How was Reanne able to get close to her?"

Mya answered before Jonarel could. "Aurora had allowed herself to be captured by the same Setarip who was holding the Admiral. She tracked him down, tried to rescue him. But Tnaryt contacted Reanne before Aurora could get him out."

The slight guilt in her voice must have given her away. His eyes narrowed. "You were not with her?"

"We were on the Suulh homeworld."

"You left her *alone*?" Outrage came through his pores.

And she got defensive. "She wasn't alone! She had Cade's team with her."

Wrong thing to say. Twin flames ignited deep in Siginal's eyes. He turned the blaze on Jonarel. "Ellis was with her?"

Jonarel remained stoic under the heat of his father's stare. "They were on Ellis' ship."

More fire. Siginal's voice came out deadly calm, promising retribution. "You allowed Ellis to take her from you?"

Star appeared, standing in front of Siginal. "Aurora chose to leave the ship. Jonarel and I made every effort to change her mind, but she refused."

Siginal's gaze burned between them. "Then you should have stopped her."

"Hold it right there!" Kire rose from his chair, a Fleet commander taking charge. "Aurora is captain of the *Starhawke*. You have no right to dictate what she can and cannot do regarding her decisions, her ship, or her crew."

Siginal's gaze bored a hole right through Kire's forehead. "I have every right. The *Starhawke* is part of my family. I am the leader."

Kire gave a sharp shake of his head. "No, you don't. You gave up that right when you gifted the ship to Aurora." He pointed at Star. "The ship carries *her* name and *Aurora's*. Not yours."

Star glanced between the two, clearly surprised by Kire's vehement defense.

Siginal released his hold on Mya's hand as he stood. From her angle, it looked very much like a David and Goliath match, but Kire didn't show one iota of uncertainty.

"The ship bears Tehar's name, but also her essence. She has given it life, and she is *my* daughter. *My* family. *My* clan." Siginal lowered his head like a bull preparing to charge. "Without her, the ship is a lifeless hulk that will never leave this planet."

The threat hung in the air like a plume from a smoking volcano.

Star flinched.

Kire stared at Signal in disbelief. "Are you saying you'll ground the ship if Aurora doesn't fall in line with the boundaries you've drawn for her?"

"Her role in future events is critical. Any deviation from the correct path cannot be permitted."

Mya's stomach sank into her toes.

"Correct path?" Celia rose to stand beside Kire. "Who are you to decide the correct path for her?"

"I am the clan leader."

"She's not a part of your clan!"

"She will be."

The certainty in his voice galvanized Mya to her feet, indignation heating her blood. "Like hell she will! You can't force her into it."

"And you cannot stop her." The full brunt of Siginal's anger hit her like the slap she'd received earlier. "Do not be a fool. Your feelings for my son will never be reciprocated."

Her mouth hinged open, the air leaking from her lungs like water through a sieve. "Whhhaaa—"

"Do you think I am blind? That I do not see how you stare at him when you believe no one is looking?"

The room spun. A nightmare. She had to be caught in a nightmare. She'd had plenty just like this over the years, dreams that ripped open her greatest fears and secret yearnings, exposing them to the light.

Daymar rose beside Siginal, pressing a hand to his chest. "That is enough."

He pulled away. "No. She needs to understand." He moved within centimeters of Mya, forcing her to tilt her head back to meet his gaze. "My son will mate with Aurora. That is certain. Whether they produce a child or not, he will be her lifelong protector, always by her side. Do not hold onto your fantasies. They will only bring you suffering."

She caught movement in her peripheral vision, knew Jonarel now stood beside her, but she couldn't have looked at him if her life had depended on it. Flames climbed her neck and suffused her cheeks, whether from rage or shame, she couldn't say.

She wanted to tell Siginal he was wrong. That Aurora would never mate with Jonarel because she was in love with Cade. That Jonarel had cast aside the burden Siginal had placed on his shoulders. And most of all, that she had no feelings other than friendship regarding Jonarel.

But she couldn't.

So, she said the only thing she could say.

"Aurora will make her own choices. And nothing you, I, or anyone else says or does will change that."

Fifty-Seven

"Aurora has no choice. Only her destiny."

Mya had never felt the urge to strike another being in her life. To intentionally inflict damage. She was a healer, not a fighter. But in that moment, every cell in her body wanted to lash out at the authoritarian, self-righteous Kraed standing in front of her. "We'll see about that."

Taking a step back, she motioned to Celia and Kire and headed out of the room.

She couldn't bring herself to look at Jonarel. She didn't want to make him choose between his father and his friends, especially in the heat of the moment. But more to the point, she didn't want to face him after Signal had stripped her naked for all to see.

She made it out to the walkway before a strong hand wrapped around her upper arm, drawing her to a halt.

She glanced down. A tanned, female hand. Celia.

"Want me to break his jaw?"

The seriousness of Celia's tone matched the cold steel in her brown eyes. She wasn't kidding. She was ready to wage a personal war against the Clarek clan leader, exacting retribution for the emotional knockdown he'd delivered.

"Arrogant bastard." Kire looked just as hostile as Celia, but without the threat of imminent violence. "Who does he think he is, deciding Roe's future and making wild accusations to upset you?"

His tone indicated he hadn't believed a word Signal had said. If she was very, very, *very* lucky, Jonarel would have the same reaction.

But Jonarel hadn't followed them out of the house. Neither had Star.

Not a good sign.

Worse yet, if Siginal's threat had teeth, her crew could find themselves stranded on Drakar for a long time.

Or maybe Siginal would drop them on Azaana rather than having them underfoot.

"Let's go back to the ship. I need something way stronger than tea."

Fifteen minutes later, they'd gathered around the circular wooden table in the kitchen nook. Mya poured tenrebac into three glasses from a bottle Daymar had sent over shortly after their arrival. Maybe she'd had a premonition they'd need it.

She set down the bottle and lifted her glass. "To Aurora."

Celia and Kire raised their glasses and clinked. "To Aurora."

The tenrebac slid down Mya's throat, leaving a trail of pleasant warmth in its wake. She took another swallow as the sensation spread through her limbs. But it wouldn't last. Even without engaging her healing field, her body would process the alcohol in minutes, breaking it down before it could give any lasting relief from the tension coiling her muscles into springs.

She'd never envied Aurora her ability to get tipsy from the tenrebac, a result of her half-human physiology. But she did now. Anything to blot out Siginal's voice in her head.

"You're the strategist." Kire motioned to Celia with his glass. "Think they'll take the *Starhawke* from us?"

She ran a finger around the rim of her glass, contemplating. "Maybe, although it would be a ballsy move for Siginal to make if he wants Aurora to cooperate with his plan."

"That's for sure. She would have hit the roof if she'd heard him just now." He sighed, leaning back in his chair. "Jon's in a world of hurt, too. Talk about a no-win scenario. If he sides with us, he's betraying his father and clan. If he sides with Siginal, he's betraying Aurora and us." He smacked his glass down, the ruby liquid slopping over the edge. "This sucks."

That about summed it up. Mya took another healthy swig of the tenrebac. "It's my fault. Jonarel told us Siginal had a plan for Aurora. I foolishly believed I could change his mind, convince him there was a better way. That hope just got blown out the airlock." And without the Kraed fleet's help, they had no hope of freeing the Suulh homeworld.

"He wouldn't stand by if the Teeli made a move into the Outer Rim, would he?" Kire glanced between her and Celia. "He'd help the Fleet defend the colonies, right?"

Mya shrugged. "At this point, I can't predict what he'll do. He clearly doesn't want the Suulh under Teeli control, but after what he said today, he seems to think he has to have Aurora under his thumb so the Teeli can't get to her. What his plan is after that, is anyone's guess."

"Yeah, about that." Kire refilled his glass then topped off Mya's and Celia's. "Roe's our best defense against a Teeli and Suulh attack, especially after she learns to control her empathic reactions. But it sounds like he's planning to lock her in a tower."

Celia took a sip. "I think he's playing a long game, hoping to put off a confrontation with the Teeli until he's established a permanent connection between his clan and Aurora."

"Why? What does it matter?"

"The Kraed are a very ritualistic race. And family means everything to them. As long as Aurora is unmated, she cannot truly be a part of the clan, no matter how much

Siginal wants her to be. But if he can get her to mate with Jonarel? Then he'll have the support of the entire Kraed nation behind him, and the assurance of her loyalty to the clan. Especially if she and Jonarel are able to produce a child."

Mya's stomach pitched, souring the tenrebac. She set down her glass. "It's unlikely they could."

"More unlikely than Reanne being half-Teeli?"

"I think so. Aurora's already a hybrid of two races. The odds of a successful mating that introduced a third biological element are astronomical. At least, without medical intervention." Hopefully that wasn't part of Siginal's plan. She'd never heard of the Kraed using genetic manipulation in conception, but Siginal's fanatical devotion to achieving his goal might push him into bringing all the technological knowledge of the Kraed to bear on the problem.

"What about sterilization?"

A chill passed over Mya's skin, the blood draining to her feet. The thought had never occurred to her. "Aurora would never allow that."

"Not even if Siginal convinced her it was the best way to protect the Suulh?"

The heat returned, riding a wave of anger. "She is the Sahzade. The protector of our people. Her line must continue!"

"But if she ended up under Teeli control, she could be forced to produce a child who never understood the concept of freedom."

The image of the Necri cages flashed into her mind. "Aurora would die before allowing that."

"Would she let others die, instead?"

Mya pushed back from the table, desperate to escape the apocalyptic vision Celia was painting. "No." She spun, heading for the doorway that led to the greenhouse.

Celia's chair scraped against the deck as she stood. "Mya, I—"

Mya turned. "Forget it. I just need some time to process."

Thankfully, Celia took her at her word.

The doors to the greenhouse parted, the moisture in the air and the babble of the winding brook greeting her like old friends. As soon as the doors closed behind her, she knelt by the path's edge and dug her hands into the rich soil. The energy of the plants reached out to her, blending and harmonizing with the nurturing energy she gave in return.

Blocking out all thought, she focused on sensation, the purity and beauty of the energy. Of the life within and without. Of her connection to all that was and would be.

Slowly her body relaxed. She pressed the leaves of two of the plants, the scent of mint and lavender joining the sweet earthy smell of the loosened soil, soothing and energizing her. She held onto that sensation as she stood, moving along the path, brushing her fingers across the surface of the plants and expanding her field.

This was her world. The world of life. The world of the Suulh.

Aurora's world.

She settled onto the bench near the door to the med bay, the tendrils of the climbing vines on the trellis dancing around her as the plants responded to her energy.

But Celia's words crept around the edges of her consciousness, like thieves intent on stealing her peace and tranquility.

Or Aurora's future.

No one had the right to take it from her. Not Siginal. Certainly not Reanne. Only Aurora could choose the path her life would follow. And whether a child would be a part of it.

She'd always assumed Aurora would have a daughter. Funny really, considering she'd pretty much given up on the idea for herself. And what would happen to a young Sahzade who had no Nedale to balance her? Yes, Mya could nurture and support Aurora's daughter, assuming she had one, but it wouldn't be the same. The tradition of the Suulh was a pairing, a daughter born to both houses, the Nedale first, and then the Sahzade.

She was the Nedale, the elder of the pair, yet she was so far from having a child it felt like a cosmic joke. What did that say about *her* adherence to tradition? She was a full-blooded Suulh, while Aurora was only half. If anyone had an obligation to carry on the Suulh line, now that she knew there were other Suulh still alive, it was her, not Aurora. So why did the idea of Aurora never having a child bother her so much?

The door to the med bay opened.

She glanced up... and met the golden gaze that had haunted her dreams for more than a decade.

"Hello, Mya." Jonarel stopped a couple meters away, his entire body telegraphing wariness.

Mya curled her fingers around the edge of the bench, the death grip cutting off circulation, but her voice came out remarkably even. "Hello, Jonarel." Now that she'd met his gaze, she couldn't look away. Thankfully years of practice helped her keep any emotion from showing through.

The puzzled look she'd come to recognize was creating small lines on his handsome face. He gestured to the bench. "May I join you?"

No. You can turn around and walk out that door before I come apart at the seams. "Of course." Unhooking her fingers, she scooted over until her hip pressed against the wooden side railing, giving him as much room as possible.

He sat, bringing her in dangerous proximity to the heat from his body and the rich scent that was uniquely his.

She leaned away, wrapping an arm around the side railing, holding on like she was clinging to the side of a cliff.

His gaze searched hers, puzzlement turning into a frown. "I owe you an apology."

Not what she'd expected. "What for?"

"My father's verbal assault. I should have anticipated his reaction, stopped him before he lashed out at you."

"It wasn't your fault." What she really wanted to know was whether he'd believed what his father had said.

"It is my fault." He reached out, grasping her free hand in both of his.

The contact sent a bolt of lightning through her system, stealing her breath.

"You are a cherished friend. I would not want my father's actions to jeopardize our relationship."

Friend. No doubt regarding where he stood. "It won't."

For a moment, his expression softened, warmth lighting his eyes.

She bathed in that warmth, tingles moving along her nerve endings.

"He should not have attacked you. I am truly sorry."

The longer he held her hand, the less sorry she became.

"I was afraid his lies had lessened your opinion of me."

The warmth vanished in a splash of cold reality. She'd gotten her wish. He hadn't believed a word. And why would he? They were just friends, after all. She'd never given him any reason to believe otherwise.

"Mya?"

She'd looked away without even realizing it, her gaze on the deck. She focused on his face. The puzzled look had returned.

His grip tightened. "You do not think less of me, do you?"

Tell him! Tell him! His touch was messing with her ability to get oxygen to her brain, but Celia's voice in her head was coming through just fine.

"Of course not." He could murder someone in cold blood in front of her, and she'd probably find a way to overlook it. "You're a wonderful friend." She worked to push the last word out, because she knew he needed to hear it, but it hurt like hell. "You're honorable, generous, and loyal."

"Loyal." His gaze dropped to their joined hands. He used the pad of his finger to trace the skin on the back of her hand like it was a labyrinth. "How does one remain loyal when family and friends are in opposition?"

Such bitterness in his voice. She released her grip on the railing and placed her hand over his, stopping the motion that was sending unwelcome heat through her veins. "Is that how you feel? That your loyalties are divided?"

"How could I not?" He lifted his head, his thick dark hair forming a curtain that framed the strong beauty of his face. "I want to help Aurora, and you. I believe in your right to knowledge, your right to choose your own path. But my father does not. My clan does not. To them, Aurora is a potential threat, one my father hopes to neutralize by keeping her within his control."

"Is that what he thinks would happen if you and Aurora mated? That he'd be able to control her?" Because if he did, he didn't know anything about Aurora Hawke.

"In the customs of my people, the clan is more important than any individual. We have thrived for millennia because all we do, all resources we have, all decisions we make are focused on the needs of the clan. That is at the heart of who we are."

"But Aurora's not a Kraed. She doesn't share your traditions."

"She shares our belief system. She fights for the good of all. She understands the importance of protecting others. That is why she is such a powerful leader of the Suulh."

"If you believe that, then why does your father see her as a threat?"

"Because she does not know the full extent of her power. But the Teeli do. So does Reanne. Aurora must not fall into their hands."

"Then why did you give her the *Starhawke*? You gave her freedom. That's when the problem with Reanne started."

"It started long before that. For years, my father has suspected the Teeli have been influencing the Council and members of the Fleet. It was becoming more and more difficult to control Aurora's assignments without drawing attention. That is why he and the Admiral arranged for her to transfer to the *Argo*, and why I returned here to build the *Starhawke*. Giving her the ship was supposed to keep her out of trouble."

Mya laughed. She couldn't help it. "Seriously? You thought giving her command of a ship would lead to *less* trouble?"

Jonarel frowned. "We misjudged."

"No kidding." And she was beginning to understand why Signal was so out of touch with reality. He was basing his assumptions about Aurora on Kraed behavioral norms. He hadn't figured out she had a yearning for freedom and independence that ran like a river through her core. She would never bend to his will, even if she agreed to his premise. "What about love?"

His brows lifted. "Love?"

"Yes, love." Saying the word took effort, but she pressed on, needing to make her point since Aurora couldn't argue for herself. "Has your father considered that criteria? You told me that Aurora loves you as a friend, but she's not *in* love with you. How could she be happy in a relationship without romantic love?" *Especially when she's already passionately in love with Cade.*

Jonarel was silent for a moment. "We encourage matings where love has already flourished. That is always the wish. But we also understand that matings between friends are sometimes necessary when such a pairing will benefit the clans."

Now they were getting somewhere. "Arranged marriages?" She'd heard of the custom, but never met anyone who still practiced it.

He tilted his head. "Yes, I suppose that description fits. It can be a very positive experience, bringing happiness to all. My parents made such a match."

Her eyes almost popped out of her head. "Your parents had an arranged marriage?"

He nodded. "They were paired based on the benefit their joining would bring to the Clarek and Terfeli clans."

"Terfeli?"

"My mother's clan of birth."

"She left her clan to mate with your dad?"

"Yes."

"Where is her clan now?"

"The Terfeli live in the hill regions bordering the wide sea far to the north. My mother is the daughter of the clan leader."

"Huh." She hadn't seen that coming. For some reason she'd believed the Kraed always mated within their own clan. "Why did she mate with your dad?"

"My mother's clan are expert horticulturists. They can grow food almost as well as the Suulh. They are also the clan that created tenrebac. They alone know the secret of how to produce it. The Clarek clan is renowned for our hunting skills, but before my parents mated, we had much more limited knowledge and skill for agriculture. My mother's joining with my father brought new skills to our clan, and a steady flow of tenrebac from her clan's bounty."

"What about her clan? Did they get anything in return?"

Jonarel's dark brows snapped down in a scowl. "Of course. The mating benefitted both clans. The Terfeli wished to increase their knowledge of engineering and technology, which had fallen far behind ours. My parents spent the first year of their mating with her clan, and they devote one lunar cycle of every year with the Terfeli, exchanging ideas and new discoveries. My father is currently helping them build and launch their first starship."

"First starship? I thought all the Kraed clans had starships."

He shook his head. "Only six of the fifteen clans have taken an interest in interstellar travel. The Terfeli are the seventh to follow that path."

"I'm going to guess your clan was the first to achieve space travel."

A gleam of pride lit his golden eyes. "You are correct. Our clan leads the fleet."

And as the leader of the Clarek clan, Siginal would logically be the leader of the entire fleet. "So, your father's position is similar to Admiral Schreiber's with the Galactic Fleet?"

"Yes."

The picture was coming into focus. Too bad it looked like an insurmountable mountain. "So, I was right. Without his approval, we don't have a prayer of gaining Kraed support for a rescue mission to the Suulh homeworld."

He gazed at her through his thick lashes, piercing her with a look that struck like a spear. "Without his approval, we do not have a prayer of leaving this planet. Ever."

Fifty-Eight

"Use the river, Aurora. Pour the emotions into it."

Aurora's breath hitched from the effort of maintaining focus as emotional pain battered her with blow after blow.

"The river is there for you. Surrounding you. Push the pain into it."

She struggled to obey, but a tsunami of sensation struck, bending her like a sapling. "I... can't."

"Yes, you can. Visualize the pain. Give it form. Then push it into the river."

A trickle of sweat rolled between her shoulder blades. She could see the pain. It had taken on the form of a silvery behemoth with razor-sharp teeth and massive arms. Kinda resembled the rock monster she'd battled with Kire. But she was making zero progress getting it away from her and into the river. It charged and swung with reckless abandon.

And vanished in an instant.

Her eyes flew open, the abrupt change startling her. She pulled in air, slowing her heartbeat and increasing the oxygen in her system.

The room came into focus, her dad's and Micah's faces at the forefront, wearing matching expressions of concern.

"Ror? You okay?"

She nodded, placing a hand over her heart to calm the baby jackrabbit kicking to get out. When it finally agreed to settle down, she lowered her hand.

Following her sessions and discussion with her dad regarding her fears, she'd had a very successful day of visualization work processing projected fear. The river had absorbed the fear well, allowing her to find her inner calm.

But today they'd begun working on the one emotion she hadn't faced—pain. And she'd crumbled like a sandcastle before the tide. "I don't understand. Why can't I maintain focus when dealing with pain?"

Her dad set his tablet aside. "Pain is the most challenging emotion for empaths because it's the most elemental. We need a frame of reference to understand and process anger, sadness, fear, loneliness, and joy. We definitely need reference for shame. But we're born understanding pain. We instinctively recognize it when we feel it. And most people will do almost anything to avoid it."

"But I'm not trying to avoid it."

"No, but compared to most people, you have a limited amount of experience processing it."

"What do you mean?"

He cradled her hand in his. "You got into as much trouble as a child as most kids, maybe more. But unlike other children, including Micah, you didn't suffer physical pain as a result. No bumps or bruises or cuts when you learned to walk and run. Your shield protected you from physical injury and the pain that comes with it."

"I... guess so." She'd never really thought about it.

"For you, physical pain wasn't normal. How often have you experienced pain from injury?"

"At the Academy and with the Fleet I've been in situations where I couldn't shield and took a hit. I've also earned my share of knocks sparring with Celia."

He released her hand. "And how quickly could you heal that pain?"

"Uh... a couple minutes or less."

"Exactly. When you couldn't shield, you could heal yourself almost instantly. Until you encountered the Suulh, you'd never experienced prolonged physical pain. And until Reanne turned them into Necri soldiers, neither had the Suulh. You're a race of self-healers. None of you were prepared to handle that type of abuse."

"Are you saying that if the Suulh were better trained to handle their own physical pain, that would make it easier on me?"

"Yes. But that won't help when you're facing Necri soldiers. Or Kreestol. They'll *want* to cause you pain, not help you avoid it. To deal with them, you have to shore up your defenses."

A dart of worry from Micah made her glance his way.

A rare frown line creased his forehead.

She rested a hand on his arm, allowing the connection to soothe them both. "It's okay, big brother." She turned back to their dad. "So how do I gain control over the pain? The river visualization wasn't working."

"Not by itself. I think for this challenge we need a slightly different approach."

"Like what?"

"Something I've been tossing around for the past few days. A new visualization technique. I think it might work well for you."

"I'm game for anything."

"Then let's give it a go." He picked up his tablet. "Close your eyes and focus on your breathing."

She dropped into the zone with easy familiarity, curiosity percolating in the back of her mind as her muscles relaxed and her subconscious awakened.

"I want you to call to mind a specific place. It can be from any time in your life—your childhood, your Academy days, your Fleet career—but this place must be significant. It must be somewhere you feel strong and powerful. Where you feel in control of yourself. Where your focus and concentration are at their best."

A flurry of images flipped through her mind, sorted and discarded until one pushed forward with perfect clarity.

"Can you see your chosen place in your mind's eye?"

She nodded.

"I want you to move into that space, taking whatever position makes you feel most in command of your surroundings."

She walked across the planked wood floor of the *Starhawke's* bridge, continuing up the low rise to the captain's chair at the center. Settling into the chair, she rested her hands on the armrests.

"Look around you, see everything in vivid detail."

Her gaze swept the bridge, taking it all in. Celia at tactical, the movements of her hands over the console as fluid as a dancer's. Kelly at navigation, her riot of red curls creating a halo as she bent to her task. Kire at the comm, the focused intensity on his face as he listened to an incoming message. Mya at the science station, the comforting pulse of her Suulh energy invisible but always there.

The inky starfield beckoned on the wide bridgescreen, with *Gladiator's* solid form visible on the port side, ready for action.

"Hear the sounds."

Jonarel's deep voice came over the bridge speaker, telling her the interstellar engines were ready on her command.

"Inhale the scents."

The crisp, subtly earthy smell of fresh air filled her lungs as she inhaled, courtesy of the lush greenhouse three decks below.

"Feel the tactile sensations."

Her fingertips stroked the smooth surface of the armrests, the display coming to life at her touch. She settled more firmly into the chair, its embrace like an extension of her own body, the deck solid beneath her booted feet.

"Connect with this place fully. Allow the strength you find here to fill you from the inside out."

Sparks of energy moved through her body, carrying a sense of power, confidence, surety.

"In this place, you are exactly who you want to be."

The energy pushed outward, engaging her field and surrounding her with calm focus.

"Have you faced danger in this place?"

She nodded.

"Have you felt pain here?"

Another nod.

"And yet, this place remains your seat of power."

The Starhawke. My seat of power. The realization struck like a thunderbolt.

"When pain and fear threaten to overwhelm you, this is the place where you need to go."

Her hands gripped the armrests, her gaze moving steadily around the bridge. Since learning of Jonarel's and Siginal's deception, doubts had plagued her regarding her ship. She'd even abandoned it. Twice. Anger and sadness had convinced her it had become a gilded cage.

Her subconscious knew the truth. It had stripped her fears to their foundation, showing her the supports that made her life whole.

"This place gives you strength. Draw on it. Trust it. Feel it flowing through you."

She stared at the image of *Gladiator* on the bridgescreen. Cade's ship, gliding alongside hers. She'd conjured it, placing it into this vision. That was no accident.

Whatever her conscious mind believed, her subconscious didn't see Cade as a weakness. Or someone she had to protect.

He'd been right all along. Being together made them both stronger. She'd allowed fear and pain to obscure that fact.

And he'd been right about something else. She belonged here. In command of her ship.

The rest was just details.

Fifty-Nine

Micah watched Aurora's expression as their dad took her through the visualization. He knew the moment she'd found clarity and focus. Her posture and the tilt of her head had changed, making her look like a Fleet officer rather than his kid sister.

And no wonder. He'd caught a few flashes of imagery that could have been from a starship, although unlike anything he'd seen before.

"Are you settled into this place?" His dad's gaze flicked to him when Aurora nodded.

Enough speculation. He had work to do.

Projecting physical pain wasn't easy or fun—his own mind resisted—but it was often helpful for his dad's students, so he'd gotten pretty good at it over the years. Thanks to his rambunctious childhood and all his years catching waves, he had plenty of personal injury experiences to draw on, although he'd always healed faster than anyone anticipated. He probably had his Suulh mother to thank for that.

"You're going to be challenged in this place. The danger here is real. If you allow fear and pain to overwhelm you, you will suffer. But you've faced those dangers before. You can do it again."

Aurora drew in a slow breath and rolled her shoulders.

"Are you ready?"

A curt nod.

His dad pointed at him.

Showtime. He conjured the memory that had blown her concentration last time, projected it through their shared connection. When he was eleven, he'd flipped over the handlebars of his bike and earned an impressive road rash on his thigh that had burned like biting fire ants whenever he'd touched it.

She inhaled as the memory took hold, but her reaction was completely different. She was handling it, her brows drawing down in concentration, her breath slow and even.

He caught his dad's smile from the corner of his eye. "You're in control. Maintain focus." His dad held up two fingers.

Next memory. Saltwater swept over his head, pushing his body down and momentarily dragging his skin across a razor-sharp coral bed. The salt attacked the deep lacerations, making his nerve endings scream.

Aurora's lips pinched, but she didn't waver. Whatever visual she'd conjured, it was working for her.

His dad added a third finger.

Micah switched to a different memory, this one from a jellyfish sting. The initial pain had been intense, and the red welt had lasted for a week.

Aurora's fingers curled and her shoulders hunched.

Was she losing control? No. Her breathing evened out.

Four fingers. His most painful memory.

Sharp and throbbing pain flared in his left thigh and shoulder, where a childhood fall from a banyan tree had left him with a huge hematoma and a dislocated shoulder.

Aurora jerked, tension drawing her body tight as a bow.

He increased the intensity of the projection, increment by increment, until he was hitting her with everything he had.

She stayed with him, clearly uncomfortable, but also in control of her reaction.

He eased off, taking her down slowly. But inside he was cheering. She'd done it.

That left one more major hurdle, although he'd need his dad's approval to act on it.

"Settle into your place of power. Allow yourself to rest."

Micah made a motion to his dad to indicate they needed to talk.

His dad nodded. "Remain in this focused state. We will return shortly."

Aurora didn't respond, but her eyes stayed closed.

Micah followed his dad to the top of the stairwell, out of sight of the loft. He kept his voice to a whisper. "I have an idea for testing Aurora's pain defense abilities in a more realistic setting."

"Realistic?"

"Rather than projected pain from a memory."

Understanding lit his dad's eyes. "Micah–"

"She has healing powers, right?"

"Yes, but–"

"Then it'll be fine."

His dad's frown made it clear he didn't agree. "Let me–"

"No. I'm connected to her. It has to be me."

His dad blew out a breath. "I don't like it."

"I know." Micah punched him playfully on the shoulder. "That's because you're a good dad."

"And you're a good brother. We'll be waiting for you."

With a nod, Micah went down the stairs to the kitchen, going right to the knife block on the counter.

Drawing out the paring knife and an old dishtowel, he headed back upstairs.

His dad eyed the knife, the look on his face asking him to reconsider.

He shook his head. This was his job. The only true test of how Aurora could handle pain from a Suulh was for her to experience it firsthand. He was the one with Suulh blood flowing through his veins.

Settling in on the other side of Aurora, he laid the towel across his lap and lifted the knife, poising it over his left hand.

The corners of his dad's mouth pulled tight. "You have faced and defeated pain in this place successfully. You can defeat any pain that comes to you now."

Aurora drew in a slow breath, her relaxed posture shifting back into a focused intensity.

His dad met his gaze, conflict clear in his eyes. With obvious reluctance, he nodded.

Micah turned the blade, laid it across his palm, and pulled.

Pain shrieked as blood welled along the clean cut.

Aurora's energy field flared to life. Her hand shot out with unerring accuracy and covered his palm, just missing the tip of the knife.

"Focus on controlling the pain!" Their dad's sharp command froze her hand. "Don't try to heal it."

Furrows grooved her brow, her arm trembling.

His hand throbbed, but he ignored it. He wanted to help her, but she needed to learn how to win this battle on her own.

"You are in your seat of power."

The trembling eased.

"In this place, you are strong."

The trembling stopped, the frown lines smoothing from her forehead.

"In this place, you are in control."

Her chin lifted, her breathing slowing.

A deep warmth enveloped his hand, the glow from her field intensifying. The pain in his palm receded like the outgoing tide, the energy pulsing in time to his heartbeat. When she finally lifted her hand away, he stared in fascination at the dried blood and his unblemished skin.

His sister had done that. Healed his wound with the touch of her energy field.

Lifting his gaze, he discovered she was watching him, a hint of reproach in her eyes.

"You could have warned me."

He shook his head. "You needed to be caught off guard. It was the only way to have a true test."

"But your hand—"

"Is good as new." He flexed his fingers to prove it.

"You're lucky you picked your hand. The energy centers in the palms make it easier to promote healing there."

"Huh." He set the knife on the towel. "Thanks for the quick fix."

Her gaze focused on the smudge of red on the blade's edge. "You aren't planning to make a habit of this, are you?" The reproach had returned.

"Definitely not." He wasn't a masochist. "This was a one-time deal."

"Good." She turned to their dad. "I'm surprised you let him do it."

"Wasn't easy. But he had a point. You needed to test yourself, and he was the only one who could channel direct pain."

Her gaze swung back to him. "Are you any good at sparring?"

He didn't trust the speculative gleam in her eyes. "Sparring? You mean like hand-to-hand fighting?"

"Yeah."

"No. I've never tried it."

The gleam grew, a grim smile curving her lips. "Then I have another way we can test my ability to handle empathic pain."

"How?"

"I'm going to knock you on your butt."

Sixty

Mya spent a good chunk of the night stewing. Jonarel had given her the insight she needed to understand the breadth of the problem, but no solutions. Well, not unless she was willing to go along with Siginal's plan to force Aurora into accepting Jonarel as her mate.

She had personal reasons for hating the idea, but she had practical reasons, too. If Aurora gave in, even with the best of intentions, the sacrifice would slowly drain the life out of her. She'd seen Aurora in wraith form after she'd come back from her confrontation with Reanne. It had been a temporary condition then, but giving up her dreams—even if it meant saving the Suulh—would kill her piece by piece until there was nothing left.

She suspected Jonarel understood that, which is why he wasn't pushing his father's agenda anymore. He'd explained the arguments in favor of the mating, but without the fire and conviction he'd had a few months ago. Or even a few weeks ago. Was he truly letting go of Aurora and facing the situation more objectively? Or did she just want that to be true so she could keep a small flame of hope burning for her own future?

Regardless, she'd made a huge tactical error by coming here. Rather than gathering support to achieve her goals, she'd stranded the crew, leaving them dependent on Siginal's good will to get them back home.

Wherever home was now. Her mind kept bouncing between images of Stoneycroft, the Suulh settlement on Azaana, and Feylahn, the original Suulh homeworld. Home used to be wherever Aurora was. But Aurora was evolving, moving beyond the traditional Suulh paradigm of Sahzade and Nedale. If Mya didn't want to be left in the dust, she needed to do the same.

Swinging her legs over the side of her bunk, she stood. "Star, where's Celia?"

The Nirunoc's voice filled her cabin. "She is in the exercise room."

"Thanks."

After changing into a pair of sweatpants and a sweatshirt, she took the lift down to the cargo deck. The exercise room took up the entire forward section, providing the crew with a cornucopia of options for cardio, strength training, stretching, and skill building. Mya's favorite spot was the elevated walking path, which tied into a VR system that could reproduce in vibrant detail any terrain in the ship's database. She'd tried a few of the walks depicting Earth and Fleet colonized worlds, as well as locations the Kraed had visited, but her favorite was a recreation of the Clarek compound. Or at least it had been. She couldn't imagine using it now.

Celia wasn't on the sparring mat or one of the interactive treadmills. The sound of splashing water drew her to the alcove for the hydrotank. The five-meter-square device provided wave resistance, allowing a swimmer to experience the equivalent of an ocean, river, or lake swim, complete with realistic visual projections on the tank walls.

Jonarel had included the tank in the ship's design because of Aurora's love of water. And Aurora had used it regularly until the meltdown with Reanne and the breakup with Cade. When Mya had suggested she take a swim to relax and reenergize during the long flight to Earth, Aurora's look of horror had chilled her to the bone. She hadn't brought it up again.

Celia's lithe form stroked along the surface of the water, her navy-blue one-piece suit and tanned limbs visible through the clear glassticine walls. When the projection system was running, the glassticine could act as a one-way mirror in either direction, allowing privacy as desired. But Celia hadn't turned it on.

Mya climbed the curving steps to the wide deck surrounding the pool, heading for one of the deck chairs. The sounds of movement in the water ceased before she reached it.

"What's up?"

Mya turned.

Celia bobbed in the center of the pool, the smooth stroke of her arms under the water keeping her stationary against the mild current. She'd probably known Mya was there as soon as she'd stepped through the training room's door.

"I didn't mean to disturb you. It can wait until you're done."

Celia shrugged. "I'm done." She touched the control band around her wrist, stopping the waves. Swimming to the edge, she bypassed the stairs and planted her hands on the deck, lifting her body out of the water with the grace of a water nymph.

Mya bit back a sigh. She didn't envy her friend her beauty and physical prowess, but sometimes she wished she could be a little more like her. Especially if it would help Jonarel see her as more than a friend.

She handed Celia the towel draped over one of the chairs.

"Thanks." Celia patted the moisture off her skin before wrapping the towel around her torso and squeezing water from her ponytail. "Rough night?" She gestured for Mya to sit before settling into one of the deck chairs.

"Yeah." A lock of hair fell in front of her eyes and she shoved it behind her ear. Normally she kept her hair short, but the rapid pace of events over the past few months had made it difficult to find time for a haircut. She'd expected to take care of it while they'd been on Earth, but it hadn't worked out that way. She'd borrowed some hair ties and clips from Celia, but she kept forgetting to use them. "I talked to Jonarel last night."

Celia's brows rose a fraction. "How did that go?"

"He believes his father's accusations regarding my romantic feelings for him were a ploy to rattle me."

"And how did you respond?"

"I agreed with him."

Celia nodded, no judgment in her eyes, only understanding. "Did he say anything about Siginal's plan?"

"A little." She filled her in on what Jonarel had told her about his parents and the clans.

"So, we're here until Siginal decides to let us go?" Celia's gaze swept the alcove. "I've been in worse prisons."

Celia's matter-of-fact tone made Mya shudder. Her friend had made references to her difficult past over the years, but Mya hadn't formed a clear idea of the extent of Celia's suffering. All she knew for sure was that Celia had been abducted as a child, held against her will until she was a teenager, and been rescued by members of the Fleet.

Celia met her gaze. "Are you going to contact Aurora?"

"No." However this played out, the last thing she wanted to do was give Siginal more ammunition. Or to disrupt Aurora's training with her father. "We'll have to find a way out of this on our own."

A gleam lit Celia's brown eyes. "A jailbreak?"

"I guess, although I don't know how. Kelly can fly the *Starhawke* just fine, but Siginal implied the ship won't function without Star." She lowered her voice to a whisper, suddenly aware of her surroundings. "And I can't imagine Star would help us escape."

A green and brown skinned form materialized beside Mya's elbow, forcing a startled squeak from her lips.

"I am the lifeblood of the ship," Star said, folding her hands in front of her and gazing calmly between Mya and Celia. "As integrated as the blood that flows through your veins. Without me, the ship would require extensive modifications to operate independently."

Mya stared at the Nirunoc, heart pounding. "Are you going to tell Siginal what we've said here?"

Star did a fairly good imitation of the puzzled look Jonarel often gave her. "Why would I do that?"

"Don't you report to him?"

"He is my clan leader, and my father. I owe him my life."

"Is that a yes or a no?"

"It is a fact."

And Star was talking in riddles. "So, are you going to tell him or not?"

"No, I will not."

"Why not?" She'd never known Star to lie, but she wasn't about to make any assumptions at this point regarding the Nirunoc's motivations.

Star lifted her chin. "Because I too struggle with divided loyalties, just as Jonarel does. But unlike my brother, I have born witness to all that has happened on this ship." Her gaze locked on Mya, making it clear she'd heard every word of the discussion in the greenhouse the previous night. And at least suspected the truth about Mya's feelings for Jonarel. "I have watched you struggle, and Aurora struggle, to reconcile the conflicting challenges you face. You both work very hard to do what is best for others, often at the expense of your own needs."

Wow. She had not given the Nirunoc enough credit for observation or empathy.

"When I chose to bond with this ship, I knew I was choosing to serve a non-Kraed captain. I had hoped that my father's vision and Aurora's would be in alignment. But experience has shown me that can never be so."

The admission shocked Mya to her core. If Star didn't agree with Signal, then what—

"I love my brother. I love my father. I love my clan. But they are not infallible. And they do not see Aurora for who she is. For who she can become."

Her words sent a trickle of dread down Mya's spine. Did Star fear Aurora's power, too? "And what is that?"

Star's eyes glowed, the intensity almost blinding.

"The greatest leader the galaxy has ever known."

Sixty-One

Star could have knocked Mya over with a touch of her non-corporeal finger after her pronouncement. "You honestly believe that?"

The puzzled look returned to Star's face. "You do not?"

"Of course I do. I just thought... well, I expected you to see her the way Signal does."

Star shook her head, her long hair swaying in imaginary air currents. "My father sees Aurora as he chooses to, not as she is. Jonarel has suffered from the same misconception." Her gaze held Mya's. "But I believe he is growing beyond those constraints."

Mya swallowed. Impossible to miss the undercurrent in her words. But now wasn't the time to discuss it. "Will you help us to leave Drakar?"

"Where do you wish to go?"

"Earth." The only person she could think of who might talk some sense into Signal was Admiral Schreiber. And Sol Station would provide a safe haven if Signal decided to send ships after them.

Star's lips pursed. "No ship has ever attempted a..." She glanced at Celia. "What did you call it? Jailbreak?"

"That's right."

"I am uncertain if it can be achieved." Star's gaze went unfocused for a moment. "I will discuss it with Jonarel. If there is a way, we will find it." She met Mya's gaze, her honey-colored eyes looking like liquid sunlight. "When we do, we will have to act quickly. My link with the Nirunoc makes it difficult to hide my movements. But I will not allow you to become a prisoner here."

As Star's image winked out, a mountain slid off Mya's shoulders and crumbled to dust at her feet. The Nirunoc was one hundred percent on their side. What an unexpected gift. But could she set them free from Siginal's iron grip? She glanced at Celia. "Am I an idiot for trusting her?"

Celia's mouth curved in a soft smile. "No." She undid the ponytail tie and ran her fingers through her hair, shaking water droplets onto the deck. "She's been watching us, but I've been watching her, too. Everything she said is true. She loves her clan, but she loves this crew, too." She secured her wet locks in a loose topknot. "And when she chose this ship, her loyalty shifted, just as Jonarel's did. It's why they've both been struggling, caught between two worlds. But I think they're starting to see things clearly for the first time."

"I hope so. We need them."

"And they need us. I can't picture either of them being happy staying on Drakar forever. Can you?"

She hadn't considered the possibility, but now that Celia had brought it up? "No, I can't." Jonarel had loved being on Earth, and he'd seemed equally delighted with his Fleet assignments, no matter where they were sent. Remaining here under his father's watchful eye seemed to be the last thing he'd want. The promise of Aurora as his mate might have been the only thing that had made the idea palatable.

Celia stood. "Have you eaten?"

"No."

"Give me five minutes to change and I'll join you in the kitchen."

Which is where Star found them forty minutes later, her image appearing beside the dining nook. "You must go to the bridge. Now."

Mya set down her tea mug. "You found a way out?"

"Yes." Star vanished before Mya could ask anything else.

She exchanged a glance with Celia as they both stood. "Here we go."

Leaving their dishes on the table, they hurried into the portside passageway and took the lift to the bridge.

Kelly was already at the navigation console, the chair's safety harness across her torso. She glanced over, her usually placid expression replaced by a mixture of tension and excitement. "This should be interesting."

Mya looked to the empty captain's chair and communications station as Celia slid behind the tactical console. "Where's Kire?"

Kelly didn't turn, her fingers flying over the controls. "Helping Clarek uncouple the docking clamps."

Mya sank into the captain's chair, tapping in the command for the safety harness. If Kelly was using hers, she'd definitely need it. "Star, what's going on?"

"She can't answer you." Kelly glanced over her shoulder. "She's busy keeping the other Nirunoc distracted."

"Distracted?" Star had indicated her connection to the other Nirunocs could pose a threat to any escape plan. "Can you get us out of here without her?"

"We're going to find out."

Mya's fingers gripped the armrests as the ship's engines came to life, a subtle vibration working up through the deck.

"Clarek to bridge." Jonarel's deep baritone filled the space, all business.

Mya responded in kind. "Go ahead."

"Docking clamps disengaged. Emergency engine startup progressing. Thrusters ready."

Which meant exactly zip to her. "Kelly?"

"Maneuvering out of docking port." The navigator's voice was steady, but slightly higher pitched than normal.

The image on the bridgescreen changed, the trees steadily receding as the ship backed away from the berth.

A hard jolt shoved Mya against the straps of her harness. "What the—"

"A tether," Kelly responded without turning. "The Nirunoc—"

The ship's motion resumed, though not as smoothly as before.

"Star cleared it," Celia called out. "But they're—"

Another hard jolt, this one rocking the ship to port.

"Another tether." Kelly didn't sound concerned, but her hand gripped the edge of the console as the deck tilted down five degrees on the port side. "Make that two."

The vibrations from the engines increased, the image on the bridgescreen rotating as the ship was dragged to port.

Mya stared at the trees, helpless to do anything. "Celia? Options?"

Celia pivoted. "Weapons charged." The unspoken question hung in the air.

The air leaked from Mya's lungs. Could she do it? Could she justify firing on the Clarek compound? She shook her head. "Not unless we have to."

The lift doors opened and Kire staggered onto the bridge, catching himself on Celia's console as the ship shimmied. His gaze met Mya's. "Status?"

"Out of my depth." Her medical training hadn't prepared her for breaking out of a docking berth. "I'm open to suggestions."

He turned to Kelly. "Status?"

"Two tethers to port. Star's unable to break them."

"Are shields up?" he asked Celia.

"Coming online in six... five..."

Kire dropped into the chair to Mya's left and strapped in. "Kelly, ready starboard thrusters."

"Aye."

"Two... one... shields ready."

"Engage shields. Full starboard thrusters."

The ship shot to port. A muffled thud reverberated through the bulkhead, halting the ship's motion with a bone-jarring jerk.

"Full reverse!"

Mya braced for another jolt. When it came, her head snapped forward as a series of deep booms filled her ears. Branches and leaves from the surrounding denglar trees fell in front of the bridgescreen like oversized confetti. Mya's heart constricted, but there was nothing she could do to protect the ancient trees as the ship fought its way backwards.

"Tethers cleared, increasing speed," Kelly called out.

Within seconds the injured trees were no longer visible, the surrounding forest blurring and then shrinking as the ship altered course, gaining speed and altitude.

A weight settled in Mya's chest. No going back now.

"We're outside the perimeter. Adjusting heading. Setting—"

A flash of light and a loud bang made Mya flinch.

"Orbital charges in the atmosphere," Celia said. "They're trying to drive us back down. Shields holding."

"Engage hull camouflage. Kelly, get us out of here!" Kire ordered as additional concussion waves rocked the ship.

Star's image appeared beside Kelly. "New course." The navigation console flashed with incoming data.

"What about the planetary defenses?" Kire asked Star as Kelly sent the ship hurtling into the upper atmosphere.

"They will not use them."

"Because they can't detect us?"

Star pivoted to face him. "Because if they did, they would destroy us."

Sixty-Two

"Three patrol ships on an intercept course. Converging on our position." Celia reported from the tactical station. "Three more ships launching from Drakar."

Six ships? Signal may not have been willing to use the planetary weapons. but he wasn't going to make it easy for them to get away.

"One of the patrol ships has cut off our jump window." Kelly said.

Mya turned to Star, who had remained by Kelly's console. "Can you alter the camouflage so we can hide from them?"

Star shook her head. "As soon as we docked. the configuration I had used became part of the Nirunoc link. I could not prevent its transfer. Security has already adapted to counteract it."

And she'd thought getting off the planet would be the hard part.

As the newest ship built on Drakar. the *Starhawke* was faster than any other ship in the Kraed fleet. Unfortunately, six to one were not good odds.

What if they didn't make it out of the system? What punishment did the Kraed impose on traitors? She should have clarified that with Star before asking her to facilitate their escape.

Because that's how Signal would see them. If it had only been her. Kire. Celia. and Kelly who'd managed to free the ship. he could have made excuses. blamed their actions on foolish idealism or childish defiance. But when Star and Jonarel had sided with the crew. they'd made it personal.

Siginal was coming for them. And if he caught them, he'd make them pay for their betrayal.

She glanced at Kire, who had moved to the comm console after they'd escaped the planet's gravity. "Any recommendations?"

"A few. First, we need a new jump window. Kelly, alter course. Head for any window that will get us out of the system and Kraed space. If a ship moves to block us, find another window. Star, is there anything you can do to help us deal with those patrol ships?"

"I have modulated the shields for maximum effectiveness against their weapons." Star's voice was surprisingly calm considering three heavily armed ships were bearing down on them. "But their firepower is significant. I cannot deflect sustained blasts for long."

"Would they do serious damage to you?" Mya hadn't stopped to think that for the Kraed, firing on one of their own ships was like striking a member of their clan. Literally. Star would be taking the hits.

"Critical damage, no. But they understand the ship's design and weaknesses. They will coordinate to disable the engines and tow us back to Drakar."

Oh. "How do you feel about firing on them?"

Star hesitated. "They are my family. As are you." She paused, her gaze moving slowly among the crew before resting on Mya. "I would prefer not to harm them. But if they will not see reason, I will do what I must."

Her admiration for the Nirunoc rose a few more notches.

Celia glanced over her shoulder. "First patrol ship will be in weapons range in seventy seconds."

"Changing course to evade," Kelly said.

"We're being hailed by the *Jasclarek*," Kire informed Mya.

"The patrol ship?"

"No, one of the three from Drakar."

Probably Siginal. She took a slow breath, trying to ease the pounding of her heart. "On screen."

Sure enough, Siginal's image appeared on the split bridgescreen. If she'd thought he'd looked fierce when they were arguing on Drakar, she'd been wrong. The warrior staring at her was out for blood. "Return to Drakar immediately."

A tremor worked over her skin, but she held her ground. "I don't think so."

His shoulders pulled back, his arms lifting like a gorilla about to pound its chest. Or like he wanted to wrap his fingers around her throat. "I am not asking. Return now!"

Instead of inspiring fear, his posturing triggered anger. "Back off, Siginal. You can't command me. And you have no right to hold us here." Heat built in her chest. "If you fire on us, you will *not* be happy with the result."

His eyes narrowed. "Your threats mean nothing. You are a healer, not a fighter."

The straps holding her in the captain's chair dug into her skin as red clouded her vision. "I am a leader, the Nedale of the Suulh, consort of the Sahzade. If you think I will not fight to defend Aurora from your machinations, you are wrong!" She punctuated the word with a jab of her finger. "You're trying to control her just as the Teeli want to, only you're wrapping your deception in the guise of friendship."

His lip curled in a snarl. "You understand nothing. She must be part of my clan. She must be protected."

"Second patrol ship closing on our position. In range in one minute."

Mya didn't look at Celia. Or note Kelly's course change. The patrol ships didn't concern her anymore. All that mattered was the Kraed in front of her. "She doesn't need your protection." *Or mine.* But she did need their support, now more than ever. "Kelly, put us on an intercept course with the *Jasclarek.* Star, arm all weapons."

Siginal's eyes widened. "You cannot order my daughter to fire on me."

"I won't need to." A cool calm settled over her, Star's words reverberating in her head. "She's perfectly capable of doing it on her own."

Siginal's lips parted, but no words came out. He stared at her in shock, his gaze slowly tracking to Star.

The Nirunoc faced the bridgescreen without flinching. "Weapons armed."

Mya rather enjoyed his dumbfounded expression. And she wanted to applaud Star. She was showing more composure than Mya could have achieved if their roles were reversed. She couldn't imagine firing on a ship her dad was on. Then again, she couldn't imagine a scenario in which she'd have to. "Your move, Siginal. What's it going to be?"

"Fifty seconds to weapons range with *Jasclarek,*" Kelly informed her.

"Their weapons are armed," Celia added.

Siginal's gaze held Star's. "Do not make me fire on you, Tehar." The words came out as half growl, half plea.

Star's reply sounded more like a warning. "Do not make me fire on you, Talta." *Talta,* the Kraed word for father.

The smack of the gauntlet brought the warrior back to the surface, shouldering the parent aside. "How can you do this? You have turned your back on your clan. On me!"

"Respectfully, I have not. I am defending those you asked me to protect."

Mya's chest constricted. Star was going to the mat for them in every way possible. She had to give her some backup. "She's right, Siginal. But there is one thing you and I agree on. You need Aurora as an ally if you want to protect your clan from the Teeli." Her gaze shifted to the other half of the bridgescreen, where the *Jasclarek* was now visible as a silver speck in the distance.

"Thirty seconds to intercept," Celia murmured.

If Aurora were here now, how would she react? What would she say? Certainty settled over her, like she was channeling Aurora's thoughts. "If you try to take us by force, she will *never* be on your side. And when she comes for us—and she will—you will lose her forever."

His eyes burned like candle flame, but she could tell her words were making him think. That was a very good thing. Up to now he'd been driven by his overblown ego.

"Is that what you want? For Aurora to be your enemy?"

The image of the *Jasclarek* on the bridgescreen grew, the *Starhawke* closing fast.

She needed to speed up Siginal's thought process. "One shot, Siginal. That's all it will take to lose everything you've worked for all these years."

His face twisted into a mask of anger. "You are making a grave mistake."

The corners of her lips lifted, but it wasn't a smile. "The only mistake I made was trusting you."

"You must—"

"I *must* do nothing. But I *will* learn from my mistakes. Will you?"

One heartbeat. Two. Three.

"*Jasclarek* in range."

"Star, fire forward cannons."

"Stop!"

She lifted a hand and held Siginal's gaze, waiting.

He looked to his left, barking a command in the Kraed language.

"Fall back." Kire translated in an undertone.

Siginal's gaze flicked to Kire in annoyance, then back to Mya. "I wish to speak to my son."

She opened a channel to the engine room. "Jonarel? We need you on the bridge."

"On my way."

Celia turned her head slightly, still keeping an eye on her console. "All six ships are holding position."

A small victory. But Siginal clearly hadn't conceded the fight just yet.

Jonarel's expression when he stepped off the lift tore a ragged gash in her heart. He looked like a man facing the gallows. He met her gaze briefly before wiping away all emotion and facing the bridgescreen. "Father."

Siginal didn't waste any time. "I expected such behavior from your friends. But from you? From your sister? How could you betray the clan?"

Jonarel clasped his hands behind his back, which allowed her to see the slight tremor in his fingers. "I want what is best for our clan. And for Aurora. But I disagree with your methods for achieving it."

"How can you? I know you want her as your mate."

"No, I do not."

Mya's heart stuttered.

Siginal blinked, like Jonarel had just said he wanted to take a spacewalk without an enviro suit. "Yes, you do. You always have."

"I did when I believed it was necessary. I no longer do."

"You love her!"

"Yes. Which is why I cannot be her mate."

Siginal's confusion began morphing into anger. "Have you lost your senses? She is—"

"In love with someone else."

"What?" The anger took laser focus as understanding dawned. "Are you talking about Ellis? Is that what this is about?"

"Partially."

"You are betraying your clan and abandoning the future so Aurora can mate with that mongrel?" Rage and disbelief warred for dominance. "I will never allow it."

"It is not your decision."

"It is my right!" Siginal's face darkened like a thundercloud. "I have protected her. Been the father she did not have. She *will* be part of our clan."

"She does not wish it."

"I don't care—"

"I do!" Jonarel's stoicism fell away, his body drawing tight with anger. "Your plan is not the only way!"

Siginal went silent, which made him seem more menacing not less, like a stalking predator whose prey had just stepped into open ground.

Jonarel didn't seem to notice. "Aurora isn't a mindless puppet. Or a piece on your chessboard. The more you tighten your grip, the harder she will fight to get free."

"You are a fool."

"I am her friend."

Jonarel's assertion—friendship over clan—had just sealed his fate. She could see it in Siginal's eyes.

"Jonarel, son of clan Clarek. Tehar, daughter of clan Clarek. You have chosen to stand against me. Against your clan."

Jonarel's spine stiffened, bracing for a gale force wind, while Star went completely still.

"If ever again you see the skies of Drakar, you will pay for what you have done."

Jonarel's sharp inhale and the flicker of Star's image plunged a dagger into Mya's heart. Signal was banishing them? Could he truly be that callous?

Unfastening her harness, she surged to her feet. "They're not standing against you. They're standing *with* us. They're fighting for what they believe is right!"

Signal managed to shut her out without moving a muscle. "As am I. A traitor is a traitor, no matter their beliefs. Or their blood."

Pain turned to rage. "And a dictator is still a dictator, no matter his beliefs. Or his blood."

She'd hoped to strike him with the barb, but he looked more annoyed than wounded.

"You have far more fire in your belly than I imagined. But it will not change the course of events laid before us. Or elevate you from your minor role."

His barb missed the mark, too. It was a weak insult, at best.

Strangely, it was Jonarel who reacted, his hands curling and his claws flashing. "We shall see, father. The rook has less power than the queen, but both can checkmate the king."

His words had the desired result, striking with the force of an arrow. Signal's upper lip pulled back from his teeth. "Yes, we shall see."

The screen went blank.

Silence settled over the bridge like fog.

Mya let out a shuddering breath, her muscles creaking as she turned to Celia. "Status on the ships?"

Celia checked the tactical display. "All six ships are retreating. We have a clear path to our jump window."

And a rocky path ahead.

"Kelly, get us out of here."

Sixty-Three

"Exiting interstellar jump in five, four, three, two, one." Cade switched *Gladiator* from interstellar engines to main engines.

The image outside the viewport changed from the streaming light of the interstellar jump to the diamond-studded velvet of deep space.

Justin tapped the controls on the co-pilot's console. "Scanning for ships."

Cade eased back on the engines. *Gladiator* drifted along like a leaf in the current as he waited for the all clear.

"Sensor deflectors activated." Gonzo said.

Cade glanced over his shoulder at the auxiliary station. "Weapons?"

"Charged and ready."

"Let's hope we won't need them." He faced forward, his gaze flicking through the exterior camera views, which were all set to maximum magnification. No flashes of light on metal. So far so good.

The seconds ticked by, the soft whir of the air circulation system the only sound in the cockpit.

Justin sat back in his chair, his shoulders visibly relaxing. "All clear. No ships or tech on scanners."

One hurdle crossed.

Cade turned to Gonzo. "Launch the drone and have it scan us when it reaches one-thousand kilometers."

Gonzo nodded. "Launching drone."

A spot of light and metal appeared briefly in the camera view before being swallowed by the blackness.

Silence descended again, though with less tension vibrating in the air.

"Drone has reached specified distance. Scanning now."

Cade pulled up the tactical readouts on his console so he could monitor the drone's transmission. The lack of data gave him his answer. "It can't find us."

"No, it can't." Gonzo smiled. "Drew did it. *Gladiator's* invisible to sensors."

Second hurdle down, and a huge improvement. Bella's friendship with Jonarel Clarek had paid an unexpected dividend. "But still visible to cameras. We'll take it slow. Recall the drone and keep watching for any sign of enemy ships."

Pointing *Gladiator's* nose into the system, he fired the main engines, moving the ship toward the star at the center.

The rendezvous was set to take place around the second planet, a superearth rocky mass with nine moons. He'd purposely entered the system from the opposite side of the star. It meant orbiting the star to reach the planet, but it gave them the protection of the star's light behind them while they observed the rendezvous. The odds of the Teeli spotting them while looking at the star would be like picking out a gnat flying in front of a searchlight.

The sound of heavy footsteps approaching in the corridor indicated Williams had decided to join them. He walked through the hatch and rested his hands on the back of Cade's chair. "How we looking?"

"So far so good. Drew's sensor deflector is doing its job."

"Of course it is." Justin grinned. "She's brilliant."

"I'll make sure to tell her you said so." Williams lightly jabbed Justin's shoulder.

"Go right ahead. She knows I love her mind."

Williams shot Cade an amused glance.

No doubt he had the same thought in his head that had popped into Cade's.

The internal comm panel pinged.

"Speaking of Bella." Justin opened the connection. "What can I do for our brilliant engineer?"

Bella's soft laugh drifted over the comm. "That's quite an opening line."

"Only the best for you." Justin winked at Williams.

"Well, your brilliant engineer wanted to let you know that the additional power load from running the deflector is making some of our operating systems sluggish. Weapons and shields are on a separate system, so they aren't affected, but navigation will respond slower than normal."

Cade sat up straighter. "How much slower?" He hadn't noticed any change so far.

"At our current course and velocity it's undetectable. But if you try to make any sudden changes, you'll feel it lag, maybe by as much as a second or two."

Which during a battle could mean the difference between a glancing blow and blowing up.

"I'm putting as many non-critical systems into low-power mode as I can to compensate, but the deflector's a major drain. If you need *Gladiator*'s full maneuverability, you won't be able to stay hidden from sensors."

"Understood." Hopefully he wouldn't have to make that choice.

"At our next station dock, I'd like to retrofit the ship to give the deflector a separate power source. That would solve the problem permanently. For now, I'll keep working on alternatives and let you know if anything changes. Drew out."

Williams stepped toward the hatch. "I'll be in the engine room helping Drew if you need me."

Justin switched off the comm and leaned back in his chair, his gaze on Cade. "You still thinking about tracking down *Gladiator's* previous owner?"

Was he? The thought had been pushed out of his mind by more pressing matters. "I don't know. Probably." If his assumption was correct that Weezel had stolen the vessel, then he had a moral obligation to search out the owner. The fact that he thought of *Gladiator* as his didn't make it legal. Or honorable. He didn't have the right to keep the ship until he checked its history.

Which meant Drew would have to hold off on the permanent upgrade. And he'd have to tackle the research project as soon as this mission was over.

But right now they needed every advantage they could get. Ironically, he had Jonarel Clarek's overprotective instincts to thank for the deflector. The Kraed had spoken to Drew after witnessing the pounding *Gladiator* had taken during the battle with Reanne's warships. He'd supplied the knowledge and resources necessary for Bella to complete the project, asking nothing in return.

Which put Cade in the Kraed's debt. Not where he wanted to be.

Finding a way to repay him was yet another unpleasant task hovering in his future. "That's a problem for another time," he said, more to himself than to Justin.

"Agreed."

Cade checked the navigation charts. "The planet will be visible around the star's corona in ten minutes. Gonzo, I want continuous sensor sweeps of the area. If so much as a dust mite moves, I want to know. Justin, start checking the comm frequencies, see if you can pick up any chatter or noise that will alert us to incoming ships."

While Justin slid on his headset and Gonzo returned to the sensor data, Cade focused on making minor course corrections to compensate for the star's gravity pull. He also monitored the exterior camera views until navigation confirmed they had a straight-line view to the second planet.

"I've got something."

Cade glanced at Gonzo. "A ship?"

"Looks like it. Just came out of a jump window, headed this way."

Cade's heartbeat picked up the pace. "Reanne's cruiser?"

"No, smaller than that. The sensor readings don't match any of the Teeli configurations we've seen before."

"So not the yacht, either."

"Uh-uh. This ship's somewhere in between, size-wise."

"An unknown guest to the party. Coordinates and heading?"

Gonzo rattled them off while Cade aligned their most powerful telescoping camera to match the ship's trajectory. The ship wouldn't be visible until it moved closer to the star, but he wanted a clear view as soon as it did. "What can you tell me about it?"

"Not much, except it's fast. Coming in like a bullet. Some kind of shielding is making it difficult for sensors to penetrate the hull. It seems to be masking its emissions trail, too. Whatever it is, it's designed for stealth."

"Of course it is. Sneak attacks are Reanne's MO."

"But it's not a Teeli design."

"Not one we know of."

Gonzo acknowledged the point with a shrug.

Cade tapped Justin on the shoulder. "Anything?" he mouthed when Justin met his gaze.

He shook his head, sliding the headset around his neck. "Silent as a graveyard."

"We've got an incoming ship, unknown origin and design."

Justin's eyes lit up, accepting the unspoken challenge. "I'm on it."

He left Justin to his soundproof cocoon while he kept watch on the camera view. He didn't have long to wait. A shape moved in the darkness, though it was difficult to distinguish from the surrounding void of space.

Gonzo's chair creaked as he leaned toward the camera display. "Is the ship painted black?"

"Seems to be." Which made identifying any particular part of it a challenge, like spotting a black cat in a dark room. Even as it filled the image, his eyes had trouble picking out any details. "Switching to infrared."

The color tones of the image shifted, but the ship still remained well blended with its surroundings with hardly any visible heat signatures.

Gonzo let out a low whistle. "Damn. That's Kraed-worthy tech."

"Close to it." But there was zero chance the ship was a Kraed design. They'd never stoop to painting a hull when they could use their technology to make a ship truly invisible.

A ping from Gonzo's console made them both turn. "Second ship incoming." Gonzo analyzed the data. "It's the Teeli yacht."

Cade checked the chronometer. "Right on time. Either the Admiral wasn't able to delay them, or they pushed their engines the whole way here."

As the yacht made its way into the system, the mystery ship settled into a high orbit around the second planet.

"Good thing they didn't decide to meet on the dark side," Cade murmured. He'd been a little worried they might. "Now all we need is—"

Justin held up a hand. "I'm picking up a transmission from the ship to the yacht."

Cade fell silent, waiting.

Justin's eyes scrunched tight in concentration, his forehead furrowing. A moment later he slipped the headset around his neck, his head falling back as he stared at the ceiling. "Oh, hell."

Not what Cade wanted to hear. "What?"

Justin's gaze met his. "Setarips."

Sixty-Four

Cade stared at Justin. "That ship's from one of the Setarip factions?"

"Yep. Judging by the distinctive hiss, it's the Ecilam."

Wonderful. He'd known Reanne was working with the Ecilam—they'd helped her take down Tnaryt—but he hadn't expected one of their ships to show up at the rendezvous. "Can you translate the message?"

"Only Bare'Kold's response. Teeli spoken with an Ecilam accent sounds like wolves fighting in a wind tunnel."

"What did Bare'Kold say?"

"He instructed them to have the envoy ready for transport in ten minutes."

"Envoy for what?"

"I'm not sure. But anything involving the Setarips is bad news."

Cade studied the image of the dark ship on the display. "Especially the Ecilam." Attacks by the Regna and Egar on human settlements were brutal, but often uncoordinated and therefore defensible. What made the Ecilam so terrifying was their surgical precision. Victims never saw them coming, and rarely survived the encounter.

With one notable exception.

Aurora.

He'd read her report regarding the battle she'd fought on the Persei Primus space station when she was the commander of the *Argo*. The Ecilam, with the help of human traitors, had overcome the station's considerable defenses and stolen a classified research project.

On orders from Admiral Schreiber, no one onboard the *Argo* except the Admiral's son Knox had been told what the Ecilam had taken. But Cade knew exactly what had been in the case. He'd even seen it in use a few months ago on Gaia. The Fleet-designed propulsion prototype the Ecilam had stolen had been the basis for the winged harnesses used to control the movements of the Necri soldiers.

But the Ecilam hadn't been the ones in charge of the ship that had attacked Gaia. That job had fallen to the Etah, an equally arrogant but far less lethal Setarip faction. After seeing the way Reanne had used and betrayed Tnaryt, it was easy to picture her playing the two factions against each other—encouraging the interstellar civil war between the bitter enemies, promising them assistance when it suited her purposes and discarding them when she no longer needed them.

It was how Reanne operated. Sociopathic narcissism. Her intellect and manipulative abilities helped her get away with it, as he'd learned firsthand. He took small comfort in the knowledge that he was now immune to her machinations.

"I'm recording all transmissions." Justin slid his headset back into place. "I might be able to sort through the Ecilam comments later if they keep talking."

Cade nodded, glancing over his shoulder at Gonzo. "Any indication either ship is aware of us?"

"Nothing so far. Deflector's holding steady."

"Good." His gaze returned to the image of the Ecilam ship, which had been joined by the yacht, though at a discreet distance, like two loyal subjects standing guard while they awaited the arrival of their queen. "Hopefully we won't have to wait too—"

"More ships just appeared on sensors."

Not long at all.

"Four Teeli warships. The fifth ship is a cruiser, and it's transmitting the homing signal Cardiff planted on Reanne's transport while she was on the Suulh homeworld. The transport must be onboard."

Making a grand entrance. Reanne had been famous for that. "Position?"

"Coming around the far side of the star."

Damn. He should have guessed Reanne would be as cautious about her approach as he had been with *Gladiator.* "Do they have line of sight to us?"

"Not any better than we have on them." A blindingly bright image projected on the viewport from one of the external cameras. Cade squinted against the glare, trying to pick out the shape of the cruiser. No luck. The light from the star was too strong, rendering the entire image into a yellowish-white splotch.

"That's what they'd be seeing looking in our direction, only we're considerably smaller."

"Keep tracking their movements. If they make any changes, we'll need to get out of here in a hurry." He turned to Justin. "Any communications?"

"The cruiser just sent a broadcast to both ships. It sounds like shuttle docking instructions."

"So, they're meeting on the cruiser?" He tapped his thumbs on the yoke, *what if* scenarios playing in his head. "How close would we need to be to pick up the audio feed from the device I planted on Bare'Kold?"

Justin's brows rose. "It's designed for mid-range terrestrial surveillance, not interplanetary transmission."

"I know. But could we pick it up if we got close enough?" He really wanted to hear what was said at this gathering.

Justin blew out a breath. "If I reconfigured the receiver to narrow band, focusing on just that one signal, and boosted the amplification, we might be able to get something if we were within ten thousand kilometers. But we'd be deaf to anything else."

"And that close, we'd lose the visual protection of the star," Gonzo added.

"Which means we'd need another form of camouflage. Any sign they've spotted us?"

"Not yet. They're continuing on their trajectory to the second planet."

"Give me a display of their projected course."

The data appeared on the viewport.

Cade merged it with his navigation data, rapidly testing and rejecting various vectors to get them where they needed to be. "This one." He highlighted one of the paths in green. "If we follow this flightpath, we'll keep the sun to our backs until we can use the planet's third moon as a buffer. After we orbit, the moon's shadow will provide visual cover." He pointed at their destination. "This point will put us ninety-eight hundred kilometers from the cruiser with line of sight but still in the moon's shadow." He glanced back at Gonzo. "What do you think?"

"Risky, but doable."

"Justin?"

"It should work."

"Then get started on those modifications. We've got a party to crash."

Sixty-Five

Micah hadn't resisted Aurora's idea to spar as much as she'd expected, but he'd insisted on a concession first. Before they met on the mat, she had to join him on a snorkeling expedition.

Thanks to the work with their father, the terror she'd been experiencing at the thought of coming into contact with saltwater had settled down. He'd reminded her that she was in control of her power, a fact her fear had overshadowed. Her gut still clenched as she watched the waves slapping the side of the boat Micah was guiding to one of his favorite dive locations, but the reaction was manageable. Especially when she watched Micah.

He was as much in his element at the helm of a boat as she was on the bridge of her ship. And he looked the part, too. Sculptors would pay good money to have him pose as the Greek god Poseidon.

He glanced at her, his enthusiastic grin coaxing an answering smile from her lips. "How could you not love this?" He swept his arm out to encompass the blue sky dotted with fluffy white clouds, the azure ocean, and the brown and green landmass of Oahu off to port.

Her smile widened at his childlike eagerness. "How much farther?"

"Only a couple kilometers. This spot doesn't have a beach nearby, and it's a little small for serious divers, but it's perfect for beginners. We probably won't encounter anyone else."

Even better. She could stay focused on her visualizations if she needed them.

An image of the *Starhawke* bridge drifted into her conscious mind, an unexpected consequence of all the visualization work with her dad. Thoughts of her ship and crew had crept in since the previous evening and had also filled her dreams, triggering a low-grade yearning to be back onboard. The pull had stayed with her after she woke. The urge to reach out to Mya was strong, but her desire to avoid interacting with Signal was stronger. Besides, she didn't want to contact her crew until she was ready to return. She wasn't there yet.

Hopefully this venture was a step in the right direction.

When they reached their destination Micah cut the motor, the rolling waves steadily slowing the boat's momentum. After checking the readouts on the instruments, he lowered the anchor, waiting until the line pulled taut before turning to her. "Let's go have some fun."

Her stomach flipped, but she managed to keep her smile in place. "I'll follow you."

He outfitted her with a snorkeling mask and a pair of flippers, giving her a rundown on proper procedures and safety precautions, including his three rules of diving. Don't be late, don't touch the animals, always keep track of your dive buddy.

The flippers felt incredibly awkward on her feet, pulling on her ankles and toes, at least until she entered the water. Ah, much better.

Micah bobbed beside her. "How you doing?"

"Fine."

"No anxiety?"

"No. I—" She paused. The newness of the experience had temporarily distracted her. Yet here she was, fully immersed in the ocean, with Micah right beside her and tropical fish visible through the crystal-clear water below. A tremor passed over her, but she focused on the image of the *Starhawke* bridge and the mantra her dad had taught her. *I control my power. It responds to my commands.*

The tremor passed. She met Micah's gaze, grateful for his reassuring presence. "I'm fine. Really."

The worry lines fled. "Glad to hear it. But if that changes, you let me know."

"I will." She swung one leg back and forth, the flipper creating a lot of resistance in the water. "I think my thighs are going to get a workout this morning."

"Don't worry. I'll go easy on you." His words had a teasing lilt, but the look in his eyes was deadly serious. "I want you to have fun."

She shifted her mask into place. "Then let's get started."

Hearing her own breathing through the snorkel was distracting, although it wasn't all that different from breathing in the closed environment of a spacesuit. It wasn't long before she forgot all about the mechanics of the dive as the underwater world came to life around her.

A quartet of fluorescent yellow fish with large crests swam near the small reef below. *Yellow Tang* flashed on the mini display built into her mask. The mask also identified Angel Fish, Groupers, Snappers, and at least a dozen other names that were unfamiliar to her.

Micah swam beside her, his movements as graceful as the fish. He made the hand signal he'd taught her for diving, asking if she wanted to get closer to the reef.

She signaled back, then took a deep breath and submerged, the flippers helping to propel her away from the surface. Micah appeared beside her, guiding her along the reef's edge and pointing out some of the shy residents tucked into the nooks and crannies. Most of the fish seemed unconcerned by their presence, paying them no more mind than any of the other aquatic creatures.

When they surfaced, she exhaled forcefully, blowing the accumulated water out of her snorkel, which sounded a lot like a whale spouting.

Micah removed his mouthpiece. "Having fun?"

She did the same. "You bet. I can see why you like this."

His delighted grin made her smile. "You ain't seen nothing yet." He glanced out toward the open water. "Let's do another dive."

"Okay."

When they were below the surface again, he touched her arm and pointed. A shape materialized from the cloudy depths in the distance, gliding toward them on elegant wings. *Spotted Eagle Ray* her mask informed her.

The ray's path curved, bringing it into a slow arc less than a meter away. She could count the spots on its back, but each flap of its "wings" showed her its pearl white underbelly.

She had to surface to get air after its first pass, but rather than moving off, it circled them four times, giving her ample opportunity to take in the majestic beauty of the graceful creature. She couldn't tell from Micah's expression whether he was communicating with the ray, but it seemed likely considering how focused the ray was on them.

As it finally glided away, two other forms appeared from around a rock outcropping. *Green Sea Turtle* flashed on her mask.

The pair swam toward them, much as the ray had, clearly curious.

She touched Micah's shoulder and mimed talking with her hands, then pointed at the turtles.

He nodded.

So, he was having a conversation with them. No wonder they were so curious. She was, too.

The turtles split up, circling in opposite directions, the sunlight through the water dancing across their enormous flippers and patterned shells. The look in their eyes captivated her—wise, serene, assessing. But her lungs were starting to burn as her body ran out of oxygen.

By the time she propelled herself to the surface, she didn't have the breath control to clear her snorkel. She sputtered and coughed as seawater and air rushed into her mouth.

Micah was beside her in a heartbeat, rubbing her back. "Breathe."

"I'm—" She gave another watery hack. "Trying."

"I meant the air. Not the water."

The splash of water she sent his way with her cupped hand spattered his face, making him laugh. "No splashing the instructor."

"No making fun of the student." Movement in the water caught her eye. The turtles were still circling them. "How long will they stay?"

Micah glanced down. "Up to them. They're fascinated by you."

"Me? Why."

"It's hard to explain, but they sense something's different about you. And that you and I have a connection."

"They can sense that?"

"Sure. Non-human animals communicate on a much more open frequency. They pay attention to things humans often ignore. From what you've told me about the Suulh, they're very interconnected with their environment. Other creatures can sense that."

"Huh." She watched the turtles making slow arcs in the water. "Let's go back under."

The turtles continued their graceful gliding movements as she and Micah joined them. One came close enough to touch, but she kept her hands to herself, not wanting to risk harming it in any way.

Unfortunately, the need for air soon drove her to the surface again. "How long... can they stay... underwater?" she panted as her lungs recovered.

Micah didn't show any signs of exertion, his breathing slow and steady. "Depends on how active they are. Several hours is common, or longer if they're resting or sleeping."

"That's amazing, given they're about our size. I didn't picture them having that kind of lung capacity."

"They're perfectly adapted to their environment."

She smiled. "So are you."

He grinned back. "Not perfectly, but I do all right." His grin faded, his eyes growing unfocused for a moment. "Oh, boy."

She tensed. "What?"

He shook his head and grimaced. "The dolphin pod just found us."

Sixty-Six

Micah glanced out to sea, where a few dorsal fins arced out of the water. He'd been hoping to avoid the dolphins on this first trip. Unlike the turtles, who were merely curious, the dolphins tended to show up with an agenda. He didn't want them to cause any problems for Aurora during her first time back in the water. "We should head for the boat."

Aurora frowned. "Why? They're not dangerous, are they?"

Her obvious reluctance to leave made him smile. She was clearly working her way past the fear that had made her avoid the ocean like it was filled with hydrochloric acid.

But she didn't know how rambunctious the dolphins could be with him, especially the two interlopers who'd broken away from the pod and were making a beeline for them.

He'd dubbed them Streak and Cutter because he couldn't get his mind wrapped around the names they used to refer to each other. Streak was the fastest swimmer he'd ever encountered, while Cutter delighted in darting around him while he was on his board. He'd first encountered them when they were juveniles, and while several years had passed, maturity had yet to set in.

"I wouldn't call them dangerous, but they can be a little rough around the edges." He could hear their excited chatter as they drew closer.

Her gaze shifted out toward the pod as a series of emotions tripped across her face. When she turned back to him, her eyes were clear and focused, her words direct and calm. "They can't hurt me."

Wow. Talk about a transformation. Not only was she unconcerned that the dolphins would trigger an unexpected and potentially lethal reaction from her, but she seemed prepared to use her shielding ability while she was in the water to protect herself. Apparently, she'd washed away all remnants of her fear. If he hadn't been so stunned, he would have given her a high-five. "Okay, then."

"Anything I should know?"

He was still catching up with her emotional shift. "Give me a moment." Filling his lungs with air, he slipped below the surface and flippered in the direction of the approaching dolphins, noting that the two sea turtles were already heading in the opposite direction. Smart move.

Good behavior. He projected the message with a subtle warning. The rest of the dolphin pod was close enough that their mothers would hear him and intercede if he asked them to.

Streak swam by, giving him a tail tap on the leg before starting a lazy circle. *Always good.*

Cutter charged past his other side just out of reach. *Really good.*

Micah rolled his eyes. Yep. Still juveniles.

Swimming back to Aurora, he rose to the surface, the dark shapes of the dolphins moving closer. Cutter executed a barrel roll as he went past.

"That's Cutter." Micah pointed to the dolphin, who'd changed course to swim under him. "And that's Streak, his cousin." He indicated the second dolphin who was swimming around them in a lazy circle.

The schools of nearby fish scattered as the two dolphins started their favorite game. Streak kicked into high gear, continuing her circle while Cutter tried to make it across the circle's diameter, dodging the human obstacles, to cut Streak off.

Aurora watched them intently. "Have you known them long?"

"Most of their lives. I encountered their pod when they were about five months old, which is why we're able to understand each other so clearly. They learned how to communicate with me while they were still developing, so it's much more natural for them."

"And for you?"

"I can understand them better than the others, which hasn't always been a good thing, especially when I'm surfing." He made a face. "When these two first started seeking me out, they thought smacking into me or flipping my board was a good way to get my attention. I learned early on how much damage a fast-moving dolphin can cause. It took a while to convince them to stop. If I'd had your shielding ability, they would have gotten the point a lot quicker."

Cutter spun past them again, narrowly avoiding Micah's thigh.

"They've knocked me off my board more times than I can count, but that's rare nowadays, unless we—" He paused, listening.

"What is it?"

"Streak wants to know if you can talk."

"If I can talk?"

"Like me. With them."

She gazed at the cavorting dolphins with obvious longing. "I wish I could."

Too bad he couldn't project their communications to her. Or could he? "Do you want to try?"

"How?"

"It's just a thought, but if you engage your energy field and surround me, maybe I could project what they're saying to you." It was a long shot, but it couldn't hurt to try, especially now that her fear of her abilities was under control.

Her eyes lit up, followed by her energy field. It enveloped him in its pearlescent glow.

He chuckled.

"What?"

"Cutter just called you shiny lady."

"Shiny lady? He can see the energy field?"

"Apparently so. He's projecting an image of how it looks from the water. It's different than what we see, since they don't see color like we do, but it's pretty."

Cutter swam closer, passing underneath Aurora so his dorsal fin grazed the edge of the field.

Her head came up, her eyes widening. "I got something! Distorted, but definitely from him. Ask him to swim through the field again."

Micah sent the request to Cutter as Aurora expanded the field several meters deeper into the water.

But Streak beat Cutter to it, darting right through the center. *Shiny water!*

Aurora squinted in concentration.

Cutter followed right behind Streak, making a tight turn at the field's edge to pass through again. *Shiny water, shiny water, shiny water!*

Micah's snort of laughter drew Aurora's attention. "They like your field," he explained. "It feels good to them. Invigorating."

She nodded. "I can sense their emotions and vague images. Also the presence of a message, but it's like trying to understand a language I never learned."

He smiled. "And just like learning a language, it takes practice. I'm thrilled the shared field idea works at all. If you can hear them, then eventually you'll be able to understand what they're saying."

"What a wonderful gift." Her eyes glowed almost as much as her field. "Thank you."

The dolphins were having a ball passing back and forth through the field. *Swim! Swim! Swim!*

He glanced at Aurora. "Do you want to try swimming with them?"

She frowned. "You said not to touch them."

He shook his head. "We won't. I meant we'd swim, and they'd swim around us."

"Oh." Her smile returned. "Sounds like fun."

"It should be as long as they behave themselves, which I think they will. They really seem to like you."

She laughed. "Or at least what I can do."

He grinned. "Now you know how I feel."

They slid beneath the surface. Micah stayed slightly behind Aurora's left shoulder so he could keep an eye on her and the dolphins. But any lingering doubts soon faded. The dolphins were reveling in the touch of Aurora's energy field and seemed loath to do anything that might cause her to retract it. They swam beside or underneath her, always at a respectful distance, shifting positions when they came up for air, and circling to accommodate her slower pace.

Aurora's composure was blowing him away. She was getting more proficient with her snorkel, no longer inhaling water, which allowed her to keep swimming as long as she stayed close enough to the surface that she could breathe. She even dove a few times so she was eye-to-eye with Streak or Cutter, clearing the water from the snorkel when she surfaced without stopping.

The dolphins seemed as enchanted by her as she was by them. They repeated *shiny* and *swim* over and over, which made him smile. He'd never seen the two so excited, or so focused.

He lost track of how long they'd been at it, but eventually a series of complex thoughtforms entered his mind, coming from the dolphins' pod.

Streak and Cutter slowed, reluctantly leaving the glow of Aurora's field.

Aurora stopped swimming, removing her mouthpiece and treading water as she watched them. "They're so beautiful."

The reverence in her voice got him. She might have made her life among the stars, but she was as captivated by his world as he'd hoped she'd be. Too bad their time together was limited. With practice, she could be an excellent free diver.

As the dolphins moved off, she gave a little sigh, like a kid who'd been told playtime was over. "Goodbye."

Streak sent one parting thought as she and Cutter glided out to sea on their way back to the pod. *Good shiny lady.*

Micah wrapped an arm around his sister's shoulder, giving her a quick hug.

He couldn't agree more.

Sixty-Seven

"Likanak finesc vadu, Ylkeet."

"In Galish, Bare'Kold." Reanne's voice coming through *Gladiator*'s speakers was unrecognizable thanks to her vocal modulator, but Cade would know that withering tone anywhere.

"You risk much, Sovereign." Bare'Kold sounded annoyed at having to repeat himself.

Cade appreciated the translation. Justin could provide him with one if there was a lag in the conversation, but he preferred being able to keep up with the discussion going on somewhere on Reanne's cruiser.

Bare'Kold's shuttle had docked while they were getting into position, but it sounded like the meeting had just begun.

"And we stand to gain much more. Our enemy is vulnerable. The time to strike is now."

"But I have been unable to get any information from Magee."

Reanne's laugh through the modulator reminded him of a rusty hinge. "Oh, Bare'Kold, you simple-minded fool. Do you honestly believe I had you take in Lt. Magee to obtain her secrets?"

Bare'Kold's voice sounded tight as a drum. "Then why did you?"

"To throw our enemies off balance. To give them a glimpse of our power. Breaking her was never the goal. Her loyalty to the Admiral is too strong. She'll take her secrets to the grave."

"Then terminate her. She has been increasingly difficult to control, especially after she saw the Admiral. You should not have allowed her to interact with him."

"You dare to question my orders?"

Bare'Kold's arrogance dropped several notches. "No, Sovereign. But I do question her value to us."

"Her value will be proven in due time. For now, it is enough that we have her and the Admiral does not. And since I am relieving you of the burden of her care, the discussion is over."

Bare'Kold was turning Magee over to Reanne? A knot tightened in Cade's gut. Whatever Reanne had in store for her, it wouldn't be pleasant.

"I have a new task for you." The muffled sound of methodical footsteps came over the comm, like Reanne was pacing. "Thanks to the incompetence of the Setarips and Teeli, Aurora Hawke has repeatedly slipped through my fingers."

Way to pass the buck, Reanne. Not that he expected any less.

"Their failure has forced me to come up with a new tactic, to use our resources in a different way. To make use of you. However, know this." Reanne's words punctuated the air like a jabbing finger. "I will not tolerate failure from you. Is that understood?"

Cade was willing to bet Bare'Kold had a lot to say on the matter. But the delegate wasn't an idiot. "Yes, Sovereign."

"Good. To defeat Aurora Hawke, we must strike a blow where it will do the most damage, where she is most vulnerable. To force her into submission."

The hairs on the back of Cade's nape stood up.

"You will take the Ecilam to Earth."

Cade almost fell out of his chair. He exchanged a startled glance with Justin before returning his focus to the comm.

Disdain coated Bare'Kold's reply. "You are asking me to transport these... creatures?"

The cold steel in Reanne's words sliced deep. "It's not a request."

"But—"

"One more word, Bare'Kold, and your presence on Earth will no longer be required. Is that understood?"

The threat wasn't implied. It was guaranteed.

Two beats passed before Bare'Kold responded. "Yes, Sovereign."

Reanne let the silence drag out before continuing. "The Ecilam are ideally suited to this task."

"And what task have you given them?"

"You do not need to know the details. When they've completed their mission, they will rejoin you at the Embassy. You will then be responsible for safely delivering them and their captives to me."

Captives? Who was she sending the Ecilam to abduct?

"The necessary containment systems have already been installed on your shuttle."

The goosebumps on his neck traveled down his arms.

Bare'Kold grunted in irritation. "Why do the captives require special containment?"

"Because they could kill you with one hand."

"One hand?" His tone changed from irritation to fear. "You are sending them to capture the Lost Ones."

"Yes. And they will succeed where your people have failed."

"What about Hawke? If she returns—"

"Do not concern yourself. Her ship is in Kraed space. She poses no threat."

Aurora was with the Kraed? He should have guessed. Clarek had probably suggested it.

But if Reanne was sending the Ecilam to Earth, and Aurora wasn't there, the targets had to be—

"And once I have control of her mother, Aurora Hawke will be neutralized forever."

Sixty-Eight

An earthy swear word left Cade's lips as an asteroid dropped into his gut. Reanne was going after Libra Hawke.

Terror vibrated in Bare'Kold's voice. "What if they break free of the containment system?"

"They won't." Even through the vocal modulator, Reanne managed to sound smug. "I'm sending a special passenger whose presence will guarantee their compliance. She's already onboard your shuttle."

Another curse word filled the small cabin, this one from Justin.

Cade echoed the sentiment. Reanne was sending Kreestol with the Setarips.

Aurora had been able to stop Kreestol, but she was a trained fighter and stronger than her mother. Would Libra fight her own sister? Could she? To his knowledge, Aurora's mother had never been in a physical confrontation. She might not even be able to summon the abilities she'd been born with.

A sound like scraping metal came over the line, the mechanical voice louder and clearer over the comm. "Do not fail me."

Bare'Kold's reply came out constricted, like someone had a hold of his throat. "I-I won't, Sovereign."

Silence followed for a few breaths, followed by the tap of retreating footsteps.

Bare'Kold muttered something in Teeli.

Cade glanced at Justin. "What did he say?"

"I'm not positive—it sounded colloquial—but based on context, I think it was either a prayer or a curse."

Bare'Kold started speaking rapidly in Teeli.

Justin slid on his headset and switched off the cabin speaker. "He's heading back to the shuttle. He's ordered the yacht to move into position to receive him."

Cade checked the tactical display. Sure enough, the yacht's thrusters glowed. A few moments later, it began maneuvering closer to the cruiser. He turned to Gonzo. "Any chance we can stop that yacht before it reaches Earth?" Preferably without killing Aurora's aunt.

"One-on-one, sure. *Gladiator* was designed to defend ships like that. But Reanne won't sit idly by when we start shooting, and I doubt the Ecilam ship will, either. If we attack, we could end up repeating the Burrow fight, but without the *Starhawke* to get us through."

"*Gladiator*'s a lot tougher than the *Nightingale*."

"Not tough enough to take on a Teeli cruiser, four warships, and the Ecilam. We'd end up disabled, captured, or destroyed."

Cade stared at the magnified forward camera display. Bare'Kold's shuttle exited the cruiser, heading for the yacht. Another shuttle, sleeker than Bare'Kold's, headed for the Ecilam ship. "Maybe we'll get lucky and the cruiser will leave first."

Gonzo snorted. "And maybe Reanne will suddenly develop a conscience and call the whole thing off."

Justin slid one side of his headset off. "Bare'Kold just got flight instructions. He's departing first. The cruiser and warships are going to hold their positions until the yacht has made the jump."

Cade blew out a breath. "Fine. We won't try to stop them. We'll send a message to the Admiral instead."

"We'll have to wait until all the ships have left the system. The outgoing signal would light us up like a Christmas tree."

"Fair enough. We'll wait until the party breaks up. The Admiral and Reynolds can handle evacuating Aurora's mom and Mya's parents before Bare'Kold's yacht makes it back to Earth." He wasn't crazy about the idea of sitting idly by while Reanne set her plan in motion, but getting his team captured or killed wouldn't help. The Admiral would still have at least three days lead time on the Ecilam. "Maybe Drew can goose the engines to—"

"What the hell!"

Gonzo's startled exclamation yanked Cade's head around. "What?"

Gonzo pointed at the aft camera display. "It just appeared out of nowhere."

Cade's gaze darted to the display. A massive shadow filled the image, blotting out the starfield and part of the moon's curve, coming up behind them. He checked the magnification. No, it really was that huge. And *Gladiator* was right in its path.

Sixty-Nine

"Nothing on tactical." Gonzo sent the display to the viewport. "No way it's a natural body. It's bouncing all our sensor scans."

Cade studied the image. "Could it be Kraed?" They were the only race with camouflage technology. And a reason to sneak up on the Teeli. Maybe Aurora had learned about the rendezvous from the Admiral and convinced Siginal Clarek to send a ship to back them up.

"No idea."

"Justin, we need the standard receiver ASAP." Listening in on Bare'Kold had just been kicked out of the top position. If the vessel was a Kraed ship, *Gladiator* was currently deaf to their hails.

"On it."

Cade checked the aft image. The shadowy vessel had moved closer, still on target with *Gladiator*.

A thread of unease wound through his belly. Without tactical data, it was impossible to judge how quickly the other ship was moving. And in the deep shadow of the moon with his ship's sensor deflector on, it was conceivable the other ship hadn't spotted them yet.

He didn't want *Gladiator* smashed like a bug on a windshield. He couldn't risk lowering the sensor deflector without announcing their presence to Reanne, but he could nudge *Gladiator* out of the approaching vessel's way.

He fired the starboard thrusters, angling *Gladiator*'s nose toward the moon. The controls responded sluggishly, with a noticeable lag, but a section of the starfield reappeared to port in the aft camera view, outlining the shadowy ship. "Gonzo, any readings?"

"Sensors still bouncing back, but I'm using the returning signals to build a 3D approximation of size and shape."

"Does it look like a Kraed ship?"

"Hard to say. It has some curves like a Kraed ship, but it doesn't look like much of anything yet."

"Keep at it." He glanced at Justin. "How much longer for the receiver?"

"Another minute."

By that point the other vessel would have caught up with them.

He checked the forward camera and tactical displays. Bare'Kold's yacht was no longer visible, but not because it had left for the jump window. It had taken up a position on the cruiser's starboard side, hidden by the larger ship's bulk. Two warships flanking the cruiser's port side, while the other two were at point in front and behind.

Reanne must have spotted the newcomer.

Hard not to. Even in the shadows, a ship that size couldn't hide.

Well, not once it dropped whatever camouflage had hidden its entry into the system.

Which made one thing clear. The new arrival *wanted* to be seen.

The Ecilam ship had also reacted. Tactical indicated they'd armed weapons, and the ship had pivoted to face the incoming vessel.

Clearly the mystery ship was no friend of the Ecilam or Teeli.

Which would make sense if it was a Kraed vessel. "Guys, I need data on that ship."

"Ten seconds," Justin said.

"Image is coming up on visual, but–" Gonzo broke off on a sharp inhale. "I'll be damned. It's a modular ship."

"Modular?" Cade's gaze darted to the aft display.

Gonzo had zoomed in on the ship, the camera finally able to pull out details. Gaps had opened in a non-linear pattern throughout the bulk of the ship, breaking it apart. In seconds, instead of one vessel, Cade was staring at seven.

And the smallest was still three times larger than *Gladiator.*

Because they needed another challenge. Or seven.

"Not Kraed."

"Not likely," Gonzo confirmed.

Which left... *who*?

The separation had also expanded the flight path, putting *Gladiator* back on a collision course with the closest of the seven ships.

"Justin?" Cade kept his gaze on that ship as he thumbed off the sensor deflector and brought the main engines up to full power. At this distance, disguising *Gladiator*'s sensor readings wasn't worth the loss of power.

"They're transmitting–"

"Incoming!"

Gonzo's shout coincided with a warning siren and three blips on the tactical display, racing for *Gladiator* with deadly accuracy.

"Countermeasures!" Cade took *Gladiator* into a steep dive as Gonzo launched the decoys.

"Countermeasures away."

A quick peek at the tactical display informed him only two of the projectiles had been diverted. One was still on target and closing fast. "Justin, hail them!"

"I can't. They're generating interference that's blocking all outgoing transmiss–"

The torpedo closed the distance and impacted, the booming echo through the hull drowning out Justin's comment.

Cade gritted his teeth. "Damage report."

"The projectile hit our communications array," Gonzo informed him.

"Destroyed?"

"I don't think so."

"But it may be boosting the jamming signal," Justin added.

"Are internal comms still working?"

"Seem to be."

"Then alert Drew. See if she can verify whether the transmitter is still functional while you work on cutting through that interference."

"On it."

Lights flared on the camera displays from the direction of the Teeli and Ecilam ships, indicating weapons fire and explosions, but Cade didn't spare them a glance. The only ship that mattered right now was the one shadowing him like the other pilot could read his mind.

He pulled *Gladiator* into an arc, doubling back away from the battle and toward the closest jump window. This wasn't his fight. His only goal was getting a message to the Admiral. Time to run.

But the other ship was faster. It shot past him like *Gladiator* was standing still and cut him off.

"Gonzo, target their engines. Let them know we're not staying for this party."

"Happy to."

Gladiator's weapons roared, striking the other ship's shields.

"Direct hit."

"Any damage?"

"No idea. Still unable to get sensor readings."

"Keep firing." Cade banked hard to port as the ship cut him off again. He punched *Gladiator*'s engines to full.

Another siren from Gonzo's console. "They're returning fire. Incoming torpedoes."

Four more projectiles headed their way. And they were too close for countermeasures. "Hard to port!" He called out the warning a millisecond before executing the maneuver, the shoulder straps of his harness biting into his skin. "Hard to starboard!"

Justin grunted, but Cade didn't dare take his gaze off the approaching torpedoes. "Full power to shields." He'd evaded one of the projectiles, and Gonzo had blasted another, but the two following behind struck hard. Debris from the torpedo casing smacked against the ship's armor plating, making the hull ring like an enormous bell.

The yoke bucked in Cade's hands. He fought to stabilize their course as warnings flashed on the displays, indicating severe power fluctuations. Whatever they'd been hit with, it had affected their systems rather than damaging structural integrity.

Not that being left adrift without power was a better option than being destroyed. "Justin, status on external comm?"

"Nothing yet."

"We may not have much time."

"I know." The addendum Justin muttered wasn't suitable for young audiences.

Cade echoed the sentiment.

The alert siren wailed. Four more incoming torpedoes.

"Gonzo?"

"I'm hitting them with everything we've got, but nothing seems to make a dent."

"Perfect." How many more ways could this situation go wrong?

And then *Gladiator*'s weapons fell silent.

"Gonzo, fire!"

"I can't. We just lost power to weapons."

"How?"

"I'm checking."

With no crossfire, the four torpedoes came at *Gladiator* with hungry maws open. Cade evaded, looping back and cutting in close to the other ship.

But his efforts to get the projectiles to change targets failed. They split around the enemy ship. Out of desperation, he fired the starboard ventral thrusters, pushing *Gladiator* onto its side. Two of the torpedoes sailed underneath the starboard wing, but the third and fourth impacted, throwing Cade back in his chair.

The blinding blast of energy against the shields lit up the cockpit, making Cade see spots.

"Shields down. Structural integrity holding," Gonzo informed him.

"How many hits can we take without shields?"

"I'd be able to answer that if I could figure out what they're firing at us."

Cade made another turn, trying to get some space between his ship and their attacker, but the navigation system fought him for control. It was like playing tug-of-war with an invisible opponent. "Navigation's sluggish. Have Drew check it on her end."

Justin followed his order as Cade continued to struggle with the yoke. "Come on, big guy, we need you." But instead of obeying his commands, *Gladiator*'s motion smoothed out and the engines dropped to a soft purr. "What the—"

Keeping one hand on the yoke, he tapped the engine controls, but the ship didn't respond. Pulling on the yoke had no effect, either. It was like *Gladiator* had switched itself to auto-pilot. "We have a serious problem."

Seventy

The yoke moved independent from any visible control. *Gladiator* slowly turning toward the enemy ship.

"Guess we won't be leaving after all." Cade muttered. He glanced over his shoulder at Gonzo. "Navigation's got a mind of its own. Anything working for you?"

"Nope."

"Justin? Tell me Drew's got a fix for us."

"Not yet. She's working on it."

Cade stared through the viewport at the other ship, which had altered trajectory to draw alongside as *Gladiator* approached. "She needs to work faster."

Their adversary matched their speed and heading, flying in perfect formation on *Gladiator*'s port wing.

The good news? The other ship wasn't firing at them anymore.

The bad news? It didn't need to. Whatever tech it had hit them with had taken control of *Gladiator*'s systems. They were hostages on their own ship.

This close, Cade could pick out a few details on the exterior camera view. The mystery ship had a freeform design that reminded him of a Kraed vessel, with a similar aesthetic appeal. In different circumstances, he might have been tempted to call it graceful. Instead, the curving lines looked menacing, like the hook of a talon or claw.

Williams' voice came over the shipwide intercom. "Anybody injured?"

Cade glanced at Gonzo and Justin, who both shook their heads. "No, we're okay up here. Bella, how about you?"

"Nothing that needs tending right now."

Justin shot Cade a look.

Interpretation—nothing broken, but probably bleeding. "Williams, would you—"

"Already on my way."

Gonzo stood. "I'll head down there too, see if I can help Drew."

Cade nodded, his gaze moving to the forward camera view and tactical display. They both seemed to be providing active feeds. "At least we're not blind."

The sensor data indicated Reanne's ship, the yacht, and two of the warships were on their way out of the system, with no sign of pursuit by the enemy ships. The six ships had focused on surrounding the Ecilam vessel, tightening the net.

So much for his hope that Reanne and Bare'Kold had been detained by the new arrivals.

The remaining two Teeli warships still showed on tactical, caught in the same spatial web as the Ecilam vessel.

Cade magnified the forward camera view.

The Ecilam ship circled the confines of the perimeter established by the modular ships like a shark trapped in a tank. However, the Ecilam were having surprising success avoiding or destroying the torpedoes launched at them. Based on their movements, it almost seemed like they knew how the other ships would attack and were countering in anticipation.

The Teeli warships, far from helping the Ecilam find an opening, seemed to be actively getting in the way, providing obstacles to the Ecilam ship's movements.

The Ecilam ship banked, opening fire on the smallest of the modular ships while making a run for the gap between it and the nearest ship. The other ship's shields absorbed the onslaught as it returned fire, but it was the

Teeli warship that cut across the Ecilam ship's bow, forcing it to alter course to avoid a collision.

The Ecilam responded by firing a heavy barrage on the warship.

The resulting explosion snapped the warship in two.

Cade flinched. No way was that an accident. The Ecilam had fired on their ally with deliberate intent. Why? Just because the Teeli warship had cut across their path like—

His stomach bottomed out. "Like they didn't have control."

Another vicious barrage from the Ecilam scattered the second Teeli warship into chunks of debris. The Ecilam ship continued to circle, using the remains of the two warships as physical shielding from the attacking ships.

He checked their heading. *Gladiator* was on course to enter the arena, their smaller size making it relatively easy to slip between the modular ships. Was his crew to be the next sacrifice in this deadly game? Without shields they wouldn't last any longer than the warships.

The modular ships pulled in the perimeter, closing the gaps and firing torpedoes. The Ecilam ship evaded, returning fire.

He calculated the time to reach the perimeter. Three minutes, maybe less. If this was going to be their end, they had to make it count for something. "Justin, tell me the external comm signal is cleared." They had to get a message off to the Admiral before the Ecilam ship turned them into Swiss cheese.

"Hmm?" Justin turned to gaze at him like he'd asked about the weather.

"The external comm signal. Have you cleared it?"

A frown line appeared between his brows. "Comm signal?"

Cade's heartbeat stuttered. "Justin? What's wrong?"

"Wrong?"

"Yes, wrong!" Cade grabbed the arms of Justin's chair and swiveled him so they were knee to knee. "Talk to me."

Justin's head listed to the side, his eyes drooping. "Can't... talk." And then his body slumped forward.

Cade caught him in an awkward hug. Reaching around with one hand, he opened the shipwide comm. "Tam! I need you up here."

"Acknowledged."

Cade gently righted Justin's limp form so he could see his face. "Justin? Can you hear me?"

Justin mumbled something unintelligible, his eyes closed.

Cade's gaze darted to the viewport.

The Ecilam ship swept under an incoming torpedo but a second smashed into its ventral shields from below, creating a corona of light.

Williams' footsteps thundered down the corridor. "What happened?" he asked as he took in the scene in the cockpit and crouched beside Justin.

"No idea. He acted drugged, confused, and then passed out."

Williams pulled a med scanner out of his kit, one beefy hand gripping Justin's shoulder, pinning him to the chair while he ran the scanner over his body. "The bridge wasn't hit?"

"Not recently. He was fine until a minute ago."

Justin gave an audible gasping inhalation, then another, like he was having trouble getting air.

"What's wrong with him?"

"Tachycardia and apneustic respiration." Williams said it calmly, but Cade picked up the worry in his voice. "We need to get him to the infirmary."

Cade stared out the viewport. In less than two minutes, *Gladiator* would be thrown into the center of the pitched battle, rendering any actions to help Justin moot.

But that wouldn't stop him from fighting for every second. He hit the shipwide comm again. "Drew, we need the external comm cleared, now!"

"Working on it."

He couldn't ask for anything more. Rising, he slid one arm behind Justin's back. "Let's go."

Seventy-One

Justin's dead weight and wheezing breath made every step to the infirmary pure torture. "Hang in there, buddy." Cade angled his body sideways so he could follow Williams through the narrow corridor. No way could all three of them fit side-by-side.

Williams lowered the med platform in the infirmary while Cade held Justin upright. He estimated they had less than a minute until all hell broke loose, but at the moment all he cared about was Justin's next breath.

Williams guided Justin onto the platform and strapped him in with the efficiency of years of experience. "Mask," he said, pointing to the oxygen mask on the swing arm.

Cade affixed it to Justin's face. "This will help." He had no idea if it would help or not but talking kept him focused. The ship hadn't given the slightest hiccup, gliding along like a fish in a pond.

A pond filled with piranha.

Williams rested a hand on his arm. "I've got this."

The unspoken message was clear. "Keep me posted."

Williams nodded.

Exiting the infirmary, Cade sprinted to the cockpit. He had to find a way to defend his ship. Change course. Save his team.

He skidded to a stop, gripping the back of the pilot's chair.

Adjusted his thinking.

No more weapons fire. No more explosions. The battle was over.

The Ecilam vessel sat quietly in the center of the six modular ships. The exterior didn't show any signs of damage, but clearly its systems had been incapacitated, ending the fight.

The ship that had captured *Gladiator* moved between its companions, headed for the Ecilam vessel. *Gladiator* didn't follow. Instead, its reverse thrusters fired, slowing the ship to a crawl.

Cade let his breath out on a long exhale.

Gladiator wouldn't be cannon fodder. Well, not at the moment.

He opened a channel to the engine room. "Drew, what's our status?"

"Not good. All the ship's systems are functional, but I can't get control."

"Any idea what's causing it?"

"Best guess is some kind of nanotech, but way more advanced than anything I've seen. Since I can't run any internal diagnostics, I'm having to use handheld scanners to get readings. Anything hardwired to propulsion, navigation, or defense is infected and won't respond, with the exception of the sensor shield. I don't know if that's because it wasn't active, or because something about the Kraed tech prevents infection."

"What about life support?"

"It's still running, thankfully, but it could go whenever these little buggers decide to switch it off."

"How did they get in?"

"Best guess? Those torpedoes they hit us with weren't designed to destroy. They were designed to deliver a payload. Our shields didn't deflect the blow, they channeled it, absorbing the nanotech like a sponge taking in water. After they infiltrated our shields, they made their way into the systems through micro-fissures in the hull."

"And took over."

"Exactly."

"How do we regain control?"

"Good question. We need a way to draw the nanotech out of the system, or to destroy it without also wreaking havoc with the systems it's connected to. Unfortunately, without knowing anything about what I'm facing, or who designed it, I'm working in the dark."

"What about the external communications? Can we send a message?"

"Nope. The jamming signal is still preventing all external comms, though the system itself doesn't seem to be infected. That's why the internal comm works fine. No sign of visible damage to the transmitter either, but to verify I'd have to crawl out on the hull."

"Any way to break through the interference so we can contact the Admiral?" Bare'Kold and his harbingers of doom would be on their way to Earth by now.

"None that I can see. Does Justin have any ideas?"

Cade swallowed. "Justin's in the infirmary."

"*What?*" Drew packed a lot of emotion into that one syllable.

"He passed out after we lost control of the ship. Tam's treating him."

Her voice rose an octave. "Is he okay?"

"He's stable." He hoped that was true.

A pregnant pause. "I'll see what I can do with the interference."

"I'll notify you of any changes." He switched off the comm and sank into the pilot's chair. He'd rather be helping Tam or Bella, but right now his team needed him to be their eyes and ears. That meant staying put.

It would be easier to accept their hostage status if they'd accomplished their mission. Instead, he felt like he was sitting on a bomb. He could hear the ticking of the clock in his head, counting down.

If Kreestol and the Ecilam reached Earth, and succeeded in abducting Aurora's mother, Reanne would have the bargaining chip she needed to bring Aurora to her knees.

He couldn't let that happen, for more reasons than he could count. If Reanne managed to turn Aurora into a Necri soldier—or worse—no one in the galaxy would be safe.

Which meant focusing on gathering information and finding solutions. No time for self-recrimination.

His gaze moved to the modular ship that had captured *Gladiator*, now visible beside the Ecilam ship on the forward camera view.

Huh, that was interesting. The two were of similar size, and strangely, similar configuration.

Setarips were notorious thieves, taking whatever they needed, usually with excessive force. Had the owners of the modular ships come to reclaim a vessel the Ecilam had stolen? But if that were true, who had the Ecilam crossed? Not Teeli, certainly. And the technology was far beyond anything humans had designed. Which left the Kraed.

Except all Setarips avoided the Kraed like the plague. Even the Ecilam wouldn't attempt to steal a Kraed ship. They weren't suicidal. Besides, the Kraed wouldn't be in this part of Fleet space without the Admiral's knowledge, and he would have told them to hail *Gladiator*, not jam communications and attack.

An enormous question mark hung like an elongated crescent moon in space. What was it Sherlock Holmes had said? If you eliminate the impossible, then whatever is left, no matter how improbable, is the truth.

Which left one inescapable conclusion.

His team had just made first contact with an unknown technologically advanced species.

Seventy-Two

Mya stared at the bridgescreen, the steady stream of light from the interstellar jump providing visual background noise to the never-ending circle of her thoughts.

What have I done?

In the heat of the moment, with the crew trapped on Drakar, and then during the faceoff with Siginal, her choices had seemed pretty damn clear. But now, in the light of cold reflection, they seemed rash, foolish, destructive.

In the space of an hour she'd managed to get Jonarel and Star banished from their home, cut herself off from the Suulh on Azaana, and created a rift with the Kraed, their best hope for assistance with helping the Suulh.

She sank deeper into the captain's chair, allowing her head to fall back, her gaze moving to the ceiling. She didn't need to be here. Star was perfectly capable of monitoring the jump while the rest of the crew slept.

But sleep had eluded her.

It didn't help that she'd imagined Jonarel in his cabin, nursing the wounds she'd unintentionally inflicted upon him through his father. His pain might as well have been hers. Was this what Aurora dealt with all the time? Feeling the pain of others like it was her own?

If so, she hadn't given Aurora nearly enough credit for mental and emotional fortitude.

Then again, maybe what she was feeling wasn't really pain at all. Maybe it was guilt. Why hadn't she taken a little more time to assess the situation? Bounced a few ideas around? Considered how her actions would impact others?

She'd been focused on Aurora, on the threat Siginal posed, but that wasn't an excuse. If anything, she'd made Aurora's situation worse.

The soft hiss of the lift doors opening drew her attention.

Kire stepped off the lift, an uncharacteristic slouch in his spine and a sallowness to his skin. He met Mya's gaze and grimaced. "You couldn't sleep, either?"

She shook her head.

He dropped into the chair to her left, pivoting to face her. "What's on your mind?"

"Jonarel. Star. Aurora. The Suulh on Azaana." She could go on, but that seemed like a long enough list to start.

"That sounds about right." He sighed. "I never imagined Siginal would react like this. They're his *kids*."

"I know." She'd always thought Libra was harsh with Aurora when she didn't follow her expectations, but compared to Siginal, she was a paragon of compassion and understanding. "Do you think he meant it? Or was he reacting in the heat of the moment?"

"It may not matter. Even if he wanted to change his mind, he might believe he has to follow through for the sake of the clan. Their system of honor and loyalty doesn't allow for a lot of flexibility or forgiveness unless Jon and Star fall in line."

"Which they'll never do." She may have acted rashly, but she seriously doubted either of them had. The speed with which they'd come up with and executed a plan to escape Drakar indicated they'd anticipated the turn of events and been prepared to deal with the situation head-on.

"No, they won't."

Mya's gaze drifted back to the bridgescreen. "What about the Suulh on Azaana?" She couldn't look at him when she voiced the fear that had settled into her stomach. Didn't want to see a confirmation in his eyes. "Will he take his anger out on them?"

"Never."

His certainty surprised her. She met his gaze. "You're sure?"

"Absolutely. I've been studying the ancient texts of the Kraed ever since our last trip to Drakar, and one of their core tenets is protecting others from harm. As a rule, they don't believe in aggression. They don't even have a word in their language for revenge. They believe in justice, not vengeance, although sometimes their form of justice can be violent."

"Like when Jonarel attacked Cade at the Academy."

"Exactly. From his point of view, he was delivering justice to an aggressor. It was Reanne who turned his reaction up to thermonuclear. But the Suulh on Azaana live under the Kraed code of protection. Even the idea of harming them would be abhorrent to the Kraed, no matter what you or Roe may do."

She let out the breath she'd been holding. "That's something."

"The hardest part for them will be not hearing from you and Roe."

"I guess we won't be making any more under-the-radar visits."

"Probably not, unless Star can figure out another way around the Kraed defense system. Even if she does, I suspect Signal will be adding new patrols and maybe some orbital defenses around Azaana, as well. His wounded pride will demand it."

"Yeah." She ran a hand along the inlaid wood of the captain's chair. "What about Aurora? Do you think she'll forgive me for screwing things up?"

"Forgive you?" Kire snorted. "For what? Siginal wants to put her in an ivory tower. You knocked that tower down. I think she'll applaud you."

"Really?"

"Really. I certainly wanted to applaud when you took him down a few pegs."

The corner of her lip twitched. "That did feel good."

"Damn right. His head is on backwards when it comes to Roe. He needs to be straightened out."

"I just wish Jonarel and Star didn't have to pay the price."

"Me, too. Hopefully it's a temporary situation. Siginal will have to see reason if he wants to protect his clan from the Teeli."

"Do you think they'd attack Kraed space?"

"With Reanne in charge, I'd believe anything. She's whacked."

"Very." A cold chill raised goosebumps on Mya's skin. "Would Siginal attack the Teeli first? Beat her to the punch?"

"I doubt it. Again, they don't believe in aggression. I think that's one of the reasons why Siginal is so focused on Aurora as his lynchpin. She's a protector, just like the Kraed. He's viewing this entire situation from a defensive strategy, how best to protect his clan, his planet. I'd be shocked if it's even occurred to him to take the fight to the Teeli."

"But Aurora's only one person. How could he expect her to protect all the Kraed?"

"I'm not sure. Maybe he doesn't. Maybe he sees her in a symbolic role. His eagerness to have the Suulh establish a new home in Kraed space supports the idea of forging a permanent bond between the two races. As a defensive strategist, he would see the great value in Aurora's abilities, and the power she draws from the rest of the Suulh."

A flicker of latent anger lapped at Mya's throat. "He doesn't think much of my abilities."

Kire grinned. "That's because he's an idiot."

His matter-of-fact delivery drew a bark of laughter from her chest.

"Seriously, it's a cultural thing. The Kraed don't like showing weakness. After they reach maturity, going to see a healer for anything that isn't life-threatening is a mark of shame."

Which explained Siginal's odd reaction to her healing of the injury Jonarel had inflicted. He'd seen her treatment as a dig or rebuke. "Jonarel doesn't believe that."

"Jon isn't a typical Kraed."

No kidding.

"He's always been fascinating by your abilities, with how quickly you can heal injury. He sees the value, the strength in what you can do. He doesn't let his ego get in the way. In fact, I've sometimes wondered if he's allowed himself to get injured on missions so he'd have an excuse to be treated by you."

She blinked. "You're kidding."

He shook his head, not a hint of irony on his face. "You don't give yourself enough credit."

"Credit?"

"For how you draw people to you. For the feelings of love and loyalty you inspire."

"I don't—"

"Yes, you do. You've just been living in Roe's shadow most of your life, so you don't see it. I know I was against Roe going off with Cade while we visited the Suulh homeworld, and I've missed having her onboard, but I think this time apart has been good for you. You're finding your power."

"And falling on my face."

He smiled. "We all do that. It's part of life. Every decision has consequences. Sometimes we know what to expect, and sometimes we don't. The point is to make those decisions, and then face the consequences squarely. That's the mark of a leader."

"Aurora's the—"

He gave her a pointed look, cutting her off. "When the boot fits, wear it."

Seventy-Three

Cade zoomed in the camera view on the closest modular ship. He needed clues, anything that would help him prepare for what was certain to be a defining moment in his life. Hopefully not the final one.

The ship's hull was unlike anything he'd seen before. It had a textured look like interlocking scales. Except these scales wouldn't have come from any terrestrial creature. More like a moon-sized dragon.

The color was also surprising. Rather than the black he'd assumed at first glance, the base color for most of the ship appeared to be a deep emerald green. Light from the star revealed a striking pattern of black and gold chevrons layered along the base. Beautiful, actually, in a deadly kind of way, like the markings on a python.

A flare of light in the forward camera yanked his attention away.

The Ecilam ship was no longer still. Its body shook as explosions bloomed along the hull like a fireworks finale.

Cade's breath caught. Had the other ship fired?

No.

The explosions continued in a lethal line on the ship's port side, engulfing the modular ship through the attached airbridge. Debris from the death throes of the Ecilam ship tore into the modular ship's hull at point blank range, ripping ragged holes in the exterior and shredding the point of connection, setting both ships adrift.

The six other ships were in motion before Cade had finished processing what he was seeing, closing the distance to their dying companion.

He was too far away to see any bodies, but they had to be floating in the debris. The structural integrity of both ships had been severely compromised, their outlines only vaguely recognizable.

An icicle dragged along Cade's spine.

The Ecilam had chosen suicide over capture, which made no sense. All previous encounters with the Ecilam had indicated they'd do anything to survive.

What horrors awaited on the modular ships that would prompt such a decision?

What did they know he didn't?

He opened a channel to the engine room. "Drew, please tell me you're making progress."

"What happened?" She'd clearly picked up on his tone.

"Let's just say our future isn't looking too bright."

"I wish I had good news. It'll be hours before I can make any headway here. But I do have one Hail Mary idea. We use the manual controls to eject an escape pod. They're independent of the main system, so they're not infected. We program the pod with a pre-set course that will take it away from the star and embed our message to the Admiral in the distress signal. Once it's out of range of the interference from the ships, the signal should be picked up by the nearest ICS beacon."

Which would direct the message to the Admiral. "What would stop the modular ships from destroying the pod when we launch it?"

"I could set a time delay on the transmission and propulsion. Let it drift away from *Gladiator* like it short-circuited, then have the program initiate the burn a few hours later. With the low energy signature at docking release, they may not notice it at all. If they do, we'll just have to hope they assume it's a malfunction and not worth investigating."

Cade glanced at the remnants of the Ecilam and modular ship, now surrounded by the six remaining ships. "How long do you need?"

"Five minutes, maybe less."

At least with their attacker focused on the debris, *Gladiator* was being ignored. Drew would get her shot. "Notify me when you're ready to launch."

Seventy-Four

The escape pod tumbled end over end in the aft camera view, quickly swallowed up by the vastness of space.

Drew's voice came over Cade's comband. "Any indication they noticed the pod?"

Cade gazed out the viewport. "Not yet." The largest of the modular ships had moved next to the two broken vessels, blocking them from view. Only two of the remaining ships were visible from his perspective, their positions indicating they were acting as sentries. He assumed the other ships were focused on salvage or gathering the bodies of their dead. They didn't seem in any hurry to leave. "They're still focused on the wreckage."

"Good news for us."

"We were due."

Williams had checked in a few minutes earlier to confirm he'd stabilized Justin, who was exhibiting all the symptoms of a mild traumatic brain injury. Williams was at a loss to explain why. He'd recommended they stop using the ship's comm system until they had more data, since that was the one variable that set Justin apart.

Unfortunately, his number one was too out of it to answer questions, and Williams estimated it could be a couple days before he'd recover enough to leave the infirmary.

That was the best-case scenario. Worst case? When their attackers turned their attention to *Gladiator*–and they would before long–they'd all need medical assistance.

But his team wouldn't go down without a fight. *Gladiator* was far from defenseless. His ship had been designed to repel invaders.

Gonzo had successfully closed the blast doors for the central room using the manual controls, isolating the airlock and gangway from the rest of the ship, while simultaneously blockading the corridors leading to the cockpit and infirmary as well as the forward and aft stairwells. If nothing else, it would buy them time.

Gonzo appeared in the cockpit hatchway, his wiry frame wrapped in flexible body armor and a rifle in each hand. He set one of the rifles on the co-pilot's seat, along with two spare power packs. "How's it looking out there?"

"Quiet."

Gonzo peered out the viewport, lines of tension on his lean face. "Wish we knew who we were fighting."

Cade grunted. "I wish we knew *why* we were fighting. We didn't start this."

Gonzo nodded, his gaze still on the enemy ships. "Maybe we'll find out." He turned to Cade. "If not, the longer we can hold them off, the better the chance the pod will reach transmission range."

"I know." Cade pushed to his feet. "I'll go suit up."

While Gonzo kept an eye on the enemy ships, Cade took the long route to his cabin—down the forward stairs to the lower level, past the galley and communal areas to the aft stairwell in the engine room. Drew gave him a tense wave as he passed, her focus on the array of objects she'd gathered on her workstation. "You need to suit up," he reminded her.

She gave him another wave, this one decidedly annoyed. "I will."

Her suit sat on the deck beside her feet. Gonzo must have brought it down, correctly assuming she'd focus on the puzzle of the nanotech rather than her own safety.

"Five minutes, Bella."

She glanced up, the anger in her eyes startling him. Drew had the longest fuse of anyone he knew, but right now she was royally pissed.

Not at him, apparently. The anger mellowed to frustration as she held his gaze. "They've messed with our ship."

"I know."

"And Justin..." Her gaze lifted as though she could see through the deck to the infirmary above. "They must have done something to him."

He'd reached the same conclusion. How was still a mystery. "Tam's watching out for him. He'll be okay." He stepped to her side, resting a hand on her shoulder and squeezing. "And Justin would want you to take care of yourself." He glanced significantly at her folded body suit.

She followed the direction of his gaze and sighed. "Yeah, I know." Setting down the tool in her hand, she snagged the suit off the deck. "He'd say the same thing to you." She gestured to his clothes.

He nodded. "Already on my way." Pivoting, he took the stairs three at a time, pausing briefly when he reached the upper deck, poking his head into the infirmary.

Justin lay on the med platform by the far bulkhead, his body in repose. The mask still covered his mouth and nose, but he seemed to be breathing more regularly.

Williams was already pulling on body armor, his gaze tracking Justin's bio readings at the same time. A rifle and power packs lay on the empty med platform closest to the doorway. Also delivered by Gonzo, no doubt. However, the items looked incongruous in a room designed for healing.

"You need anything?" Cade asked.

Williams glanced over. "Besides answers to my questions and a stiff drink?"

"Yeah."

"No."

Cade lifted his chin in Justin's direction. "Any change?"

"He got agitated a few minutes ago, so I sedated him to keep him calm. Rest is the best treatment I can offer for now."

He wanted to ask if Williams had any theories on the cause, but now wasn't the time. He motioned to his comband. "Holler if you need anything."

"I will."

Cade changed into his body armor in record time, exiting his cabin and retracing his steps through the engine room to the cockpit. Drew was still working at her table, but he was pleased to note her armor was on, and she'd holstered a couple pistols at her hips.

When he reached the cockpit, he found Gonzo seated in the co-pilot's chair. "Anything to report?"

Gonzo gestured to the tactical display. "The readings on the Ecilam ship and the debris from the downed modular ship are almost gone. Whatever system they're using to work salvage, it's efficient."

"They've cleared all the debris?" That seemed hard to believe, given the short timeframe. "Those were not small ships."

"It's possible that the largest modular ship is designed to store massive objects, more like a garbage scow than a battle cruiser. But I'm still not able to scan through their hull to confirm my suppositions."

"I'm surprised the external scanners still work. The nanotech has had plenty of time to take them over."

"What would be the point? *Gladiator*'s external scanners can't provide those ships with any data they can't get on their own, and we can't get any info about them, either."

"True." He settled into the pilot's seat, placing his weapons close at hand. "Let's just hope the escape pod makes it far enough out before—"

"The ships are moving."

Cade's gaze snapped to the forward camera. Sure enough, the two sentry ships were in motion, and another of the modular ships appeared from behind the large central ship. "I think we just ran out of time."

Gonzo thumbed on his comband. "Drew, Williams, the ships are heading our way."

"Acknowledged," Williams replied.

"Time?" Drew asked.

Cade did a quick calculation based on their heading and apparent speed. "Four minutes. Maybe less."

"What's the plan?"

"Gonzo and I will take point fore and aft, hold them off as long as we can."

"What about me?"

"That depends. Any chance you can reclaim control of engines? Or weapons?"

"Any chance you can buy me three hours?"

"No."

"There's your answer."

Apparently Drew got snarky when she was angry. "Then I want you in the infirmary with Williams to protect Justin. Whatever happens, do what you can to buy time. And stay alive."

Her reply was a lot more subdued. "Understood."

Gonzo rose, remaining by Cade's chair. "That goes for you too, mi amigo."

Cade met his gaze, silent understanding passing between them. Despite what he'd told Drew, this could be the last time he'd see his team. Was this how Leonidas of Sparta had felt facing the Persian army?

He reached out a hand.

Gonzo clasped it, forearm to forearm. "There's nowhere else I'd rather be."

He returned Gonzo's firm grip. "There's no one else I'd rather have on my side."

Gonzo held his gaze for a three count, took one last look at the approaching ships, and exited through the hatchway.

Seventy-Five

I'm sorry, Aurora.

The irony of Cade's situation wasn't lost on him. Aurora had ditched him because she feared for his safety. But in protecting him from herself, she'd sealed his fate. Instead of being onboard the *Starhawke* with her right now, he was facing whatever awaited him inside the modular ships.

He couldn't help feeling like he'd let her down. Not just because their message might never reach the Admiral. Even if it did, and her mother evaded the trap Reanne had set, Aurora would still probably blame herself for his death. He didn't want her to. It wasn't her fault. As he'd told her, his job required continually putting his life on the line.

He also didn't blame her for sending him away. He understood her reasons, her emotion-based logic, even if he disagreed.

Unfortunately, he had no way to tell her.

And no time to dwell on it.

He turned his attention to the approaching enemy ships. All six had moved into flight formation, coming right at him. At this range, they could obliterate *Gladiator* in the blink of an eye if they wanted to.

But he doubted they would. They seemed to have a very different goal in mind.

Which did nothing to ease the tension between his shoulder blades.

As they drew closer, they slowed, their motion drawing them tighter to one another, eliminating the gaps.

The scale plating on their hulls began to shift, slithering like snakes across the surface.

Fascinating, really.

And scary as hell.

The hulls of the ships expanded outward like a mechanical inhalation, the shifting scales touching and locking together until the seams between the ships disappeared, forming a monstrous whole.

With the unusual coloring and scaled hull, he couldn't shake the image of a giant coiled cobra with hood extended, its body poised to strike.

And *Gladiator* was the mouse paralyzed by fear.

And nanotech.

"They've reintegrated the ships," he informed his team. "Still on approach."

An oval opening appeared on the lower half of the enormous ship, a cool yellow light filtering out.

The deck beneath his boots vibrated as *Gladiator*'s engines kicked in, propelling the ship toward the aperture. He zoomed in on the image, but the yellow light didn't do much to illuminate the interior. Logic told him it was a bay of some sort. "We're heading to a docking bay."

"Any details you can give us?" Gonzo asked.

"It's difficult to see inside. The opening is large enough to accommodate *Gladiator*, but just barely. I don't think that's an accident."

"What do you mean?"

"Their ship's hull moves like snakeskin, completely pliable. They may be able to control the size of the opening." And *Gladiator* was right at that opening, the reverse thrusters firing to slow their momentum. "We're passing inside."

The yellow glow surrounded him, filtering into the cockpit as the opening closed behind the ship, creating an eerie sensation of being swallowed whole. "They've sealed us inside. The ship fits, but the bulkheads are only three meters away." Or was it four? They seemed to be shifting as he watched.

The thrusters continued to fire on their own, bringing the ship into a hover and slowly lowering it to the deck. He searched his surroundings. "The interior has the same scaly look as the hull." And the same deep emerald green coloring. "No visible hatches."

"Any signs of life?"

"Not yet."

Gladiator settled to the deck with the lightness of a butterfly. "Nice landing," he muttered, snagging his rifle and rising. The green light that indicated the gangway lock was engaged winked out. "They just unlocked the gangway security. I'm moving into position."

"Roger," Gonzo replied.

"We're ready," Drew added.

The blast door cut off the corridor right before it reached the central room. A tactical panel built into the starboard bulkhead allowed him to monitor the security cameras on the gangway and above the blast doors. Gonzo had a similar panel in the aft corridor. So far, the nanotech hadn't taken steps to disable them.

Gonzo had rigged several traps in the central room—some lethal, others designed to incapacitate. Additional devices were positioned all over the ship, all tied into their combands so anyone on the team could activate them.

Drew had done something similar with a couple handheld scanners, placing them in the central room near each blast door to give the team some tactical data on whoever showed up. "The exterior is reading as a breathable nitrogen-oxygen atmosphere," she informed them.

Cade peered at the images coming through from the video feed on the gangway. "Any sign of movement?"

"Nothing yet," Gonzo replied. "No, wait. Aerial drone just appeared lower left."

"I see it." But he didn't know what to make of it. The egg-shaped object had the same emerald-green coloring and scaled appearance as the ship, but no defining features. He couldn't spot any visible propulsion, either. "Explosive device?"

"Not according to Drew's scanners."

The drone hovered at the base of the gangway for several moments before continuing up the ramp.

"Drew? Any thoughts?"

"The scanner readings indicate it has a transmitter and receiver. Maybe some form of communication device?"

That sounded promising. He tracked the path of the drone up the ramp, switching to the central room feed when the drone stopped near the ramp's interior control panel.

"It's transmitting something," Drew said. "I'm not sure—" She and Gonzo swore at the same time. "Jamming signal."

"I've lost the signal for the explosives in the central room," Gonzo said. "Correction. I've lost signal on all the explosives."

Cade tensed. "Could the drone trigger them?" He didn't want his team wiped out by their own traps.

"Possibly."

"Start disabling all the ones in your area."

"On it."

"But my scanners and our combands still work," Drew said. "The jamming signal is very focused on—"

A voice flowed out of the ship's internal speakers, making Cade jump and startling Drew into silence. The syllables were unintelligible but strong, and spoken with the authority of a command. The texture of the sounds wasn't like anything he'd ever heard before. Not a human voice, definitely.

"Uh, did anyone understand that?"

"Not a clue," Gonzo replied.

"No," Williams said.

"No idea," Drew said, "but it confirms the nanotech has moved into the internal comm system. The transmission came from the drone."

Good thing they'd switched to using their combands.

He tapped the comm panel next to the tactical display to open a shipwide channel. The panel obeyed the command, so the nanotech hadn't shut them out of the system. Yet.

"This is Commander Cade Ellis of the Fleet ship *Gladiator*. Why have you captured my ship?" He doubted their captors would understand Galish, but without Justin's help, it was his only option.

Silence greeted his statement for one breath, two, then the voice responded with another string of unintelligible sounds, followed by the same command as before, delivered with more force.

Definitely didn't understand Galish. "Drew, can you run that through the ship's translator?"

"If the nanotech will let me." A couple seconds passed. "The translator isn't finding any matches."

Justin, we need you. Cade tapped the comm panel to reply to the drone. "We can't understand you. You've seized control of our systems and prevented–"

The distinct hiss of air escaping made him whirl around, his gaze sweeping the area to locate the source. Then his ears popped. "Drew, Gonzo, are you–"

"We're losing atmosphere," Drew confirmed. "The nanotech is venting it out of the ship."

"Is the entire bay depressurizing?"

"No, just the—" She broke off in a coughing fit. "It's just behind the blast doors." Deep inhale. "The central room still has atmo." More coughing.

Cade's lungs protested the thinning air as well. "They want—" Cough. "The blast doors—" Cough. "Open."

Gonzo wheezed, his voice barely recognizable. "What do we do?"

Their enemy had proven they could kill them without presenting a target.

Which didn't leave him a choice.

"Open the doors."

Seventy-Six

The hydraulics on the manual release opened the door in seconds. Cade sucked in air, fighting the hacking cough that wanted to double him over. He needed to keep his focus on the drone.

The hiss of lost atmosphere ceased. With the blast door eliminated, he now stood eye to eye with the device as it hovered in the opening for the gangway. Well, eye to optical sensor. He had no doubt he was being watched.

He spotted Gonzo in the shadows of the opposite doorway, the barrel of his rifle aimed at the drone.

"Cade?"

"No aggressive moves. This thing still controls your explosives."

Gonzo slowly lowered the rifle.

"How many did you disable?"

"All the ones in the bunk area and by the infirmary. Everything in the lower decks and by you is still armed."

Which left a lot of firepower at the drone's disposal.

Cade moved cautiously into the central room, his gaze never leaving the drone.

The drone responded by drifting closer. The strange alien voice came over the ship's internal speakers again. This time it sounded a little less domineering, but no less assertive.

"Any idea what it's saying?" Gonzo murmured.

"Only a hunch." Experience told him their enemy had correctly identified him as the leader. And that the command being given was directed at him. Holding his arms away from his body, he set his rifle on the table to his left. "I'm going to see if I can leave the ship with the drone."

"By yourself?"

"Yes. I need you to disable the explosives. And I want Drew working on that nanotech." He removed his smaller weapons from their holsters and added them to the rifle on the table, still keeping his gaze on the drone.

When he straightened, it drifted back toward the gangway.

Drew's voice came over his comband. "You're taking a big chance."

"That's the job. You're in charge while I'm gone. Gonzo, after you disable your devices, keep an eye on the gangway, but play nice as long as they do, understood?"

"Understood." Drew and Gonzo said in unison.

Cade faced the drone. No weapons. No plan. Just a hope and a prayer. He spread his arms and gestured to the opening behind the drone. "Lead the way."

Seventy-Seven

The drone hovered at Cade's eye level a meter in front of him, effectively blocking his view of what lay directly ahead. But as he walked through the bay along *Gladiator*'s port side, he got a close up of the surrounding space.

The bay was remarkable for its complete lack of functional delineation. Most bays had tie downs, docking clamps, consoles or control panels at strategic points. The interior of this bay was seamless, smooth walls of interlocking emerald scales the size of his palm. Which is why he didn't see the doorway that peeled back like a veil in front of him.

The drone passed through the opening. When Cade hesitated, the voice emanated from the device in a clipped command. Whether the sounds translated to *come* or *follow* or *don't stop* he couldn't say, but he obeyed the clear intention, stepping out of the bay into a passageway.

The bulkheads here continued the same pattern of emerald green scales, while a repeating black and gold geometric pattern undulated along the deck, echoing the markings he'd seen on the ship's hull.

But the bold colors weren't what caught his attention. As the drone moved forward, the curved bulkheads flowed with it, shifting in an ever-changing maze. A bulkhead that had been within arm's reach would slide away and realign to create part of a new passageway or close off a previous one.

Only the repeating pattern on the deck remained constant, but since it looked the same from all directions, and he'd been watching the drone and bulkheads rather than the floor when he exited the bay, he'd lost his frame of reference.

He couldn't chart a path back to his ship, or even say for certain in which direction he'd need to go. He checked his comband but couldn't get any sensor readings to provide a clue, either.

Welcome to Wonderland, Alice.

The drone didn't have any problem navigating. It continued at a steady pace through the passageways.

The shifting walls made a subtle rustle, like a snake slithering through dried leaves. It was the only sound that accompanied his footsteps.

Where was the crew? The presence of life support systems and artificial gravity indicated the ship wasn't run exclusively by drones and automation, but the battalions of heavily armed soldiers he'd anticipated had failed to appear.

Then again, with bulkheads that moved like living beings, did the ship need a large security force? Or any security at all? If he attempted to attack his drone guide, he had no doubt he'd quickly find himself enclosed in an impenetrable cell, and possibly deprived of air until he blacked out.

The drone's forward motion ceased.

He stopped next to it. A second later the bulkheads converged. He reacted on instinct, spinning to put his back to the drone and dropping into a battle-ready pose. But the green-scaled walls halted half a meter away, forming a perfect cylinder just wide enough to accommodate him and the drone.

And then the deck rose.

He wobbled, adjusting his balance as the force of the upward acceleration pressed against his boots. "Going up," he murmured. He glanced at the drone, which had remained at his eye level. Either its independent propulsion system could perfectly match the motion of the unconventional lift, or it had somehow tied into the mechanism before it began moving.

He counted to twelve before the motion slowed and stopped. By his calculations, that should place him somewhere in the center of the ship's mass, or close to it.

The walls rolled away with the same quick efficiency, revealing the first seemingly solid structure he'd encountered on the ship—a circular door set into a thicker circular frame made of the same material as the bulkheads but with a more elaborate decorative pattern of emerald, gold, and black across the surface.

The drone floated past him, a series of clicks and whirs emanating from its interior. A moment later, the door rolled back into the bulkhead, revealing a darkened room of indeterminable size.

Cade's hand dropped to his holster—for all the good it did. He'd left all his weapons on *Gladiator.*

Relaxing his arms by his sides, he took a deep breath. Every minute he was onboard and alive bought another minute for the escape pod to reach its transmission point and send the warning message to the Admiral.

He needed to keep that thought fixed firmly in his mind, no matter what he encountered in the darkness.

A now-familiar command reached out to him from the interior, repeating the same order he'd been given when he hesitated to follow the drone out of the bay. However, the voice sounded subtly different—fuller, more resonant—because it wasn't coming from the drone's speaker.

His captor was waiting for him.

Taking a deep breath, he stepped into the dimly lit space.

Seventy-Eight

An interconnecting geometric pattern of green and gold light flared to life to his left, the sudden movement making him pivot. The light pattern glided in a five-meter-long stream across the bulkhead, rippling as it moved clockwise. A second matching pattern appeared behind it, then a third and fourth, all at a perfectly equal distance from each other, the head of one endlessly chasing the tail of another in a fluid circle around the room two meters above the deck.

The effect was hypnotic. And disturbing.

Primitive instinct had him shifting his weight to the balls of his feet and widening his stance, preparing for an attack.

The voice spoke from the darkness—low, soothing—the tone reminding him of how he'd talk to a frightened animal. The acoustics in the room made it difficult to pinpoint the source of the voice, but as his eyes adjusted to the dancing light, he picked out a solid shape ten meters in front of him. He straightened, consciously relaxing his shoulders. "Who are you?"

He didn't expect the speaker to understand him, but his voice could still convey intention.

The voice responded by giving the command he now recognized, which sounded something like *shreenef* and seemed to mean *move forward* or *follow*.

The drone drifted in the direction of the speaker, the green and gold lights glinting off the curved surface and reflecting on the deck, giving the patterned surface the look of a dance floor in a themed nightclub. If the situation wasn't so serious, he might have questioned whether he was dreaming.

He stepped forward, the shapes in the room taking on more definition as he closed the distance. He could make out what looked like a raised dais and a seated figure. A *large* seated figure.

Chills raced over his skin. Not only was he outmatched technologically, but it appeared his captor was a giant. Maybe it was an illusion, manipulation of light and shadow to give the appearance of size.

The drone cut in front of him, bringing him to an abrupt halt. This time it lowered to chest height so he could still see the seated figure clearly. Well, as clearly as the strange low lighting allowed, which wasn't much at all.

The figure spoke, the tone indicating a question, but the words were still unintelligible except for the last one.

"Did you just say Teeli?"

The figure rose. Definitely not a trick of light and shadow. The being's sheer size locked his boots to the deck as it strode toward him with measured, fluid steps. It stopped on the opposite side of the drone, forcing him to tilt his head back to keep his gaze on the creature's face. The drone began to glow, generating a circle of light that illuminated both of them. What he saw was... breathtaking.

The shape of the creature's head reminded him of a python, only with a larger, elevated cranium and a clearly defined neck. The emerald plating on the ship exactly matched the coloring of the smooth scales covering the creature's head, nose, and across its elongated cheeks to its front-facing eyes.

He couldn't look away from the hypnotic intelligence in those eyes—the color of mesquite bark, with black pupils in a curved diamond shape.

His mouth ran dry. "You're a Setarip." But unlike any he'd ever encountered.

The gold and black pattern on the deck perfectly matched the scale pattern on the creature's chin and throat. A golden braid of metal secured a cloak over the Setarips shoulders, the subtly reflective fabric that draped to the ground the same jewel-toned green as the Setarip's scales.

The Setarip spread the fabric of the cloak to reveal what looked like a form-fitting body suit made of small interlocking scales in the same shade of green that covered the rest of the creature's scaled skin. The texture emphasized the toned muscles underneath, as did an intricate insignia across the chest.

The Setarip lifted its head with aristocratic bearing, its gaze boring into his as it spoke. He only understood one word in its reply.

And it rocked his world.

"Yruf?" Was it possible?

The mysterious Yruf faction was more legend than fact, known only by the bits and pieces of information the Fleet had gathered from encounters with the other four Setarip factions. But looking at this imposing creature, he was willing to believe.

A slender tongue flicked from its mouth, like a snake's. The Yruf repeated the question it had asked before, the one that contained the word Teeli. It lifted an arm the size of a bamboo stalk but as supple as a blade of grass, the smooth scales covering its hands decorated with the same beautiful geometric designs as its face. It gestured with a graceful arc of its long arm to his hair.

He touched his head. In the low light, his blond hair might be mistaken for Teeli white, especially after all the sun-bleaching it had gotten while he was on Burrow. He shook his head. "I'm not a Teeli, if that's what you're asking." He pointed at his chest. "Human."

The Yruf drew in a slow breath, those hypnotic eyes holding him in their grip. But it didn't respond.

He tapped his chest again. "Human." He pointed at the Setarip. "Yruf." He tried to say the word the way the Yruf had, extending the vowel sound and adding a puff of air at the end, almost like he was imitating a dog woof.

The creature's tongue flicked out again. A million thoughts seemed to be streaming behind its eyes, but he couldn't begin to guess at the conclusions the Setarip would draw from his bumbling attempts at communication. What he wouldn't give to have Justin by his side. Or Celia Cardiff. She was amazing with non-verbal communication.

Maybe he should try asking the Yruf a question. But what? He'd only been able to understand two words the creature had said, and only because he'd already known them. What simple idea could he convey?

An image of Bare'Kold and his yacht flashed into his mind. Too complicated. He pictured the pod, falling through space, the timer counting down to engage propulsion. He had to buy more time. "You." He pointed at the Yruf. "Take me." He pointed at himself and then the doorway. "To my ship." He made an awkward pantomime with his hands of his ship.

Wrong thing to say, apparently. The Yruf's demeanor changed. Its head bobbed side to side in a movement that made him take an involuntary step back—out of striking distance.

Even without special skills, he knew suspicion when he saw it. And heard it. The creature's next question had the word Teeli in it again.

He shook his head forcefully, irritation welling. Too bad they hadn't captured Bare'Kold. Then it would be easy to show the Yruf the difference between a Teeli and a human. He pressed his palm to his chest. "Human."

No help. If anything, his protest agitated the Yruf even more. It lifted its arms.

And he became aware they weren't the only ones in the room. Four figures not quite as large as the one in front of him but no less imposing detached from the shadows, moving to his side with alarming speed and stealth.

The glow from the drone revealed coloring almost identical to the Yruf before him. All were clad in scale-patterned body armor that looked like it could deflect a rifle blast with ease. But it was the lethal-looking weapons in their long-fingered hands that made him lift his arms, palms out, in what he hoped was a universal gesture of surrender.

The Yruf leader made a motion to the guards, who surrounded Cade with weapons poised, as though daring him to make a move.

He held perfectly still, his gaze on the leader. "I didn't mean to upset you," he said in the softest, most non-threatening voice he could summon.

The Yruf's head bobbed again. Was that how they expressed agitation? Aurora would know. Too bad she wasn't with him right now.

The Yruf stared at him in obvious frustration, like he was a puzzle box it couldn't unlock. Its tongue flicked out several times before it motioned to the guards.

The drone moved toward Cade. He stepped back to keep it from smacking into his chest. Two of the guards closed the gap behind the drone, cutting him off from their leader. The drone continued to push forward, backing him up toward the doorway. He could sense the other two guards keeping pace behind him, enclosing him in a lethal circle.

He made sure his hands stayed at shoulder height. Light spilled into the room as the door opened behind him, but he could no longer see the Yruf leader behind the two guards. The increased illumination did give him a much better view of his captors—at least the two he could see.

Except for subtle variations in their markings, they could be clones. Their heads and necks were slender and graceful like their leader's, their features stunning compared to the other Setarips he'd seen. They most closely resembled the Ecilam faction, although their coloring was far more dramatic, and they had a refinement to their physiques the Ecilam lacked.

And a good half meter of extra height. His neck was going to ache from maintaining eye contact.

As soon as he'd backed out of the room and the door had rolled closed behind the guards, the drone rose to eye level again, blocking his forward view. The guards adjusted their positions, allowing the drone to pass through.

"Shreenef." The command was accompanied by a nudge to his shoulder blades which was a lot gentler than he expected.

He would gain nothing by resisting. He was alone, with no idea where he was in relation to his ship, or how to get back there.

He started after the drone, the bulkheads once again shifting around him. He counted forty-seven steps before the drone halted. So did he. When the walls converged, he didn't even blink, keeping his gaze on the drone as what passed for a lift on this ship took them down.

But only to the count of six, not twelve. They weren't returning to his ship.

The bulkheads pushed back, creating a wide passageway. The drone resumed its motion, the four guards following to the side and behind Cade, their footfalls barely audible on the deck.

After another sixty-three footsteps the drone halted, dropping back down to chest height, halting Cade, too. Another lift?

No, end of the line.

In the blink of an eye the guards retreated and the walls moved in, surrounding him in a cylinder about the size of *Gladiator*'s main room, but with no openings of any kind.

A prison cell.

Movement in his peripheral vision made him turn. A three meter by two meter platform at knee height had risen from the deck. A moment later a more rounded shape rose to the same height. Water flowed into a basin at the top. Hydration and sanitation station, perhaps? A quick check confirmed that's exactly what it was for.

"At least I won't have to pee in a corner." Not that the cell had any corners. Even the platform bed was all rounded edges.

Striding to the spot where the passageway had closed off, he placed his palms flat on the wall and pushed until his muscles strained. Nothing. If he'd hoped the fluid nature of the bulkheads would make them weak, he had another think coming. Using his fingernails, he tried prying at the scales. Might as well have been working on steel.

He turned and surveyed his cell. "Way to go, Ellis. No help to your crew, and certainly no help to yourself." Except that wasn't exactly true, was it? He'd bought time for the escape pod.

He checked the chronometer on his comband. Thirty-seven minutes since he'd left *Gladiator*. Not long enough for the pod's timer to trigger propulsion, but it was a start. He tapped the comm link. "Drew, can you hear me? Gonzo? Williams?"

Dead air. Not even static greeted him.

"No way to talk to my crew." His gaze moved up to the drone, which had risen to the ceiling in the exact center of the cylinder, nestling into an alcove that seemed designed to hold it. "And no privacy."

How long did the Yruf plan to keep him here?

Seventy-Nine

"I'll go easy on you. I promise." Aurora gave Micah a saucy grin as she stepped onto the sparring mat her dad had set up in the front room.

She needed this workout. She'd been antsy ever since shortly after the dive with Micah. Her free-floating anxiety was probably a holdover from facing her fears of the water. And all the images of Cade that had been haunting her ever since.

"Don't worry about me." Micah shot back, joining her on the padded surface. He stretched his arms over his head, making the muscles of his chest pull taunt underneath his snug T-shirt. "I'm a lot bigger than you."

"Size isn't everything." Celia was living proof of that. They were almost identical in height, but Celia was the deadliest fighter she'd ever encountered. She'd taken down Cade and Siginal Clarek in matches. And taught Aurora many of her methods for turning her size into an advantage.

"It is when you can't shield." Micah waggled his eyebrows like a melodrama villain.

"We'll see about that."

"Children. Focus, please." Their dad stood just off the edge of the mat, arms folded. He was dressed in a T-shirt and lounge pants just as they were, but he managed to make it look like a coach's uniform. "The point of this exercise is to teach Aurora to control her empathic reactions when fighting with a Suulh."

"That's right." Aurora nodded, then crooked her finger at Micah. "Heeeeere, Suulhly, Suulhly, Suulhly."

The taunt worked perfectly. With a cocky grin, Micah lunged for her, trying to catch her around the waist. She spun out of reach and followed up with a roundhouse kick to his derriere. The blow connected, knocking him off balance.

And triggered an echo in her glutes, making her stumble.

"Uh-huh. As I said." Her dad gave her a pointed look. "You need to focus."

Her good humor fled, chased away by memories of her battle with Kreestol in the river.

Micah's expression grew serious as well, his gaze on her. "What do you want me to do?"

"Do you know how to throw a punch?"

"Sure. I took karate lessons as a kid."

"Then let's start there. You punch, I'll block."

"And before you do either," her dad interjected, "get your visualization firmly in place. You need to be in control of anything you sense from Micah."

"Right." Drawing in a slow breath, she focused on the *Starhawke's* bridge, and the emotional stability it gave her.

Micah met her gaze. "Ready?"

"Yeah."

He moved in closer, arms lifted, fists closed.

His first jab came in slower than she'd expected. She could have avoided it by dodging, but the point of the exercise was physical contact. She deflected it instead, feeling the double hit of her arm against his and the echo of discomfort from him. But she was able to push both aside immediately. "More force."

His mouth turned down, but his next punch came at her a lot faster. Another deflection, another burst of discomfort.

Micah kept the punches coming, each with a little more force than the previous one. She continued to block, her arms complaining about the abuse. But it was giving her exactly what she needed. With each strike she was able to anticipate the pain more easily, and to channel it away while maintaining focus.

Micah backed off, his breathing not as steady as it had been when they'd started.

A quick look confirmed her forearms were red where she'd blocked the punches. His hands were red, too. She motioned him forward. "Come here a moment." Resting her palms near his elbows, she engaged her energy field. With the augmentation she received from him, the redness and resulting aches vanished in a couple seconds.

Micah's brows lifted. "When we finish, you need to tell me how you do that." He flexed his fingers, working the muscles of his hands and forearms.

"That trick only works with you. Normally it would take a minute or two for me to repair the damage to someone else's cells, but with you, it's like I'm healing myself. Actually, it's even quicker than when I'm healing on my own."

"See?" He gave her a playful punch on the shoulder. "I knew I'd come in handy."

She returned his smile. "Ready for something more robust?"

"Meaning what?"

"Meaning this time, I'll be hitting back."

"Ah." He glanced at his hands. "At least I won't be in pain for long."

"And I'll be dealing with the same pain you are."

"True." A frown creased his forehead. "I wish there was a way I could block you from feeling my pain."

"That would defeat the purpose. I need this practice. Besides, if you were ever really hurt, I'd want to know."

He cocked his head. "Would you? I mean, if we weren't near each other? Would you still sense it?"

"I think so, though maybe not if I was lightyears away. My ability gets weaker with distance. But now that I know what our connection feels like, I think I'd be able to recognize it, especially from anywhere on Earth. I may have sensed some of your previous injuries and just had no idea why I suddenly felt uncomfortable."

His lips quirked. "So, are you saying if I want to get your attention, all I need to do is injure myself?"

She shot him a mock glare. "Please use a comm device."

His chuckle made her smile.

"All right you two." Their dad made a rolling motion with his hand. "Back to work."

This time when Micah threw a punch, she blocked and kicked, connecting with his lower torso. Her abdominal muscles contracted in response but she kept moving, blocking his next punch and delivering another blow. The cycle repeated again and again, her body echoing the aches in his, challenging her concentration.

"Remain focused on your place of power."

The reminder from her dad helped steady her. She visualized the sparring mat sitting in the center of the *Starhawke* bridge, with her friends as spectators. The image held. When her next few blows struck, channeling the pain away took less effort.

Micah's next punch got through her defenses, colliding with her shoulder.

She rolled with it, jabbing him in the stomach with her elbow.

And knocking the air from her own lungs.

She staggered, pressing her palm to her chest as the visualization vanished.

Micah rubbed his solar plexus. "That stung."

"I know. Sorry." She moved closer and rested her free hand over his, the healing energy pouring from her palm. Instantly the pain abated, their breathing coming into sync.

"So, what did you learn?" Her dad stood with his arms over his chest, watching them.

"That when I react instinctively during a fight, I lose my grip on the visualization."

He nodded. "Why?"

"Because..." She replayed the sequence of events. "Because I've sparred enough that I don't necessarily have to think about each move. Muscle memory steps in. But the visualization isn't part of that process."

"Which tells you what?"

"That I need to make the visualization second nature just like I have with my combat skills."

"Exactly. Start again."

Eighty

"Let me out of here you mangy reptiles!" Cade slammed the side of his fist against the green-scaled wall of his cell.

No reaction from the bulkhead, but a starburst of pain radiated through his hand. He welcomed it. The pain proved he wasn't catatonic.

He turned his face up to the drone, raising his voice. "I want to see my crew. Now!"

The drone wasn't impressed. It didn't make a sound. In fact, he wasn't even sure the damn thing was powered on.

He stalked around the perimeter of the enclosure. Thirty-nine hours. That's how long he'd been stuck in this spartan cubicle. Almost two days. His patience had long since worn through. He had no idea what had become of his ship or his crew, and the Yruf leader had made no attempt to contact him through the drone. The unending silence was driving him insane.

A low hiss made him turn.

The bulkhead had pushed into the room, creating a dimple in the perfect circle. He waited, knowing exactly what would happen next. Sure enough, a few seconds later the dimple parted like a curtain and reassembled behind a circular pedestal with a metal bowl in the center.

Feeding time.

He'd been served three other meals since taking up residence, always in the same manner and with the same food. The brothy mash in the bowl was palatable but unremarkable, bland in both taste and texture. It looked and tasted like what you'd get if you soaked Fleet field rations in warm water. He'd questioned the wisdom of eating it, but had finally decided he needed to keep up his strength.

He hadn't suffered any ill effects, so at least the Yruf weren't intent on poisoning him. But he had no way of knowing if the same applied to his team.

And what about Justin? Was he still in *Gladiator*'s infirmary? Williams had seemed confident he'd recover with proper care, but that assumed the Yruf hadn't pulled his crew off the ship. Tam might not be in a position to treat Justin anymore.

Snagging the bowl and spoon-like implement off the pedestal, he sank down on the spongey surface of the platform bed beside his folded battle armor and shoveled a bite into his mouth. There had to be a way out of here. He just needed to figure it out.

During the first day, he'd tried pleading with the drone in the hope the Yruf leader was listening and might reconsider his incarceration. When that had garnered no response, he'd switched to systematically testing every centimeter of his cell's walls for weaknesses he could exploit.

And come up empty. Which had led to his current state of agitation and mounting anger. It didn't help that he hadn't been able to sleep much. He'd been haunted by nightmares involving his crew—enormous snakes swallowing them whole—mixed in with dreams of Aurora trapped in a cage with Reanne standing over her, holding the key.

He hoped that fear was unfounded. The Admiral should have received the recorded message from the escape pod the day before. By now, Libra Hawke and Mya Forrest's parents could be under the Admiral's protection. Where exactly he would take them was unclear—possibly to President Yeoh—but he definitely would have contacted Aurora through Siginal Clarek to alert her.

Bringing the *Starhawke* back to Earth would be unwise, but the Kraed had plenty of other ships they could send under diplomatic flags. Or under cover of their hull camouflage. It would be a fairly simple matter for a Kraed shuttle to land unobserved and pick up Libra and the Forrests. The only wrinkle would be the time needed to reach Earth from Drakar. The *Starhawke* could do it in five and a half days. That was about three days too long. Maybe Clarek's clan had a ship that was closer or faster.

He swallowed the last bite of food and set the empty bowl back on the pedestal. As soon as he stepped away the bulkhead shifted to encircle the pedestal, blocking it from view. He glanced up at the drone. Definitely being watched. He spread his arms wide. "I'd really like to see my crew."

No response.

He had the urge to kick the bed, but channeled his frustration into a more productive activity. Dropping into a plank position, he started doing push-ups. Exercise helped him think.

The rustle of the bulkhead moving told him the pedestal had been removed and the room returned to its normal state. "Efficient bastards."

"Cade?"

The unexpected voice startled him so badly he lurched into a low crouch, his heart pounding. The sight that greeted him took a moment to sink in.

Where the solid bulkhead had been a moment ago, now there was open space that doubled the size of his enclosure. And standing in the center of that space was Drew.

"Bella!" He crossed the distance in three strides, grasping her by the shoulders to assure himself she was real. "Are you okay?"

"Fine." She gazed past him, taking in the platform bed and sanitation station in his cell. "Have you been here this whole time?"

He nodded, releasing her. "All but the first half hour."

Her blue eyes widened. "I had no idea." She gestured to the matching setup in her half of the cell. "I've been here thirty-three hours."

He blinked. "And you never heard me?"

"Not a peep."

Which meant the bulkheads were not only flexible, but soundproof. They'd been separated by centimeters and hadn't had a clue. "What about the others?"

"I don't know. They took Gonzo first, three hours after you left. Sent a drone like the one that came for you, and made it clear they wanted one of us—only one of us—to go. You'd told us not to fight unless we had to, so he volunteered."

"How did you know it only wanted one of you?"

"When I tried to follow, the nanotech dropped the emergency bulkhead for the gangway in my face." She touched a finger to her nose. "Almost clipped me on the way down."

"And then a drone came for you?"

"Three hours later."

He glanced at the ceiling in her cell, where a drone just like the one keeping him company sat in a matching alcove. He turned in a circle, looking at the bulkheads defining their prison with new interest. "So Gonzo could be in a cell on the other side of these walls."

"It's possible."

"What about Justin? How was he doing?"

"Still on oxygen, but his heartbeat had stabilized. Tam was keeping him sedated so he could rest."

Cade's gaze drifted to the drones again. "If they sent a drone for him after they took you, he wouldn't have left Justin. He would have resisted."

"I know." The worry in her eyes reflected the tension building in his chest. "Do you think they'd use force to remove Williams? Have the guards drag him off the ship? Or cut the air again so he'd pass out?"

"I don't know. Maybe." And they wouldn't learn the answer until their captors revealed it. "Did you meet the leader?"

"Yeah. Yruf Setarip, right?"

"That's my guess."

"Crazy." She shook her head, her gaze sweeping the cell. "I didn't see that coming. Yruf, Teeli, and Ecilam were the only words the Setarip said I understood. It also seemed very intrigued by my hair." She touched the short brunette locks. "It acted like it expected me to do something, but I have no idea what."

"It mistook me for a Teeli." He pointed at his blond hair. "I explained I was human."

"And it understood you?"

"I don't think so. It definitely didn't trust me."

"Not surprising, considering they've been fighting a civil war with the other factions for centuries. I doubt they trust anyone."

"Good point."

She surveyed their surroundings. "So, what's our next—"

The rustle of a moving bulkhead behind him cut her off. They both turned.

"Gonzo!"

Gonzo sat on a bunk identical to his on the opposite side of the expanded cell. He leapt to his feet and hurried toward them. "Cade! Drew! Boy am I glad to see you."

They exchanged a round of quick hugs.

"Have you two been together this whole time?"

"No." Cade quickly filled him in.

Gonzo gave a report of his time with the Yruf leader, which hadn't produced any useful results, either. "My goatee seemed to confuse the heck out of them. The leader tried to rub it off. When I resisted, I ended up here." He motioned to his cot, where his folded battle armor sat at the end like Cade's. "Been here ever since. Any idea what happened to Williams and Byrnes?"

"Not yet." Cade's gaze swung to the far edges of their triple cell. "But I'm hoping they're behind those bulkheads."

Eighty-One

The next ten hours passed easier for Cade. Knowing at least half his team was okay helped. But worry about Justin and Tam still gnawed at his gut.

Drew and Gonzo were passing the time debating the possible mechanics behind the Yruf ship's unusual functionality.

"But how can they maintain structural integrity without load-bearing walls?" Drew pointed to the bulkhead. "It's an artificial gravity environment. Even if there's some kind of magnetic or electrical force that's capable of moving the walls, they still need to support the weight of what's above."

"Maybe all the walls on all decks move in unison."

"Impractical. They'd need—"

Cade zoned out of the discussion. From his seated position with his back to his bunk, he could make out the individual scaled pieces that made up the bulkhead. He willed them to separate and show him Justin and Tam. He could picture them so clearly—Justin lying on the med platform, Williams suited up for the upcoming confrontation.

Were they still on *Gladiator*? Was Justin still alive?

He was concentrating so hard on the image that when the rustle of the moving bulkhead reached his ears, he mistook it for wishful thinking.

"Cade, we have company." Gonzo's voice held a note of warning.

He turned his head. The four guards who had escorted him to his cell were back, standing in the opening in the bulkhead with a long corridor visible behind them.

Cade rose to his feet as movement in his peripheral vision caught his attention. All three drones had descended from their positions in the ceiling and had moved with unerring accuracy to hover in front of their respective charges.

One of the guards lifted a long-limbed arm and pointed down the corridor. "Shreenef."

Drew and Gonzo glanced at him.

He nodded. "Put on your armor. We'll go with them. Let's hope they're taking us to Byrnes and Williams."

The walk through the shifting passageways didn't distract him from that single-minded focus. Even the ride on the unconventional lift, which had expanded to accommodate all seven of them and the three drones, didn't get more than a glance. He still counted—four decks up by his estimation. Not *Gladiator* or the throne room.

The drones led the way, hovering at chest height in front of him, Drew, and Gonzo as they moved along a short passageway with the guards to the side and behind. The bulkhead shifted in front of them, opening to reveal a large chamber lit with a soft but vibrant golden glow, like the light from a thousand candles.

At the center of the chamber, Justin lay on a raised platform.

Cade rushed forward, heedless of the drone that barely got out of his way. The guards didn't try to stop him, either. He reached Justin's bedside just as his number one turned his head to meet his gaze.

"Hey, Cade." Justin's voice was low, weak, but the best sound he'd heard all day.

"Hey, Justin. Fancy meeting you here."

Justin's smile lacked strength, but it was there.

"How're you doing?"

Justin sighed. "Better now that you're here."

Drew appeared on Justin's other side, a drone hovering over her right shoulder. She rested her hand on Justin's arm. "You don't seem surprised to see us."

He shook his head. "I'm not. I asked them to bring you here."

"And they understood you?" Cade asked.

Justin's smile showed a hint of his usual spark. "Obviously."

A beefy hand landed on Cade's shoulder. "Good to see you're still in one piece."

He turned to find Williams standing behind him, no longer in battle armor but looking no worse for wear. The accumulated tension in his chest eased. "You, too. Are you okay?"

Williams nodded. "We had a few bumps at first." He indicated the four guards standing watch in a row in front of the resealed bulkhead. "They arrived on *Gladiator* with a drone and tried to separate us, but I made it clear that wasn't an option. After some tense moments, they moved us both here and I started working with their doctors to treat Justin. The situation got a lot better when he started talking again."

Cade turned his attention to Justin. "You've been communicating with them?"

"A bit. Williams started the process. He made sure he understood what the doctors were planning to do before he'd let them treat me. He didn't want them to accidentally kill me."

Williams snorted. "What kind of a doctor would I be if I'd turned you over to Setarip medical care without lifting a finger?"

"A bad one."

"That's right. I didn't even know Setarips had doctors." He turned to Cade. "Thankfully the Yruf know their medicine."

"So, you figured out who they are?"

"Byrnes did."

Cade's gaze swept the room. "Where are the doctors now?"

"They left shortly before you arrived," Justin said.

"Have you found out why they're holding us?"

"No. We're still communicating on basic terms." Justin winced, placing a hand on his forehead and closing his eyes. "To be honest, this is the longest I've talked since I came to."

"Are you in pain?"

"Not really. Just dizzy and nauseated."

"He needs to rest." Williams folded his arms and gave Cade a stern look.

He got the message. Stepping away from the platform, he motioned to Williams to join him. "Any idea what caused this?" he asked in an undertone.

"Based on how they treated him, and the fact he's the only one affected, my theory is an ultra-low frequency tone channeled through *Gladiator*'s communication system. Justin would have been the only one exposed to it for any length of time, and it would have been inaudible."

"Was it part of the jamming signal?"

"No, it would have needed a direct connection. Justin said the first torpedo that struck the ship affected the communications system. I'm guessing it delivered a transmitter that attached to the system and started the signal."

"But Justin didn't collapse until later."

"It's a cumulative effect. It would have taken ten to fifteen minutes to reach a debilitating level."

"So, his condition is temporary?"

"Yes, although he may feel the effects for several more days."

"Would that type of signal only affect humans that way?"

"Unlikely, although the specific effects would depend on physiology. Why do you ask?"

"From what we've seen, we're the first humans the Yruf have encountered. That means that signal was designed with someone else in mind."

"The other Setarip factions?"

"Maybe." Or possibly the Teeli. However, he didn't want to bring that potentially explosive term into the discussion. For all he knew, the Yruf could hear every word he was saying. He didn't want to upset them again. "How soon could Justin manage a conversation with the Yruf, enough to convince them to release us?"

Williams glanced at the platform. Gonzo and Drew were stationed on either side, keeping watch over Justin, whose chest rose and fell in the rhythm of sleep. "He's weak, and still having trouble focusing. It took a lot out of him to convey his wish to have you three here, and until you showed up, I wasn't convinced he'd gotten the point across."

"How much is he able to translate their words?"

"Less than he'd like. His condition isn't helping. He gets confused easily. Anxious, too. I think that may be the real reason they brought you here. It was the only way to calm him down."

"So, they do care whether he's okay?"

"They seem to. They act more assertive than aggressive. And intrigued. I caught them staring at me on multiple occasions. One of them even ran a hand over my head. The lack of hair seemed to fascinate them."

Cade's lips quirked up. "That's because you look the most like them."

That earned him a withering glance. "I should take that as a compliment. They're stunning."

"That they are." He gazed at the guards, who had not moved a muscle since they'd arrived, but were clearly keeping a close watch on his team. "Any recommendations on the best tack to take for opening a dialogue?"

Williams followed the direction of his gaze. "Don't bother with the guards. Even Justin couldn't get them to respond. But the doctors tried to communicate as best they could given our limited understanding of each other." He pointed at his comband. "I've made notes and recordings, and added the words Justin figured out."

"What about the Yruf? Were they trying to translate your words?"

"Not really. Their method of communication is different, though I'm not sure exactly how. Justin might have an answer when he's feeling better. I do know they don't seem to use very many words, even when talking with each other."

That fit with his experience talking to the leader.

"I changed my strategy to fit, using a single word whenever possible to convey an idea."

"Which means Justin will have to do the heavy lifting." He sighed. "At least it explains why the rest of us failed to make any inroads with the Yruf leader."

"You've met her?"

"Her?"

"Yep, if you're talking about the gigantic one whose coloring matches the guards and decor."

Cade nodded.

"She visited us several hours ago, after Justin started talking. She seemed very pleased that he was trying to accurately reproduce some of their words in context."

"I'll bet. How did he figure out she's female?"

"Actually, that's my assessment. From a genetic standpoint, the Yruf most closely match the Ecilam. In that faction, the females are the larger, more colorful sex, though the difference isn't as dramatic as what we've seen here."

Cade gave the guards a sidelong glance. "They all look pretty much the same to me."

"Then you haven't met any of the males, yet."

"All those guards are female?"

"Uh-huh."

Mental adjustment made. "When did you become an expert on Setarip physiology?"

"Remember that Setarip attack on Persei Primus?"

How could he forget? Aurora had led the team that had confronted the Ecilam and the human traitors. Reading the reports had given him heart palpitations. "Sure."

"The Admiral asked me to investigate the toxin used to kill the leader of the assault and the injured Ecilam. I discovered during my research that all the Ecilam fighters who'd been left behind were female. The station personnel also recovered several bodies from the destroyed Setarip ship, including three males. They were all significantly smaller than the females and more neutral in their coloring. The markers in their genetic code made it clear those traits were common."

"And you're theorizing the same is true here?"

"The same physical characteristics are easily identifiable. Two of the doctors checked all the boxes for the male traits, while the third ticked all the female ones. I'd need to run a med scan to be absolutely certain, but I believe the Yruf leader and the guards are female."

Cade's gaze strayed back to the guards. Two of them were watching him and Williams with keen intensity, the rounded diamond-shaped pupils of their hypnotic eyes seeming to draw him in.

He looked away. "Did Justin gather any intel on the leader that might help us?"

"She wants answers, but he could only guess at the questions. Who we are, for one. And why we're here. She seemed concerned that Justin might be a Teeli."

Cade nodded, lowering his voice to a whisper. Williams' use of the T-word had brought a third guard's gaze to them. "She had the same issue with me. I think it's the hair. I doubt the Yruf have ever seen blond hair, but they seem familiar with white. They may think we're just a variation of the same species."

"Which will not work in our favor. It's clear their leader is not a fan."

"Then I guess we have our priority one—convincing them we're Human."

Eighty-Two

Three more days of sparring with Aurora had left Micah physically and mentally exhausted. But the result was well worth the effort.

His sister was getting stronger. He could see it in the way she responded during their matches. In the beginning, she'd been tentative, flinching every time they made contact. Now she came at him with assurance, the look in her eyes calm, focused.

She apologized every time she inflicted pain. He reassured her that he could take it. He'd gladly suffer far worse if it enabled her to learn the skills she needed to fight their aunt and the Suulh without debilitating herself.

He'd prefer she never faced them again, but given the history she'd shared, that seemed unlikely. Her former roommate would see to that. How anyone could hate Aurora was a mystery. Then again, Reanne Beck sounded like she didn't have both oars in the water.

The warm spray from the shower felt good on his skin, easing any lingering tension. He was staying over at his dad's house for Christmas Eve so they could get a jump on the beachside festivities in the morning.

That was another benefit of the sparring matches. Aurora's confidence in her ability to control her empathic reactions had spilled over into her issues regarding her energy field. Not only was she excited about the beach party tomorrow, but she'd agreed to let him give her a surfing lesson. What a change from the terror that had held her captive when she'd arrived. He couldn't wait to get her out in the water and see what she could do.

Stepping out of the shower, he ran a towel over his hair before wrapping it around his waist. The scents of baking bread and Italian spices filtered up from below, where his dad was fixing dinner while he and Aurora got cleaned up.

He paused near his bed, glancing toward the interior balcony of Aurora's room, visible through the French doors in his. What would it have been like to grow up with Aurora? How different would his life have been if he'd been able to spend time with her, to learn from her, and teach her in return?

She'd arrived less than two weeks ago. Every fiber of his being told him they'd only begun to scratch the surface of their connection. Yet how much longer could she stay? She hadn't said anything about leaving, but he'd caught a wistfulness in her eyes the previous night when she'd been gazing up at the stars.

In addition to the insights she'd given him regarding their aunt and Reanne, she'd also told him about her ship, and the crew she'd assembled, as well as her goal to free the entire Suulh race from Teeli enslavement. Expecting her to stay here was beyond foolish. Her future was up there among the stars. And his was... not.

Shoving the maudlin thoughts away, he dressed in a long-sleeved shirt and jeans and padded downstairs to the kitchen. His dad stood at the stove, alternately stirring pots of simmering red sauce and bubbling pasta.

Aurora was already perched on a barstool at the counter, her hair in her customary braid, still damp from her shower. She flashed him a bright smile. "Merry Christmas Eve!"

"Merry Christmas Eve to you, too." He wrapped his arms around her from behind and gave her a hug, breathing in the citrus scent of her soap as their energetic connection filled him with joy.

She set down the napkins she'd been folding and wrapped her arms over his. "You feeling okay?" Concern shone in her green eyes.

He pressed a soft kiss to her temple. Her worry only made her more precious. "I'm good." He released her and struck a superhero pose, fists on hips. "It takes more than a sparring match to take down Micah the Magnificent."

She laughed, just as he'd hoped, and tossed one of the napkins at him.

He plucked it out of the air and returned it to her with a deep bow. "I believe you dropped this, milady."

"I believe I did." She was still grinning as she gathered up the folded napkins and headed down the hall to the pool deck.

He moved to the counter beside the stove where his dad had set out salad fixings and a cutting board. He picked up the knife and started chopping. "I'm really going to miss her."

His dad's stirring hand stilled. "Did she say something about leaving?"

"No, but it's coming. I can feel it."

His dad's silence said more than a denial.

He couldn't let it go. "She's learned what she needs to know, hasn't she?"

"The core concepts, yes. She'll improve with practice, but there's only so much we can provide here. She needs to work with other Suulh."

"I know." He brought the knife down with more force than necessary and it skidded across the wooden board. Only his quick reflexes prevented him from slicing open his arm.

He set the knife aside and took a deep breath. He wanted to find a way to spend more time with her, but having her heal a knife wound wasn't what he'd had in mind.

"Sure smells good in here." She strolled in from the hallway, her gaze finding his like a heat-seeking missile. Her tone was light, but he couldn't fool her empathic abilities. She knew something was bothering him.

"The bread should be ready." His dad handed her a padded oven mitt.

Picking up the knife, Micah resumed chopping. The yeasty aroma of the garlic bread surrounded him as she set the golden loaves on the raised section of the island beside the stove. "We'll talk later," she murmured as she walked behind him to the cupboard and began gathering plates.

Later. Yes, later was good. Right now he just wanted to enjoy their first Christmas Eve together since they were kids.

Birdie and Kai arrived soon after. During the meal, Aurora shared anecdotes from Christmases past, many featuring the girl he'd known as LeeLee, but who Aurora called Mya. That took some getting used to—hearing his childhood nickname and associating it with someone else. But the pictures she painted of LeeLee matched the kind, thoughtful girl he remembered. She'd clearly filled in as a surrogate sibling for his sister, even more than Birdie had for him.

"And she's now the doctor on your ship, right?"

"Yes. But she also spends a lot of time in the greenhouse. Plants are her passion, one she shares with Celia."

"Celia's your security chief?"

"Uh-huh. She's remarkable. We met while I was on the *Argo*. I'm damn lucky that she agreed to leave the Fleet to serve on the *Starhawke*."

Their dad lifted his wine glass in a small salute. "The fact that she did is a testament to how lucky she felt to be offered the job."

"I suppose." Her gaze drifted to Micah. "She's the one who taught me how to spar."

"Then maybe I need to meet this woman. Get some pointers for our next match."

Her lips curved. "She wouldn't be as gentle as I am."

That sounded like a challenge. "Don't think I can handle it?"

"I think you'd spend a lot of time on your butt. I sure did. She won't even step on the mat with you unless she knows you're serious about learning."

"Sounds intriguing."

"That word fits my entire crew." The wistful look was back in her eyes. "I can't wait for you to meet them."

His heart thumped in his chest. Bam, bam, bam. Meeting her crew would coincide with her leaving. "Like I said before, you invite me, and I'll be there."

Her gaze turned assessing. "When do classes resume?"

"Two weeks." But right now he wished it was two months.

"Then I'll contact Mya after Christmas and make arrangements. I want to get you up there before your break is over."

He smiled at her enthusiasm, but the part of him that was still a four-year-old boy started to cry.

He'd been right. In her mind the timetable had already been set. In less than two weeks, she'd be gone.

Eighty-Three

Mya didn't hear the greenhouse door open, but some sixth sense told her Jonarel had entered. She set down her pruning shears on the potting bench and turned.

Sure enough, his muscular body filled the pathway, the greens and browns of his skin fitting in perfectly with the cornucopia of plant life surrounding him.

He'd made himself scarce for the past few days, as had Star. She'd assumed they were both nursing the emotional wounds they'd suffered from standing against their father and clan. And perhaps coming to grips with what it would mean for their futures.

He approached slowly, almost cautiously. She couldn't read his expression, which in itself was unusual. Normally he was an open book, at least to her. He stopped within arm's length, his gaze moving over her like she was a new species of flower he'd never seen.

Thank goodness he hadn't believed his father's accusations. She could imagine how awkward and stilted their interactions would become if he had. She'd seen it firsthand after he'd made his intentions clear to Aurora. Such polite behavior overlaying coiled-spring tension would drive her mad.

She clasped her hands behind her back to quell the urge to reach out and touch him. "What can I do for you?"

One dark brow lifted. "Do for me?"

"Yes. Is there something you need?" He must have some reason for being here. If he'd only wanted food, he could have fetched it without coming over to her. He wasn't the type to wander or engage in casual conversation.

"I find myself in a quandary."

"I can imagine."

His gaze grew thoughtful. "Can you?"

"I think so. Maybe not to the extent you're dealing with, but I understand the painful pull of divided loyalties." She'd been fighting that battle most of her life.

"Yes. That you do understand very well."

And standing this close to him, she was fighting another battle. But he clearly needed a friend. She'd just have to set her feelings aside. Good thing she had plenty of practice.

His gaze shifted to the potting table behind her. "Herbs?"

"Yes. These are from Azaana." She'd gathered them while the settlement was being built. Tending to them and interacting with their energy always made her feel connected to the Suulh. But all the extra attention had caused the plants to overflow their containers.

He reached past her, picking up the largest of the containers with one hand like it weighed no more than a feather. With his other hand, he traced the leaves of the plant. "You fill everything you touch with life."

"Uh... thanks." She couldn't get a bead on his tone. He said it like a compliment, but melancholy laced every word.

Setting down the container, he pivoted, his gaze slowly tracking around the room. "I designed this ship for Aurora."

She couldn't tell if he was talking to her or himself. "I know."

He continued to turn, his back now to her. "I thought of her, imagined her walking the passageways, taking command of the bridge."

Mya's molars ground together. She should be used to these kinds of talks by now. Unfortunately, they still made her bleed. "And she loves this ship."

"Yes." Now he was in profile, his strong jawline and cheekbones highlighted by the tendrils of brown twining across his dark green skin. "But not the designer."

Kick to the gut. The only thing harder than knowing Jonarel was in love with Aurora, was knowing the pain he suffered because Aurora wasn't in love with him. "I'm sorry."

His head turned, his golden gaze meeting hers. She still couldn't read his expression. "Sorry for what?"

"Sorry that you're hurting."

He faced her fully, bringing all that masculine muscle and beauty even closer.

She resisted the urge to step back. "I want you to be happy."

He tilted his head, his full mouth softening. "I know. You have always wished that for me." He spread his arms to encompass the room. "And I have always wished this for you. I designed the ship for Aurora, but when I created this space, I thought only of you."

Whoa, baby. She did *not* want to let her imagination run wild with that comment.

"You breathed life into my vision. You made this room the heart of the ship."

Her fingers twisted painfully behind her back. She really didn't want to talk about hearts right now, not while hers was playing the bongos in her chest.

He leaned closer.

Her hands dropped to her sides and curled into fists as she fought to remain still. But when his fingers brushed her cheek and cupped her jaw, she almost levitated off the deck.

"And time and again you have breathed life back into *me.*"

She had no idea where he was going with this, but if she didn't get some breathing room fast, she was going to hyperventilate and pass out. "I'd do anything to help you."

"Anything?"

Did he just take a step closer? Was the room getting hotter? "Of course. You're my friend." *Just a friend, just a friend, just a friend...* The mantra wasn't helping with his gorgeous body overloading her senses.

"And I am yours."

How could such simple words cause so much pain? He had no idea he was torturing her. "I'm glad." He was definitely closer. Way, way, waaaaay too close.

And then he removed the gap entirely, wrapping his arms around her and pulling her in for full-body contact, short-circuiting her brain. The gesture was a familial Kraed hug, the kind she'd received from Siginal on many occasions.

Coming from Jonarel, it felt *completely* different.

He rested his cheek on top of her head, his warm breath brushing across her hair, making every nerve ending in her body vibrate. "Tell me, Mya. What would make you happy?"

You.

Thank the stars that this close, he couldn't see her expression. "I am happy."

His arms tightened a fraction, pressing the muscled wall of his chest against her.

She fought to keep her breathing steady as the assault on her senses did funny things to her heartbeat.

"Not as happy as I wish you to be."

Stellar light, please stop this! Any second now she would start shaking from the strain, and she had no way to explain her reaction to him.

"You give to everyone, yet accept nothing for yourself." His lips brushed lightly across her forehead, leaving a trail of searing heat as he leaned back so he could see her face.

She kept her gaze averted.

"What do you want, lovely Lelindia?"

His use of her real name startled her. She met his gaze. Bad move. The look in his golden eyes drew her like a magnet. He was close. Too. Damn. Close.

Reason and self-preservation vaporized, blasted by an urge she couldn't resist. One moment she was staring into those beautiful eyes. The next she'd lifted onto tip-toe and pressed her lips to his.

Eighty-Four

Stop!

Her brain blared the warning at the same instant Jonarel's muscles froze.

But it was too late. The sweet taste of his lips had already registered, his luscious scent surrounding her. For that one moment, euphoria flowed through her veins.

Icy reality chased after it with razor-sharp teeth as the horror of what she'd just done hit her. She jerked back, but didn't move a millimeter, not with his arms still locked around her.

"Mya?"

She didn't look at him. *Couldn't* look at him. Heat flooded her face. "Let me go."

Her command fell on deaf ears. If anything, his grip tightened. "Mya, look at me."

Her lower lip trembled, her body following suit. "I can't."

"Why not?"

He couldn't possibly be that dense. "Because I'm mortified."

Silence. His hold on her shifted, but not to let her go. Instead, he locked her in with one arm and used the other to cradle the back of her head, his fingers starting a gentle massage against her scalp that was deliciously hellish. "Why?"

The clear confusion in his voice made her look up. She braced for the pity she expected to see, but it was conspicuously absent from his golden eyes. That was something. Instead, he was looking at her with puzzlement.

Maybe she could salvage the situation. If he hadn't figured out why she'd kissed him, she could come up with another plausible excuse. "I surprised you. Sorry. I meant it as a thank you."

The massaging of her scalp stopped. "A thank you?"

"You've been incredibly supportive of me." At the moment, he was the only thing keeping her upright. Her bones felt like liquid mercury.

His eyes narrowed a fraction. "You were expressing gratitude?"

She couldn't out-and-out lie to him, so she settled for a non-committal. "Ummm."

His gaze searched hers.

She fought to keep her expression pleasantly neutral, but staring into his eyes made that a Herculean task.

His expression shifted to something new, something she couldn't interpret. "Then I wish to express my gratitude as well."

She figured out what he intended to do a millisecond too late. Her lips parted to call a halt just as his mouth settled firmly over hers. The sensation blew every fuse in an instant, his lips moving over hers, fireworks igniting at each point of contact. But when the tip of his tongue slid along her open lower lip, her body went supernova.

So did the *Starhawke*. Or at least it should have. Her entire universe contracted to Jonarel. Only Jonarel.

The delicious sensations flowed through her body like warm honey. He pulled her closer, or maybe she pulled him. She lost track of where he ended and she began. But she hadn't lost track of where his talented tongue was stroking hers, the taste of him making her shudder.

When he pulled back, breaking the connection with her mouth, she whimpered.

A deep rumble from his chest reached her ears. It took a moment to realize it was a Kraed chuckle. She'd never heard him make that sound before.

"Gratitude?" he murmured as his lips brushed across her cheeks, the bridge of her nose, and her forehead before returning to hover just above her mouth, his breath warming her skin. "Tell me the truth, Lelindia."

Drugged by his touch, it took effort to lift her eyelids, but she managed it. The heat in his gaze stole her breath. She swallowed, trying to find her voice. "Not... gratitude."

He brushed his lips across hers once, twice, like butterfly wings, coaxing her in a way she couldn't resist. "What then?"

"You." She leaned toward him, wanting more, but he pulled back just out of reach.

"What do you want from me? This?" He allowed their lips to touch briefly before retreating again.

She growled in frustration. "More."

He kissed her again, his tongue turning her inside out. They were both breathing hard when he lifted his mouth. "How much more?"

No reason to fight, no reason to hide. He'd stripped her bare. "Everything."

The heat in his eyes intensified, scorching her. "Everything?"

"Everything."

They stared at each other for seconds, minutes, hours. She couldn't tell. Time stood still as they balanced on the edge of the knife blade, the tactile pleasure of his body pressed to hers and the desire burning in his eyes blocking out everything else.

His chest rose and fell with his unsteady breaths. "That can be arranged."

Eighty-Five

She squealed when he swept her off her feet, but unlike on Drakar, this time she didn't fight to get down. As he carried her through the door into the med bay she wrapped her arms around his shoulders and placed kisses along the warm skin of his neck.

His steps faltered.

She tensed, turning. But no one was in the med bay.

His stride grew more fluid. "You may want to resist until we reach your cabin," he murmured.

A bubble of laughter rose in her chest. "Am I distracting you?"

He didn't respond until they'd entered the lift and the doors had closed behind them. "Yes." Then his lips found hers.

A whole new sensation, kissing him while he held her. Never in her wildest dreams had she imagined such a moment. Well, okay, maybe in her *wildest* dreams.

He broke the kiss as the doors parted on the crew deck, home to both their cabins, side by side to their right. But hers had the advantage of being closer.

The door opened for them without prompting. Some part of her mind registered that Star had to be responsible, but she didn't care whether the Nirunoc knew what was about to happen or not.

Jonarel carried her into her bedroom, stopping beside her sleeping nook. He set her gently on her feet but kept their bodies in close contact. His fingers wove through her hair, sending tingles down her spine and warming her core. "Lovely Lelindia."

She'd never considered herself particularly lovely, but the look in his eyes made her a believer.

He, on the other hand, was beauty incarnate. No sculpture, painting, or tapestry could compare.

Cradling her face in his large hands, he brought his mouth to hers, his touch softer, more reverent than it had been in the greenhouse or the lift.

She matched the shift in mood, running her hands up his broad back and tunneling her fingers into his long locks. His hair brushing over her skin felt even more delicious than she'd imagined.

His lips left hers, tracing a path along her jaw to the sensitive spot behind her ear, then continuing down the column of her neck. She trembled, her fingers gripping the material of his tunic as his hands moved to the hem of her sweatshirt.

"Lift your arms."

She obeyed as he broke contact long enough to tug the sweatshirt over her head.

Tossing it on the chair near the bedside, he turned back to her, a hint of amusement in his eyes when he beheld the long-sleeved tunic still tucked into her lounge pants. "I have not accomplished much."

"I can fix that." She reached for the shirt, but his hands closed over hers.

"No. You are my gift. I wish to unwrap you."

The oxygen level in the room dropped and moisture gathered behind her eyes. No dream had ever been so magical.

He cupped her face again, his kiss as sweet as his words. This time when he moved the hem of her shirt up, cool air swirled around her stomach and back. After he pulled it over her head, she glanced down at the boring, unadorned, flesh-toned bra covering her breasts. Smallish breasts at that, especially compared to Aurora's. If she'd known this would happen she would have... what? Tried to find something sexier? She almost laughed at the absurdity.

But the laughter vanished in the blast of heat from his gaze when he turned back to her.

Whatever faults she found with herself, he seemed quite pleased by what he'd revealed.

Reaching out with one hand, he traced the line of her collarbone before placing both hands on her shoulders and stroking down to her fingertips. Lifting her hands to his mouth, he kissed each finger, then ran his tongue along the tips.

She trembled.

"Are you cold?"

She shook her head. "No."

A look of masculine pride spread across his face. "Are you warm?"

"Very."

Releasing his hold on her hands, he knelt in front of her, bringing her chest to eye level. How... convenient.

He unfastened her bra and drew it away a centimeter at a time, exquisite torture. "So lovely." But that was nothing compared to the touch of his hands on her skin. And his mouth.

She closed her eyes, unable to handle the visual overload, although the image of him on his knees in front of her, his dark green skin a sharp contrast to her pale breasts, burned through her eyelids. She'd never had a fever, but it felt like she was working on a volcanic one now. Her body was on fire.

And then suddenly, it wasn't.

Or more accurately, a coolness that was every bit as intense as the heat enveloped her.

Jonarel's sharp inhale snapped her eyes open.

A rich green glow surrounded them in a cocoon, dancing over their skin like fairy light.

He stiffened, breaking contact with her breasts. "Have I hurt you?"

He'd misinterpreted the touch of her energy field, thinking she'd summoned it to heal an injury. She smiled, brushing her fingers through his hair and drawing his mouth back to her skin. "I've never felt better."

"Then why—"

"My energy field isn't only for healing. It's a form of connection."

The tension eased from his face. "So this response is natural for a Suulh?"

"Yes." She'd learned that fact from her parents, but she'd never experienced this with the boy she'd lost her virginity with, or the two men she'd dated before meeting Jonarel at the Academy. That it was happening now both stunned and thrilled her.

Aurora had mentioned something similar happening with Cade. It's how she'd learned Cade could see Suulh energy fields.

She brushed her thumb across the velvety softness of his full lower lip. "Does it bother you?"

His brows lifted. "Bother me? Your energy is life itself."

And right now, the mix of warm and cool was having a very erotic effect on her bare skin. But he was still fully clothed. She sank to her knees in front of him and tugged on the hem of his tunic. "Then enjoy it," she whispered, peeling up the material to uncover the rippling muscles of his chest. She'd had this visual before when she'd treated him for injuries, and also when they'd been on Sanctuary. But this was the first time she'd had the right to touch him without professional detachment.

She used her fingertips to trace the fascinating pattern of brown lines that wove across the expanse of forest green skin, then followed the same path with the tip of her tongue. His shuddering breath emboldened her, her attention moving lower.

He stopped her as her hands reached for the clasp of his pants. "Not like this." Encircling her wrists with his fingers, he drew her to her feet, scooped her up, and settled her on the mattress of her sleeping nook. "My turn." He made quick work of her shoes and socks before sliding his fingers under the waistband of her pants.

Heat poured through her core as he stripped them away, his gaze following the movement of his hands. "Lelindia. My lovely Lelindia."

She shuddered at his words and the look in his eyes as he stepped back, gazing at her like she was a priceless work of art.

He managed to undo the elaborate fastenings of his boots without breaking his concentration on her. When he removed his pants, breathing became a real challenge.

"You're..." Nope, couldn't finish the sentence.

He stood before her, a god of the forest revealed in all his glory. She could now confirm that the brown tendrils on his skin continued... everywhere. And there was absolutely no doubt that he wanted her as much as she wanted him.

But he wasn't moving. In fact, a wariness had crept into his golden eyes. "Do I frighten you?"

"Frighten me?" She barked out a laugh. When he still didn't move, she sat up and held out her hand. "Jonarel, you are everything I've ever wanted and more."

The wariness vanished, replaced by the heat that filled her with yearning and promised exquisite pleasure. Taking her hand, he slid onto the bed like a panther, moving over her with fluid grace and a protective confidence that curled her toes. But that was nothing compared to when skin met skin in the most intimate caress, sending shockwaves along her nerve endings that triggered her energy field once again, locking them in its embrace.

He gazed down at her, his eyes and skin luminous against the green glow. "And you are the greatest gift I have ever received."

Eighty-Six

Cade had ample time to consider what Williams had told him.

Justin slept most of the next day and a half, waking only briefly the two times the doctors had come to check on him. Williams had confirmed the doctors were giving him something to induce sleep to keep him relaxed and speed the healing process.

At least they seemed genuinely focused on his recovery.

Despite their strongly negative opinion of the Teeli, the Yruf couldn't have had many in-person encounters with members of the Teeli race. If they had, the doctors would have been able to identify Cade's team as a separate species. In basic physiological terms, humans and Teeli shared a lot of similarities, but a bioscan should have pointed out their obvious differences.

Then again, to a species that had a reptilian look like the Yruf, distinctive mammalian traits might blur together.

The bigger question was why the Yruf had chosen to show up now. Why this rendezvous? Had they followed the Ecilam from Teeli space? If so, what was their goal? Certainly not conquest. The other Setarip factions had been raiding outposts, settlements, and space stations in this sector for decades to gather supplies for their civil war, but the Yruf's appearance hadn't involved a cascade of violent destruction typical of a Setarip attack. They'd seemed more intent on immobilizing and capturing the Ecilam rather than obliterating them.

Just like they'd captured his ship. They could have easily blown *Gladiator* into a billion dust particles, but instead they'd subdued them non-violently.

And what about their behavior toward his team? Williams was right—they were assertive, not aggressive, using their technology to minimize the chances of an escalation of hostilities.

His gaze moved to the guards, who were still doing an amazing statue imitation while keeping a close eye on his team. If the Ecilam ship hadn't exploded, and the Yruf had successfully captured the Ecilam crew, how would they have treated them? With the caution and respect they'd shown his team? Or with the vicious ruthlessness of bitter enemies who'd been at war since long before he was born?

For reasons he couldn't explain, he had trouble picturing the Yruf choosing the second scenario. Which was a strange conclusion. They were Setarips. Their race seemed biologically pre-conditioned for murder and mayhem.

"Cade?"

He turned.

Justin was propped up on his elbows, his blond hair tousled over his forehead and a few days beard stubble shadowing his jaw, but his gaze was clear and focused. Drew, Williams, and Gonzo stood beside him.

Cade strode over to the platform. "Sleep well?"

"Yeah. Whatever they gave me made me dead to the world." He glanced around the room, his gaze resting briefly on the four bunks, large sanitation station, and the small table that had been added to the décor the previous day after the bulkhead had realigned. "Anything happen while I was out?"

"You mean besides Gonzo's dance of the seven veils?"

"Ha. ha." Gonzo's fist connected lightly with Cade's arm. "That was nothing compared to your Madame Butterfly aria." He placed his hand over his heart. "I wept."

"Like a baby," Cade deadpanned. "It was very touching."

Justin grinned as he sat up and swung his legs over the side of the platform. "Why do I miss all the fun?"

A familiar rustling sound made Cade turn. The bulkhead behind the guards had parted. But instead of the doctors, the imposing presence of the Yruf leader appeared. The room's golden light reflecting off her emerald scales made them almost luminescent.

Her gaze locked on Justin as she stepped forward.

"Not all the fun," Cade replied.

One of the male Yruf doctors entered behind her. This one was Cade's size, much smaller than the leader or the guards, with geometrically patterned scales in neutral shades of tan and beige.

"This should be interesting," Williams murmured as he tapped on his comband.

Cade glanced at the screen. Looked like Williams was bringing up the translation program he and Justin had started. The date that flashed also caught his eye. Christmas. Not exactly the venue he would have chosen for a celebration.

Two of the guards accompanied the Yruf leader as she and the doctor strode to the platform. When the Yruf leader halted a couple meters away, the guards took up positions on either side of her with their weapons in hand but not pointed at Cade's team.

The doctor continued to the med console attached to the head of the platform. He studied the readings, then turned to Justin and Williams.

"Respiration?" Williams' comband translated the Yruf word the doctor had spoken.

Justin took a couple slow, deep breaths, then gave a little cough. He said something to the doctor Cade didn't understand but which the comband translated as *eight*.

"Eight?" he asked Justin.

Justin nodded. "Conveying a complex concept like bad or average or better wasn't going to work given our linguistic challenges, so I used a number system to rate how I felt. The doctors were able to understand that kind of comparison scale and I was able to quickly learn their numbering system."

Interesting. Even half out of his mind, Justin had figured out a workable solution for communication. Hopefully during this interchange he'd come up with more of them. The fate of the team—and possibly their mission—depended on it.

Cade shifted to the foot of the platform as the doctor moved next to Justin, a slender object in his hand. He passed it over Justin's chest, strange symbols appearing on the med console. The doctor consulted them for a moment before moving the object in an arcing motion from ear to ear over the top of Justin's head.

"Head?" The comband translated the doctor's one-word question.

"Nine," Justin replied in the Yruf language, the comband translating. He glanced at Cade. "I'm glad my marbles no longer feel like they're being hit by a shooter."

Williams rested a hand on Justin's shoulder. "You're in better shape than I'd expected. The first time they checked you out, before you could talk, you would have been at two or less."

Justin's grin resurfaced. "Can't keep a good man down."

Cade watched the reaction of the doctor and the Yruf leader to the banter. They seemed intrigued but puzzled, the way he might look if he were trying to understand the meaning of the trumpeting of elephants or the songs of whales.

The doctor continued to scan Justin's body, his calm, relaxed manner very similar to the way Williams treated patients. Might explain why they'd been able to work together to help Justin, despite the language and species barriers. After a few minutes, he set down his tools and turned to the leader. He spoke to her, but the comband remained silent, unable to translate any of his words.

She reached into a fold of her cloak and pulled out a circular disk the width of her palm. Holding it flat in front of Justin, she pressed it with one slender finger. A solid three-dimensional miniature image of a circular object appeared above it.

Cade's heart stuttered in his chest. "The escape pod."

It was perfectly rendered in every detail. No way was this an image taken at a distance. Or in the pale light of open space.

He pointed at the image. "How did you get this?"

The Yruf leader glanced at him briefly but didn't respond, returning her attention to Justin.

She held the disc a little lower so it was right in front of Justin's eyes. She spoke, her words coming out slowly and distinctly with long pauses in between. But the comband still didn't translate them.

She waited, her gaze on Justin.

He glanced at Cade. "Any idea why she would have an image of one of our escape pods?"

Right. Justin had been incapacitated when Drew had set up the launch.

Drew answered for him. "I rigged one as a transmission device and sent it off before we were brought onboard. It was supposed to send our message to the Admiral when it got out of range of the Yruf jamming signal."

Justin's eyes widened. "Oh."

"Can you find out how she got this image?" Cade asked. "And when?" *And please let it be recently.*

"I'll try, but those aren't simple concepts to convey. I'm guessing she wants to know what it is, or what it does." He turned back to the Yruf leader.

She jiggled the disc a bit and repeated the same series of words.

Justin's eyes narrowed in concentration. "I don't know the words, and I can't get a lock on their syntax. It's very unusual, like they're only speaking every third or fourth word in a sentence." He angled his head toward Drew but kept his gaze on the Yruf leader. "Bella, do you have an image of *Gladiator* on your comband?"

"Of course. I took scans of the whole ship before we left Weezel's junkyard."

"I need it."

She moved to his side, already tapping on the device. An image of *Gladiator* projected above the band.

Justin pointed at the escape pod image, then at the location on *Gladiator*'s belly where the curve of the pod's exterior was visible.

Drew enlarged the image of the ship so the matching details showed clearly.

The Yruf leader studied the two images, her thin tongue flicking between her lips. Tapping the disc again, she changed the image.

Cade swore. They were now looking at the interior of the pod through the open hatch. Any hope that it was the one still attached to *Gladiator* vanished. The timer Drew had installed to delay the propulsion and transmission was clearly visible.

The leader's gaze locked on him, her pupils dilating, taking in his reaction. One of the guards had also moved closer, her weapon no longer in a relaxed position.

"Tone it down, Cade," Justin murmured. "I don't think the Yruf respond well to strong displays of emotion."

"Sorry." He focused on his breathing, slowing it down as he met the anxious gazes of his team. The same question buzzing in his brain looked like it was circling theirs as well.

If the Yruf had control of their escape pod, had the warning to the Admiral been sent to Earth?

The leader watched him for a few moments before returning her attention to Justin, but the guard kept her gaze and weapon on him.

Justin pointed to the transmitter in the pod. "It sends an audio signal." He made a wave motion with his hand in the air, then touched his finger to his ear.

More flicks of the leader's tongue. She changed the image again, showing a less defined miniature of another vessel Cade recognized.

Bare'Kold's yacht.

She motioned to Justin's ear, then to the yacht.

Justin swallowed audibly. "Uh, this could get tricky."

"Why?"

"I think she knows we were receiving an audio signal from Bare'Kold's surveillance device."

A chill passed over Cade's skin. "That's why she thinks we're Teeli." The leader's sharp-eyed gaze fixed on him. He barely suppressed a flinch. "She was monitoring us while we were monitoring Bare'Kold."

"And came to the conclusion that because we were receiving a signal from a Teeli ship, we were Teeli, too. Or at least working with them."

"How do we explain the truth?"

"Good question." Justin frowned. "We." He used his arm to indicate the team as Williams' comband translated the Yruf word. "No Teeli." He crossed his arms at the wrists, then pointed at the yacht.

The leader's dark tongue flicked out between her lips.

"Does she understand you?" Gonzo asked.

"I hope so. Assuming my translation is correct for *we*. I'm more confident about *no*."

The leader's gaze slowly moved from Justin to the other members of the team, settling on Cade last.

Keeping a tight rein on his emotions and the nightmarish visions driving those emotions, he repeated Justin's gestures, ending pointing at the yacht.

The leader lifted her head, her pupils dilating again while her tongue flicked in and out.

Cade slowly lowered his arm, waiting with all the patience he could muster.

Breaking eye contact, the leader turned to the doctor. A quiet exchange ensued, Williams' comband translating only a few words, including *no, Teeli,* and *head.*

"Head?" Bella darted a glance at Justin.

"Not sure," he murmured, all his attention on the two Yruf.

Their behavior indicated a debate of some kind, though the most respectful one Cade had ever seen. They never interrupted each other, and their voices and body language remained calm and relaxed.

The doctor's attention shifted to Justin, his gaze sweeping up and down before moving to the display for the med platform. In the middle of his next comment to the leader, Williams' comband chirped the word *four* before falling silent again.

"Four what?" Cade asked.

Justin held up a finger, indicating he needed Cade to hold that question.

The Yruf leader also looked Justin up and down, assessing. She spoke once more to the doctor, her tone indicating they'd come to some consensus. The immediate conflict resolved, her gaze moved to Cade, her stare drilling into his head with a none-too-subtle warning.

He did his best to look benign, though he doubted he pulled it off.

Her flicking tongue seemed to agree with him.

With a last look, she stepped away from the platform. As the bulkhead peeled back to allow her to leave, the guards closed ranks behind her, blocking the opening.

Cade almost laughed. What did they think his team would do, rush the door? Even if they got outside the room, it wouldn't do them any good. They'd still be lost and unable to reach their ship. Or the escape pod.

"Any idea what they were discussing?" he asked Justin.

"I'm not certain, but I think at least some of it was about me."

On cue, the doctor faced Justin, resting a long-fingered hand on his bicep and exerting gentle pressure.

"What's he doing?" Drew asked Williams.

"Probably wants to see if Justin's able to stand."

Justin glanced at Williams. "Should I?"

"If you feel up to it."

Justin's bare feet slid to the deck. He wobbled but the Yruf doctor kept him stable as Williams moved to his other side.

"How do you feel?" Williams asked.

"Like I'm on an ocean liner." Justin took a slow breath. "But I'm okay."

The doctor took a step away, his hand still on Justin's arm.

"I think he wants me to walk."

Williams nodded. "Then let's walk."

Cade watched with the rest of the team as the strange trio took a slow turn around the room. Justin looked fairly steady on his feet, considering, but he also had two support pillars standing by as he shuffled along.

Cade moved next to Gonzo and Drew. "Any way you two could track down where they have our escape pod stored?"

Drew and Gonzo exchanged a look before shaking their heads.

"I hate to throw in the towel without trying," Drew said, "but I haven't been able to figure out how any of their tech works, let alone how to circumvent it. I've tried every trick I can think of with my comband to gather data, with zip to show for it. I've studied their medical equipment, too, but it's like analyzing mutated Kraed technology on steroids. I'd need my tools and several weeks to even find a starting point."

"I've been checking out their weapons." Gonzo gave a subtle head nod toward the guards. "They're an unusual design. I don't think they're used at distance, like a firearm, but then again, the bulkheads don't look like they should move, either. If I thought we had a chance of getting back to the ship, I'd be willing to find out."

"By allowing yourself to be attacked?"

He shrugged. "There's a lot more than my life at stake here."

"And we're a long way from reaching *Gladiator*. Besides, it's still possible our transmission was sent before they captured the pod."

"True." Drew nodded. "The outgoing signal may have been what attracted them to it in the first place."

"Which means no heroics until–" He cut off as Justin shuffled back into his peripheral vision with Williams and the doctor, headed for the med platform. "How're you doing?"

"No dizzy spells, so that's a plus." Justin's eyelids had begun to droop, though. He didn't resist as the doctor eased him back onto the platform.

Cade leaned in. "Justin? You okay?"

"A little tired." He yawned. "But it felt good to be on my feet again. I'll rest for a bit and then go another round."

The short walk had apparently taken a lot out of him.

"Williams and I..." Another yawn. "Talked about–"

"I'll fill him in." Williams laid a hand on Justin's arm. "You take a nap."

"Aye-aye, sir." Within seconds, Justin dozed off.

Cade faced Williams, brows lifted.

"None of this is random," Williams explained as the doctor checked Justin's vitals once more. "The leader's appearance, showing us the pod, the doctor wanting Justin to walk. I think if Justin can get on his feet, she'll take him to the pod."

Which was the opportunity they needed. "And he can find out whether our transmission was sent."

"Exactly."

"What can we do to help?"

"Let him rest. He needs to regain his strength. But he's healing quickly. He might be ready to go in half a day or less."

Half a day. Hopefully it would be soon enough.

Eighty-Seven

"That's for us?" Aurora stared at the enormous tent visible from the beach walkway.

The cloud-white awning stretched over at least fifty meters of sand. Crisp white linens covered circular tables with folding chairs that filled the back section on both sides of the tent, with long rectangular tables bisecting the middle. Rows of multi-colored beach chairs sat toward the front, facing the water, which was only about twenty meters from the tent's edge. Centerpieces of tropical flowers on every table added to the festive décor.

"That's for us," her dad confirmed, leading the way to the tent.

Micah nudged her with his elbow. "Not what you expected?"

"Uh... no." Kai had warned her, but she'd never imagined something this opulent.

Ceramic platters filled with fruit and finger foods lined one of the rectangular tables. Glass or metal cylindrical towers of what looked like fresh fruit punch, iced tea, and coffee sat on another table, along with row upon row of ceramic mugs with festive holiday beach and ocean scenes painted on them.

The few people already gathered under the tent called out greetings of Merry Christmas and Mele Kalikimaka as they approached. She recognized two of the guests from Micah's birthday party, although she couldn't recall their names.

If the number of chairs was any indication, she'd be meeting a lot more people today.

Her dad introduced her to the catering manager, Naia, who was putting the finishing touches on the table decorations. "Naia's been handling this event for the past eight years. None of this would be possible without her."

The woman's plump cheeks creased in a wide smile. "I wouldn't miss it. No better place to be on Christmas."

Aurora nodded. "I agree. This is amazing."

Her dad's blue eyes sparkled. "And this is only the beginning."

An hour later, she understood what he meant. The tent had filled with people, although the feel of the interactions was more like a huge family reunion rather than a party. Smaller children chased each other around on the sand while peals of laughter and excited conversation filled the tent.

Kai and Iolana had arrived early on, and she and Micah had tag-teamed Aurora, introducing her to guests and giving her a rundown on how they knew the various attendees. In addition to their close friends, she'd also met a lot of local business owners her dad and Micah had befriended and teachers from the school where Iolana and Micah had graduated.

She spotted a group of teenagers gathered just outside the tent with their surfboards, their gazes shifting in her direction.

Micah appeared by her side a moment later. "Ready for your surfing lesson?"

Aurora swallowed as anxiety threw darts into her abdomen. Swimming in a quiet cove with Micah and the dolphins was one thing. Wading into the crowded surf was a much larger hurdle.

Iolana stepped up to her other side and gave her a sideways hug. "Of course she is."

She stared out at the waves, counting at least thirty people in the immediate vicinity, with many more near the water's edge. A tremor worked down her spine.

"Ror?" Micah's hand clasped hers, channeling a burst of excitement into her bloodstream. "You can do this."

Her gaze met his. He was projecting his feelings to her, not to override her own, which she could now control, but to show her he didn't have any fear. Which was the point, wasn't it? He and Iolana were both eager to be out in the water with her, even though they knew perfectly well how dangerous her abilities could be in that environment.

Was she going to be a coward, knocking aside the gift of their unconditional faith and trust?

No way.

She lifted her chin. "Let's do this."

Eighty-Eight

Micah kept a close eye on Aurora as they approached the water. He'd given her the longboard he used with all beginners.

Her steps grew tentative as the gap to the water's edge closed, her chest rising and falling rapidly. But she didn't stop, even when her knuckles whitened where she gripped the edge of the board.

Birdie kept pace on her other side. She looked totally relaxed, but he recognized the stubborn set of her jaw. She wasn't about to let Aurora back out.

They'd discussed their game plan during a vid call the previous day. He'd worked with nervous students before, but their anxiety had stemmed from either not wanting to look foolish or worrying they'd get injured. Aurora's fears were entirely different, emanating from her subconscious, which made them harder to predict. He didn't believe for a moment that she posed any threat, and consciously, she seemed to have accepted that as well.

But the widening of her eyes and the hitch in her breathing told him her conscious mind was fighting a battle with her less rational half.

The teenagers who'd gathered for his coaching session entered the water, working their way past the initial waves until they could get on their boards and start stroking toward deeper water.

As the sand under his feet switched from loose and dry to damp and hard-packed, he reached out with his free hand and clasped Aurora's elbow. She jerked in response, the quaking beneath his fingertips making him grind his teeth. He hated that she was suffering, but there was only one way to get through this.

He projected his calm assurance and confidence. "You can do this," he murmured, pausing to attach his leg rope to his left ankle and help Aurora with hers.

Her muscles tensed as the waves rushed up the sand to meet them and swirled around their feet and ankles. She planted her feet, immovable as a redwood, exhaling audibly.

He rested his hand on her shoulder blades, waiting, offering quiet support.

Her eyes closed and her breathing switched to the rhythm she used during meditation.

Another wave rolled in. But instead of flinching away as the water swept past her feet, Aurora relaxed, as though the pull of the surf was drawing the tension out through her skin.

Her eyes opened as the third wave danced around them. What he saw in their green depths made him smile.

"Last one in's a rotten egg." She took off so quickly he almost lost his balance, his arm swinging through the empty air as she charged into the water.

He exchanged a startled look with Birdie before racing after Aurora. He caught up with her as she was laying her board on the water, looking it over nose to tail like she'd find instructions written on the surface. He set his down beside hers. "Do you have any idea what you're doing?"

She grinned. "Not a clue."

Her smile lit up his world. "May I make a suggestion?"

"Absolutely."

"To start, you'll want to get comfortable lying on the board, figuring out the sweet spot for your weight distribution. That's best done in waist-high water."

"Oh." She glanced down, where the water was lapping at her chest. "Okay." She started to back up, but the waves caught the board and pushed it against her, making her stumble.

He snagged the nose of her board and lifted it, aligning it so that it was facing out to sea. "If you hold it like this, then the waves will glide right under it when you're walking."

She took hold of the board as he instructed, her balance immediately stabilizing as the waves stopped pushing the board. "Good tip. What's next?"

"Now you're going to lie down on the board and stroke across the water parallel to the sand. You'll want to shift your body forward and backward until you find the spot where the nose stays down without dipping into the water, and where you can still use your feet to kick."

Birdie moved next to Aurora. "I can help her with this part. Why don't you go work with the kids for a while?"

He glanced at Aurora.

She made a shooing motion with her hand. "Go on. We'll meet you out there when I'm ready."

He hesitated. "You sure?"

"Yep." She hopped up on the board's tail, which tipped the nose into the air. She gave a little yelp and scooted forward, overcorrecting as the nose dipped under the water. Her laughter washed over him. "Oh yeah. This could take a while."

The laughter convinced him she wasn't having second thoughts. "Alright. Holler if you need me."

Birdie gave him a thumbs up. "Will do."

He climbed on his board and stroked out to where the five teenagers waited. They were all eager to show him what they'd been working on.

As they made their runs, he kept an eye on the shallows, where Aurora and Birdie were paddling around. Aurora had found her positioning, and Birdie was showing her the most effective way to stroke through the water.

Aurora must have sensed his emotional shift, because she glanced his way and waved.

He waved back, his chest constricting. She was doing it, conquering her fear and having fun.

After checking in with the teenagers, he caught the next wave and hopped off his board near where Aurora and Birdie were paddling. "You ready to try belly boarding?"

Aurora's brows rose. "What's belly boarding?"

"Catching the wave while lying on the board. It's easier to get a feel for moving with the water when you're not having to think about balance."

"Makes sense." She gestured to the incoming surf. "What do I do?"

He took her through the instructions, then he and Birdie demonstrated so Aurora could see what they wanted her to do.

"Your turn."

She waded out into the waist-high water, keeping the nose of the board up and turning it as a good wave came toward her. She hopped up on the board in time, but wasn't angled quite right and got a late start paddling. The wave left her behind.

She grimaced. "That didn't work."

"You're a beginner. Cut yourself some slack. I'll go with you this time." They walked into the water together. "Make sure your board is facing the shore, and as soon as you feel the wave pick you up, start paddling. That will keep you moving with the wave."

"Got it."

They positioned their boards. "Get ready. Now!"

His body went through the motion on autopilot, which allowed him to keep his focus on her. This time she caught the wave, a delighted giggle escaping her lips as the bubbling foam propelled them toward where Birdie waited.

"That was fun!"

He grinned at her enthusiasm. "Then let's see you do it again."

She successfully caught the next five waves in a row. With most newbies, he'd end things there, but she was progressing quickly and seemed eager for another challenge. Her yoga training would probably help her with the next step.

He turned to Birdie. "Would you be willing to work with the teens while I help Aurora with her standing position?"

"Of course." She winked at Aurora and hopped on her board. "See you soon."

Motioning to Aurora, he headed for shore. "For this next part, we'll work on the sand."

She followed. "On the sand?"

"Yep." Lifting his board, he carried it to a section of damp sand and unstrapped his leg rope. "Go ahead and remove your leg rope." He drew the outline of two boards on the sand, side by side. "That's your board." He pointed to the one closer to the water. "The stringer, the center line on the board, helps to guide foot positioning. Ideally, when you pop up, you want that line running between your feet."

"Or I'll overbalance and fall off."

"Uh-huh. When you catch the wave, your hands will go to either side of the board and you'll lift your chest up to make room for your legs. Like this." He lay on his sand board and demonstrated the pose.

"That looks like up dog."

"Up dog?"

"It's a yoga pose."

"Ah. Then this should feel familiar. After you've lifted your chest, you'll bring one leg forward and keep one leg back with the stringer in between, like this." He popped into the position.

"Kinda like warrior one. Which leg comes forward?"

"That's up to you. Most likely one side will feel more natural and stronger than the other. You want your feet roughly shoulder width apart. Give it a try."

She moved to her sand board and followed his example, flowing into the standing pose without the awkwardness and instability that characterized most beginners. Her yoga practice and sparring work were serving her well.

"Try it with the other leg forward."

She switched sides, her right leg forward, but this time she wobbled, her arms pinwheeling.

"Does that feel weaker?"

"Yeah."

"Then you've found your side. The leg rope always gets attached to your back leg."

"Got it."

"Work the pose on your strong side a few more times."

She moved through the motions with ease, nailing the upright position with assurance, her feet and torso in nearly perfect form. If she'd started surfing when he had, there was a good chance she would have been his toughest competitor.

Of course, hopping up on sand was quite a bit different than on a board in the water. He'd waxed the board this morning, giving the surface plenty of grip, so that would help. The rest would be up to her.

Eighty-Nine

Micah was an open book.

Aurora hid her smile as she practiced the standing pose on the sand board.

He was clearly impressed with her form, but she'd also picked up on a trill of competitive drive creeping into his emotional field. She'd seen enough of his interactions with Birdie to know he'd challenge her to keep moving forward, but he also enjoyed his status as king of the surf.

"That's really good. Want to give it a try in the water?"

"You bet." She attached the leg rope to her right ankle and followed him down to the water's edge.

He paused to watch two of the teenagers as they surfed an incoming wave, their boards sweeping across the wave rather than riding it straight in as she had during her bodyboarding sessions.

When the force of the wave petered out, Micah called out instructions to the teens, who acknowledged with a wave before turning their boards to paddle back out. He returned his attention to her. "You'll catch the wave just like you did with the body boarding. After you pop up, you'll want to crouch low. That will help with balance and stability. If you do fall off—which you probably will—try to land on your feet with knees bent, or belly flop. You want to avoid landing on your shoulder, your head, or with straight legs."

She lifted one brow. "Because I might get hurt?"

"Yeah. It's—" He paused, catching her meaning. "Well, no, I guess you wouldn't. But it's still a good practice to protect those areas. And to be aware of other surfers nearby."

"Understood." That last part was a top priority. She'd conquered the irrational terror that had held her captive. The specter of unintentionally electrocuting every living being in the water no longer held sway. But she didn't want to accidentally run into someone while her shield was engaged, either.

He smiled. "Let's see what you've got."

Grasping her board, she strode into the water until it lapped around her waist. A wave rolled toward her. She adjusted her grip, pivoted her board and caught the wave. As soon as the motion carried her forward, she moved her hands, lifted her chest, and brought her legs up.

But unlike the sand board, this one wobbled underneath her, throwing off her foot position. She crouched, but her center of gravity pulled her to one side. Adjusting her foot bought her an extra second before gravity circled her torso and dragged her over. Pushing off with her feet, she landed with a splash, the wave continuing on without her while the one right behind it hit her thighs, pushing her forward a couple steps.

"Good first run!" Micah called out. "Go again."

She picked up her board and headed back out. The next wave produced a similar result, but on the third attempt, she managed to stay up, albeit with a lot of arm waving and leg adjustments. She made seven more runs, with mixed results, before Micah motioned her over.

"Your form is good, but your focus is off. Remember, wherever you point your front arm and direct your gaze, that's where you'll go. If you look down at the water, or allow your arm to drop toward the water, your body will follow."

Which perfectly described what she'd been doing.

He lifted his board. "Let's catch this next one together. But before we do, I want you to engage your energy field, wrap it around the two of us, and open yourself to receiving what I'm projecting."

"Like with the dolphins?"

"Yep. Another experiment."

"Okay." The last one had certainly turned out well.

After aligning their boards she engaged her field, expanding it to encompass him as the wave approached.

"Get ready. Go!"

She heard the words, but she also felt an energetic push that propelled her onto her board. She started paddling, the wave catching her. She lifted up, rising to her feet on the waxed surface. She didn't look at Micah, but she could sense him as clearly as if she could see him. Or more accurately, like he was standing on the board with her. She kept her focus down her arm toward the shore, but her body made millimeter adjustments as if guided by an unseen hand, keeping her stable on the board.

Euphoric joy surrounded her and filled her from head to toe as they coasted along the wave, her body as perfectly balanced as if she was practicing on her yoga mat. She could sense her emotions blending with Micah's, as synchronized as the water droplets that made up the rolling wave, flowing together without beginning or end.

As the wave lost momentum, she hopped off into the ankle-deep water. Pivoting toward Micah, she dropped the energy field.

His eyes looked lit from within. "It worked! Could you hear me?"

"Hear you?"

"Yeah. Could you hear my instructions? I projected my thoughts like I do with the dolphins. You reacted like you could."

"Hear? No. But I felt you making adjustments to my form."

"You felt it?"

"Yeah. It felt like you were right with me, moving my body into position."

"Huh."

"Not what you expected?"

"No. I could tell when you were out of position and I'd think of the correction. You'd immediately make the change. But now that you mention it, I'm not sure I was seeing it so much as feeling it. Like you were on my board and we were balancing together. Interesting."

"Very." The connection that bound them obviously had layers they had yet to explore.

"You've never felt anything like it before?"

"Not like that. It was almost like our subconscious minds linked."

He nodded. "I think that's exactly what happened. We were both focused on the same task, connected by your field, and open to each other. In that moment, we were able to function as a single entity."

Goosebumps lifted the hair on her arms. "That's... different."

The tremor in Micah's emotional field indicated he was a little spooked, too. "You sure that's never happened with another Suulh?"

"No. Not even Mya. Or Mom." Opening herself that fully to her mother would have been impossible with the chasm that stood between them. She'd never make herself that vulnerable. And while she'd blended her field with Mya's before, it wasn't the same. She'd never felt Mya was an extension of herself.

This connection with Micah had been effortless, instinctual, primal. The closest she'd ever come to a similar sensation of seamless interconnection had been with Cade, when their focus was entirely on each other and the outside world faded away.

A gleam lit Micah's eyes. "Want to try again?"

She accepted the challenge. "Okay."

They set up for the run, going out a little deeper into the water before she engaged her field. Calm focus surrounded her. Catching the wave took almost no effort. Instead of concentrating on her movements, she felt the cool lap of the water across her feet, the salty air brushing her cheeks, the sun warming her skin.

She glided along as the euphoria she'd experienced last time returned, a laugh bubbling out of her throat like champagne from a bottle. She heard an answering rumble from beside her, Micah's laughter blending with hers as they swept along the surface of the water.

A piercing whistle and clapping greeted them as they hopped off their boards into the surf. She glanced over her shoulder and discovered Iolana and all five teens were straddling their boards watching them. Iolana stuck her fingers in her mouth and let out another sharp whistle of appreciation.

More clapping joined in, this time from the direction of the tent where their dad and Kai were watching them.

Heat climbed up her neck, but she grinned and waved before turning to Micah. "That was amazing!"

He shone like a star. "You're amazing."

"*We're* amazing." She wrapped her arm around his waist and squeezed. "Thank you."

He squeezed back. "You're welcome." The huskiness in his voice paralleled the powerful emotions she sensed welling inside him.

And because they were so completely in tune in that moment, the meaning behind those emotions cut right into her heart. She held his gaze. "This isn't the end. I promise."

Moisture gathered in his eyes. He blinked, then pulled her close in a one-armed bear hug. "I love you, sis."

"I love you too, big brother."

Ninety

After a break for lunch served buffet style under the big tent, Aurora settled into one of the beach chairs at a smaller tent near the water's edge, with Micah and Birdie on either side of her. Her dad and Kai stood just in front of the tent, ready to officiate the upcoming surfing competition, while Micah and Birdie acted as judges.

"Did you and Iolana ever participate in the competition?" she asked Micah.

"We used to when we were teenagers, back when Dad did all the judging." He grinned. "Now we get to be the big finale instead."

Because it was a family event, they'd created a spectrum of activities that enabled everyone to participate, starting with the youngest competitors. Having spent the morning learning the basics, Aurora had a new appreciation for how good many of the surfers were.

In between the first and second round of competition, two tandem surfing pairs performed an exhibition of acrobatic lifts while riding the waves.

Aurora nudged Micah with her shoulder. "Have you and Iolana ever tried that?"

He shook his head. "She never had any interest."

"Ha! Interest had nothing to do with it," Birdie chimed in. "I'm too much woman for Stone. Even with his bulging muscles, I didn't trust him not to drop me in the drink."

Micah rolled his eyes. "What she means is most women who participate in the sport are short and acrobatic.

Birdie was one of the tallest girls in our graduating class. And she was never interested in gymnastics."

"Why bother swinging on bars or rolling around on mats when you could be out here?" She gestured to the open water.

Micah conceded the point as the performance drew to a close. "Ready for round two?"

Birdie nodded. "All set."

The surfers took to the waves again. Aurora found herself cheering with the crowd during each run and holding her breath whenever a surfer toppled from their board. She also enjoyed Micah and Birdie's easy banter. Their insightful comments about what they were seeing helped her understand the criteria they were using for judging.

Her dad and Kai joined them under the tent after round two ended. Her dad winked at her as he sat in one of the beach chairs. "Time for the surf dog competition."

"Surf dog?"

"Yep. It's our most popular event." He gestured to where a group had gathered with their canines, each dog outfitted with a life vest and a dog-sized surfboard.

Aurora stared, taking it all in. "Oh, my goodness. I had no idea."

"A lot of the dogs on this island love surfing." Birdie pulled up the list of entrants. "Some surf with their humans, but this competition is for dogs only."

"And you can help us judge this one," Micah added.

"What are the criteria?"

"Staying on the board, for one. They also get points for any special tricks."

"What kinds of tricks?"

"Could be any kind of unusual movement. You'll know it when you see it. It's a little easier for them to maneuver on the board since they have four feet rather than two."

"And a lower center of gravity," Birdie added.

"I suppose so. Any other criteria?"

"I'll be judging them on difficulty of the wave. And Birdie will give them a score based on surfing style."

Aurora's lips twitched. "This should be very interesting."

Big understatement. The first entrant was a golden retriever named Daisy wearing a sunshine-yellow life vest that matched the yellow daisies painted on her board.

Aurora laughed as the dog caught the wave. "She's in puppy pose!"

Micah glanced at her. "Puppy pose?"

"A yoga posture." The dog's front legs were stretched out low to the board, head up and butt high in the air. "Seems to be working for her." The wave was a little rough, but the dog rode it like a champ all the way in.

The audience cheered, and the golden barked in response before hopping into the water with a splash.

Birdie consulted the list. "Next up is a bulldog named Sharkey."

"Bulldog?" Aurora glanced at her. "They aren't water dogs, are they?"

"Not normally. But with a name like Sharkey, I'm guessing this guy's an exception."

Sure enough, the dog turned out to be a real crowd-pleaser. Not only was he wearing a color-coordinated shark's fin attached to the top of his life vest, but as soon as he caught the wave, his pudgy body spun around so he was surfing backwards, looking over his shoulder at the crowd with his tongue lolling out of his mouth in a happy grin.

"That's what I mean by tricks," Micah told Aurora over the whistles and cheers.

The parade of aquatic pooches continued, wrapping up with a triple entry of a Bernese Mountain Dog, Irish Setter, and a Border Terrier that rode in together on a single board, looking like the personification of large, medium, and small.

First prize went to Sharkey, but all the dogs received bags of goodies and toys to take home. Aurora laughed as the Bernese Mountain Dog she'd just given a prize to swept his tongue over her cheek in a big kiss.

Throughout the festivities, Aurora watched Micah almost as much as the surfers. He had the focused intensity of a born teacher, analyzing and making notes while scoring the contestants. No doubt each one would receive valuable insights that would help them take their skills to the next level.

After the final round of competition, Micah and Iolana stood, reaching for their boards. "Showtime." He gave her a big grin before setting out for the water with Iolana.

Her dad and Kai moved to the seats they'd vacated. "This is my favorite part," her dad said as he settled in next to her.

"What are they going to do?"

"Not sure, although it will probably involve the dolphins."

She'd forgotten all about the dolphins. She hadn't seen any sign of them while she was in the water. "Are they out there?"

"Oh, sure," Kai said. "The pod's always nearby on Christmas day, whether we see them or not."

As if on cue, she spotted a fin poking briefly out of the water behind the breaking waves before disappearing under the rippling surface.

Micah and Iolana were already halfway to the same spot, dropping under the waves and then continuing to paddle out. Duck diving Micah had called it.

"You having a good time?" Kai asked her.

"The best."

"Glad you came?"

"Oh, yeah." She turned and gave her dad a kiss on the cheek. "Thanks for the invitation."

His soft smile warmed her heart. "It's an open invitation anytime you can make it."

The understanding in his eyes warmed the rest of her. What a change to have a parent who supported and encouraged her to go after what she wanted, rather than throwing massive monoliths in her way.

"Iolana's ready." Kai pointed out toward the water.

Iolana was on her board, head turned as she watched the incoming wave. As she popped up onto her feet, two dolphins leapt out of the water behind her, their silvery skin sparkling in the sunlight as they crossed each other in the air and slid back into the sea.

Cheers erupted from the crowd. Iolana crouched lower, picking up speed on her board, making it dance across the cresting wave. Shouts and whoops urged her on as she rode the wave with the assurance of a creature of the sea.

Aurora rose to her feet, clapping and cheering with everyone else as Iolana glided in with the whitewater.

Iolana hopped off her board and bowed, waving to the crowd before pivoting to face the water.

Aurora's gaze moved out to the ocean as well, where Micah sat on his board, as relaxed as if he was having a cup of tea. She spotted two more fins near him. When he shifted position, his head turning to the incoming waves, a hush fell over the crowd.

Aurora dug her toes into the sand as anticipation curled in her belly like a cat ready to spring.

Micah caught the wave, his body moving with the fluid grace of a sea creature. As she'd anticipated, several silvery forms appeared on either side of him, riding the wave as he took the board on a looping path up and down the wave face.

One of the dolphins shifted position as Micah turned the board and crouched. The dolphin cut sideways and leapt out of the water directly over Micah's head, the droplets from the dolphin's underbelly and tail sprinkling Micah's face, making him laugh. She couldn't hear the sound, but she could feel her brother's surge of joy as he took the board in an arcing turn.

That had to be Cutter.

Another dolphin broke from the group, surging in front of the wave like a torpedo shot from a submarine.

Streak.

Micah crouched again as the dolphin surged out of the water, passing over Micah in the opposite direction as more droplets rained down.

This time she did hear Micah's delighted laugh as he rode the whitewater in.

The dolphins, however, turned back and disappeared below the surface.

Aurora's palms burned from clapping by the time Micah hopped into the water, joined Iolana, and bowed.

He was immediately mobbed by the other surfers who blocked him from view. But she didn't need to see him to know he was in his element.

"Pretty impressive, huh?" Kai asked her.

"Incredible." Seeing the two dolphins with him had made it extra special. She'd carry the memory of this moment close to her heart. She'd need it during the times when necessity would put physical distance between them.

Her dad wrapped his arm around her shoulders. "He loves having you here."

He wasn't just talking about the party. "I know. I love being here, too." But that didn't change the fact that she had a starship waiting for her.

Ninety-One

Mya had never felt so relaxed in her life. She'd had the most incredible dream about Jonarel, one so real that—

Her train of thought collided with a brick wall as she discovered she wasn't alone in her bed.

And she couldn't move.

Dark green arms the size of tree branches enfolded her torso, pressing her back against a mountain of warm, equally green skin. Her legs were similarly incapacitated by a muscular thigh curled over hers.

Jonarel's thigh.

Because he was in her bed.

It hadn't been a dream.

She blinked rapidly, the only way to release the building tension. *What have I done?*

It had seemed so natural, so right at the time, but things looked quite different now that her brain wasn't fogged by a sensual haze. She'd had *sex* with Jonarel. And it had been glorious. She'd never known her body could feel such pleasure.

But now what? He was in love with Aurora. A quick search of their conversation the night before gave no indication anything had changed in that area.

Yes, he was in her bed, not Aurora's, but unlike her, his behavior wasn't necessarily tied to his feelings. He'd responded to her obvious attraction in the way any hot-blooded Kraed would. They were a sensual species. She'd always known that. She seemed to be the only one who'd seen how hard Jonarel had fought to conceal that side of his nature while living among humans. How hard it had been for him to hide his desire from Aurora.

So, what had happened last night made perfect sense. She'd always been his source of comfort, the one he could be himself with no matter what. Giving in to his bottled-up emotions after she'd made it clear she was very open to the concept had a certain logic.

But there was no future in it. Even if he wasn't in love with Aurora—a hugely important if—he had already defied his clan to support Aurora's autonomy. If he announced he was taking Mya as his mate, he'd probably be banned from Drakar forever.

Not that he'd even consider the idea in the first place. The sex had been amazing, but neither of them had said anything about an emotional investment. He clearly found her desirable, but that was a far cry from being in love with her.

Which left her with a decision to make. Did she want their physical relationship to continue? Judging by his actions last night and the way he was curled around her now, he'd be fine with the idea.

Was she? She'd been swept away by her core desires the first time, but that wouldn't be the case if things continued. The harsh glare of reality shone like a spotlight on the situation, revealing all the sharp corners and jagged edges she'd ignored.

She couldn't ignore them now.

A deep rumble vibrated against her back, almost like a purr. He shifted, pulling her closer and nuzzling her neck. He murmured something in what she assumed was the Kraed language that sounded like *trick-call-a*.

"What?"

He brought his mouth next to her ear, his breath sending shivers over her skin. "Good morning."

"Morning." The *good* part was still up for debate.

At least in this position she didn't have to look at him. The last thing she wanted was his pity. If he figured out she wanted more than physical pleasure, she was doomed. And she didn't trust herself to hide her emotions. Not after what they'd shared.

His tongue traced the curve of her ear, spreading warmth through her traitorous body.

She couldn't do this. Pleasure had turned to pain. She needed space. Fast.

She pulled away as far as the restraint of his arms would allow, snaking one hand out to grab the top blanket. "I need to get up."

He stilled. "Why?"

Because this is killing me. "Nature's call."

"Oh." He released her with obvious reluctance.

She moved like lightning, sliding out of bed and snatching up the blanket in one motion, wrapping it around her torso as she darted to the bathroom and closed the door. She leaned her back against it, fighting to control her breathing and her racing heart.

This was ridiculous. She was running from Jonarel. Hiding from him in the bathroom like some adolescent girl with a crush. She was a doctor for crying out loud! Her professional bedside manner could act as her shield.

As long as she was in the bathroom, she made use of the facilities and took a peek in the mirror. The woman staring back at her looked like a woodland fairy—hair disheveled, eyes bright, skin flushed. All she needed was a ring of leaves woven into her hair to complete the picture.

Instead, she grabbed her brush and corralled her hair into some semblance of order. If she'd kept the short cut she was used to, it wouldn't be a problem. One of the many items she'd neglected on her to do list.

She splashed cold water on her face, took a couple deep breaths, and secured the blanket firmly around her body like a toga.

She could do this. Dr. Forrest was back in the house.

But so was a very naked Kraed.

She tripped over her own feet when she caught sight of him lounging in her bed, only one leg covered by the sheet. The rest of him was beautifully, gloriously on display.

Her throat tightened as heat bloomed. Her mind might be fighting to keep a professional detachment, but her body remembered the feel, the taste, the tactile joy she'd found with him.

And it wanted more.

He held out his hand.

She didn't move.

His dark brows drew down. "Lelindia?"

"Yes?"

"What is wrong?"

Wrong? Where should she start? "I should get dressed. Check in with Kire."

His frown deepened. He glanced at the chronometer near her bed. "We have many hours before we will reach Sol Station."

"I know." She turned toward her closet, welcoming the distraction as she pulled out underwear, a tunic, and pants. "But I have other things I need to take care of." *Like not throwing myself back into your arms.*

The rustle of the sheets told her he'd gotten up, but she still squeaked when his arms closed around her. He moved with the speed and stealth of a jungle cat.

Gently but insistently he turned her around to face him. "Lelindia, what is wrong?"

At least the clothes in her arms provided a buffer to his bare skin. But she couldn't avoid looking at him as he cupped her jaw and tilted her head back.

She needed to set boundaries quickly, before her resolve crumbled. "Maybe you should call me Mya, instead."

Confusion flickered across his handsome face. "Why?"

"Using my real name seems too... intimate."

A flash of heat lit his golden eyes, but she couldn't tell if it was desire or anger. "It is meant to be intimate."

Maybe a little bit of both. "But we're going to be interacting with the crew, and I'd rather they didn't know."

The muscles in his arms flexed and his jaw tightened. "You regret what we shared."

"No!" Whatever else he thought, she couldn't let him believe that. It would be a lie. She was in hell right now, but it was a price she'd been willing to pay for experiencing heaven. "I just don't think we should continue."

Now his face looked like granite. "Continue." Not a question. A command.

"Last night was wonderful. I don't regret it. We both obviously needed... comfort. But carrying on a physical relationship would be complicated. It's not like we're going to get emotionally involved with each other." She couldn't get more emotionally involved with him. She was already in over her head. Nowhere to go but down.

His arms dropped to his sides. "I see." He backed away and began dressing. "I am glad I could bring you... comfort."

She didn't need her Nedale gifts to see the tightening of his muscles that indicated emotional stress. She'd hurt him, the last thing she'd ever intended. "It really was wonderful." Even to her ears, it sounded lame.

His derisive snort gave her his views on the comment. He sat on the bed and began lacing up his boots with more speed than she would have thought possible. "Now your curiosity is satisfied."

"Curiosity?" What the hell did that mean? And then her stomach plummeted into her feet as understanding dawned. "You think I slept with you because I was *curious?*"

He was on the second boot and working quickly. "You cannot help it. Alien life fascinates you, flora and fauna. You must have wondered what it would be like to have sex with a Kraed."

She wanted to deny it, but he was right on both counts. He just didn't understand that the only Kraed who fascinated her was him. And she couldn't tell him that without revealing how she felt.

Better to temporarily wound his pride than earn his eternal pity.

He met her gaze, clearly taking her silence for confirmation. His golden eyes looked flat as wheat, his expression an impassive mask. He stood, filling the compact room with the strength of his presence. "Do not worry, *Mya.*"

His emphasis on her name made her flinch.

"No one on the crew will ever know."

And then he was gone.

The clothes tumbled to the floor as she pressed her hands to her heart. At that moment, it felt like it would never beat again.

Ninety-Two

The soft light of the setting sun sparkled on the water from the west, painting ribbons of gold over the surface.

Most of the guests, including Aurora, took advantage of the rows of solar showers and adjoining dressing compartments to wash away the accumulated saltwater and sand and change into clean clothes. Showering outdoors was a new experience, with the tangy sea air brushing her skin and the happy chatter of the other guests surrounding her. But rather than feeling self-conscious with only a thin panel of wood for privacy, she reveled in the connection with her surroundings.

After securing her damp hair in a braid and pulling on the flowing sea green beach dress her dad had presented her with that morning, she joined Micah and Iolana in the buffet line. The tent had been taken down, leaving the tables open to the sky, where the first glimmers of emerging stars peeked through the fading sunset. Torches lined the area, casting a vibrant glow and making the silver platters sparkle. The aromas from the table made her stomach rumble as she filled her plate.

"And don't forget dessert." Micah pointed to a table that looked more like an artistic sculpture than a food display, with confections arrayed on multiple levels of snowy-white linens and silver trays. "Dad made sure there were plenty of dark chocolate options for you. And him."

"He's a chocoholic, too?"

"Big time."

Sure enough, amid the assortment of traditional Hawaiian treats she spotted dark chocolate brownies, fudge, and a decadent chocolate cake drizzled with chocolate ganache. She snagged bite-sized pieces of each, as well as a few other goodies that caught her eye.

Her dad and Kai sat at a round table in front of a raised platform. She spotted her dad's dessert plate, which looked remarkably similar to hers, full of dark chocolate treats. He glanced at her plate and gave her a wink as she sat down.

As the other guests filled the nearby tables, a group of young women stepped onto the platform. They were wearing matching floral dresses with flowing skirts, leis around their necks, and bands of flowers woven into their long dark hair. Three musicians moved behind them—a woman with a ukulele, a man with a guitar, and an older man with a standing bass.

They began to play, the woman singing a lovely melody while the dancers flowed into synchronous motion, hips swaying side to side, arms outstretched as they expressed with their bodies and movements the story behind the song. The effect was hypnotic, the murmur of the crowd ceasing as all attention focused on the stage.

But as the dancers continued their graceful harmony of motion, a soft ache settled into her chest. The movements reminded her of the lyrical quality of the ceremonial Suulh language. In fact, if she unfocused her eyes a little, she could easily believe one of the dark-haired women was Raaveen.

Her fingernails dug into her thighs. How long had it been since she'd spoken with the young woman she'd left in charge of the Suulh settlement? Almost two months? She'd been in contact through Justin until she'd landed on Tnaryt's ship. Since then? She hadn't been able to summon the energy to broach the subject.

Now that felt like a glaring omission. She didn't even know if they'd finished work on the settlement. Or if Raaveen's father, Ren, was continuing to heal. Mya would have those answers by now. If her timetable was accurate, the *Starhawke* would be on the way back to Sol Station.

Her heartbeat picked up. She missed her ship. She missed her crew. And she missed the sense of forward motion that came with each new mission.

She'd needed this time with her dad and Micah. She'd needed the peace and light that she'd found in their company, all that they had taught her. But she'd conquered her fears. And she was well on her way to controlling her physical and emotional reactions to the Suulh.

Her crew needed her. The Suulh on Azaana needed her. The Suulh on the original homeworld needed her. And thanks to her dad and Micah, she was finally ready to face the challenges before her head-on.

The ache shifted, growing sharper, more insistent.

But reaching for one meant letting go of the other. It meant leaving with no guarantee of when she'd be back.

A hand circled her wrist. She met her dad's concerned gaze.

What's wrong? he mouthed.

She glanced skyward, where the stars were steadily claiming the expanse of deepening purple and blue. Reanne was out there somewhere, plotting her next attack.

His gaze followed hers, understanding dawning in his eyes. He gave a slow nod, acknowledging the unspoken truth her emotional state explained better than words.

It was time to return to her ship and crew.

And track down the psychotic former friend who wanted to destroy her.

Ninety-Three

Cade had just finished a bowl of lukewarm mash when the Yruf leader reappeared with the doctor.

All conversation among his team ceased as the leader walked straight to Justin, her guards flanking her as before, though not as close.

Cade set down the bowl and switched on the Yruf translation program he'd copied from Williams' comband. Standing, he approached the med platform where Justin had been reclining, talking to Bella.

Justin slid off the side of the platform next to Bella, bringing him face-to-chest with the Yruf leader. He tilted his head back to meet her gaze as the doctor checked his vitals.

The leader looked him up and down, as if cataloguing the changes in his appearance. Justin had been able to wash up at the large sanitation station at the back of the room, which took care of the basics of hygiene, but his beard stubble was getting thicker by the hour, making him look as scruffy as Cade and Williams. Gonzo was the only one who'd been spared. Thanks to his existing goatee, he just looked like he was switching to a full beard.

The Yruf leader lifted a hand, her long fingers brushing across the bristle on Justin's face.

He didn't move, his focus entirely on her.

She tilted his head to the side, running a finger along the point where his beard met his hairline. Her demeanor indicated fascination.

"I'll bet she's never seen a beard growing in before," Williams said as he came up next to Cade. "It might help our case. Teeli don't have them."

Her gaze darted to Williams. "Teeli?"

Williams used the crossed wrists gesture and the Yruf word for *no.* "No Teeli." He ran a hand across the dark scruff on his own face, which rasped under his palm.

Her tongue flicked in and out for several moments before she returned her attention to Justin. Lowering her hand, she spoke, Cade's comband providing a translation for two words, *head* and *walk.*

Justin listened intently, then smiled and gestured to himself, head to toe. "Nine," he said in the Yruf language, the comband translating to Galish.

"What's she asking?" Cade asked.

"How I'm doing, I think. And whether I can walk."

The Yruf leader seemed satisfied with his response. She turned to the doctor, who had finished his scans. A very short interchange followed, before the doctor stepped away.

The leader withdrew the same circular disc from her cloak she'd brought previously and projected the image of *Gladiator*'s escape pod. Whatever she said to Justin next wasn't translatable at all.

But they'd been anticipating this scenario, and the team had come up with a strategy. Holding the Yruf leader's gaze, Justin responded in her language, pointing first at himself, then Cade, then the image of the escape pod. "One, two, walk," the comband translated.

Her gaze shifted to Cade. It felt like she was looking into his soul.

He forced his mind and body to remain relaxed, his emotions calm. He needed the leader to let him go with Justin. If the escape pod hadn't sent its message, every second would count. They'd need to convince her to launch it. Or better yet, let the team return to *Gladiator*.

Justin believed Cade had the best chance of doing that. Cade hadn't been prepared for that little insight. But Justin had explained that he'd been watching the leader's reactions and analyzing the way the Yruf communicated. His theory was that there was more to her attitude toward Cade than they understood. And that it might hold the key to their freedom.

But the only way to test that theory was to orchestrate time together with the leader, where Justin could observe her interacting with him.

Her scrutiny continued for several breaths. He had the odd sensation that she was somehow in his head. But that was crazy.

Her gaze shifted to Williams. "Two," the comband translated, as she pointed at him.

She wanted Williams to go with Justin instead.

"No." Justin placed his hand on Cade's shoulder. "Two."

Flick, flick of her tongue. Justin was taking a chance by insisting, but Cade trusted his judgement implicitly. If he believed Cade needed to be there, he'd support him one hundred percent.

The leader must have realized Justin wouldn't budge. She glanced between the two of them, then said the one word he knew without a translator. "Shreenef."

"I guess we're going," he said to Justin.

"Yep."

As the guards moved beside Cade, Bella reached out and caught Justin's hand. "Don't get lost, Byrnsie."

"Me? Never." He grinned, bending down to kiss the top of her head. "We'll see you soon."

"You better." She gave him a playful swat. "Don't make me come find you."

"Yes, ma'am."

As Cade and Justin followed the Yruf leader out of the room, four more emerald-scaled guards awaited them on the other side of the shifting bulkhead, along with two drones. The drones dropped to chest level as the group strode along the winding passageway behind the imposing figure of the leader. With the four guards on either side and behind, it was like being at the center of a circle of evergreens. Christmas, indeed.

"How did you know she'd agree?" Cade asked in an undertone, indicating the Yruf leader.

"Because I finally figured out what's so unusual about their language. The words they speak are only part of the whole. I thought maybe they were using non-verbal cues to fill in the blanks, but I wasn't seeing any. What I did see was the focused concentration they have when they communicate. I think they're projecting mental images."

"You mean telepathy?"

"Not exactly. They're not reading each other's thoughts. At least, I don't think so. It's like the words they speak provide a framework, and the imagery fills in the details."

"How can you know that?"

"Because I've witnessed something similar with the Suulh. Raaveen, Paaw, and Sparw would communicate that way, with the same kind of focused look. I was never able to see the imagery they used, but while we were captives of the Meer, I got pretty good at picking up the direction of their thoughts."

"But how did knowing that convince you she'd let me come along?"

"Because you—"

Justin broke off as the leader halted the group. The bulkheads closed in, creating the circle of the lift.

The momentary lessening of pressure from the deck indicated they were descending, and Cade's count when they stopped told him they might be on the same level where *Gladiator* was being held.

As the bulkheads rustled open to expose a passageway, the leader strode forward, Cade and Justin following behind. "I think we're close to *Gladiator.*"

Justin nodded. "That's what I expected." He met Cade's gaze. "I know you want to get to the ship, but try not to think about it. If I'm right, your thoughts might be what's making the leader nervous."

"*My* thoughts? Why me?"

"You mean why not the rest of us? I'm not sure." Justin frowned, his gaze drifting to the leader. "Have you ever tried communicating with Aurora through imagery, the way she and the other Suulh do?"

"No."

"Not even when you were at the Academy together?"

"Definitely not. She did everything she could to keep her abilities hidden from me. If I hadn't been able to see her energy field, I'm not sure she would have revealed any of her secrets."

"Hmm. What about that? You're the only one on the team who can see their fields."

"Are you trying to say I'm a Suulh?"

Justin's lips twitched. "No. But I think you're much more receptive and empathic than you think. It might be part of what drew you to Aurora in the first place. Her energy spoke to you."

A lot more than her energy spoke to him.

"Maybe that's part of the equation. If the Suulh were here, they might be able to speak with the Yruf." He was silent for a moment. "I think the Yruf are picking up on images you're unconsciously projecting. Without the context of words, some of them might seem threatening."

"Great. You're saying I'm threatening them without realizing it?"

"Possibly."

"So what do I do? Send happy pictures?"

"Not necessarily. Even if you consciously sent images you believed were positive, they might not mean anything to the Yruf. Or worse, they might have an unintentional meaning that causes friction. You don't have any shared experiences or a common frame of reference with the Yruf."

Cade frowned. "I'm not following."

"Let's say you projected an image of the Fleet insignia or Earth, which means something very specific to us, but absolutely nothing to them. You could show it to them a hundred times, and they're not going to understand the meaning. To get the point across, you'd have to come up with an equivalent image that has the same emotional or intellectual context for them. But without knowing the details of their culture and history, that's a virtually impossible task."

"And they don't know any more about us than we do about them."

"Exactly. The Yruf are alien to us in every way, as we are to them. I'm doing my best to communicate with them, but I may never get to the point where I truly understand them, because I can't see their mental imagery."

"You've done well so far."

"Because we've been dealing with simple concepts all related to me—my health, the team, the escape pod. Abstract concepts like trust, honesty, and integrity are a ballgame played on a rogue planet. Everyone's flailing in the dark."

Flailing in the dark was an apt description for how he'd felt ever since they'd set foot on this ship.

"But you may be able to bridge that gap."

"How? You just said any image I think of could potentially cause conflict." His gaze shifted to the guards, who were all watching him, not Justin or the leader. "Maybe I shouldn't have come with you."

Justin shook his head. "I disagree. You're our leader. And our best hope. But you may have to tap into mental muscles you've never worked before. Don't focus on what you're projecting. Instead, focus on opening yourself to what they're projecting."

He was *not* onboard with that. He didn't want the Yruf playing with his head.

The leader turned, her steps slowing and her neck curving in a way no human's could, her gaze resting on Cade. She came to a stop, halting the entire group. She said something, but the comband couldn't translate.

Cade stared back at her, a weird jolt running through his body as an image that might have been the escape pod flashed in his mind. He blinked twice before meeting Justin's gaze. "I think we're here."

That wasn't disturbing at all. Communicating the Yruf way might be their best option, but that didn't make it a good one.

The bulkheads to their right shifted, creating an opening two meters wide. Light spilled out, the glow more like sunlight than the dusky light of the passageways. Two of the guards stepped through the opening first, followed by the leader and the two drones. Cade, Justin, and the other two guards brought up the rear.

The chamber on the other side was close to the size of a typical shuttle bay, but devoid of the markings or hardware that would be found on a Fleet ship. Cade pivoted slightly to take in the space, his gaze resting on the circular object sitting on the deck like a giant boulder. The escape pod looked distinctly out of place in the rich-toned, geometrically patterned space, the hatch still open, exposing the interior.

He took a step toward the craft, bumping into the drone still hovering in front of him. It let out a bleat of protest, pushing back with enough force to rock him back on his heels.

Justin rested a hand on his shoulder, steadying him. "Easy."

The rustle of the bulkhead made him turn. It had moved up behind them, creating a curved pocket with the two of them at the center. The four guards now stood facing them at the other end, weapons aimed at him, not Justin. Both drones were making whirring noises that seemed more than a little ominous.

The Yruf leader stood behind the guards, her face visible over their heads. Her emerald green scales shone like polished gems in the warm light, making them look almost wet. But there was no warmth in her eyes.

He held his hands up, palms out. "Sorry."

Flick, flick of her tongue. She spoke to the guards. Two moved closer to Cade, though far enough away he couldn't reach them if he tried. The other two stepped back toward the escape pod, which was still visible through the gap in the curved bulkhead.

"Shreenef," the leader said to them.

The drones moved forward in the direction of the pod. Cade and Justin followed.

Cade kept his hands where the Yruf could see them and fought to keep his thoughts from winding into a coiled spring as they approached the pod.

Justin managed to look as though nothing more than idle curiosity drew him.

Cade couldn't muster that level of nonchalance, but he focused on taking slow, even breaths. Getting the Yruf riled up again would ruin their chance at obtaining the pod's transmission logs.

The leader stopped in front of the open hatch, blocking the entrance as she turned to face them.

Cade studiously ignored the urge to check his comband, not really wanting a reminder of the passage of time. He worked to keep his mind blank, but a meditative state did not come naturally to him. Unfortunately, if Justin was right about the Yruf's reaction to any mental images he was conjuring, monitoring every thought was a necessity.

The leader faced Justin, her words slow and deliberate. But Cade's comband couldn't translate any of them.

"What's she asking?"

Justin took a few seconds to answer, his gaze still on the leader. "I think she wants to know the escape pod's function before she'll let us inside." He gave Cade an apologetic look. "I'm not sure how to explain it to her. I don't think they have anything similar on this ship."

"No escape pods? That seems unlikely on a ship this size."

Justin shook his head. "Not after what Gonzo told me about the salvage job they did. Or if you think about how this ship functions. Several modular ships forming a united whole. Moveable bulkheads on all decks that can react in a heartbeat. Why would they need escape pods?"

"In case of emergency."

"But their ship design could handle emergencies like hull breaches, engine explosions, and life support failure relatively easily, isolating a damaged section and realigning the rest of the ship to compensate. We need escape pods because our ships can't do that. But for them, abandoning ship makes no sense."

He glanced at the leader, who was watching them intently but patiently. "So, she's concluded the pod serves a nefarious purpose because she can't imagine a benign one?"

"That about sums it up. Until we came along, the Yruf had only dealt with the other Setarip factions and the Teeli. None of them are exactly known for providing a positive role model."

Cade rubbed his forehead with his fingertips. A headache was building steam. "Then what do we do?"

"Ready to try a little Yruf communication?"

No. The taste he'd gotten in the passageway, if that was in fact what he'd experienced, hadn't put him in a more receptive mood. "I want to try something else first." Calling up a stored image file on his comband, he projected it.

The Yruf leader's gaze snapped to the image of the blue and white sphere, her pupils dilating and her tongue flicking in and out.

Cade pointed at it. "Home." He pointed at the escape pod. "Pod." Then he pointed at each in succession. "Pod home."

The Yruf leader's demeanor shifted as she stared at the image. She went from looking suspicious to intrigued. Her head lifted, her hypnotic diamond-pupiled gaze meeting his, capturing him like a fly in a web.

She said a word, softly, reverently, but that wasn't what held him immobile. Images flickered like ghosts before his eyes. Or were they in his mind? He couldn't be sure.

A blue and white planet very similar to Earth. Two orbiting moons. Glorious sunsets, lush greenery, azure seas. He could smell the salt air, feel the brush of the wind through his hair.

And then it was gone.

He inhaled sharply as the harsh smell of scorched earth and charred flesh hit him. Desolation lay before him in an endless sea of blackened ruin. Somewhere in the distance, a plume of intense red and orange erupted, followed by another and another. And then he was yanked backwards, pulled through space into orbit, watching in horror as the violent death spasms of the planet reached a crescendo, the atmosphere igniting and burning away.

Cade clutched his chest as pain struck, an aching emptiness that resonated to his core. Loss. Terrible, unending loss.

"Cade! Cade!"

A shaking broke apart the images like shattered glass.

He sucked in air as his eyes focused on the intense gaze of the Yruf leader.

"Cade?"

Justin.

His neck creaked as he turned his head.

Justin's blue eyes clouded with worry. "What happened? You okay?"

How long had it been? A day? A millennium?

"The leader's been focused on you for the past minute like you held the secrets of the universe."

Only a minute? He tried to speak, but his throat wouldn't work. He swallowed, tried again. "I just experienced the destruction of the Setarip homeworld."

"What?"

Cade blinked several times, reorienting. "She just showed me their homeworld. Before and... after."

"After the civil war started?"

"Yeah." He swallowed hard. "If I'm right, their planet used to look a lot like Earth. Blue oceans, white clouds, green landmasses. Beautiful. But by the time they were forced to abandon it, their war had turned it into a lifeless hunk of rock. I think they even burned off the atmosphere."

"Too bad they didn't find a non-violent way to solve their differences."

The human race had certainly faced a tipping point of their own in the not-too-distant past. Thankfully they'd tossed aside their bickering and worked together to save their planet.

The Setarips hadn't been so fortunate.

The Yruf leader held his gaze, but he didn't feel like he was being pushed. Just observed. She reached her long fingers out to the image hovering above his comband, stopping just short of touching it, as if it was a precious jewel she didn't want to damage.

Justin pointed to the image, and repeated the single word the Yruf leader had spoken previously.

Her gaze moved to him, then back to the image. She repeated the same word.

"I think that means home," Justin said.

Cade studied the leader, mentally conjuring the image she'd shown him of the Setarip planet before the destruction. He repeated the word she'd said as best he could.

Her gaze snapped to his, this time creating a physical sensation of connection. She repeated the word again, along with another that his comband translated.

Yes. Home.

"You're right. It means home."

"She told you that?"

"In a way." He wasn't sure he could explain the experience in words. His gaze shifted briefly to the pod before returning to the leader. "We're protecting our home," he told her.

"I can help with that." Justin spoke in Yruf, Cade's comband translating. *One, two, guard home.*

Cade glanced at Justin. "Guard?"

"It's the word the doctors used to refer to the guards. Closest thing to protect I could come up with."

The Yruf leader straightened, looking between the two of them with an expression he'd never seen before. Like they were rational beings she could relate to. Her neck moved in that eerie snake-like way, allowing her to look over her shoulder at the pod without turning her body. She remained that way for several long moments, before turning back and focusing on Cade.

Guard?

Cade pointed at the pod, but called to mind an image of the Ecilam ship, Bare'Kold's yacht, then Earth. *Guard home Ecilam Teeli,* the comband translated. Their words were coming easier to him. He followed the phrase with the scorched image of her homeworld.

The leader's pupils dilated so wide her eyes looked black. She said something the comband couldn't translate except for the word *home.*

He didn't know exactly what she'd said, but he felt like she was understanding the danger the Ecilam and Teeli posed.

Guard home he said, gesturing again to the pod.

After a few more flicks of her tongue, the leader stepped to the side, her long arms disappearing into the folds of her cloak.

Cade released the breath he'd been holding. "I think we're in."

He kept his gaze on the leader as they approached the opening to the pod, but she didn't try to stop them.

Climbing into the pod took extra effort, because the Yruf hadn't angled the opening the way a human crew would have. The deck was at a ten-degree pitch from level and a fifteen-degree incline.

The Yruf probably hadn't climbed inside. Too tight a fit. As it was, once he was in, he had to hunch his shoulders and duck to keep from banging his head.

Justin crouched in front of the controls. "They completely shut down the pod's systems."

"Even the backup generator?"

"Yep. I gather they didn't want any surprises when they brought it onboard."

"Any idea when that occurred?"

"No. We'll find out as soon as it boots up. Assuming it does. I'll start with the backup generator." He braced one hand against the bulkhead. "It'll come online quicker than the main power."

While they waited, Cade inspected the pod's interior. Everything seemed normal, but then again, he'd only been in it once before. Drew had coached every member of the team on the system controls shortly after they'd acquired *Gladiator* so they'd all be capable of operating the pods in an emergency situation.

"Systems online. Checking the logs."

The pod didn't provide enough room for them both to see the display panel clearly, but he pushed his back against the bulkhead so he could peer over Justin's shoulder.

14:05 *Navigation and communications online.*

14:16 *Course and destination set.*

14:24 *Systems detached from umbilical.*

17:01 *Engines online.*

17:02 *Programmed course and destination verified. Engines engaged.*

17:10 *Error. Navigation and communications offline.*

17:13 *Error. Primary system power failure. Backup generator engaged.*

17:15 *Error. Backup generator failure.*

Tension wound around Cade's chest like a boa constrictor. He checked the time stamp again. No mistake. The pod had powered down within minutes of coming online following the pre-programmed drift period.

No way was that a malfunction. The Yruf had spotted the pod and captured it.

Justin turned his head, the flat look in his eyes showing the same realization, and the inevitable conclusion that followed.

The message to the Admiral hadn't been sent.

And Bare'Kold's yacht had already reached Earth.

Ninety-Four

"Can you send the transmission now?" Cade felt every second passing with each beat of his heart.

Justin switched on the transmitter, checked the readings, and shook his head. "No. The jamming signal is still preventing all communication." His gaze shifted to the hatch opening, where the Yruf leader stood, watching them. "They may project the signal continually, or she may have ordered it turned on before bringing us down here. And even without it, we'd have to launch the pod or get *Gladiator* out of the docking bay to send a transmission. Our signals won't penetrate their hull."

"Getting her to release the pod would probably be easier. But without a lock on our current coordinates, I'd have no idea what course to set or which way to transmit the signal."

"And no way to confirm if the signal was actually sent or received." Justin rubbed a hand over the bristle on his jaw. "*Gladiator*'s a better option."

"But *Gladiator*'s systems are overrun with nanotech. We'd have to convince the leader to remove the nanotech, too."

"*You'd* have to convince her."

Cade grimaced. "That's supposed to be your task."

"I would if I could, but you're the one with the direct connection."

"Lucky me." He glanced toward the hatch.

The Yruf leader was still watching them, the flick of her tongue working overtime. If he had to take a guess, he'd say she looked worried.

"Shreenef," she said, one of the drones moving into position behind her shoulder.

"Guess our time is up." Cade pushed away from the bulkhead and moved to the opening.

Justin followed. "You have a plan?"

"Working on it." He'd rather focus on that than what could be happening right now on Earth.

By the time he climbed out of the pod, the four guards had formed a loose semi-circle behind their leader. The drones hovered overhead rather than descending.

The leader faced him, waiting.

Tapping on his comband, he brought up the image of *Gladiator* Drew had shared with him.

The leader's gaze shifted to it briefly, her expression growing wary.

How could he clearly convey the threat to Aurora's mom from the Teeli and the Ecilam? Of the threat to them all if Reanne succeeded in bringing Aurora under her control?

Was Reanne planning to turn Libra Hawke into a Necri? And if she did, would Aurora fight her own mother? Or be forced to abandon her mother to that existence rather than become a slave to Reanne's twisted schemes herself? The alternative—bowing in subjugation to Reanne—would turn Aurora into the most feared monster in the galaxy at the end of Reanne's leash.

Reanne and Aurora. That was the crux of the issue. And where he needed to focus his imagery.

Drawing in a slow breath and holding the leader's gaze, he called to mind the image of Aurora crossing the river, her hands bound, the Ecilam behind her with weapons drawn, the cloaked figures of Reanne and Kreestol standing on the opposite bank.

He couldn't explain how, but he felt the leader tense, an emotional shift like recognition and alarm.

"Sooovereeeign."

His heart thumped in his chest. Had she just said what he thought he'd heard? He repeated it, just to be sure. "Sovereign?"

"Sooovereeeign." Her diamond-shaped pupils seemed to swallow him whole.

She knew about the Sovereign? A sick feeling settled into the pit of his stomach. Had he missed the most devastating answer to why they were being held captive? Were the Yruf working for Reanne?

An image appeared in his mind. He immediately recognized the figure standing before him, the long brown cloak concealing any identifying attributes of its wearer. She appeared much smaller, but he realized that was because he was seeing Reanne as the Yruf leader had seen her. He sucked in a breath. "You've met the Sovereign?"

She shouldn't have been able to understand his question, but the next image answered it. The scene rolled forward, not smoothly, but in halting steps and leaps. He saw two other figures appear beside Reanne, one cloaked—Kreestol—and one Ecilam who was almost as tall as the Yruf leader. A female, based on Williams' observations. Her scales were fluorescent green rather than emerald, and monochromatic over her entire face, but it was the look in her eyes that caught his attention. Chilling, arrogant, malicious.

The emotional resonance that came through from the Yruf leader was quite different. She gazed at the Ecilam female with a sense of longing, of hope.

The acid in his stomach started to churn.

The next image showed the Sovereign standing right beside the Yruf leader, a dark-gloved hand clasping the leader's long, slender one. A millisecond later the image blew apart like a cyclone, replaced by an image of the Yruf leader kneeling in supplication at the Sovereign's feet, her beautiful cloak and body armor replaced by shapeless, colorless rags that covered her from neck to ankle, shoulder to fingertip.

Cade swayed on his feet, the deck shifting under his boots. Something solid connected with his shoulder, supporting him.

"I've got you. Stay with her."

The image returned to the Yruf leader's perspective as she pulled her hand away from the Sovereign's and stepped back.

"She saw a vision," Cade murmured, more to himself than Justin. "She saw what was in Reanne's mind."

The feeling of longing intensified as the Yruf leader faced the female Ecilam, but the next image showed the Ecilam ship detaching from the Yruf ship and flying into the black. A deep sadness replaced the longing, and a tremendous sense of loss.

The image faded from his mind until he was gazing into the Yruf leader's eyes again. She was blurry, like he was looking at her through water. He blinked, then swiped his eyes with his sleeve. Moisture coated the material.

Justin gripped his shoulder. "What was the vision? What did she see?"

The Yruf leader's pupils dilated, making her eyes appear black, the only outward sign that the shared experience had affected her, too.

He couldn't look away. "Reanne planned to betray her, to turn her into a servant. But when Reanne touched her, the connection enabled the leader to see what was in her mind."

"Wow. I doubt Reanne expected that."

"I'm not sure she even knew. I think Reanne was using the Ecilam female as a bargaining chip, somehow. The Yruf leader wanted something from the female."

"Wanted something? Like a prisoner exchange?"

"No, I don't think so." He shook his head. "Her emotions were primal, painful, devastating. She cared about the Ecilam female but couldn't draw her away from Reanne. When she discovered the truth of Reanne's plan, she was forced to send them both away."

"Send them away? I thought they were at war with each other."

He stared at the Yruf leader, seeing her through new eyes. "I don't think the Yruf have ever wanted to defeat the Ecilam. I think they want to bring them back into the family."

Ninety-Five

"Family?" Justin sounded completely confused. "What do you mean, family?"

He wasn't entirely certain himself, but it felt right. He broke eye contact with the leader, facing Justin. "We've always believed the Setarips were five warring factions, all intent on each other's destruction. But what if we're wrong? Especially when it comes to the Yruf. I didn't sense any hostility toward the Ecilam from her. I think she wants to broker a peace with them. That's why they followed the Ecilam ship here. Not to destroy its crew, but to talk with them."

"But you told me the Ecilam destroyed their own ship to avoid capture. Why would they do that if the Yruf only wanted to talk?"

"What if they didn't?" His mind whirled, disjointed pieces coming together to form a picture. "What if Reanne destroyed the Ecilam ship the same way she destroyed the Etah ship on Gaia?"

"Why?"

"For the same reason she's killed off everyone she's used to achieve her goals. To keep them from sharing what they know about her plans. Only in this case, she had an added motivation—not wanting the Ecilam to align with the Yruf. She's been using the Etah and Ecilam as her personal minions. She may be using the Egar and Regna too, for all we know. Losing control over the Ecilam, especially at this critical time, could have serious consequences. Far better to kill them before they could be compromised."

Justin's lips pressed into a line. "Sounds like Reanne's twisted logic." He glanced at the Yruf leader. "But how would she get away with it? That can't be the only Ecilam ship. Wouldn't the other Ecilam turn on her?"

"Not if she blamed the destruction on the Yruf. That would increase the hostilities and drive them farther apart."

Justin closed his eyes briefly and shook his head. "Yep, that fits." He met Cade's gaze. "What's our next move?"

He glanced at the Yruf leader, who was watching him with an openness he wasn't used to. "Maybe I could use memories to explain why we're here, and why we need to contact the Admiral."

"You said she saw Reanne's vision for her. Maybe you can show her that Reanne's plan for Aurora is very similar. And how horribly that would impact all life in this part of the galaxy."

"Right." Minor task. No problem.

Uh-huh, sure.

Taking a deep breath, he faced the Yruf leader, meeting her gaze, the sensation of connection returning.

Concentrating on that connection, he called up a memory of Aurora standing on the bridge of the *Starhawke*, giving the Yruf leader a good long look at her while he allowed his feelings of respect and admiration to flow through. He wasn't sure if she could read his emotions the way he'd gotten hers, but it would certainly help his cause if she could.

The sense of connection grew, prompting him to move to the memory of the Necri cages as they'd looked when his team had first boarded the Setarip ship on Gaia—cramped, filthy, dank—and the horror and disgust he'd felt when the reality of their lives had sunk in.

When he morphed the image to the Necri gathered around Aurora in the engine room of the Setarip ship, their combined energy creating a protective shield as the autodestruct device that should have annihilated the ship exploded, the Yruf leader inhaled sharply.

The sound reached his ears while his mind stayed with the image, allowing it to slowly shift into a montage of happier moments with the Suulh as they began to shed their Necri existence and heal. He showed her the greenhouse they'd built on Burrow, the Suulh's first moments of wonder and excitement on Azaana, and the circle ceremony in the central building, where Aurora's energy had once again mingled with the Suulh's, this time with breathtaking joy and beauty.

His throat tightened as the memory took hold, reminding him of how perfect that moment had felt, of how much hope he'd had for his future with Aurora. He'd felt invincible.

If he dwelled on that memory for too long, he'd lose focus. Shifting gears, he returned to the memory of the battle at the river, starting with the same moment when Aurora had picked her way across the water in shackles, the Ecilam behind her with weapons drawn until she sank to her knees in front of the cloaked Sovereign.

He sensed the Yruf leader's mental grip tighten, urging the scene forward. He didn't resist, allowing her to witness the moment when Aurora had struck Reanne in the leg, making her howl. As Aurora rose to her feet and began fighting Kreestol, the Yruf leader made a humming sound, the images now moving in slow motion under her control.

The thought should have terrified him, but it didn't. In fact, he felt completely calm, almost peaceful. He knew he could break the connection if he chose to—she didn't have control of him—but that would be counterproductive. They needed this. He'd do whatever it took to convince her to help them. Even letting her sift through his memories like photos in an album.

The fight ticked forward frame by frame. She seemed to be analyzing Kreestol's attack and Aurora's defensive strategy. When Aurora and Kreestol plunged into the water, the scene became a blur as he and Justin rushed down to the river's edge to help Aurora. A flash of pearlescent white from the water was followed by utter blackness.

He sensed her confusion at the abrupt end to the memory, but how could he explain that he'd almost died? Instead, he called up his next memory—Aurora's beautiful face above his, water dripping off her nose and chin onto his skin as she gazed at him with fear in her eyes. The scene played forward until Aurora brushed a gentle kiss over his lips and stood, leaving him and Justin by the river as she raced off.

He skipped over his and Justin's slow trek after her, pausing only on the image of the Sovereign's ship gliding above the treetops, headed for the cruiser in orbit. Next, he showed Aurora in her catatonic state on the shuttle ride back to the *Starhawke*, looking like the life had been sucked right out of her.

He sensed more confusion from the Yruf leader, and also sadness. Or maybe those were his emotional memories rising to the surface.

Which left him with one more memory set to impart. Jumping to the recent past, he showed her snippets of the arrival of Bare'Kold's yacht, the Ecilam ship, and the Teeli carrier for the rendezvous, followed by Justin's collapse while working the comm, and the launch of the escape pod after *Gladiator* had been disabled.

They were imperfect messengers, especially given the complete lack of shared history between Humans and Yruf, but it was all he could do to make his point.

The image of the pod faded, replaced by the leader's hypnotic gaze.

He stepped back, the crick in his neck letting him know he'd been staring up at her for a while.

She dipped her hand into her cloak and pulled out the disc she'd used before. Holding it up, she projected a vid.

His heart stuttered. The vid was of Aurora and him, laughing and bantering while they worked on repairs in *Gladiator*'s cockpit. Justin had taken it while they were in Weezel's junkyard. It had been stored in *Gladiator*'s database ever since. Cade had watched it more times than he could count during the long flight to Earth after Aurora had refused to see or speak to him.

The Yruf must have pulled it from the ship's memory files.

The vid ended with Aurora spotting Justin in the hatchway, grinning like a kid, and tossing a rag at him.

Cade reached out a hand to touch the frozen image of Aurora's laughing face.

"*Guard?*"

His comband translated the leader's word, but he would have recognized it anyway. He'd heard the term often enough. He wasn't sure if she was asking if Aurora was a guard, or if Cade was guarding her, but the answer was the same for both.

"Yes. Guard." He grimaced. He'd done a bang-up job so far. When Aurora had needed him most, he'd failed her.

He projected the image of Earth on his comband. "Home."

The Yruf leader gazed at the image.

His gaze moved to the one of Aurora, a yearning stronger than he'd ever felt in his life pulling at his chest. *Where are you, Rory?*

The leader's expression softened in a way he'd never seen, her eyes becoming luminous. Facing one of the drones, she said something that the comband couldn't translate.

The drone rose, disappearing through an opening in the ceiling.

The leader turned, motioning to the bulkhead to Cade's right. It immediately separated, peeling back to reveal a bronze-toned ship sitting on the other side.

"*Gladiator.*" Cade took an involuntary step forward before halting and glancing at the leader.

"Shreenef." Without waiting for him to react, she strode across the deck toward *Gladiator's* lowered gangway.

Cade and Justin didn't need the prompt. They followed close on her heels.

The remaining guards moved to flank them, but without the same sense of implied threat that had been the norm. If anything, they seemed to be urging Cade and Justin forward.

The remaining drone sailed overhead, gliding up the gangway in front of them. The leader swept up the incline, her cloak swirling behind her in an emerald curtain. For such large beings, the Yruf moved with surprising stealth. Cade's and Justin's boots thumped on the metal decking, but the leader and the guards barely made a sound.

When they entered the main room, two Yruf he'd never seen before were waiting for them, one male and one female. The female's base color was a similar green to the leader's but her scales were covered in gold splotches like she'd been splattered by a bucket of gold paint, giving her a mottled appearance. The male was distinctive for his lack of color. White covered most of his scales, with thin ribbons of black creating a repeating oval pattern.

The leader spoke briefly with both of them before sending them to the aft corridor. The drone followed behind like a child's balloon on a string.

"Engineers?" Justin asked Cade.

"That would be my guess."

Two of the guards took up positions at the top of the gangway as the leader faced Cade and Justin.

"Shreenef." She motioned to them before heading to the narrow corridor leading to the cockpit. She had to duck to keep from hitting her head, but the tight fit didn't slow her down. Cade followed, Justin behind him, the other two guards bringing up the rear.

"We're not all going to fit," Justin murmured.

One of the guards stopped at the stairwell, but the other kept coming.

Despite the confines of the small cockpit, the leader managed to maneuver into the cramped area behind the two seats, her shoulders and neck contorting in a way that freaked him out. She pointed a hand at the comm unit and the yoke. "Guard," the comband translated.

Cade and Justin exchanged a look before moving forward.

Cade settled into the pilot's chair and checked the console while Justin picked his way past the Yruf leader and slid into the co-pilot's seat. "Looks like they shut the ship down cold. It'll take time to power up the system."

But no sooner were the words out of his mouth than the display lit up like a Christmas tree. "Or not. Their engineers must be putting the nanotech to work."

Justin picked up the headset like it had fangs and cleared his throat. "Uh, if I put this on, what are the odds I'll end up comatose again?"

Cade glanced at him, a stab of anxiety punching him in the gut. "I don't know." His gaze shifted to the Yruf leader, who was watching them intently, but calmly. The anxiety eased. "But I seriously doubt they're going through all this just to land you in the same fix."

Justin nodded, settling the device over his ears.

Cade checked his display. The system was already coming online without any direction from him. "How long until you can transmit our message?"

Justin frowned, checking the readings. "The system's almost ready, but we can't send anything until we get off the ship."

"And we can't leave without our team." Cade pivoted to face the Yruf leader, who had moved to the hatchway behind his seat, completely blocking the opening. "We need—"

The sound of footsteps in the main room cut him off. He counted three sets.

"Cade? Byrnsie?"

Drew's voice.

"In here," Cade called out.

He could hear her approach, but couldn't see her past the wall of green in the hatchway. The Yruf leader didn't seem inclined to move, and he'd guess the guard was right behind her.

"You okay?" Drew asked.

"Fine. You?"

"Yeah. What's going on? The guards gathered us up and hustled us down here hauling our battle armor and yours."

"Gonzo and Williams are with you?"

"We're here," Williams and Gonzo called out from the direction of the main room.

His team was onboard. That was a good beginning. "Get ready for takeoff."

"Takeoff? Really?" Drew sounded surprised, but hopeful.

"Yeah. You'll find two Setarips below getting the systems online."

"On it."

As her footsteps padded down the stairwell, the leader's gaze captured his, that sensation of connection taking hold again. She pulled the disk from her cloak and held it in her palm, two images appearing side by side—Earth and Aurora.

"*Guard.*" A command, extracting a promise.

He held her gaze. "I will."

Ninety-Six

"What's the status on that nanotech?" Cade asked Drew through the comm.

Her reply came through the cockpit speaker. "Not a trace to be found. Whatever their engineers did, we're back to normal here. Better than normal, actually. According to the readings, system efficiency is up twenty percent. We're good to go."

Justin glanced at Cade, giving him a crooked smile. "Parting gift?"

"Guess so." The Yruf leader had left five minutes earlier, taking the drone, engineers, and guards with her. Gonzo was seated at the auxiliary station behind Justin, while Williams helped Drew run diagnostics on the engines in preparation for takeoff.

The exterior hull had opened up as soon as the Yruf had cleared the bay, the stars beckoning him into the black. The navigation computer was working on identifying their current position, but the process would go quicker once they were able to see more than the thin slice of the starfield.

"Engaging thrusters." *Gladiator* lifted off the deck, a slight flutter in Cade's belly letting him know his ship's artificial gravity had taken over. As soon as he'd guided the ship through the opening in the Yruf hull his gaze shifted to the aft camera view. An oval of golden light showed for a moment before being swallowed up, leaving nothing but starlight in its wake. The Yruf ship was, for all intents and purposes, invisible.

"That's unnerving."

Cade turned to Justin.

"If you didn't know it was there, you could fly right into it."

"They'd never let that happen." The Yruf valued life. He knew that as surely as he knew his own name. They'd never intentionally destroy another ship. He'd analyze why he was so certain later.

Shifting his attention to the navigation charts, he checked their position. Blinked, and checked again. No mistake. "I'll be damned."

"What?" Justin and Gonzo said in unison.

"We're only about an hour away from Earth."

"Really?" Justin leaned over, scanning the data on Cade's console. He met Cade's gaze. "Why were the Yruf heading toward Earth?"

He shook his head. "We'll figure that out later. Right now, we need to get that message sent."

Justin straightened. "On it."

As Justin followed his order, Cade calculated the interstellar jump. The sooner they got there the better. They'd lost enough time already.

Justin slid off the headset. "Message sent."

Cade blew out a breath. "How long before we can expect a reply?"

"Forty-five minutes at our present position, but a fraction of that as we get closer to Earth."

"We'll hit our jump window in three minutes." He'd already set the ship's flight path. But as *Gladiator* hurtled through space, those three minutes stretched into the longest of his life. If it would have helped, he would have gotten out and pushed. "Bringing interstellar engines online."

His heart hammered against his ribs until the view of the starfield disappeared in a blur of light and the interstellar engines took over. He sank against the back of his chair and closed his eyes.

"You okay?"

He opened one eye and found Justin peering at him. "Yeah." He sat up, scrubbing a hand over his face, his palm scraping his beard stubble. "Just didn't dare believe until that moment that we were actually going to make it back."

"I know what you mean."

Gonzo turned from his station. "So, now that we've got a little time on our hands, let's discuss why the Yruf were heading toward Earth, and how we're going to warn the Fleet."

"Warn the Fleet?" Gonzo's comment seemed like a non-sequitur. "Warn them about what?"

Gonzo stared at him. "The Yruf."

Apparently Cade didn't give him the reaction he wanted, because he increased the volume.

"Setarips! You do recall being captured and imprisoned, right?"

Ah, he got it now. Gonzo hadn't been privy to what had transpired in the bay. "They're not going to attack Earth."

Now Gonzo looked worried, like Cade had been infected with an alien virus. "Why would you believe that? They're Setarips."

"Life-loving Setarips. They don't want to attack anyone, including the other factions."

Gonzo looked at Justin. "Back me up here, buddy."

Justin shook his head. "They were never aggressive with us."

"They put you in a coma."

"I'm not sure that was intentional," Cade countered. "Williams doesn't think the ultralow frequency would affect them in the same way. For them, it might act more like a tranquilizer or sedative. I don't think they anticipated the damage it could inflict on human physiology."

"Then why transmit it?"

"They needed to incapacitate us. But Williams believes they were concerned about potential side effects on an unknown species, which is why they limited the frequency to the external comm signal. Drew confirmed their nanotech could have been monitoring our bio signs. When Justin went down, they must have decided not to use the signal on the ship's internal comm to knock out the rest of us."

Justin nodded. "I agree with Cade. They didn't want to hurt us. They wanted answers. You should have seen how the leader communicated with Cade in the bay. It was amazing, like they were in each other's heads."

Gonzo's disbelief changed into serious concern. "And you think that's a *good* thing? What did they do, scramble your brain, too?"

Cade took a deep breath rather than letting fly with a retort. They'd all been through the wringer, and Gonzo was just trying to do his job. "She showed me the destruction of her planet, Christoph. And I found out she's as concerned about the Sovereign as we are."

"Reanne? How could you know that?"

"She projected images to me of her homeworld, and of her meeting with Reanne. We have a common enemy. That's why she let us go. So we could protect the Earth. Not because the Yruf plan to destroy it."

Gonzo didn't look convinced. "Why would you believe anything she showed you?"

"It wasn't just what I saw. It's what I felt." Cade struggled to put the sensation into words. "There was an honesty to how we communicated. A complete openness. I would have known if she was making it up. In fact, I'm not sure the Yruf are capable of lying."

Gonzo sank back in his chair, his gaze on Cade as he slowly stroked his beard. "You're one hundred percent certain of that?"

Cade did an internal reality check, just to be sure. "Yes, I am. I'd bet my life on it. I'd bet *all* our lives on it."

Gonzo sighed. "All right. That's good enough for me. But it still doesn't explain why they were heading toward Earth."

"I think I can answer that, too." He pulled up the logs for their flight path from Earth to the rendezvous point. "Their nanotech would have given them access to all *Gladiator*'s data. I know for a fact they pulled our vid files." The image of Aurora's laughing face drifted across his vision. He pushed it away. "I'm guessing they accessed our logs after we were captured. Investigating where we'd come from would have helped them figure out if we posed a threat."

"If *we* posed a threat? Correct me if I'm wrong," Gonzo said, "but they could park that ship in orbit around Earth and we'd never know it, right?"

"Probably not." The Fleet's satellite sensor network was a lot more sophisticated than anything *Gladiator* had to offer, but he still doubted the network would have the ability to detect the Yruf ship.

"You're not making me feel better."

"I know." And he wished there was a way to share the depth of his experience. For now, Gonzo and the rest of the team would have to take his word on faith. "You'll just have to trust me. And prepare for a rapid turnaround at Sol Station."

He checked their ETA. One hour, eight minutes. "Best case scenario, we'll be picking up Libra Hawke and the Forrests for transport, probably to Azaana. Worst case?" An image of Aurora in chains filled his mind. He gritted his teeth. "We'll be chasing after Bare'Kold's yacht again. Only this time we'll have to catch it."

Ninety-Seven

Aurora rolled over in her bed, pounded her fist into her pillow, and settled her head in the divot. Not that it mattered. She couldn't sleep.

Making the decision to leave had stripped off the superficial gloss that had coated her existence for the past two weeks like wax on a surfboard, keeping her firmly rooted with her father and brother. Now that it had been wiped away, staying still was untenable.

Micah was in his room across the loft. Judging from the agitation in his emotional field, he was fighting insomnia as well. Her dad was out by the pool where she'd left him a couple hours ago contemplating the stars. And no doubt contemplating what exactly he would say to her mother when they arrived at Stoneycroft.

Micah was coming with them, which helped ease some of the sense of loss creeping up on her. She'd promised to show him the *Starhawke* before the spring semester started, and that was a promise she intended to keep.

Of course she'd also promised her dad she'd contact Cade before leaving Hawaii. She couldn't lie to herself. That was a major factor in her tossing and turning. She hadn't been able to stop thinking about him for hours, as though he had his own private broadcast channel in her brain. But she dreaded that first communication.

He had every right to be angry with her. She'd shut him out when he'd done nothing wrong. She'd have to do a lot of groveling, and a lot of explaining. But she wanted to do that in person, not through a comband vid call. Which meant convincing him to meet her.

The question was, where? She couldn't invite him to Stoneycroft. That situation would be tension-filled already. But she didn't want to wait until she returned to the *Starhawke*, either.

Then again, she might not have a choice. Now that she was tuning into her connection with him again, she had the distinct impression he wasn't on Earth. The Admiral hadn't contacted her to tell her he'd sent Cade on a mission, but that didn't mean anything. He preferred to deliver important information in person. He certainly wouldn't tell her in a comm message that he'd sent the Elite Unit off planet. And she'd made it clear she wasn't responding to Cade's attempts to contact her directly.

Flipping onto her back, she pulled the pillow over her head and pressed it to her mouth, letting loose with a screech of frustration. She'd made this mess, and she'd have to—

A sledgehammer of fear slammed into her, stopping her mid-scream. She shot up in bed and scrambled to her feet. *Micah? Dad?* She was halfway to her door when another blow struck, even more powerful than the first, doubling her over.

Planting a hand on the wall to steady herself, she threw the meditation image into place, visualizing the *Starhawke* bridge surrounding her. The image held, the fear swirling around her like a thick dark cloud, just out of reach.

She pushed into the loft, each step taking conscious effort.

"Aurora!" Her dad's voice, followed by the pounding of footsteps on the stairs.

The emotions weren't coming from him.

Micah threw open his door a moment later. A quick flick of connection confirmed he wasn't the source, either.

That only left one person who could affect her so strongly.

She saw the same realization in her dad's panicked gaze as he rounded the corner into the loft and came to a halt.

"It's Mom."

"I know."

And then the fear cut off abruptly, replaced by pure rage.

Her dad's eyes widened, his breath hitching.

Air wasn't coming easily to her, either. "What's happening?"

He closed the distance between them, pulling her into a brief hug before leaning back so he could see her face. "We're going to find out."

She lost track of the sequence of events after that, although an avalanche of pain struck at some point, along with a sick feeling that started to drain her until she pushed it back with the visualization. She used her comband to contact her mom. No response. She tried Marina, too. Nothing.

Somehow she got dressed and threw her few belongings into her bag while battling the maelstrom of emotions pounding her. The rage continued unabated, making it difficult to breathe. She'd never sensed anything remotely this strong from her mother before, even when they were in the same room. Feeling it across an ocean edged her toward emotional overload. Only her dad's training kept her moving forward.

He was waiting for her, a small pack slung over his shoulder, when she returned to the loft.

"Can you get me to the transport station?" She'd do whatever it took to claim a seat on the next flight headed for the mainland.

"Of course."

Micah strode out of his room, a matching pack in his hands.

The meaning of those packs hit her. "We can't all go. It'll be hard enough to get one seat. Three will—"

Her dad put a hand on her shoulder, propelling her forward. "I already have a plane standing by."

"How could you—"

"I'll explain later. Let's go." He shepherded her and Micah down the stairs and out the front door, where a streamlined transport waited.

"A chariot?" The vehicles were part ground transport, part airshuttle, designed to fly in and out of residential areas. And very pricey to rent.

Her dad dropped his pack in the cargo area before settling into one of the seats. "Our plane is waiting."

Apparently that was all the explanation she was going to get for now. Questions and doubts assailed her, but she accepted his calm command of the situation like a drowning woman grabbing onto a life preserver. As the vehicle lifted off, gliding over the deserted streets, she blocked out her surroundings and tuned into the emotions pummeling her. Sharp spikes of rage struck with no discernable pattern, mixed in with shots of mind-numbing fear. Was she sensing Marina and Gryphon, too?

She couldn't imagine any scenario in which they'd generate this degree of emotion. Even during their worst arguments, she'd never sensed anything close to this. Which meant they were facing an external threat.

Visions of the battle with Kreestol at the river flashed before her eyes, chilling her blood. *Please, no. Please,*

please, please no. She'd warned her mother about Reanne,
but her concerns had been dismissed.

She didn't want to be right.

Pulling up her sleeve, she tried contacting her mom
and Marina on her comband again. Still no response.

Her dad glanced at her, a question in his eyes. She
shook her head.

Micah pressed his thigh against hers, offering his
silent support. She leaned into him, craving the strength and
comfort he gave her as she struggled to stay focused. He
slipped an arm over her shoulder, drawing her against the
protective curve of his body.

The chariot picked up speed as it passed over the
highway, heading toward the transport station. But rather
than landing near the main terminal, it continued to an open
hangar for smaller craft.

A small jet sat out on the tarmac, the stairway
lowered and the engines already rumbling. The chariot
touched down next to it. She followed her dad out of the
vehicle, her gaze moving to the words stenciled on the side
of the plane.

Far Horizons Aerospace.

She was familiar with the company. Their education
grant had paid for her Academy tuition. In addition to planes,
they were a major supplier of Fleet shuttles and ships. Had,
in fact, been a vital part of the planning and construction of
the *Argo.* But she wasn't aware that they offered private
transportation services. "You hired a private plane?" Renting
the chariot was extravagant, but this plane would cost a
small fortune, especially on such short notice.

He headed for the stairs, where a uniformed woman
waited. "The plane is mine."

"Yours?" Her steps faltered. "Then why—" The
question lodged in her throat as her breath caught. All the

vaguely incongruous pieces that had been nagging her finally clicked into place, forming a seamless whole.

The house. The gifts. The Christmas luau extravaganza.

"*Far Horizons*? You *own* it?"

He murmured something to the uniformed woman before turning, tension in the lines of his face. "That's right." He moved to her side, placing a hand at the small of her back and guiding her to the stairs.

She climbed them in a daze, her dad and Micah right behind her.

She had to be dreaming. That was the only explanation for the abrupt shift in reality. No way could her father be the owner of the oldest and most prestigious aerospace company on the planet. He just couldn't. He was a university professor. End of story.

She watched him as he gave instructions to the pilot before returning to her side. Same greying blond hair. Same blue eyes. Same inner strength and calm assurance. Except now that strength and assurance took on a completely different meaning. "How?"

His gaze held hers. "I'll explain later. For now, you need to get buckled up."

A bubble of hysterical laughter climbed her throat. She didn't need to buckle up. The plane could crash and she'd probably walk away unscathed. But sitting down sounded like a brilliant idea. Her legs weren't feeling all that steady anymore.

She moved to a pair of seats and sank into the one by the window. Her dad took the one directly across, facing her, while Micah stood between them, his gaze uncertain. She motioned him to the seat beside her. Maintaining her mental focus would be easier with his help.

If she hadn't spent so much time controlling her emotional reactions over the past week, she'd already be a puddle of goo on the floor. But so far she'd been able to manage her mother's high-octane emotional state without getting pulled under.

Micah rested his arm next to hers, the gentle connection intensifying her empathic senses while simultaneously increasing her concentration. She closed her eyes, drawing in deep breaths as the chair vibrated, the engines rumbling as the plane streaked down the runway and lifted off.

Finally in the air. The familiar sensation of flight soothed her, adding tactile reinforcement to her *Starhawke* bridge imagery.

The red haze of rage coming from her mother flared, feeling more like the inferno that had yanked her out of bed rather than the steady, controlled burn of the past few minutes. A sense of loss had mushroomed in direct proportion, as had the sharp bite of pain.

"She's protecting someone."

She opened her eyes, meeting her dad's troubled gaze. "How do you know?"

A soft smile like the ghost of a long-forgotten memory crossed his face. "Trust me, I know. Are you getting any images from her?"

She shook her head. "We've never communicated that way. Mom denied her Suulh abilities."

"What about Marina? Could you send a visual message to her?"

"I don't know. I've never tried." To her knowledge, only she and Mya had taken advantage of that particular Suulh skill. "But I'll give it a shot." Closing her eyes again, she focused on Marina's energetic resonance, sending an image of herself and the plane.

She waited, but the seconds ticked by with no response. "I'm not getting anything." She sent the images again, but they fell into a void. Either her message wasn't getting through, or Marina was unable to respond. "How long before we land?"

"About twenty-five minutes."

Her eyes flew open.

Another micro-smile softened the thin line of his lips. "This is no ordinary plane."

Obviously. She'd expected the journey to take at least three hours. "Where will we land?"

"A small airport near the coast. I have a chariot meeting us there that will get us to Stoneycroft in five minutes."

She glanced at her chronometer. That would put them at Stoneycroft a little after four, local time. It was half a day sooner than she could have hoped for if she'd gone through Fleet channels, but it still seemed like an eternity as the firestorm of emotions continued to blast her. What nightmare would they find when they arrived?

The surge of anger from her mother abruptly abated, like someone had cranked the dimmer switch. But rather than a sense of relief, the change sent a rod of tension through her body.

Her dad looked equally distressed. He stood, moving into the aisle. "I'll be right back."

As he headed for the back of the plane, she focused on the emotions from her mother. What she sensed scared the stuffing out of her. They needed to get there now!

Her dad was doing everything he could, but one other person might be able to get there quicker.

According to the timetable Mya had sent her two weeks ago, the *Starhawke* could be en route home, or even waiting at Sol Station. If the Fates were kind, it was the latter.

Turning to her comband, she opened a channel to her ship.

No connection.

Damn! But Mya could still be close. The problem was how to communicate with her. Assuming Reanne was behind whatever was happening at Stoneycroft, she'd also have minions watching the secure Fleet communications passing through the Sol Interstellar Communications System. Anything directed at the *Starhawke* through the ICS would be relatively easy to tag, providing Reanne with more ammunition.

The Kraed comm system was secure, but it would require the signal to reach Drakar before being rerouted to her ship. The delay defeated the purpose.

Which left one viable alternative.

The intensity of emotions from her mother continued to pummel her like waves against rocks, but her visualization was allowing her to manage the empathic influx. Reaching out into the cosmos for Mya's unique emotional vibration while surrounded by the chaos wouldn't be easy, like hearing the melody of a music box playing in another room while standing in the midst of a brass band trumpeting a Sousa march. And they'd never tested the range of their Suulh connection, partly because they'd rarely been separated. Communicating from orbit to planetside, or from ship to ship within the same star system was relatively simple. Across a lightyear or more might be a different story.

But she had to try.

Ninety-Eight

Mya stood at the viewport in Aurora's office, gazing at the streaming starlight of the interstellar jump. Half a day had passed since Jonarel had left her room, but she hadn't seen him. Most likely he'd enlisted Star as his ally to make sure they didn't cross paths.

Not that she blamed him. In his eyes, she'd used him for selfish purposes and discarded him. But it was the only choice she had. She wasn't a Kraed. She didn't have his ability to enjoy a physical relationship without getting emotionally involved. It wasn't in her DNA. A sex-only affair would tear her apart.

The Kraed were masters at compartmentalizing, especially when it came to sex. Emotions weren't a factor unless a pair were promised as mates. She'd learned that from discussions with Siginal and Daymar while at the Academy. Not that she'd been paying close attention. Or had asked any questions. Well, maybe a few.

For the Kraed, physical intimacy was simple and natural. They didn't attach stigmas to it or look down on short-term liaisons. On the contrary—they encouraged it. Most pairings lasted a few weeks or months. Jonarel would have engaged in such activities while he was on his homeworld working on the *Starhawke*. Siginal's plan for him to mate with Aurora wouldn't have prevented him. In Kraed culture, until the promise was made and accepted, both partners were free to enjoy experiences with others, and did so regularly.

But she was fairly certain Jonarel hadn't been with anyone since he'd brought the *Starhawke* to Earth. Knowing his devotion to Aurora, he wouldn't have considered such a move for fear that Aurora would misinterpret the seriousness of his intentions toward her.

The only reason he'd encouraged Mya last night was because he'd given up hope of joining with Aurora. He was free to do as his chose. And he had. Oh yes, he certainly had.

But then she'd rejected him after a night of intense passion without giving him a logical reason for ending the affair, something a Kraed would never do. Of course he was confused and hurt.

Crossing her arms, she pivoted to face Aurora's desk. "What do I do now, Sahzade?" She'd made a royal mess of everything, just as she'd feared she would. And she couldn't talk to anyone about it, either. Not even Celia.

Oh, her friend would understand and be sympathetic, but she'd also *know*. And Jonarel was way too perceptive to miss that fact. If he discovered Mya had told Celia, after claiming she didn't want any of the crew to know, it would be yet another wedge between them.

Aurora would understand too, if she were here. Assuming Mya found the courage to tell her. She might be forced to after they were back together. Aurora would want an explanation for the strange emotions she and Jonarel would be giving off when they were around each other.

Maybe she'd—

A clenching sensation in her stomach blindsided her, driving up into her chest and pushing the breath from her lungs. She flung her arms out as she lost her balance, staggering like a drunken sailor until her hand came in contact with the bulkhead. *What the hell?*

A quick internal check didn't provide any answers. Nothing physically wrong with her, but the clenching sensation continued, pulling at her.

What is going on? The feeling was vaguely familiar, tickling a memory she couldn't quite place. But it spurred her to action.

Shoving away from the bulkhead, she walked to the office door and onto the bridge. "Status?"

Kire turned from the captain's chair. "Still on course to Earth." His smile turned to a frown as she drew closer. "Uh, you okay?"

"I don't know." She rested a hand on her belly, her gaze on the bridgescreen, which showed the same star stream as the viewport in Aurora's office. "How long until we arrive?"

Kire checked the display on the captain's chair. "One hour, twenty-three minutes."

Too long. Far too long. Why that thought blazed across her brain like a meteor she couldn't say, but it resonated with every cell in her body. "Can we get there faster?"

His frown shifted to concern. "What's wrong? Something with Roe?"

She focused on the sensation in her gut, but couldn't come up with any answers. She wasn't getting any images from Aurora, which would have given her a clue. Then again, they weren't exactly around the corner from each other, either. At this distance, an urgent cry for help from Aurora might trigger a reaction like this. "I don't know. Maybe. I just know we need to get there as quickly as possible."

Kire thumbed open the comm channel. "Bridge to engineering."

Jonarel's deep voice filled the bridge. "Go ahead."

"Jon, how much quicker can we reach Earth?"

"The engines are running at optimal efficiency now."

"I understand that. But Mya's got a feeling we're needed on Earth ASAP."

A pregnant pause preceded his reply. "Tehar and I will work on it."

"Understood. Bridge out." He turned to Mya. "Maybe you should sit down." When she didn't move, he stood and took her elbow, guiding her to the chair to his left and settling her into it. "Can I get you anything? Tea, maybe?"

She shook her head, unable to look away from the bridgescreen. *Faster. Please go faster.*

Linear time untethered for her after that. She had a vague impression of Celia crouched beside her, asking questions, and Kire hovering beside her chair, but her focus remained on the image on the bridgescreen and the increasing severity of the tension in her belly, like a giant hand squeezing her insides. Just like when she'd—

Her brain stalled, recognition dawning. *Gaia.* She'd felt this way on Gaia when the Necri had attacked.

But why was she feeling it now? Azaana was days away and the only Suulh on Earth were Aurora, Libra, and her parents.

A chill danced over her skin. *Aurora.* Had Reanne tracked her down? Was she in danger?

Fear coursed through her veins, freezing her in her chair. If Reanne had captured her—

As if saying her name had conjured her, she sensed Aurora's presence calling to her, faintly at first, but growing more distinct with each second.

She reached out, desperate to find her. *Sahzade?*

Mya!

The power of Aurora's response shot through her like lightning, a knowing that transcended her logical mind, joining them on an elemental level.

I need you.

The words drove a spike of fear into her heart, but it dissipated as quickly as it had struck. Aurora wasn't the one in danger. Every fiber of her being told her that with absolute certainty. She could feel her resolve, her focus, her determination.

But that left a question the size of Mt. Everest in front of her. She projected an image of the *Starhawke*'s bridge. *I'm coming.*

The reply was almost immediate. An image of Stoneycroft filled her mind. She inhaled sharply, that sense of knowing pulling everything into sharp focus.

Home.

The single word from Aurora expelled the air from her lungs, her stomach bottoming out. It explained everything. Why the feeling had been so intense. Why it had reached her across the vast distance of space. Why she desperately needed to reach Earth.

Her parents were the ones in danger. Their pain was drawing her to them. And yet the call had to be unintentional. Neither her parents nor Libra would willingly draw her into danger.

But she would answer the call, nonetheless.

As the connection with Aurora faded, she lurched out of her chair, anger and frustration firing her blood. "Kire? How soon?"

He met her gaze, apparently startled by the heat in her words. "Uh, Jon estimates we'll reach the system in thirty-five minutes."

An eternity, but they'd cut the time by more than half. "Engage the hull camouflage and tell him I want a shuttle ready to launch as soon as we arrive. We're going to Stoneycroft, and we won't be using proper channels."

Ninety-Nine

"Cade?" Justin's voice drifted down the corridor from *Gladiator*'s cockpit to the central room.

Cade swallowed the mouthful of dried fruit he'd grabbed—the first non-mash food he'd had in days—as he hurried to the cockpit. A quick check of their food stores had confirmed the Yruf had taken their Fleet ration bars, using them to create the mash they'd fed the team while they were captives. "What is it?"

"We just received a message from Reynolds."

"Reynolds? Not the Admiral? Did she—"

"It's not a reply. They didn't have time to receive our message and respond yet."

The muscles between his shoulder blades laced up and pulled tight, the tension radiating along his entire spine. Reynolds had been under orders to maintain comm silence until the team returned or contacted her. Her decision to override those orders could only mean one thing. All hell had broken loose. "Put it on speaker."

Reynolds' voice filled the cockpit. "Ellis, I sure hope you're hauling ass to Earth when you get this. The Admiral and I are on our way to pick up a transport to northern California. We believe there's been some kind of attack at the Hawke- Forrest house."

Cade echoed Justin's muttered oath. Their message hadn't arrived in time.

"The Admiral received a call ten minutes ago from Brendan Scott, owner of Far Horizons Aerospace. Turns out he's Aurora Hawke's father."

Cade's jaw hinged open, his mind stalling. Brendan Scott was Aurora's dad? How could that be? Her father had died decades ago.

"He has Hawke with him."

The second sucker punch hit him in the gut, driving the air from his lungs. No. Aurora couldn't be on Earth. She was on Drakar. With her ship. Far, far, away.

"They're headed to the house, too. They'll beat us there, and from what Scott said, Armageddon could be waiting for us. We could really use backup on this."

His heartbeat shot into the stratosphere, his worst nightmares roaring like an inferno. And Aurora was heading right into the flames.

"I contacted the *Starhawke* and Siginal Clarek through the Kraed network, but no response yet. Notify me as soon as you get this. Reynolds out."

He was in full command mode before the subtle hiss from the speaker cut out. "Send a reply." He dropped into the pilot's seat and tapped his comband. "Drew, I need you to find a way to draw more speed from *Gladiator*'s engines."

"What happened?"

He gave her a two-sentence summary.

"I see." A brief pause. "Well, I have good news. The changes the Yruf nanotech made to our systems upgraded our engine efficiency. We should be able to push them beyond normal limits without running into any problems."

Finally something going their way. "Keep an eye on them, let me know if anything changes."

"Will do."

He made an adjustment to their speed. The ship trembled a little at first, then smoothed out.

Justin turned. "Reply sent. They should get it shortly after our initial message arrives."

"At least they'll have more information about what they're facing." But was it too little too late? "Get Gonzo up here. As soon as we drop out of the jump, I want him to start scanning for Bare'Kold's yacht. We don't want it slipping past us."

"Understood."

He checked the navigation readings. Their arrival time had already improved. But not enough. He opened a channel to the engine room. "Any chance you can coax more speed?"

"Ordinarily, I'd say no." Drew's voice had a harder edge than normal. *Focus voice* Justin called it. "But I can live with a little shimmying if you can."

"I can. Do it."

He didn't have to wait long. Within moments the vibration through the deck increased, the yoke trembling in his hands and a subtle roar drifting up from the lower deck. But he trusted Drew to take the ship to its limits and no further. More speed wouldn't do them any good if the engines failed.

He glanced at Justin. "Anything from Reynolds?" It was a pointless question. If Justin had received a message, he would have put it on speaker immediately. But filling the silence kept the anxiety clawing at his chest from taking hold.

"Not yet." Justin met his gaze. "Did you know?"

"Know what?"

"That the owner of Far Horizons was her dad?"

"Not a clue. She told me her dad died when she was a child."

"Could Reynolds be wrong?"

"Not if Aurora's with Scott." The impossibility of Brendan Scott being her father also made a weird sort of sense. Aurora was a woman of power and mystery. Why should her father be any different?

He'd met Scott once during his flight training, a year before he'd started dating Aurora. He'd liked him on sight, impressed by the man's talents as a pilot. Scott had taken a liking to him, too. In fact, Scott had told him he reminded him of his son, Micah, who was the same age. Which meant Aurora had just inherited a brother along with her non-deceased father.

But it was Scott's strength of character that had made a lasting impression. Brendan Scott had held the world in the palm of his hand, yet he was the most humble, compassionate person Cade had ever met. Well, with the exception of Aurora.

Which begged the question of how he'd been able to turn his back on his daughter, allowing her to believe he was dead. She'd been in emotional freefall the last time Cade had seen her, a broken shell of the woman he knew and loved. He could only imagine the toll learning about her father had taken on her.

Scott had a lot to answer for.

Why was she with him now, and not on the *Starhawke*? And why had her crew left Earth without her? He couldn't imagine Mya abandoning Aurora, especially considering her emotionally compromised state. She was the textbook definition of a mother hen. And Clarek would crawl over razorblades to stay by Aurora's side. He wouldn't willingly leave her alone on Earth.

Yet that's exactly what they'd done, taking off for Kraed space without their captain.

Why?

"Message coming in from Reynolds."

His focus snapped back into the cockpit. "On speaker."

Reynolds' words came out like machine-gun fire. "Got the intel on Bare'Kold and the Ecilam. It confirmed what the Admiral already suspected. Just wish we'd known sooner." A brief pause. "The satellite images of the house show a conflagration. Damn thing looks like a bonfire. Scott provided the Admiral with contact information for the Forrests, but we're not getting any response."

The vise around Cade's chest tightened.

"Scott has arranged for one of his company shuttles to meet you at Sol Station. It'll be waiting at the closest shuttle bay to *Gladiator*'s docking berth. You're already cleared to dock at C1. Far Horizon's security will get you onboard, but you'll be crewing the shuttle yourself."

So, he'd be piloting them to Stoneycroft, avoiding any time-consuming discussions regarding their purpose or destination.

"Emergency personnel are working to contain the fire. No reports yet on casualties. Scott and Hawke should be arriving shortly. We're still at least thirty minutes out."

He thought the recording had ended, but after a long pause, she said one word, her voice uncharacteristically strained.

"Hurry."

Cade's fingers curled over the yoke as he met Justin's gaze. If Reynolds was worried, they really were facing Armageddon.

One Hundred

By the time the plane touched down, Micah was ready to crawl out of his skin. The looks his dad and Aurora kept exchanging ramped up the tension minute by minute.

As they rose from their seats to exit the plane, he leaned down to whisper in Aurora's ear. "Is Mom okay?"

She met his gaze, hers deeply troubled. "I don't know. What I'm getting from her now... it's very weak."

Silence descended as they entered the waiting chariot and lifted off, each lost in their own thoughts. A red light flashed on the console not long after, followed by a woman's voice. "Flight approval overridden due to emergency no-fly restriction. Switching to alternate terrestrial roadway."

Micah turned to his dad. "What does that mean?"

His face looked grim. "It means we're taking the long route."

The chariot touched down on the roadway below. The full moon and dense forest cast the surroundings in menacing shadows and eerie slices of moonlight, making it difficult to imagine he'd once lived and played here as a child.

Aurora gripping the doorhandle, her gaze locked on the view of the winding road out the front windshield. "I smell smoke."

The ominous words sent his heart rate skyrocketing.

As the vehicle slowed and turned off the main road, the flicker of orange light joined the moon's glow, illuminating the surrounding trees. When the chariot rounded a bend in the driveway and the trees parted, his harsh inhale matched Aurora's.

"No!" A sharp point of pain shot the single syllable from her lips.

Directly ahead, flames leapt ten meters in the air from the roof of a domed structure. The blaze's glow obliterated the moonlight and painted the nearby trees in ribbons of red, orange, and gold. Firefighting personnel raced like ants across the scene, their large vehicles hunkered down by the stone blocks of the foundation. A sheriff's vehicle was parked sideways, preventing access to the circular driveway in front of the house.

His dad and Aurora were out of the vehicle before it came to a stop. One of the sheriffs moved into their path but Aurora darted around her as nimbly as a cat and kept running toward the structure. Firefighters tried to grab her next, but she dodged them too, climbing the front stairs and disappearing from view.

His dad wasn't so successful. The sheriff's partner had one palm planted on his dad's chest and the other hand wrapped around his bicep as they argued.

Micah took three steps toward the house before the other sheriff intercepted him.

"You can't go in there."

"This is my mom's house!" He hadn't meant to shout, but that's how the words left his mouth. Moisture filled his eyes, and not because of the smoke.

The woman darted a glance over her shoulder. "Is your mom inside?"

"I don't know. But my sister's in there." He stared in the direction Aurora had gone. She was nowhere to be seen.

"She's the one who ran inside?"

He nodded.

"We'll do what we can to get her out. You need to wait here so no one else gets hurt."

Micah!

The call punched directly into his brain, but it was his sister's voice.

Micah, I need you!

He didn't think. He just reacted. Pivoting away from the woman blocking his path he sprinted toward the house, Aurora's voice guiding him forward.

Emergency personnel moved to stop him as he raced across the pavement, but a pearlescent ribbon reached out from the doorway. As soon as he touched it, it surrounded him, deflecting the outstretched hands. He leapt up the stone stairs and charged through the open front door.

The air shimmered in front of his eyes, but the shield blocked out the heat from the flames. He skidded to a halt just inside, staring at the scene before him.

Aurora stood in the center of the room near what might have been a kitchen island, her gaze turned up to the burning beams of the domed ceiling as they rained sparks down on the pearlescent glow of her shield.

The visual was bizarre and otherworldly, but that wasn't what had brought him to a standstill.

His kind, loving, compassionate sister looked like an avenging Valkyrie, her face twisted into a mask of fury that stole the breath from his lungs.

One Hundred One

"Reanne!"

Aurora's enraged screech roared louder than the flames that surrounded her.

But no one answered.

The fire consumed every flammable object in sight, the damage too thorough to be accidental. The central room was unrecognizable, the furniture obliterated and buried under the debris raining down from above. The curving stairway looked like a gateway to Hell, holes gaping in the treads like hungry mouths. Flames ate away at the second-story gallery on both sides.

Her gaze swept skyward, where the domed ceiling stood partially open to the sky. Water from the firehoses streamed down, pattering the floor, creating hissing steam where it landed.

Fury engulfed her chest, hotter than the flames climbing the walls. *Micah!* She shot the message like an arrow. *I need you!*

His emotional shift was immediate, as was the sensation of movement in her direction. But he'd have to make it past the firefighters to reach her.

She pivoted back to the front door and flung a narrow channel of her shield in his direction. She couldn't see him through the billowing smoke, but she didn't need to. She felt the surge of power when he plowed through the shield and kept coming. But the firefighters who made a grab for him couldn't breach the unyielding, invisible surface.

The power built as he raced toward her. Maintaining her shield took no thought or effort, freeing her to enter the main room and face the real threat—the attack Reanne's minions had launched on her mom, Marina, and Gryphon.

Her gaze moved to the inferno consuming the gallery in front of the Forrest wing. She could sense her mom and Marina up there, but their emotions and energy were getting weaker with each breath. She couldn't sense Gryphon at all, even as she expanded her search through the rest of the house. Micah's presence glowed like a beacon in the entryway as he moved toward her, but the only other emotional resonances nearby belonged to the emergency personnel. No indication of the attackers who'd started the fire. Or Gryphon.

She swallowed, pushing down the fear that gripped her throat in an iron claw.

Moving to the base of the stairway on the Hawke side, she inspected the glowing wood of the treads. Calling them unstable would be generous, but the right side looked more solid than the left. She glanced over her shoulder, meeting Micah's gaze. "They're upstairs."

His gaze followed the curve of the stairway and the flaming railing of the gallery. When he looked back at her, she didn't sense a single thread of doubt.

"Lead the way."

One Hundred Two

When the picture resolved into the glitter of stars on black velvet, Mya's fingers dug into the arms of her chair, propelling her to her feet. She'd paced like a caged tiger until the nervous looks from Kire and Celia had convinced her to sit. But now that they'd reached the Sol system, sitting was no longer an option.

Celia followed her to the lift, Kire's voice trailing after them. "Jon, Mya and Celia are heading down to you."

"On my way."

The ride in the lift passed in a blur, as did the walk to the shuttle. Before she reached the cockpit, her body went ramrod straight as an image blasted into her consciousness. "No!"

Flames soared into an inky sky, illuminating giant redwoods in a nightmarish glow.

"Noooo..."

Voices spoke to her, but she couldn't understand them. Only the flames existed. And then she was racing into them. "Sahzade, no!"

Something shook her body hard, dispelling the image. Burning golden eyes and dark green skin replaced the flames and trees, matching their intensity.

"Mya, what did you see?"

The urgency in Jonarel's voice cut through, as did the strong grip of his hands on her shoulders. "Stoneycroft. It's on fire."

His eyes widened.

"Aurora ran inside."

His grip tightened for a second, then he was gone.

Celia appeared in front of her, her gaze calm. "Let's get you strapped in." She guided Mya to the co-pilot's chair like she was a puppet, fastening her harness as the shuttle lifted off and exited the bay.

Mya closed her eyes, trying to bring back the image, but it was gone. *Sahzade, what's happening?*

She sent the message as a desperate plea, but got no response. Her breath hitched as another possibility occurred to her.

Reanne.

A warm hand closed over hers, making her jerk. Her gaze darted to Jonarel.

He had his other hand on the controls, his body coiled for battle even when seated. "What are you seeing?"

"Nothing. The image is gone. But—" She had to clear her throat to push the words past her fear. "What if Reanne did this?"

The muscles of his jaw flexed, his lips lifting off his teeth. "Aurora will handle it."

"But what if—"

He squeezed her fingers. "She will be all right."

Was he assuring her, or himself?

One Hundred Three

Aurora's raw power held Micah transfixed. He climbed the rickety, burning stairway, following right behind her, yet his body was completely untouched by the heat or smoke of the inferno. The fire could have been a projected image for all it affected them.

But it was definitely having an effect on the house. Boards creaked and gave way, smoke billowed in thick clouds, and pieces of the ceiling collapsed, lighting up the shield. He ducked instinctively the first few times the shield flared, but by the time they'd carefully picked their way up the staircase to the edge of the gallery, he'd accepted the impenetrable safety his sister's shield provided from falling objects.

The floor was another matter. He didn't want to think about what might happen if it gave way. The bottoms of his feet felt a little toasty now that they were on the upper level. Aurora probably didn't have a way to form the shield solidly underneath their shoes without creating a slick surface that would make them slide.

The micro-gaps in the shield also let in a little smoke, the ashy scent prompting him to cover his nose with his sleeve. The smoke in the gallery was so thick he couldn't see much besides the flames and the pearlescent glow of his sister's shield.

Aurora didn't seem the least bit concerned by the flames or the smoke. She paused near an opening in the wall to their right, tilting her head like she was listening, her gaze going unfocused. She glanced at him. "I think they're in one of the bathrooms. Come on."

Pushing into the smokescreen pouring out at them, she disappeared through the opening. After a few steps he figured out they were in a hallway. Aurora led him through a doorway to the right, which turned out to be a bedroom. The bed was a rectangle of flame in front of them.

Aurora gazed at the flames for a heartbeat before hurrying through an archway to the left. "Mom? Marina?"

He followed her into the room, spotting a sink through the haze. A bathroom.

Aurora took a few more steps before halting. She reached out to touch a rock wall on the far side of a shower and tub enclosure. "Mom!"

The alarm in her voice made his heart pound.

She whirled around. "They're in the shower enclosure on the other side."

He backed up, giving her room to get past him. "How do we get to them?"

"This way."

They retraced their path to the hallway. Aurora was practically running now, but she came to a screeching halt when they reached the next doorway.

He stared over her shoulder, as horrified by the sight as she was.

The bedroom wasn't just on fire. A huge chunk of the floor was missing, and what little was left had been a feast for the flames.

The stairway had been tricky. This was impassable.

One Hundred Four

The fury burning in Aurora's chest battled with a surge of panic.

The floor to Marina and Gryphon's bedroom was an open pit, flaming debris drifting down to their home office in the room below. The interior wall to her right was still partially intact, but the burning boards of the floor between where she stood and the opening that led to the bathroom wouldn't support her weight. Definitely not Micah's.

"What do we do?" Micah asked.

Her mind raced. The bathroom didn't have any other access points, except for the exterior window in the small reading room that joined the bedroom to the bathroom.

She didn't have time to go outside and check it out. Her mother's energy was fading fast. She had to get them out now!

She backed up, looking in the direction they'd come. The wall of the hallway that joined Mya's room with Marina and Gryphon's also formed part of Marina and Gryphon's walk-in closet, which opened into the bathroom. If she got into the closet, she could access the bathroom from there.

Which meant breaking through the planked wood wall.

She'd never tried anything like this before, wasn't even sure if it would work. Or if she could do it without bringing down the whole house. The structural integrity was already shot. But she was out of options.

She motioned to Micah. "Get behind me, and rest your hand on my lower back." She'd need the connection for the power and control it would offer.

He didn't question her. When his hand made contact, the energy coursing through her flexed its muscles like a wrestler getting ready for a match.

She pointed to a spot on the wall. "I'm going to take it out here."

"Okay." No doubt. No concern. His trust and complete faith in her gave her courage.

She could also feel her mom's and Marina's emotions, though not with the clarity she sensed Micah's. They knew she was here. She was sure of it. But she wasn't getting the overwhelming fear she'd anticipated. Only a sense of anticipation. And hope.

She could do this. *Had* to do this. Taking a slow breath, she focused all her attention on the wall. "Here we go."

Pulling her arms back like a batter preparing to hit the next pitch, she channeled a ball of energy down her arms and into her hands. On the downswing, she sent the ball slamming into the wall at the same point where her shield struck the surface.

The boom that resounded through the hallway battered her ears, making them ring. Timber exploded against her shield like shrapnel.

But she'd made a hole. The wall looked like it had been struck by an oversized cannonball, a charred circular opening half a meter across revealing the closet's interior.

"Go again."

She glanced back at Micah. The smokey gloom in the hallway made it difficult to see his expression clearly, but she could feel the intensity of his emotions.

"You've got this."

She looked back at the hole. Now that she had an idea of the result of her previous strike, she could better gauge how much juice to put into the next blow.

Getting back into position, she gathered the energy, pushing it down into her hands before swinging forward.

This time the impact made the floor shake under her feet. A section of the ceiling collapsed, dropping on top of the shield and sliding to the floor, the flames lighting up the meter-wide hole in the wall.

Smoke rushed through the opening. She followed it in, stepping over the lip into the fire-lit gloom.

One Hundred Five

She'd done it. His little sister had broken through a wall!

He stayed with her as she crawled inside, ducking to avoid the remnants of shelving dangling in front of the opening. He struggled to find his footing on the other side, stepping on chunks of wood and softer piles of clothing scattered on the floor.

A rectangle of orange light appeared across from the hole Aurora had created as she opened the door to the walk-in closet. Smoke concealed the opening like fog, obscuring his surroundings.

His fingers curled into the fabric of Aurora's jacket, letting her guide him through the haze as she stepped through the doorway.

"Mom! Marina!"

"Aurora." The voice was more frog than human, thick and deep, followed by a hacking cough.

Aurora rushed forward, pulling him with her. After a few steps she turned right and crouched. "Mom?"

He sank down beside her, barely making out the stone confines of a large shower enclosure. But what was clear as day was the pearlescent shield creating a bumpy blanket over the huddled forms on the floor, pale green threads running through it.

A pair of bare male feet and pajama bottoms marked the edge of the shield near where Aurora knelt.

Aurora inhaled sharply. "Gryphon! What happened to him?"

The froggy voice came again, a little stronger this time, from a petite figure lying near the opening. "He's unconscious."

"Unconscious?" Aurora shook her head, as though denying the statement. "Marina? Are you—"

"Weak." The reply came from deeper within the enclosure. "But I'm okay."

His heart thumped in his chest. By process of elimination, the woman with the froggy voice, the one within touching distance, was his mother.

Aurora's spine straightened, her gaze switching back to their mother. "Can any of you walk?"

"No." His mom sounded apologetic.

Aurora looked back at Micah. "Let's see if we can fix that."

He wasn't sure what she had in mind, but when she reached a hand back to him, he took it. And felt their connection shoot to a whole new level.

"Mom, lower your shield."

The glow in the enclosure winked out, replaced a nanosecond later as Aurora expanded her shield to fill the shower enclosure, drawing them all within the same safety bubble.

Aurora placed her free hand on their mother's bent knees, the glow of her energy field intensifying.

Micah stared at the point of contact, afraid to look anywhere else. His mom was *right there!* The mother he'd believed was dead. He hadn't thought about it as he'd followed Aurora into the flames, but this tiny moment of calm in the storm brought him up short. What would she think? What would she say? Would she be glad to see him? Would she even recognize him?

Aurora's shield had pushed the smoke out of the way, clearing the haze surrounding them. He lifted his gaze to his mother's face.

She was looking right at him. "Hello, Micah."

One Hundred Six

Aurora concentrated on sending healing energy into her mom's airways and muscles, revitalizing them the best she could. She also sensed her mom's emotional turmoil, and Micah's trepidation. She would never have chosen this as their first meeting, but the universe had other plans.

What surprised her was the warmth in her mom's voice when she spoke Micah's name. "Hello, Micah."

His surprise mirrored hers, his anxiety receding. "Hi, Mom." A beat of silence. "Fancy meeting you here."

The quip startled a laugh out of Aurora, which was echoed by her mother, although it quickly turned into a hacking cough.

Aurora moved her hand to her mom's chest, calming the spasms. And was startled to see her mother grinning at Micah.

"I see you've got your father's sense of humor."

Micah grinned back. "Definitely."

Aurora stared. Her mother was joking? At a time like this? Maybe she'd taken a blow to the head during the attack and gone loopy.

She shifted her focus from her mother to Marina and Gryphon. Marina had claimed she was okay, but now that she could see her better, she knew the lie in those words. She also had a sick feeling about what had brought her to this condition. She'd seen greyed out energy fields before, knew what caused them.

She still couldn't sense Gryphon at all, even though he was right beside her. Marina had her hand on his chest, air rasping in and out of his lips in time with the rise and fall of his ribcage. But it looked like Marina was functioning as a living ventilator, willing each breath into Gryphon's body. He wasn't producing any energy field of his own.

A hand settled over hers, drawing her attention back to her mother.

Her mom gave her hand a gentle squeeze. "That's enough for me. You two need to help Marina."

Because time wasn't on their side. "Can you stand?" She and Micah would have to carry Gryphon out of here. She needed her mom and Marina on their feet.

Her mom pushed to her hands and knees, then rose to a tottering crouch. Micah steadied her with a hand on her arm. She nodded at them both. "Well enough."

That would have to do. Already the flames had spread through the wall behind Micah and across the ceiling. The air inside the shield was going to get more contaminated the longer they were up here. At least now that they were on the slate floor of the bathroom and not moving, she could keep the smoke from seeping in.

Shifting to her right, she placed her hand on Marina's shoulder, bracing for what she knew was coming as their energy fields merged.

Helping Mya heal the Suulh refugees from their Necri existence had prepared her for this, as had her father's training. But that didn't stop tears from dampening her eyes as she gazed at Marina's sweat-soaked face, sensed the pain and anxiety coursing through her.

Marina reached to remove Aurora's hand, her gaze on Gryphon's face. "Gryphon—"

"Needs you."

Marina's hand stilled, her gaze lifting to Aurora's.

Aurora surrounded Marina in the most nurturing, calming energy she could generate. Healing wasn't her strong suit, except when it came to herself and Micah. But her energy would strengthen Marina's. "I'll help you so you can stabilize him. Then we'll get out of here."

The fear in Marina's dark eyes receded, a hint of her self-assurance returning.

The green of her energy field deepened a couple shades as Aurora continued to funnel energy to her. The color change passed along Marina's arm to Gryphon's chest and around his body. The effect of the healing field was very muted compared to what Aurora was used to seeing from Marina, but the longer she fed her energy, the richer the color became.

A crackling and hissing drew Aurora's attention upward. A moment later the flaming remnants of what had been a skylight frame dropped through the smoke, smacking into her shield and clattering to the floor. The smoke made it impossible to see the extent of the damage, but it was a good guess the ceiling was about to give out.

They were out of time.

She looked back at Gryphon. His breathing still grated like gravel, but he seemed to be doing it on his own again. "Can we move him?"

Twin frown lines appeared between Marina's dark brows, her gaze darting to the smoke above her head. "If I keep a connection with him, we should be able to go now."

The way she said *should* made it clear there were a multitude of ways Gryphon's condition could deteriorate. But if they stayed in the house any longer, it could collapse around them. She didn't want to find out the hard way whether her shield could protect them from an implosion.

Releasing her hold on Marina, she turned to Micah, assessing his muscular frame. He was a little shorter than Gryphon, but broader through the chest and shoulders and a lot more muscled. "Do you think you can–"

"Carry him?" He was way ahead of her. "Yeah, I should be able to manage."

"Then let's get going."

One Hundred Seven

Gryphon was a lot heavier than he looked.

Micah grunted as he lifted the tall man over his shoulder in a fireman's carry. Marina moved to his side, placing her hand on Gryphon's back once Micah had gotten him settled.

He'd never tried to carry anyone when they were dead weight. Another experience he hadn't anticipated. With Aurora around, his life seemed full of them.

"You okay?" Aurora asked.

Her concern lightened his load. Compared to her, he had the easy job. She was the one keeping the fire and smoke from killing them, which had to be wearing her out. Instead, she was worried about him. "I'm good."

She held his gaze for a moment before switching her attention to their mother. "You can go between us so—"

"I'll bring up the rear."

Aurora's eyes widened, her brows lifting. "Really? It would be safer—"

"I'll guard our backs." The authority in the statement matched the way he'd heard Aurora speak, as did the way his mom lifted her chin. Now he knew where she got it.

Aurora's lips parted, the look in her eyes indicating she was going to object, but all she said was, "Okay," before turning toward their exit point.

His mom glanced up at him as she slipped past. "Stay close to her."

Whether she said it for his sake or Aurora's, he couldn't tell. But it was good advice. He nodded. "I will."

Aurora's shield formed a shifting, curving bubble around their bedraggled group. He followed her out of the bathroom and through the rectangle of the closet doorway.

In the short time since they'd passed through here, the fire had made hay. The opening Aurora had created in the wall now looked like a hoop of fire only partially obscured by the billowing smoke.

Climbing through the first time had been relatively easy. Now he hesitated.

Aurora halted right in front of the flaming circle, her hand closing around his wrist as she turned and leaned toward him. "With me. We'll go slowly."

Her shield pulsed with renewed vigor, expanding out to perfectly fill the opening. The flames guttered and died around the edges, although the raw wood still glowed orange-red.

He followed Aurora as she stepped over the lip, maintaining her grip on his wrist. He bent his knees and ducked down, Gryphon's weight pressing on him, threatening his balance. Two sets of hands on his back steadied him as he stepped through, one giving him a sensation of soothing coolness while the other gave a jolt of energetic warmth.

As he straightened, his mom and Marina moved beside him, placing him at the center of their energetic triangle with Aurora at the head. He doubted they'd ever been in a situation even remotely like this before, yet they were working together like a well-oiled machine.

Aurora had to shout to be heard over the cacophony of the roaring fire, the clatters and bangs of the emergency personnel battling the blaze outside, and the crackling and popping of the wood. "You still good?"

"Yeah!" Using his head, he motioned her in the direction of the stairway.

She squeezed his wrist but didn't let go, guiding him along the curved hallway, past the doorway to the first bedroom they'd encountered, and through the opening to the gallery.

The curtain of smoke danced out into the open space of the central room, allowing him to see the destruction the fire had wrought since he and Aurora had climbed the stairs.

Huge chunks of the gallery had collapsed to the lower level, burying the furniture underneath. The water from the firetrucks had created pools on the hardwood floors that reflected the flames still battling for dominance over the stairway and the back half of the house.

Fear injected his veins as he eyed the flaming staircase. He wasn't an engineer, but common sense told him the compromised structure wouldn't support his and Gryphon's combined weight.

Aurora's grip tightened as she moved next to him, her shield pulsating.

He leaned forward, putting his mouth close to her ear. "Is there another way down?"

She shook her head. "No."

He swallowed, his gaze still on the stairs. Gryphon wasn't getting any lighter, and the staircase wouldn't get any stronger. "What do you suggest?"

Her forehead creased as she looked between the stairs and their group.

Their mom stepped forward. "I'll go first. Test it out."

Aurora's lips parted, shock written all over her face. "What?"

"I'll go first," their mom repeated, louder this time. "I already survived a fall once tonight. Even if the stairway collapses, I'll be fine."

"But... but..." Clearly his sister was having trouble processing.

Their mom rested her hand on Aurora's shoulder. "I'll be fine."

Aurora stared at her for a long moment, her internal struggle as obvious as the shield surrounding them. But eventually she nodded. "Okay."

Their mom's gaze shifted to him briefly before she turned and walked to the top of the stairway near the outer wall, Aurora's shield opening and closing to let her through.

His mom's shield wasn't nearly as bright as Aurora's. It didn't look as sturdy, either. But she was the lightest person in the group and didn't need Aurora's shield to keep the smoke and fire at bay. She was the logical choice.

She'd made it down four steps when the stairway gave a tortured groan. One minute it was attached to the wall, the next it dropped like an elevator, slamming to the ground in an eruption of flames and jagged wood that blew apart like fireworks.

One Hundred Eight

The beautiful blue expanse that was Earth took form rapidly as the Kraed shuttle hurtled through space, leaving the *Starhawke* far behind. Mya didn't have to ask to know Jonarel was pushing the engines to the limits, and that he'd engaged the hull camouflage to conceal them from the Fleet's satellite sensor network.

As the lights outlining the western coast of the North American continent appeared below, her mind raced forward. "Where will you land?" Stoneycroft was in the middle of a redwood forest. It wasn't like they had a landing platform near the house. And even if they did, by now she'd expect emergency vehicles to be swarming all over the place.

"Do not worry."

Again, his complete confidence calmed her fears. She took him at his word, watching as they descended into the atmosphere and continued toward the coast. The populated areas were easy to pick out, but Stoneycroft was located near a little hamlet, not a major city. Huge swaths of blackness spread out to the east. "How can you see?"

"Darkness does not hinder me."

Right. Kraed eyesight was enhanced in darkness, like a cat's.

But he wouldn't need that skill to locate Stoneycroft. The glow of the fire guided them like a searchlight, the orange and yellow flames and rolling plumes of grey smoke rising into the moonlit sky.

Jonarel took the shuttle in a high pass, angling it so she could look down on Stoneycroft. Or more accurately, the remains of Stoneycroft.

The air refused to remain in Mya's lungs.

Sections of the central dome had caved in, glowing embers on the remaining supports creating an intricate pattern that gave a vague outline of the original structure. But the half-moon living quarters on either side were far worse. It looked like a fire-breathing dragon had taken a bite out of each. The firefighters were battling intense blazes that had already decimated her parents' bedroom on the Forrest side. In the Hawke wing, the space that had been Aurora's bedroom was now a vacant shell. "Oh, Sahzade."

"Where is she?" Celia's voice, right behind her.

She glanced over her shoulder. Celia clutched the back of the co-pilot's seat to keep her balance, her gaze out the viewport.

Mya focused on what her Suulh senses were telling her. And shuddered when she got her answer. "Down there. Maybe inside." Aurora's powerful energy pulsed nearby, drawing her like a magnet. She thought she detected her mother's unique energy, too. She turned to Jonarel. "We have to get down there."

He nodded, the shuttle banking away from the house.

Apparently he'd been waiting for her order. She didn't pay much attention to what happened next, her gaze on the aft camera view of the house, but somehow he set the shuttle down in the trees about three hundred meters from the house in an area where it shouldn't have fit.

As she exited, the interior of the shuttle seemed vaguely different, too. She didn't stop to figure out why. Only one goal mattered. Finding Aurora and her parents.

"Stay with me." Jonarel's hand closed over Mya's, his broad shoulders barely distinguishable from the trunks of the redwoods in the ambient light from the moon and the smoking remains of Stoneycroft. He gave her hand a gentle tug.

She didn't have to be told twice. Not only could he take her through the woods quicker than she could navigate on her own, but his very warm, very reassuring presence blocked the chill, both outside and within.

Celia kept pace with them as they hurried through the forest in a more or less direct line back toward the house. When Mya stumbled over a branch, Jonarel caught her effortlessly, setting her back on her feet before continuing on.

A few moments later the outlines of the rear deck showed through the trees, the heat from the fire chasing away the winter chill, making the surroundings feel like midsummer, not Christmas.

Jonarel paused, his head tilting like he was listening.

"What is it?" she whispered.

"I smell Setarips."

Not listening. Scenting. Her heartbeat stuttered, her gaze darting around the trees. She'd been right. Reanne had orchestrated this attack. "Where are they?"

His golden eyes glimmered in the scattered light. "Gone." He stared off to the west. "Fleeing like cowards."

She clutched his hand. "My parents—"

"Were not with them. But another was."

Her heart thumped. "Libra?"

He frowned, lifting his head to scent the air again. "No. But similar."

She didn't have to ask if it was Aurora. No way would Jonarel confuse her scent with anyone else. He could probably track Aurora like a bloodhound. And Mya could sense her nearby, though she didn't have Aurora's gift to pinpoint exact locations. Was she still in the house?

Lifting her gaze, she caught a glimmer of pearlescent white through the wide-panel windows along the exterior wall. Her throat constricted. The smoke-covered glow was coming from the second floor of the Forrest wing, near the staircase. It also looked weak.

She pointed to the glow, even though Jonarel and Celia couldn't see it. "She's inside."

And then the glow plummeted. A crackling crash and the explosion of glass drowned out her cry of alarm as the back windows along the deck shattered. Flames leapt behind the broken frames.

"Sahzade!" She took a step and then halted. The strong pull of Aurora's energy continued unabated. What the hell was happening?

Instinct prompted her to send out a mental flare. *Sahzade?*

The response was immediate. And strong. *Mya! My mom.* An image of Libra, her shield surrounding her amid the flames, falling as the staircase collapsed.

Libra had been the one she'd seen, not Aurora. And she'd just dropped five meters onto a broken staircase. *I'm here!*

She'd taken three steps toward the deck before a powerful grip on her fingers stopped her.

"Where are you going?" Jonarel's golden eyes blazed as much as the firelight.

"They need me!"

"You cannot walk into a fire!"

"Yes, I can!" It would hurt like hell, but as long as she didn't get stuck anywhere, she could heal any damage from the fire or smoke as quickly as it occurred.

She tugged at their joined hands, but she might as well have been caught in a steel trap for all the good it did.

"No," he insisted. "It is not safe."

She laughed without an iota of humor. "Of course it's not safe! And my parents are in there!"

She knew that with absolute certainty. She understood Aurora's need to protect better than anyone. The visual Aurora had sent made it clear she was still on the second floor. The only reason she would have stayed up there and sent Libra to the staircase alone was if Mya's parents needed her protection.

And now there was no way down.

Jonarel's grip eased, but not enough for her to escape. "Then I will go with you."

She recoiled in horror. "No! The fire could kill you."

He pulled her closer, his voice rumbling from deep within his chest. "Not if I am with you."

Conflicting emotions slammed against each other, locking her in place as she stared into his eyes. A hand on her arm made her jump.

"Go, Mya." Celia's voice was remarkably calm. "Take Jonarel and help Aurora." She tapped the comband on her forearm. "I'll do what I can from out here."

That tipped Mya off the fence. Without another word, she engaged her energy field and hurried up the stairs to the deck, Jonarel right behind her.

The heat intensified, pouring out of the remains of the wide window to the right of the door.

She peered into the smoky ruin. "Libra! Where are you?"

No answer.

"Libra!"

Jonarel's fingers tightened on hers. "I heard her, saying your name."

Mya couldn't hear anything over the crackle of the burning wood, but she trusted Jonarel's superior senses. "Where?"

"This way." Moving with assurance, he stepped over the remains of the windowsill and then crouched low while he waited for Mya to join him.

The natural cooling effect of her healing field kept the heat from charbroiling their skin, but the smoke was a tougher opponent. It gnawed at her eyes and airways, working to break down her cells almost as quickly as she healed them. It didn't help that she was focusing most of her attention on keeping Jonarel unharmed.

He lifted her over a jumble of burning boards like she weighed no more than a feather. When he set her down on the other side, she caught sight of Libra's familiar pearlescent shield through the rising smoke. "Libra!"

Aurora's mother turned her head as Mya and Jonarel made their way across the glowing remains of the staircase to her side. "Mya?" Her gaze moved to Jonarel, her eyes popping wide. "Jonarel?"

"We're here." Mya crouched, Jonarel beside her, bringing her hand and energy field in contact with Libra's shield. Immediately the shield expanded to envelope her and Jonarel, her green energy winding ribbons through the pearlescent white. The heat and smoke abated with it.

"I thought I'd imagined your voice." Libra gazed at her like someone who's afraid they're dreaming and doesn't want to wake up. She was lying partially on her side, her right leg pinned under one of the fallen support beams. Mya saw signs of minor trauma in both legs and her back, consistent with a fall, but nothing serious. Her shield had protected her.

The beam across her leg was another matter.

"I tried to move it, but it's too heavy." Libra gestured to the beam, then pointed up to the ragged edge of the gallery above them. "Aurora's still up there, with your parents and Micah."

"Micah?" She hadn't anticipated that.

"He's carrying your dad."

Her heart thumped. "Carrying him? Why?"

Libra held her gaze, her voice softening. "He and Marina are in pretty bad shape. You need to hurry. Get them out."

"What about you?"

"Unless you have a forklift, I'm not going anywhere."

She didn't, but she had the next best thing.

She turned to Jonarel. He was already moving to straddle Libra's legs, positioning himself so he could get his hands under the downed beam.

"Can you keep his hands shielded?" She didn't want to think of the kind of damage the burning wood could do if he touched it without any protection.

Libra blinked rapidly, clearly startled by Jonarel's looming presence. "Uh, yeah."

Mya focused on channeling as much healing energy into Libra's shield as she could, making it stronger as Jonarel slid his large hands under the beam on either side of Libra's leg.

His shoulder, back, and leg muscles flexed under the close-cut material of his tunic and pants, the raw power in his body visible as he forced the beam up centimeter by centimeter.

Libra pulled her leg back, slipping her foot out the narrow gap Jonarel had created between the beam and the floor.

Mya helped Libra stand as Jonarel set the beam back on the floor, his chest rising and falling with his breathing as he straightened.

One problem solved. Four more to go.

Her gaze swept the gallery, looking for answers. "How are we going to get them down?" Aurora could manage the drop, and possibly Micah too, if he was with her. But if her parents were as bad off as Libra had indicated, the fall might kill them.

"I will get them down."

Mya turned to Jonarel. "How?"

He held up a hand. The claws extending from each of his fingertips gleamed in the firelight.

She stared at him. "You want to *climb* up there?"

He stared back. "The exterior wall will support me."

Fear surged in her chest. "And the smoke and fire will drop you."

His dark brows lifted. "I am sturdier than you believe."

Oh, she knew full well how sturdy he was. But he wasn't invincible.

"Do you have a better option?" he asked.

She chewed on her bottom lip, scrambling for an alternative. And came up empty. But if he was going, she had one caveat. "I'm going with you."

His brows snapped down. "No, you—"

"It's logical. I can help you during the climb, minimize any damage. Then you can carry my mom and dad down while I stay with Aurora." No one else could carry them both at the same time, but she had no doubt Jonarel would manage. He'd hauled her up a tree, multiple times, like she was a leaf.

Saying Aurora's name worked like a charm. The worry in his golden eyes cleared. Aurora was the one person he trusted more than himself to protect her. "Very well."

Mya turned to Libra. "When he gets back, get my parents out of the house. Celia's waiting outside. She'll know what to do. Aurora and I will join you as soon as we can."

Libra's gaze flicked over Mya's shoulder in Jonarel's direction, but she nodded. "Be safe."

"We will."

Turning to face Jonarel, she gazed at the back wall of the house and sent Aurora a mental message. *Sahzade, we're coming.*

One Hundred Nine

Aurora tracked the movement downstairs through the emotional currents of her mother, Mya, and Jonarel. The pain she'd felt from her mother after the fall had eased shortly after Mya and Jonarel had arrived.

She wasn't surprised Jonarel had insisted on entering the danger zone with Mya. No way would he have let her go in alone.

She sensed Celia's presence as well, but she was still outside, no doubt monitoring the situation and communicating with the *Starhawke*.

Micah had laid Gryphon down near the exterior wall where they were all huddled, one of the few places in the house that hadn't been claimed by the fire, although the boards under their feet still creaked ominously.

Aurora had helped Marina provide healing energy to Gryphon, but it wasn't working very well. She suspected the damage Marina had suffered from the Necri was preventing her from fully accessing her abilities. And as she and Mya had learned, treating the unnatural results of Necri energy was a serious challenge. They'd struggled during the healing sessions with the Suulh refugees.

An emotional shift from Mya and Jonarel made her lift her head, her gaze moving to the drop-off where the staircase had collapsed. Moments later, Mya sent her a mental message.

Sahzade, we're coming.

She stood, focusing on their movements. When they left the protection of her mother's shield, needles of pain struck as they were exposed to the heat and smoke, but she could sense Mya's energy fighting back, healing the damage as it was inflicted. Her mother stayed below, but Jonarel and Mya were getting steadily closer, like they were climbing a ladder along the side of the wall. A moment later a dark shape encased in an emerald green glow rose above the lip of the gallery, attached to the wall like an enormous spider.

Jonarel landed with the grace of a panther on the gallery floor a couple meters away. Mya slid off his back, rushing forward.

Aurora enveloped them both in her shield as Mya grabbed her in a bone-crushing hug.

"Sahzade, are you okay?"

Aurora squeezed back. "Better now that you're here." She released Mya. "Your parents need you."

As Mya crouched beside Gryphon and Marina, surrounding them in her healing energy field, Micah stood, moving out of the way.

Aurora turned to Jonarel, but his gaze was on Mya, not her. "Thank you for bringing her."

He glanced at her briefly before returning his attention to Mya. "She insisted."

O-*kay*. That was different. *Totally* different. Like universe-shifting different. He'd never focused on Mya before, at least not when he was around her. And certainly not when they were in a dangerous situation. He'd always acted like her personal bodyguard. Now, that concern was focused on Mya, instead.

Fascinating.

But she'd have to analyze the change later. "Getting Gryphon and Marina out is our top priority. Can you carry them down?"

He nodded, his gaze still on Mya. "That is my plan."

Great, he'd already worked out the logistics. "Can you take them both at once?"

He finally looked at her full-on. The sensation was surreal, like seeing someone after a ten-year absence. He was still Jonarel, but different in a million undefinable ways. What exactly had happened while she was gone?

He answered her question with a question. "You will protect Lelindia?"

He had to ask? And when did he start calling Mya *Lelindia*? "Of course I will."

He held her gaze, his expression and emotions in serious lockdown. But one thing was very clear. He wasn't concerned about *her* safety. What a concept.

Mya stood, rejoining them. "I think my dad's stable enough to move, as long as my mom can go with him." She gazed at Jonarel, hope and fear pouring off her in equal measure.

Jonarel clasped Mya's hands in his. "I will keep them safe."

Wait a minute. Were they—

Jonarel moved to Gryphon's side before she completed the thought. Grasping Gryphon's arms, he hauled him onto his shoulders as Micah had done, although Jonarel made it look easy. He positioned Gryphon so his legs and arms dangled in front of his chest. Then he crouched beside Marina. "Climb onto my back. Lock your arms around my neck, and your legs around my waist."

Marina did as instructed, while Marina helped her get secured.

Micah moved next to Aurora, leaning down so his mouth was by her ear. "Who is this guy?"

"Jonarel. My engineer."

"*He's* your engineer?"

She could understand his skepticism. At the moment, Jonarel looked more like a professional bodybuilder crossed with a tiger. "I'll fill you in later."

The floor groaned as Jonarel stood. His gaze met Aurora's, the unspoken message clear. The structure would not hold much longer.

He faced Mya. "I will return for you."

"Return? But—"

And then he was gone, two bounding leaps taking him to the wall, the claws in his hands and feet digging into the wood as he disappeared from view.

"Whoa."

She echoed Micah's sentiment. She'd never been in a spectator position during one of Jonarel's feats of athleticism. Impressive. And a little unnerving.

But her reaction was nothing compared to the cavalcade of emotion coming from Mya. Fear. Anxiety. Surprise. And something deep and powerful that she doubted Mya was ready to define.

One Hundred Ten

A loud crackling pop yanked Mya out of the trance Jonarel's disappearance had put her into.

"Mya!" Aurora's hand gripped her upper arm, pulling her backward.

The crackling continued, growing louder, like the rumble of an avalanche all around them.

She stumbled, and then shrieked as the floor in front of her gave way. Her feet went out from under her as strong arms circled her waist, holding her in midair.

"We've got you."

She whipped her head around, staring into eyes that were both familiar and foreign.

"It's okay, Leelee, we've got you."

Recognition clicked. "Micah."

"Yeah." He set her on her feet but the pressure around her waist kept her pinned against his body. He gave her a weak smile. "Long time no see."

On some level she'd known he was there when she and Jonarel had reached the gallery, but she hadn't acknowledged him. Seeing her parents had overwhelmed her.

Her dad's condition had scared the stuffing out of her, the degree of cellular necrosis pushing her toward panic. But the familiar signs of Necri energy had given her a starting point, helping her stabilize him enough to move him.

More creaking and popping. She looked past Micah, to the rest of the gallery along the Forrest wing. Not much left, except a ragged two-meter by six-meter section that ended before the opening to the hallway. That left them standing on the rickety peninsula.

"Anyone have a plan for this?" Aurora asked.

She turned her head. Aurora stood on her other side, her left arm wrapped over Micah's right, so that they were caging her in with their bodies and the shield. Their backs were to the exterior wall.

"Well," Micah said, craning his neck to peer over the edge, "either we jump, or we fall."

"I agree." Aurora met Mya's gaze. "Jumping seems like the better option."

Jumping sounded like a terrible idea. "Shouldn't we wait for Jonarel?"

"We may not have time."

She sighed. "Just so you know, I hate this."

Her comment brought a tiny smile to Aurora's lips. "Noted." She looked at Micah. "On three, we run to the edge and leap. I'll manage the shield. You keep a tight hold on Mya, okay?"

Micah nodded.

Aurora turned to Mya. "Give me all the juice you can."

"I will."

"Okay. One, two..."

A dark shape dropped out of the smoke, landing directly in front of them.

Mya's startled yelp stuck in her throat as she stared into the blaze of Jonarel's golden eyes.

"I will take her." His deep growl left no room for argument. Neither did the warning look he shot Micah.

Micah and Aurora let go, their arms replaced by Jonarel's strong hands. His *burned* hands. The damage shone like neon to her senses as he swung her onto his back. "Hold on."

She engaged her energy field, catching a glimpse of the shocked look on Aurora's face right before Jonarel bounded off the floor. launching them into the air. She pressed her face into his back and her body against his as the falling sensation sent her stomach into her throat. But as quickly as it started it stopped. the downward motion slowing.

She didn't look. didn't want to know how he was getting them to the ground. Instead. she focused her attention on her healing energy. channeling it to his hands and feet.

His momentum shifted forward and he started to run. A crash behind them jerked her head around.

Aurora's shield glowed like a curving moonbeam as flaming debris shot in all directions. Mya saw movement in the glow but the smoke quickly obscured it as Jonarel carried her across the deck. leaping down the steps and bounding into the trees beyond.

One Hundred Eleven

"Are we jumping?" Micah shouted over the crackling wood as his childhood friend and her bizarre protector vanished into the smoke.

Aurora stared after them for a heartbeat, then turned to him. "No. Now that it's just us, I say we surf the shield."

He blinked. "Surf the shield?"

She nodded. "If I energize the molecules between us and the ground with my energy field, essentially creating a powerful updraft like a wave swell, I can project the shield on top of it, giving us a surface to glide along. I'd rather slide than plummet."

He couldn't argue with that. "How many times have you done this before?"

She shot him a look that was part challenge, part chagrin. "Never."

And that's why he loved her. "I'll follow you."

She lifted her hands, the pearlescent glow of her energy field expanding past the edge of the drop-off. She looked at him, her face tense with concentration. "Ready?"

He placed his left hand over her right, the field glowing like moonlight. "Let's do this."

As one, they ran toward the edge, following the shimmering pathway. When his shoes hit the point where the floor ended and the shield began, he slid. So did she. But rather than fighting it, he leaned into it. Just like a wave, only this one took them in a looping path down and to the right, mimicking the curve of the missing stairway.

Aurora stayed right with him. He didn't look at her, his attention on where they were going, but their connection told him everything he needed to know, as did the stability of their path. If she'd been worried she couldn't manipulate her energy field and shield to keep them from dropping like rocks, she'd blown that fear away.

As the floor rushed up towards them, the shield blasted a path through the hunks of burning wood, sending them flying. Friction pulled at his feet as they slid onto the ground level, Aurora's energy field expanding to provide a buffer and slow their momentum. They halted half a meter from the wall.

An ominous creaking made him look up. The remaining chunk of the gallery was right above them. It sagged and buckled, then collapsed with alarming speed.

He ducked, but Aurora was quicker. Her shield shot up to meet the threat as she clenched his hand in hers and pulled him toward the back wall. They leapt through a smashed window into the night air, their feet hitting the deck outside. Tightening her grip on his hand, she raced for the stairs, barreling past several stunned firefighters, her shield bumping them as they passed.

Before he knew it, they were in the trees.

Aurora didn't slow, but her shield and their connection kept him from taking a header as they ran.

"Where are we going?"

"Mya needs me."

Not exactly an answer, but a moment later he spotted the same rich green glow emanating through the trees that he'd seen LeeLee produce in the gallery.

The trees blocked out a fair amount of moonlight, painting everything in splotches of intermittent light and shadow. He made out Gryphon's tall form stretched out on the ground, unmoving. LeeLee and Marina knelt on either side of him, their hands on his head and torso, while his mom sat beside Marina, her pearlescent energy field mingling with Marina's.

The walking tree-cat with the yellow eyes that Aurora had identified as her engineer hovered just behind LeeLee. Another figure, an athletic woman Aurora's height, stood off to one side, her gaze sweeping the area and coming to rest on him.

The shadows made it difficult to see her face, but he instinctively halted under her intense scrutiny, and probably would have raised his hands in a gesture of surrender if Aurora hadn't tugged him down with her as she knelt beside LeeLee.

"Sahzade," LeeLee said with obvious relief, her gaze remaining on her father.

"I'm here." Aurora placed her left hand over LeeLee's.

Micah felt a jolt pass along their connection that made his stomach twist. He instinctively pulled away, but Aurora squeezed his hand.

"It's the Necri damage." She took a slow breath, her pearlescent energy field weaving in with the emerald green as she turned to him. "That's what feels so wrong."

Necri? Aurora had told him about the dark side of Suulh energy, but he'd never expected to encounter it. "That's what did this to him?"

She nodded. "Mya and I have seen something similar before, though not quite like this."

He swallowed, staring at the still form of a man he barely remembered. The pull of emotion tightened his chest, nevertheless. "Will he live?"

"Yes." Marina answered him, her green field flaring for a moment as if to emphasize the point.

Aurora met his gaze, a question in her eyes. "We can help."

"How?"

"Allow me to open us fully to the connection with Mya. Let her have all we can give."

His stomach twisted for a different reason. "Will we get like him?"

Aurora smiled softly. "No. Helping him won't hurt us, just make us uncomfortable. And tire us out."

"Oh." He felt the sentry woman's gaze zero in on him like a sword point. He lifted his head, staring back at her shadowy form in the darkness. If this was a test, he wouldn't fail.

"I'm in."

One Hundred Twelve

Cade moved with the efficiency of long practice, docking *Gladiator* and shutting down the systems in record time, his emotions as locked down as his ship. The transfer to the Far Horizons Aerospace shuttle passed in a blur of security uniforms and bulkheads. By the time he guided the shuttle through Earth's atmosphere, heading toward the west coast of the North American continent, the icy calm began to thaw, allowing tendrils of anxiety to punch through.

Ever since they'd left *Gladiator*, Justin had been maintaining a connection with Reynolds. She'd informed them that the *Starhawke* had arrived in the system ahead of them. Emoto had made contact with the Admiral, who'd filled them in on the situation with the Setarips. The *Starhawke* was now patrolling under camouflage, watching for any sign of Bare'Kold's yacht.

That information had brought a grim smile. No way could Bare'Kold outrun Aurora's ship.

Reynolds had also let them know that Mya, Cardiff, and Clarek had taken one of the Kraed shuttles to Stoneycroft.

He had mixed feelings about that, but any help for Aurora was welcome at this point, even from Jonarel Clarek.

"Reynolds just reported she and the Admiral are on site with Scott."

Cade glanced at Justin, tension radiating up his spine. "What's the status?"

"The fire's still going, but she made contact with Cardiff. The Setarips failed. Aurora got her mom and Mya's parents out of the house."

His fingers tightened, his heart not daring to believe what he'd heard. "The Ecilam didn't get them? They're safe?" After all they'd been through, he couldn't seem to accept good news.

"Yeah."

The monolith on his shoulders slid to the deck, but a steel rod quickly took its place. "What about Aurora? Is she okay?"

"Reynolds didn't specify, which I assume means yes."

She'd done it. Averted disaster despite his late warning.

Releasing his breath on a sigh, he said a silent prayer of thanks. But as he returned his attention to the flight path for their landing site, a small municipal airport east of the coast, a new cord of anxiety snaked through his muscles.

He'd been so hell-bent on rushing to the rescue that he hadn't given any thought to what would happen when they got there. Now, he couldn't think of anything else.

Stopping Bare'Kold's mission had been his focus for days, the point of light he'd been racing toward. He'd failed to reach it in time, yet by some miracle the Ecilam attack had been foiled anyway. Aurora hadn't needed his help after all.

Which left him rushing to the scene to do... what?

He banked the shuttle, taking them inland, his gaze moving to the moonlit treetops visible outside the viewport. He checked the display. The glow of lights in the distance aligned with the coordinates they'd been given.

His gut clenched. Aurora was down there. They were about to come face-to-face for the first time since she'd kicked him to the curb in the *Starhawke's* conference room. Much as he yearned to see her, talk to her, this wasn't what he'd had in mind. Her mother had just been attacked by

Setarips, her family home torched. If she'd been emotionally raw before, she'd be doubly so now. His arrival wasn't going to improve the situation.

She'd made it extremely clear during their last encounter that she didn't want to be anywhere near him. Opposite ends of the galaxy would have suited her just fine. And while he'd had a different take on the situation, she'd been unwilling to hear it, shutting him out completely.

For his own protection. Oh, the irony.

Ordinarily she was too much of a professional to allow her personal feelings to show in a public forum, but there was nothing ordinary about this scenario. He couldn't begin to predict how she would react to his presence. Not well, that was certain.

One Hundred Thirteen

The queasiness in Aurora's abdomen made her glad she hadn't eaten recently, but she didn't care about the discomfort. Gryphon's breathing was evening out, and his eyes had closed in a restful sleep, rather than the creepy, heavy-lidded glazed look he'd had since she'd arrived.

The energetic connection with Mya and Micah rooted her in place, allowing her to channel energy from their surroundings and pour it into Mya's hands, giving her what she needed to bring Gryphon back from the darkness he'd been dragged into.

They'd never attempted a Necri healing this intense before, and it was taking a toll. Sweat trickled down the side of her face despite the winter chill, but she ignored it. Gryphon needed them. All of them. She'd rest later.

What she couldn't ignore was how the connection with so much Suulh energy was magnifying the growing sensation of a very familiar presence drawing near.

Cade.

She could track him effortlessly, which is how she knew he'd flown in and landed at the same airport where she'd arrived a lifetime ago, and was currently making his way in her direction.

She'd broken her promise to her dad that she'd contact Cade before they left Hawaii. Apparently the universe was going to rectify that transgression.

Her father was still out in front of the house, but he'd been joined by the Admiral and Reynolds. She'd sensed them as soon as the healing session began. They all appeared like little tracking dots in the map of her mind, which was a new experience. She'd always been able to sense individual emotional fields before, especially for people she'd spent time with, but nothing like this. Each one was crystal clear, distinct, like pieces on a chessboard.

And then there was Cade. He shone like a sun in her mind's eye, a beacon of warmth and light that called to her. But she still had no idea what she'd say when he arrived. *I'm sorry*? That didn't begin to cover it. *I'm an idiot*? Better, but still not enough.

The truth was, she knew exactly what she wanted to say. She was just terrified that he'd throw it back in her face.

A gentle squeeze on her right hand brought her back to her surroundings. She met Micah's worried gaze.

Are you okay? he mouthed.

She nodded, gave him a weak smile, and mouthed *later*.

He nodded back and squeezed her hand again.

Her gaze moved to her mother, who was sitting across from her, beside Marina. Their hands were joined just as hers and Mya's were, all the energy they were generating flowing into Gryphon's chest and surrounding his body in a beautiful tapestry of pearlescent white and emerald green. But her mother was looking at her and Micah.

What she saw, she could only imagine. They probably looked a fright after the race here and the battle with the fire. Then again, her mother wasn't exactly pulled together, either. She was in her Christmas-themed pajamas, the ones with the red and green reindeer prancing across a snowy-white background. But the white wasn't very white anymore, and the fabric clung to her sweaty skin.

But that wasn't what stunned her. It was her mother's emotional state. She was calm, almost relaxed, the low-grade anxiety and fear that typified her field conspicuously absent, the exact opposite of what she'd expected. Her mother had just faced one of her worst nightmares, yet here she sat, more composed than she'd ever seen her.

Her mother met her gaze, a soft smile slowly turning up the corners of her mouth.

Instead of fear and anxiety, what she sensed was a joy that bordered on excitement. Bizarre. Then again, she'd never been good at figuring out her mother before. Why should sitting in the forest in the wee hours of the morning during a Suulh healing session change that fact?

The other puzzle stood over her left shoulder, behind Mya. Jonarel's behavior since he'd arrived had shattered all her pre-conceived notions about their relationship. And when he'd swung Mya onto his back and leapt off the gallery without a backward glance? She'd seriously wondered if she was dreaming.

Not that she objected. If he'd transferred his overprotective instincts from her to Mya, that would ease her burden considerably. What she didn't understand was why. He'd been her shadow since the day they'd met thirteen years ago, hovering, tracking, always with a yearning look in his yellow eyes. He'd made it clear he wanted to pair bond with her, something she'd considered for about two seconds when he'd kissed her during their stay on Drakar.

But she'd known he wasn't the right one for her. Or her for him, no matter what he believed. Or what his father wanted.

She'd tried to explain that fact, to convince him to let go, move on.

Her abrupt disappearance might have convinced him she was serious. But that didn't explain his unusual behavior. Or the emotions she'd felt blasting from Mya. Something had happened between those two, something monumental. She was more than a little curious to find out what. And whether they planned to do anything about it.

One Hundred Fourteen

Mya's head drooped, her gaze on Aurora's hand resting over hers, their joined energies feeding her dad's healing.

The necrotic tissue in her dad's body was restoring, the cell walls repairing, the systems flowing. His body was finally able to take in the oxygen it needed and feed it to his blood as his lungs resumed their necessary function, albeit reluctantly. He'd still require a lot of healing work, and his recovery would be slow, but the death rattle was gone and he was resting comfortably.

Still, she hesitated to call a halt to the healing session, even though she was fairly certain if she closed her eyes, she'd fall into a deep sleep herself. The problem she was wrestling with was the inevitable moment when she'd turn around and face the Kraed male standing centimeters behind her. The one who had returned to a *burning building* to pull her out.

But that wasn't the most astounding part. He'd rescued *her* and left Aurora to fend for herself! Never in a million years would she have envisioned that scenario. What did it mean? Was it his overprotective instincts kicking in, pinpointing her as the weakest link, the one most in need of help? Or was it something more?

She wasn't ready to find out, not after the rollercoaster this night had turned into. But she wasn't sure she could put it off, either.

A fluctuation in Aurora's energy caught her attention. She turned and found Aurora staring over her shoulder in the direction of the house. "What's wrong?"

Aurora's gaze darted to Jonarel and her mother before she answered. "The Elite Unit is here."

Even in the moonlight, she picked up on the anxiety in Aurora's eyes. Translation? Cade was here. And Aurora was jumpy as a frog.

She waited for a growl or grumbled comment from Jonarel. It didn't come. When she glanced over her shoulder, she discovered he was staring right at her with an intensity that made her stomach flip.

She whipped her head back around, her heart jackhammering in her chest. He definitely was *not* concerned about Cade Ellis right now. Which helped her move forward.

Ending the flow of energy, she met her mother's gaze. "We need to get Dad to the *Starhawke*, if that's okay with you."

Her mom looked even more exhausted than she felt. "As long as it's okay with Aurora."

Aurora made a waving motion with her hand, her attention still toward the house. "Go ahead. I can catch a ride later."

Catch a ride? She wasn't sure what that meant, but Aurora clearly wasn't ready to leave yet. She turned to Libra. "Do you want to come with us?"

Libra shook her head, her attention in the same direction as her daughter's. "I'll stay, too. At least for now," she added in a murmur, almost to herself.

Taking a breath to bolster her courage, Mya stood and faced Jonarel. "Can you take us back?"

His words, combined with the look in his golden eyes, made her toes curl. "It would be my pleasure."

Her face grew hot and she quickly looked away. At one time she'd been able to conceal her feelings from him. Now, that felt like an impossible task. Which put her in very dangerous waters, indeed.

Jonarel crouched beside her father, gently lifting him off the ground and draping him over his back as he had before.

She glanced at Celia, who had been keeping watch over them during the healing session. "Are you staying or going?"

Celia's gaze remained on Micah and Aurora. "I'll stay."

She knew that look. Her friend was analyzing Micah, determining if he was friend or foe. And whether Aurora needed backup.

She already knew the answer, but Celia always made up her own mind on such matters. "Contact Kire if you need anything."

She nodded, following as Aurora, Libra, and Micah headed in the direction of the fire's glow.

Leaving her alone with her parents and Jonarel. A shiver passed over her skin, but it wasn't from cold. "Let's go."

Jonarel led the way back to the shuttle, his pace much slower than normal. Her mom might think it was because he was carrying her dad, but she knew better. He'd figured out they were both ready to drop, and was making the trek as easy for them as possible.

How he located the shuttle with unerring accuracy in the darkened forest was a question she'd ask another time. For now, she was grateful that he took charge, helping her lay her dad out on the shuttle's mobile med platform and strap him in before moving to the cockpit.

She started to sit in one of the cabin seats, but her mom stopped her with a hand on her arm. "I'll stay with him. You can go with Jonarel."

I don't want to go with Jonarel. Well, that was a lie. She *always* wanted to go with Jonarel. But she was afraid of what idiot comments might pop out of her mouth while she was in her current condition.

Still, arguing with her mother would only put a finer point on the matter. "Okay."

Sliding into the co-pilot's seat put her uncomfortably close to Jonarel, her senses picking up on every nuance of his muscular body. And highlighting the burns on his hands, arms, and feet. "You're still burned!" She'd been so blown away by the breathless way he'd rescued her, and then the rush to reach her father, that she hadn't made sure his injuries had been completely healed.

He shrugged as the shuttle powered up and lifted off, rising above the treetops with ease. "I will heal."

"Of course you will. As soon as we get to the ship, I'll treat you."

"No."

"No?"

He met her gaze, the look in his eyes making her nerve endings sizzle. "You must take care of yourself."

"I'm fine."

A frown tightened the muscles around his mouth. "You will be, after you rest."

"But I can—"

"Lelindia." He said it softly, but hearing that name from his lips silenced her instantly. "You need to rest."

Wanna join me? The quip almost got out before she dragged it back. But the longer he held her gaze, the more the idea took hold. And the more she wanted the possibilities it unfurled.

He'd just saved her life, injuring himself in a show of heroics that made a pretty clear statement about where he stood regarding her. And Aurora.

The question was, what was she going to do about it?

Taking a deep breath. she plunged in.

Lowering her voice so her mother wouldn't overhear. she leaned closer. "Maybe we can do both."

One Hundred Fifteen

The flashing lights of emergency vehicles appeared through the windows of the transport as it pulled to a stop in front of the uniformed officer blocking the driveway.

Cade stared at the glowing wreckage of what had once been a house. He recognized the configuration, not because he'd ever been to Stoneycroft, but because it mimicked the design for the main building on Azaana. Seeing the glowing shell punched him in the gut. He felt the loss as keenly as if it were his own. "I'm sorry, Aurora."

"What?"

He waved Justin's question away. "Nothing." But guilt settled into his chest like a snake coiling up for winter's hibernation. If he'd been able to communicate with the Yruf sooner, if he'd been able to send the warning message before being captured, this scene could have been prevented.

As his team exited the transport, he spotted three familiar figures standing off to the right, away from where the emergency personnel worked to contain the blaze. Admiral Schreiber and Brendan Scott had their heads bent together in deep conversation while Reynolds stood several meters away, monitoring the situation.

She moved toward him as he approached the officer blocking the path.

"I'm sorry, sir," the officer said. "Only authorized personnel allowed beyond this point."

"They're with us," Reynolds said. "This is my C.O., Commander Cade Ellis. We were expecting them."

The officer turned to Reynolds. "Does the Fleet always send a team when one of their own has a house fire?"

So, the emergency personnel had been informed about who lived here. "They do when that house is home for a captain and chief medical officer," Cade said. "I'm guessing you'd do the same for yours."

The officer gave him a sharp look, his attitude respectful but cautious. "You're cleared to join your party on the perimeter." He pointed to where the Admiral and Scott waited. "No one approaches the house."

That was said with more force than normal. Aurora was clearly the reason, since she'd already slipped past them and pulled her mom and Mya's parents out of the house. He wished he'd been here to see it. When Aurora made up her mind to do something, no one stopped her. Even when she was running into a burning building. "Understood."

As his team moved across the driveway, Scott's gaze settled on him, an enigmatic expression on his face. Did Scott remember him? Or had Aurora told him something about their history together? Would either scenario help his cause, or hurt it?

"Good to have you with us," the Admiral said, taking in their ragtag group. "I understand it's been an interesting journey."

To say the least. Cade ran a hand over the scruff along his jaw. "We'll fill you in later."

"I look forward to it. In the meantime, allow me to introduce you all to Brendan Scott." The Admiral handled the introductions, ending with Cade. "I understand you two have already met."

Scott nodded, shaking Cade's hand, his grip firm but relaxed. "Yes, I've had that pleasure."

No sign of anger or reproach. That was a good start. "Same here." Now that he knew who Scott was, it was surprising he'd never noticed the resemblance to Aurora, especially around the eyes and nose. "It's been a few years."

"Yes, it has." Scott released his hand, an assessing light in his eyes.

What exactly he was assessing, Cade could only guess. He could think of a dozen items just to start. This wasn't exactly his finest moment. Might as well ask the most pertinent question, the one burning a hole in his chest. "Where's Aurora?"

"With her mother." Scott glanced over his shoulder in the direction of the trees behind the house. "In fact, I believe they will be joining us soon."

Cade started to sweat. Seeing Aurora was going to test him no matter what. But seeing her with her family and his team watching? He'd dropped into his own private Hell.

A hand on his shoulder startled him.

Scott leaned closer but kept his gaze toward the woods. "Relax. She's nervous, too."

Cade stared at him, another piece of the bizarre jigsaw clicking into place. Scott was an empath, just like Aurora. He hadn't been analyzing Cade's appearance. He'd been analyzing his emotions.

He closed his eyes for a moment, silently cursing. Scott had been sensing everything he'd been feeling since he'd arrived. Everything he'd been feeling about this man's *daughter.* "Sir, I didn't mean to—"

"It's okay." Scott smiled and gave his shoulder a squeeze before folding his arms over his chest. "She was going to contact you today, anyway. And call me Brendan."

One Hundred Sixteen

Longest walk ever.

Aurora's senses were on overload as she led the way through the woods on the east side of the house. Not only was she getting a cavalcade of emotion from Cade, but she was processing what her mother, father, and brother were feeling, too. Which made for one heck of a confusing mishmash of emotional input.

At least no one was angry. Or afraid. Anxiety dominated, but the kind that borders on excitement rather than fear. Micah was the calmest of the five of them, which made sense. He'd already handled his most challenging moment, coming face-to-face with their mom. The last time she'd glanced back to check on them, they'd been walking side by side with the kind of comfortable silence that spoke of nurturing and healing. The future of their relationship looked bright, indeed.

She wasn't nearly so certain about what her mom and dad would face. Or how Cade would react to seeing her. She couldn't make sense of his emotions. Then again, she wasn't sure she could make sense of her own emotions right now, either.

The solar lanterns that lined the driveway appeared through the shelter of the trees, as did the lights from the emergency vehicles parked in the elongated oval in front of the house. Firefighters still moved around the perimeter, but with the more measured pace of a job winding down.

She didn't look at the house, didn't need to see on the outside what she'd witnessed from the inside. It was gone. She'd already accepted it as much as she could for now. Instead, she focused on the cluster of people waiting for them.

Her dad and Cade stood side by side, facing in her direction. They wouldn't be able to see or hear her little band yet, but her dad would be sensing them. Especially her mom. She imagined her presence triggered the same kind of red alert for him that Cade did for her.

That thought gave her some clarity, providing a distraction as she emerged into the light.

Cade took a step forward, then hesitated. So did her dad. She halted as well, uncertain how to proceed. And realized her mom and Micah had stopped beside her, with Celia on her opposite side.

They stood there like gunslingers in an old western, two outlaw gangs ready for a shootout on a dusty street. It was her dad who broke the standoff, taking two steps closer, his gaze locked on her mother. "Hello, Libra." His voice was thick as mud.

"Hel—" Her mother couldn't even finish. She cleared her throat. Loudly. "Hello, Brendan." But she stood still as a statue.

She'd been a fool to think she'd plumbed the depths of her parents' emotional bond. The intensity of the feelings pouring off them nearly knocked her off balance. She could practically see the band drawing them together.

But they were resisting. Out of habit? Certainly not because it was what they wanted. Or needed. "Oh, for goodness sakes." She placed a hand on her mother's back. "Enough already." She gave her a little push.

That's all it took. Her mom stumbled for a step, two, and then her dad was moving. Opening his arms, he gathered her mom into a hug of pure joy.

One Hundred Seventeen

Cade watched the scene unfold between Brendan and Libra, a lump lodged in his throat. He knew what that kind of love felt like. Had experienced it with Aurora, who was standing several meters away, her gaze on her parents.

The perimeter lighting created a soft halo around her blonde hair, the breeze blowing wisps from her braid. She looked far more composed than he'd anticipated.

A tall, muscular blond man stood beside her, his gaze also on the pair. Her brother, he guessed, based on the family resemblance. Cardiff stood slightly behind him.

Brendan finally eased his grip on his wife, leaning back and cupping her face in his hands. "You cut your hair."

She gave a hiccupping laugh. "You grew a beard."

His chuckle blended with her soft laughter, the sound a spot of sunshine in the smoky pre-dawn air.

Cade watched Aurora's reaction. A gentle smile turned up the corners of her mouth, making her look softer. More approachable. He took a few steps toward her, stopping when she turned to face him, bracing for what he'd see. "Hello, Aurora."

The smile disappeared but she met his gaze without hesitation. "Hello, Cade."

He saw wariness there, but the haunted look that had plagued her since the showdown with Reanne was visibly absent. "You look..." *Beautiful.* "Good." He winced. What an inane thing to say, given their circumstances.

A spark of amusement flickered across her face. "The beard's a new look for you."

His hand went to his jaw. He probably looked like a caveman. "Temporary, I assure you." He didn't want her to think he'd given up personal hygiene after she'd kicked him to the curb. He gestured to his grungy clothes. "We just got back from a mission."

Her brows lifted. "And came straight here?"

He glanced at the house. "The situation called for it." He couldn't say anything more with the emergency personnel in earshot. And he was acutely aware of his team watching, too.

"I see." She held his gaze for a long moment, no doubt reading his emotions.

He didn't try to suppress them or catalogue them. Where she was concerned, he was an open book. He couldn't seem to find any other setting.

Her expression gave nothing away, but somehow he got the sense that she was happy to see him. That surprised the heck out of him, considering how they'd parted. And where they were standing. Had she really planned to talk to him today?

Breaking eye contact, she gestured to Brendan. "I see you've met my father."

Cade's gaze switched to her dad. He and Aurora's mom now formed a united front, although Brendan's expression was far more welcoming than Libra's. "Actually, we've met before."

Aurora blinked, her head swiveling between him and her dad. "You know each other?"

"We do," her dad confirmed.

"We met during my flight training." He clasped his hands behind his back, fighting the urge to pull Aurora into his arms so he could hold her the way Brendan was holding her mother. "He ran a clinic for a small group of Academy pilots."

Her jaw worked. "I see." She shot her father a look that clearly said they'd be discussing that topic in more detail later.

Brendan didn't look the least bit quelled by his daughter's ire. Instead, his smile grew. Interesting.

Aurora's brother stepped forward. "Well, my dad may have met you, but I haven't." He stuck out his hand. "I'm Aurora's brother, Micah."

Cade accepted Micah's firm grip. "Cade Ellis. Nice to meet you."

And he meant it. The way Micah was looking at Aurora indicated a deep emotional connection. Whatever their history, he had no doubt Micah loved his sister. That gave him high marks in Cade's book. The smudges on his skin and clothing indicated he hadn't sat idly by during this crisis, either. Yet another reason to like him.

"Likewise." Micah's gaze was assessing, but with curiosity, not judgment.

The judgment was coming from Aurora's mother. She didn't say anything, just watched him with a none-too-subtle warning in her eyes.

That was fine. He understood he had a long road to walk if he wanted to earn her respect after the way he'd treated her daughter at the Academy. He could handle the frost from her, especially since Aurora's dad and brother seemed to be on his side. He just needed Aurora to give him a chance.

The Admiral stepped up beside him. "Now that we're all here, we may want to consider moving this gathering to a more suitable location."

Aurora and Brendan nodded. "Agreed," they said in unison.

Like father, like daughter.

Aurora glanced toward the sky, uncertainty in her eyes. "Normally I'd offer my ship, but—"

"Excuse me, folks."

They all turned.

One of the firefighters approached, her cheeks streaked with soot and sweat. "I'm Captain Lee, the battalion chief. The fire's ninety percent contained, and we're working on securing the structure. But I have a few questions I'd like to ask you about how this started." Her gaze flicked to Aurora and Micah. "And how you both got in and out."

The woman's tone was businesslike, but Cade caught the underlying anger and concern. She knew the conditions weren't normal. And neither was whatever she'd seen Aurora and Micah do when they'd evaded the members of her company and entered the house.

Libra stepped forward, facing the woman. "Then you'll want to talk to me. This is my house."

Captain Lee pulled out a small datapad. "And your name?"

"Libra Hawke."

"Hawke? Any connection to the plant nursery Hawke's Nest?"

"Yes, I'm the owner."

"Oh." That seemed to improve the captain's attitude. "My daughter loves that place."

Libra smiled. "So do I."

"And this is your home?"

"Yes."

"Do you live alone?"

"No. But the other two occupants aren't here."

Interesting spin on the truth. He hadn't given Libra Hawke enough credit for verbal gymnastics.

"And their names?"

"Marina and Gryphon Forrest."

"And where are they?"

"Visiting their daughter."

On the *Starhawke*, no doubt. Or on their way there. Another adept dodge.

"But you were here when the fire started?"

"I was."

"Were any of these folks here at the time?" She gestured to the group.

"No."

The captain's gaze swept the semicircle, coming to rest on Aurora. "You were the first to arrive, as I recall."

"That's right."

"And your name?"

"Aurora Hawke. I'm her daughter."

"Daughter." Captain Lee glanced from Aurora to Micah. "And you are?"

"Micah Scott. Her son."

"I see." The captain gazed between the two of them, the tightly leashed anger on her face softened slightly by understanding. "Is that why you ran *into* the house? To find your mom?"

"Yes."

"And how did you make it out unharmed?"

Aurora's calm, closed-lip smile would have made any Fleet commander proud. "Just lucky I guess."

Captain Lee's brows lifted. She kept up the stream of questions to Aurora and Libra, and occasionally Micah, but without drawing any details from them.

He particularly liked Libra's answer to the question *do you know how the fire started.* "Once I saw the flames, I was focused on getting out." He couldn't wait to hear the full story on that one. But he was absolutely certain nothing they told the captain was a lie, just a misdirection or shift in point of view.

And it worked. Captain Lee finally gave up, but not before gathering contact information from Aurora and her mother, and letting them know the department would be in touch after they'd assessed the extent of the damage.

The Admiral cleared his throat, a hint of amusement in his eyes as Captain Lee walked away. "As I was saying, let's find a more suitable location, preferably with showers and beds for those that need them. I can take Mr. Ellis' team back to my house." His gaze moved from Aurora to Brendan and back. "Would you like to join us, or meet on the *Starhawke?*"

Aurora pressed her lips together. "Neither." Her gaze slid to her mother first, then her father. "Can we meet at your house?"

A look passed from father to daughter, carrying a meaning Cade didn't quite understand. "My house it is," Brendan said, turning to Libra. "If that's acceptable to you?"

Libra's eyes widened, but she nodded. "That's fine."

Brendan turned to the Admiral. "I'll have my plane come back for you and your team. Is early evening soon enough to meet?"

"Absolutely."

As Brendan and the Admiral worked out the logistics, Aurora stepped toward Cade.

"Can I talk to you for a moment?"

His heart thumped. Whatever she'd been planning to say to him before, she wanted to tell him now? Did he want to hear it? "Of course."

She held up a hand in the direction of her family, fingers splayed. "Give me five minutes."

Her dad nodded. "We'll be here."

Cade followed Aurora around the curve of the driveway and out into the woods to the east. Not long after they'd entered the trees, they came across a well-worn path that meandered deeper into the darkness.

Aurora halted, turning to face him. Her eyes were mostly in shadow, making it hard to read her expression. "There's something I need to say."

Thankfully his face was in shadow, too. She wouldn't see him gritting his teeth. "All right."

She drew in a slow breath, then blew it out. "I was wrong."

He stared at her, certain he'd misheard. "What?"

"I was wrong. Cutting you off like that, sending you away with the idea it would keep you safe... I was wrong. It was unfair and unkind and...." She trailed off, taking another deep breath. "I hope you can forgive me."

"Forgive you?" His brain was still stuck on *I was wrong.*

"I know it's asking a lot. I hurt you. Horribly. And I'm sorry. So very, very sorry."

Air became a rare commodity. Her words were everything he wanted to hear, but that was the tip of the iceberg. Deep inside, he could feel what she was feeling. Actually *feel* it.

"I know it will take time, and I'll do a lot of groveling because—"

He cut her off, startling a squeak out of her as he closed the gap between them, captured her face in his hands, and brought his lips down on hers.

One Hundred Eighteen

The brush of Cade's lips on hers sent tingles racing over Aurora's skin. The scratch of his beard was a new experience, creating dozens of tiny points of contact.

But it wasn't enough. Not as his emotions washed over her.

Tunneling her hands inside his jacket, she locked them behind his back and pulled him flush against her. He groaned in response, shifting the angle of the kiss to deepen it. She welcomed him, allowing her touch to express what her words couldn't do justice.

By the time she pulled back, they were both panting. "I'm sorry, Cade. I'm so—"

"Shhh." His hands caressed her hair as his lips glided over her face, touching down with featherlight softness. "I should be honored, really. Now I understand how much you really love me."

She rested her palms on his beard-covered cheek, leaning back so she could look into his eyes. "More than I thought possible. I would do anything to keep you safe." She stroked her thumb over his lips, her body warming at his sharp inhale. "Except give you up."

His eyes closed. When they opened, a shimmer made them glisten. "That's the nicest thing anyone has ever said to me."

"It's the truth. I thought I was strong enough to push you away. But I'm not."

He turned his head, kissing her palm. "You're wrong. You're much stronger. Loving me, knowing what we know, takes more courage than sending me away. Even for my own good."

She'd never considered that possibility. And now that she was in his arms again, she couldn't imagine her world without him in it. "You make me stronger. My dad helped me see that."

"Really?" His brows lifted. "I wasn't sure he'd even remember me."

"He clearly does. Not that he told me. He acted a little strange the first time I mentioned your name, but I thought maybe Marina had shared some info with him. I had no idea you knew each other."

"I met him before I met you."

"Huh." She leaned up, brushing her lips over his. "Sounds like one way or another, we were destined to come together."

He captured her mouth with his, giving her a toe-curling kiss. "Count on it."

One Hundred Nineteen

Micah watched Aurora as she headed into the woods. He wasn't clear on exactly what was going on between his sister and Cade, but he'd liked the man on sight. Or maybe he'd been sensing how Aurora felt about him through their connection. Regardless, their discussion seemed long overdue. If it could lighten his sister's load, he was all for it.

"We haven't been introduced."

He turned toward the slightly accented female voice. The woman his sister had identified as Celia stood at his elbow, watching him. "No, we haven't."

In the shadows of the forest, she'd been intimidating. Now that he could see her in the light, she was breathtaking. He couldn't look away if he wanted to. Which he most certainly didn't.

He held out his hand. "Micah Scott."

She clasped it with a grip that made him wonder if she could break his fingers. "Celia Cardiff. I'm Aurora's security chief."

Security. Right. Aurora had told him about her, although she was nothing like what he'd pictured. Why someone who had the face and body of a goddess would choose to work in security escaped him. Her dark-haired, olive-skinned beauty reminded him of Birdie, but ramped up to a jaw-dropping degree. And the sharp intelligence in her dark eyes captivated him.

She pulled gently but firmly on her hand.

A flush crept up his neck when he realized he'd been holding on for far too long. He released her with a sheepish smile. "So, how long have you known my sister?"

"Since she was commander of the *Argo*. She came to me for training."

And he should have known that because Aurora had already told him. He really needed to get his brain in gear. If this was the woman who had taught his sister to fight, he'd do well to stay on her good side. "You're an excellent teacher."

She cocked her head. "What makes you say that?"

"I've been sparring with Ror recently. She's been kicking my butt."

A flash of approval lit her dark eyes. "Glad to hear it."

That look stunned him, knocking all reasonable thought from his mind again. "Uh-huh." What was he even responding to?

"She's a hard worker. Dedicated. Disciplined."

"Yeah." *Enough with the monosyllables, idiot!*

Her gaze grew speculative. "What do you do?"

"What? Oh, um, I'm a professor. Marine biology."

That seemed to surprise her. "I didn't realize muscles were a requirement for marine biology."

Muscles? "What?"

"Your muscle definition. Is it a result of your job, or something else?"

She'd noticed his muscle definition? That was kinda sexy. Or maybe she'd been sizing him up as a potential security risk. In that case, not so sexy. "I'm a surfer."

Again with the head tilt, this time combined with what he could only describe as a visual full-body scan. "A good one, I'll bet."

She could tell that by looking at him? "I do alright."

Her eyes narrowed.

He started to sweat. This was feeling like an interrogation, not a conversation. He couldn't get his balance. He needed to get the focus off him. "Do you surf?"

Her dark eyes gave nothing away. "I do alright."

Maybe he could use surfing as an ice breaker. Talking certainly wasn't working for him. "Since you're coming to my dad's house, maybe we can find a few hours to hit the waves."

"That would be up to Aurora."

Right. He had no idea what her job description entailed, but he had a feeling she wasn't a nine-to-five kind of employee. He gave her a small grin. "Well, I do have a little pull with your boss."

All signs of emotion left her face. "I'm sure you do."

Soooo, he'd just belly-flopped on that test. In fact, she seemed to be questioning whether he should be allowed anywhere near Aurora. That sucked.

Oh, he admired her loyalty. This woman definitely had Aurora's back. But what the hell had he done to earn her mistrust? She'd only laid eyes on him, what, an hour ago? How could she see him as a threat?

And speaking of threats, what about that hulking, clawed male who'd hauled LeeLee out of the fire? He was part of Aurora's crew. The engineer, no less. Where did Celia stand regarding him?

He was about to ask her when Aurora and Cade reappeared.

Holding hands. And wearing matching smiles.

Their talk must have gone *really* well. That took some of the sting out of Celia's scrutiny.

However, when they got back to the house, he was going to maneuver some alone time with his sister. Questions were mounting, and he wanted answers.

One Hundred Twenty

The shuttle ride to the *Starhawke* should have lulled Mya to sleep.

Maybe it would have if the look Jonarel had given her after her last comment hadn't warmed every cell in her body. He hadn't replied, but the flex of his muscles and the way he kept glancing at her spoke volumes.

The melodic chime of the ship's homing beacon guided them in, the ship's hull camouflage making it invisible until the shuttle was drawn up into the bay.

Her senses were fully alert to the Kraed male beside her as he powered down the shuttle, but before she could focus on him, she needed to get her dad settled in the med bay.

Kire had contacted them on the comm to make sure they were okay before they'd even landed. Since he and Kelly were the only crewmembers besides Star onboard the *Starhawke*, they were still on the bridge, watching for any sign of Bare'Kold's yacht or other Teeli vessels entering or leaving the system. He'd told Mya to notify him if she needed help, but she'd assured him she and Jonarel had the situation under control.

The portable med platform in the shuttle functioned as a detachable hover stretcher, allowing Mya and her mom to move her dad to the lift and up to the bay with ease. She prepared an IV for him while Jonarel transferred him onto one of the permanent platforms.

She turned to her mom. "Do you need an IV, too?" It seemed an odd question to ask a Nedale, but she'd never expected her mom to face a Necri attack, either.

"No, I'm okay."

Her mom didn't look okay. She looked exhausted. Her dark hair hung limp around her shoulders and her filthy Christmas red pajamas reeked of smoke. "We can set you up in one of the guest quarters."

Her mom shook her head. "I'll be staying right here."

"But—"

"At least until your dad's awake." She clasped his hand, her green energy field working down his arm to his chest.

Mya placed a hand on her shoulder. "Mom, you need to rest. He's stable. And once we've both had some sleep, we can give him the healing he needs."

Her mom stood very still, gazing at his closed eyes and slack jaw. "I was so scared." Her shoulders started to shake, a drop of moisture dampening the sheet. "I thought he was going to die."

Mya wrapped her arm around her mom's shoulders and held her in a sideways hug. "I know. I was scared, too." She looked over at Jonarel, who was watching them from a few meters away.

He'd taken away her fear. Made this moment possible. She owed him so much.

What she saw in his eyes made her stomach flip. She'd seen that look before. But he'd always been looking at Aurora.

She swallowed, returning her attention to her mom. "He's going to be okay. He just needs time. So do you."

He mom sighed, a hitch in her chest. "What I really need is a shower."

Mya smiled. "It just so happens we have one. And you don't even need to leave the med bay." Taking her mom by the shoulders, she guided her to a small door in the corner of the room. Touching the panel, she opened the door, revealing a compact shower space. "Not as luxurious as the ones in the guest quarters, but more convenient."

Her mom looked at the shower with longing, then down at herself. "I don't have any other clothes."

"I've got you covered. While you get cleaned up, I'll run to my cabin and fetch you a change of clothes. You'll have the med bay to yourself, so don't worry about privacy. I'm going to get some shuteye." She studiously avoided looking at Jonarel. "If you need anything else, just ask Star."

"Star?"

Right. She'd never explained about the Nirunoc to her parents. "Uh, Star, do you have a moment?"

Star appeared beside her dad's med platform. "Of course."

Her mom jumped back, her hand going to her chest.

"It's okay, Mom. This is Star. Star, this is my mom, Marina, and my dad, Gryphon."

Star stepped forward, her expression welcoming. "It is a great honor to meet you, Marina."

Her mom shot Mya a look before focusing on Star. "Are you... real?"

Star laughed. "Quite real, although I am not like you." She passed her hand through the edge of the med platform and back out. "I am a Nirunoc from Drakar, part of Jonarel's family. When he gifted this ship to Aurora, I chose to integrate with it, to help them along their path."

Her mom was hooked. She could see it in her eyes. "So, you're part of the ship now?"

"I am the ship. And more. If there is anything I can do to make your time with us more comfortable, please let me know."

Her mom looked like she wanted to ask more questions, but she settled for a simple, "Thank you."

Star nodded before vanishing.

Her mom spoke to Mya in an undertone. "Does she do that a lot? Appear and disappear?"

Mya smiled. "Not as often as she used to. She doesn't like to startle the rest of the crew."

"I see." Her mom turned back toward the shower. "I guess I'll–"

"I'll go get your clothes." Giving her mom a quick hug, she headed for the doorway.

Jonarel moved to her side, following her through the door and into the lift.

The last time they'd made this trek together, it had been the beginning of the most sensual night of her life. The memory reignited the warmth in her blood. As did his reaction to her bold statement earlier. Hopefully they were still on the same page.

She kept her gaze on the lift doors, not trusting herself to look at him. "Do you want to wait in your cabin or–"

"I will wait in yours." The words held a subtle challenge.

She turned her head, meeting his gaze. "Worried I'll back out?"

The glow in his eyes didn't look like worry. "Not worried." He leaned toward her, his breath caressing her cheek. "Determined."

She gulped. If she'd believed she was in control of this situation, she was dead wrong.

The doors parted and they stepped out onto the crew deck. Her cabin was the first on the right, the door swinging open as they approached. *Thanks, Star.*

Mya hurried to her bedroom, snagging a change of clothes for her mother with lightning speed while Jonarel remained in the front room. She practically ran past him. "Be right back."

She wasn't sure if the lift moved faster than normal with a little help from Star, or if that was her imagination, but she made the trip down and back to her cabin like she'd sprouted wings.

She halted when she exited the lift, resting a hand on her chest to calm her galloping heart. This was it. Time to lay her cards on the table. No more hiding. No more assumptions.

When she entered the cabin, Jonarel was exactly where she'd left him, gazing at a picture of her with her parents that Aurora had taken during one of their trips home.

He turned as she approached. "Their bond to each other is very strong."

She nodded. "They've been in love since they were teenagers."

His expression shifted slightly, his gaze more focused. "They are blessed to have found each other."

"Yes, they are."

He stepped closer, the warmth from his body tantalizing her senses. "Children learn how to love from their parents."

She tipped her head back, meeting his gaze. "I suppose they do."

"The love between your parents nurtures them, makes them stronger." His voice dropped to a low purr as he gazed into her eyes. "Tell me, Lelindia. Are you capable of such love?"

The look in his eyes locked her feet to the floor. She couldn't move if the ship blew apart around her. "Um..."

"I believe you are." Another step closer. "As am I."

Her knees weakened, threatening to drop her to the floor, but he held her in place with the intensity of his gaze and the magnetic pull of his body.

Her voice came out on a whisper. "It was never just sex between us, was it?"

The warmth in his golden gaze grew, blazing a trail through her veins. "No, it was not. Was it for you?"

The slightest hint of hesitation in his words, a flicker of vulnerability in his eyes, loosened her tongue. "How could it be? I've always loved you."

He closed his eyes, his brow furrowing as he frowned.

Her stomach bottomed out. She'd read it wrong. Whatever this was, he didn't—

"I have been a fool." His eyes snapped open and her breath caught.

There. Right there. That was the look she'd been dreaming of for years.

And then he sank to his knees in front of her. "Forgive me, my lovely Lelindia."

Huh? "For what?"

"For being blind. For causing you pain."

"Pain?" She wasn't in pain. In fact, she was losing the thread of his words as she tumbled into the depths of his golden eyes.

Lifting his hand, he brushed the back of his fingertips along her cheek.

And her healing senses flashed an emergency alert as the burn damage to his hand shone like a stoplight. "Jonarel!"

She was the fool. *He* was the one in pain. Her focus on the emotions ping-ponging between them had pushed his injuries to the back of her mind. And his, apparently, though she couldn't imagine how.

Circling her fingers around his wrist and turning his palm toward her, she engaged her healing field, the deep green glow enveloping them both.

He inhaled sharply, but not from pain. She'd already blocked his pain receptors before she focused on the cellular damage. Which was significant. Yet he'd carried her through the flames without showing the least sign of discomfort. Either he'd been on an adrenaline rush, or her field had dampened the effect.

His selflessness brought tears to her eyes.

Dropping to her knees beside him she lifted his other hand, resting it in her palm so she could bring the full force of her energy to the burns, expanding the field to also treat the burns on his feet. He'd carried her *father* with his hands and feet like this! What had he been thinking?

"Do not cry, *checana*."

She lifted her head, her tears tracking down her cheeks and dripping off her chin. She couldn't brush them away without letting go. No way was she doing that. Not until he was healed. "Checana?"

"It means beloved."

Beloved? He was calling her beloved?

But rather than accepting it, her annoyingly practical brain called up a point of order and sent it sailing out her mouth. "I thought the Kraed word for beloved was *checala*." She'd heard Siginal call Aurora that often enough. But never her.

Not that it had bothered her. Much.

"Checala is used when spoken to a member of one's family."

Okay, that fit. Aurora was the only one Siginal had wanted to become a part of his family. "And checana?"

Instead of answering, he lowered his head. Her heart beat like a bass drum, her breath catching as his lips brushed across hers in a seductive kiss that brought a whimper from her throat.

The rumbling sound of pleasure he made in response was sexy as hell.

His lips moved to the soft shell of her ear, the feather-soft contact making her shiver. But his whispered words stole the breath from her lungs.

"Checana is only said to one's mate."

One Hundred Twenty-One

By all rights, Aurora should have been exhausted. She'd had a high-octane night without a moment's sleep. Instead, she felt hyper-stimulated to the point of effervescence. The promise of seeing Cade tonight might have had something to do with that.

Thanks to the speed of her dad's plane, her family and Celia would touch down in Hawaii in time to greet the sunrise. But at this moment, she had nothing to do. The restlessness was driving her nuts.

She needed a distraction. "Tell me about Far Horizons Aerospace."

Her dad shifted in his chair, being careful not to jostle her mom, who sat next to him, wearing a set of loaner clothes from Aurora's pack and her dad's jacket. She'd fallen asleep with her head resting on his shoulder and her fingers entwined with his. "What do you want to know?"

"Everything."

He glanced out of the corner of his eye across the center aisle to where Celia sat.

She knew exactly what that look was asking. "Celia's as close to me as Kai is to you. I trust her with my life. And my secrets."

Micah's emotions flickered, drawing her gaze, but he was staring out the window at the moonlight on the water.

She turned back to her dad and Celia.

Curiosity dominated Celia's emotional field, but the analytical look in her eyes and a wariness in her attitude indicated she was building a security profile on Aurora's dad too, figuring out where he fit in the new paradigm.

Her dad didn't seem to mind. "Fair enough." He focused on Aurora. "Our family has owned the company since it was founded in the twenty-first century, but I have very little to do with the day to day operations. I made that choice after I met your mother."

She didn't sense any remorse, despite what such a decision must have cost him. Her gaze moved to her mom. She'd never seen her looking so peaceful, or relaxed. It was sweet. And a little unsettling. Who would have guessed that having the world collapse would make her mom calmer? "Why was that an either/or situation?"

Her dad's lips brushed the top of her mom's head, his voice growing softer. "Because she was terrified, and with good reason. She loved me, more than I ever thought anyone could, but she didn't want to be connected with the owner of the most well-known aerospace company on Earth. Once she told me who she was, where she came from, I understood why. If I'd remained in that role, she would have become a public figure, associating with Fleet officers, members of the Galactic Council, possibly even the Kraed and Teeli. It would have put her in danger, something I'd do anything to prevent."

"How did you two meet?"

He shook his head. "That's a story for another time. Suffice to say I already had good people in place to manage the company for extended periods. I simply made what was designed to be a temporary situation, permanent."

"What about now?"

"Now I advise the R&D department, but the company is in the hands of my management team. Very few people know I'm the owner. This plane is one of the few visible ties I have."

She nudged Micah in the ribs with her elbow. "You knew all this? And didn't tell me?"

He shrugged. "It's not a secret. But we've built our lives separate from the company. The topic doesn't come up very often."

"You're not involved with Far Horizons?"

"It never appealed to me."

How strange. It intrigued the heck out of her. Not running the company, but having the ability to influence the development of future space technology. If hers and Micah's positions had been reversed, she would have insisted her dad take her with him to the labs and shipyards.

A lightbulb went off. Suddenly her driving urge to explore the galaxy took on a whole new meaning. She'd believed it was due to her alien origins, but it turned out she came from a long line of space travelers. No wonder she and her dad had sat on Stoneycroft's porch together, gazing at the stars.

The knowledge also gave her a whole new respect for her human heritage. The nebulous, unfocused forms related to her human half had solidified into terra firma. She had ties to a company whose origins dated back more than a hundred and fifty years. Her ancestors had helped to develop and construct the first colony ships. How many people could say that?

That fact rooted her to Earth. She'd always loved her home planet, but after learning about her alien origins, she'd felt like an uninvited guest, not a resident. Learning her dad's history had changed everything. She was part of the family that had helped shape Earth's future. She belonged to this world just as much as the Suulh homeworld. Maybe more.

"Do Kai and Iolana know?" she asked her dad.

"Yes, although it's not something we discuss. I suspect the topic will come up more now that they've met you."

"What about you? Do you have any interest in getting more involved with the company in the future?"

His brows lifted. "Do you?"

She made a non-committal noise, but the bubble of excitement in her chest gave a stronger answer. "I don't know. Maybe. I'd at least like to learn more about it. I researched the company after I got my grant for the Academy, but–" She cut off as her subconscious connected two dangling threads. Her dad was the owner of the company that had paid for her Academy tuition. "Did you have something to do with that?"

"With the grant for your tuition?"

"Yes."

"Yes and no. The company has been sponsoring the grants since the Academy opened. I made sure Marina had the information so you could apply, but I had nothing to do with the selection process. That was all you."

He wouldn't lie to her, but still... "What if I hadn't been selected?"

He gave her a crooked smile. "I would have found another way to get you the money you needed."

"I never stood a chance." The slightly muffled words came from her mom, who opened her eyes, meeting Aurora's gaze. "He wanted you to go since you were a baby. Every time he took you outside to look at the stars, you cooed and laughed."

She wasn't sure what to make of the comment. Or the lack of fear or bitterness in her mom's emotional field. "He and I have a lot in common."

Her mom startled her with a smile. "Yes, you certainly do."

Who was this stranger sitting with her dad? "And you're okay with that?" Her mom had always hated her passion for space travel.

Her mom sighed, snuggling closer to her dad and closing her eyes again. "I am now."

It took Aurora a moment to pick her jaw up off the floor. Her dad seemed to be in a similar state. They stared at each other, both with the same question and neither with an answer.

What could possibly have happened during the attack at Stoneycroft that had flipped her mom's internal compass one-hundred-and-eighty degrees?

One Hundred Twenty-Two

Cade's team excelled at quick recovery and power sleeping. By the time Brendan Scott's plane picked them up at the airport at four-thirty that evening, everyone was well rested, fed, showered, and de-scruffed.

The Admiral had told them to hold off on giving their report so Aurora's family could hear it, but Cade informed him of the most personally relevant outcome of their mission—Reanne Beck had taken Lt. Magee to Teeli space.

"I'm sorry, sir." Cade sat with the Admiral at the back of the plane, staring out at the water below. "There was no opportunity to prevent it."

The Admiral nodded. "I understand. It was not your job to bring her back."

"I know, but—" He really hated admitting defeat. "Reanne's not exactly a compassionate jailer."

"And Magee is no wilting flower. We all understand the risks when we accept a life in the Fleet. So did she."

He knew what the Admiral was saying, believed in it, but that didn't stop him from wishing he'd gotten his hands on Reanne Beck months ago on Gaia. He'd been *right there*, in her office, talking to her. But he hadn't known who, and what, she was then. If he had, things would have turned out quite differently.

The aquamarine waters of Hawaii appeared far sooner than he'd anticipated. Before he left the islands, he'd have to ask Brendan for the specs on this plane. Or for a chance to check out the cockpit.

For now, he had three goals. Find out what had happened when the Setarips had attacked Stoneycroft, report on their encounter with Reanne's ship and the Yruf, and spend as much time as possible with Aurora.

The ground transport that met them at the airport took them to the base of Diamond Head, turning onto a steep inclined driveway that gave them an excellent view of the ocean to the south.

He looked to the right, watching for a glimpse of the house.

He'd prepared himself for a palatial mansion. The owner of Far Horizons Aerospace would have tremendous wealth at his fingertips. But the house that appeared, partially built into the hillside, seemed modest compared to his expectations. Much like the Admiral, Brendan seemed to have favored location and a smaller footprint over the more sprawling or towering homes in the area.

Aurora greeted them at the front door, looking fresh as a tropical flower in a sea-green shirt and pant combination that brought out the green in her eyes. Her hair was back in her customary braid, but her feet were bare. The overall effect was softer and more relaxed than the tailored blue, brown, and green outfits she favored. And made him want to pluck her off her feet and lay one on her.

"Come in." She swept a hand to her right, where a low wall and short stairway led to a living room with a view of the ocean. Three couches arranged in an elongated U-shape and a row of three dining chairs along the fourth side provided ample seating. "Make yourselves comfortable. My dad's in the kitchen, whipping up some snacks in case anyone's hungry."

Based on the aromas drifting out from the back of the house, she wasn't talking about crackers and nuts. "Does he need any help?"

Aurora grinned. "Oh, he has plenty of help already." The murmur of voices reached them from the hallway. "A few too many cooks in the kitchen."

On cue, Celia Cardiff appeared from the hallway, carrying a platter of bruschetta. She was dressed very similarly to Aurora, only her shirt and pants were a pale blue and her dark hair was pulled up in a loose ponytail. Her feet were also bare. "Follow me," she said, leading the way down the stairs to the seating arrangement.

His team and the Admiral followed her as Aurora headed back to the kitchen. Cade trailed after her. The sight that greeted him at the end of the hallway stopped him in his tracks.

Brendan was clearly the ringleader, debating with Aurora's brother about spices as they stood side by side in front of the stove. They each had kitchen utensils in their hands, which they used to emphasize their points. Aurora's mom was loading food onto additional platters, a bemused look on her face as she handed one of the platters to Aurora.

He'd never pictured Aurora in such a domestic scene.

With her family.

Laughing and joking.

Family had always been a tense subject for her. This scene was the opposite of tense.

The debate cut off as Brendan glanced to the hallway. "Cade!" He motioned him forward. "Welcome to our home."

Our home? He darted a glance at Aurora and Libra, but neither of them seemed inclined to contradict the statement. "Thank you for having us."

Brendan waved the thanks away. "It's me who should be thanking you. I understand your team went through hell getting a warning off to the Admiral about the attack."

He didn't dare look at Aurora and Libra now. "Not in time."

Brendan set the wooden spoon down and fixed Cade with a pointed look. "I'm certain you did everything humanly possible."

That much was true, but guilt still weighed him down. "I wish it had been sooner."

"So do we," Libra said, walking toward him with a platter in her hands. "But we can't control the actions of others."

She held out the platter, but he was too stunned to take it. He didn't see any accusation or anger or blame in her eyes. In fact, what he did see was a grudging respect.

He finally took the platter from her. "I'm sorry you lost your house."

Sadness flickered in her eyes, but her gaze moved to her husband and son and the sadness vanished. "Good things can come from bad."

He blinked, his gaze sliding to Aurora.

She gave him a soft smile, motioning him forward. "Come on, let's get these to your team."

He followed her down the hallway, but she slowed halfway, turning toward him.

"What was that?" he whispered.

Her smile reappeared. Leaning in, she brushed her lips briefly across his. "My mom's had an attitude adjustment," she whispered back.

He brought his mouth back to hers, making firmer contact. If he'd imagined this moment while on the Yruf ship, he never would have believed it was possible. "So I see," he murmured, lifting his head and gazing into her eyes. "She seems more accepting of us."

She nodded, her smile widening. "It helps that my dad adores you. His opinion carries a lot of weight with her."

"Adores me?"

She nodded. "Oh, yeah. I asked him why he didn't tell me he knew you, and he said he didn't want to influence my decisions. But it turns out you made quite an impression during that training session. He kept tabs on you after you met. He was quite surprised when you accepted a position as a pilot for the Rescue Corps. He thought it was a waste of your talents. Finding out you're the leader of the Admiral's Elite Unit has thrilled him to no end."

"Huh." If these kinds of revelations kept coming, he really would believe he was destined to be with Aurora.

One Hundred Twenty-Three

Having Cade sitting beside her on her dad's couch was surreal, but Aurora drank in the sight of him. He'd shaved off the scruff, which made her very aware of his mouth. Not that she'd minded the beard. She'd take him any way she could get him.

But having her parents, especially her mom, happy that he was here? Priceless.

Micah sat on her other side. Her dad, mom, and the Admiral sat in the chairs across from them, with Justin, Drew, and Williams on the couch closest to Cade, and Gonzo, Reynolds, and Celia on the one by Micah.

She'd noticed that Celia had chosen the spot closest to Micah, which was not an accident. Her friend had been keeping a very close eye on him whenever they were in the same room. She was still curious to know why, but since she'd spent most of the morning and afternoon sleeping, she hadn't had a chance to find out.

She'd spoken briefly with Justin after she and Cade had delivered the platters of food, getting the latest information he had regarding the Suulh on Azaana. She expected Celia would have more to report after her trip to Kraed space, but the full story might have to wait until Aurora returned to the *Starhawke* and could speak with Mya. She wasn't sure exactly when that would be just yet.

The Admiral cleared his throat, ending the rumble of conversation in the room. "Let's begin with your team's report, Mr. Ellis. It should give us context for what followed. And be sure to include what we learned before you took *Gladiator*."

Cade set his plate on the end table and rested his elbows on his knees, his gaze on Aurora. "It started with a meeting with President Yeoh and a discussion with Admiral Payne. And ended with the Yruf."

"The Yruf?" She hadn't seen that coming.

He nodded. "That's where we spent the past few days, on their ship."

"You were captives?" The very idea chilled her blood.

"Yes, but it's not what you think."

The story that followed sent her on a rollercoaster ride through the web of manipulation at Fleet HQ, the treachery of Reanne's plan to send the Ecilam to kidnap her mother, and the revelation of the Yruf, who turned out to be potential allies rather than adversaries.

Her head was spinning by the time he finished. "So, the Yruf aren't like the other Setarip factions?"

Cade shook his head. "They're peaceful. Benevolent, even. I believe they're trying to bring an end to the Setarip civil war."

"And you were able to communicate with them telepathically?" That point had sparked all kinds of emotions. And questions.

"Not telepathy. I think it's more like what you and Mya have done in the past. Sharing imagery."

She and Mya could now share more than just imagery, but she didn't need to go into that, either. "But you were the only one who could do it?" She glanced around the circle, getting nods of confirmation from his team, including Justin, who was the team's trained communicator.

"Why you?"

Cade glanced at Justin. "Justin has a theory that it's somehow tied to my ability to see Suulh energy fields. But I have no idea how."

"I think I can answer that." Her dad crossed his ankle over his knee, his gaze intent. "Tell me, Cade, what emotion am I feeling right now?"

Aurora felt the wave of sadness that washed over them.

Cade frowned, his gaze searching her dad's face like he was trying to read a distant billboard.

"Close your eyes."

Cade glanced at her, then did as her dad asked.

"Now tell me."

The sadness grew, strong enough that she triggered the defenses her dad had taught her.

Cade opened his eyes, his frown deepening. "You're sad."

The emotion dissipated. "Or to be more accurate, I'm *projecting* sadness. And you could sense it."

Aurora stared at her dad, then back at Cade, understanding dawning. "You're an empath."

His frown was gaining traction. "No, I'm not." He sounded defensive.

Her dad sighed. "And probably got negative feedback for that ability when you were a child, I'll wager."

"I—" Cade paused, the frown morphing into a look of confusion. "My mom called me overly emotional," he murmured, only loud enough for her to hear. His gaze returned to her dad. "You think I'm an empath?"

"Yes, although an untrained and abused one. And while you've fought against your receiver abilities, suppressing them, you nurtured your ability to project."

"Project?"

Stellar light. She got it. Cade could see Suulh energy fields because he was like her dad—a projector *and* receiver.

It explained so much. Not only regarding the energy fields, but why he'd always been so easy for her to read, why she could track him at great distances even though he wasn't a Suulh. He was a strong projector and she was an empath with a Sahzade-given built-in GPS.

Just like my mom and dad.

She struggled to focus as her dad continued.

"We can discuss it later. Suffice to say, your natural talents would give you a distinct advantage in communicating with the Yruf." His gaze shifted to her, the message in his eyes clear.

She would have the same advantage.

Not that she wanted to go looking for the Yruf anytime soon. She had enough on her plate at the moment, thank you very much.

Like finding out about the attack on Stoneycroft. "Mom, you're up. What happened when the Ecilam attacked?"

Her mother's chin lifted, an echo of the anger Aurora had sensed this morning wafting off her. "I can't give you all the details, especially regarding what happened to Marina and Gryphon. They were attacked at the same time I was, but not in the same way." She drew in a slow breath, clasping her hands in her lap.

Aurora's dad rested his hand on top of hers, offering silent support.

"I couldn't sleep, so I was heading for the kitchen to make tea when they surrounded me outside my bedroom. They trapped me in a net and carried me to the stairs."

Five seconds in, and Aurora was already getting chills.

A cold smile curled her mom's lip. "That didn't work out so well for them. After I got loose, I ran to your room." She held Aurora's gaze. "My plan was to climb out the window and down the oak tree, then slip back into the house to help Marina and Gryphon."

Her mother was going to climb down a tree? She couldn't even imagine it.

"But there were more Setarips outside. They used some kind of explosive device to blow in the window and most of the wall. Then they blasted the room with flames. That's when the fire started."

Aurora swallowed past the constriction in her throat. It wasn't hard to picture her childhood room as it probably looked now.

A warm hand slipped under hers. She glanced at Cade as he gently twined his fingers with hers, holding her hand in a comforting grip.

"I jumped out the opening. I tried to grab the branch of the oak tree, but I hadn't counted on how slippery my shield would be. I had to keep it solid to block out the fire, so I fell." She met Aurora's gaze. "Maybe you can give me some pointers on correcting that issue."

Aurora's mouth popped open in surprise. "Uh, yeah, sure. I'd be happy to." Her *mother* was asking her for *shielding* advice?

"I knew Marina was still inside the house, but I couldn't sense Gryphon. I went back in through the door off the deck and got through the Setarips blocking the stairway."

She *really* wanted to know what her mom meant by *got through the Setarips*, but didn't want to interrupt the narrative.

"When I reached Marina and Gryphon's bedroom, I found them both crumpled on the floor. Marina's energy field was a sickly grey-green, and Gryphon looked..." She swallowed convulsively, a shimmer in her eyes. "He looked dead." She swiped at the moisture that ran down her cheek, taking a slow breath.

Aurora could imagine the horror of that sight. She'd had the same reaction when she'd seen him lying like a corpse in the shower enclosure. Gryphon had been like a father to her mother, even though he was only ten years older. And Marina... well, she meant as much to her mother as Mya meant to her. She remembered how she'd felt when Mya had collapsed in the orchard on Gaia. One of the scariest moments of her life.

"I went to them, but they weren't alone. One of the Setarips was in the room. It closed the door behind me, blocking the way. And then I saw... her." Her mother's gaze locked on hers. Pain flowed off her like a river. "I saw my mother."

One Hundred Twenty-Four

"Your mother?" Micah had kept silent up to this point, but his mom's startling revelation pulled the question from his lips.

Aurora stiffened by his side. "Our grandmother's alive?"

"Yes."

He didn't like the way she said it. "Is she... okay?"

Her gaze rested on him for a moment before moving to Aurora. "She's a Necri."

Aurora's eyes closed, her body going still. But she didn't seem surprised.

He sure as hell was! From what Aurora had told him, the Necri were Suulh who'd been turned into deadly monsters. "But... a Necri? How?"

His mom looked apologetic, like somehow it was her fault.

"She's the one who attacked Marina and Gryphon, isn't she?" The question came from Aurora.

Their mom nodded. "She tried to attack me, but it didn't work. I felt a pull, but then it was almost like my energy rebounded to her. She just froze, completely immobile. Even when the Setarip prodded her, she didn't react. It finally hauled her out of the room like a sack of grain."

Aurora leaned forward. "What happened to the Setarips? How did you get trapped in the bathroom?"

"When I didn't go down like Gryphon and Marina had, they changed tactics. Tried the flames and netting again, tried blowing us up. I had to protect Marina and

Gryphon. They couldn't move. We were trapped as the fire took hold."

"What did you do?" Micah was picturing the nightmare he and Aurora had run into. Hearing his mother's side of the story made it worse, but he wanted to know the extent of the threat she'd faced. And how she'd survived.

"I blasted the Setarip in the doorway, not so we could get through—there were more of them in the hallway— but to buy time. I dragged Marina and Gryphon into the reading room that joined the bedroom and bathroom. I thought about going out the window, but the drop would have killed Gryphon. Possibly Marina, too."

What an impossible choice. His heart ached for her.

"It didn't end up mattering. The Setarips came through the window. All I could do was shield. I was so tired. But then..." She paused, her fingers going white with tension as she looked to their dad, then back at them. "Then I sensed you. All of you. You were coming for me. And I had to protect you."

Tears spilled down his mom's cheeks, but she didn't swipe them away this time. "I took them out, the ones who came in through the window. But it took me out, too. I collapsed. When I woke up, I was in the bathroom. Marina had pulled Gryphon and me in there. I guess my energy blast had re-energized her enough that she could stand and move us. And that's where we stayed." She drew in a shallow breath, letting it out on a sigh. "Until you saved us."

Micah's heart pounded in his ears, the loudest sound in the room. His mom had almost died today. Or been captured. Repeatedly. Only her strength and determination had kept her alive.

Aurora rose, walking slowly to their mom's chair. Kneeling, she clasped their mom's hands in her own. "Sounds to me like you saved yourself."

His mom made a watery sound that was part sob, part laugh. "I had to. Because I knew you would come. My stubborn, obstinate, beautiful, powerful daughter would come to protect me. And no matter what the Setarips did, no matter how bad the situation was, you would handle it. Like you always do."

He couldn't see Aurora's face, but he heard the small sound she made. Her shoulders shook and she bent her head, resting her forehead on their joined hands.

He didn't check, but from the subtle throat clearing and sniffing, he guessed there weren't many dry eyes in the room. His certainly weren't.

No one said a word as the silence stretched out. His sister finally lifted her head, holding onto their mom's hand as she stood. "I'm so glad you're here."

His mom seemed surprised by the comment, but the smile that lit up her face was a wonder to behold. "I'm so glad *we're* here."

One Hundred Twenty-Five

Cade had never been a fan of Libra Hawke before today, and the feeling had been mutual. She'd caused Aurora pain and suffering most of her life, an unpardonable offense. He'd done no better, but at least he'd admitted his failings and was working hard to make amends.

It looked like Libra had finally turned a corner, too. Her speech to Aurora had been a pretty clear mea culpa. And she'd made it in front of most of the people Aurora called family and friends. That went a long way toward clearing the red in Libra's ledger, at least in his book.

Aurora swiped at her eyes. "Uh, can we take a short break?"

The Admiral stood. "We certainly can." The gruffness in his voice was a clear tell that he'd been affected by the scene between mother and daughter, too. He rested a hand on Aurora's shoulder and walked with her up the short stairs to the main level.

Cade stood to follow, but stopped when Libra's diminutive form blocked his path.

"May I speak with you?"

She'd never voluntarily started a conversation with him in her life. He wasn't about to rebuff her now. "Of course."

He walked with her to the door at the back of the room that led to the poolside patio. Stepping outside, the ocean breeze greeted him, the tang of salt and cry of sea birds soothing away the rough edges of the past week.

Libra strolled to the curved edge of the pool before turning to face him.

He stopped a meter in front of her and waited.

Clasping her hands together, she lifted her chin, looking him in the eye. "You and I have never been on good terms."

Direct and to the point. He respected that. "No, we haven't."

"I've always believed you were a bad influence on my daughter. And that your presence in her life would only cause her pain."

Respect was moving toward irritation. But she had a point. "I made mistakes. She got hurt. But that was ten years ago. I'm not the same person, and neither is she. I would never intentionally hurt her again."

Her eyes narrowed and her lips thinned. "Twenty-four hours ago, I wouldn't have believed you. But it's been an enlightening day. My daughter and my husband have made it clear they both think very highly of you. Coming from two incredibly sensitive empaths, whom I love dearly, that counts for a lot."

Not exactly a ringing endorsement from *her*, though. "But?"

"But, as you have no doubt noticed, I'm an extremely protective woman, especially when it comes to my family. And slow to trust."

Light dawned. "You want to know my intentions."

"To put it bluntly, yes. Aurora feels everything deeply, just like her father. She doesn't know how to have temporary relationships. When she loves someone, it's with her whole heart. That kind of bond can bring great joy, but it can also bring great sorrow."

He studied her, this petite momma bear who had the power to knock him into next week if she chose. Her story regarding the Setarips had made that clear. But she didn't want to hurt him. Or see him leave. She wanted him to keep bringing love and joy into Aurora's life. He knew that with a certainty that surprised him.

Maybe it was the empathic senses Brendan insisted he had. Or maybe it was his years of training reading nuance and tells. Either way, the knowledge was a gift, one he'd do well to cherish and protect.

"I've been in love with Aurora since the day she walked into my life. And I will be in love with her until the day I die. What happened at the Academy, the way I behaved—" He blew out a breath and shook his head. "I understand why you hated me. Blamed me. I hurt Aurora. Badly. Reanne's influence had a lot to do with it, but that's not an excuse."

"Reanne?" Now the momma bear was on her haunches, although the threatening stance wasn't directed at him.

"That's right. She used her manipulative abilities on me. Clarek, too. Pitted us against each other so she could get us out of the way, have Aurora to herself."

He didn't see any actual sparks fly, but if Reanne Beck had been standing beside him, she would have been reduced to a pile of ash by the look in Libra's eyes.

"The good news is that I'm now immune to her influence. Or the influence of any Teeli. I have such a negative association with the feeling that goes with their manipulations that it can't affect me anymore. That's why I'm not worried about hurting Aurora ever again. The only way I will not be by her side for the rest of my life is if that's *her* choice, not mine."

Libra took a slow breath, the fire and brimstone fading from her eyes. "You really do love her, don't you?"

"More than life."

A small smile tilted up the corners of her mouth. "Believe it or not, I know what that feels like."

He nodded. "I do believe you." He'd been feeling it from Aurora's family ever since he'd arrived, even though he hadn't acknowledged it until right now.

Her small smile turned self-mocking. "This is the part where I would usually make you promise to keep Aurora safe. But I've finally realized she's perfectly capable of handling that on her own."

"Yes, she is. She's the strongest person I know."

"That she is."

"But I can promise you something else instead."

"And what's that?"

"I promise you that Aurora will always feel loved and cherished."

Libra's veneer of ice broke through. To his surprise, her smile looked exactly like Aurora's.

"You know what, Cade? I believe we're going to get along just fine."

One Hundred Twenty-Six

By the time Aurora sat down on the couch between Cade and Micah, she'd restored a modicum of balance to her emotions. Her mother's admission had knocked her feet out from under her. Never, in a billion years, had she imagined her mom would show such confidence in her. Such support. And such a lack of fear.

The shift in her own worldview was taking some getting used to. Her mom believed in her. Believed in her power. What a concept.

Now that they'd tackled the two toughest components of the debriefing, she was ready to hear about the *Starhawke*'s trip to Drakar. She turned to Celia. "Mya didn't give me any details as to why she took the ship and crew to Kraed space. What did you learn while you were there?"

The tremor in Celia's emotions surprised her. And didn't bode well.

Celia glanced at the Admiral. "You had indicated that Signal was in charge of the secret expeditions into Teeli space when the Teeli applied for Council membership. Mya wanted to learn what he knew about the Teeli, see if we could figure out how Reanne managed to gain power over their forces." Her gaze returned to Aurora. "She also wanted to ask the Suulh about any interactions they'd had with Reanne and Kreestol."

Based on the underlying thread of Celia's emotions, the news hadn't been good. "What did you find out?"

"You'll want to get Mya's take on all this, but the Suulh definitely had dealings with Reanne as the Sovereign.

She's the one who manipulated them into going onto the Etah ship that attacked Gaia."

Aurora nodded. "I'd suspected as much."

"They were also under the mistaken impression that you were Kreestol's daughter."

"Kreestol?" Her mother sat ramrod straight. "Why would they think that?"

"They weren't aware Kreestol had an older sister."

Her mom puffed up with indignation, but deflated just as quickly. "No, I suppose they wouldn't. It's been a long time." She said the last part to herself.

"What about Siginal? Did he give you any leads?"

Celia shifted in her seat, an unusual sign of agitation. "Not exactly. The visit didn't go as we'd hoped."

Knots started forming in her belly. "What happened?"

"Mya didn't want Siginal dropping in on her while we were at Azaana, so she asked Jonarel and Star to hide the ship from the Kraed security network. They pulled it off, keeping us camouflaged until we were approaching Drakar. Siginal wasn't happy with the deception. And he really wasn't happy that you weren't onboard."

Cade snorted.

She gave his foot a tap with her heel. He really needed to get over his dislike of the Clareks. "But you met with him?"

"Yes. Twice. The first time, things got a little heated and he accidentally backhanded Mya. Jonarel went ballistic and punched him in the chest. Cracked a few ribs in the process."

Aurora's jaw dropped. "He struck his own father?"

Celia nodded. "Apparently injuring a guest is a serious offense in Kraed culture. Jonarel reacted accordingly."

Aurora wasn't buying it. The look in Celia's eyes was telling her there was a lot more to the story that she was holding back. And what about the way Jonarel had behaved toward Mya during the fire? That certainly hadn't been about enforcing cultural norms.

"What about the second time you met?"

"Siginal was very contrite. At least at first. He told us what they'd learned about the Teeli caste system. You'll hate it, by the way. Then he dropped the first bomb. Apparently, the Teeli aren't just after you and Mya. They want the potential of your children."

The knots multiplied throughout her torso, her entire body revolting at the image Celia's words brought to mind. "*Our children?*"

Cade's arm circled her shoulders, drawing her close. Her gaze moved to her parents, who were staring at her with matching masks of horror. But it was Micah's soothing touch that calmed the horse galloping in her chest.

He clasped her hand in his, giving her his strength. "Not in this lifetime."

She could feel his outrage, but it rippled like a wave on top of the calm bedrock of certainty underneath. He wasn't speaking with bravado. He was telling her that it *would not* happen. Ever.

She looked into his eyes, gratitude washing away the toxic emotional residue. "Thank you."

He nodded, but didn't release his hold on her hand.

Celia's gaze dropped to their clasped hands, her eyes narrowing.

Aurora took a breath and let it out slowly. "Well, that's horrible. What other gems did Siginal have to impart?"

Celia's mouth pinched.

Oh, stars. "That's not the worst of it, is it?"

"Siginal is determined that you will mate with Jonarel. When Mya argued with him, told him it was your choice, he grounded the *Starhawke*."

"*What?*!" She stared at Celia, certain she'd heard wrong.

"He said you don't have a choice."

"Like hell!" Cade was on his feet, rage blasting off him like flames. He pointed an accusing finger at the Admiral. "Did you know about this?"

The Admiral stood as well, but with less haste. "I have always known Siginal's wishes, but it is a point on which he and I have disagreed. I believe Aurora *does* have a choice. Selfishly, I have secretly hoped she'd choose you."

Some of the heat went out of Cade's anger, but Aurora's was building like a volcano. Her voice remained surprisingly calm. "If he grounded the ship, how did you manage to get off Drakar?"

Celia's closed-mouth smile was wicked, and a little smug. "He didn't count on Jonarel and Star siding with you. And us. They executed a jailbreak that got us off the planet."

The Admiral sighed deeply. "Jonarel will pay a heavy price for that decision."

Celia met his gaze. "He knows. So does Star. Siginal pursued us, but had to back off when Mya threatened him."

"Threatened him?" Aurora frowned. She'd never heard Mya threaten anyone, let alone a hostile Kraed flexing his muscles. "Threatened him with what?"

Celia's gaze swung back to her. "You."

"Me?"

"She told him that if he used force to stop us, he would make you his enemy. And when you came for us, he would lose everything."

Her brain took a few moments to process that. "Huh." Mya had played it well. Perfectly, actually. And she'd told the truth. If Siginal had chosen to hold her ship and crew captive, she'd have opened the gates of Hell to get them back.

But it left them in an awkward situation regarding the Suulh. Azaana was in Kraed space. Not to mention they'd need the support of the Kraed to defeat the Teeli. The way Reanne was chipping away at key members of the Fleet, she couldn't assume that when the Teeli finally made their move, the Fleet ships and crews would all be on her side. They might as easily fire on the *Starhawke* as the Teeli warships.

She'd need to talk to Jonarel, Star, and Mya when she got back to the ship, see what recommendations they had for dealing with Siginal. She sure wasn't going to fall in line with his plan. And wonder of wonders, it looked like Jonarel was through being Siginal's pawn, too.

She turned to the Admiral, who had resumed his seat. So had Cade, though he was as pliable as a brick wall. "Do you have a plan for how you want to proceed?"

He ran a hand over his smooth head as he gazed at her. "Will you be returning to the *Starhawke?*"

The question surprised her. "Of course."

A small smile played across his mouth. "I did not want to assume, now that your family is back together."

Oh. Her gaze moved from her parents to Micah. "We haven't really talked about it."

The original plan she and her dad had discussed was out the window now that Stoneycroft was a smoldering wreck and her mom was here. Would her mom want to stay here? Or was this temporary? And what about Marina and Gryphon? She couldn't imagine her mom being separated from them for any length of time. It was surprising she'd gone this long without any contact.

She squeezed her brother's hand, meeting his gaze. "I promised you a tour of the ship. Assuming you still want to go."

"I'm with you."

Interesting choice of words. And his emotional field was even more puzzling. She couldn't quite pinpoint what she was sensing from him.

"I'd like to go, too," her mom said. "Check on Marina and Gryphon."

Her mom's request startled her. "You mean, go to the ship? In space?" she added, just to clarify.

Her mom smiled. "Yes, I would like to go to *your* ship, in space."

"That makes three of us." Her dad wrapped his arm around her mom's shoulders and squeezed, but his gaze was on her. "If that's okay with you."

"Of course it is." Her brain leapt to the logistics. "I can have the ship dock at Sol Station and—"

"Not so fast." The Admiral held up a hand, palm out. "We still have the issue of Admiral Payne's involvement with the Teeli to work through. Before the *Starhawke* makes her presence known in the system, we need a strategy to deal with that threat."

"Good point. I'll have Jonarel bring a shuttle down instead." She looked to her dad. "If you're okay with him landing in your driveway."

"The driveway?" He frowned. "He could do that?"

"He landed it in the woods this morning. I'm pretty sure he can land one of those shuttles anywhere, and no one will know."

Her dad's eyes gleamed. "I'll be eager to see this shuttle of yours. And meet Jonarel."

The Admiral clapped his hands together and stood. "Excellent. Then why don't we call it a day and convene here tomorrow morning at oh-eight-hundred."

Her dad stood as well. "Sounds good. I've arranged accommodations for you and your team at a nearby hotel. I'll have the transport here in a few minutes."

"Thank you."

As her dad and the Admiral headed to the stairs and the rest of Cade's team stood, Aurora turned to Cade. "I guess this is where we say goodnight."

"Guess so."

"Not necessarily," her mother said as she approached them. "Why don't you stay here tonight, Cade?"

Aurora blinked. Looked at her mother. Looked at Cade. Back at her mother. "Did you just invite Cade to spend the night with me?"

Her mother's brows lifted. "Is that a problem?"

"Uh, no. Not a problem. Weird, but not a problem." She glanced at Cade. He wasn't nearly as floored by the offer as she was. Why?

"Mother's prerogative," her mom said. "Am I correct that you'll sleep better if he's here?"

"Definitely."

"Then he should stay." Her mother smiled, turning to Micah. "And I'm going to enjoy the pleasure of tucking my baby boy in for the night."

Micah's lips parted in dismay. He shot Aurora a plea for help. "Uh, Mom, I think—"

Their mom laughed, making Aurora jerk in surprise. "I'm kidding, sweetheart. You're not four. But I wouldn't object if you'd walk with me up the stairs."

Micah grinned at her. "It would be my pleasure."

As Aurora watched her mom and brother head for the stairs, Justin moved to the low wall separating the living room from the foyer. "Cade, you with us?"

"No, I'm staying here."

Justin's gaze moved between Cade and Aurora, a smile lighting up his face. "Well, alrighty. See you in the morning."

Cade gave him a brief wave before turning to Aurora.

She placed her hand on his arm. "What is up with you and my mother?"

He batted his lashes at her. "Whatever do you mean?"

"Cut the act, Ellis. Why's she being so nice to you?"

He slid his arms around her and pulled her against his body, all those solid muscles distracting her. "We had a talk. I told her how I felt about you. She believed me."

"That's it?"

"Mostly. I also told her if I ever left your side, it would be your choice, not mine."

"Oh." His hands had started a lazy massage on her back. Another distraction, but she didn't mind. In fact, she loved everything about this moment. "So, she knows this is the real deal?"

"Uh-huh." He leaned down, his lips brushing lightly over hers. "And so do you." He pulled back, gazing into her eyes. "I love you, Aurora. Everything I have, everything I am... it's yours. Always. And no sadistic half-Teeli or egotistical Kraed will change that, no matter what they believe, no matter what they do. I. Am. Yours."

If he wasn't anchoring her, the bubble of joy in her heart might have floated her right to the ceiling. "And I will never again be foolish enough to turn my back on what we've found, even if I believe I'm acting with the best of intentions. Because I love you, too. Only you. With all my heart. Now, and always."

He pulled her closer, his lips touching hers once more. "That makes me the luckiest man in the universe."

One Hundred Twenty-Seven

Mate.

Half a day had passed since Jonarel had said that word to her, and Mya was still processing. Or more accurately, waiting to wake up.

True to his word, after she'd healed the burn damage—*all* the burn damage—Jonarel had stripped them both down and tucked her into bed, using his body as a sheltering cocoon. She hadn't slept so well in years. Maybe ever.

And when she'd woken up, they'd enjoyed more... aerobic activities.

Now she was on her way to the med bay to check on her parents, borrowed clothes in her hands from Jonarel for her dad, while he went to the bridge to relieve Kelly. She'd join him shortly so Kire could get some shuteye.

Stepping through the med bay doors, she crept forward as silently as possible, not wanting to disturb the two sleeping figures.

Her mom had donned the clothes she'd left for her and had also stripped off her dad's dirty clothes and given him a sponge bath by the look of it. His chest was bare, and all the ash and dirt had been washed from his face, hair, and chest. She no longer smelled the smoky residue from the fire.

Her mom had also pulled the portable med platform next to her dad's bed, climbed onto it, and fallen asleep with one hand resting on his chest and the other curled around his hand.

A little color was coming back to her dad's skin, though he was a far cry from healed. Her mom was in better shape. Her body's natural healing instinct would have kicked in even while she slept, accelerating the process.

She set the change of clothes on the nearest med platform. Her mom woke while she was changing out the IV.

She blinked, a frown furrowing her brow. "Lelindia?"

"Hi, Mom." Hearing her mom use her birth name had a very different effect than when Jonarel said it. "Sleep well?"

Her mom pushed to her elbows, her gaze sweeping the room. Recognition dawned as sleep peeled back the curtain. "We're in the med bay."

"That's right. You've been out for half a day."

Her mom yawned, her gaze shifting to Mya's dad. "He looks better." A slight hitch in her voice indicated she was evaluating the cellular damage as Mya had. "He hasn't woken up, has he?"

Mya shook her head. "Star would have alerted me." Or maybe not, depending on whether Mya was otherwise engaged with Jonarel. "Do you feel up to another healing session for him?"

Her mom slid off the med platform and stretched. "Absolutely."

Mya moved to one side of her dad's bed while her mother positioned herself on the other. Resting their hands on his chest and against his temples, they engaged their energy fields. The touch of her mom's energy brought an instant sense of calm and ease, as it always did. Blending her own energy with it, she focused on the Necri damage, reinforcing cell walls, healing sites of minor trauma, encouraging her dad's heart and lungs to move oxygen-rich blood through his body.

As the minutes ticked past, her dad's breathing grew stronger, and his eyelids began to flutter. Not long after he blinked them open, frowning at the ceiling, then at the emerald green energy surrounding him. He turned his head toward her mom. "Marina?"

Her mom leaned forward, brushing a kiss on his forehead. "Welcome back, my love."

"Back?" He turned his head and spotted Mya. "Lelindia? What are you...?" His gaze swept the med bay. "Where am I?"

"On the *Starhawke*," Mya answered, disengaging her energy field and resting a hand on his forearm when he reached for the IV. "We brought you here after the Necri attack."

"Necri attack?" The furrows on his brow thickened. "What Necri attack?"

"You don't remember?" Her mom peered at him, worry etched on her face.

"No, I—" He stared at her, his eyes slowly widening. "Someone was in our room. I saw a cloaked figure leaning over you. I lunged, but struck a pearlescent shield." He swallowed. "The face under the cloak looked like... like..."

"Sooree," her mom supplied.

His eyes now resembled saucers. "Sooree? That was real?"

Her mom nodded. "Setarips brought her. She attacked you, draining the life energy from your body. I fought against it, tried to save you." Her voice grew hollow. "But there was so much pain. Ours and hers. I couldn't stop her. She drained me, too. Then the house caught fire." Her hand curled into a fist. "It's gone. Our beautiful home is gone."

Moisture gathered in their eyes as they stared at each other.

Mya was having trouble holding it together, too.

"But you're alive," her dad said, his voice gravelly. "*We're* alive. How?"

"Libra."

"Libra?"

Her mom nodded. "She fought them back."

"She did?" Disbelief filled both syllables.

And no wonder. Libra was scared of her own shadow. Or more accurately, her Suulh abilities. Mya hadn't seen her use her energy shield since Aurora was two.

Her mom gave him a shaky smile. "You would have been so proud. Our little Libra became a true Sahzade today." She lifted her gaze to include Mya. "She kept us alive until Aurora came. Aurora and Micah got us out of the bedroom, and then Jonarel carried us out of the house, and Lelindia brought us here."

Her dad looked totally bewildered. Or overwhelmed. Hard to tell the difference.

"Is Libra okay?" he asked.

"She's fine." Mya answered. She'd had several messages from Celia, informing her of what was happening planetside. "She's with Brendan, Micah, and Aurora at Brendan's house."

Her dad looked even more confused. "She's with Brendan?"

"He's the one who got Aurora to the house in time to rescue you."

And without Aurora there, she and Jonarel never would have been able to save her parents. Or even known where in the house to look for them. She didn't have Aurora's ability to pinpoint the exact location of a particular Suulh. And Jonarel wouldn't have been able to hear or smell them through all the fire and smoke. "She's the one who alerted me."

"Thank the stars for Brendan." The confusion slowly faded, replaced by a strange smile she couldn't interpret. "I knew that boy would never let her go."

She wasn't sure if *her* referred to Aurora or Libra. Maybe both.

But now seemed like a good time to make her exit, give her folks time alone. "I need to get to the bridge. Dad, I've left a change of clothes for you, and Mom can show you how to use the shower. Are you two okay here for a few hours?"

Her mom nodded. "We'll be fine."

Mya pointed through the currently transparent privacy wall to the door leading into the greenhouse. "The greenhouse is through there. You can gather anything you two would like to eat. If it needs to be cooked, the kitchen is on the far end."

Her dad's eyes lit up at the word *kitchen.*

"But you still need to rest," she said, emphasizing with a hand on his shoulder. "Don't push it."

His soft smile warmed her heart. "Yes, doctor."

She rolled her eyes and headed for the door. "I'll check on you a little later."

"Lelindia?"

She turned at his soft call. "Yes?"

All humor had left his eyes. "Thank you."

A lump rose in her throat as she gazed at him. At them both. She'd almost lost them, forever. "You're welcome."

Her throat was still a little thick when she stepped onto the bridge. Kire sat in the captain's chair, his chin propped on his fist like he needed the extra structural support. Jonarel, on the other hand, looked like a jungle cat preparing to pounce from a branch as he sat at the navigation console.

His golden gaze warmed as he turned, a subtle smile curling his lips. The look in his eyes made her want to stroll over and crawl into his lap, but she forced herself to walk to the captain's chair instead.

Kire lifted his head. "How are your folks?"

"They're going to be okay. Dad's awake, and I told Mom to raid the greenhouse for food."

"Has she seen it yet?"

"The greenhouse? Not yet."

He grinned. "Then I may have to wander down there before I take my break. I'd love to see her expression when she steps through the door."

"I'm sure they'd be delighted to see you."

He pushed up from the chair, sweeping his hand toward the seat. "It's all yours."

She nodded, settling into the chair he'd vacated as he crossed to the lift.

As soon as the doors closed, Jonarel pivoted his chair so he was facing her. "I thought he would never leave."

She bit back a smile. "Why? Was there something you wanted?"

He crossed the distance separating them between one breath and the next, his hands on the arms of her chair, caging her in. "Yes. You."

Despite his predator's stance, his lips came down on hers with exquisite tenderness, the kiss drawing a sigh of pleasure from her mouth. She gazed up at him as he pulled back. "How do you do that?"

He tilted his head. "Do what?"

"Know exactly what I want?"

This time he did smile, the beauty of it striking her like an arrow. "Now that I know what is in your heart, you are very easy to read."

And now that she wasn't hiding her feelings, she wasn't giving off mixed signals. "Read away."

His eyes glowed with banked fire. "Oh, I intend to." He gave her one more tender kiss before pushing away. "But not right now."

He returned to his station, which gave her the advantage. She could watch him and the data regarding movement of ships in the system at the same time.

This was going to be the most enjoyable work shift she'd ever had.

One Hundred Twenty-Eight

After Jonarel landed the *Starhawke*'s shuttle in front of her dad's house the next morning, the hug he gave Aurora when she greeted him told her everything she needed to know about the change in their relationship. His hug was warm, friendly, and delightful, without the slightest trace of the awkwardness, passion, or romantic inclinations that usually made her tense up.

She might as well have been hugging Micah.

She stepped back, giving him a once over. "You look really happy."

His yellow eyes seemed to glow from within. "I am."

Which would have been weird considering what she'd learned about the altercation with his clan, had she not also suspected something serious was going on between him and Mya. Would the good doctor be glowing when she saw her, too?

She and Cade had discussed the possibility last night as they'd cuddled in her bedroom. He'd been as surprised as she'd been at the potential pairing, but the longer they'd discussed it, the more certain she'd become she was right. Jonarel's current behavior seemed to confirm it.

The shift made this situation so much simpler. She caught his hand in an easy grip, tugging him toward the house. "Come on, I want you to meet my dad. And my brother, without all the fire and smoke."

She led him to the kitchen, where Celia and her brother were cleaning the breakfast pans and loading the dishwasher while her dad supervised.

Micah glanced over his shoulder, giving a little jolt when he saw Jonarel. He quickly dried his hands on a towel and faced him, his gaze wary.

She couldn't blame him for his anxiety. If the first time she'd seen Jonarel he'd been leaping down from a burning wall after scaling it with his clawed hands and feet, landing like a panther, she'd be a little intimidated, too.

"Micah, Dad, I'd like you to meet Jonarel, my engineer and good friend."

Micah was clearly off balance, but her dad acted like he met heavily muscled Kraed every day. He reached out a hand to Jonarel. "A pleasure to meet you, Jonarel. I'm Brendan."

Jonarel accepted the handshake. "The pleasure is mine."

Micah stepped forward next. "I'm Aurora's brother." But he kept his gaze on Jonarel's hand as he extended his. Probably checking for Jonarel's claws.

Jonarel clasped his hand with obvious gentleness, his emotions indicating he would allow Micah to set the tone of the interaction.

The tension eased from Micah's stance, his usual exuberance returning. "I didn't get a chance to thank you yesterday for your part in the rescue. Aurora and I would have struggled to get Marina and Gryphon out of the house safely without your help."

Jonarel inclined his head. "I would do anything to help Lelindia's parents." His gaze slid to her, and he flinched slightly. "And Aurora."

She grinned, sharing a look with Celia, who was leaning on the counter, watching the interplay with interest. Aurora thoroughly enjoyed being the afterthought in Jonarel's mind rather than the main feature. And he'd just called Mya

Lelindia again, a clear sign they'd gotten cozy. Only her parents called her that.

Love looked good on him, when it was reciprocated. "You were awesome." She couldn't resist teasing him a bit. "I'm sure Mya was very grateful as well."

She'd never seen a Kraed blush—dark green skin didn't allow for it—but if he could have, he would have. All the other tells were there.

He cleared his throat. "Yes, she is."

She stifled a snort, not wanting to make him uncomfortable, but this scene was a dream come true for her. She rested her hand on top of his and looked him in the eye. "I'm *really* glad."

His eyes narrowed. "You are?"

"Thrilled."

He tilted his head, then nodded. Message received. "She will be glad to see you, too."

"Oh, yes. We'll have *lots* to talk about."

He didn't growl, but he looked like he wanted to. She just gave him an innocent smile.

Micah looked confused, but her dad and Celia seemed to be following the subtext just fine. And enjoying the heck out of it.

Her mom appeared in the archway from the hall. "Jonarel!" She rushed forward, giving him a big hug and an even bigger smile. "How are Marina and Gryphon?"

"Doing very well. They were sharing a meal with Lelindia when I left."

Her mom cocked her head, catching the odd use of Mya's birth name, but she didn't comment on it. "Thank you for taking such good care of them."

Aurora sensed Jonarel's discomfort at the show of gratitude, but he hid it well. "You are welcome."

And then came the acid test. Cade stood in the archway, watching Jonarel and her mother.

Aurora sent a silent plea to Cade to stay cool. He'd agreed to remain upstairs until after she'd introduced Jonarel to the rest of her family. But the two couldn't avoid each other forever.

Jonarel turned, his gaze resting on Cade. He looked him up and down, but she wasn't sensing any anger, resentment, or hostility from him. In fact, he seemed puzzled, like he was as surprised by the absence of those emotions as she was. He nodded his head in a casual, almost friendly gesture. "Ellis."

Cade's brows lifted, the hint of a smile on his lips. "Clarek." He stepped forward, moving to Aurora's side.

Jonarel watched him, but his emotions didn't change. The territorial protectiveness he'd exhibited around her since the day they'd met was conspicuously absent. In fact, she'd go so far as to say he seemed pleased by Cade's presence.

Hallelujah! The long cold war was finally over.

One Hundred Twenty-Nine

Micah stared at the visible section of the *Starhawke* shuttle's interior as he followed Jonarel toward it, Aurora by his side. His mind was struggling to make sense of what he was seeing. The slice where the ramp sat looked somewhat comparable to the shuttles his dad's company designed, although the detailing was very unusual. Were those wood floors?

But that's not what was working his brain. It was the fact that the rest of the shuttle wasn't visible at all. He could see the rocks and vegetation, as well as the mini-waterfall that made up the back section of the driveway and the hillside beyond. It was like the ramp was a portal into another dimension.

"Kinda freaky, isn't it?"

He glanced down at Aurora. "You could say that."

"But it comes in really handy on stealth missions."

"I'd imagine so." He still couldn't believe Jonarel had managed to land the shuttle without causing an uproar in the neighborhood. But apparently no one had heard a thing. Including him. "Just how silent is it?"

"It could hover a meter away and you'd never know it."

Wow. That was a little scary.

"All Kraed technology?" his dad asked as they walked up the ramp. He sounded excited rather than anxious.

"Modified Kraed technology combined with Fleet standards. Jonarel wanted the rest of us to feel at home." She motioned to the cockpit. "Why don't you take the co-pilot's seat, Dad? I'm sure Jonarel would be happy to answer your questions."

His dad's eyes brightened. "You don't mind?"

Aurora shook her head. "Go for it."

He glanced at their mom. "Is that okay with you?"

She smiled. "As she said, go for it."

As their dad moved forward, Micah's gaze swept the main cabin, which contained twelve seats in three rows of four.

Aurora pointed to the far chairs in the first two rows. "Mom, Micah, why don't you take the window seats. Enjoy the view." She glanced over her shoulder as everyone else filed in. "You too, Admiral. The rest of us get to see this sight on a regular basis."

Micah did as instructed, settling into the far chair in the middle row while his mom sat directly in front of him. Aurora and Cade sat next to her, but Celia claimed the seat beside him.

Perfect. Now he was *really* anxious.

"First space flight?" she asked as the shuttle lifted off.

Only the downward pressure and changing scenery alerting him that they were airborne. The shuttle could have been at a standstill from the lack of noise and vibration. "Is it that obvious?"

"To most people, no. But I'm more observant than most."

He believed that. She'd been *observing* him far too much. He couldn't get a bead on her. She was keeping a close eye on him, and he had no idea why. Maybe he should ask. "Are you always this focused?"

"Focused?"

"Yeah. I feel like you're analyzing my every move."

She held his gaze. "I am."

At least she was honest about it. He noticed Aurora turning her head slightly, listening in. Maybe she'd noticed Celia's behavior, too. "Why?"

"Because it's my job."

"Am I a security threat?" He said it like a joke, but she didn't smile.

"I don't know. Yet."

Turned out honesty wasn't always nice.

Aurora twisted in her chair so she could see Celia. "Why would Micah be a threat?"

His mom and Cade had turned, too, his mom looking like a disgruntled badger.

Celia didn't seem the least bit concerned by the attention, or his mom's glower. She answered Aurora's question calmly. "From what I've seen and heard, he has a strong connection with you, and the potential to influence you. It's my responsibility to make sure that influence doesn't present a danger to you or the crew."

Aurora's eyes narrowed, her gaze shifting from Celia to him and back again. "How long until you figure that out?"

Celia lowered her chin like she was initiating a staring contest. "As long as it takes."

Aurora stared back for several beats before focusing on him. "Celia always makes her own evaluation of anyone we come in contact with, and I respect that. However, if she gives you any grief, let me know." She waited until he nodded before turning back to face front.

His mom gave Celia a parting glare before turning around. Cade shot him a look of sympathy, making him wonder if he'd been under Celia's microscope at one time, too.

He chose to look out the window. He wasn't used to being under suspicion and didn't like the feeling one bit. Sure, he had a powerful effect on Aurora, but it wasn't a threat. They'd just spent the past two weeks proving that.

The one upside was that Celia's views had effectively squashed the seeds of attraction he'd felt. She might be beautiful, smart, and athletic, three things that flipped his switches, but she had some serious trust issues to work through. That wasn't his style.

The murmur of conversation resumed around him. He could hear his dad in the cockpit, firing questions at Jonarel. The view out the windows shifted as the shuttle gathered speed, shooting up through the cloud layer.

Aurora turned again, but this time with excitement in her eyes. "I love this part!" She pointed out the window.

He turned, his breath catching as the image shifted, the curve of the planet growing distinct, the blue of the ocean calling to him on an elemental level.

"Isn't it beautiful?" Aurora murmured.

"Yes. Yes, it is." Pictures didn't do it justice. And he'd seen the best of the best, thanks to his dad. But nothing could have prepared him for the breathtaking vista of the blue-white planet as it became a vibrant sphere among the dark blanket of stars.

The shuttle banked, following the curve of the Earth to the west, away from the sun.

"We're meeting the *Starhawke* on the dark side of the moon." Aurora pointed to the pale orb in the distance. "That way you'll get to see her without Sol Station knowing we're in the system."

The eagerness in her voice was infectious. His mom seemed to have caught it, too. She'd turned so that her palms were pressed against the wide windows, watching as the moon grew steadily larger.

That's when the reality of where he was sunk in. He was in space! Headed for the moon! He'd never imagined seeing the Earth or the moon from this perspective. Now that he had, he couldn't look away.

"This is why I want to be out here." Aurora whispered.

He nodded, the pull of the vista keeping him fixated. "It's incredible." He wouldn't want to live in space, as she did, but he could certainly understand the appeal.

As the shuttle flew around the curve of the moon, the sunlight dimming, a soft chime sounded in rhythmic beats. He turned to Aurora. "What's that?"

She gave him a Cheshire Cat grin. "Homing beacon. Right now we're invisible to the ship, and she's invisible to us. The homing beacon makes sure we don't crash into each other."

That threw a little ice water on his excitement. "Could that happen?"

She shook her head, all teasing gone. "No. Star could prevent it. She has a... unique way of communicating with the shuttle. And she'll be dropping the camouflage any moment." Aurora gestured out the window. "There she is."

He turned, and his mouth popped open in a perfect O.

Shimmering in the semi-darkness was a frozen waterfall crafted of black velvet and glittering diamonds. Smooth lines and graceful curves blended into a harmonious whole that defied categorization. "*That's* your ship?"

"Uh-huh."

"Oh, Aurora," their mom whispered in hushed tones, "it's *beautiful.*"

"Yes, *she* is."

He detected a slight emphasis on the gender pronoun.

"All Jonarel's doing," Aurora continued. "He designed her and oversaw her construction."

They glided closer, the ship dominating his view. He gawked, his gaze trying to go everywhere at once. This wasn't a ship. It was a work of art.

And he'd changed his mind. If he was flying on *this* ship, he might be able to live in space.

One Hundred Thirty

Her family's reactions had been everything Aurora had hoped for. And they hadn't even seen the inside of the ship yet.

Her dad had been talking with Jonarel non-stop during the shuttle flight, and his enthusiasm had bubbled over into her. Not that she needed the boost. She was finally home.

As the shuttle rose into the bay, she reached for the release on her harness.

"Lelindia is on her way to meet us," Jonarel called into the main cabin as he powered down the engines.

She was already on her feet. Cade was almost as fast, but her mom and dad took a while longer, partly because her dad was still asking Jonarel questions. Celia and Reynolds stepped out of the way so Micah could join the rest of the family as Aurora led them down the ramp into the bay.

"Sahzade!"

The happy cry reached her as Mya hurried toward her from the bay's entrance.

"Mya!" Aurora picked up the pace too, meeting her halfway in a laughing, stumbling hug.

"I'm so glad you're back," Mya whispered in her ear, squeezing her tight.

"Me, too. It's good to be home."

They released their grip on each other, stepping back as the Admiral and Cade's team gathered around them. Sure enough, Jonarel moved beside Mya in the exact same posture he used to take with her.

Mya's cheeks tinged pink as Aurora looked between the two of them. She held Mya's gaze, smiling softly and lifting her brows slightly.

Mya's blush deepened.

Oh, yeah, they'd have *so* much to talk about.

Mya broke eye contact and gave Aurora's mom a hug, but hesitated in front of her dad.

He made the decision for her. Closing the gap, he pulled her into his arms. "I've missed you, firefly."

Firefly? The nickname rang a distant bell in her memory.

"I've missed you, too." She hugged him back with equal enthusiasm.

"The little girl I knew grew up."

She laughed as she stepped back. "That tends to happen."

Her dad's eyes sparkled. "So it does."

Micah stepped in next, claiming a hug from Mya, too.

Aurora noticed her mom's eyes looked a little damp. She slipped an arm around her shoulders.

"I've missed this," her mom said, a soft smile on her lips.

"Yeah. Me, too." So much more could be said, but not now. "Let's go see Marina and Gryphon."

Fitting everyone onto the lift was a tight squeeze, but they managed.

When the lift doors parted, Cade touched her shoulder. "My team will meet you in the observation lounge, if that's okay."

"Sure." No point in everyone tromping into the med bay.

Cade's team and the Admiral headed for the observation lounge while Aurora's family, Mya, Jonarel, and Celia walked down the corridor to the med bay.

Kire was waiting for them outside the doors. He opened his arms and Aurora stepped into them. "Good to have you back, Roe."

"Good to be back."

While she introduced Kire to her dad and Micah, her mom, Mya, Jonarel, and Celia slipped into the med bay, headed for the inclined med platform where Gryphon lay, talking to Marina.

A weight she hadn't known she'd been carrying tumbled to the deck at the sight. Yes, she'd gotten reports that Gryphon was on the mend, but her last mental image was in direct conflict with that assurance. Seeing him up and animated again was an emotional balm.

"Brendan!" Gryphon called out as Aurora walked into the bay with her dad, brother, and Kire. "How the heck are you, boy?"

Boy? She had trouble imagining anyone viewing her dad as a boy, but apparently Gryphon did.

"Doing well now, old man," her dad responded with a grin.

Okay, now the interchange made sense.

"Glad to hear it." Gryphon's gaze moved to Micah, his eyes widening. "Oh, my goodness. Is this strapping young man really Micah?"

Her brother's grin matched their dad's. "That's me." He accepted Gryphon's outstretched hand.

Gryphon's gaze moved past Micah's shoulder and settled on her. He smiled, but there was a seriousness to his eyes and emotions that spoke of the trauma they'd just been through. "You keeping these two scoundrels in check?"

"I'm doing my best."

Gryphon hooked a thumb over his shoulder to where her mom stood beside Marina. "You need any help, ask these two. They were pretty good at it once upon a time."

Marina rolled her eyes, but her mom smiled.

Aurora grinned back at her. "I'll keep that in mind." She leaned in, giving Gryphon a soft kiss on the cheek. "I'm glad you're on the mend."

He nodded. "Thanks to you and Lelindia."

She gestured to the group gathered around his bed. "It was a team effort. Speaking of which." She stepped back. "I need to steal Mya and Celia away for a few minutes."

Mya shifted her weight, very obviously *not* looking at Jonarel, who stood beside her.

Celia, on the other hand, looked like she was trying not to laugh.

Gryphon took their reactions in, amusement sparking in his eyes. "Sure, sure. You have a ship to run."

"Yes, I do." She nodded, working to keep a straight face as she turned toward the greenhouse. "We'll be back in just a bit."

One Hundred Thirty-One

Mya had a fair idea what Aurora's little chat would be about as the three of them entered the welcoming space of the greenhouse. Sure enough, Aurora pounced immediately.

"What happened between you and Jonarel?" She clasped her hands like a kid waiting impatiently for a treat. "I want all the details!"

Mya turned to Celia for backup, but her traitorous friend lifted her hands and bumped her shoulder against Aurora's. "Don't look at me, I'm with her." She nodded toward Mya. "Spill it."

She sighed, although it was mostly for show. She'd been eager to share this with her friends since it had occurred, but they'd both been planetside. "We, um, got together."

Aurora's eyes sparkled with mischief. "You mean *together*, together?" She waggled her eyebrows.

Mya couldn't hold back anymore. Her smile burst forth. "Yep."

"Whoop!" Aurora shot a fist in the air and spun in a circle. "I *knew* it! Oh, Mya, that's wonderful." Aurora grabbed her in an exuberant hug. "When did this happen?"

A flush crept up her neck. "The first time was during the flight to Earth."

Celia snapped to attention. "So *that's* why you went all silent. I was wondering."

Mya nodded. "I thought it was just sex for him. You know, a Kraed thing now that he'd given up any hope of mating with Aurora."

Aurora nodded. "I was hoping that wasn't the case."

"When I realized I couldn't do that, I shut him out." Her smile returned. "Turns out I was wrong. He wants me as his checana."

"Checana?" Aurora looked at Celia, who shrugged. "What's that?"

"It means beloved, like checala, but only refers to one's mate."

Aurora let out another whoop. "Oh, Mya, I am so happy for you. For both of you. No wonder he was so calm this morning. He didn't even mind being around Cade."

"Really?" That was hard to believe.

Celia held up a hand. "I can attest to that. Not a bit of manly posturing between those two. It was unnerving."

"Yeah, but in a good way. And speaking of unnerving." Aurora turned to Celia. "What's with giving my brother the third degree?"

Mya looked at Celia as well. "You've been interrogating Micah?"

"I've been *cautious* with Micah. Totally different."

"Cautious about what?" Aurora folded her arms over her chest. "He's my brother for goodness sakes, not some stranger off the street."

Celia folded her arms as well. "A brother who's half-Suulh and has the ability to ramp up your power, correct?"

Aurora conceded the point. "Yeah."

"Does he have any other unusual abilities? Because I'm guessing the answer's yes."

Now Aurora looked a little uncomfortable. "He can communicate with animals. Telepathically."

"Uh-huh." Celia gave Aurora a pointed look.

"Really?" Mya asked Aurora. "Since when?"

"Since birth, I guess. He just didn't think anything of it until he was older and realized the other kids couldn't hear the animals the way he could."

"And you don't think that makes his presence near you worthy of caution?" Celia asked.

"No, I do not." Aurora widened her stance. "He's not a threat. I've never known a gentler soul. And he can't turn me into a threat, either. I've learned a lot about myself, about my abilities, while I was gone. If anything, Micah helps me to stay focused and under control." She pointed a finger at Celia. "In which case, you should be completely onboard with team Micah."

Celia huffed, looking away.

It was the looking away that tipped Mya off. Celia never looked away when she was challenged. "There's something else, isn't there? Something you haven't told us."

Celia took a moment before meeting her gaze, a hint of vulnerability lurking behind her usual confidence. She glanced at Aurora before answering. "I've felt strange ever since he came on the scene."

"Strange how?" Mya prompted.

"Like how I feel when my subconscious perceives a threat my conscious mind hasn't grasped yet."

Aurora dropped her arms to her sides, stepping closer. "So that's what you've been trying to do with all the scrutiny? Get your conscious mind to process what you're feeling and why?"

She shrugged in a non-committal way. Also an unusual Celia behavior. "I figured if I stayed close to him, monitored his actions, let my senses take it all in, I'd figure out what was bothering me. But so far, I've got nothing. Just this weird feeling that something's not as it should be."

Aurora looked to Mya, but she shook her head. She'd known Micah since he was born, and she agreed with Aurora.

Unless he'd changed dramatically as he grew up—which his behavior didn't seem to indicate—he was the least threatening person she could imagine, especially when it came to Aurora.

As a child, he would have done anything for his little sister, and had. There was no reason to believe that had changed. "Maybe it's the half-Suulh thing," she offered. "How did you feel when you first met Aurora?"

"Cautious," Celia admitted, her gaze moving to Aurora. "I could tell there was something different about you, something you were hiding."

Aurora gave her a weak smile. "And you proceeded to knock it out of me."

Celia's smile was even weaker than Aurora's.

But Mya thought she had a point. "Exactly. You two started off sparring together, which gave you a chance to test each other out, get to the core of each other's being. And let's not forget that lovely few days we spent together of Persei Primus." She'd love to forget those traumatic days, except that they were responsible for bringing Celia into her life, bonding the three of them together. "It was a trial by fire. With Micah, all you've been able to do is observe, rather than really interact."

Aurora brightened. "Maybe what you need to do is get him on the mat. He's been sparring with me a bit. He could handle a session if you go easy on him."

Celia looked like she was mulling the idea over, testing it for weak points. Or trying to figure a way out of it. "Maybe."

"It's worth a shot." Aurora put her arm around Celia's shoulders and squeezed. "And keep in mind he's only here for a visit and a tour. As soon as Gryphon's well enough to travel, they'll all be leaving."

Celia grunted.

But Mya's mind moved to the adjacent point. "Do you have any idea where our folks are going to stay when they leave?"

Aurora shook her head. "I'm guessing my mom will want to stay with my dad, although she'll have to decide what she's going to do about Hawke's Nest. I haven't asked her about that, either. I'm sure my dad would be happy to have your folks stay with him, too, at least in the short term."

"They'd have to decide what to do about the clinic." Which wouldn't be easy. Her mom and dad loved working with their patients, most of whom they'd known for years.

"Yeah." Worry crept into Aurora's eyes. "I'm not comfortable with the idea of their going back there alone."

Mya sighed. "Neither am I."

"Ironic, isn't it?" Aurora gave her a wry smile. "Now we know how they usually feel about us."

A position she'd never expected to be in. "It might help if we figured out what we're doing, first."

Aurora nodded, turning toward the doorway to the med bay. "Then let's get the ball rolling."

One Hundred Thirty-Two

Cade loved being back on the *Starhawke*. But more than that, he loved being *welcome* on the *Starhawke*. Sitting around the carved wood oval table in the observation lounge with Aurora by his side felt right.

It was also the first time he'd been in this room with her and Clarek without having the Kraed shooting death darts from his eyes. He could get used to that, too.

Instead, Clarek's focus was on Mya, who was sitting beside him. He wasn't looking directly at her, but the subtle cues in his body language, which Cade was used to seeing projected toward Aurora, were now directed at Mya.

Cade looked down at the table, hiding a smile. Aurora had been right. And if this meeting was any indication, his days of worrying about Clarek's overprotective behavior toward Aurora were over.

Justin leaned in, his voice low. "What's so funny?"

Apparently he hadn't hidden the smile as well as he'd thought. "I'll fill you in later."

The rest of his team sat to Justin's right, then Cardiff, Mya, Clarek, and the Admiral. Micah sat to Aurora's left, then Bronwyn Kelly, the *Starhawke*'s pilot, and Kire Emoto. A holoscreen behind Mya and Jonarel provided a live feed of the med bay, where Aurora's and Mya's parents were listening in.

The Admiral folded his hands on the table, his gaze sweeping around the group. "We have reached the point where decisions must be made, priorities set. I suggest we start with how we will handle the situation with Admiral Payne and her family, and the probable trap Reanne and the

Teeli will set for the *Starhawke* at the site of the scientific expedition."

His gaze moved to Aurora. "The Teeli believe your crew will resume the mission when you return to Sol Station around the first of the year. Obviously, that's not an option in practical terms, since Reanne will no doubt try another ambush, or send the Setarips to do it for her."

Grumbles of agreement circled the table.

"I can put the Teeli off for a few days, but we'll still need to come up with a response for the Teeli ambassador, be it Bare'Kold or whomever Reanne sends to replace him. Do you have any recommendations for how you would like to handle this situation?"

Aurora was silent for a moment, her brows drawn down in a frown of concentration. "What if accepting the mission was an option?"

"What?" Cade stared at her. "You can't be serious."

She held up a hand. "Hear me out. What if we could turn the tables? Make the trap meant for us an ambush for them, instead?"

The Admiral's brow furrowed. "We could not send any Fleet ships into Teeli space."

"And my father would not provide any assistance, either," Clarek added.

Aurora nodded. "I know, but we may have an ally who could help us. One whose goals parallel ours." She looked at Cade. "The Yruf."

Hadn't seen that coming. In fact, he hadn't given the Yruf much thought since leaving their ship. He'd been a bit preoccupied. "Why would they help us? And how?"

"You said last night that their goal is to bring an end to the Setarip civil war. That they tried to capture the Ecilam ship rather than destroying it. You also said their hull camouflage and sensor dampening rivals ours, and that they were able to put Justin in a coma without setting foot on the ship." She glanced at Justin. "Glad you're fully recovered, by the way."

Justin lifted two fingers in a mini-salute.

She turned her attention back to Cade. "The Yruf would be ideal backup for whatever nasty surprise Reanne has in store for us."

"Okay, I can see your point. But why take the risk at all? What do we stand to gain by playing into their hands?"

"You mean besides helping the Yruf end the reign of terror the Setarips have been wreaking in Fleet space for decades? And gaining a powerful ally whose actions could weaken Reanne's grip on the other factions?"

Cade's lips pressed together. She was making too much sense considering he hated the idea. "Yeah, besides that."

"Then how about the potential to capture Teeli warships? Or maybe even a cruiser. Maybe *Reanne's* cruiser." Her eyes gleamed with a light he knew all too well.

"We wouldn't succeed. Reanne always destroys any ship that's disabled. Probably even hers, although I'm sure she has an emergency escape plan for herself."

"Well, *we* might not succeed, but what about the Yruf? You indicated they were distraught when the Ecilam ship they'd captured was destroyed, along with everyone onboard. I'm guessing they'll learn quickly from their mistakes. You also said they gathered all the debris. They're probably already analyzing it, working on a way to neutralize whatever auto-destruct Reanne had implanted."

The Admiral chuckled, drawing their attention. "I like the way you think. And I agree." His gaze moved to the other members of Cade's team. "So now the question becomes how do we contact the Yruf ship?"

Justin and Bella exchanged a look. "We might have a few ideas about that," Justin said. "Some of their technology has a Kraed feel to it, so maybe you could offer some input?" He looked at Clarek, who nodded.

The Admiral smiled. "All right. That's a good beginning." He focused on Aurora again. "Next is the issue of Admiral Payne. Whether your idea is workable or not, her family is still at Reanne's knife point." He glanced at Mya. "And her grandson may not survive much longer in the ICU without intervention. I'd like to offer Payne and her family an alternative to Reanne's machinations."

Mya sat up straighter. "What happened to him?"

"He suffered head trauma from a supposed accident." The Admiral gave her a brief rundown.

"So, if anyone goes into his room to treat him, Reanne will kill him?" The anger in her voice was stronger than anything Cade had heard from her before. In fact, Mya projected more strength in general, like she was more comfortable in her own skin.

"That's correct."

She chewed her bottom lip. "Even if he died, I could bring him back as long as I got to him quickly. And as long as the physical trauma wasn't too great. But we'd have to get him, and me, out of the hospital without being stopped." She looked at Cade. "Is that possible?"

He turned to Williams. "What do you think?"

Williams leaned his forearms on the table. "It wouldn't be easy, but with the right plan, it's doable. The real trick isn't getting out, it's not being seen, either by the staff or the cameras that monitor the patients."

"And we'll need a safe house for the family," Reynolds said. "Somewhere Reanne wouldn't think to look for them."

"How many people are we talking about?" Gonzo asked.

"Assuming Payne goes with them," the Admiral said, "it would be five. Her son and daughter-in-law have a little girl as well."

Aurora spoke up. "Wherever they go, it would need to be viable as a long-term solution, in case the situation with Reanne and the Teeli isn't resolved anytime soon. Reanne will hold a grudge against Payne forever."

"That she will," the Admiral agreed. "Ideally, I'd like to see them off planet. Maybe in one of the Rim colonies."

"What about Gaia?"

They all turned to face the holoscreen, where Libra had moved closer to the camera. "Would that be a possibility?"

Aurora answered her. "It's still pretty close to Earth."

"I know, but they could have support there. Protection."

"They could? How?"

Libra glanced back at Mya's parents before answering Aurora's question. "When we left our homeworld, we weren't alone. Six other Suulh went with us. They all chose to remain on Gaia when we came to Earth."

Aurora slapped the table with her palm. "*That's* why you and Marina acted so strange when Mya and I first told you about our mission to Gaia. You thought maybe we'd encountered the Suulh you'd left there."

Libra nodded.

"Are you still in communication with them?"

"Yes. Wolf and Skye have been visiting us every three years to touch base ever since the Teeli first arrived in this system."

Aurora looked at Mya. "Did you know about this?"

Mya frowned. "No, although those names seem familiar."

"You were only three the last time you saw them, at my mating ceremony." Libra looking a little contrite, glancing back at Brendan before retuning her attention to Mya. "After that, we would meet with them in town rather than at the house, at least until you both left for the Academy."

Aurora's lips pursed, but she seemed to be taking the news well.

Cade was beginning to wonder just how many more secrets Libra Hawke had in her bag. "And you think they'd be willing to shelter Payne's family indefinitely?"

"Without question."

Aurora looked at him, then at the Admiral. "What do you think?"

"I think the idea has merit." He turned to Cade. "Gather whoever you need to tackle the Yruf plan while the rest of us work with Aurora and Mya's parents. We need to create an extraction for Payne's grandson that will get the family safely relocated to Gaia." He stood. "And remember, the clock is ticking."

One Hundred Thirty-Three

Aurora's brain felt like mush by the time the Admiral called it a day. But she was very pleased with the progress they'd made on formulating a workable plan. The real question was whether they could convince Payne to agree to it.

And then execute it.

She'd noticed that Micah was uncharacteristically quiet through all the discussions, his normal exuberance decidedly tempered. His emotional field was subdued as well.

When her group left the med bay, she suggested taking him on a tour of the ship to get him alone. Her parents had decided they'd wait for their tour until Gryphon and Marina could join them.

He'd agreed, but without the excitement he'd shown when they'd first discussed it. Was Celia's behavior toward him responsible?

She decided to start on the lower levels and work their way up. Since Micah wasn't much of a tech guy, they made it quickly through engineering before moving on to the training and exercise room.

He paused just inside the door, his gaze sweeping the room as he whistled softly. "Wow, this is not the kind of gym I expected."

That reaction was a little more like it. "When you live in space, keeping your body functioning optimally is critical. The Kraed have perfected it, and we're the beneficiaries."

He eyed the large mat on the floor. "Is that where you and Celia spar?"

She nodded. "As often as we can. I like to keep my skills sharp, and she always has something new to teach me."

"Hmm." He strolled further into the room, looking up at the elevated running track. "She doesn't like me, does she?"

"It's not that she doesn't like you. She's just naturally cautious."

He shot her a look over his shoulder. "She's not cautious with Mom and Dad. Or Gryphon and Marina."

"I know." And she couldn't explain Celia's odd behavior because she didn't fully understand it. Or what vibe Celia was getting from Micah that was putting her on edge. "Just remember I'm the captain. She answers to me."

That earned a weak smile. "Good thing. Otherwise I think I might be floating home."

"You would not." She clasped his hand, sending a soothing energy pulse along his arm. "I don't know what's up with her, but I suspect it has more to do with her than you. I'm sorry she's gotten under your skin."

He shrugged, his gaze moving toward the back of the room. His muscles tightened and his back straightened, but with excitement, not anger. "Is that a *swimming* tank?"

She grinned as he practically dragged her across the room to the bottom of the stairs. "Sure is. I'm in there a lot, too. Well, I was before..." She waved her hand. He could fill in the rest. "But I'll be back in as soon as I get the chance."

He started up the stairs and she followed. "It's not very big." His gaze swept the relatively tight dimensions of the pool. "You wouldn't be able to get in more than a few strokes edge to edge."

"That's where you're wrong." Kneeling, she touched the control panel at the edge of the pool, activating the wave feature. "It can be adjusted to simulate most water conditions." She gave him a rueful smile. "Well, maybe not surfing."

He was studying the pool with keen interest. "Maybe not. Although with the right board and conditions..." He trailed off, walking the length of the tank and back.

Seemed as good a time as any to bring up the pertinent question. "Is that why you've been so quiet today? Because of Celia?"

"Huh? Oh. Uh, no."

She stepped closer. "Than what is it? You've said more in the past five minutes than all the time since we docked."

He glanced at her, but his gaze drifted back to the water. "I know. And I'm sorry. You were so excited to show me your ship." He sighed. "I've just been processing."

"Processing what?"

"The reality of all this." He swept an arm around the room. "You talked about your life while we were at Dad's, but coming here, it made it so much more real."

"And that's a bad thing?" She had to guess, because his emotions were a confusing muddle.

"No. Not at all." He finally faced her. The seriousness in his gaze surprised her. No hint of a smile. No teasing. "You're fighting for things I never even imagined. The fate of an entire race. The integrity of the Fleet. The end of the Setarip civil war, for goodness sakes!"

He ran his fingers through his hair and stared up at the ceiling. "I was sitting there, listening as you calmly talked about using yourself and your ship as bait to lure this Reanne lunatic, and all I could think about was how I couldn't imagine leaving in a few days. Not knowing what you plan to do."

Her heart ached at the pain and sadness surrounding him. "This is my life, Micah. Ever since I chose to join the Fleet and found out about the Suulh. And Reanne. I have to do this. I have to fight back."

"I know." He looked down at her, a sad smile curving his mouth. "And I understand. It's who you are. Protecting others from danger is what you do. I get that now, too."

"And you hate it."

"No, I don't hate it. I'm proud of you. And incredibly honored to have you as my little sister."

"But?" She could feel him holding back, blocking her from seeing whatever monster he was wrestling with.

He shook his head. "Not a but. The reason I've been quiet is because I realized I can't go back to my life the way it was. Too much has happened. Too much has changed."

Now an asteroid was sitting in her stomach. "What are you saying?"

Reaching out, he clasped her hands in his. The zing of connection lit her up like a searchlight.

"I'm saying that you have a huge battle ahead of you, one that needs to be fought. And there's only one place I can imagine being."

She held her breath.

"Right here, with you."

She stared at him, unable to form words.

A slow smile spread across his handsome face. "You look stupefied."

That broke her paralysis. "You can't be serious." But she knew he was. She could feel it.

The smile vanished. "I've never been more serious in my life. Whatever happens with this mission, you're going to need every resource at your disposal. If I stay, I can give you a *huge* advantage."

"But at what cost? Your job? Your future?" *Your life?* She couldn't imagine putting him in harm's way. And if

Reanne found out about him? She couldn't even let her mind go there.

"Don't get me wrong. I love my job. And I'll miss being ten minutes from the beach. But I love you more. And there's no way I can go back to teaching classes and surfing with Birdie knowing you're up here battling with alien races and a deranged psycho. Not going to happen."

"But, Micah—"

"No more buts. You won't change my mind."

She wouldn't. She could feel that, too. And stars save her, she didn't want to.

He gave her a classic Micah grin, pulling her into a hug.

She engaged her energy field, the warm feeling of connection filling her with hope.

He rested his cheek on top of her head. "Face it, sis. Whatever happens with this mission— with Reanne—one thing is certain. You and I will face it together."

Together.

The word reverberated in her mind as something deep within shifted into alignment, stabilizing her like a cornerstone.

Since she was a child, she'd been searching, without knowing for what or why. She'd thought she'd filled the void when she'd become captain of the *Starhawke* and assembled her crew, especially after Cade had come back into her life.

But the nagging sense of loss, of emptiness, hadn't abated.

Now she understood why. *This* had been the missing piece. Losing Micah had torn her apart in ways she was only beginning to see clearly. And while they'd each built lives from the rubble, on some level she'd known what she'd lost.

Connection was in their blood, the very basis of what it meant to be Suulh. Sahzade and Nedale. Mother and daughter. Sister and brother. Lifeforce to lifeforce, forever entwined, nurturing, healing, protecting.

The universe had brought her to this point. She'd be a fool to turn away now.

Leaning back, she looked into Micah's eyes, so similar to her own. "All right, big brother. Together it is."

Separately, they were strong. But together?

Together they could move the stars.

Captain's Log

Meeting Micah

I've been thinking about Micah Scott for years. The scene where Aurora and Micah meet on the beach has been spinning in my mind in one iteration or another practically since the series began, waiting for me to get far enough in the timeline to write it.

But first I had to plant the seed with the name Aurora used to call him as a child, My-a. And then I had to keep that secret for three books, even though I knew exactly who he was, what had happened to him, and where he'd gone. I couldn't share any of it with you, or Aurora, until now, but when Micah came on the scene, it was all worth it.

Writing about Micah and Aurora's relationship has been pure joy. I never had to worry about what they were going to say, or how things would turn out. I just rested my fingers on the keyboard and let them take over

It didn't hurt that I had a wonderful reference point for Micah — my own big brother. All those sterling qualities in Micah? They came from him. And while he's never admitted to actually talking to animals, he certainly has a connection with them, and with the ocean.

But what really brought this home for me was what happened eight months before I started writing this book. My big brother was hit by a drunk driver.

When I got the call from my mom, letting me know he was in the ICU with a serious head injury, I froze. I couldn't move, couldn't function for the first ten seconds or so. The one thought that kept racing through my mind was, *He can't die. He hasn't read his story yet.*

Well, my brother must be half-Suulh, because he made a full recovery that would make Lelindia/Mya Forrest proud. And while he focused on healing, I focused on getting his book written so he could finally read it.

Now that you've read it, too, when I say Micah is a very special character for me, you can truly understand why.

Like Aurora, my world is a brighter place because my big brother's in it.

Do They Really Have Dog Surfing?

Yes. Yes, they do.

While researching the surfing scenes for this book, I came across videos that showed these fun-loving canines doing their thing. If you head over to my Pinterest page, you can check out the images and videos that inspired the competition scene.

If, after reading this story, you and your canine decide to get into the surfing scene, or if you're already seasoned pros who've had many adventures on the waves, send me a pic and I'll share it!

Puzzling out the Yruf

The Yruf are another element that I've known about since book one but had to wait to bring out in the open. But unlike Micah, I knew very little about them until their ship uncloaked behind *Gladiator*'s stern. Even that was a surprise to me. I had no idea their technology was more advanced than even the Kraed, or that their ship would turn out to be modular, with moving bulkheads.

In fact, in a few early versions of scenes for this book, I had them attacking the Ecilam with murderous intent. And threatening to blow up Cade's ship. But it didn't feel right. First of all, I had them speaking and understanding Galish. That made no sense, considering no human had ever encountered an Yruf. And the aggressive, vicious attitude didn't fit with the fascinating ship and the history I'd envisioned for them.

So, I sat down and started asking myself some tough questions. Why hadn't the Yruf attacked human settlements as the other four Setarip factions had? Why had their ships never been seen in Fleet space? What part had their faction played in the destruction of their homeworld?

The answers to those questions radically altered the way I viewed the Yruf, and how they reacted to the situation I had drawn them into. The plans they revealed to me were far more fitting for their intelligence and ingenuity than my preconceived notions.

I'm excited to learn even more about them in book five!

Ecilam Attack

When I reached the climactic fire scenes in this book, I hit a bit of a snag in the writing. I'd thrown my main characters into a situation where they had to react to events none of them had witnessed, and they seemed to be flailing as badly as I was. I quickly realized the problem. I didn't have a clear view of what had occurred during the Ecilam attack and resulting fire, either.

That led to the bonus feature short story GUARDIAN, told from Libra Hawke's point of view during the attack on Stoneycroft. Not only did writing it give me the details I needed, but it allowed me to see the changes in Libra's character that resulted. What I uncovered made the scenes in this book so much richer, and led me in directions I hadn't anticipated.

You'll find a copy of this bonus feature starting on the next page.

Enjoy the journey!
Audrey

P.S. - I always write to music, and I select a different piece of music for each story, one that feeds the mood I need to get the words flowing. If you'd like to experience this story the way I did, listen to the soundtrack for *The Rock* while you read.

GUARDIAN

A Starhawke Rising Bonus Feature

One

This is ridiculous.

Libra Hawke punched a fist into her pillow as the grandfather clock near the base of the staircase in the central room chimed twice. She'd been lying here, staring at the curved ceiling of her bedroom, for three hours. But sleep refused to come.

The soft glow of the full moon through the windows outlined the curved footboard of her sleigh bed. The bed Brendan had commissioned for her when they'd begun construction on the house, handcrafted by a local artisan from salvaged wood. It was a beautiful piece of furniture, one she treasured. In its loving embrace, she usually found peace and solace.

But right now, it felt like a prison.

She flipped onto her side, putting her back to the window, and closed her eyes. She needed to sleep, dammit. She'd be opening Hawke's Nest in seven hours and expected the usual post-Christmas flurry.

She'd worked late into the evening on Christmas Eve, too, putting together last-minute arrangements for a few long-time customers. She'd told herself it made good business sense. This was her busiest time of the year. But that hadn't been the real reason she'd stayed.

She hadn't wanted to come home to an empty house.

Not that she was alone. Marina and Gryphon had done their best to keep the holiday spirit going from the moment she'd walked into the central room, with festive meals she hadn't tasted, holiday tunes she'd barely heard, and gifts she couldn't remember. She'd made it through Christmas

Day by force of will. All she'd been able to think about was her family.

Aurora. Micah. Brendan.

They were together for the first time since... since everything had fallen apart. And she was the one left behind.

She could feel the distance that separated them, though not with the accuracy she once had. When she'd first met Brendan, she'd been grateful for her ability to sense exactly where he was, to pinpoint his location with her eyes closed. It had been a game, giving her a sense of safety she'd desperately needed. But when she'd sent him and Micah away, safety had changed to longing. She'd endured the discomfort, cherishing the connection her ability gave her to sense them, even at great distances.

With Aurora, it had been different. Always. Aurora wanted to push boundaries, explore, journey out into the world. She'd resisted the constraints on her mobility and freedom, challenged the rules Libra had set to keep her close. To keep her safe. Monitoring Aurora's whereabouts had been a constant source of anger and frustration, for both of them. And a battle she was destined to lose.

Inevitably, Aurora had grown up, becoming stronger and more stubborn with each passing year. When she'd been accepted to the Academy, Libra's gift for sensing where she was had turned into a curse.

The hundreds of kilometers that had separated her from her daughter during Aurora's Academy years had pulled her like a strained muscle, always aching, always painful to the touch. She'd seriously considered moving to Colorado to be closer to her, but Marina and Gryphon had talked her out of it. They'd warned her that it might harm her relationship with Aurora. She didn't care. Her daughter's safety came first. But then Marina had made the point that her presence might draw more attention to Aurora, the one thing she feared most.

So she'd stayed at Stoneycroft.

But conceding that point was a walk in the park compared to when Aurora had accepted her first starship assignment.

Libra had thought she'd known sadness, loss, loneliness. But having her daughter light years away, facing untold dangers? It had ripped her right in two.

Every second, every hour since, fear and anxiety had warred within her, and she'd been helpless to do anything to ease her suffering. As the years ticked by, and Aurora's visits home became more infrequent, she'd numbed her senses, blocking out the gift of connection, isolating herself from the knowledge it brought.

But that hadn't stopped her from doing everything she could to protect her daughter. She'd extracted a promise from Mya and Jonarel to watch over Aurora, to defend her, to shield her, to keep her safe.

And most of all, to bring her home.

But when Aurora had finally returned to Earth, it hadn't been the joyful reunion she'd imagined. Instead, her enraged daughter had forced the truth out into the open, condemning Libra for a crime she'd committed out of love.

The irony scraped her heart like a razorblade, bleeding it drop by drop. In protecting her family, she'd lost them all.

Over the past two weeks, she'd felt pulses in the connection, her senses reawakening like a surging wave. At first, she'd tried to keep it at bay, the pain of what she'd lost too overwhelming to bear. But as memories resurfaced and emotional dams broke, she'd lost the fight. If this connection was what she had left, she would cling to it for all she was worth.

Which was why she'd only managed two hours of sleep on Christmas Eve, and was staring into the moonlit darkness now. A long-buried instinct whispered of shifting currents and approaching swells. Change was in the air, as tangible as the scent of pine from the wreath over her headboard.

All I wanted to do was protect you.

Her husband. Her son. Her daughter. They were everything—her sun, moon, and stars. She'd believed her choice was the only option, the only way to keep them safe. But it hadn't worked, had it? Aurora had still found a way to attend the Academy. Had roomed with Reanne Beck, the one person on the planet with a link to the Teeli.

The odds were astronomical, yet seemed strangely inevitable, as if the universe was determined to pull them together. Just as Aurora had seemed destined to become captain of her own ship. And find the Suulh.

She shuddered, pushing the thought aside before the tremors could take hold.

Smacking the pillow again, she pushed the covers aside and sat up. Maybe some warm chamomile tea would silence the phantom whispers in her head.

Pulling her booted slippers over her socks, she stood and grabbed her bathrobe. But she'd only taken a few steps toward the door when a queasiness crept into her belly.

She paused, resting her hand on her abdomen. Residual anxiety? Lack of sleep? Probably both. Marina could make her right as rain in a heartbeat, but she wasn't about to wake her. The tea should do the trick.

Out in the hallway she paused again, pressing her palm against her skin as the sensation intensified. What was going on? She was used to occasional physical discomfort— she'd stopped using her shielding and healing abilities the night she'd sent Brendan and Micah away—but this didn't feel like indigestion or muscular tension. It felt... *other.*

Fear crept under her skin, making her tremble. "Marina?" The whispered name sounded loud in the quiet house. She glanced to the left, where the gallery led to Marina and Gryphon's bedroom. Should she go check on them?

No. She was being ridiculous, letting her anxiety about her family and lack of sleep get to her.

Pulling her bathrobe tighter, she turned right, continuing along the hall toward the stairs. Moonlight filtered down from the skylights, lighting the way, but a faint scratching sound halted her in her tracks near the open door to Aurora's room. *Just a tree branch against the window. Get a grip!*

Apparently Aurora's dire warnings about Reanne had infiltrated her subconscious after all, making her jump at shadows. Marina would get a laugh when—

And then a shadow moved.

The shriek that rushed up from her chest was cut off by the constriction in her throat as multiple shadows converged on her. Fear struck at her heart, the pearlescent glow of her energy field bursting to life like a solar flare.

Arms reached out for her, passing through the field and grasping at the fabric of her robe. She spun wildly, but they were coming from all sides, penning her in. A sicky-sweet odor filled her nostrils as a harsh tug forced her hands behind her back.

Fear ramped up to terror as the moonlight revealed the scales covering the arms and clawed hands of her attackers. Her heart stuttering as a reptilian face right out of a nightmare loomed over her.

She stood perfectly still, frozen in place, each breath a feat of will. *A dream. Only a dream. Only a—*

And then cold metal snapped around her right wrist. Not a dream.

The fear blew apart as white-hot rage roared through her veins.

She yanked against the pull on her hands, separating them as the metal grazed her left wrist but didn't make contact. She struck out wildly, connecting with something solid that gave way. She swung again, pivoting and lunging at the dark shapes around her.

The grips on her body and clothing detached, her attackers moving against the walls to form a tight circle with her at the center.

Setarips. Had to be. A race of ruthless killers. She counted six total.

But why had they backed off?

A glance at her hands gave her the answer. Not by choice. Her shield had pushed them away.

It was pale, weak, a phantom version of the glow she used to be able to generate, but it was there, surrounding her body a few centimeters from her skin.

She turned slowly, trying to keep all of them in her line of sight. Movement in her peripheral vision made her snap around just as one of the Setarips fired a weapon.

She ducked instinctively, but it didn't matter. A weight settled over her, wrapping around her head, arms, and torso.

Her feet were jerked out from under her. She hit the floor with a thump, although her shield cushioned the blow. More grasping hands, this time holding onto the thick mesh covering her from head to toe like a fishing net, obscuring her vision.

She struggled, but what little leverage she had she lost as they lifted her off the floor and carried her down the first flight of stairs. But rather than turning left toward the central room, they continued forward to the stairs going back up.

To the Forrest wing.

To Marina and Gryphon.

No!

Sahzade?

Marina's voice, in her head, confused. Distant. Like she was at the far end of a long-abandoned tunnel.

Run! She shrieked the mental warning as she kicked out, the smooth surface of the shield forcing the net to move, her foot connecting with what felt like a chin. A snarl confirmed she'd made contact. She kicked again, fury and fear warring for dominance. But the Setarips kept climbing the stairs.

She had to stop them. Had to protect Marina and Gryphon.

The burning anger ignited, lighting up the parts of herself she'd kept closed off and shuttered for decades. Power surged through her body, focusing her mind, but channeling that power took all her concentration. She lost track of her surroundings except for the six figures carrying her.

Her energy blast shot out, striking like a bolt of lightning.

Agonizing screams echoed off the domed ceiling of the central room.

For a millisecond she was weightless. Then she dropped like a stone, landing haphazardly on top of the Setarips and the upper steps of the stairway. The sudden fall knocked the air from her lungs, but she forced her limbs to move, finding the opening in the net that had bound her. Pushing it aside, she scrambled away from the Setarips on her hands and knees, the metal around her wrist letting go and clattering on the stairs.

She was almost to the landing when visible light flared and a tug yanked her back. She darted a glance over her shoulder. One of the Setarips had grabbed the loose sash of her robe, which wasn't surrounded by her shield. Its clawed hand was scraping the edge of her shield, creating the light flares, while it clung to the strip of material.

Two of the Setarips behind it weren't moving, but the other three were already rising and turning in her direction.

Her body felt heavy, drained. Another blast was out of the question. Maintaining her shield was already a struggle.

If she couldn't fight the Setarips, she'd have to draw them away from Marina and Gryphon.

Shoving the robe off her shoulders and slipping free, she lurched to her feet. As she scrambled up the stairs to the gallery that would take her back to her bedroom, the Setarips close behind, she flung another mental command at Marina.

Down the stairs! Hurry!

If she could clear the Setarips off the stairway and keep them occupied in the Hawke wing, Marina and Gryphon could escape.

But Marina didn't respond. Instead, the queasy feeling returned with a vengeance, making her gasp.

Marina?

Nothing.

A claw scratched the back edge of her shield. She wasn't going to reach her bedroom before the Setarips caught up with her.

Aurora's door stood open to her left. Changing strategy, she skidded through the gap, slamming the door behind her before the Setarips could react.

She dropped her shield, conserving her strength while she dragged Aurora's dresser in front of the door. Spinning around, she scanned the room for potential weapons, or any other objects she could move in front of the door. The desk. The legs scraped across the wood floor as she shoved it up against the dresser.

Her heart pounded in time to the banging on the other side of the door. Why hadn't Marina responded?

Fear wound through her rage like a snake through grass. She had to get to Marina and Gryphon, had to help them.

The Setarips were blocking the interior path. She'd have to go outside.

Moonlight flooded the room through the large window as she shoved the casement open. Cold air snapped at her through the loose flannel of her pajamas.

Wood splintered behind her, the doorframe groaning in protest.

She smacked the screen, sending it flying into the night, then grasped the window frame, reaching for the branch of the large oak that grew beside it.

Long-buried instinct triggered her shield a heartbeat before an invisible force shoved her across the room, knocking her into the front edge of the desk. She collapsed to the floor as debris rained down in a chaotic horde, large chunks that whacked against her shield, the wall, the floor, then smaller pieces that fell like hellish confetti.

She stared at the far wall, not believing what she was seeing.

The window was gone. So was the support structure around it and a section of the ceiling, opening the space to the sky. The bed had been knocked against the interior wall, the comforter littered with wood fragments.

They'd destroyed Aurora's room!

Two dark figures climbed through the ragged hole. More Setarips, although their reptilian forms were covered in a dark mesh, easily visible as moonlight flooded the room. They advanced on her, their weapons pointed at her head and chest.

They opened fire. Literally.

A wall of flame lit the room like a solar flare. She flung her arms up, but it was her shield that stopped the deadly assault of heat.

The furniture behind her wasn't so lucky. The desk and dresser both crackled and popped as the weapons continued to discharge, superheating the wood.

She lowered her arms, squinting, trying to make out the figures of the Setarips through the glare. They'd shifted positions so that the flames were coming at her from two angles.

Which left the path to the opening in the outer wall unprotected.

Shoving to her feet, she raced toward it, leaping over the shattered glass and debris, catching hold of the oak branch swaying in the night breeze.

The glow from the flame weapons followed her, lighting the way and forcing her to maintain her shield. The shield's slick surface prevented her from getting a grip on the tree and she slipped, falling to the ground with a jarring thud that made her teeth click together. Pain radiated along her left leg and ribcage but she forced herself to her feet. A quick glance over her shoulder revealed the two figures standing at the edge of the destroyed wall, backlit by the growing fire in the interior.

And then the Setarips started to climb down the wall like spiders.

That got her moving. Fighting to keep her balance against the pain in her leg, she ran along the path to the deck at the back of the house, the moon lighting her way. She pulled up abruptly after climbing the stairs.

The glass-paneled door on the right side was wide open.

Had Marina and Gryphon made it outside?

A quick check of her internal senses pinpointed Marina. Still inside, upstairs in the Forrest wing. But the connection felt off, warped. And she couldn't tell if Gryphon was with her or not. She couldn't get a sense of—

The crack of a stick behind her made her spin. The two Setarips, coming around the house.

Barreling through the open door, she ran up the first flight of stairs as quickly as her panting breaths would allow.

And met the four Setarips she'd fought previously blocking the path to the second landing.

Stumbling to a halt, she glanced over her shoulder. The other two Setarips were right behind her.

She had a split second to make a decision. Her body cried out for oxygen, her muscles shook. If she ran at the Setarips, could she knock them aside with her shield? Would it hold?

One way to find out.

One of the Setarips lifted the netting weapon. She charged at that one, her shield slamming into the weapon and then the Setarip. The Setarip crashed into its nearest companions, clearing a small space.

She was a small woman. She darted through as claws scraped her shield.

Turning the corner on the second landing, she pounded up the last set of stairs to the Forrest wing. Her slippers slid a bit on the hardwood floor as she picked up speed. They hadn't been designed for sprinting.

She could sense Marina in the bedroom. And maybe Gryphon, except—

She raced along the hallway, passing Mya's room and barely slowing as she flew through the open doorway of Marina and Gryphon's bedroom. But the sight that greeted her as she stumbled to a halt took a moment to register. Even then, her brain refused to accept what the moonlight shining through the window revealed.

Gryphon, prone on the floor beside the bed, his large body deathly still, his head pillowed on Marina's chest. Marina, her back against the exterior wall, one arm cradling Gryphon while her other hand lay over his heart, her energy field barely covering them in a thin layer of sickly greyish-green.

What the–? "*Marina?*"

Her gaze met Libra's in slow-motion, but her head didn't move, as though she didn't have the strength to lift it. Her eyes widened, her lips parted, a single syllable barely audible on her weak exhale. "*No.*"

A soft click as loud as a shotgun blast made Libra turn.

A Setarip loomed in front of the closed bedroom door. This one was head and shoulders taller than any she'd seen so far, it's coloring dramatic. Even in the moonlight, the fluorescent green scales that covered its face and neck seemed to glow.

Libra pivoted, facing the Setarip, blocking Marina and Gryphon from view with her body while her shield provided a more substantial barrier.

That's when she registered the second figure in the room.

It stood to the Setarip's left. At least she thought it was standing. Its form was hard to make out, its hunched posture difficult to reconcile in the play of grey light and shadow. Not a Setarip, certainly. Maybe not even bipedal. A large dog?

It moved, shuffling steps that brought it beside the Setarip.

Not a dog.

Fabric surrounded the creature, like a blanket or cloak, a hooded section covering what might be its head.

"No."

The fear and pain in Marina's whispered word swept away Libra's shock and reignited her anger. What had the Setarips done to them? How had they taken down the strongest healer of the Suulh?

She locked gazes with the Setarip, her anger surging through her blood, giving her strength. "What do you want?"

Its reptilian tongue snaked out. It didn't make a sound, but the malicious look of glee in its creepy eyes indicated it was laughing at her.

Well, she could do something about that.

Drawing in a slow breath, she sent a focused blast of energy at the Setarip.

And stared in shocked horror as it was deflected by a grey and silver version of a *pearlescent* energy shield!

Visible light flashed where the two collided. Streaks of energy radiated around the room, scorching the rumpled comforter on the bed and the upholstered chair in the corner.

Libra backed up a step, her gaze locked on the cloaked figure. The shield had come from it! "Kreestol?"

Aurora had warned her. She hadn't listened. Hadn't wanted to.

The figure didn't speak, just shuffled fully in front of the Setarip.

"Kreestol?" Aurora's descriptions hadn't prepared her for this. She knew her little sister had been warped by Reanne Beck, but she'd believed the change was mental, not physical. The creature in front of her wasn't even recognizable as a Suulh. "I don't want to fight you."

She knew this twisted version of her sister understood Galish, because Aurora had talked to her. Tried to reason with her. And failed.

"*No.*" Marina's voice was weak, but the force of intention behind the word came through. "*Sooree.*"

Sooree? Sooree!

Libra's heart stopped dead, her body freezing as her veins turned to ice. Her mind rebelled. No. It couldn't be. Couldn't—

The creature took a lurching step toward her, the hood sliding back.

Libra stumbled in the opposite direction, bringing her shield in contact with Marina's energy field. The result was instantaneous. One minute she was standing, the next she'd dropped to her knees, the strength sucked from her body.

She planted her palms on the floor, forcing her head up.

And wished she hadn't.

The hairs rose on the back of her neck as the moonlight from the window behind her struck the creature's face.

So familiar.

So horribly different.

Grey stretched skin covered hollow cheeks and sharp cheekbones. Thin lips twisted in a perpetual scream. Clumps of pale, stringy hair hung like tattered cobwebs. And grey-blue eyes stared back, completely devoid of emotion.

Not Kreestol.

Her mother.

Two

She'd had fantasies about seeing her mother again. But not like this. Never like this.

The vacant eyes looked right through her. Not a hint of recognition. Or life.

She was staring into the eyes of a walking corpse.

"Leebaae." Marina's voice, stronger now. Speaking the name Libra had refused to answer to ever since Marina and Gryphon had taken her from their homeworld when she was a child.

"Leebaae, Sooree." Not talking to her. Talking to her mother.

But the words had no effect. Instead, the corpse creature that was her mother lifted her hands, palms out, her greyed energy field hanging around her like a shroud.

"Libra!" Marina's strangled warning came at the same moment her own internal alarm shrieked like a banshee.

Falling back on her heels, she slapped one hand on Marina's thigh and raised the other in front of her, palm out in a mirror image of her mother. Her energy shield solidified, ribbons of pale green threaded through the pearlescent glow.

The blow struck.

Invisible hands latched onto her bones, her muscles, her skin, pulling her forward, leeching energy from her. Her shield flickered, growing thin and translucent.

Marina's energy wrapped around her, pulling her back.

Protect. Defend.

The push-pull tore at her. She fought to break free, to hold onto her strength. Drawing on every bit of energy she could summon, she flung it at the caricature of her mother.

And then the tug-of-war abruptly stopped.

Her bones turned liquid. Slumping to the floor beside Marina and Gryphon, she tried to make sense of what she was seeing from the weird angle.

Her mother looked like a grotesque Halloween statue, completely still, staring out the window without seeing it. Her misshapen body was slightly more upright but otherwise unchanged.

The Setarip stepped forward, prodding her mother with its clawed hand.

The ragged curtain of her mother's hair swayed, but she didn't move, didn't react at all.

The Setarip prodded her again, harder, a snarl curling its fluorescent green lips.

No response. It was like her mother really *had* turned to stone. Only an occasional blink of her eyes revealed any sign of life.

The Setarip's gaze shifted to Libra as it backed to the doorway, its large body coiled with violent potential.

She stared back, watching for the Setarip's next move in this deadly game.

It opened the door and two more Setarips entered the room—the mesh-covered ones with the flame weapons. The taller Setarip stepped forward, lifted her mother off her feet like a sack of grain, and carried her through the doorway. The other two Setarips came toward her, leveling the barrels of their weapons at her.

She rolled flush against Marina and Gryphon, enveloping them in her shield as the Setarips unleashed the wall of flame. It struck her shield, but the pearlescent glow blocked the fire and most of the heat.

The bedside table and the bed ignited, the hellish orange glow overtaking the ghoulish grey shadows of the room. The Setarips stopped the onslaught and stepped back through the open door as the bedding fueled the flames, pushing them up the headboard toward the beamed ceiling.

The tall Setarip reappeared in the doorway. The firelight made it easy to see the malevolence in its yellow eyes as it stared at her huddled group on the floor. It didn't look happy.

Neither was she. She could hear Gryphon's labored breathing—the painful rasp and wheeze of every inhale and exhale—but she didn't dare take her gaze off the Setarip to check on him. If Marina couldn't help him, nothing she did would improve his chances. She kept her focus, and her body, between them and the Setarips.

The tall Setarip hissed over its shoulder without taking its gaze off her.

She inhaled slowly, the blending of her energy with Marina's calming her racing heart. Her mind was another matter. The Setarip blocked the only exit. The heat and smoke from the fire made the air between them shimmer and wave. Her shield was keeping the three of them safe from the effects, but how long could she maintain it?

Another Setarip joined the tall one in the doorway. She recognized the weapon in its hands. It had discharged the netting they'd used to capture her before.

She wouldn't make the same mistake twice.

As the Setarip stepped into the room, she expanded her shield so that it connected with the wall above them, creating a slope.

The Setarip fired, the net whirling toward her and striking the shield. But instead of surrounding them, it slid to the floor in a heap before snapping back into the weapon, unable to wrap around the flat surface of the shield.

More angry hissing from the Setarips, barely audible over the crackle of the flames.

She darted a glance at the fire. It had consumed the bedframe, the wall above it, and was licking along the curve of the ceiling as it spread. The Setarips had moved into the hallway, the heat driving them out, although they seemed less affected by it than she'd expect. Their scales must be providing insulation and protection.

The malice in the tall Setarip's eyes never wavered as it stared at her during the mini-huddle with the other two Setarips. When it broke up, the tall Setarip and the one with the net weapon disappeared from view, leaving her alone with the mesh-covered Setarip.

Were they in for another wall of flame? The damage to the room from the first blast was growing exponentially. Only the chair in the far corner wasn't burning.

But instead of lifting its weapon, the Setarip pulled an object out of a concealed pocket. It crouched, sliding the object across the floor to the edge of her shield before darting out the doorway.

She reacted without thinking, smacking the object with her shielded hand, sending it careening under the bed. Then she wrapped her body around Marina and Gryphon.

The explosion that followed shattered all the windows, made the floor shake like an earthquake, and blew what was left of the bed apart, raining down chaos. Her shield flashed repeatedly as large chunks of wood smashed into it.

She lifted her head. Part of the interior wall was gone, too, giving her a smoke-filled view out to the corridor and the gallery beyond. She pushed onto her elbows. Was that a—

No. Not a potential exit. The floor in front of the opening was gone, too, now a cavernous maw with a five-meter drop to Marina & Gryphon's office below.

The shattered windows vented some of the smoke into the night, but the incoming drafts fanned the flames, shooting them up into the ceiling.

Her fingers curled and her jaw clenched. They were destroying her home! *Their* home. The one they'd built together.

The floor and ceiling creaked and groaned, the sound both a lament and a warning.

She'd rushed in here without a plan, playing right into the Setarips' claws. And if the Setarips didn't capture them, the fire eventually would.

She had to get Marina and Gryphon safely out of this room, away from the Setarips. But how?

Three

Marina's pale energy field continued to pulse around her, but Gryphon's harsh breathing was getting worse, not better. Whatever healing Marina was doing wasn't enough for him. Possibly because she was too weak herself.

Because of *her* mother. The Necri monstrosity that had sucked the life—

The green-scaled form of the tall Setarip took shape through the smoke in the doorway, crouching low.

She gave herself a mental slap. No distractions. No time to feel. If they made it out of this alive, then she could face her demons. "Your move, greenie," she gritted out, sweat trickling down her cheek. The heat of the fire wasn't affecting her through the shield, but the strain of maintaining it was wearing her down.

Her only consolation was that she'd foiled the Setarips' initial plan. She'd also figured out what the Setarips had been trying to do with the explosive. Rather than dragging them out of here, they'd been trying to collapse the floor and send them crashing to the ground level. Or blast them out through the exterior wall.

She and Marina could have survived the five-meter drop. Probably. But Gryphon would have died.

And judging by the calculating look in the Setarip's eyes, it was going to find another way to make that happen.

She couldn't afford to stay on defense any longer.

Drawing in a steadying breath, she gathered and focused her energy, producing one powerful blast directed at the Setarip.

It struck like a cannonball, knocking the Setarip into the corridor and slamming it against the opposite wall.

As it collapsed to the floor, a wave of heat hit her. The attack had drained her shield. She pushed it back into place, lowering the temperature but not blocking out the heat entirely. She checked to make sure the shield was enclosing Marina and Gryphon before shifting to her hands and knees.

And got her first good look at Marina.

Her thick dark hair was a disheveled mass plastered against her head by sweat. Even in the warm glow of the fire, her skin looked sallow, her eyes dull. She still had one arm cradling Gryphon against her body while the other remained over his chest, pulsing faintly with a grey-green glow.

Gryphon was so much worse. If not for his tortured breathing, he could be dead. His eyes were half-open but glazed over, unseeing. His mouth was slack, his large body completely limp.

Rage pounded through her, making her blood burn, but she reined it in. She needed to make every second count.

She touched Marina's shoulder, shuddering as the queasiness she'd experienced before returned with a vengeance. But as soon as she made the connection, her shield pulsed with new life. She channeled that strength back to Marina.

Now she understood Aurora's words regarding the Suulh-Necri. Had seen it for herself. If her mother had hit Marina with a normal energy blast, Marina could have handled it easily. The Nedale couldn't be harmed by Sahzade energy. It invigorated them.

But the attack her mother had launched earlier was an unnatural corruption of Suulh energy. And had produced devastating results on Marina and Gryphon.

But not her. She'd figure out why later.

"Marina, hold onto Gryphon." She didn't wait for Marina to respond. Grabbing hold of Gryphon's limp hands, she rose to her feet and pulled.

He barely moved. As dead weight, his size was working against her, especially with Marina clinging to him.

The ceiling crackled and the floor groaned, the fire devouring everything it touched with wild abandon.

Frustration made her anger surge. "Come on!" Using her physical connection to Gryphon as a guide, she spread her shield along his body to Marina's like a second skin.

It worked. The shield provided a slick surface, eliminating the friction with the floor. She scooted them across the wood planks, through the arched opening, and into the compact reading nook between the bedroom and bathroom.

Her hip bumped against the back of the small couch, halting her. But it was far enough, at least for now. The flames hadn't made it across the ceiling or through the archway yet, and the bend in the interior wall blocked the three of them from sight of the main doorway. The Setarips would have to come right up to the archway—if they dared.

Pained, angry shouts from the hallway reached her through the opening. Her lips twisted in a grim smile. The Setarips were getting more than they'd bargained for.

She sank to her knees, giving her back and shoulders a moment to recover as she fought to catch her breath, her gaze traveling around the tiny room. The outside window had been blown out by the explosion, bits of glass littering the floor, but the couch and two wingback chairs were still upright.

Now what? The Setarips were in the hallway, blocking the only exit. The fire was coming at her from the same direction. The only other way out of the reading room was through the broken window. But how could she get Marina and Gryphon to the ground safely in their present condition? Inside the house, it was a five-meter drop. Outside it was six meters because of the sloping hill.

She needed an answer to that question, and soon. It was getting harder and harder to maintain her shield. Even resting, she could feel her strength waning.

A loud crack and groan of wood preceded a thunderous crash and flare of light from the bedroom. She leapt to her feet as the floor shook.

A quick peek through the archway confirmed part of the ceiling had collapsed near the far corner, taking another chunk of the floor with it. The fire had really sunk its fangs in. It wouldn't be long before it reached them.

"Sahzade."

She turned, meeting Marina's gaze. "Yes?"

Marina drew a shaky breath. "You must... go."

"Go?" The word had no meaning.

"Leave... us."

Oh, hell no! Anger shot through her veins. "Are you insane?" She knelt, placing her hand on top of Marina's, covering Gryphon's heart. "I am *not* leaving you."

"They want... you. You must... escape."

"And leave you and Gryphon here to die? I don't think so. We're in this together."

"No, you—"

"Whether you like it or not!" she snapped. She'd had plenty of arguments with Marina over the years, and she'd won most of them. This one was over.

She rose to her feet.

The broken window was venting black smoke, creating nightmarish faces that taunted her. Below, a six-meter drop to rocky ground. The archway at the opposite end of the reading room led into the bathroom. A dead end.

Take your pick. Bad or worse?

Marina and Gryphon's closet was also through the far archway. There wasn't an exit in that direction, or access to the rest of the house, but maybe she could use their clothing to create a rope and lower them to the ground through the broken window. She could also get water from the sink and shower to soak the walls and floor in the reading room, maybe slow down the fire.

She took hold of Gryphon's clammy hands and pulled him and Marina closer to the bathroom, away from the heat and smoke. Then she quickly shoved the couch and two chairs in front of the archway to the bedroom. It wasn't much of a barrier for the Setarips, and might only feed the flames, but it made her feel better.

Until the exterior wall blew in.

Four

The strength of the blast knocked Libra on top of Marina and Gryphon. Chunks from the wall slammed into her shield and bounced away. Smoke swirled and danced in front of her eyes, the full moon adding its haunting light to the disturbing scene.

Behind her, the shattered glass from the window crunched under booted feet.

She didn't have to turn her head to know Setarips had crawled through the opening.

She tried to push herself up, but her muscles wouldn't obey her commands, stranding her where she'd fallen. She clung to Marina, struggling to maintain her shield.

Leave us alone!

But the scream echoed only in her mind.

She was out of gas. Out of ideas. Out of time.

Passive resistance was the only hope she had left.

A popping sound was the only warning she received. But she'd heard it twice before, and her subconscious had correctly identified it as a threat. Before the net settled over them, she'd already expanded her shield to connect with the floor in an inclined flat plane.

The net smacked against the surface and slid to the floor just as it had the last time, bringing her a moment of satisfaction.

The Setarips' claws scraped against her shield, trying to grab hold of her, Marina, or Gryphon. The shield held, though she could feel the pressure pushing against her, weakening her. It wouldn't be long before they'd break through.

Rage simmered in her veins as she watched the three Setarips—the one with the net weapon and the two in mesh—circle them in the remains of the room, just at the edge of the shield.

She had to do something. *Anything!* Was there an option she'd overlooked? A tactic she hadn't considered?

She hadn't been trained for this. In fact, her every move since childhood had been designed to prevent exactly this scenario. But it had found her anyway.

Aurora's insistence on leaving Stoneycroft to join the Fleet should have been a call to action. But instead she'd hidden away, denied the reality, downplayed the risks. Her daughter had been the one facing the threats, preparing for the fight to come.

What would she do in this situation? How would she—

A new awareness shot to the surface like a lightning bolt, her thoughts triggering her internal GPS.

Aurora.

Horror slithered under her skin, sinking into her bones. Her throat constricted.

Her daughter wasn't in Hawaii anymore. She was headed this way, moving quickly.

And she wasn't alone.

Brendan was with her. And Micah, her precious baby boy.

No! No, no, no, no, no!

The primal scream of fury that erupted from her throat filled the room, overtaking the roar of the flames and angry hissing of the Setarips.

These monsters would NOT harm her family!

Conscious thought fled, but the next thing she knew, she was standing, facing the Setarips.

They lifted their weapons, but not quickly enough.

Her energy blasts struck, flinging one into the furniture piled in the archway. It crashed through and fell on the other side. The two mesh-covered Setarips were thrown up and over the lip of the exterior wall, tumbling out the ragged hole into the night.

She stared at the crumpled Setarip, but it didn't move, even as a burning piece from the ceiling fell on top of it and its clothing burst into flames.

Her gaze moved to where the other two had disappeared. The moonlit trees of the forest were barely visible through the thick clouds of smoke. One heartbeat. Two. Three.

Nothing moved.

Her vision wavered, the floor shifting under her feet. She sank to her knees, catching herself on one outstretched hand as the room spun. Then everything went black.

Five

A soothing coolness wrapped around her like a gentle breeze on a hot day. It called to her, drawing her back from the void she'd fallen into, as did the voice that followed.

"Libra. Libra, wake up."

A hand on her shoulder, shaking her.

"Libra, *please.*"

The fear in that voice pushed her eyes open. She blinked several times, making out a shape in the dancing orange light. Marina, leaning over her, her face glistening with sweat.

Heat pressed in on her, but not as bad as it had been when she'd passed out. And she way lying on something cool and textured. It took a moment to orient herself. She was in Marina and Gryphon's bathroom, stretched out on the slate floor in front of the sinks.

The flickering orange glow came through the archway to her right. The fire must have made its way into the reading room.

The smell of ash coated her airways, making her cough.

Marina crouched below the thickening haze, keeping her hand on Libra's shoulder. "Can you move?"

Her body protested in a hundred ways, but she rolled onto her side and pushed to a semi-seated position. Her gaze fell on Gryphon's large body beside her. "Gryphon?"

Marina's gaze darted to her mate. "He's... still alive." She swallowed. "But—" She shook her head, leaving the rest unsaid.

Libra finally registered the green glow that surrounded all three of them. It was still washed out and weak, not a healthy rich emerald green, but no longer the sickly grey-green it had been. Marina looked more vibrant, too.

The energy surge that had taken out the Setarips must have recharged her. "You dragged us in here?"

Marina nodded. "This was the only option."

"Any sign of the Setarips?"

"No."

"What about the one in there." She gestured in the direction of the bedroom.

"Dead. Its body started to break down into a gelatinous goo."

Completing the image of a monster from her worst nightmares. "How long was I out?"

"Hard to say. Ten minutes, maybe."

Long enough for any remaining Setarips to make their next move. If they could. The only way to reach them now was through the inferno. It was also the only way out.

She made a slow scan of the bathroom. Gryphon had crafted the exterior walls out of rock rather than wood. The shower enclosure was rock, too, the stonework continuing to the ground level, forming part of Marina and Gryphon's meditation space below and a grotto feeling up here.

The rock would provide some protection from the fire as long as she could keep the heat from cooking them and the smoke from asphyxiating them. She was a little afraid to test her shield and learn the answer.

But that wasn't the most pressing concern on her mind. "Aurora's on her way."

Marina's eyes widened. "She is? Did you—"

"No. I never would have sent for her." She wasn't even sure she could if she wanted to. "It must have been Brendan. He's with her. Micah, too."

"They're all coming?" Guarded hope replaced the desperation on Marina's face.

She could forgive her for that. If Brendan was the one lying on the floor rather than Gryphon, fighting for each breath, she'd be desperate, too.

But her daughter was at risk.

"How soon?"

She closed her eyes, focusing on the connection. And was startled by the answer. "They're over the mainland already." Brendan must have pulled out all the stops.

His ability to sense her every emotional nuance had drawn them together from the beginning. And distance didn't seem to matter. Even across the Pacific, her rage must have felt like an air raid siren going off.

And he'd responded without hesitation.

A tremor passed over her that had nothing to do with the Setarips and the fire.

But bringing Aurora and Micah? That was reckless. Unconscionable. Better that he let her die than allow any harm to come to either of them. For all she knew an entire pack of Setarips could be waiting in the forest, biding their time, poised to strike.

Her stomach pitched with fear. *Aurora, no. Stay away.*

But her daughter wouldn't hear her. Even if she did, she'd ignore the warning.

Despite her best efforts, her daughter had become the Sahzade, protector and leader of the Suulh. She was driven to defend her people. Her family. Whatever it cost her.

But Libra didn't want her to pay that price. To suffer pain and loss. *The way I have.*

She'd tried to protect Aurora. Protect them all. But she'd failed. And now they were in danger because of her.

If only she'd listened to Aurora, taken the threat from Reanne Beck seriously, this wouldn't have happened. They'd all be safe.

They'd ALL be safe!

Understanding struck like a blow, tilting her world on its axis, a window flying open that she hadn't even realized was there.

If only she'd *listened* to Aurora.

She'd always viewed Aurora's obstinate behavior as a form of rebellion. She'd laid a safe path out for her, but her daughter had turned her back and walked the other way.

But it wasn't Aurora who'd been rebelling.

It was her.

Rebelling against who she really was. Against the people she came from. Against the role she was meant to play. Instead of standing up to the Teeli threat, she'd sent Brendan and Micah away, crushing her heart in the process.

So she'd hidden. Avoided. Denied. And attempted to mold Aurora into the same coward she'd become.

"Libra?" Marina leaned closer, peering at her. "What is it?"

Thank goodness her daughter had resisted. Had fought for who she was even when the deck was stacked against her. If she'd followed her mother's example, they'd both be cowering in this bathroom. Or worse.

She met Marina's gaze. "We need to give Aurora all the time we can to reach us."

Marina sat back on her heels, staring at her like she'd sprouted a second head. "Are you serious?"

Libra nodded.

Marina kept staring at her, her mouth hanging open. "But... the fire. The Setarips. She'll be in danger."

Something that was almost a smile curved Libra's lips. "She's the Sahzade. She can handle it."

Six

Marina continued to look at her like she wasn't in her right mind, but she didn't care. "We need to move Gryphon to the shower enclosure."

Marina nodded, the stunned look in her eyes replaced by determination.

Libra tried to get to her feet, but her legs wouldn't cooperate. "I don't think I can stand."

Marina crouched beside her. "Can you kneel?"

Shifting her weight, she rolled to her hands and knees. A little wobbly, but not bad. "Yeah, I think so."

"Okay, you push, I'll pull."

Marina grasped Gryphon's hands while Libra crawled to his bare feet. Working together, they dragged him across the floor into the walk-in shower.

His breathing was starting to sound more like a rattle than a wheeze, which scared the stuffing out of her.

Marina sank down by his side, resting her hands on his chest and surrounding him in her green energy field.

Libra's body trembled, her arms ached, and sweat soaked her pajamas. She laid down beside Marina, her head spinning from the oppressive heat.

The shower was slightly cooler than the rest of the room. But the smoke was collecting in an expanding cloud above them with nowhere to go but down.

Gryphon gasped, startling her.

"I've got you, my love," Marina murmured, bending down and brushing a kiss on Gryphon's cheek. "I've got you. Breathe for me."

His next breath rasped in, out, like sandpaper coated his lungs.

Tears burned Libra's eyes. She'd been a cowardly fool, and now Gryphon was paying the price.

Reaching out, she rested her hand on Marina's knee. The physical connection calmed her immediately, as it always did. She engaged her energy field, which responded better than she'd expected but not as vibrantly as she'd hoped. It wasn't anemic like Marina's, but it had an unusual gossamer quality that didn't bode well.

She'd have to work with what she had.

Drawing a slow breath, she allowed it to flow over Marina and Gryphon, weaving in with Marina's energy, enclosing the three of them in a nurturing web.

So far so good. But generating the field was the easy part. Now came the real challenge.

Concentrating on the flowing energy, she summoned her shield.

Nothing happened.

Oh, no.

Panic surged, rushing to her nerve endings like fire ants. If she couldn't shield, they'd never survive. Marina couldn't sustain all three of them, not long enough for Aurora to save them. They'd all end up incinerated. Or die from smoke inhalation.

And she'd be to blame.

No. That can't happen. I won't let it happen.

Her family was coming. Aurora, her brave and powerful daughter, was coming. She could feel how close they were. They were moving slower now, like the plane was on its approach for landing.

Aurora would help her. Save her. She believed it with every fiber of her being. She just had to hold off the fire until she got here.

Using the image of Aurora as a focal point, she summoned the shield again.

This time the pearlescent glow solidified, encasing them behind its protective wall, blocking out the heat and smoke.

The shield would hold. It had to.

Because she had a lot to say to her family before this day was over.

Audrey Sharpe grew up believing in the Force and dreaming of becoming captain of the Enterprise. She's still working out the logistics of moving objects with her mind, but writing science fiction provides a pretty good alternative. When she's not off exploring the galaxy with Aurora and her crew, she lives in the Sonoran Desert, where she has an excellent view of the stars.

For more information about Audrey and the Starhawke universe, visit her website and join the crew!

AudreySharpe.com

CPSIA information can be obtained
at www.ICGtesting.com
Printed in the USA
LVHW010147121220
673920LV00001B/10